Gemini Girls
Footsteps in the Park
Maggie Craig

Marie Joseph was born in Lancashire and was educated at Blackburn High School for Girls. Before her marriage she was in the Civil Service. She now lives in Middlesex with her husband, a retired chartered Engineer, and they have two married daughters and eight grandchildren.

Marie Joseph began her writing career as a short-story writer and she now uses her Northern background to enrich her bestselling novels. Down-to-earth characters bring a vivid authenticity to her stories, which are written with both humour and poignancy.

Her novel **A BETTER WORLD THAN THIS** won the 1987 Romantic Novelist's Association Major Award.

OMNIBUS

Marie Joseph

ARROW

Arrow Books Limited
20 Vauxhall Bridge Road, London SW1V 2SA

An imprint of Random House UK Ltd

London Melbourne Sydney Auckland
Johannesburg and agencies throughout
the world

First published in 1991 by Century

Arrow Edition 1992

1 3 5 7 9 10 8 6 4 2

Printed and bound in Great Britain by
Cox & Wyman Ltd, Reading, Berks

ISBN 0 09 910211 0

Gemini Girls

MARIE JOSEPH

For Sarah and Emily,
my twin granddaughters

CHAPTER ONE

Libby Peel knew she had no right to be there. But then Libby was not over-concerned with rights and wrongs. All she knew was that on that warm summer evening her whole being throbbed with the excitement of finding herself where she was not supposed to be.

The market place of the Lancashire town that May evening in 1926, on the very eve of the General Strike, was certainly no place for a slightly built girl, her long brown hair bundled up beneath a small straw hat. But Libby felt not even the faintest twinge of fear.

Here was where she was meant to be, right here in the middle of it all, not merely sitting at home with her hands folded in her lap, waiting for things to happen. She found she was almost jumping up and down on the cobblestones as the blood pulsed through her veins with a wildness she had no desire to control.

Mr Baldwin, the Prime Minister, an obstinate, short-sighted, pig-headed little man, in Libby's opinion, had turned up his nose at the idea of any further dealings with the miners—*earthworms*, as a lady member of the aristocracy had called them.

So the strike was on . . .

Already the trains had stopped running, the town's evening newspaper had printed its last 'Special Pink', and to Libby's disgust, the government had seized the monopoly of any further news bulletins, giving of course their side of the case. Even before it had begun, the fight was unequal.

The militant speaker, balanced precariously on a makeshift platform, was a weaver from one of the town's cotton mills, possibly even from the mill owned by Libby's father. The stocky little man was waving his short arms about, yelling at the top of his voice. 'They say the weavers are in the second line. That's all. The bloody second line!' His face glistened with sweat, and his whole body seemed to swell with indignation. 'That's what they say we are!' He pointed a finger, stabbing the air to emphasize his next words. 'But *what* bloody second line? Second lines are called up second, and we are ready *now*, lads. Think on! *We're* ready now!'

The crowd surged forward roaring its approval.

'So what the 'ell are we waiting for?' The speaker put up a clenched fist as a man tried to pull him down from his perch. 'What about Chorley? Now there's a town not waiting for some bloody second line! And don't forget that Chorley's not supposed to be a trade union town. Fertile as bloody granite from a socialist point of view is Chorley, and yet their weavers are ready to walk out to a man. Aye, missus, that's right. To a woman an' all. So where does that leave us, eh?' He dropped his voice a fraction, sensing the crowd's sympathetic attention. 'I'll tell tha lot summat for nowt. The maister at my mill has a son, a great 'aporth of a son what plays golf three mornings a week when he's supposed to be working. Oh, aye, he does that. An' he's a member of the Manchester Exchange, and gets there on a railway contract paid for by the likes of us, while his father's weavers have to feed their families on bread and jam, with sixpenn'orth of fish of a Saturday night when the chip shops want to get rid. Bloody disgraceful!'

Libby stared down at the cobbles. So the man wasn't from her father's mill after all. Oliver Peel's only son, her brother Willie, had been killed in France at the very end of the war. There were no days for Willie at the Manchester Exchange. Willie's life had ended with a flash of gunfire, and life at Westerley, the big house on the outskirts of the town, had never been the same since then.

For the first time since mingling excitedly with the milling crowd, she felt apart from them, and with the feeling came the first twinge of unease. In spite of the third best coat and the plain straw hat, Libby began to realize just how conspicuous she was. She tried to move and found that she was hemmed in as surely as if she had been nailed to the ground.

'We're still a country of down to earth, moderate thinking people,' she had told her twin sister Carrie before sneaking out of the house and starting on her long walk into town. 'It's no use, Carrie, I can't, I just can't sit here at home while everything is happening. I have to be there to *see*.'

Carrie, a mirror image of her twin, had tried hard to dissuade her. Libby frowned, thinking just how conspicuous the two of them would have been standing together in the market place. Most people knew the Peel twins when they were together, even if they were sometimes unsure which was which.

'I am me!' Libby would shout in one of her childish tantrums. 'And she is her!'

Carrie was slightly smaller than her twin. Libby's small brown mole at the left side of her mouth was on the right side of Carrie's, and Libby was right-handed to Carrie's left-handed awkwardness.

Libby was outspoken and sure, while Carrie was quiet and often — very often — not so sure, but this time she had surprised her sister by her vehemence.

'Father will kill you if he finds out where you've gone. He says that dignity for the middle classes is all-important just now, and what is there dignified about going down town all alone and listening to the agitators?'

'Pooh to dignity!' Libby had said, slipping out of the side door. 'There's nothing dignified about being hungry.'

But all the same, remembering Carrie's words, her heart contracted with fear. Oliver Peel sober was a force to be reckoned with, and Oliver Peel in his cups was as bad as a raving lunatic.

'I hate him,' she thought. 'He is my own father and I loathe him.' She kicked viciously at a harmless cobblestone, then turned to apologize as her kick landed on the shin of the man standing next to her.

He stared at her with open curiosity, a tall man with black hair and a thin pale face, flushed now with an excitement to match her own.

'No place for a lass on her own.' The stranger tut-tutted in cheeky disapproval. 'And you *are* on your own, aren't you, lass?' He grinned so that the craggy seriousness of his features broke up into lines of almost boyish mischief. 'Finding out for yourself what the peasants think?'

It was so near to the truth that Libby's large brown eyes fell before his steady gaze. The crowd, pressed from the back, surged forwards towards the speaker's rough platform, and at once the man took her arm and pulled her close to his side, bending down to speak into her ear. 'What the heck *are* you doing here, for heaven's sake, then? Looking for a chance to hop up there yourself and put the other side to us ignorant workers?'

Libby tried to pull away, but he held fast, and because she was privately glad of his supporting arm (although she would rather have died than admit it) she flared into instant characteristic retaliation.

'I work too,' she told him. As the crowd swayed her hat was knocked sideways, causing the slipping bun of her long hair to wisp down her back.

'In a shop?' The stranger grinned. 'No, come off it, lass. You'll be telling me next you've been out picking coal from the surface Burnley way.' He lifted one of her gloveless hands and pursed up his lips at the sight of the engagement ring on her third finger. 'What's your man doing letting you come down here?' His eyes twinkled. 'Or doesn't he know?'

Libby blushed a fiery red as tears of humiliation pricked behind her eyes. 'I'm a teacher.' With as much dignity as was left to her, she clung to her hat with her free hand. 'And I know why I am here. *I* know.' She tilted her chin. 'There are children in my class who haven't got a pair of clogs to their name, even in the winter, and if their father is lucky enough to have an egg for his tea, they are allowed to dip a finger of toast in it.' Her eyes met his. 'I'm on *your* side, can't you see?'

Tom Silver, a compositor on the town's weekly newspaper and the youngest Father of the Chapel in the county, wrinkled his hawklike nose at her.

'All the same,' he said wickedly, 'I wouldn't mind laying bets that you have never had to queue up with your brothers and sisters for a dip in your father's soft boiled egg. That's a fact, isn't it lass?'

Libby widened her eyes to stare furiously into the teasing, laughing face so close to her own. She was tightly pressed against his side. She could actually feel the restrained violence emanating from his body. This man was making her feel ridiculous; he was enjoying himself. She did not know him at all, and yet she was being held so close to his side that they might have been lovers. She tried to turn away from him, but at once he swung her round again, and now she could see the irregularity of his front teeth, and the way his brown eyes were flecked with green. He pursed his lips into a mocking semblance of a teasing kiss, and she jerked her head backwards so that the hat slipped even farther sideways.

The part of Libby that was all Oliver Peel made her temper flare. 'If I told you who my father was you wouldn't speak to me like that, whoever you are. But I won't tell you because you wouldn't believe me!'

'Then don't bother, lass.' Tom Silver laughed outright into her upturned face. 'Tell you something, though. If you really are a teacher, I wouldn't like to be in your class.' His next words were drowned by a man built like an ox who had pushed the speaker bodily from the platform.

'This is the day we have been waiting for, lads!' The puffy face beneath the greasy cap sharpened with wild enthusiasm. 'This is the hour when the oppressed throw off their shackels and make a stand for what is theirs by right! As Mr Bevin says: "We are not declaring war on the people. War has already been declared by the Government, urged on from behind by sordid and selfish capitalism!" '

'Good man, Bevin.' Tom Silver pulled hard at Libby's arm as the crowd swayed forward dangerously. 'Come on, lass. There's going to be a free-for-all. The Bolshies want a fight. I am going to get you out of here somehow.'

But even as he turned, a tram rumbled by along the wide street flanking the market square, clearly visible to the inflamed crowd. Driven by a moustached man of immense dignity, an ex-army officer by the look of him, it stopped with a rattling shudder for the passengers to dismount.

Grasping his opportunity to incite his listeners, the speaker wheeled round and pointed an accusing finger at the man standing on the driver's platform.

'The tram men met at nine o'clock this morning, and they are out to a man,' he yelled. 'Come on, lads. Let's have 'im, the filthy scabby blackleg! Let's have them bloody whiskers out by the bloody roots!'

Libby found herself swept off her feet, in spite of Tom Silver's protective arm. She watched in horror as stones were prized up by knives from the cobbled ground and hurled towards the tram. As windows shattered into a hail of splintered glass, the passengers scrambled out, a few of them mingling with the crowd as if uncertain which role would afford them the greater safety. The driver was hauled from his platform to face his accusers with the same courage he had undoubtedly shown on Flanders Field as he faced the enemy lines.

'By tomorrow,' the speaker shouted, cupping his hands to his mouth in an attempt to recapture his audience, 'over one and a half thousand looms will be stopped in this town!' His voice rose to a pitch bordering on hysteria. 'The bloody government have ignored us once too often. We've got 'em lads, and by the time we've finished, there won't be a machine working, a train running, nor a single poor bugger eking out a miserable existence on what them in Parliament calls a living wage. Listen to me, lads! We've got 'em. I tell you, we've got 'em, and there's nowt they can do to stop us. Listen to me!'

But it was too late. The crowd, desperate now for action and not words, were fighting for the sake of fighting.

'It only takes a handful of bother-makers.' Tom Silver put both arms round Libby as stones flew like a hail of bullets.

Then someone shouted 'The police! The police are here!' and the crowd scattered. Its movement changed like a field of corn rippled by a sudden wind. For a brief moment Libby was actually lifted off her feet, so that she saw a line of policemen crossing the cobbles, truncheons raised.

Tom Silver dragged her with him to the rough platform. 'Stop there, and keep your head down. Don't run, for God's sake!' he told her, then hoisted himself up and raised both arms above his head.

'The police won't interfere!' He was yelling at the top of his voice. 'They are sympathetic, you fools! They are on our side. Drop those stones! Drop the stones, men, and they won't do a thing. Please! Listen to me!'

But again it was too late. Libby held both hands over her head in a futile gesture of protection as the missiles flew. The police advanced slowly, in a determined line of dark blue, and she heard what sounded like the thud of a truncheon on a man's head.

'Run for it, love!' A woman with a brown shawl clutched beneath her chin ran past. 'They'll nab anybody, so run like 'ell.'

Libby could only stand there, transfixed with terror, as the crowd dispersed, the irons on clogged feet ringing metallically. The younger ones were laughing, the older element cursing, and a few sober-suited clerical types walked quickly away, hands in pockets, as if embarassed by the whole situation. But the hard core of the militants lingered to hurl abuse and stones before they too melted away.

Even as Libby hesitated, a stone whizzed past her head to hit Tom Silver full in the face.

She saw it land, saw the way he put up a bewildered hand to his forehead, saw the blood gush and his features shrivel into a white mask before he fell from the platform to lie in a twisted heap on the ground.

A shout went up from the fleeing crowd. 'The police are attacking the people!'

'That's not true!' Libby heard her own voice yell back, then she knelt down by the still figure crumpled on the cobblestones.

He was quite unconscious, and she saw that the deep gash had missed his left eye by a fraction. He was a strange grey colour, and she pulled his lolling head on to her lap, trying in vain to stem the flow of blood with a white handkerchief pulled from her sleeve.

'Do you know this man, miss?'

The policeman was very young, very correct, his truncheon held almost self-consciously in his hand as he stared down at her.

Libby looked up into his round face and shook her head. 'No, I don't know him. I don't know him at all. He was just standing next to me in the crowd.' Her voice broke on the verge of lost control. 'But he wasn't doing anything wrong. He wasn't fighting. He was trying to calm them down. He *was*!' she added, as the policeman replaced his truncheon and took out his notebook.

'So the victim is unknown to you?' he asked, pencil poised.

Libby shook her head slowly from side to side. If she was watching this, she told herself, on the screen at the Olympia picture palace, she would laugh out loud and think how funny it was. It was like a Charlie Chaplin film: a man lay dying on the pavement as a policeman slowly and seriously took down the particulars in his little notebook. It was incredible, but it was happening. And the stranger, the man who had cheeked her and tried to protect her, looked terrible. He was shaking now, shivering jerkily as a thin trickle of blood oozed down his nose to mingle with the steady flow from the gaping wound so close to his eye.

The evening air was still and warm, unusually heavy for that part of Lancashire, a promise of the long hot summer to come. Libby, without stopping to think, unbuttoned her long fawn duster-coat and laid it over the still figure.

'He must be kept covered. Warm. For the shock,' she whispered, then turned startled eyes as the policeman blew his whistle in a long, piercing blast.

He nodded. 'Everything is being taken care of, miss. Now don't you fash yourself.' He licked the point of his pencil. 'May I have your own name and address, miss? I take it you was a witness to the assault.'

Libby was controlling her impatience with great difficulty. If the policman did not put his flamin' notebook away *now*, this very minute, she would snatch it from his red hand and throw it as far as she could. But she gave him the information he wanted, unaware of the raised eyebrows as it was taken down neatly on a flipped-over page. She lifted her head and saw with surprise that the market square was now completely deserted. The large crowd had disappeared, the £5 fine for disturbing the peace a deterrent to even the most aggressive.

'What about the ambulance?' Libby's voice was sharp, but the policeman merely held up a hand as if directing the traffic.

'On its way, miss. We had it stationed down the bottom end of Victoria Street. The *motor* ambulance, miss,' he said, his voice tinged with more than a touch of pride as the newly acquired petrol-driven van chugged over the pavement and across the cobblestones.

'Thank God for that.' Libby got to her feet and watched as the unconscious man was wrapped in a red blanket and laid on a stretcher.

'You coming with him, miss?'

She accepted her blood-stained coat from an outstretched hand, and shook her head. 'No. He's in good hands now, and I don't know him personally . . . it was just that — just that . . .'

But the doors were being slammed and the policeman was waving the ambulance away, directing it over the empty square with as much concentration as if streams of traffic converged from every direction.

'Wait!' Libby bent down and picked up a small leather-backed book. 'This must have fallen out of his pocket.'

She held it out in front of her, but the ambulance was already back on the road, and the policeman, his duty done to the letter, walking stolidly away in the opposite direction.

'Ah, well . . .' Libby shook her head. Then, as she pushed the book down into the deep patch-pocket of the coat over her arm, she turned and saw a familiar figure striding towards her — Harry Brandwood, the man she was to marry.

'Oh, Harry!' She tried to smile as she almost ran towards him. 'Oh, thank you for coming to find me. You've no idea! They were like wild animals . . . oh, if only you'd been a few minutes earlier, you could have done something!' She clutched his arm. 'And that policeman! He took my name and address. You don't think they'll get in touch with my father? If my father even finds out I've been down the town, he'll go mad. But I *had* to come.'

Her brown eyes were full of tears, her hair half hanging down her back, and her blood-stained coat trailing on the cobblestones. Dr Harry Brandwood loved this wayward girl with all his being, but she angered him at times with her impulsiveness, her intense way of identifying with matters beyond her experience. Had he been a violent man, he would have taken her across his knee and given her a good beating. He took Libby's hand and started to walk quickly across the square, his face set into stern lines.

He had often told himself that *Carrie* Peel was the twin he should be marrying. Carrie, with her softness, her gentle smile, her understanding. But Carrie was milk and water to Libby's full-bodied red glowing wine. Mirror images of each other they might be, but Libby's mirror was clear and sparkling where Carrie's was soft mother-of-pearl.

Already the crowd was gathering again, eager for more words, more action. The overturned platform was set right way up, and two men fought for the privilege of being the first to put his point of view.

Angrily, Harry hurried Libby along.

'I've got the car over there, down King William Street past the shops.' He was taking such long strides that Libby was forced to make small running steps to keep up with him. Now they were in for one of their frequent quarrels, and this time he didn't care. This time she had gone just too far.

'I don't suppose there's much point in asking you what you were thinking about coming down town on your own at a time like this, is there?' He opened the car door and half pushed her inside. 'And I don't want to listen to any more nonsense about you *having* to be there. You could have listened to the wireless like any other normal woman, or read the bulletins.' He ran round the car to climb in behind the wheel. 'Have you any idea of what might have happened?'

He started the car and fought the gears in a fury of frustation. 'When Carrie told me where you'd gone, I could not believe it.'

Libby scrubbed at the bloodstain on her coat, making no impression at all. 'It means less than nothing to Carrie that the whole country is on the brink of revolution.'

'Revolution?' Harry's pleasant face darkened. 'What kind of Bolshie talk is that?'

'Harry Brandwood! You might have the reputation of a good doctor — for the rich of course — but you walk about with your eyes and ears closed.' Libby raised both arms to try to pin the long fall of hair back into place. 'Damn this hair! I'll have it bobbed. This week! Tomorrow!' She jammed the hat on again. 'Do you realize that in this town alone, and almost every other town in the north, come to think of it, there is a choice of three jobs for the boys coming up to school-leaving age? They can go in the mills to work for someone like my father, or they can go as railway clerks or porters, or be apprenticed if they're lucky — or they can go down the mines.'

She dropped a hairpin and scrabbled for it on the floor of the car. 'Do you know, Harry, the brightest lad in my class went as a pony drawer out Burnley way just before the lock-out? He was asthmatic and yet down he went, breathing coal dust into his lungs and crawling on his belly like a mole. You have no idea! I heard that if there's a fall the owners want the ponies out before the men. It's true!' Her eyes blazed. 'There was a girl in the top class at school — Nellie Sharp — and sharp was the right word for her. She had a mind like a razor, and yet because the money was needed at home, do you know what she is doing now? Standing by the belt at the mine

19

and picking the coal over! I saw her once and she showed me her hands, full of blisters and going septic. She told me she has to walk to work across the fields, and it takes her half an hour each way, an' if she gets soaked then she has to stay in the same clothes all day! For seven shillings a week, Harry! And you shy away from the word revolution? You must be blind!'

Harry was bone tired. He had spent forty minutes since a hastily snatched dinner trying to convince a pampered woman there was nothing wrong with her. And above all he was a reasonable man. Struggling to keep his voice low and even, he said, 'Stop and think, darling. How can going on strike help in the long run? People like your father won't suffer, not on a day-to-day life or death basis, but his workers will. I know there *is* exploitation, and there always has been. But conditions *have* changed, and will go on changing. But not this way!'

Libby was still trying to rub at the stain on the coat held on her lap, her small face scarlet with fury. 'Oh, Harry! Can't you even *begin* to see? If the parents got living wages, then there would be no need for them to send their children out to work, *any* work, the very day they leave school. It's a vicious circle. You won't face up to reality, Harry. You never have.'

Even the patience of a man as much in love as Harry Brandwood could exhaust itself. Driving away from the centre of the town now, he turned the car into a quiet street off the main Preston road, and switched off the engine.

'But I was facing up to reality ten years ago, wasn't I, Libby?' His hands left the wheel to hold her fidgeting fingers tightly in a grip that made it impossible for her to break away. He spoke softly and calmly. 'I've never been one for talking overmuch

20

about what I went through or saw out there in France, but believe you me, I saw enough of what you call *reality* to last me a lifetime.'

His mouth set in a grim line as, just for a moment, he was back at the front again. Captain Harry Brandwood, mentioned in dispatches, twice wounded and twice returned to the front line . . . In that quiet street of respectable terraced houses, he was back in the aftermath of battle as he knelt in the Flanders mud trying to ease the last dying moments of soldiers, some of them barely old enough to be called men. Lads from his Lancashire regiment screaming for their mothers through shattered lips. In his mind he felt his feet slip from the duckboards, saw a man's open mouth as he disappeared beneath the sticky stinking mud, weighted down by the pack he had carried for two days without sleep.

'Oh, yes,' he said grimly. 'I've had my share of reality, Libby Peel.'

Libby frowned, not liking her thunder stolen in that way. She tried another tactic. 'Then why don't you take a practice in the town where folks *need* your help? Wouldn't that make more sense than blindly moving into your father's shoes when he retires? Didn't the war make you want to come home and fight for the men who were forced to return to nothing? Some of them daren't call a doctor in because they know they can't afford the shilling a week they would have to pay the doctor's man every Friday night.'

Harry let go of her hands then to stare unblinking through the windscreen. He loved this girl sitting by his side so much that he was preapred to accept the hurtful things she said. She loved him too, he knew that, but sometimes he suspected that she used him as a personal sounding board for her own

21

ideas and emotions. Just as he needed *her* to shake him from his own admitted and sometimes deliberately self-induced complacency.

Libby was strong in both mind and body, and when they married at Christmas she would be a doctor's wife to be proud of. Once he had got her away from that mixed infants' school with its asphalt playground, once he had got her away from her friend Margaret Bottomley with her half-baked socialist ideas, Libby would conform.

Or would she? Harry sighed. 'Remember, Libby, love. The world is made up of winners and losers, and always will be.' He started the car. 'And another thing. The rich can suffer too.' They were on the main road again now. 'This morning I stood by the bed of a child dying of diptheria. I was helpless to do more than watch.' His face crumpled in sadness. 'That child's father owns enough shops to line the Arcade twice over. But no power on earth and no medicine we know could have prevented that child choking to death on its own spittle. So don't get too carried away, Libby. I do sometimes come face to face with what you call realism. Even if my patients do pay through the nose for the privilege of seeing their loved ones die.'

Libby had nothing more to say for the moment. Now that they were getting nearer to home she was forgetting wider issues for the time being. At Westerley her father was waiting. Somehow he would be sure to have found out where she had been. Libby chewed at her bottom lip. Her father could sit at his desk in the billiard room all evening, and still know exactly what was going on everywhere else in the house.

And oh, dear God, if he had drunk too much whisky then his anger could leap and crackle like a fire out of control. Libby closed her eyes, seeing it all . . .

Her mother would cry and clutch her heart, but Carrie would defend her twin even if her body shook with terror. It was all so petty, so shameful, so degrading to have to stand there like a child instead of a grown woman of twenty-two, listening to her father's bigoted, sarcastic flow of invective that made her suspect at times that he might be going mad. Like his sister before him, ending her days in a private clinic, plucking with nervous fingers at the bedclothes as she tried in vain to remember who she was.

Libby sat up straight, tilting her chin defiantly, and when Harry risked a sideways glance he saw that her eyes were as bleak and hard as moorland stones.

'Let's hope the *maister* has drunk enough whisky to soak up most of his temper,' she said without much hope.

Oliver Peel had been born in 1862. His grandfather had built Bridge Mill, a four-storey building with a vast weaving shed. A self-made man rather than an established landowner, Abraham Peel had been a weaver himself, had stood at his looms with the noise deafening him, vowing that someday he would move on to what he called 'better things'.

He had achieve this by marrying into money, and from then it was all plain sailing. A fair-minded man, he had given birth to a fair-minded son, Benjamin, who in his turn had fathered Oliver. But with the death of Willie Peel, Oliver's only son, in France, the fair-mindedness had ended.

Westerley was built in Georgian style. There were five wide steps up to the front door leading into a mosaic tiled hall. In the dining room hung an enormous crystal candelabra, and the lounge at the front was liberally dotted with potted ferns. On the first floor were the main bedrooms, with boxlike rooms for the servants at the top of the house, and though Libby on entering the house glanced longingly at the wide staircase, Harry urged her towards the drawing room door.

'You may not have been missed,' he whispered, but in that first glance Libby knew the worst had happened.

Her mother, Ettie Peel, cowered like a small pale ghost in the corner of the chesterfield, with Sarah Batt, Ettie's maid and companion, positioned behind her mistress, hands clasped together beneath her high pouter-pigeon bosom. Carrie stood over by the window, her brown eyes wide and anxious as she tried to send out a message of unspoken sympathy and apology for giving the game away. And last but not, dear God, least, Oliver.

He stood in front of the fireplace, legs straddled wide apart, black eyebrows drawn together over the high ridge of the distinctive Peel nose, his glance sliding over Libby as if she did not exist.

'Ah, Harry, lad.' He nodded into the fold of his treble chin. 'There's been a message for you. Over the telephone. Urgent. It was a Mr Bebbington.'

'Oh Lord, I know what that means.' Harry took an instinctive step backwards. 'But her baby's not due until the end of the month.'

Oliver nodded. 'So he said. But it seems her time's come on sudden like, and she won't see nobody but you, not even your father.' His loud voice boomed in anger as he shot a venomous glance at Libby. 'And if you hadn't had to go traipsing after that one there you'd have been here to take the message a good half hour ago. As it is you'd best be off.'

Libby swivelled her eyes sideways and saw the

expression on her fiancé's face — a farmer's face, she often thought. It was a mixture of indecision, anxiety and a professional obedience to his calling. 'I have to go,' the expression said. 'Please try to understand, sweetheart.'

'Yes, you must go at once, Harry.' Libby made no move to go into the hall with him as, reddening uncomfortably, he made his excuses and left, leaving behind him a silence that grew and lengthened, lasting until the sound of the car's wheels on the gravel path outside died away.

And all the time Oliver's dark eyes never left his daughter's face. He was drunk enough to sound sober, but too drunk to sound reasonable, Libby calculated. Trying hard to meet his gaze, she felt her legs tremble and her heart begin to race and she despised herself for her weakness.

She was twenty-two years old, she reminded herself silently. A qualified teacher, engaged to be married to the son of the town's most distinguished doctor. She could walk out of this house and never come back, without taking a thing with her. Harry would marry her next week if she asked him to. They could be married quietly, and his mother and father could retire to their bungalow waiting for them at Lytham St Annes. And she need never set eyes on her father again.

Libby held her head up high, as the silence in the room grew even more menacing. Oh, no, she would never do that, not to her little mother sitting there quietly, nor to Carrie, the sister who was more than a sister. She would stay and stand her ground.

At last Oliver spoke. 'All right then. Now tell me where you've been. Take it slowly, then I can take it in, because when your mother told me I couldn't rightly believe it.'

'He got it out of me love.' Ettie's voice was a whimper. 'And don't go blaming Carrie. She only told *me* to set my mind at rest.'

'You *know* where I've been.' Libby heard the tinkle of a hairpin as it escaped her slipping bun to fall on the polished surround where she stood by the door.

'I would like to hear it from your own mouth.' Oliver was using his voice now to full dramatic advantage, so that it hissed like a whiplash.

Suddenly Libby could bear it no more. 'Oh, Father!' she burst out. 'Please don't make such an issue out of nothing. I only went down the town to see for myself what was going on. I knew there would be speakers on the market place, and I wanted to hear what they had to say. Father! They were decent, hard-working men in the main, and they are fighting for their very existence. I'm a *teacher*, for heaven's sake. Isn't it right that a teacher should know both sides of things?' She glanced round her wildly. 'All I see here, in this house, is *one* side, and I've got to see both. Can't you understand?'

'The miners should have learned their lesson five years ago. Or *last* year, come to that, when Baldwin settled things down.' Oliver's face was now dangerously quiet. 'What I want to know is, were there any of my weavers there? Because if there were . . .' He rolled his big head from side to side. 'They don't know which side their bread's buttered on. It only needs *one* man, one ignorant bother-maker to shout the odds, and they'll all be following him, like sheep. There's only half of them turned up today, and tomorrow, if I know owt, I'll be faced with idle looms, and three bloody contracts unfulfilled. I could tell you summat about strikes, lass, if you asked me. *And* about the unions. Do you know how much the union spent way back in 1896 to keep that strike going?' Clasping the lapels of his smoking jacket with both hands he rose up on to his toes. 'Eight hundred and fifty pounds a week! So how much do you think they've got in the kitty now?' He snorted. 'Enough to put me out of business if it goes on long enough, and you, *you* have the effrontery to creep from the house to side with them!'

'No!' Libby took a step forward. 'No, that's where you're wrong, Father. I didn't go down to take anybody's side. I went because I wanted to listen to what they had to say. I have a right to know, to make up my own mind.'

Oliver's florid face turned purple. 'Right? Did you say *right*?' Let me tell you something, lass. As long as you live under my roof you have *no* rights. If you'd been born sooner you'd have been like them daft women chaining themselves to railings for the vote. And for what? To vote for something they know nowt about!' He raised a clenched fist. 'One son. One son was all I had, and he had to go and get himself killed, leaving me here in a house full of women, with even the cat a bloody female!'

'Oliver . . .' Ettie Peel made an involuntary movement as if to get up. 'Please don't bring Willie into it. You know how it upsets me.' She laid a hand over her heart. 'It's not my fault, and it's not Libby's fault she's not a man. She's high-spirited, that's all. No harm's been done.'

'No harm?' Oliver turned on his wife. 'No harm for a daughter of this town's best-known mill owner to be seen mingling with the scum of the earth, down on the market of an evening looking like a night woman? What did you do down there, Libby Peel? Jump on a soapbox and encourage that rabble to walk out on their wicked employers? I must be the laughing stock of the whole town.

"How can he control his workers when he can't control his own daughter?" That's what they'll be saying over their ale. Oh, aye, they can always find money for ale even when their families are supposed to be starving.'

'Some of their children *are* nearly starving, Father.' Libby spoke quietly, 'There are a dozen children in my class alone with rickets, and that is a direct result of not getting proper food. Half of them with head lice, and not because they're dirty, but because they have to sleep four and sometimes five to a bed.' Forgetting all self-control, Libby raised her voice. 'It's *time* they rebelled. And I'll tell you something else. I hope they all come out, and I hope they stay out long enough to make you and your like see sense! That's what I hope!'

One minute Oliver was standing, back to the fire, then the next, without seeming to move, he shot out a big hand and struck Libby hard across the face.

Too shocked to retaliate, Libby felt tears of outrage and shame fill her eyes, and saw in the same moment her mother crumple forward, to be saved from falling to the carpet by the swift action of Sarah Batt who, moving like lightning, came from behind the chesterfield to take her mistress in her arms.

'I am all right.' Ettie spoke in a whisper, her face white as chalk, her lips a strange blue colour. 'I never thought to see the day when in my own house . . .' Her voice faltered as Sarah helped by Carrie, led the trembling woman from the room.

Oliver stood irresolute for a moment. Before Libby too turned to follow the little procession upstairs their eyes met, and the glance was shot through with mutual dislike, a hatred that was almost tangible.

'Go and see to your mother,' he muttered before striding into the hall and flinging open the door of

28

the billiard room opposite. 'And just keep out of my sight for a bit, that's all.'

For as long as Libby could remember her mother and father had slept in separate rooms. The carrying of twins and their difficult birth had left Ettie a semi-invalid. Libby could never remember a time when, bursting in from school full of the day's doings, she had not been shushed into silence by the frail little woman half lying on the chesterfield in the big front room.

Now Ettie was drooping, ashen-faced, as between them Sarah Batt and Carrie helped to undress and get her into bed.

'Shall I send for Dr Brandwood?' Libby hovered, helpless, one side of her face scarlet, the tears of humiliation still prickling behind her eyes.

Sarah shook her head. 'I don't think so, miss. She's just upset, that's all. It affects her like this. I'll go down and fetch some hot milk. It usually settles her nicely.'

Neither Libby nor Carrie thought there was anything unusual in Sarah talking to them over her mother's head as if Ettie was not only blind and deaf but mentally retarded as well. Sarah's devotion to her mistress was complete, and although the reason was never mentioned it was fully understood.

At twenty-six, Sarah Batt had the figure of a young matron and the face of a twelve-year-old child. Hair as red as a lick of flame sprang from her childish forehead above eyes as blue and shining as bluebells. Coming to the family straight from school, she had disgraced herself by having a baby in 1918, fathered, it was understood, by a soldier who had had his way with her on one of her rare evenings off. The child, a boy, was being brought up by Sarah's parents in a village five miles the other side of the town, and in deference to Sarah's sensitivity the matter was never referred to. The entire episode had warranted a mere five months' absence by Sarah from Westerley, and if Sarah pined for the boy she saw only once a month on her weekend off, the longing was never expressed, not even by a sudden unexplained clouding of the blue eyes or a droop of the wide smiling mouth.

When Sarah came back upstairs bearing a tray with hot milk in a glass and a couple of water biscuits on a tray, Ettie was being ministered to by a twin on either side of her bed, one patting her hand and the other smoothing her brow.

'You must try and understand your father better, she was telling Libby in a weak voice. 'It's not just this strike upsetting him. He's not a young man, and with Willie gone . . .' Her lip trembled. 'With Willie gone there's nobody to take over.' She sighed at the skin forming on the top of the hot milk, only to have the offending layer spooned away by Sarah Batt before the sigh was over. Tears formed in her eyes, and as if following an unseen signal Libby and Carrie nodded to each other, leaned over to kiss their mother good night and left the room.

There was a dividing door between the twin's bedrooms, usually left open so that they could call out to each other, but conferences, shared secrets, long unrewarding discussions about their parents — 'Was Mother really as ill as all that?' and 'How much longer could Libby stand being in the same house as her father?' — always took place in Libby's room.

'That's it! Finished!' Libby declared the minute the door on to the wide landing was closed. 'If it hadn't been for Mother I would have left, for good!' She threw herself down on her bed, twisting round so she could see her reflection in the dressing-table mirror.

'I can't stay here now until the wedding at Christmas. He might have reduced Mother to a nothing, but he's not doing it to me.' She touched her cheek as if still feeling the flat-handed slap. 'He's mad, that's what he is, and it's no use blaming Willie's death for his behaviour. It's eight years since it happened. Eight years since the war ended, and I am sick and tired of being blamed for not being a boy to take over at the mill.' She sat up suddenly. 'How does he know that Willie would have wanted to, anyway? He hadn't shown much aptitude for it when he rushed off to enlist. Why should his being killed have suddenly turned him into a plaster saint?'

Carrie sat down on the dressing-table stool. 'Nobody knows how Willie would have turned out. But he was special, you know that.' She picked up a small leather-framed photograph of a fair young man in army officer's uniform gazing seriously into the camera. 'He only went into the mill for Mother's sake, because that was what was expected of him, and because he knew Father would have created. It was his *kindness* I remember best. Do you remember the time he talked Father into letting us ride bicycles? And how nice he was to Sarah? I think she had a bit of a crush on him. I've seen her blush sometimes when his name is mentioned.'

Libby wasn't really listening. She was still shaking inside from the aftermath of the scene downstairs. It was all very well for Carrie to sit there, calm and reasonable so that it was impossible to know what she was really thinking. Carrie was *too* calm and reasonable, especially lately. It seemed at times as if she was away in some far-off place, dreaming her own dreams, thinking her own thoughts, so that nothing happening around her really touched her. She would come home each day from the private school by the park where she taught History and French, to sit with her sewing, going occasionally to concerts in the town with a friend who still wore black for her sweetheart who had been killed at the front. Carrie, in her twin's opinion, was halfway to being a spinster herself. And she didn't seem to care, which was worse.

'What will you do here when I'm married?' Libby heard herself ask the question suddenly.

'What do you mean? What will I do?' Carrie stared down at the pink flowers blooming on the carpet. 'Stay here, of course. What else could I do? I like my job, and I've got my friends and my music, and you're not exactly going to the other side of the world. Not even to the other side of the town.'

For a long moment the sisters stared at each other, a look compounded of a love that was closer than any mere affinity. Libby, perhaps for the first time, was seeing clearly how it would be for Carrie when she had gone. How it would be for herself, too.

No more bedroom conferences, no more shared amusement at mealtimes when their eyes would meet in silent laughter. No Carrie to run to when she was mixed up and frustrated. No Carrie for Libby to lead, sure that her sister would follow.

'Oh, I *wish* Harry had fallen in love with you instead of with me!' Libby kicked off her shoes. 'You would make a much better doctor's wife that I can ever hope to be. You *tolerate* fools, Carrie, where I . . . where I want to spit in their eye.'

'If you really wish that, then you don't love him.' Carrie went to pick up the scattered shoes, laying them neatly side by side. 'You're not marrying Harry just to get away from Father, are you? Because if you are, that's despicable. He's far too nice for that.'

'I think you love him more than a little yourself,' the demon on Libby's shoulder prodded her to say.

'All right, then, you can have him. I hand him over to you, as of now.'

To her astonishment, instead of flaring up in indignation, Carrie went as pink as the carpet flowers. Turning her back and sitting sideways so that all Libby could see was her straight back and her brown hair twisted into a knot at the nape of her neck, she whispered, 'Suppose you fell in love . . . oh, what I mean is, suppose, just for the sake of supposing, you fell in love with someone not at all suitable — what would you do?'

'Marry him,' Libby said promptly. 'If he wanted me, that is. But then I would never fall in love with anyone who didn't love me. It would be a waste of time.' She started to unpin the heavy weight of her hair, too self-obsessed to realize that her twin was in real distress, that Carrie's fingers were twisting together in an agony of despair. 'I happen to love Harry, not because he is a good doctor with a thriving practice to take on when his father retires, but because I enjoy being made love to by him, especially when he is angry with me. His kisses are exciting when I know he really wants to hit me, like Father hit me downstairs.' She took her brush from the dressing table and began to sweep it through her hair. 'I'm longing to know what it's *really* like when you're married. Aren't you? I wonder if it's as wonderful as it says in books?'

But Carrie, her shoulders heaving, got up suddenly from the stool and rushed through into her own room, closing the dividing door behind her with a soft click.

As she was standing right behind the door, Libby could hear her crying as she turned the door handle, only to realize that the bolt had been shot into place on the other side. With the width of the oak-panelled

33

door between them Libby spoke softly, urgently. 'Carrie! Open the door! Come on. Stop being silly.' She pushed as if by sheer strength she could force her way through into the other room. 'Carrie! I had no idea. I didn't know . . . look, we have to *talk*. I always knew you liked Harry, but I never dreamed . . .'

'It's not Harry.' The whispered words sounded as though they were hurting Carrie to say them. 'Please go away. Libby. I can't talk to you. Not just now. Tomorrow perhaps, but not tonight. There's been enough.' There was a slight pause. 'When Father hit you it was as though he was hitting me, and in a strange way it hurt me more than I think it hurt you. I just want to be alone. *Please*, Libby.'

Libby rattled the door handle in a last protest, then stepped back. What Carrie had just said made indisputable sense. To chastize one twin was to chastize the other, to hit one twin was exactly the same as hitting the other. It had always been so, and always would be, because the bond between them was stronger than could be explained rationally. It was probably the only inexplicable fact that Libby could accept.

But who? When? Where? She tried to bring to mind half a dozen of Carrie's admirers, dismissing each one with a shake of her head. Carrie had never been serious about any man. Libby knew her through and through. Sometimes the ten minutes' difference in their ages stretched into years as far as worldliness and experience went. And yet . . . She moved to the door again.

'You're all right?' I won't go to bed till I know you're all right.'

'I'm all right. Truly.' Carrie's voice was weary, but she had stopped crying. Knowing for once when she was beaten, Libby began to pull the stockinette blouse over her head. It was nothing. Probably some man had stared at Carrie on the tram on the way to school, and, knowing her sister's romantic mind, Libby assumed she had blown it up into a grand passion, fired now by the distressing scene downtairs. Libby raised her voice. 'Meet me after school downtown tomorrow and we'll have our hair cut off, shall we? I dare you.'

'Without telling Father?'

Libby sighed with relief at the normality of her twin's breathless voice.

'Without telling Father. He can't stick it back on again once we've done it.'

'Maybe.' Libby saw the door handle begin to turn, held her breath, then sighed as Carrie changed her mind. She rubbed at the beginning of a headache throbbing between her eyes. Enough was enough for tonight. Too much had happened in too short a time. Now she was alone for the first time since coming back home, she could hear the shouts and angry voices of the men down on the market place. She saw the tall, thin man with black hair fall from the platform, his face as grey as dust, the blood running down his cheeks from the wound on his forehead.

'Oh, God. My coat!' She looked wildly round for a second, then remembered dropping the fawn duster-coat on a chair in the hall as she came in with Harry. The bloodstains down the front would be the start of another violent inquisition by her father if he found it.

Pulling the loose blouse over her head again she opened the door quietly. If she could creep downstairs without being seen she would be safe. She hesitated, peering through the crack in the door.

The house was quiet. Sarah Batt would be in her own room, the little room at the end of the landing, once used as a sewing room but now given over to Sarah so that she could be as near as possible to her mistress. Mrs Edwards, the live-in cook, as deaf as a post, would be snoring her head off in her room on the upper floor, and Martha Cardwell, the maid of all work, had gone to bed long ago to read one of the new confession magazines to which she was addicted. And Oliver . . . he was still downstairs in the billiard room. Libby knew that because the hall light was still on. If she went down now, if she crept down, picked up the coat and ran back, all would be well. Libby bit her lip. It was possible that Oliver would never see it, but then Sarah Batt or Martha might pick it up early in the morning, see the mud and the bloodstains on it, and oh, dear God, she was in no mood for explanations. She moved to open the door, then stepped back quickly as the light streamed out from the billiard room into the hall with its shaded wall fixtures.

Oliver Peel was coming up to bed.

Still as a mouse, Libby waited until she heard his unsteady progress up the stairway, heard him stumble past her door. Opening it a crack she saw him turn, not into his own room at the end of the landing, but towards the shorter flight of stairs to the upper floor, pulling himself up by the banister rail, unfastening his waistcoat buttons as he went.

There was no mistaking it. No mistaking where he was going. Libby put a hand over her mouth. Her heart was beating rapidly as if she had run a race, and she felt sick. She could have been sick right there.

Instead she tiptoed to the foot of the short flight of stairs, heard the click of the door — but whose door? Mrs Edwards, a thin sparse widow of at least forty-five, hiding her deafness with wild and mostly inaccurate guesses at what was said to her? Or little

Martha Cardwell, sixteen, no more, with her giggles and her pathetic efforts to please?

Was she pleasing Oliver Peel right this minute, sitting up in her narrow bed in her nightdress, waiting for him to come to her?

But her father was *old*. He was . . . he was . . . Libby ran downstairs, making no sound, needing to run somewhere, even if it was only to fetch the coat, which now seemed less important.

Back in her room she sat on the edge of her bed, holding the coat pressed to her cheek, rocking backwards and forwards, trying to come to terms with what she had just seen. Oliver Peel was a strong, virile man, with a full-blooded man's appetite. As his wife had lived the life of a semi-invalid since the birth of her daughters, it followed that what he needed he must find. Libby stopped the rocking and let the coat drop to the floor.

With trembling fingers she began to undress, kicking the coat to one side and dislodging the little leather-backed book from the pocket. It meant nothing to her at that moment, but when she was in bed and before she had put out the light, she opened it at random.

'My heart leaps up when I behold a rainbow in the sky; So was it when my life began; so is it now I am a man.'

Libby rippled the closely written pages and read on:

'The day is placid in its going, to a lingering motion bound, like the river in its flowing; Can there be a softer sound?'

Then scribbled at the bottom of the page; 'Wordsworth's poems, each time I read them, seem to be so simple, so fresh, it is as though the dew were still on them . . .'

The book lay on the coverlet as Libby put both hands to her face to feel the tears slipping down her cheeks. Had he copied them out, the tall thin man, at a time when he felt unhappy? And had they helped him, as they were undoubtedly helping Libby now, to release the tensions of an emotion-filled hour with the comfort of tears?

CHAPTER TWO

The lane leading to the main road from Westerley was May green, fields glittering yellow with buttercups stretching away to one side, flanked on the other by the dark brown of ploughed earth. In the soft spill of sunshine the air was scented with hawthorns, and the horse-chestnut tree on the corner had patterned the grass verge with pink petals.

It was a morning for slow lingering, but both girls pedalled away furiously, the wheels of their bicycles turning in unison. Carrie's face was pale beneath the upturned brim of her hat, and Libby was unusually silent.

'Thank goodness Father got away before we came down to breakfast. I couldn't have borne a scene before breakfast.'

Libby put up a hand to hold on to her hat, dislodged by a sudden gust of wind, and the bicycle veered dangerously close to her sister's front wheel.

'I'm not afraid of Father,' she shouted. 'I admit I might have been at times, but not any more.'

She pressed her lips tightly together at the memory of him creeping soft-footed up the stairs to the upper floor, her concentration slipping again.

'Careful!' Carrie wobbled towards the kerb. 'See, there's no tram there. We were right to get our bicycles out. The men *must* have come out on strike.'

'They've got pickets down at the depot.' Libby

started to freewheel as the road sloped downwards. 'They're to get seventeen shillings and sixpence strike pay. How about us going into the recruiting station at the Public Hall and volunteering as conductors? It would be a bit of a lark, wouldn't it?'

'Whose side *are* you on?' Carrie shouted the words back over her shoulder. 'Last night you were talking Bolshie, now you're on the other side. Come on, our Libby. Whose side are you on, really?'

'Both, I suppose.' Libby was loftily unperturbed. 'I was talking to a man on the market place last night. He wasn't a Bolshie, but he knew the miners couldn't go on and on talking. After five years of trying they've had enough!'

For the next mile or so they pedalled on in silence. Carrie was busy with her own tremulous thoughts. Soon she would leave Libby to turn into the rhododendron-fringed drive of the Park School. Already pupils wearing the scarlet blazers and caps with black velvet trimmings were hurrying in twos and threes along the wide pavements. The majority of them were girls from the big houses on the out-skirts of the town, their fathers the business men, lawyers, bankers and professional men who could afford the fees to have their children privately educated. Soon she would wheel her bicycle into the shed at the back, hurry through the back door of the red-brick building and up the wide oak-panelled stair-case to the staff room, taking off her hat as she went, her heart beating in anticipation and hope that Mungo McDermot, the English master, would be their alone. Anticipating the smile on his lean face as he turned and saw her.

When it actually happened it was almost like the re-run of a film, except that this morning he broke their rigid rule to take her in his arms and kiss her mouth.

It was not a very long kiss, and, terrified of being caught, Carrie did not respond. Instead she pushed him away and went to stand at the other side of the room with the width of a table between them.

'You mustn't do that here! You promised!' Her face was full of fretting anxiety. 'I passed Mr Eccles on the stairs, and Miss Clayton has arrived. I saw her bicycle in the shed. I came on mine,' she added desperately, trying to channel the conversation into some sort of normality. Mr Eccles, the headmaster, had once sacked a woman teacher on the spot for coming to school in too short a dress, only to have her reinstated the week after by the intervention of her father who was on the board of governors. Besides, Carrie knew she was no Libby, defiant just for the sake of being defiant. What was happening between her and Mungo McDermot sent the blood flowing nervously through her body with an emotion that was half fear and half thwarted passion. She steeled herself against the slumbering desire in his eyes, making a determined effort to change the subject.

'Isn't the strike awful? Libby went down to hear the speakers on the market place last night, and she says it will go on for months. Father's workers are joining in unofficially before they are even called out. Libby says she doesn't blame them.'

Mungo wasn't in the least interested in the strike or in what Libby Peel might say or think. Ever since the day he had seen the two sisters together, walking home from church in the dusk, and had raised his trilby hat to one of them without being completely sure it was Carrie, he had disliked intensely the inescapable fact that she was an identical twin.

To Mungo, Carrie Peel was unique — she had to be. He felt the familiar stirring of desire as he watched

41

her take off her short jacket and saw the high swell of her breasts straining against the button fastening of her cotton dress. His Carrie was as clean and fresh as bleached linen, and when he held her close she smelt of sun-warmed apricots. He took a step forward, only to see her back away as she picked up a blue-covered register and held it in front of her like a shield.

'I hate it when the evenings grow lighter,' he whispered with one eye on the door. 'But I have to see you alone. Meet me after school.'

There was no need to tell her where. As the long cold winter had turned into spring they had found a place and made it all their own. It was an old summer house, nestling behind a high brick wall in the grounds of an eighteenth-century manor house, too neglected and overgrown with ivy and trailing weeds to be of interest even to stone-throwing boys. There had been talk for years of turning the manor into a school or a nursing home, but with every passing year it grew more derelict, seeming to sink deeper into its shroud of ivy.

There was an inside bolt on the door of the tiny summer house, an ancient bamboo lounging chair, a relic of glories long since past, and two small windows over which Mungo sometimes fastened pieces of corrugated paper. Once through the rusty gate and inside the summer house they were totally private and excitingly alone. As it was no more than a quarter of a mile from Westerley, and as no one ever thought to query the time a teacher stayed late after school, it was the perfect rendezvous.

'I can't meet you today,' she whispered frantically. 'I'm meeting Libby in town.' She put up a hand to the tidy bun at the nape of her neck. 'We are going to have our hair cut short.'

'Oh, no!' Mungo forgot to be circumspect, raising his voice as he leaned across the table. 'I won't allow it! Not your beautiful hair!' He had noticed the way she had said 'our' hair, not 'my' hair, and his hands clenched into fists as he thumped them on the table. 'Let your sister do as she likes, but you stay the way you are.'

'Then I will never again mistake one of you for the other,' was what he really meant. 'Tomorrow then,' he whispered as Miss Clayton, the gym mistress, burst into the room, bouncing on her crêpe-soled plimsolls, her shiny face eager with suspicion as she darted quick glances from one to the other.

'Good morning, Miss Peel. Good morning, Mr McDermot.' She walked over to the cupboard, her shoes making little sucking noises on the parquet floor. 'What's the matter with *him*? He looks as if he's lost half a crown and found a sixpence.' She stared at the door as it closed behind Mungo. 'Bit shirty, is he, because we teachers haven't struck?'

'He isn't always very well, Miss Clayton.' Carrie walked towards the door with the register, deciding to tell Libby she had changed her mind about her hair, yet knowing that when the time came she would follow her sister and submit to the scissors like a sheep submitting to the shears.

In the mean streets surrounding Libby's school no birds sang. There was no rhododendron-fringed drive leading to the squat two-storey building, its grey stones weathered with grime, just a square asphalt playground penned in from the street by iron railings. The children wore mostly hand-me-downs, and the only sport was drill, with the pupils marching round and round the playground, swinging their arms to the shouted instructions of whichever teacher happened to be on duty at the time.

The three classes for the younger children were held in one big room, split into sections by sliding glass doors, and because Libby's class of seven-to-eight-year-olds was at the far end it could only be approached through the two outer rooms.

Margaret Bottomley, the infants' teacher, was already at her desk, sorting through a pile of grey colouring paper, her neat head with its two earphones of plaited hair bent industriously over her task.

'Well, did you go?' She pulled at the drooping skirt of her brown jumper suit, torn between the desire to look modern and the shame of showing her fat knees. 'I heard there was a bit of a to-do. You would have been far better coming with me to the Labour meeting. They let us in with the men. You'd be surprised how much money they've collected from their ha'penny a week door-to-door collections. We're going to win, Libby, make no mistake, this time we're going to win.' She lowered her voice. 'There's a rumour that Ellen Wilkinson might be coming up to give us a talk, and you know what they say about her? She's a woman for women all right.'

Libby wrinkled her nose at the sour smell which always seemed to be at its worst in the infants' classroom. It was the smell of neglect, of ammonia, of clothes not washed often enough, and made worse by a flannel of cress growing sourly from one of the high window ledges.

'I can't join, Margaret, not while I'm living at home.' She rubbed the side of her face reflectively, remembering with shame the sharp sting of her father's flat-handed slap. 'I'm with you all right, but I can't openly flaunt my faith.' She stared down at the bare boards of the classroom's slightly sloping floor. 'It's different for you. You're independent.'

'You mean I live at home with a mother who couldn't care less? You mean I haven't got a man? Not a father nor a fiancé to keep me in line?' Margaret Bottomley's thick neck flushed an unbecoming red. 'Especially a father who is a capitalist.' She glared at Libby with an expression of contempt. '*You* are only playing at it, Libby Peel! You think you can identify, but you can't. *You* didn't have to leave school at thirteen, then work in a factory by day and swot at nights for years and years to get your place at college. Then when you were there you didn't have to exist on a grant so small you were patching the inside of your shoes with cardboard. Libby Peel, it took me six years to be a teacher, so no wonder I am *independent*!'

She banged the register down on her desk, and made no attempt to pick up a pen when it rolled to the floor. 'You should be thinking of joining the Conservative Club, not the Labour movement. Stanley Baldwin's more of a Labourite than you!'

'Have you heard of a man called Tom Silver?'

Libby had no idea what had made her say that. All she knew was that somehow she had to put a stop to her friend's chip-on-the-shoulder tirade. She liked and admired Margaret Bottomley, knew that her life was drab, her out-of-school activities given over to caring for a querulous invalid mother and her newly found burning enthusiasm for the women's section of the Labour Party. But the flushed quivering face with its thin tight lips filled her with distaste.'

'I met him last night,' she went on miserably. 'He was hit by a flying cobblestone, and I thought that as he seemed to be . . . as he was so obviously wrapped up in the cause . . .' Her voice trailed away.

'Tom Silver? Tom Silver?' Miss Bottomley pursed her top lip so that her incipient moustache darkened into ugly prominence. 'I should think I do know him. He's been victimized twice for what he believes. He'd die for his members.' Tom Silver would. He's a Father of the Chapel, and turned down the offer of a job as Secretary of the Trades and Labour Council not long ago. Was *he* speaking, then?'

'No.' Libby turned her head towards the windows as the playground bell clanged out. She was furious with herself for mentioning the name she had seen written inside the front cover of the small notebook, and could not think why it had just popped out like that. Now Margaret Bottomley would worry at it like a puppy with an old slipper until she found out more. For someone who boasted she could get along without a man, thank you very much, Margaret took a marked interest in them, Libby thought uncharitably. She imparted a bit more information with an obvious show of reluctance.

'I don't think he was too badly hurt, though he looked awful. He was knocked unconscious, and his face was bleeding.' Her eyes half closed at the disturbing memory of that grey face and the blood trickling down the side of his nose. 'He dropped a book. I've got it at home as a matter of fact.' She sighed. 'His name and address were in the front.'

The children were marching into their classrooms now, to stand by their desks for morning prayers before the slides were dragged across by the boy monitors from the top class. Miss Thomson, a large John Bull type woman, was easing her ample behind on to the piano stool, but Margaret would have her say, and Libby knew it.

'Bring the book tomorrow.' The pale eyes shone with eagerness. 'I have to go up to the infirmary in the evening to visit a friend. I'll take it off your hands, find Tom Silver and explain. Save you posting it on.'

'I hadn't quite decided . . .' Libby turned away, knowing that as far as Margaret was concerned the matter was settled. She moved through into her own classroom.

She paid no attention at all to the religious doctrine gabbled by the children. She sang 'Fight the Good Fight' with her head held high, her lips moving without any sound coming from them. Damn and blast Margaret Bottomley with her interfering nosiness! Libby closed her eyes as the morning prayer washed over her. She hadn't even finished reading the poems penned in that neat firm handwriting. And the ones she had read seemed to be such an antithesis of the man himself. She remembered his teasing laughter, his scorn of her middle-class ignorance and all he thought she stood for, and she remembered the feel of his arm holding her in tight protection against the swaying crowd. She had thought . . . she must have thought subconsciously that she would return the book herself. To thank him, that was all, merely to thank him for helping her, and maybe to show him that she was serious in her need to identify with the strikers. It didn't matter, of course, what he thought of her, one way or the other, but it would have been — it might have been interesting, at least.

'Amen,' intoned the headmistress, and Libby went to take her place on the raised dais which supported her desk. She waited until the children were seated, hands on heads, patiently obedient.

'Take out your arithmetic exercise books.'

As the dividing glass slides were dragged back into the closed position, thirty-eight children banged back their desk lids. Libby began to set out the sums on the blackboard while the ink monitor, a smug boy wearing round spectacles and an air of gloating power, walked round the desks with a tray, dropping the grey inkpots into their waiting wells.

The squeaking of the chalk on a greasy patch of blackboard set Libby's jangled nerves quivering. She felt suddenly penned in, trapped, as if out there through the high windows things were happening, wonderful, terrible things that could change the course of the country's history. She made a mistake and rubbed at it furiously with the board duster. Banners were being paraded, open-air meetings held, blacklegs routed, picketing organized, collections raised for those without a few pennies put by. Miners, railwaymen, transport workers, engineers, weavers and spinners, all united in the common cause.

And the only futile pathetic gesture of defiance she, Libby Peel, was going to make that day was to have her hair cut short at half past four . . . She pressed too hard on the chalk and it broke into two pieces in her fingers, causing her to whip round in anger at the girl in the front row who had dared to laugh.

'Do you two know what you look like?' Oliver Peel's lips curled with sarcasm, and his words had a slurred edge to them.

He had been drinking before dinner, Libby concluded, shutting himself away in the billiard room straight from his return from the mill, scarlet-faced and glowering. Carrie shot her a warning glance, so with difficulty Libby held her tongue.

Because each twin possessed an identical unruly cowlick at the hairline, Libby's on the right and Carrie's on the left, the hairdresser had trimmed the front of their glossy hair into fringes, club-cutting the rest to jaw length so that it swung forward into their cheeks.

Mesmerized by the two faces staring at him from the long mirror, he had snipped away, first at one head then the other, matching each snip so that the end result had been to make the two girls look even more alike than when they had first walked into the newly thriving salon in the town's main street.

'Like two bloody peas in two bloody pods,' he was to tell his wife that night. 'Till the cheeky one smiled, then you could tell the difference. But before that there *were* no difference!'

Now Oliver faced them across the dining table, with Martha Cardwell serving the roast lamb in her usual fluttery manner, her movements jerky and disconnected. Had a glance passed between the peak-nosed girl and Oliver as she hovered by his shoulder with the jug of mint sauce? Libby shivered with distaste. Or was Mrs Edwards, out in the kitchen sliding the milk jelly on to a platter, counting the hours till her maister crept up the stairs again? Disgust sharpened her voice so that Carrie looked up in dismay.

'What *do* you think we look like, Father?' Calmly Libby passed the dish of chopped carrots to her sister, ignoring Carrie's eye signals. 'At least it won't take hours to dry now. When we went up to Mother's room she said she thought it looked rather nice.'

'Then your mother's a fool!' Oliver tucked a white linen napkin into the front of his waistcoat, threading it between two buttonholes, then picked up his knife and fork. 'Right then, Libby Peel. Since you ask me I will tell you what you look like.' He pointed his knife at each twin in turn. 'You look like a couple of street women! A pair of whores. All you need is a feather boa apiece, stuff on your faces and your skirts even shorter than what they are. And I'll tell you something else. You wouldn't get past the Town Hall without being picked up by two men who have nowt else to do at the moment but roam the town looking for trouble!'

'Father!' Carrie blushed bright red, but Libby waited until Martha had walked out of the dining room. Turning her head to make sure the door was safely closed, she leaned forward and said softly, 'Martha Cardwell has her hair cut short, Father. Even shorter than ours. Do you think of her like that? Does Martha look like a whore, Father? Is that why the word came to your mind?'

Carrie gave a little gasp, but Libby kept her gaze steady on her father's face. For a moment their eyes locked, then Oliver was the first to turn away. His high colour deepened to purple and his left eyelid began to twitch. For a startled moment Libby was sure he was going to hurl the contents of the gravy boat straight at her.

'Get on with your dinner.' He was blustering and she knew it. 'There's been enough bother down at the mill today without you riling me. You'd be smirking the other side of your face if you knew how many contracts I stand to lose. Aye, and it would be jam butties for your dinner, not roast lamb. You'd soon lose them Bolshie ideas if you had to get your snouts in the trough along with the rest of them. I've had enough, more than enough, for one day.'

As the meal continued in uneasy silence, Libby knew she had guessed right. It was to Martha's bed her father crept at night when the house was shrouded in darkness and his family slept.

Triumphantly she speared a sliver of lamb on the prongs of her fork, telling herself that never again would she walk in terror of this man, this shouting bully of a man who just happened to be her father. She watched him carefully as he gulped his food without chewing, controlling his emotions with difficulty. Refusing the Lancashire cheese which followed the pudding, he threw down his napkin with an obvious gesture of relief and walked quickly to the door, slamming it behind him. The slam was echoed by the banging of the door of the billiard room.

Libby smiled at her sister. 'Well, that wasn't too bad, was it?' She pulled a dark wing of hair forward, laughed as it barely reached her nose, then squinted down at it. 'The only way to defend oneself against a bully is to *attack*. I'm always telling you that, Carrie.'

'All the same, I wish you hadn't said that.' Carrie rolled up her napkin and slid it tidily into the silver ring marked with her initial. 'Father will never forgive you. He's not stupid, you know.'

'Aren't you going to have any cheese?' Libby helped herself to a crumbly wedge, then stretched out a hand to the bowl of fruit. 'It shut him up, anyway.'

'It wasn't just an innocent remark, though, was it?'

Libby froze with a grape halfway to her mouth. Oliver's reaction to her words had in no way spoilt her enjoyment of her meal, but what Carrie had just said, and the *way* she had said it, made her push her plate aside, her appetite gone.

'I don't quite know what you mean.'

'Oh, yes, you do.' Carrie's eyes were downcast. 'I saw the way you watched Martha when she was serving Father, and I guessed what was going on in your mind.' She twisted the rolled napkin round and round in her fingers. 'I've known for a long time what was going on. My bedroom is directly underneath Martha's and Father's voice and laugh aren't exactly on the quiet side.' She breathed on the silver ring and

51

rubbed at it with her fist. 'So you see,' she added softly.

'But you never said!' Libby stared at her twin in disbelief. 'You kept it all to yourself!' She twisted round in her high-backed chair. 'Why? I thought we always told each other things. Especially anything as important as that.'

Carrie shook her head. 'Not always we don't, Libby. And besides . . .' She glanced over her shoulder towards the door. 'I don't think it *is* all that important, if you must know.'

'Not important?' Libby forgot to keep her voice down. 'Not *important*' Our father making love to the housemaid? A girl young enough to be his daughter, his granddaughter, even! You must be mad!'

Carrie put a finger to her lips as the door opened to reveal Martha Cardwell, cap awry, tripping over what could only have been the pattern in the carpet as she came forward with a tray to clear away.

'Mind if I side the pots now ?' She hovered uncertainly. 'I've been a bit run off me feet all day with Mrs Peel having all her meals in her room along with Sarah, and Mrs Edwards getting off early to the second house pictures. She's gone to see Zazu Pitts at the Olympia.'

'That's all right, Martha.'

It was Carrie who smiled at the tall clumsy girl, Carrie who led the way down the hall and into the big front lounge, there to carry on the conversation as if they had never been interrupted.

'Listen, Libby. Our mother has been an invalid since we were born. That is over twenty years ago, and in all that time — for as long as we can remember, anyway — Father has seen to it she's been taken care of. He even let Sarah come back after she'd had her baby because he knew how fond

52

of her Mother was.' She patted the cushions on the chesterfield for a bemused Libby to sit down beside her. 'Think, Libby. Father used to be a keen Rotarian and a Mason, but he seemed to lose interest in them after Willie got killed in France. Do you ever stop to think what it's like for him down at the mill? Father isn't a man who can easily trust, so he takes on far too much, and it's sometimes as hard being a boss as a worker, you know.'

'Hah! Talk about middle-class righteousness!' Libby's voice rang with scorn. 'I suppose you'll be saying next that Father's workers have a struggle to keep fed because of their own inadequacy? Bosses have been saying that for hundreds of years. Anyway, what has all that got to do with. . . ?'

'Everything. You know as well as I do that the boom in cotton didn't last long after the war. Father was a broken man because of Willie, and Mother being the way she was, and it was only natural that his weavers turned against him when he had to reduce their wages by forty per cent four years ago. Of course they were bitter, so they set against him.' She patted Libby's hand. 'Father is an anti-union boss, so they are only loyal to him for fear of losing their jobs. It's clear to me. Six of one and half a dozen of the other, so why can't you make allowances for him?'

'Allowances for that?' Libby jerked her head upwards. 'And why tell me what I know already? Father tells us often enough, but a lot of it is his own fault. Father treats his workers as if they were the scum of the earth. No wonder they hate and loathe him. He treats you and me and Mother as if we were the scum of the earth, too, just because we're women. His sun rose and set with Willie, and just because he hasn't a son to follow him into the mill he takes it out on us.'

Carrie agreed. 'But have you ever stopped to think how lonely he is? He needs comfort. All men do, even the toughest of them. Can he turn to Mother? To you and me?' Her cheeks grew pink. 'He is a *man*, Libby. A strong normal man, and he has to get it — affection, love, softness — from somewhere.'

'You mean lust.' Libby hardly knew how to contain herself. Carrie was so serious, so intense, pointing out the reason for things as if she were ten years older and not ten minutes younger. She got up to stand in front of the fireplace. 'You'll be saying next that they are in love! Our father and that — that unfinished girl who started as one of his weavers. He brought her here, Carrie, I distinctly remember him bringing her here himself and telling Mother she was half-starved and having to sleep four to a bed at home. The great philanthropist! Him! Our father treats his weavers as if they were mere extensions of their machines. They're not even human beings to him! And now he's using Martha, that's all. *Using* her, Carrie. So how can you defend him? What's got into you, for heaven's sake? And, oh God, don't cry, please don't do that.'

Libby went to sit beside her sister, her own throat tightening. It had always been the same. If one twin cried then the other followed suit. She placed an arm round Carrie's shaking shoulders and drew her close.

'You're not upset just because of Father, are you?' She whispered as she had whispered through the closed dividing door between their rooms the night before. 'What is it, Carrie? Is there someone — some man you are trying to tell me about? Someone at the tennis club? The church?' Her darting mind considered one acquaintance after another, dismissing every one as impossible. So many of the boys they had known had gone straight to France from university, never to return. And those who had come back seemed remote and strangely indifferent, as if what they had seen had marked them for ever. Libby frowned. There was more here than met even her penetrating eye. She had seen nothing, suspected nothing — she had dismissed Carrie's strange behaviour of the night before as trivial.

'It's not a married man, is it, Carrie? You wouldn't be such a fool as that?'

Carrie raised a face stiff with pain. 'Being a fool doesn't come into it. Not when you love someone as I love him.' Tears rolled down her cheeks as she groped in her pocket for a handkerchief. 'His wife has no feeling for him. None at all. She is unbalanced, Libby. Insane.' Her voice broke on a sob. 'Sometimes he has bruises on his face, and once his eye was closed right up. She *attacks* him, Libby, and he is so gentle, so sensitive, he just has to take it. He didn't go to the war because he . . . because his beliefs wouldn't let him fight back. He just lets her scream at him. Oh, Libby, it's so awful.'

'You mean he was a conchie?'

Carrie bit her lip and nodded. 'Yes, he was, but what he had to face took as much courage as if he had rushed out of the trenches with a fixed bayonet. For what he believed to be right he went to *prison*, Libby. And now that dreadful so-called wife of his keeps reminding him of it, taunting him. The war has been over for eight years but she will never let him forget that he stayed at home. They were newly married and she *wanted* him to go. Imagine.'

'And he stands there and lets her hit him? Oh, my sainted aunt!' Libby opened her eyes wide in disbelief. 'What kind of a man is he, for heaven's sake?'

'He's good. That's what he is.' Carrie jumped up from where she sat, twisting the handkerchief round and round in her fingers as she had twisted the napkin ring not ten minutes before. Now there was a desperate pleading in her voice. 'Try to understand, Libby. At least *try* to understand. He has no one, not one person in the world to turn to.'

'Only you.'

'Only me. She has even tried to turn his son against him, a boy who was born at the end of the war, deaf and dumb, as if fate hadn't been cruel enough.'

'I thought you said he was in prison?'

Carrie flapped a hand from side to side impatiently. 'He was sent home because of his health. His lungs. He had a mild form of consumption, and he's so thin and so pale. Oh, Libby, you don't know. You just don't know. His wife sleeps in a separate room, and he told me once that if only he could wake up one morning and see the face of a woman who loved him on the pillow beside him, he would think he had died and was in heaven.'

'*Your* face?' Libby found she was holding her breath. 'You're not . . .' She hardly knew how to go on. 'You wouldn't be such a fool as to . . . oh, Carrie, you wouldn't?'

'I don't know!' Carrie's voice rose to a wail. 'He needs me so much!'

'And like Father, he's only human?'

Libby was so angry she wanted to grab her sister by the shoulders and shake her until her teeth rattled. 'Oh, Carrie, you silly, stupid — I don't know what!' For once words failed her. 'Do you want to end up like Sarah, with an illegitimate child? Do you? Because that's what will happen if you let him, whoever he is, have his way with you. If he can't control his own wife, then he'll hardly be able to control himself any other way.' She fought the blush rising to her cheeks. 'Oh, Carrie. I'm engaged to be married. Harry . . . we're getting married at Christmas, and he . . . we want it to be the first time for, well for *me*.' Harry was in the army and, well, it's different for a man. Biologically different.' She gave up, and threw up both hands in a wild gesture of exasperation. 'Besides, where would you go? Not to his house, I'm sure. In the back of a car?'

'Stop it!' Carrie backed away as if physically trying to ward off anything else her sister might say. 'You're so — so *clinical*. You don't know what loving means, to talk like that. You might be going to get married, but you don't know! Oh, I wish I'd never told you.'

As the door bell rang she was running upstairs to shut herself in her bedroom, and when Harry Brandwood was let in by a dishevelled Martha with a dish towel over her arm, Libby was waiting for him in the lounge with hands outstretched in a dramatic greeting.

'Oh, Harry. I can't tell you how glad I am to see you.' She turned her face into the comforting smell of his tweed jacket. 'Father slapped my face last night, and now I've quarrelled with Carrie. She looked at me just now as if she hated me, and I can't tell you anything about it because it's a secret, a terrible, terrible secret.'

Harry, an expression of resignation on his round ruddy face, held her close and stroked her hair. 'Now then, love. You've quarrelled with Carrie before, but you know the arguments between the two of you never last. What were you doing? Waving the red flag at her? You know Carrie has no social conscience, and I told you last night the strike will succeed or it will fail, and there's nothing you can do about it.' He smiled into her hair. 'And if your father slapped you I'm sure it was only a little smack and you must have provoked him.' Suddenly his voice trailed away as he realized something about his beloved was very different. Gently he pushed her away. 'Libby! You've had your hair cut off!' His blue eyes twinkled. 'It's lovely, darling. Absolutely lovely. Spiffing. You look about seventeen years old.'

Libby put up a hand and touched the swing of her cropped hair. The appeal to her vanity and the admiration in his eyes steadied her as nothing else at that particular moment could have done.

'Do you really like it?' She gave him a trembling smile. 'I wasn't sure . . .'

'I love it and I love you, and I wish I could take you out somewhere so that I could show you off, but I'm on my way to see yet another patient with strike fever.'

'Strike fever?' Libby widened her eyes, then snuggled close again.

Harry's voice was teasing. 'Remember last night when you told me it was only the downtrodden poor who suffered? Well, it seems you were wrong, Libby Peel. I can't speak for the majority of the rich bossmen in this town, but one coal owner who shall be nameless worked himself up into a mild heart attack this afternoon. One of his miners actually stormed his way into the pit office and declared that the outcome of this strike would be the nationalization of the whole of the coal industry. Result — one poor downtrodden boss practically foaming at the mouth, in need of urgent medical attention.' He put up a finger. 'No, not a word. I haven't finished yet. And I'm off now to minister to Mrs Amos Birtwistle at Gawley Hall, prostrate with a migraine because her dress for the tennis party on Saturday is holed up somewhere in a siding, and likely to remain there till the railways start running again. So you see.'

He was so solid, so reassuring, such a comfort that

Libby actually smiled properly before surrendering to one of his pleasantly thorough kisses.

Harry relaxed. His Libby wasn't always as easily calmed down as this, and she had seemed to be genuinely upset. He surfaced for a moment, then bent his head to kiss her again. And Carrie with a terrible secret! Docile, gentle Carrie with a secret too terrible to be told — how Libby liked to dramatize everything! Her twin was as open as a spring-lit day, so passive as to be merely a shaded echo of her sister. He touched the tip of Libby's nose with his finger.

'I think Mrs Amos Birtwistle is quite taken with me, especially when I assured her that with her grace and charm she was bound to be the belle of the tennis court with or without the missing dress. If she invites us to the party on Saturday, shall I accept? I'm free after lunch. I hope.'

Libby walked with him to the door. 'Oh, yes, please Harry. I've never been to Gawley Hall, and we haven't worn our new tennis dresses yet.' She patted the new fringe. 'They are an exact copy of Suzanne Lenglen's, with orange bandeaux to go with them.'

'We?' Even as he asked the question Harry knew what the answer would be.

'Me and Carrie, of course. You'll wangle an invitation for her as well, won't you darling? It's just what she needs.'

Harry ran down the steps to his waiting car, seeing himself for one slightly hysterical moment arriving at Gawley Hall with two Libbys in tow, identical in white dresses with orange bandeaux round their short dark hair.

'Love me, love my sister,' he muttered good humouredly, then turned to wave before driving back down the drive and heading the car towards the road leading away from the town.

As soon as Libby went back into the house she remembered her intention of going down to the tram depot at the weekend to volunteer as a driver. She started upstairs, then hesitated for a second with one hand on the banister rail. Ah, well . . . She tossed her head, enjoying the feel of her hair bouncing freely. It had been a crazy notion anyway, especially in view of the fact that she was on the side of the strikers. And she was. Most definitely. She was thinking about them at that very moment, walking with earnest workworn faces to their meetings, tightening their belts in determined preparation for the long weeks and months of struggle to come. Oh yes, there would be lots of ways she could help, she decided vaguely. If the teachers remained uncommitted she could drive a tram during the long summer holiday, in an impartial way of course, not really identifying with either side. And besides, going to Mrs Amos Birtwistle's party wasn't going to influence the outcome of the struggle one way or the other. And the orange bandeau might need a tuck in the back now that her hair was short.

When she saw Tom Silver's notebook lying on her dressing table where she had left it before going down to dinner she picked it up, held it for a moment while running her fingers over the binding, then almost without volition pushed it deep into her school purse. Margaret Bottomley would take it to him at the infirmary tomorrow, report on his progress, and that would be that.

Tom Silver, tall and dark with his teasing eyes and strong arms . . . he had thought her beliefs shallow. He had openly laughed at her, and made a kissing movement at her with his lips. She felt her cheeks grow pink at the memory. And if he *had* copied out bits of poetry, bits that reached out for rainbows and soothing comfort, then it didn't make him anything out of the ordinary. He probably only did it for effect anyway, like a lot of working-class men who fancied themselves as amateur botanists, going on hikes into the country on Sundays with shabby haversacks on their backs.

Libby opened a drawer and, taking out a strip of brightly coloured material, slipped it over her head so that it covered the fringe and showed her eyes in the mirror, bleak with surprising despair.

Snatching it off she threw it from her, then stared down at the purse with its bulge showing where the notebook lay.

He was rude and mocking and arrogant, and she would never see him again. And she didn't care. . . . Well, of *course* she didn't care. For heaven's sake, why should she?

CHAPTER THREE

It was very hot in the summer house in the late afternoon. Mungo had taken off his tie, and was feverishly trying to unbutton the front of Carrie's cotton dress even as she pushed at his hands, begging him to stop.

She wanted him to; at least part of her wanted him to, but he was, as usual, in too much of a hurry. She needed, first of all, to be reassured that what they were doing was right, wanted to hear him saying once again that as neither of them was hurting anyone, where was the harm?

'She isn't getting suspicious about you having to stay late at school? Surely she must be?' Carrie always referred to Mungo's wife, Beatrice, as 'she', finding herself unable to say the name. Her eyes clouded over with worry.

Mungo's mouth fastened hungrily on her own, forcing her lips apart. Then when he surfaced he said bitterly, 'She wouldn't give a damn if I never went home again.' His hand slid inside Carrie's dress as he pulled down the strap of her underskirt. 'Oh, God, how I love you, sweetheart!'

With a frantic determination Carrie tried to stop thinking about the wife whose existence she had never really admitted to the reasoning part of her mind. There was an ache deep inside her, a quivering, burning sensation, but when Mungo's hand crept lower she pushed him away and sat up, hot and distressed. She pulled the ribbon strap over her shoulder.

Groaning, he pulled her close again. 'I *have* to, darling. You can't keep tormenting me like this. Nothing will go wrong. I *promise*. I give you my word.' He closed his eyes so that she saw the long eyelashes fan out on his cheek above what looked like a recent scar.

'She did that?' Carrie's fingers were gentle as she traced the tiny half-moon shape.

'Yes. And this.' He turned his head so that she saw a scratch running down from beneath his left ear. 'She wasn't quite drunk enough last night. Properly drunk she has no fight in her, but halfway gone she can fight like a hell-cat.'

'Have you ever tried hitting her back?'

'The boy,' he said softly. 'I have to endure in silence because of the boy.'

'But he's deaf!'

Mungo shook his head sadly. 'I did retaliate once, and she ran into the boy's room and showed him the marks on her wrist, faint marks which faded while he was staring at them in horror.' His head drooped, and when he raised his eyes Carrie was dismayed to see that they swam with tears. 'She pointed at her wrist, then at me, then she clung to the boy as if he were the only thing standing between her and a further attack. And Edwin suddenly rolled on his back making terrible noises. It was dreadful. I sometimes catch him watching me warily as if he were just waiting for me to turn violent again.'

Carrie put her arms tight round him then and rocked him as she would a child, pity welling inside her. 'Oh, my love . . . oh, my love,' she whispered.

Mungo relaxed against her with a sigh. 'So you see, for Edwin's sake, I have to endure. Because he can't hear or speak it's impossible to know what he's thinking, but he watches me. I feel his eyes watching me.'

'And you would never leave her?'

It was a question to which Carrie knew the answer. This lonely man could never bring himself to desert a handicapped child. And his wife would never leave her home and give up the husband who was no more to her than a meal ticket.

Carrie pressed her lips close together in an attempt to hold back her own tears. Being in love, she had always believed, was meant to be a joyous thing; a meeting of eyes, a sharing of private jokes, laughter on a summer's day.

She remembered Libby coming into the house wearing her engagement ring for the first time. Holding out her hand, turning it so that the light caught the three diamonds, whirling round the room, skirts flying, hugging her twin, shouting 'You next Carrie! You next!'

But *this* love, this powerful overwhelming obsession, weighed on her like a spreading net, enmeshing her in strands of despair. Mungo was there in her thoughts from the moment she opened her eyes in the morning. She would sit with her mother in the evenings and imagine he was there sitting in a chair, smiling at her, telling her of his love in his beautiful voice.

Sometimes she would try to tell herself it was hopeless. She would steel herself to tell him the same. Then the next day, at school, she would see him, brown hair waving back from his high forehead, shoulders stooped, and she would be engulfed in a wave of tenderness so great that she would have to hold herself back from running to him.

'We can't go on meeting like this without something happening,' he was saying now, making no attempt to touch her again. 'I tell you, Carrie, the way I want you is killing me. And being alone like this, in our own little hideaway, I — I haven't got that much control, sweetheart.' He ran a finger round his unbuttoned stiff collar as if he were choking. 'A more ruthless man would insist, but I'm not like that. I love you so much I'm prepared to wait for you to come to me.' His smile was tinged with sadness. 'I'm a very patient man, Carrie. A deeply frustrated man, but a patient one.'

Carrie felt as if she were choking too, but her emotion stemmed not from frustration, but because she knew Mungo was waiting for her to make up her mind. The heat inside the tiny building was sticky; she could feel the perspiration sliding down her sides. And they had been there for longer than usual — the light had shifted as it seeped through the cardboard shutters. She sighed. Ironically it was Mungo's very restraint that made her hesitate. If he had taken her forcibly, *made* her give in by bruising her mouth with kisses, she would have . . . oh, God, at least she *thought* she might have . . .

Slowly she began to button up her dress. It could never happen like this — with Mungo waiting patiently for her to decide. She didn't want to decide; she wanted the decision to be taken from her, and now he was going to be angry again. She could see his face working as though he had a tic.

'But I will,' she whispered as he buried his face against her. 'It's just that, just that . . .' Her voice tailed away as she remembered.

She could still recall the look on Sarah Batt's face on the day she had admitted she was going to have a baby. A shy schoolgirl of fourteen. Carrie had come into the kitchen at Westerley to see Sarah sobbing uncontrollably, trying to hide her rounded stomach by holding her clasped hands over it, then running upstairs to pack her bag and leave Westerley. True, Sarah came back, but her child was being brought up by his grandmother and only visited by his mother once a month. And Sarah was so ashamed of her past that she flatly refused to talk about her son. It was as though what she had done in a moment of passion eight, nine years ago had filled her with a shame that would linger for the rest of her life. Carrie shivered.

'What are you thinking about, darling?' Mungo's voice was gentle, and though normally Carrie would tell him exactly what she was thinking, this time she shook her head.

Just how did you tell a man as unworldly, as sensitive as Mungo that every time he wanted to make love to her *properly* she became a fourteen-year-old schoolgirl again? A girl in a pudding-basin hat gazing in horror, pity and fascination at a housemaid with tears running down her cheeks and her arms wrapped round her swollen stomach.

'I think we must go soon,' she whispered. 'It must be very late.'

'To hell with time,' Mungo muttered, taking her into his arms again.

They were eating earlier than usual that evening at Westerley because Oliver had to go down to the mill again.

'They should rechristen Bridge Mill,' he thundered, striding into the house around six o'clock. 'Moscow Mill it should be called.' Then he shouted through the swinging door leading to the kitchen, 'Look sharp with it, you two lasses. I want to be away in half an hour at the most.'

'Where's Carrie?' He came into the lounge with

a glass of whisky in his hand, then he narrowed his eyes at Libby. 'I can't make out why she's always stopping on late. You can get home in good time, it seems.' He jerked his chin upwards. 'Is your mother coming down for her dinner tonight?'

'Why don't you go up and ask her yourself?' was what Libby wanted to say, but the most important thing was to stop him going on about Carrie. So she took a deep breath and let it out again with a sigh. If her father found out that Carrie was meeting a married man after school, a man who had stayed at home during the war instead of going out to France and being killed like Willie, then murder would be done. Libby was sure of it.

'Why have you to go back to the mill, Father?' She assumed a bright expression. 'Is the strike affecting you badly?'

Oliver swilled the whisky round and round in his glass, then took a deep swallow. His ill-humour was such that Libby guessed he was prepared to release his frustration, even to the extent of discussing the situation with her.

'If I have to fill the mill with tramp weavers I'll keep those looms running,' he almost growled. 'And if I have to run the place without tacklers, than I'll do just that.' He went to refill his glass. 'They reckon there'll be well over a thousand looms stopped as a result of the strike whichever way it goes. But what can you expect when the union representative's a damn Bolshie? This strike is right up his street, isn't it? He hasn't got enough up top to remember that his bloody union has fought and lost two strikes in the last year against necessary wage cuts. Don't the stupid fools realize we're in a period of economic chaos, and that cotton exports are one of the hardest hit? Haven't they the sense to see that the cotton which used to go to India is either produced there, or got from Japan?'

He went to stand with his back to the fire. 'It's like what it was at the beginning of the war. Then everybody got excited and jumped about, desperate to do something. It's a sort of hysteria. Why, one of my tacklers told me his wife has started her own soup kitchen already, making broth and getting cheap offal from the butcher. All her neighbours are collecting coppers for her, and they've got enough to take round to the co-op bank.' He snorted. 'And they have the nerve to say they are starving!'

Oliver patted his stomach. 'Where the devil has Carrie got to? We'll have to start without her if I'm to get back. I'll have a word with Joe Postlethwaite next time I see him.'

'Joe Postlethwaite?' Libby was still stalling for time. 'I've never heard you mention that name before, Father.'

'On the board of governors at Carrie's school. I'll have it out with him about the extra hours his teachers have to work. Teachers' hours are supposed to be civilized, they're not miners or factory workers. Go into the kitchen, Libby, and tell them we want to start. I can't hang about like this another minute.'

'They're not miners or factory workers! Oh, dear God . . .' Libby was muttering to herself as she walked down the long passage to the door leading to the kitchen. 'Oh, Carrie, why do you have to be so stupid? Why? And where *are* you?'

'Miss Carrie's just wheeled her bike round the back. She says she had a puncture and had to walk all the way home with it.'

Mrs Edwards was putting the finishing touches to a pink blancmange, and Libby was sure the look she gave her was knowing. 'I'll go upstairs and tell

Mother,' she said, and left the kitchen before any more could be said.

'Carrie's just come in,' she told Ettie, and saw the relief on her mother's face as she got up from her dressing table.

'I'm much better today, dear,' Ettie said wistfully. 'I am so glad we will all be sitting down to a meal together. Your father is so busy, and Carrie has so much extra work to do at school these days, then you are often out with Harry . . .' She pulled at the strands of faded hair covering her forehead. 'I sometimes feel that you have all made separate lives for yourselves, and just come home to eat and sleep.' She smiled at Sarah hovering in the doorway. 'I can manage the stairs myself, Sarah. I mustn't let people think I am an invalid.' She left the room.

Libby sat down on the edge of the bed, her hands for once still in her lap. Then suddenly her mood changed as she watched Sarah pick the hairs from Ettie's tortoiseshell brush and stow them away in the hair-tidy on the dressing table. With her head on one side, her restless mind ticking over, she studied the matronly solid figure through narrowed eyes.

'How can you stand it, Sarah? I mean having to be with Mother all day long? It would kill me. Do you never feel you want to break away to go and do something quite different?'

'Oh, no, Miss Libby. I'm right fond of your mother and I like looking after her. We have a nice understanding, me and your mother,' Sarah bustled forward to strip the green satin cover from the bed, twitching at it in a pointed way so that Libby was forced to stand up.

It was an unspoken rule that Sarah's 'trouble' of eight years ago was never referred to, but now the worry of Carrie's behaviour filled her twin with an anxiety that bordered on a terrible half-acknowledged fear. Surely Carrie wasn't going to make the same mistake that Sarah had made all those years ago?

'How is your little boy, Sarah?' Libby asked the question, not quite admitting the association of ideas, even as she told herself that Carrie would never . . . not with a married man. Not out in the fields . . . she shuddered. 'We never hear anything about your son. How old is he now, Sarah?'

'Eight, Miss, coming up.' Sarah had her back turned as she shook out her mistress's nightgown and laid its crêpe-de-Chine folds over the top sheet.

Libby persisted. 'What does he look like? Is he dark? Red-haired like you? Small for his age? Big for his age?' She smiled. 'I know. Why don't I get the doctor to drive me over to your parents' cottage on one of your weekends off, so you can introduce him? It seems so silly that none of us have seen him. There's no shame, Sarah, not to my mind anyway. You mustn't feel there is.'

'No!'

Libby blinked as Sarah turned round, her face contorted with what seemed to be fear. 'He's to be let be. He's happy as he is with his grandma and grandpa, and me going home regularly. I won't have him *shown*! I won't!' She gripped a corner of her apron in both hands and twisted it round. 'An' if you insist I will give up me job, and then where will your poor mother be without me?' The blue eyes filled with tears. 'There's only me what cares about her, really. *He* doesn't . . .' — this with a jerk of her head towards the door — 'an' you and Miss Carrie, you're so full of each other you don't need nobody else.'

She started to back out of the room. 'In all this time your mother has never once asked me a thing like that. She knows when to let be. She cares about folks' feelings, while you . . .' Overcome, Sarah rushed out of the door, leaving it wide open behind her.

'Oh, my sainted aunt!' Libby opened her eyes wide at her reflections in the tripled mirror over Ettie's dressing table, then, shrugging her shoulders, she went out on to the landing.

There she bumped into Carrie, warm and pink, with hastily brushed hair, and verging on hysteria in her twin's opinion.

For a second they stared at each other; in another second they would have had their arms round each other as Carrie's obvious distress communicated itself to her sister. But Oliver's loud voice boomed up the stairs.

'Will somebody tell me what you two are doing up there? The soup is on the table, though why anybody wants soup on a warm evening like this I don't know!'

'And I heard you come in, Carrie,' he added, as soon as they were all seated round the big dining table. 'Teachers are supposed to finish at four o'clock, aren't they?'

Silently, with head bowed, Carrie spooned her soup. Silently Libby watched her, noticing the way her twin swallowed with difficulty, left hand trembling as she lifted the spoon to her mouth.

'I'm sorry, Father.' Carrie dabbed at her mouth with the large damask napkin. 'We had a meeting and I couldn't get away.'

'Meeting?' Oliver hacked away at the joint of beef placed in front of him by the young maid, Martha Cardwell. 'Don't tell me the teachers are going to be the next to come out on strike?' He passed a plate over to his wife, then went on carving. 'There's bound to be Labourites amongst your lot. You know what

71

will happen if you come out, don't you? If I know Joe Postlethwaite and his committee, he'll have the bloody school closed, and there won't be a job to go back to when this lot's finished. Joe won't have any truck with sympathy strikes. The miners might have a grievance, a slight one at that, but nothing that can't be settled with negotiation. God damn it, you don't know when you're born!'

'It was nothing like that, Father.'

Libby held her breath as she calculated that Carrie was close to breaking down. And if she did, if she were foolish enough to burst out crying and rush from the room, then God help her. Even Oliver's pre-occupation with the strike and his worries about the mill wouldn't stop him from rushing after her and shaking the truth out of her.

Quickly she came to one of her swift decisions. Drawing Oliver's fire to herself, she said, 'Maybe if you hadn't put your weavers working on piece rates at a lower return last year, they would have been content to stay at their looms. They are bound to make comparisons when the rates vary from mill to mill. Now they could be grasping their chance to show their disapproval, wouldn't you say, Father?'

When Oliver dropped the lid of the vegetable tureen on to the table with a clatter, widening his eyes before letting fly with a spate of angry words, Libby knew her ploy had worked.

'It's all right now,' her eyes signalled Carrie. 'He'll be on his way out down to the mill soon, then you can give way.'

'But not before,' she prayed silently. 'Dear God, not before!'

Tom Silver, sitting up in his high bed in the long ward of the town's infirmary, saw Margaret Bottomley the minute she came through the doors, but couldn't quite place her. Her face, with its eager, thrusting jaw, was familiar, but he couldn't for the life of him put a name to it, so he leaned his head back against the piled pillows and closed his eyes.

'Mr Silver?'

He opened them again to see her standing by his bed, pale eyes shining, her upper lip with its shadowy moustache quivering with enthusiasm.

'Yes?' He sighed. Now he had placed her. She was one of the band of supposedly liberated women who tried to talk like men. And this one even looked like a man. Peevishly, because his head was aching and he had been told that morning that his immediate discharge was out of the question, he sucked in his bottom lip and tried to look even more ill than he felt.

But Margaret pulled up a little hard chair and sat down, pulling her skirt over her knees. As if he wanted to stare at her legs, Tom thought with distaste, then widened his eyes as she opened her purse and took out the little brown leather book. Forgetting his act of invalidism, he sat bolt upright.

'How the. . . ? Where on earth. . . ?' He held out his hand, only to have his wrist tapped playfully.

'Don't say you hadn't missed it, Mr Silver?'

Women with faces like that shouldn't try to look coy, he thought uncharitably, shrinking away from her unwelcome touch.

Margaret wrinkled her nose. 'Your little scribblings are safe with me, Mr Silver. I guessed the book meant a lot to you, so at the first opportunity I have returned it to you.' She tapped the book with a gloved finger. 'It was handed to me, so I thought it was the least I could do.' She smiled. 'I must say you look in better shape than I expected you to. My . . . my informant told me that the last sight she had of you

73

was when you were stretcher-bound, being handed into an ambulance.'

Tom put a hand up to his bandaged head. 'Oh, yes. The market square. It must have dropped out of my pocket.' He winced with the effort of sitting upright, and sagged down against the pillows again. 'The crowd got a bit out of hand and decided to use me for target practice, and the next thing I knew was when I woke up in this bed. The damnable thing is I can't find out what's going on.' A sudden stab of pain drained the colour from his already pale cheeks. 'I have been trying to get hold of the reports from union headquarters, but from what I hear even the reports contradict each other.' He frowned, then winced as the frown pulled at the stitches in his forehead. 'My lads will be counting on me. They'll be at sixes and sevens without me there. And there's nothing I can do, lying here like a wet lettuce.'

He suddenly looked much older than his years, as if the whole responsibility of running the strike had been his alone. 'Those men throwing stones, they weren't helping. If we succeed, and we *have* to succeed, it has to be done through patience, not by force. Violence never gets anyone anywhere.'

'Oh, I do agree.' Margaret was too insensitive to realize that the grey-faced man was talking more to himself than to her. She beamed. 'They say Ellen Wilkinson could be paying us a visit up here. Imagine! She's a real fiery speaker, and she knows what she's on about when she talks about the injustices done to the workers. There'll certainly be a full house if she does come. I know I'll be there, that's for sure.'

Tom was very tired. He did not feel like talking politics with this woman. He reminded himself that she had brought the book back out of kindness, so, speaking slowly as if every word pained him, he thanked her, closed his eyes and waited for her to go.

'It wasn't exactly me who rescued your book, Mr Silver.'

Margaret did not want such an interesting encounter to end like this. It was a long time since she had talked so intimately with a good-looking man like Tom Silver. He was a real charmer, in a masculine way of course. There was a touch of the Byron in the way his hair fell forward over his forehead like that, and his eyes were the most unusual shade of grey. Not flint grey, or steel grey, but a soft gentle grey, like rain clouds.

With difficulty, because her plump knees were already touching the bed, she moved forward. It was growing dark outside, and because the trams were so unreliable she would have a long walk home. She sighed. The very minute she turned her key in the door her mother would call out, 'Margaret? Is that you?'

As if it would or could be anyone else! She would have to take her mother's nightly cup of cocoa upstairs, then help her out of bed and on to the commode, averting her eyes from the yellowed toenails and the stick-thin legs. And oh, how she hated the lack of modesty that seemed to have afflicted her mother in her old age. Sometimes Margaret saw in the little body slumped on the commode a picture of how it would be with *her* one day, except that she, Margaret Bottomley, would had never known a man's touch, would be all alone.

'It was Miss Peel — Libby Peel, who asked me to bring your book back,' she said, not quite truthfully, and was rewarded by a sudden flash of interest in the grey eyes, and the semblance of a smile.

'Ah, yes, the teacher who wanted to see how the other half lived, all fierce and unenlightened. She got home safe then? I've wondered about her.' He kept his eyes tight shut, but this time he was not escaping. Instead he was recalling the small girl with the silly straw hat. He was remembering the earnest way she listened to the speakers, and the softness of her, small-boned and somehow fragile, as he held her tight against him when the crowd swayed and the stones began to fly.

'She teaches at the same school as me. Her father owns Bridge Mill.' Margaret gave the information reluctantly, sensing that her captive audience had somehow dismssed her more surely than if she had got up and walked away down the ward. It was always happening. A pretty face, a shapely leg, and she, Margaret Bottomley, might as well not exist.

She hurried on with a bit more information. 'Libby, Miss Peel, is getting married at Christmas to a doctor. Dr Harry Brandwood, in practice with his father up Park Road.' She laughed a trill laugh at variance with her bulk. 'I know exactly what you mean about Miss Peel being unenlightened, Mr Silver. It would be impossible for the likes of her to understand the present conflict, or the needs of the workers. The Peels of this town won't go short of a bob or two, no matter how long this struggle lasts. *Her* family have never known what it is to want. It's still Them and Us, Mr Silver, and always will be. When the likes of you and me say we are hard up we mean we are *hungry*. When Libby Peel thinks she is hard up she means she has spent her monthly dress allowance in the first two weeks. *She's* never had to turn a skirt, nor steam a hat to stop the brim from curling, and she's never had to be the sole support of her mother from the day she left college.'

It was with a deep sigh of relief that Tom heard the bell clang out heralding the end of visiting time. He knew he should have been feeling pity for the sallow-faced woman now gathering gloves and bag together, because a lot of what she had just said was right. It *was* still Them and Us, and as far as identifying with hardship and poverty went, well, he had no difficulty there, God knew. But he hoped, oh, he hoped most fervently that he would never spit out his grievances with his lips twisted into a bitter line. His mission, if mission was the right word, was to improve the lot of his men, to help lift the lower-paid workers from despair, not sink them down into a sea of envy and spite against those who had more.

And now the ache in his head was worse. There was a sour taste in his mouth as the depression closed down on him again. The pudding-faced lass, she was looking for justice, and he could have told her that justice was merely a word. Because if things were just and fair and the scales of fortune balanced out the bad with the good, how was it that he had come back from France unscathed? And why had his young wife, the girl he had married on his last leave, been blown to pieces in an explosion at the grey spread of munition factory buildings where she worked?

No, there hadn't been much justice there, by all that was holy.

And yet, at that very moment, what wouldn't he have given to be sitting at the wheel of a car, the kind of car Libby's fiancé was sure to own, with her by his side, the wind loosening that brown hair of hers, blowing it across her eyes as she laughed and pleaded

77

with him not to drive so fast? If that was envy, then he was guilty of it all right.

Reaching for the little brown book, he opened it at random and read:

'How pleasant as the yellowing sun declines, and with long rays shades the landscape to mark the birches' stems all golden light, that lit the dark slant woods with silvery white. . . .'

And was comforted.

CHAPTER FOUR

'Forget the past; look to the future,' the King said when the strike was called off on 12 May 1926.

'GREAT WORKERS' VICTORY' the *Daily Herald* declared with banner headlines, but Libby was not too sure about that.

'So much for your revolution,' Harry had teased. 'Now, if there really had been a revolution, a real Lenin-flavoured uprising, then the government would have completely lost control. And far from doing that, the government were in control all the time, from start to finish. He smiled. 'The bluff failed dismally, Libby. You must agree there.'

'The miners haven't given in. They never will give in,' Libby had retorted, but some of the fire had gone from her in the past few days. Carrie's refusal to go to the tennis party and her subsequent moping about the house with a white face and haunted expression had, of course, affected her twin. Harry knew this, but was determined not to probe. His beloved would tell him all about it, whatever it was, in her own good time.

He was, above all, a patient man.

Far more patient than Mungo McDermot, who at every opportunity tried to catch a few minutes alone with Carrie at school.

'Why won't you meet me in the summer house?' His face was lean with suffering. 'I can't go on like this.'

'I've told you why!' Carrie, with one eye on the door of the staff room, put the width of the table between herself and Mungo's wandering hands. She blushed and hung her head so that all he could see was the parting in her shiny brown hair. 'That last time we nearly . . . we almost . . .'

The break in her voice told him that tears were not far off, and his own voice was suddenly hoarse. 'But we didn't, did we? We stopped just in time.'

'What we did was just as bad.' Carrie felt a hot flush of shame wash over her as she remembered the urgency of his hands, the weight of his body, the searching open-mouthed kisses, and her own frantic struggles. 'The next time I might give in, and oh, Mungo . . . I must never give in. It's wrong and besides, I'm scared, so terribly frightened.'

'I would never hurt you, darling, in any way.'

He was saying that just as the door opened and Carrie, blushing scarlet, made a pretence of collecting books together. She reached for her register with a trembling hand. Then, as Miss Clayton, walking as though her heels were sprung, bounced into the room, Mungo walked out, his thin shoulders drooping in the jacket that always seemed too big for him, a neglected, lonely-looking man, with brown hair straggling over his collar.

'I wonder if his wife will come to Open day?' Miss Clayton, cold eyes shrewd beneath the cap of her Eton-cropped hair, flopped down in a chair. She produced a packet of cigarettes and a box of matches from the leg of her knicker elastic and blew a perfect smoke ring into the air. 'Have you ever met her, by the way?'

'No, I've never met her.' Carrie longed to escape, but knew that if she did so it would only arouse suspicion. No teacher worth her salt ever emerged from the staff room unless she was on mid-morning duty at the drinks table set out in the hall if it was raining and outside if it was fine. So she compromised by walking over to the window and staring out.

Under the long verandah pupils were queueing at a trestle table for mugs of cocoa, hot or cold milk, still lemonade and biscuits. She saw Mungo, head bowed, standing behind the table, supposedly checking that each pupil dropped two pennies into the round tin provided. But it was obvious that his mind was in some faraway place as he stared down, then lifted his head as if he sensed she might be watching him.

'She's a lot older than him.' Miss Clayton addressed Carrie's unresponsive back. 'And she wears the trousers, from what I've heard. Though I believe she's good to that poor little lad of theirs.' Carrie heard the clatter of a tin ashtray falling from the table to the floor. 'She won't let him go into an institution anyway, so she can't have much of a life cooped up with a child like that all day. Not much fun for her.'

'Nor for him,' Carrie said, then bit her lip as if she wished the words unsaid.

'For old McDermot?'

'He isn't old.' Carrie turned round, knowing she was saying too much, but powerless to stop.

'Our Mr McDermot is nearly forty, if he's a day.' Miss Clayton flicked ash in the vague direction of the ashtray. 'He gives me the creeps, but then maybe he's your type?' She narrowed her eyes. 'I must say you seem to be pretty thick with him, but he looks to me as if he'd been grown in the dark. Like a mushroom, with a big white head and wobbly legs. How he ever had the nerve to stand up and be counted and declare he was a conchie during the war I just can't think. I wouldn't have thought his guts were as strong as my garters.' The cropped head went to one side. 'Wasn't your brother killed in France?'

Carrie nodded.

'Then how *can* you be so friendly with a little squirt like that? Maybe you're sweet on him? Is that it?'

Carrie felt her face flame, and knew that she had gone scarlet. 'I am not sweet on him! What a thing to say! I just feel pity for him, that's all.'

'And pity is akin to love, so they say.' Miss Clayton stretched out her legs in their black lisle stockings and checked that the seams were straight. 'Good God, Carrie, there's no need to look so flummoxed. Your murkey secret is safe with little Angela.' Smiling, she licked a finger and made the sign of the cross on her throat. 'But I'd watch out for that wife of his, if I were you. God, I wouldn't like to meet her up an alley on a dark night. She's a fat woman with a face like the back of a fish cart, and shoulders on her like an ox. Get the wrong side of *her*, and she'd flatten you as soon as look at you.'

She sat up suddenly as Carrie moved blindly towards the door. 'Where are you off to in such a hurry? Our cocoa will be here soon. Steady on! The fire bell hasn't rung, has it?'

But Carrie, the small heels of her court shoes tapping on the wide polished stair treads, was flying as if pursued by devils. The monitress, on her way up with the tray, had to step quickly to one side to avoid being knocked over. Her face was a study as she watched the quiet Miss Peel hurtle past her.

Carrie hesitated by the door leading out to the playing fields; then she turned left into the corridor leading to her form room, her heart beating like a drum.

Angela Clayton *knew*. That blab-mouth had guessed, so it followed that the rest of the staff knew too, and oh, dear God, if it ever got to the ears of the headmaster then heaven help both her and Mungo.

Sitting down, she stared at the rows of desks and at the far wall with the map of the world with the Empire filled in with red crayons. Soon it would be Empire Day. The Union Jack would be flown from the flagpole in the grounds, and the children would be decked out in costumes representing the various countries. They would march round the field singing 'Land of Hope and Glory', and Mungo would recite a patriotic poem in his beautiful voice. She would be expected to play her part, and the truth was she did not care. The sun could set on the Empire, never to rise again, and she wouldn't give a damn. At the moment Carrie could not see an inch farther than the horizon of her own immediate distress. She shivered. It would have to be left to people like Libby to worry about the Empire, and the miners and their lock-out, and the men who would lose their jobs as a result of the strike.

Libby never got involved in anything over which she could not retain absolute control. Libby had fallen in love suitably, she would marry Harry, stop work and throw herself whole heartedly into the role of doctor's wife, while she Carrie, would still be making up her mind whether to share her life completely with the man she loved. And if she did surrender, she would have to forget that he had a wife and a handicapped son, and she would have to live in monthly terror in case anything had gone wrong.

Burying her face in her hands, Carrie tried to face up to a future as bleak and grey as the gathering clouds outside.

Libby, at that very moment, was opening and

reading the letter which had arrived at Westerley by the morning post. She had seen it on the hall table when she came down for breakfast, recognized the handwriting immediately, and pushed it deep into the pocket of her skirt. Surprised at the way her heart beats had quickened, she had said nothing to Carrie. If her twin could have secrets, then so could she.

'I will never be another Sarah!' Carrie had said through clenched teeth the last time Libby had tried to question her. 'But I can't talk about it. This is something I have to solve for myself, Libby. Can't you see?'

But no, Libby could not see, and when Harry had told her to leave her sister to get on with her own life, she had turned on him in fury.

'So you think I should just sit back and let Carrie make a mess of her life! Is that it?'

'Yes.' Harry had been adamant. 'You can't live your sister's life, and she cannot live yours. Some time the division has to come.'

'But how is it possible to divide two halves that are really one person?' Libby asked that in all seriousness, leaving Harry shaking his head in honest bewilderment.

'A pity I'm not marrying both of you.' He had pushed out both elbows, moving his head from side to side as if he were glancing from one bride to another. 'I take thee, Libby and Carrie Peel,' he had said, and the comical expression on his ruddy face had forced a smile on her lips.

Now she was furtively hiding the letter beneath the covers of a book as she sat alone at her desk during the mid-morning break. Outside the children were chanting their games in the square of concrete playground beyond the tall windows.

'The big ship sailed through the Alley-alley O, the Alley-alley O . . .'

Libby smiled to herself. All through prayers and the first lessons, she had been acutely aware of the letter in her pocket. Through the glass partition she had seen Margaret Bottomley standing on her raised platform beating time as her class sing-songed their way through their multiplication tables. And she had felt a strange sense of triumph that he had written, not to Margaret, but to her.

Taking out the single sheet of paper, she read:

Dear Miss Peel, I would like to thank you for returning my notebook by one of your teaching colleagues. It used to be a habit of mine to copy out verses of poems which appealed to me, and the book is doubly precious because I had it with me in France. As you can imagine, the words flowed like honey through a mind distracted by so much that was distinctly unpoetic. I am afraid I haven't written in the book lately. I am distressed by the premature ending of the strike and afraid for the miners in their determination to go on fighting. It will be a long and bitter struggle for them, and who knows what hardships their families will have to face? Yours sincerely, Tom Silver.

There was a PS at the end. 'One good thing came out of the strike, due to the suspension of the press. Six hundred and ninety-seven extra books were issued from the public library. Somehow that is a cheering thought, *n'est-ce-pas*?'

Libby read it quickly, then again more slowly. She looked at the address. Number 14, Meadow Street. She sighed. What a name for a street where no grass grew, a street backed by the tall menacing chimney of her father's mill. A street of Victorian houses, left to rot and grow shabby as their original owners moved out to the semidetached villas spreading from the centre of the town. Lodging houses, let into rooms. . . . With a quick decisive movement Libby reached for the register with the list of addresses at the back.

Yes, she was right. Meadow Street was where most of the 'theatricals' lodged. Two of the children in her class were living there temporarily at number 20, and attending the school whilst their Troupe of tiny Tappers played in the *Paint Box Revue* at the Palace Theatre. They were undersized girls, with straight hair club-cut into fringes, and were the envy of the rest of the class in their black patent-leather bar-strap shoes and their short white socks. Frowning, Libby folded the letter and pushed it back into her pocket. Then for the rest of the long day she imagined him, tall and thin, coming home from work to one of those shabby houses set in a street where babies played bare-bottomed in the gutter, and housewives gossiped on unwashed doorsteps, arms folded across their pinnies.

No wonder he scribbled verses in his little brown book, verses about streams where fish darted like pins spilled from a paper, where birds sang, and green fields starred with daisies stretched as far as the eye could see.

'What's been eating you all day?' Margaret Bottomley was waiting for Libby at the school gate at the end of an afternoon which had seemed endless. 'You've had your lot sitting with their hands on their heads at least twice. Have you had a row with the doctor, then?'

Libby smiled sweetly. 'Harry and I are always agreeing to differ, if that's what you mean, but we don't count them as rows. He likes me to have a mind of my own.'

'He's an unusual bloke then.' Margaret sniffed. 'I went to a meeting in King George's Hall last night. Councillor Smith was talking about the lock-out. He seemed to think they had a first-rate organization going for them. He actually gave it out that any man in dire need could go to the public office for assistance if needs be. Then he urged them to put their pride in their pockets and think of their children. A real stirring speech it was. You should have been there.'

Libby shook her head. 'You know I can't go to Labour meetings, not while I'm still living at home. Harry might be tolerant, but my father certainly is not.' She glanced up at the sky. 'I'm only putting up with it until I get married at Christmas. Father lost a big contract on account of the transport difficulties in the second week of the strike, and we are all having to suffer for it.' She started to walk away. 'I'm with you in principle, Margaret, you know that, but I'm either too much of a coward, or too canny, to flaunt my beliefs openly at the moment. It just isn't worth it.'

Margaret felt suddenly very cross as she mentally calculated the cost of Libby's simple dress and coat. The plain tailored lines set off her figure to perfection, and the fawn leather of bag and shoes picked up the narrow binding round the neck of the navy blue linen outfit. Not for Libby Peel the necessity to keep a dress and coat like that for best. *Her* wages did not go to pay the rent and the coal bill, or to keep a sick mother on the tasty food her delicate stomach craved. Mrs Peel was an invalid too, but she was waited on hand and foot by a maid. And it wasn't fair. Nothing in this rotten world was fair.

'Tom Silver got his cards when he went back to

work after coming out of the infirmary,' Margaret said. 'The management said it was because the compositors and the machine minders were going to have to go on short time anyway. But it's obvious that Tom Silver was victimized. He knows it, and they know it.' The expression on the plain face darkened with disgust. 'The worst thing is that it's doubtful whether any other paper will take him on. The bosses don't like trouble-makers, especially now when things were going from bad to worse. Mr Silver was there at the meeting last night, looking absolutely awful. He never spoke, just sat there, quiet and on his own. They say his nerves have been shot ever since he came back from the war. So where's the justice? I ask you, Libby! Out there in France, fighting for his country, losing his wife, and now this.'

She was talking quickly as they walked down the street, head jutting forward oblivious to the effect her words were having on Libby. When she turned at last and saw the expression on Libby's face, noticing how she had paled beneath the brim of her neat straw hat, she stopped dead on the pavement. 'You all right?'

Libby took a deep breath as her hand went instinctively over her bag where the letter was now hidden away. Oh, that proud man! He had written to thank her for the book, and he hadn't said a word about losing his job. Not a word. 'But he wasn't like the others.' Her voice came out hoarse. 'He was just standing here, Margaret, that night, listening quietly. He tried to stop them rioting. He wasn't there to make trouble. It wasn't like that at all.'

Margaret's pale blue eyes were fishlike in their curiosity. So there was something that could ruffle Libby Peel. 'Nobody said Mr Silver had got the sack because of that night, Libby. They've been laying off men from the compositors' room for a while now, and they say the rest will be going on short time. No, it was because he was the Father of the Chapel, and a troublemaker in their eyes. Now the strike's over I bet their next union man will be a little chap without the strength to waft a fly off his rice pudding.'

'The management don't choose.'

'Hah! But they have ways and means. I'll tell you something for nothing, Libby. This strike has done the workers more harm than good, you'll see. They are back where they started, and probably farther back than that.'

Margaret was on her orange box again, stabbing the air with a finger and for once Libby made no attempt to interrupt. She was back in control of her emotions, and now she was asking herself why the news of Tom Silver's dismissal had affected her as if she had been dealt a blow to the stomach. He was just a stranger, and yet when he had made that cheeky kissing movement with his lips she had wondered how it would be if he had really been making love to her. Oh yes, she had thought about it often. In the middle of the night, lying awake, she had imagined it. . . . He had come into her life briefly, and she had thought that was the end of it, but now, hearing that he was in trouble, Libby knew she would have to see him again. 'I'll leave you now, Margaret,' she said, and walked away, her feet dragging and her thoughts awhirl.

Libby's opportunity came on 23 May, the day before the Empire Day celebrations at the school.

With a little moan, Britannia fainted over her trident at the dress rehearsal as she was being wheeled round the playground in a go-cart trimmed with flags and flowers made of crêpe paper. The part had been given to one of the two theatrical girls working in the town that week and attending Libby's class, a girl who had a loud, carrying voice and an air of dramatic confidence which gave her speech a weighty significance.

After lessons were over and when the girl came to, the headmistress beckoned Libby over.

'Would you mind taking her home, Miss Peel? She lodges at number twenty, Meadow Street. I don't think there's much wrong with her but overtiredness.' She shook her gunmetal-grey head. 'You know my feelings about these half-timers, but I suppose their parents think they know what they are doing.' She stared with distaste at the patent-leather shoes. 'I suppose pushing them on the stage does guarantee that they are dressed well and eat three meals a day, but what they can ever hope to achieve in the way of a good education beats me.' She smiled her watery smile. 'Meadow Street is near your father's mill, isn't it? Maybe you can get a lift back home with him?'

Libby nodded. The headmistress had obviously never heard that Oliver Peel *walked* to and from his mill — never realized that the family did not own a car, only hired one when circumstances necessitated such extravagance.

'Of course I'll take her home,' she said, and in the cloakroom she pushed the child's arms into the sleeves of a blazer and pulled on a panama hat, adjusting the elastic underneath the trembling chin.

'Right then, Amy. Off we go.' And taking the small hand tightly in her own she set off down the sloping street.

In that particular part of the town well over six thousand houses had been built in the period from 1878 to 1918. They were terraced houses, spotlessly clean in the main, a semicircle of mopped flagstone in front of each door, with a step and window bottom edged with a flourish of cream or yellow stone.

But Meadow Street was different. At one time the three-storeyed houses had been lived in by professional gentlemen. There was a flight of steps up to the front door, and a basement kitchen where maids had once worked. Now the original owner had moved to new houses on the outskirts of the town, leaving the street to fall into shabby disrepair, the houses let off into single rooms with the landlady and her family occupying the ground floor.

Libby handed over the white-faced child to a middle-aged woman who answered the door of number 20. She told her, in her teacher's voice, that on no account must Amy be sent back to school until she was feeling better.

'I think she may be sickening for something,' Libby said, then before she could give herself time to think she turned and walked quickly back down the street to number 14.

This time the woman who answered her knock was wiping her hands on her apron, red puffy hands that looked as if they had been immersed in soap and water for a long time. Her eyebrows flew up towards the scragged-back hairline of her greying hair as she stared at the well-dressed young woman standing on her door step. He mouth dropped open in a round 'O' of surprise as she waited for Libby to speak.

'Mr Tom Silver?' Libby's recently authoritative manner deserted her completely as she spoke his name. 'Is he in, do you know?'

The woman nodded. 'Aye, he's in. Top floor, the door opposite t'stairs.' She stood back, mouth still agape, as Libby thanked her and climbed quickly up the uncarpeted stairs, wrinkling her nose at the smell of stale cooking and a sweeter smell she failed to recognize.

She was horrified. The house was worse than anything she had expected, far worse. Brown paint peeled off doors, and the banister rail felt greasy to her touch. Heart thudding now like a drum in her chest, she knocked at the door across the top landing and waited.

When it opened almost immediately and she saw Tom Silver standing there, she put a hand to her mouth. The man was ill. He had been discharged from the hospital, but the line of purple stitch marks on his forehead stood out like swollen veins against the pallor of his skin.

His surprise was as great as that of the blowsy woman downstairs, and all the more apparent because he tried to conceal it.

'Well, well! Miss Peel?' He pretended to look round. 'Where's the basket?'

Libby blushed. 'Basket? What basket?'

He put a hand as if to support himself against the door frame. 'The basket of goodies brought by the lady of the manor to succour the starving poor. That's what you've come for, isn't it, to dispense a little charity?'

Libby's blush deepened. 'As a matter of fact I *had* to come this way. A few doors down the street. A child in my class was taken ill at school and I have just brought her home, and I thought . . . I thought that as I was so near I would call and see how you were.' She was gabbling, unsure of herself for once. 'I got your letter last week, but you didn't say . . . you never mentioned losing your job.' A door opened along the landing and a tousled curious head peered out. 'I just wanted to say how sorry I was,' she finished desperately, 'and to say that if it was because of what happened that night I am willing to write to your editor . . . to your manager and explain. Many I come in?' she added, with a sideways glance along the landing at the half-open door.

'Welcome to my humble abode.' Tom Silver held the door back for her to enter. Then with an exaggerated gesture he took a handkerchief from his pocket and dusted off a chair. 'I'm right out of sherry unfortunately, but I can offer you a cup of tea if you don't mind it being in a mug.'

'Stop it!' Libby sat down gratefully, trying to still the trembling of her legs. 'Why must you always mock me?' She lifted her chin. 'I bet you didn't mock Margaret Bottomley when she brought the book back to you. I know you didn't because she was full of it.'

'Full of what?' Tom sat down opposite her and raised a quizzical eyebrow. 'You're trying to tell me she was impressed by my charm? Sorry, love, but if you've come on her behalf then you're wasting your time. Miss Bottomley is just not my type.'

Libby clenched her hands into fists. She glanced round the room, at the single bed in the corner, the tiny fireplace, the round table covered by a skimpy cloth, the rows of bookshelves, and the curtain concealing what was a makeshift wardrobe. 'Look, Mr Silver, I'll say what I have to say, then I'll go.' She bit her lip. 'You are obviously far from well. That cut on your head might be healing, but you were concussed, and concussion can do funny things. You're depressed and bitter, and I want to help if I can. It was awful, your coming out of the infirmary to find you job had gone. You didn't deserve that. It wasn't fair.'

'But life isn't fair, is it, Miss Peel?' He smiled. 'You've had your hair cut. Take off your hat and let me see.'

Mesmerized by the steady gaze of the dark eyes Libby did as she was told.

'It's lovely,' he said at last. 'It suits you. Before, it swamped your face, now it shows up your bone structure. You will never look old with cheekbones like that.'

His eyes were the strangest eyes she had ever seen. Piercing, dark and yet kind. She shifted in her chair. This interview was not going at all the way she had planned it should. She had expected him to be, well, *grateful* for her concern and offer of help, and instead he was so much in command of the situation that she felt about eighteen, being interviewed for a place at teaching college. She coughed nervously.

'With your permission I will go and see your boss at the *Weekly Times*. If he did what he did because he thought you were behaving in an unseemly manner that evening . . .' Her voice tailed away at the sound of her stilted phrases. Oh, God, what a mess she was making of things . . . she could see his face darkening in anger.

'You will do no such thing, Miss Peel!' I absolutely forbid you to go to my place of work. My recent place of work.' He slapped his knee hard with the flat of his hand. '*I* could have gone cap in hand if I had wanted to. I could have told them things they don't know. Things *you* don't know.' He waved a hand to encompass the shabby room. 'God knows I wasn't earning much, but when I was on full time it paid the rent of this room, and I was able to send fifteen shillings week to my late wife's mother.' He nodded. 'So you know about my wife, then? I'm not surprised. I don't suppose there's much your Miss Bottomley doesn't ferret out.'

He leaned back, closing his eyes for a second

as if the effort of talking was too much for him. 'My ex-mother-in-law lives alone, crippled with arthritis, and I have done what I could over the years. Her next move is into an institution, but with my contribution she was able to keep her independence. Now . . .' He spread his hands wide. 'And don't go putting me down in your book as a benevolent man, because I'm not. I am of the opinion that we are like animals when it comes down to basics. I helped my ma-in-law because I like her, I like her a lot, and if things had been different she would probably have been living with us.' He got up and walked over to the window. 'Do you know, they hadn't even the decency to call me into the office! Just sent a note by the office boy. Out! Finished!'

Then suddenly he turned and smiled, and at once his face looked young and boyish. 'You've given me the opportunity to let fly, and now I've done. It had to come out, and now it's said and over with. Thank you for coming. Even if it *was* on your way.'

When he opened the door he was grinning, and as she walked past him, carrying her hat, he reached out a finger, and gently flicked the dark wing of hair away from her cheek.

'Goodbye, lass,' he said, and closed the door gently behind her, leaving Libby to stumble down the dark stairs, knowing she had been well and truly dismissed.

She was alone with Harry Brandwood in the lounge that evening. Carrie had gone up to her room, saying she had a headache, Oliver was in the billiard room with his papers and the whisky bottle, and Ettie was upstairs with Sarah.

'Come here, Libby.' Harry caught her hand as she walked past his chair and pulled her forcibly on to his knee. 'For a courting couple we don't get many chances to be alone like this. Let's make the most of it, eh?'

His kiss was sensual and lingering, and Libby slid her arm round his neck and responded dutifully. Then as his hand moved to her breast she jerked away.

'Don't! Someone might come in. I don't think Carrie has gone to bed, and Father . . .' She sat bolt upright and put up a hand to tidy her hair.

Immediately Harry pulled her close again, covering her face with kisses. 'And what if they do, sweetheart? We're engaged to be married. Remember?' His face was hot, and his light brown eyes hazy with love. 'Love me?'

Libby sighed and turned her cheek into the comfort of his tweedy shoulder. Oh, yes, she did love this man. She had loved him for a long time now, all through the slow months of his wooing, accepting his devotion gladly. Whenever she needed him, he was there, he always would be there, steady as a rock. Once she had teased him and said he should have been christened Peter, not Harry, Peter, the rock.

And the other one, that thin tall man with despair in his eyes and a smile on his lips, alone in that room he called home with his pride, his tenacity. He would survive. Tom Silver would never submit to the indignity of unemployment which turned decent hard-working men into grey shadows as they trudged from one place to another, begging for work. His pride would sustain him, it had to. There was nothing she could do.

And the next time Harry kissed her, her fierce

response was all he desired, more than he had hoped for, and whatever had been troubling her was gone. He knew his Libby. All sunshine one minute and shadows the next. Passion rising in him like a lick of flame, Harry wrapped his arms tightly round his bride-to-be as their kiss deepened.

CHAPTER FIVE

In July Sarah Batt's father died suddenly in the kitchen of the little cottage five miles from Westerley. Bending over to tie the laces of his boots, he ended his life as quietly as he had led it, his eyes wide open as if he too had been shocked by the suddenness of it all.

'Mrs Peel says I must stay for as long as you need me, Mam.' Sarah, eyes sunk into the hollows of her plump cheeks, stared down at her father's peaceful face with the broad hands crossed over the white shroud. 'The schools have broken up for the holidays, and Miss Libby and Miss Carrie will be able to see to her.' She leaned farther forward towards the plain wooden coffin. 'Who laid him out, Mam?'

Nellie Batt crossed herself devoutly before covering the waxen face. Physically an older version of her stout and capable daughter, with the same red hair and pale freckled skin, she was still in a state of shock. Only a small part of her accepted that her husband was dead, and she still expected him to come in from the fields, wiping the mud from his boots on the scraper at the door before going over to the slopstone to wash his hands.

'Why, Mrs Warburton, who else? She allus does the laying out, you know that, our Sarah.'

'Then she's missed his fingernails.' Sarah pointed. 'See, Mam, they're mucky. She might have cleaned them out with the tip of a knife or something. It looks bad.'

'That's soil, not muck.' Mrs Batt's flat voice rose in indignation. 'Your dad allus had black nails, especially the thumbs, with pressing his cuttings down into his pots, and with filling his pipe.' She glanced over to the rack of pipes on the wall. 'I don't know what I'll do with them now; there's two hardly used, but I've got rid of his walking stick and his best jacket and toursers. A tramp came knocking not an hour before you got here, and I gave them to him. I think he thowt it were Christmas Day when I handed them over.' She turned away. 'You'd best go up and say goodnight to Patrick. He said he would stop awake till you came, an' knowing him he'll be lying there waiting for you. He's going to miss his grandpa, that child is,' she added, making no reference to her own feelings, which Sarah guessed were as cold and numb as her husband's still body.

Wiping her eyes, Sarah climbed the narrow twisting staircase leading up from the living room, then turning right at the top she went into the back bedroom and saw her son sitting bolt upright in bed staring at the door.

Patrick Batt, the living proof of Sarah's disgrace, was eight years old, and looked two years older. Tall for his age, he was a beautiful boy with hair as yellow as buttercups, the exact colour of Ettie Peel's as a child. His blue eyes slanted upwards at the corners and were set over a high-bridged nose. The Peel nose, Sarah thought now, struck forcibly with the uncanny resemblance of her son to his father, Willie Peel. Willie Peel, who had crept up the back stairs at Westerley and seduced her, lying in her arms and sobbing away his terror at the thought of having to go back to the hellhole that was France in that last year of the war.

Now it was his son's turn to shed tears of anguish in Sarah's arms. Over his bowed head she cursed the fate that had moulded him into such an exact copy, and even in her own sorrow she vowed that never, never would the Peel family find out the truth.

'Grandpa is with Jesus and Mary,' she soothed. 'Walking in a lovely garden where the sun always shines, and roses are in bloom in winter. His bad leg will never hurt him again. *Nothing* will hurt him. Jesus will see to that.'

'An' I will see to Grandma.' Patrick raised a small stricken face, the drama of the situation thickening his young voice with resolution. 'I made her a pot of cocoa and cut a slice of bread an' put jam on it, an' I can chop wood . . . and things,' he finished. 'Will Grandpa really have gone to heaven without making his confession?'

'Your grandpa had nothing to confess, love' Sarah said firmly. 'He never said a wrong word, not in the whole of his life. He was the kindest, best man that ever breathed. Jesus will be glad to have him up there, I can promise you that.'

Then, as her tears rolled down her cheeks into the thatch of thick golden hair, she closed her eyes and sent up a private prayer of gratitude for the father who had pulled her close into his arms on the day she had arrived home, bringing trouble to their doorstep, and had promised her that her coming baby would be brought up to hold his head high.

When Patrick was six years old, astounding the teacher at the village school by his ability to read and write, she was back at Westerley, lavishing care and devotion on Ettie Peel.

'If they were to find out, they would claim

him,' her father had said quietly one day, the pipe in his hand smoked out, his eyes suddenly bleak. 'Illegitimate or not, they would want him, not having a son of their own. Would be only natural.'

'Over my dead body!' his wife declared, rocking her chair so violently that it was in danger of tipping over. 'Why don't you come home, Sarah, and break with the Peels for good? Tongues would soon stop wagging here, and our backs are broad enough to stand it, anyroad. You could get a job in one of the big houses and the Peels would be out of our lives for good.'

Sarah shook her head. 'They will never be out of my life, Mam even if I never saw them again. Patrick is his father born again, and being born on the very day his father was killed, he *is* Willie Peel born again, can't you see?'

In their religious superstition her parents did see at once, but what they could never understand was their daughter's obstinacy in wanting to remain at Westerley. It was no use trying to make them realize that Sarah's devotion to her mistress was the selfless love of a daughter-in-law, the protective caring for a woman whose grandson she now held in her arms, trying to comfort his childish grief.

'Lie down and try to get to sleep.' She tucked the covers up to his chin. 'We have to be very brave for Grandma's sake, an' I know you will look to her, love. I'm going downstairs now to talk to her, and tell her all the things she likes to hear about Miss Libby and Miss Carrie, to take her mind off. That's what she needs, her mind taking off.' She kissed the flushed cheek, and felt herself jerked forward as two thin arms came from beneath the flannelette sheet and gripped her tightly.

'Are they really like two peas in a pod?' Patrick

was stalling for time, willing her to stay. Sarah sat down on the bed and nodded, telling the tale he never tired of hearing.

'It's like one person, except that there's two. If they have their backs turned there's no difference, and even when they're both looking at you it's hard to tell. Same noses, mouths, eyes and hair, and most of the time they dress alike because they like nothing better than foxing folks, especially Miss Libby.' Sarah put out a hand and gently closed her son's eyes, seeing as she did so Mrs Warburton from the end house doing the same for her father when she was called to do the laying out. She bit her lip and fought back the threat of tears. 'Miss Libby is noisier than Miss Carrie. Always wanting her own way, and acting like a baby sometimes instead of a grown lady. An' worrying her mother with always arguing with her father; not a bit like Miss Carrie, who's all for a quiet life.'

'Miss Carrie's your favourite.' Patrick's voice slurred on the edge of sleep.

Sarah stood up carefully, then began to back away. 'Yes, she is that. An' you know why? Because Miss Libby's always ferreting her nose into things that don't concern her, that's why.'

'An' Mr Peel?' The voice was whisper-soft now.

'Like a bull. A big, black, roaring bull. Put him in a field an' you wouldn't tell the difference.'

Sarah closed the door, letting the latch drop quietly into place. Then, with every stair creaking under her ample weight, she went downstairs to her mother, who was waiting for her, staring into the fire.

'Without a hand stretched out to me when life is too unbearable for me to carry on, I will die. Without *you* I will die.'

Mungo McDermot had done the unforgivable and

telephoned Carrie at Westerley, throwing her into a blind panic, telling her that he would wait at the summer house all day for her to come to him. 'And every day until you do,' he had finished, his voice hoarse with anguish.

'I can only stay for ten minutes,' Carrie told him, wrinkling her nose at the damp earthy smell in the little shuttered meeting place, bewildered at her claustrophobic reaction and the unresponsive stiffening of her body as Mungo held her close.

'Beatrice is always like this in the school holidays. She cannot abide me about the house.' He looked thinner than ever, all eyes, with a nervous tic throbbing at the side of his cheek. 'I interrupt her routine, she says.'

When his hand strayed to the loop-button fastening of Carrie's thin summer dress, she jerked away, then gripped his hand tightly to prevent it from straying further. At what moment, she asked herself, had she stopped loving him and seen him as he really was? A weak man who would have taken her virginity, maybe got her with child, with no intention of ever leaving his wife — just to gratify his own desires. The puritanical phrases milled round in her brain, as years of submission to a domineering father, combined with religious beliefs and a girlish naïvity towards the facts of life, rose to the surface and killed her infatuation stone dead.

'I don't believe you can't get out to meet me,' Mungo was muttering, his head bent, the thin spot on the crown of his head filling Carrie not with tenderness as before but with distaste.

She was very dignified that July morning, filled with pity as she wondered how she could tell him that she no longer loved him, that somehow love had died, forcing her to see him as he really was.

'You don't understand,' she said softly, trying to spare him. 'We are a close family. We don't, my sister and I, just leave the house without saying where we are going. If I said I was going for a walk or a bicycle ride it would be more than likely that Libby would say she would come with me, and besides, Sarah, who looks after Mother, has gone home for a while because her father has died.'

Sarah, this new, clear-headed Carrie now thought, who once gave in to a man like you and even now, eight years later, is too filled with shame to want to talk about her illegitimate son.

'You must not! You must never touch me like that again!' Carrie forgot to be kind as Mungo's open-mouthed kiss descended, covering what seemed to be the whole bottom half of her face and filling her with nausea. Jerking away, she stood up, pulling her dress down and fastening the top buttons with shaking fingers. 'It's wrong! I'm not like that. I thought I was, but I'm not. You wouldn't do that if you had any respect for me.'

'You don't love me,' Mungo stared up at her, his mouth working convulsively. 'You led me on, and now you think you can cast me aside . . .' He waved a limp wrist to encompass the gloomy interior of the summer house. 'You have been the one bright star in my apology for a life, and now you tell me I mustn't touch you. Oh, God . . .' He dropped his face into his hands. Shaking with hard sobs he rocked himself backwards and forwards, moaning, whimpering, saying her name over and over again. 'Carrie, Carrie, oh, Carrie, my own sweet love.'

She had never seen a man cry before. She had seen her father incoherent with rage, heard his voice bellow as his face contorted with anger, and she had shrunk from the sight. But nothing, nothing had prepared her for this. Mungo's lack of control shocked her so that all she could do was stand there and watch him disintegrate from a man into a pitiable object devoid of dignity and self-respect.

And she had done this to him.

'If you leave me,' he was saying now, the words ragged and torn with anguish, 'if you leave me, then I will kill myself. I will do away with myself, I swear.'

Carrie felt the sweat break out all over her body, felt it run down her sides and stand in cold beads on her forehead. With one part of her she was kneeling down by his side, comforting, wiping his tears away, soothing, promising, but with the other part — the part that was in control — she was watching him with the aloofness of a bystander.

'You will *not* kill youself, Mungo.' Her calm voice was the one she used to tick off a naughty child at school. 'People who threaten to do that never do. You have your boy to think about. He needs you more than any normal boy, and your wife . . .' she made herself go on, 'she needs you too, for support . . .' Her voice tailed away. How hypocritical can you be, Carrie Peel? Never once, in all the time of your loving, did you give a thought to his wife and her needs. She backed towards the door. 'I'm going now, Mungo. I'm sorry . . .' Pull yourself together, she wanted to say, but that would have been too cruel. 'When you think about it calmly you will know there was never any future for us. Mungo . . . no!'

With a sudden movement he pulled her to him. Through the thin material of her dress she felt his body, every hard inch of it, pressing against her, devouring her with its closeness. One hand squeezed her breast, whilst the other held the back of her head, his teeth sharp against her tightly clenched mouth, his tongue probing, daring with insistence.

105

With all his strength he was straining and writhing, forcing her body to meet his demands and Carrie realized that to fight back would only inflame him the more. She went limp in his arms — not stiff, just totally unresponsive, some inborn instinct telling her this was the only way.

When he pushed her from him she fell painfully on to the rotting floorboards, hurting her knee, embarrassed almost to the point of faintness. Staggering to her feet, she opened the door and escaped into the warm sunshine. She was shaking as if with a violent fever, but she forced her trembling legs to obey and tottered towards the hole in the hedge and out on to the main road.

'Carrie! Come back! Don't leave me! Carrie . . . Carrie . . . Carrie . . .' Mungo's voice called out to her.

With head bent and taking small slow steps, Carrie set off for home, her knee throbbing and her heart pounding. If she could get into the house without anyone seeing her; if she could lock herself into the big bathroom and sink into a tub of hot water, then maybe she could wash away the memory of the morning. She shuddered as she thought of what might have happened. But now that it was all over she could tell Libby how foolish she had been, and some day they would laugh about it together, with their arms round each other, stifling their giggles as they had done for as long as she could remember. Libby, the sensible one, who would never have got herself into a mess like this. Libby the strong one. 'Oh, Libby . . .' Carrie muttered, trudging on, near to home now, to her other self who would listen and understand. . .

'It will be clogs to clogs in three generations. You mark my words.' Oliver Peel left the house in high dudgeon one August morning, bemoaning the fact that the postman was later than usual. 'The cotton trade is finished in this town; there's three mill chimneys with no smoke coming from them, and the way things are going Bridge Mill will be next.'

Used to the morning ritual, Libby and Carrie hovered in the hall, one twin handing her father his walking stick and the other his newspaper and bowler hat. Carrie, pale but composed, had stopped skimming hastily through the paper, holding her breath as she ran her finger down the obituary column in dread of seeing Mungo's death reported.

The fact that Libby, once she had give the tearful tale her full attention, had called Mungo's threat moral blackmail and had laughed his threat of suicide to scorn, helped to assuage the biting fear in Carrie's mind. It was no use saying that she felt responsible, that remorse was eating at her soul, waking her in the night sweating and shaking. Remorse was a wasted emotion. Libby had always maintained that; what people did of their own accord was their own responsibility. 'Not that circumstances don't sometimes push them over the edge,' she had conceded rather loftily, 'but in the main we work out our own salvations.'

Oh, to be like Libby, sure of herself, restless, with quicksilver reactions, taking over in a crisis and doing what had to be done without weighing the consequences. Like now.

'I'll take the post down to the mill,' Libby volunteered when it finally dropped through the letter box. Father obviously thought there was something here he wanted to see.' She held up a long buff envelope. 'This one looks a bit sinister. Maybe it's a summons. If he treats his workers with the contempt he holds for them I wouldn't be surprised.'

Ettie Peel appeared round the bend in the stairs, a loose wrapper over her nightgown. 'But there is going to be a storm, dear. The air is heavy with it.' She came down the remaining stairs slowly, feeling for each tread with a slippered foot. 'I think I have one of my heads coming on and, oh, I wish Sarah would come back. I know it's selfish of me, but I miss her so much, and she always knows what to do. Thunder terrifies me. It reminds me of the sound of guns, and then I get to thinking about Willie . . .'

Immediately Carrie went to her mother, leading her gently into the lounge.

'I'm here, Mother. I won't leave you.' She lowered her voice. 'And Libby needs to do something. The long school break leaves her with so little to do, especially this year when Father decided there was too much going wrong at the mill for us to take our usual holiday at Lytham St Annes.'

'But what will she do if the storm breaks?' Ettie, to whom worrying came as naturally as breathing, allowed herself to be led to the chesterfield.

'Tell her to ring for a taxi cab. Father can charge it to the mill.'

Ellie raised a small piteous face. 'Why does your father insist on walking everywhere? He may have this notion of showing the world something or other by not having his own car and chauffeur, but he doesn't stop to think that it makes me a prisoner in my own home. It's all very well for him to say I have Miss Gray to dressmake whenever I need a new outfit, and that all we need is delivered to the door, but, oh, how I would long just to walk round the shops one day. You know. I could manage to walk through the Arcade if I took it easy.'

She frowned and put up a hand to the hair that was once a bright buttercup yellow and now was faded and streaked with grey. 'And another thing. Why isn't Libby showing more interest in her trousseau? The wedding is in four months' time, and she hasn't even looked through the catalogue sent from Manchester. All that sewing and fitting to be done, and once she goes back to school there'll be so little time. And why does she insist on working next term? She should have left in July and spent the time in preparations. She told me one day she wouldn't care if she got married in her best blue jacket and skirt, and you know how your father has set his mind on a proper wedding with all the trimmings. Dr and Mrs Brandwood would be so upset if we made it seem like a hole and corner affair. Harry is their only son. It would be dreadful if we let them down.'

Carrie went over to the drinks cupboard and poured her mother a glass of her favourite tonic wine. 'Drink this, Mother. I know it's early, but who cares? And try to stop worrying about Libby. She knows what she's doing. She'll probably get the tram and take her umbrella, and she won't melt even if it does rain. Libby would burst if she didn't get out of the house at least once a day, you know that.'

'I wish Sarah would come back,' Ettie said, sipping the wine and refusing to be cheered. 'What if her mother decides she needs Sarah at home now Mr Batt had died? She has a heart condition, Sarah once told me, and that boy . . . he must be a handful now, and surely the village won't hold it against Sarah any more. It's nineteen twenty-six, not nineteen hundred. People are more liberal-minded these days, even about illegitimacy. But Sarah never speaks about her son, and I respect her silence. She's such a *good* girl, Carrie, and she isn't always wanting to go to Mass like most Catholics.' Ettie took another pensive sip.

'Now that would set the cat amongst the pigeons. Your father would never hold with that. I can never understand him having Sarah back, not with his high principles. I would have thought a fallen girl would be the last person he would want in his household, so it proves he isn't as strict as he appears.'

Carrie turned away. Oh. Mother, poor trusting helpless Mother, she was thinking, if only Ettie knew the reason for her husband's supposedly liberal-mindedness. It would be the pot calling the kettle black for him to condemn Sarah, when all the time he was creeping up the back stairs to gratify his frustrated desires. She sighed and glanced through the tall window to where the trees stood motionless against a lowering sky. 'I think I will take a glass of wine with you, Mother,' she said, remembering having read somewhere that more suicides took place in stormy weather than at any other time.

'Oh Mungo. Please God you didn't mean it and that Libby was right,' she said silently as she watched the dark red liquid fill the glass.

If it rains, then it rains, Libby told herself, boarding the tram and settling herself in the seat nearest the exit. She would get off at the stop before Meadow Street and approach the mill that way. It would save going over the canal bridge, she decided, refusing to admit that her real reason for going into town was that she might possibly see Tom Silver.

And if he saw her, she had a genuine excuse for being in that street on Tuesday morning, wearing her most becoming dress and loose jacket with its false ermine collar. He might say something sarcastic, but she would brandish the letters and explain she was merely being a dutiful daughter and delivering them to the mill.

The tram was clattering its way past the Corporation Park gates now. Along the wide pavement groups of unemployed men walked slowly, hands in pockets, heads bent, shoulders dropping. She saw one stoop and pick up a discarded cigarette from the gutter, examine it closely, then toss it aside in disgust.

Meadow Street was completely deserted when she turned into it. No landladies gossiping on doorsteps, no children throwing balls up against the walls chanting 'onesy, twosey, threesey, foursey'. Nothing but closed doors and a menacing boil of thunder clouds over the rooftops. Out at Westerley, where the view was not blocked by rows of terraced houses, the sky was yellow with sheet lightning, and even here the very air seemed charged with electricity.

Libby began to run. She forgot about looking for a chance encounter with Tom Silver; all she wanted now was shelter and the safety of her father's office at the top of the sloping mill yard. Suddenly there came a blinding flash, followed by a crash of thunder, and as she turned into the short street fronting the mill she heard a scream. She looked up at the tall chimney, surprised to see it still standing. Then, as she tore through the mill gates, she saw a young girl lying face down on the cobbles, arms spread wide.

By the time Libby reached her a crowd of women weavers, clogs ringing on the stones, had poured out from the weaving shed. One women, her hair brushed up into an old-fashioned cottage bun, knelt down and lifted the unconscious girl into her arms. 'She's been struck!' she cried aloud. 'Me daughter's been struck! Oh, Mary, Mary, love! I'm here! Your mam's here. Oh, God, look at her eyes. What's happened to her eyes?'

'She's been blinded by the flash. See, she's staring

straight at us, but she can't see nowt. Another weaver, helping to support the girl in a sitting position, waved a hand in front of the strangely staring eyes, getting no response.'

'Can you see *anything*?' Libby, heedless of her best outfit and of the rain now pelting down, took the limp hand in her own as she stared into the panic-stricken face.

The girl, no more than fourteen years old, a thin waif of a child with a black fent apron over her short-sleeved blouse and skirt, opened her mouth wide and screamed. Her loud, piercing shrieks brought more weavers running from the shed to stand in a circle round the little kneeling group.

'I can't see! Oh, Mam, I can't see!' The hand snatched itself away from Libby's grasp and began to claw the air. 'There were this big flash and I fell down and now I can't see. Oh. Mam! Help me! Help me, somebody! Help me!'

'We must get her inside.' Libby recognized Jimmy Earnshaw, her father's tackler, a small wiry man with a moustache too big for the rest of his face. She turned to him eagerly. 'It's probably only a temporary thing, but we can't do anything out here. Bring her into the office out of the rain.'

Gently the hysterical girl was helped to her feet, hands stretched out at either side.

'Tha'll be awreet, lass. Take it steady.' Jimmy Earnshaw, a former weaver with the expertise of a qualified engineer necessary to his role of tackler, a man who could tune a machine just by listening to the sound of it running, glanced at Libby. 'I never thowt to see you here, miss. You come to see the maister?'

Before Libby could answer, she looked up and saw Oliver Peel coming down the yard from the office block. Bare-headed in the pouring rain, his black hair already sleeked to his skull, he advanced towards them, head lowered like a bull charging a fence.

'What's going on here? Why have you left your looms?' Ignoring Libby, he spoke directly to his tackler. 'Get this lot back, Jimmy. What do you think I'm made of? Bloody money? The hooter hasn't gone, has it? Go on, the lot of you, before I send you all home.'

'This child's been hurt, Mr Peel.' Libby cringed as the man seemed to shrink in size. She almost expected him to doff his cap as he answered his employer apologetically. 'We was bringing her into the office before sending for the doctor. She's lost her sight.'

At that the girl began to scream again, and now her mother put both arms round her and rocked her backwards and forwards. 'If you won't send for the doctor, Mr Peel, then I'll take her home,' she said, facing Oliver with the rain running down her face mingling with her tears. 'An' we'll neither of us come in no more.'

'You can't afford to stay at home,' Oliver stated calmly. He pointed back down the yard. 'Anybody not back at their looms in one minute goes home.' He turned to the tackler. 'Jimmy, take their names and bring the list to me. They'll get their pay docked for the length of time they've been out here, every man jack of 'em.'

And with that he turned on his heel and walked back to his office.

'The callous bugger!' A woman with the wizened face of a monkey muttered in a low voice as she turned to walk back into the weaving shed. 'He knows we dursn't risk our jobs, the bloody sod.'

'One of these days I'll swing for 'im and gladly.'

The faces, pale from lack of sunshine and weary from standing at the looms in the humid atmosphere of the weaving shed, reflected a hatred so powerful, so intense that it was almost tangible. Libby, unable to credit what she had just witnessed, stood irresolute for a moment. Then the young girl pressed the palms of her hands over her eyes, held them there for a moment, and, raising her small pinched face to the rain coming down like stair rods, sobbed her relief.

'Mam! I can see! It's come back. The black has gone. I can see again!'

'The Lord be praised . . . oh, my little lamb, the Lord be praised.' The mother's arms were once again round her daughter. 'It were the shock, little love, just the shock.'

'Take her home, Maggie.' Jimmy Earnshaw touched the woman on her arm. 'I'll square it with the maister. Just thee get her home and coddle her for a bit. I'll make it reet.'

'Nay, tha won't!' Libby recoiled from the venom in the strident voice. 'We're going back to our looms like what he said. I'll see to her. It won't be the first time I've done the work of two.' She lifted a clenched fist and shook it in the direction of the mill office block. 'But I'll not forget, and one of these days I'll get even, if it's the last thing I do. If her sight had gone for good he'd have done nowt but bother about his bloody profit-making. I spit on him!' She rooted round in her mouth and ejected a stream of spittle on to the cobblestones. 'I spit on his immortal soul! May he rot in 'ell, the unfeeling sod!'

'I still think tha should tek her home, Maggie.' The tackler took off his cap, revealing a bald head at variance with the flourishing moustache. 'See how she's shaking. She's as white as a piece of bleached fent. She'll not find the strength to stand at her loom.'

'I'm all right now, Mam.' The little girl, smaller than Libby had been at eleven years old, leaned on her mother for support and walked unsteadily down the yard. But her mother hadn't finished, not quite.

'He knows I've got four more at home like 'er, an' me husband laid off since the strike. He was right when he said we can't afford. He holds the trump card, an' him an' his sort allus will. If I go home now he'll lock me out tomorrow, an' if tha doesn't keep tha' mouth shut, Jimmy Earnshaw, tha'll be locked out an' all.' Then, without a single glance in Libby's direction, she led the trembling child back down the yard and into the weaving shed.

'I'll have to go after her, miss.' The tackler wrung out his dripping cap and replaced it on his head. 'If them looms 'as been left there'll be 'ell to pay.'

Libby nodded once, then walked away in the opposite direction. First she passed through the outer office, with the trio of clerical workers on their high stools and the large safe in the corner containing the account books. Looking neither to right nor left she walked determinedly through the tiny room where the manager sat at his desk, and into the inner sanctum, her father's private preserve. This room was carpeted, with a desk, a telephone, and a smaller safe on the wall. She opened the door without knocking and walked straight in.

'Did you *see* me out there?' she demanded. 'Or did you take me for one of the herd? Father! I'm asking you a question!'

Oliver Peel had taken off his jacket and draped it over one of the chairs set in a semicircle by the window. There was a glass by the files on his desk and it was obvious that he had been drinking.

He jerked his head towards the closed door. 'Keep your voice down, for God's sake. I've enough on my plate trying to keep that lot in order without it coming out that I can't control my own daughter.' He opened a drawer at the side of his desk and slid the empty glass into it with a furtive movement not lost on Libby. 'What are you doing here, anyway? What are you doing traipsing down the town on a morning like this? Have you seen yourself? You look like something the cat's brought in. Why aren't you at home seeing to your mother?'

Opening her purse, Libby took out the letters and threw them down on the desk. 'You missed the post this morning, so I brought these. Doing you a favour, I brought the post down to you. That's all.'

She was still identifying with his weavers, staring at their maister with hate-filled eyes.

'You saw what happened to that child.' Libby gripped the front of the desk and leaned forward, her face almost level with her father's. 'She might have been killed, and if she had been you would have had her covered with a length of your flaming cotton and left her there till the twelve o'clock hooter blew.'

Oliver stood up, his six-foot frame towering over her. Outside, the sliding rain hissed across the yard.

'But she wasn't killed, was she, now? She wasn't even blinded like she was making out to be. She was out in the toilets where she had no right to be, and when the flash came she had the hysterics.' he picked up a fat ledger, balanced it in his hand, then dropped it with a thud on to the desk. So don't you think you can came down here, madam, and tell me how to behave. And as for bringing her in here . . .' He waved a hand round the room. 'I don't have weavers in my office. I never have and I never will.'

'Even when they are hurt and frightened half

to death, Father?' Libby's voice was dangerously quiet.

'Even when they *think* they are hurt, and want to make out they are frightened.' Oliver said the words slowly, and as he spoke Libby saw the way the veins bulged on his forehead and his already high colour deepened to a purple hue with two bright spots on his cheekbones.

And all at once the compassion which was more inherent in her twin's make-up than her own rose to the surface. As they glared at each other she saw suddenly the way it was for Oliver Peel. A man who had to do everything for himself, never for a moment believing that anyone else could take the responsibility weighing so heavily on him. The threat of closure of the mill, the crippling competition from overseas markets. And then coming home every evening to a house peopled with women, and wife who had retreated both physically and mentally into a dim, complaining world of her own. Libby glanced over to the corner where once at a small desk her brother had bent his yellow head over his ledgers, and she thought how on the dark gloomy morning Willie's brightness of expression and his sweet temperament would have lightened the atmosphere with a touch of gold.

'Father . . .' she began. 'There are four more weeks left before I go back to school. I'm good at figures, you know that. Isn't there something I could do to help? I'm bored at home, I *need* to do something. I know I'm not a man, but I'm quick and practical. I could hold the fort on the days you go to the Cotton Exchange at Manchester. I learn fast and maybe even after I'm married I could come in in the mornings. Answering the telephone for Harry won't be enough for me. Already I dread being alone in that big house with nothing to do but arrange the flowers and entertain Harry's friends. I'm *wasted*, Father! I want to help!'

For a moment she thought he was actually going to explode. His deep-set dark eyes narrowed into slits in the puffiness of his face, and when he reached for a paperweight she thought for one wild moment that he was going to hurl it through the window.

'What bloody nonsense!' What typical rubbish!' He sat down heavily. 'Oh, yes. I can just see me having a woman working alongside of me, ferreting about, getting in my way. And I can see Harry letting you.' He jerked his head towards the door. 'You've wasted enough time for me already this morning, and now you try to tell me it's time I packed it in. You think that because I'm reaching retirement age, I'm finished. You're like your mother, always telling me it's time I sold out and went to live with her in a bungalow at Southport.' He snorted. 'I know better than most that this industry is in a steady decline, and it will get worse before it gets better. But let me tell you something, madam. Cotton is in the blood, it's in my blood like it was in my father's, and his father before him, and like it would have been in Willie's. If he had lived.' He seemed to slump deep into his leather desk chair. 'But with my son gone I have to carry on, and I *will* carry on. I'll keep that chimney smoking and that machinery going if I have to die in the doing of it, and without any help from anybody, least of all from you.' He jerked his thumb towards the door. 'And you can take yourself off, and get back to the house where you belong, and heaven help this man of yours when he finds he's married to an interfering woman who thinks she has the mind of a man.'

With tears stinging behind her eyelids Libby

groped her way blindly towards the door. She had known and accepted for as long as she could remember that her father had a cruel streak in him, but his cruelty was — or had been — not so much in what he said but in the way he said it. He could wither her mother with a glance from beneath his bushy eyebrows, and he could reduce Carrie to tears with his sarcasm. But now, since the strike of three months ago, he had taken what he termed his weavers' 'disloyalty' personally, blaming the slow trickle of orders directly on them, incurring their hatred to the point where it threatened to explode into violence.

As she stumbled through the outer office not a head was raised from the fat ledgers. The three clerks, legs wound round the spindles of their high stools, carried on writing, struggling to see in the far from adequate light, even their backs showing fear and apprehension as to what might be coming next. Not one of them turned as Libby opened the door and stepped outside into the deluge, remembering too late that she had left her umbrella in Oliver's inner sanctum.

'And I'm not going back for it,' she muttered aloud. 'He's my father, and he's sent me out in this rain wearing a summer dress and a short jacket, and he *doesn't care*. He cares for nothing but his profits and his blasted mill.'

The gutters in Meadow Street overflowed as the drains failed to take the onslaught of water. The sky hung low and grey over the chimney tops of the terraced houses. The curtain of rain hit the flagstones and bounced back again as she hurried along, unaware of the spectacle she presented of a girl obviously out of her environment, with muddied knees from where she had knelt on cobbles, her ruined upturned straw hat tipped crazily to one side.

'Well, well!' She stopped suddenly, whipping round as the voice called from an open doorway. 'Miss Peel!' What on earth. . . ?'

Tom Silver stepped from the doorway and planted himself in front of her. 'You'd better come in.' He took her elbow and guided her towards the door of number 14. 'You're soaked to the skin, lass. Come on, come on. I don't know where you think you're going, but you can't go anywhere like this.'

At the kindness in his voice Libby felt the tears, held in check, brim over and run down her face to mingle with the rain. She shrugged away from his solicitous grasp even as she allowed herself to be led over the doorstep into the dingy lobby, and up the stairs to the room at the top of the house.

'I can make you a pot of hot tea, and the first thing we must do is get those shoes and stockings off and get them dry. Come on. Off with that jacket, then give me your hat.' He produced a towel and handed it over. 'Look, you stop where you are an I'll go down and cadge a bucket of coal from Mrs Barton.' He nodded towards the tiny empty grate wearing its summer embellishment of a pleated paper fan. 'I stopped my coal recently, but she's a good sort. I won't be more than a minute.'

Libby heard him clattering his way down uncarpeted stairs, and for the first time felt the cold seep through her. The little room was as damp and cheerless as the grave, with the rain slanting down against the window and the faded oilcloth slippery to her feet.

When he came back he knelt down, screwed up a newspaper, placed a firelighter on top, arranged a heap of coal and applied a match, then covered the front of the grate with another paper spread wide. He nodded as the flames roared up the chimney, and from a coal scuttle by the side of the fireplace he took a bundle of wood and added it to the already leaping flames. Then he placed a small tin kettle on the gas ring and applied a match, nodding again and stepping back as it spluttered into life.

'And now those stockings.'

Embarrassed and confused, Libby lifted her head and shook it from side to side. 'I can't take my stockings off. Not here!'

'Then I'll have to take them off for you.' He grinned. 'Come on, lass. I'll hang them over this tidy here and they'll be dry in a minute.' He draped her jacket over the back of a chair and set it to one side of the blaze. 'You're shaking like a leaf. Don't look so worried, there's nothing going to happen. I'm not going to go mad at the sight of a bare leg. See, I'll turn my back and promise not to turn round till you give the word. Right?'

'They'll dry on my legs.' Libby tried to stop her teeth chattering. 'And I'm not shivering because I'm cold. I've just come from my father and I'm upset. He's upset me, that's all.'

She put a hand to her mouth. Now why had she said that? She hardly knew this man watching her so gravely, and yet at that moment she wanted nothing more than to put her head down and wail, and feel his hand on her hair and hear the soothing tone of his voice.

'Get those stockings off!'

Tom turned away to reach two mugs down from a shelf, then from a cupboard beneath he took out a small brown teapot and a packet of tea. 'And if you want to cry, then get on with it. Tears held in do nobody any good, and you've got a towel there to wipe them away.'

There was no mockery in the words, just a gentle

understated consideration for her feelings. So, sniffing audibly, Libby unfastened her suspenders through the folds of her wet skirt, and peeled off the dirty, wet stockings.

'And your frock,' Tom said firmly. Still with his back to her he reached out and took a dressing gown from the rail at the foot of his single bed. 'There's not many folks round here sport dressing gowns, but this one was bought special a few years back when I went to a conference in Cambridge.' He threw it over. 'There were a few women delegates there, and I didn't want to shock them going along the landing in the nude. I don't wear pyjamas,' he added, and she suspected there was a hint of teasing laughter in his voice now. 'And there's something not quite right about a man going to the bathroom in his raincoat with a towel over his arm, wouldn't you say? Now give me the word to turn round when you're ready. I never have liked this view of Mrs Barton's back yard, with your father's mill shutting out what light there is. On a day like this it's enough to make even an optimist like me feel he's reached the very depths of his existence.'

Stepping out of her dress and pulling the rough blanket wool of the dressing gown round her, Libby told herself dramatically that the depths of her own existence had been reached the moment her father had let her walk out into the torrential rain. Oliver Peel had no love for her — the hatred and contempt he felt for her had shown in his narrowed eyes — and he had no love for Carrie either, mentally regarding them as one since the day they were born. Her mother he tolerated, that was all, his servants and workforce he treated with contempt, and some day he would get his just deserts. She was sure of it.

'Do you believe the devil can get into people, Mr

Silver?' She held out her hand for the proffered pot of tea. 'I mean, so that they're angry all the time and you can hardly ever remember them speaking normally?'

Tom pulled up the little hard chair from the table by the window, turned it with its back to the fire and arranged her dress over it. 'Don't you think it's time you called me Tom, and let me call you Libby? You can't come out with a question like that to a stranger.' He sat down on the edge of the bed, holding his own mug of tea with both hands curled round it. 'Are you trying to tell me that you think your father is going mental? Because if you are, it's that doctor fella of yours you should be discussing it with, not me.'

Libby gave a visible start, then glanced down at the ring on her finger. She had forgotten all about Harry. In the whirl of her disordered thinking he had never come into the picture.

'When Harry's there my father seems almost normal,' she said slowly. 'He doesn't talk much to Harry, but on the other hand he doesn't ignore him altogether. Once when I told Harry my father had hit me, he seemed to think I had asked for it.'

'And had you?'

'No! All I want is to be treated as if I had a *mind*, a will of my own. I want to be treated as if I'm capable of being more than just a silly girl with nothing else to think about but getting married and setting up home. I *care* about people, Tom.' She said his name quite naturally. 'I sometimes feel that when I marry in December, I'll just be moving from one safe cocoon to another, and it stifles me. I should be happy, and I'm not.' She raised her head and stared into the fire. 'What's wrong with me? I mean to say, what am I doing here, sitting on this chair in your dressing gown, talking to you as if we had been friends all our lives?' She blinked back the threat of tears. 'And I'm selfish, too. My life is mapped out for me, safe and predictable, but what about yours? I haven't even asked you if you've had any luck in finding another job yet.'

Tom grinned, the couldn't-care-less grin that had infuriated her the last time they met. But now she realized it was merely a ploy to cover his despair. He shrugged his shoulders. 'When you go to see the clerk at the labour exchange you tell him you haven't been able to find work, and after a while you have to give three places each day where you've looked and failed, or they knock you off the list. Otherwise you are classed as not being genuine in search of work.'

'Then what?'

'Well, there is always Poor Law Relief, and if they send the relieving officer round and he finds you have any coal, or furniture that will sell, or too much food on the shelves, then you have to sell it all before you can get relief.' He shook his head. 'But I'm not making out a case for myself. No, it's the married men with families who have to feed their kids on bread and jam if they're lucky and they've managed to pay the rent.' His face set hard. 'Talk about a land fit for heroes! I've seen men standing in line down at the labour exchange, men who were in the thick of it in France, and they have to listen to some clerk who sat out the war on his bottom laying the law down to them. It makes me despair . . .'

Libby watched him, her cheeks glowing with a colour that owed nothing to the fire now leaping in the tiny grate. When he went out of the room later while she pulled on her dry stockings and the creased dress, she prayed that he would hint that he wanted

124

to see her again. But when she thanked him for his kindness he merely bowed his head and stood aside to let her pass.

When she stepped out into the street the wetness on her cheeks could not have been mistaken for the rain, for by now the storm had rolled away in a tumble of grey clouds over the chimney tops.

CHAPTER SIX

Carrie suspected that Libby wasn't paying much attention to what she was saying, but then Carrie was used to talking to blank faces and glazed eyes at school. She had accepted a long time ago that whilst she was an adequate teacher she had none of her sister's flair for making a lesson come alive. Still, she had to talk to her and at the moment, as they sat at the table in the window of the first floor café overlooking the town's main shopping street, Libby was a captive audience.

'Mungo just won't take no for an answer,' she said splitting a scone and spreading it with butter. 'He keeps trying to get me alone and he stares at me, even when there are other teachers in the staff room. Great smouldering stares they are, and now, instead of making me feel sorry for him, they just make me feel sick. It's as though I can see him now for what he is, whereas before . . . I must have been out of my mind.'

Libby had insisted on waiting until the window table was vacant and now she leaned over to peer down into the busy Saturday afternoon street thronged with shoppers.

'Looks can't kill,' she said, proving to a suspicious Carrie that she *had* been listening after all.

'He's so obviously unhappy.' Carrie, feeling better now she had her twin's attention, spread red plum

126

jam over the butter on her scone. 'And I really am sorry for him, but what can I do?' She removed a crumb from the corner of her mouth. 'When I look back to the summer, I can't believe it was *me* behaving like that. All that rushing about, terrified in case anyone saw us together, and do you know, you won't believe this, but I had an awful pain low down in my stomach most of the time.' She shook her head. 'It's true, Libby. It was just like colic. I used to lie in bed thinking about him, then when I woke up in the morning he was there immediately in the front of my mind. And you know, I never once allowed myself to realize just how . . . how *weak* he was. He looks *weak* , all pathetic and cow-eyed. And I thought I *loved* him! Oh, I must have been *obsessed* ! I can't believe it was me behaving like that.' She giggled. 'You know those pointed shoes we bought and regretted? Well, on the days I was seeing Mungo I sometimes wore them, and they were as comfortable as bedroom slippers, yet now I can't bear them on my feet. And when I think . . .' she shuddered, 'when I think how nearly I gave in to him . . .' She poured milk into the two cups by her side before lifting the heavy silver-plated teapot. 'I could have ruined my whole life, and he would never have married me, never left Beatrice.'

'Beatrice?' Libby swivelled her glance away from the window for long enough to accept the cup and saucer from her sister's outstretched hand.

'His wife.' Carrie took another scone from the plate lined with a fluted paper doily. 'They still fight. He came to school yesterday with a bruise the size of a half-crown underneath his eye, and he was all white and shaky. He looked dreadful.'

'I never liked the name Beatrice,' Libby said, moving the curtain with one hand to see better.

Carrie, exasperated now to the point of uncharacteristic irritation, put out a foot underneath the table and stepped none too gently on her sister's shoe. 'Libby Peel! You're miles away! Listen! I am asking your *advice*. Mungo managed to get me alone for a minute yesterday, and he said if I don't see him just once more to talk things over, he'll do it.'

'Do what?'

'Kill himself. Commit Suicide.' Carrie looked round the crowded café and lowered her voice to a whisper. 'He's desperate, Libby. He's rung me up twice at home, and if Father ever answers the telephone he'll demand to know who it is, and if it comes out, well, anything could happen.' She bit her lip. 'And I know this sound selfish and dreadful, but supposing Mungo does, well, you know, and leaves a note saying he's done it on my account, and then it gets into the paper? He's capable of it. He told me I would regret it if I didn't meet him.'

She stared open-mouthed as her sister suddenly pushed back her chair, grabbed her handbag and rushed towards the wide staircase leading down out of the café and into the street.

'Libby! Where are you going? What on earth. . . ?'

Conscious of the inquisitive stares from the other tables and the sudden lull in the teacup chatter, Carrie gathered up her own bag. Covered with embarrassment, she walked as casually as she could to the check out till at the far end of the mahogany counter, where she handed over the bill and a ten shilling note to the middle-aged woman in a pink overall.

For weeks, Libby had seen Tom Silver's dark head everywhere — in the tram, walking down the street. Now he was really there — across the road by the bank, standing on the wide corner pavement talking

128

to someone. He was hatless, his long black hair flopping over his high forehead, probably the only man she knew who went everywhere without a hat. Coatless too, in spite of the cold wind that had apparently blown the September Indian summer straight into winter.

Dodging the traffic, her own coat flying open, dropping a kid glove as she went, Libby ran straight up to him, her legs as wobbly as if she was just getting over the flu. Her feelings were in such a turmoil that she was incapable of caring about anything but the fact that he was there. After the weeks of longing he had finally materialized, just when she had thought she would never see him again.

'Tom!' Ignoring the man in a trilby hat talking earnestly to him, she actually clutched at Tom Silver's arm, feeling the bone hard through the thin serge of his shabby navy blue suit. 'How are you? I was over there . . .' she pointed back at the café, 'and I saw you. How *are* you? Have you found a job yet? You've been ill, haven't you? Oh, I can tell you've been ill . . .'

The man in the trilby hat, small ferret eyes missing nothing, mumbled that he would walk up to the Town Hall and wait there. Tom dismissed him with a nod, while Libby took no notice of his going at all.

'Libby Peel.' Tom looked down at her, at the flushed cheeks, at the rise and fall of her breasts beneath the soft blue wool of her high-necked dress. 'Come on, we'll walk a bit. It's too cold to stand here.' Taking her by the elbow, he turned her round and guided her firmly up the side street, round the corner and into the shelter of a wide shop doorway.

And Carrie, emerging from the café, flustered and disbelieving, stood on the wide pavement looking up and down, searching for her sister and seeing nothing.

Eventually she went back up the stairs to the café and asked the pink overall behind the till that if her sister came looking for her, would she please say that she had gone home?

'I'll do that, love,' the woman said, then moved to the end of the mahogany counter nearest the stairs, the better to see Carrie stumbling down, small and bewildered, out into the street again.

Tom Silver was no fool. Since his wife had died he had known two women, and both times he had been the one to break off the relationship, knowing that there was something in him that stopped him committing himself completely. And now here was this lovely, intelligent young woman, all pride forgotten, staring up at him with her feelings shining from her brown eyes and trembling to his touch.

'What is it, Libby?' he said gently, then immediately regretted the question as her face crumpled and the dark eyes swam with tears.

'I don't know.' She twisted away from him. 'I just wanted to know how you were.' She shivered, and made no move to stop him as he began to button up her coat. 'I've been thinking about you being out of work . . . and everything, and I couldn't bear not knowing.' She seemed unable to take her eyes from his mouth. 'I wanted to come and see you, but it . . . I couldn't.'

As he lifted her hand with the diamond ring on the third finger, she realized for the first time that she had lost a glove. Not that it mattered; not that anything mattered now that he was here and she was standing close to him, with the keen wind blowing discarded cigarette packets and scraps of paper round their ankles.

He smiled the smile that had haunted her for weeks. 'Not married yet?'

She shook her head, seeing the way his collar was frayed at the edges and seemed too big for his thin neck. 'The wedding's in December, the day after the school breaks up for Christmas.' Her voice faltered, and it was as though the next words said themselves. 'But I can't get married, Tom. It wouldn't be right.' She took a deep breath, then put out a hand as if to steady herself. 'Can I see you again? Please?'

She was so small, so vulnerable, so obviously distressed. He stretched out a hand and lightly touched her cheek, then felt a sense of shock as immediately she held his hand in place against her cheek and turned her mouth into its palm.

'Look, lass, we can't talk here.' He glanced over her shoulder, away down the street. 'That man I was with — he has a small jobbing printer's business out Hoghton way, and there might just be a chance he could be taking me on.' He smiled. 'It won't be the same as my last job, nothing like, just wedding invitations and business cards, that kind of thing, but I can't afford to miss the opportunity.' He gripped both her arms so that he was holding her away from him. 'But I see that it's important that we talk, so when can I meet you?' He took a step forward so that Libby was forced to take a step backwards. 'See, there's a meeting of the Labour Council, an open meeting on Monday, at seven o'clock. I know Margaret Bottomley will be there as a representative of the women's section. Why don't you come along with her, then when it's over I'll take you home and we can talk?'

He looked round as if searching for a better solution. 'It's the best I can think of right now. Will you do that?' His voice was urgent even as he consoled. 'And don't do anything rash till then. Promise?'

He was embarrassed; Libby could sense his

embarrassment, even as he tried to be kind. The enormity of what she had just said and done struck her like a sudden blow to the head. With her nerves jangling, she nodded wordlessly and held out her hand.

Solemnly, as if they had met unexpectedly and discussed nothing more important than the blustery weather for the time of year, they shook hands. 'Promise?' he said again. 'We'll have that talk first. Right?'

As they walked away in opposite directions, she turned her head and saw that he was running, loping along at the edge of the pavement, to rejoin the man who might offer him a job. She waited until he reached the corner by the Co-op emporium, hoping he would turn and wave, but he ran on, leaving her to make her way back to the café, then on to the tram stop and Westerley.

When Libby walked through the front door she saw Sarah Batt sitting on the high throne-like chair in the hall, being comforted by Carrie and her mother.

'She just broke down.' Ettie, still in her housecoat, with her faded hair hanging down her back, looked relieved to see Libby. 'She's been like this all week, not herself, and going in her room to cry, and I can't get a word out of her.'

Carrie gave her sister a look which said that any explanations about what had happened down town could wait. 'Down at the mill, fortunately,' she said, interpreting Libby's glance towards the door of the billiard room.

At once Libby knelt down on the dark red and blue patterned carpet, so that her eyes were on a level with Sarah's pinkly puffed eyelids.

'Right! Now you have to tell us what's wrong,

Sarah, because if you don't then there's nothing we can do to help, is there?'

Sarah's plump face set into lines of obstinacy as she made to get up, only to feel Libby's hands on her arms forcing her back. She sighed and gulped back a fresh flow of tears. It was no good. She knew Miss Libby of old, and Miss Libby wasn't one for taking no for an answer.

'It's my boy.' The words were dragged up from deep inside her. 'When I went home last weekend he was coughing fit to burst.' She picked up the corner of her afternoon apron and twisted it into a point. 'He's been off colour for weeks now, an' nothing me mother gives him seems to help. 'She's been scooping the top of a turnip, filling it with honey, and putting brown paper under his vest, and even letting him sleep downstairs with the steam kettle going, but nothing helps.' Her voice thickened with anxiety. 'I'm that frightened. I should have had three brothers, but everyone of them were took off with the cough . . . with the consumption,' she added, saying the dread word aloud. 'An' it runs in families. It *does*, an' nobody can tell me no different, an' me mother knows it as well. I could see the fear on her face.'

'Nonsense!' Libby spoke with firmness. 'You must be talking about — what — thirty years ago? Doctors know more about it now. Besides, your boy lives out in the country with all that fresh air and milk and eggs and cream. It's an environmental disease, Sarah. What your son's got is more like a touch of bronchitis. Some of the kids in my class have that, but they're sleeping four to a bed mostly, and not getting enough nourishment. It's different in your son's case.'

'*Why* is it different?' Sarah's indignation dried her tears. 'What do you thing me mam has to live on? There are no soup kitchens in the country like what there were down in the town when the strike was on. And with the fire going day and night, who's to fetch and chop the wood now me father's gone to his rest?' Worry was making Sarah forget her place, and once started there was no stopping her. 'I was warming a pat of butter at the fire on Sunday morning, and it slipped off the dish on to the coals, and you know what me mother did? She sat down and cried for ten minutes without stopping, an' *you* talk about milk and eggs and cream! Oh, aye, and fresh air. Well, I grant you that's cheap enough, but it's the only thing what is.'

'Oh dear,' Ettie put a hand to her head and swayed, overcome as usual by any unpleasantness. 'We never thought . . . we had no idea.'

'No. Your sort never have, do you?' Sarah was burning her boats with a vengeance, all the pent-up anxiety releasing itself in a flood. 'How do you think I feel when I see good meat on the table every day of the week an' knowing there's nothing I can do about it? Many's the time I've wished I could just send even the gravy to them. Just the gravy, never mind a nice thick slice off the joint. I'd think God had stepped down from his heaven if I saw my lad sink his teeth into a meat butty. Do you know that?'

'Take Mother upstairs.' Libby spoke almost to herself, but at once Carrie obeyed.

'Do this,' her twin had said when they were children. 'Do that,' and at once Carrie had obeyed. 'Do this,' her father had said. 'Do that,' and again she had done what was asked of her. For wasn't Libby the one looking into the mirror whilst she was merely the reflection? Even her first attempt at writing had come out back to front, only decipherable by holding it up to a looking glass. And now Libby was again taking charge. So, gently persuasive, Carrie led the distressed little woman up the wide stairs, leaving her sister to deal with a Sarah they knew little about, a Sarah with a life of her own far from the confines of Westerley.

'Poor Sarah,' Ettie raised a piteous face to her daughter. 'We forget they have feelings, don't we?'

'Now what we are going to do,' Libby was saying downstairs in the hall, 'is this. I will get Doctor Harry to drive out and see your boy this evening.' She stood up. 'The doctor is very good with children. He will examine your son, and whatever is necessary will be done. You must go too,' she added, 'then if there is nothing to worry about Harry will drive you back here. If you are needed, then you must stay there. Mother will have to do without you for a while. It might even do her good. She relies on you far too much. I would come as well, but Carrie is going to an organ recital in King George's Hall with a friend, so I will have to stay at home with Mother.' She waved a hand impatiently. 'It's ridiculous that Mother won't stay in the house alone, but there it is. I can't think what she's going to do when I get married and Carrie tries to lead a life of her own. Why some women allow themselves to become so helpless I don't know.'

All the time Libby had been talking, arranging, organizing, Sarah's mind had been whirling round and round like a moth caught in a gas lamp. The thought of seeing Patrick again without waiting for her next weekend off was an opportunity she could not bring herself to refuse. Then to have him examined by a clever doctor like Doctor Harry — and he must be clever when it cost folks a mint of money just to see him for a few mintutes — oh, dear Mother of God, how could she refuse? She twisted her apron into a harder knot. Libby's doctor would know what to do. Sarah bit her lip so hard that a blood blister formed. And it would be all right because Doctor Harry had never seen Willie . . . he hadn't been coming to the house when Willie was alive, so he would never put two and two together. Men weren't like that, anyroad. But if Patrick died because she was too frightened to accept help — oh, dear sweet Jesus! She couldn't lie awake, not one more night, imagining the worst. She was nigh out of her mind with worry; it was eating her away, and she could take no more.

'Can you do that?' Libby was saying into the telephone. 'I know it's a lot to ask, Harry, but you must see . . . We were staying in tonight anyway. You can be there and back in two hours.'

Like a butterfly Libby had flown straight from one crisis to another, persuasive, sure of her fiancé's cooperation. It was as though she had never met Tom Silver down the town, never trembled at his nearness and asked him to meet her again. First things had always come first with Libby. Besides, Harry was the rock she had clung to for a long time now, and it was unthinkable that he would let her down.

She raised her voice impatiently as he made objections. 'This is something I'm asking you to do for *me*, Harry. For all of us.'

'He's coming.' Libby replaced the receiver and turned to march into the kitchen with Sarah following like a devoted dog at her heels. 'I'll get a basket of things together whilst you go up and get your coat and hat. We're lucky that it's Saturday and the doctor doesn't have an evening surgery. So things are working out already, aren't they.

Then, infuriating Mrs Edwards in the kitchen by taking things off the pantry shelf without so much as a by your leave — the boiled ham that was for the Sunday tea and the eggs for the deep custard to go with the stewed damsons — Libby filled a basket to the brim. It was as if the episode of less than an hour ago had happened to another person altogether, a wild woman who had completely taken leave of her senses.

It was cold in the pantry with its stone floor and deep shelves. It smelled of apples, pickled onions and spices. Mrs Edwards watched in grim silence, arms folded across her one-piece bosom.

'Sarah's mother is ill,' Libby told her. The lie came easily. Sarah's secret was Sarah's secret, and her silence about her son had been respected since long before Mrs Edward's time. Libby walked briskly out of the kitchen, watched balefully by the disgruntled cook. Now she had to start again with tomorrow's menus, and if they thought she was going to put herself out then they had another think coming. Oliver Peel was stingy enough with his money as it was. If he had to make do with cheese and onion pie for his Sunday tea instead of a nice thick slice of boiled ham, then he could like it or lump it. Mrs Edwards thumped the mixing bowl down on the table so that the spoons jumped into the air to fall back with a tinkling clatter.

'A straightforward case of bronchitis,' Harry said, coming back to Westerley exactly two hours later, ruddy-faced and cheerful. He jerked his head towards the door of the lounge. 'Sarah has gone straight up to your mother. I think she feels a bit guilty now about all the fuss, but worry's a funny thing. It grows like a fungus once you let it catch hold.' He sat down on the chesterfield and patted the cushion by his side. 'Come here, love, and let me look at you. Let me hold you, and touch skin that isn't sweaty, and look into eyes that aren't bloodshot . . . Oh, God, its been one hell of a week. Half my patients have flu, or think they're going to have it, and my father is slowly passing some of his patients over to me. Not that it does my ego any good.' He laughed his uninhibited laugh. 'They take one look at me and ask straight off where my father is. You have to be at least fifty before some of them class you as a real doctor.'

Libby stayed exactly where she was. 'What was he like, Sarah's son? I've often wondered. She won't talk about him, ever. She must have been genuinely worried to agree to you going out to see him. Is he like Sarah, all red hair and big teeth and a bit, well, you know, a bit slow?'

Harry shook his head, reached into his pocket for his pipe, held it out for permission, then started to fill it.

'I was surprised. Really surprised. He's a little corker, that lad.' He puffed for a while and threw the spent match into the fire. 'Bright as a button, with an intelligence far beyond his years. He more or less confided in me that both his grandma and his mother worry their guts out about him. He'd got hold of a *Pears Cyclopaedia* from somewhere and he was reading it when we got there, sitting up in bed and going through it alphabetically, reading it as if it were a book of fiction, and understanding most of it if I'm any judge.'

'And his chest?'

'Rattly, granted, but nothing a week in bed and warmth won't cure.' The pipe was going nicely now and Harry leaned back, a man at peace with the world. 'Whippet breed definitely, not like Sarah and her mother with arms and thighs on them like a couple of lady blacksmiths.'

'Then you went for nothing really?'

He shook his head. 'I went for *you*, love. For your sake, and that's enough for me. Now come here, and let's forget young Patrick Batt. Let's talk about the wedding and decide where we're going for our honeymoon, and what changes you're going to make in the house, and important things like the kind of flowers you are going to have in your wedding bouquet.'

Libby moved reluctantly to sit by him and he put his arms round her. When she stiffened in his grasp he rubbed his cheek against hers as if to force a sign of responsiveness from her. When he kissed her she clamped her mouth so tightly shut that he pushed her away to stare at her in bewilderment.

'What's the matter, love? Look, Libby, I'm too tired and old to play games. I've told you, it's been one hell of a week.'

She twisted round to stare into the fire. 'Harry — I'm so very, very sorry, but I can't marry you. I know it's a terrible thing to say now at this moment, but better now than later. I'm sorry.'

'*What* did you say?' Roughly he pulled her round, holding her so that her arms were pinioned. Then he kissed her roughly. 'Do you know what you just said? Do you? As he felt her lack of response he drew back. 'Stop play-acting, Libby! Stop it!' The colour in his cheeks slowly drained away as he stared at her in wide-eyed amazement. 'You *mean* it, don't you? What brought this on?' He made a move towards her, then as she shrank away his temper flared.

'What is it *now*? Is it because you still want me to move my practice down into town and work a clinic for the under-privileged? Because we've been over that, Libby, over and over.' His face darkened. 'You can keep your Bolshie ideas after we're married. You can go to your meetings, and you can wave a red flag as often as you like, but I won't be intimidated.

If I want to treat patients who pay me in a lump sum instead of sixpence a week to the doctor's man, then that's my affair. My father worked all his life to build that practice up, and I intend to carry on where he leaves off. You've got it all wrong, Libby. A newborn baby with a dislocated hip is just as pathetic as a baby bowed with rickets, and a child can die of diptheria without being half-starved into the bargain. Wake up, Libby! Stop setting yourself up as some sort of saviour, because it doesn't suit you. Beneath all that idealistic talk you're still *you*, knowing which side your bread's buttered and accepting it. So come here, and never let me hear you say you won't marry me ever again. If you leave me I'll be just as bereft as if I was an out-of-work labourer in a flat cap standing on street corners. I bleed, too, Libby. Never forget that!'

They were both very tired. Libby had held the afternoon's emotions in check from the moment she walked through the door. Then for more than two hours she had sat with her mother, listening to Ettie wondering plaintively how it would be at Westerley without Sarah.

'I feel in my bones that Sarah needs to be with her mother and the boy. She says her mother hasn't picked up since her father dropped dead. One of these days she won't come back from her weekend off. I feel it in my bones,' she had said again. 'And there's Carrie. She's bound to meet the man she wants to marry before long, and that will leave *me* here alone in this big house with your father.' Ettie had shivered and stared with watery blue eyes into a future that looked as bleak as the Lancashire moors.

Harry had been called out to a patient at five o'clock that morning, and had left his dinner to drive out with Sarah — and now he was faced with Libby's rejection. But he felt his anger evaporating as he saw the way she held herself still, as if she wanted to say much more and was determined not to do so.

'Let's not quarrel, love, I know things aren't easy for you here. Maybe it's not such a good idea my popping round every day. Weddings are nerve-racking things.'

'There isn't going to be a wedding.' Libby's expression hardened. 'I'm sorry, Harry, but I can't help it. To marry you would be a terrible mistake, feeling the way I do.' She started to pull the ring from her finger, only to have her hand taken in a firm clasp.

'I won't listen!' Harry pushed the ring back, then squeezed her left hand hard. 'I have to drive my parents over to see their new house tomorrow; on Monday I have an evening surgery and two consultations, so we'll have to leave it till Tuesday.' He gave her a quick sideways smile. 'On Tuesday I'll pick you up from school at four o'clock, and we'll drive out somewhere for a meal. Then if you still feel the same you can tell me.' He released his tight hold on her hand and gave it a little shake. 'And now I'm going, but remember this.' Gently he cupped her face in his big hands and as he smiled at her she saw the hurt bewilderment in his brown eyes. 'I love you more than life itself. I'll never let you go, not if I have to chloroform you to get you down the aisle.' He glanced round the big room with its overstuffed furniture and preponderance of potted plants. 'I want to get you away from this mausoleum, with your father drinking himself to death across the hall and your mother thinking herself into invalidism upstairs. You were meant to be happy, Libby, and happy is what you're going to be.'

Without attempting to kiss her he walked to the door, a thick-set brown man in his tweedy speckled jacket, a well-fed confident man with his comfortable life mapped out for him. So different from the tall gaunt man with his hair blowing untidily in the wind, running along the pavement for the chance of a job he would hate even if he were lucky enough to get it. They were such worlds apart that Libby felt she could not bear to dwell on the comparison.

When Tuesday came it would all be settled. One way or the other her life would never be the same again. She bowed her head as the silent tears ran slowly down her cheeks.

The hall was already full when Libby took her seat with Margaret Bottomley at the back. The women were in the minority, but the rows of men sat united, their faces serious and intent, some of them leaning forward the better to hear the speakers on the platform.

'This town is in a bad way.' The speaker, a miner, spoke with a fiery delivery that belied his puny appearance. 'And what do our bosses care?' He raised a fist and shook it. 'I'm no Marxist, and neither are most of the men who think like me, but we have one thing in common in this fight of ours. We are all asking for a fair wage for a fair day's work. They — the bosses — can go on living in their big houses for all we care. We don't covet what they've already got. No! All we want is a fair slice of what's going. We just want what's ours by right, and that's a decent standard of living. Is it wrong wanting that?'

Libby could see Tom Silver's dark head four rows in front. He looked down now and again and she guessed he was making notes. He was so naïve, she thought tenderly, believing better conditions would come through the Labour Party. It was men like her father who made the conditions. the rich and the educated. Why couldn't Tom Silver see that? She looked round, startled, as a heckler seated directly behind her, jumped to his feet, shouting and waving his arms about.

'Nay, nay. Of course it's wrong wanting just that! You lot would be satisfied with half a loaf, but I say we deserve a *whole*! Labourism? You lot are nowt but Tories in a different hat. You want to be definite one way or another!'

'He's a Communist,' Margaret whispered. 'He even went so far as to stick one of their posters on the board outside the police station last week. Cheeky blighter. The police will have him if he doesn't watch out.'

Libby turned and saw the eager, screwed-up look of dedication on Margaret's face. She looked harder and saw an unhappy woman, and in a revealing instant realized that political argument could never be the centre of her own existence. It was exciting, it was fascinating, but it wasn't enough. She shivered, holding her arms close round her as if to ward off a sudden freezing wind. What *was* there to satisfy this restless feeling always bubbling up inside her. Would even Tom Silver be able to give her what she wanted, when she wasn't sure herself?

She wrinkled her nose at the smell of closely packed bodies and cheap tobacco, then drew herself slightly away from the woman sitting on her other side. Shifting her position on the hard bench, Libby closed her eyes and willed the meeting to end.

When Tom sat beside her on the slatted seat on the top deck of the tram and paid her fare, she knew the pennies he was counting out in his hand represented more to him than mere coinage. She could see her reflection in the window, all eyes beneath the tiny cloche hat, the fur collar of her wrapover coat snuggled up to her chin.

The shiny material of Tom's jacket looked as if it would disintegrate at the slightest tug, and his bony knees had poked blisters in his trousers. He was a man who did not care very much how he looked, she guessed, but surely, in the time he had been in full employment, he could have provided himself with a coat? His shabbiness caught at her throat, irritating her and at the same time making her feel ashamed of her own warm clothing.

He was talking about the meeting, laughing at the affectation of a Councillor Tomlinson, a big-stomached man who persisted in wearing a cloth cap.

'He never wanted to be a councillor; it's just that he truly believes that his ideas, if they could be put into practice, would improve the lot of working people. I think he must have read every book, every pamphlet, every paper on what the Party stands for. You'll never catch old John out, not on any point of order. He has a case for housing, wages, anything you can think of, and there's no putting him down.'

'He stood up well to the heckling,' Libby said confusedly. They were nearing the terminus now, and they might have been two casual acquaintances returning from the meeting making conversation about what had taken place. She followed him between the rows of seats to the platform, held on to the rail until the tram pulled up, then with a nod of thanks accepted the arm he held out to help her down.

'Now,' he said, as they walked down the wide road towards the lane leading to Westerley, 'what's all this about, Libby?'

He made no move to touch her, not even when her heel caught in a patch of uneven ground. He's proud, she thought, feeling her heartbeat quicken.

He's going to leave me to make all the running, and oh, dear God, what do I say? I can't tell him that all I want is to be near him. She tried to see his expression, but now they had left the well-lit road and were turning into the lane where deep shadows filled the long spaces between the lamps. His face was no more than a pale blur.

They walked on in silence for a while, then she stopped suddenly. 'This is where I live,' she told him. Through the gap in the hedge down the long, winding drive was Westerley, with lights gleaming from the downstairs windows and from the upstairs front bedroom where Ettie would be reading, trying to get to sleep.

Tom stuck both hands in his pockets and whistled softly. 'And there's just you and your mother and father live in that mansion of a house?'

'And my sister.' Libby felt her face burn at the implied sarcasm. 'And the maids,' she added defiantly. 'Mrs Edwards, and the maid of all work, and Sarah who looks after my mother.'

'I never knew you had a sister.'

'I used to have a brother, too, but he was killed in the war.' She brought up her eyes to meet his and saw that he was watching her carefully.

'What do you want of me?' he asked abruptly.

She was trembling now, rather frightened, but when he suddenly pulled her to him and held her so close that there was no point at which their bodies did not touch, and then put his mouth over hers, she responded to him with an almost animal-like ferocity.

'There!' His voice had a challenging all-male aggressive ring to it. 'There, Libby Peel. Is *that* what you want? Did you want to find out if my kiss was less clinical than your doctor lover's? Were you for finding out the difference, then?'

When she hit him, an open-handed slap on his right cheek, he threw back his head and laughed out loud. Pulling her to him again he ran his hand down her back, down her spine, lingering on her buttocks, so that she felt it as intimately as if she had been unclothed.

'Would you marry me, Libby? Would you come with me and be my love in that room you saw? Would you stop in there all day long and cook my tea on the gas ring, and manage on less than you spend on frocks and shoes, and silly hats like the one you've got on now? Because I tell you straight — not a penny would I take from that father of yours.'

She could feel every inch of him. It was as though she was being made love to, there in the dark of the wild night with the wind tossing his words away and the lights of Westerley shining out behind his head like some incongruous backdrop to a Victorian drama.

'I . . . I . . . You're frightening me!' She struggled to break free, but it was as though she were being held in a vice.

'Right!' Suddenly he let her go. 'If you really want me, then go inside. Go into the house this minute and pack a bag, and come out to me.' He thrust both his hands in his pockets. 'I'll wait ten minutes, and if you don't come then I'll know you've changed your mind. Go on now! Make it snappy! I'll be waiting.'

Without further words he turned and walked a few yards down the lane to stand in the shelter of the high hedge, a dark waiting blur, with head held high and the collar of his jacket upturned against the seeking wind.

While he waited he strained his eyes against the darkness, dimly assessing the rolling meadows and the dark blue haze of hills in the distance. Dear God, he thought, this is one gamble that has to come off.

146

Then, because even in the worst of times his northern sense of humour never quite deserted him, he admitted to himself wryly that he had always been a gambling man. Even in France on the Somme, coming unexpectedly face to face with a real bloody German, he had accepted that the best form of defence was attack. He could smell the acrid musty smell of the mud and dead bodies as he remembered the German, a lad of no more than seventeen years, lowering his bayonet in that one weak moment of indecision. Then his jaw tightened as he remembered too the look of bewilderment on the young face as the German realized that his indecision had cost him his life.

But the war had been over now for eight years come next month and Tom Silver was still fighting. Now the war was against misery and poverty. The grit of the unmade road crunched under his shoes as he walked back to the place where he could see the big house, a cocoon of warmth and light, a haven for those who could afford to be sheltered inside its walls.

What he had just done was cruel, but then he had always accepted that there was a cruel streak in him. He narrowed his eyes and held his breath for a moment as he saw a curtain move at an upper window. That lass, Libby Peel, with her half-formed ideals and the longing in her eyes for something to give a touch of drama to what she considered to be the boring pattern of her days . . . that lovely, lovely lass was no more for him than he was for her.

Tom turned away, back down the lane with his slogging soldier's walk, to the main road and the terminus where a tram stood ready for its rhythmic clanging journey back into town. But tram rides cost money, and anyway he needed to walk. He needed to despise himself a little for the way he had behaved and, besides, walking took longer and kept him out in the air, away from the room at the top of the house that smelled of the misery he swore to eradicate some day.

And the Libby Peels of this world had no place in that scheme of things, no place at all.

CHAPTER SEVEN

By the middle of November, with the wedding of Libby Peel to Doctor Harry, son of Dr Henry and Mrs Brandwood, only five weeks away, Carrie found herself trapped in the school's basement cloakroom by the man she had been avoiding for weeks.

'You have at least to *talk* to me, Carrie! You owe me that!'

Mungo's face was violin-shaped with self-pity, and a faint bruise showed up in a yellowish tinge at the side of his jaw. 'I need a friend so much, Carrie, someone to *understand*. And who else is there but you?'

He stood before her in the narrow passageway between the rows of hanging coats, felt hats and shoe bags, holding out an arm so that she was trapped between him and the wall. He was so close she could feel his breath on her face; so close that she could see the despair in his eyes, and so close that even his hoarse whispering came to her like a shout.

'Mungo!' She tried to duck beneath his arm, but his hand came down and clamped itself on her shoulder. 'Someone might come down! Mungo! Don't be so stupid. The bell will go any minute, and if they find you down here with me . . . oh, God, Mungo, let me go!'

His mouth was against her ear. 'You're driving me mad, Carrie. It's hell coming here day after day when you won't even look at me properly. I'm not made of stone. Carrie! Two people can't have meant what we did to each other, and then act like strangers!' He made a sound halfway between a groan and a sigh. 'Is there someone else? Tell me. Have you met someone else?'

'No!' Carrie jerked her head away only to have her chin grasped and twisted round again. 'No Mungo! There isn't anyone else. I've told you over and over, you're *married* and I . . . I no longer love you.' Her brown eyes were pleading. 'There was no future for us, you know that, and now you must get on with your life and leave me to get on with mine.' Tears of frustration sprang to her eyes. 'You have to be a man, Mungo and accept that it's all over.'

'Never!' To her horror, he brought his head down and fastened his mouth over hers. His hand slid down her back to hold her close. The more she struggled, the more his thwarted passion flared, and when he felt her lack of response he began to kiss her closed eyelids, her nose, her cheeks, whispering incoherent broken words of love.

'Carrie . . . Carrie . . . oh, my love. I *need* you, I must have your love. Oh, dear God, please be kind to me, please!'

When the voice of the headmaster sounded behind them, Mungo released his hold of her so abruptly that Carrie felt her knees give way. Grasping at a school gaberdine raincoat to save herself, she slid down to sit on the narrow bench in front of the row of pegs, knocking a shoe bag to the floor. Shaking so violently she could actually see her legs trembling, she looked up and met the furious, incredulous stare of the small man respected and feared by both teachers and pupils alike. Mr Eccles's eyes glittered behind the rimless spectacles worn habitually halfway down his hawklike nose.

And at that very moment the clattering of outdoor shoes on the flight of stone steps leading down to the basement heralded the onrush of Form Four hurtling in from their PT lesson, followed by Miss Clayton, with a scarlet band round her short hair, her cheeks polished red by the cold wind.

'Come with me! Both of you!' Mr Eccles nodded first to Mungo, then to Carrie, before leading the way with his small head poked forward and the back view of his trousers hanging loose over what seemed to be a non-existent behind.

'What's up?' Miss Clayton caught at Carrie's arm, then stepped back as Carrie brushed her impatiently aside.

'Now then. No talking!' Miss Clayton bellowed the command automatically, her eyes fixed on the trio disappearing up the basement steps.

'Snogging behind the coat racks, I bet.'

The gym mistress whipped round just too late to catch the girl responsible for the whispered words.

Upstairs in his study overlooking the rhododendron-fringed drive Mr Eccles MA faced the two cringing members of his staff.

'Never,' he said, in his reed-thin, trembling voice, 'never in the whole of my career have I been faced with a situation so degrading, so shameful, so repugnant.' He lifted his small pointed chin. 'I am not going to ask you what was going on because I could see only too well.' Taking out a white handkerchief he mopped his forehead. 'Teachers have a very special responsibility to their pupils, a grave and serious responsibility to show an example, to be themselves beyond reproach. And yet I find you . . .' here words failed him for a moment, 'doing what you were doing

151

in *my* school, in class time . . .' Picking up a lined ruler from his desk, he threw it down again. 'What were you doing out of your classroom, Miss Peel? Just for the record, of course.'

Carrie seemed to be finding difficulty in forming her mouth round the words. 'One of my girls had come upstairs without changing into her indoor shoes, and as they were in the middle of copying something from the blackboard I went to fetch them for her.'

It was the truth. It was a typical Carrie gesture, the self-effacing Carrie who was used to fetching and carrying.

But Mr Eccles waved her explanation aside with a downward motion of his long thin hand. 'And you, Mr McDermot? What is your excuse?'

Mungo gave an eloquent, all-revealing sideways glance at the trembling girl who looked as if she might faint at any minute. The truth was that he had seen Carrie through the glass panels of his classroom door, hurrying on some errand, and decided it was too good an opportunity to miss. Telling his class to read over the poem they had been analyzing, he had simply followed her. Now his mind was too numb with the implications of what was happening to attempt any alternative explanation. So he remained silent . . . a silence that grew and lengthened as Carrie lifted her head to stare at him in bewildered terror. Surely Mungo would admit that he was to blame? Even though it almost certainly would not help, surely as a gentleman he would at least try to absolve her from *some* of the blame?

Mr Eccles's mind was made up. As well as his genuine disgust at the scene he had just witnessed, there were wider issues to consider. For instance, an almost forgotten meeting of the town's Rotarians when

Oliver Peel, with a few snide remarks, had made him look like a fool. The fact that at the last meeting of the board of governors he had been advised to cut his staff or raise the school fees to an unacceptable level. His instinctive dislike of Mungo McDermot, who had refused to fight in the war whilst the headmaster's eldest son had been wounded. And lastly, the seconds he had stood there down in the basement cloakroom, a Peeping Tom, enjoying a vicarious thrill at the sight of the man and woman locked together, writhing together in what appeared to be an embrace of such unbridled passion that his own loins had tightened with an almost physical pain. For that alone they stood before him damned.

'You can get your things and go,' he said quietly. 'You will be hearing from the authorities in due course, but I will not have either one of you in my school again. In another minute the children would have seen the disgusting spectacle, and I will not have their minds sullied by your depravity. The rumours will be bad enough as it is, but for the time being I will take your form, Mr McDermot, and Miss Clayton will see to *your* pupils, Miss Peel.' He jerked his chin towards the door. 'Now go! Do what you have to do in a field or behind a hedge somewhere, but leave my school. Now, this minute!'

As Carrie turned to obey, Mungo came suddenly to life. As she looked back for a brief moment she saw him leaning across the wide desk, mouthing incoherent words lost to her. Then she ran across the wide landing into the mercifully deserted staff room. She collected her coat and hat from the cupboard, then ran back down the stairs and out into the damp cold of the November morning.

She was not, she told herself, a totally innocent

party. What had happened was only the culmination of what had been going on during the long summer afternoons when she had lain with Mungo in the summer house, responding to his caresses. If this was to be her punishment, then she would face it as bravely as she could. No, let Mungo plead to be forgiven, let him grovel before Mr Eccles and beg to be reinstated. She, Carrie Peel, would leave with dignity.

Then, as the tram clattered its way towards her and she moved into the middle of the road to board it, the terror she had held in check suddenly exploded inside her. Groping her way between the rows of seats like a blind woman, she sat down to find she was shaking so much that she could hardly get her fingers round the coins in her purse.

Somehow she would have to find the courage to tell her father. That same night she would have to face him and say, 'Father, today I was sent home from school because the headmaster, Mr Eccles, found me down in the basement cloakroom in the arms of one of the teachers, a married man.'

She made small sideways movements with her head as if to shake the inevitable from her as the tram clattered and rocked away from the town, dropping off its passengers, leaving her at the end to sit there alone, head bowed, too terrified even to cry.

'You must tell Father the truth.' Libby put an arm round her sister's shaking shoulders. 'You must tell him how this man has been making your life a misery for a long time. How he has been following you round at school and forcing his attentions on you, and how he overpowered you this morning so that the headmaster jumped to the wrong conclusions. You must get that all out before Father has a chance to shout you down.'

Carrie's voice filled with bitter scorn. 'But it wouldn't be *true*, Libby! Oh, yes it was exactly like I said this morning, but Mungo wouldn't have pounced on me if I hadn't been going with him all the summer. He's not a maniac.' She started to cry again. 'He's gentle, really, and, oh God, it'll be even worse for him. He has a wife and child to support. How will he get another teaching post now? He's finished, Libby — this will finish him. I know.'

'I thought you said you'd stopped loving him?'

'I *have*!' Carrie wailed. 'I don't know how I even *thought* I loved him! But that doesn't mean I can't be sorry for him. 'She shivered. 'Oh, that awful Mr Eccles! When I heard his voice, all the blood inside me froze. I'll never forget that moment for as long as I live!'

When she saw Libby turn away, her shoulders shaking, she thought at first her twin was crying in sympathy. Then to her amazement she saw that Libby was laughing.

'Oh, Carrie . . .' Libby turned round, tears of laughter brightening her brown eyes. 'Don't lose your sense of humour, love. It isn't the end of the world. You'll get another teaching post in a better school, one like mine, where you can give the kids a peep at a world they never knew existed. Not teaching kids who are only passing time till they marry the son of one of their father's friends, or go straight into father's firm.' She came and knelt down by the side of the bed, putting her hands on Carrie's knees. 'Oh, I can just see that dried-up little man standing there with his little prissy mouth wide open and his eyes standing out like chapel hat-pegs. He hasn't got a bottom has he? When I saw him on your last Sports Day I couldn't believe it, but I swear that underneath his pants and his combs — he's sure to wear combs — there's nothing, just a flat, empty nothing.'

Carrie drew a shaky breath. 'I've often wondered myself what he sits on,' she said. Then as they rocked together, Libby added, 'and if Father goes too far — if he goes on about morals, then I'll remind him of what I saw that night. "And just which pot is calling the kettle black?" I'll say. I will! I'll be away from this house soon anyway, so what does it matter?'

When Oliver Peel, without knocking, banged back the bedroom door with a slam that almost jerked it off its hinges, he saw two faces turn to him. Two identical faces, with the laughter he had heard as he stood outside wiped from them as if their old nanny had taken a damp flannel and washed the merriment clean away. Straddled in the doorway like a huge black bull, nostrils dilated, face flushed to an apoplectic purple, he bellowed, 'Where does he live? That's what I want to know!' He took a step forward as the two faces registered first dismay, then a cringing terror. 'That was Eccles on the telephone, feeling it was his duty, the sod, to break the news to me first before we get what he called the official letter. But he thought it unethical to give me the name and address of the man responsible for this filthy humiliation.'

With one movement he shot out an arm and flung Libby to one side. 'And you can keep out of this, madam! This is one time when you don't speak for your sister. One time when she stands on her own two feet, instead of acting like your bloody shadow.' Taking Libby by the arm he frogmarched her towards the door. 'But she's not your bloody shadow, is she?

Tarred with the same brush she might be, but she's capable of getting up to her own nastiness, isn't she?'

Furiously Libby tried to break free from the iron grip, only to hear Carrie's voice ring out loud, clear and commanding. 'Go, please, Libby. I want you to. Please . . .please.'

Oliver's whisky-laden breath fanned hot on her face as Libby immediately stopped struggling, but before the door was slammed in her face she called out, 'Don't tell him, Carrie! Whatever you do, don't tell him!'

Then she was outside on the landing, breathing hard, clenching her fists and muttering to herself. 'If he lays a finger on Carrie I'll kill him myself. I swear it. He isn't fit to live! He's cruel, vicious, and I hate him so much I wish he was dead! If he dropped dead right this minute I would jump on his dead face, then go down and enjoy my dinner! I would! I swear it!'

'Your sister isn't coming down for her meal.' Oliver took his place as usual at the head of the table. Libby pushed her chair back and half rose to her feet, but he motioned her back with a wave of the hand holding the carving knife.

'Oh, dear . . .' Ettie Peel took a long, deep breath, then held a hand to her heart. 'What has Carrie been doing?' She gave a piteous glance in her husband's direction. 'I heard shouting, but I thought it was Libby. It's not like Carrie . . .' Her voice wavered.

'Tell her.' Oliver ran the carving knife up and down the sharpening steel. 'Tell her if you wish. The matter is out of my hands now until I choose to do something about it. Go on! Make your mother ill. It's up to you.'

Libby held her anger tight inside till she felt her

blood must surely be at boiling point. She saw the way her mother's lower lip trembled and the faint bluish tinge to her lips, and pity, overcoming the anger, forced her back to her chair again.

'It's nothing, Mother.' To her own surprise, her voice came out quite calm. 'Carrie had a bit of an argument with the headmaster at school today, so she's thinking of changing to another teaching job. It was time, anyway. She's far too good for that tinpot private school where parents too well off to know better send their kids.'

'Oh, dear.' Ettie Peel helped herself to one small boiled potato. 'But it *will* be nice to have Carrie at home till the wedding. There's so much to do. Oh, I wish she could meet someone like Harry.' She dribbled a spoonful of mashed carrots on to her plate. 'The man who is going to be your best man, Libby — he's not married, is he? Wasn't he at university with Harry years ago?'

'He's married to his mother,' Libby said clearly, venting her anger by being deliberately provocative.

'Oh, dear,' her mother said, refusing the gravy. 'I see,' she said wistfully, not seeing at all.

'I don't know what Father said to her, but she didn't tell him Mungo's name or where he lived.' Libby ran out to the car as Harry drove up to the front of the house. 'But we're going there now. We have to warn him that Father is on the warpath. Otherwise there'll be murder done.' She climbed into the passenger seat. 'Come on then. I'm not exactly looking forward to it, but it has to be done. Father will get his address somehow, and the sooner Mungo McDermot knows what to expect the better.'

Harry raised his eyebrows. 'But what about his wife? He's a married man, isn't he? You can't just barge in and confront him, Libby. His wife won't know anything about his . . . dalliance with Carrie. Surely you see we can't interfere? It's none of our business, love.'

'What happens to Carrie *is* my business. What happens to Carrie happens to me.' Libby's small chin jutted forward. 'Carrie told me that Mungo's boy is kept at home because he's deaf and dumb, so if we can't get Mungo alone I'm going to say I've come about the possibility of the boy attending school.' She nodded twice. 'But we *have* to get Mungo alone. It will all blow over in time, but for the moment he has to lie low.'

'You can sit outside in the car if you would rather,' she added as they drove down the long tram route to the town, turning left eventually at Libby's direction. 'It's off here, I think. Number twenty-two. I used to come down here for piano lessons when I was a little girl.'

'I didn't know you played the piano.' Harry said this with the air of a man who had long ago accepted the fact that he did not know much about anything at all.

'I don't. It was a complete waste of time,' said Libby, peering through the car window at the numbers on the doors of the terraced houses set behind tiny front gardens.

'Heaven preserve me from bossy women,' Harry whispered fondly as they stood on the short paved path waiting for an answer to their knock.

'Why? Do you know any?' Libby answered sweetly, as the door opened almost at once.

Ten mintutes later Harry started the car and drove back down the street. 'So where did that get us?' he asked. 'That woman had been drinking, did you know that? Brandy, I would guess, and by the colour of her I would also guess that her liver is part rotted. She's going to be in trouble if she doesn't watch out.'

Libby wrinkled her nose fastidiously. 'She *was* awful, wasn't she? Grotesque. I thought hard drinkers stopped eating? But there wasn't much evidence of that — she must weigh at least fourteen stones.'

'Glands.' Harry was more relaxed now the mission was completed. 'But the boy was pathetic, wasn't he?' He signalled to turn right. 'You know, you could be right about that child needing help. He isn't mentally retarded, not at all. He was taking it all in. He was lip-reading, that lad, *and* making sense of it too. And don't ask me how. A child born deaf like that is only dumb if he is never taught to speak, and if that boy has never learned to speak then how could he lip-read?' He stopped to allow a man and a woman to walk out into the road to board the tram. 'But his mother soon put *you* in your place when you tried to suggest schooling, didn't she?'

Libby wrinkled her nose again. 'She smelled, Harry. Her clothes and the house weren't dirty, but *she* smelled . . .urgh! No wonder her husband looks elsewhere.' She turned sideways. 'Where do you think Mungo is? She doesn't know anything yet, does she? When she said he hadn't been home from school, I didn't know what to say. Heaven help him when he does decide to return. Carrie says she hits him, and I can well believe it. I wouldn't like to meet her in a dark passage at night. I bet she packs a hefty punch.'

Harry, driving with his usual caution, was well content. This was the Libby he had fallen in love with and would love till the day he died. Bossy, outrageous, funny, taking up causes with enthusiasm, then dropping them as suddenly. Helping, caring Libby — naïve at times and immature, childlike even, though she would flare into instant indignation if he said so. But that didn't come from inherited characteristics, but because of that man, her father. Harry sighed. If ever a man was in need of psychiatric treatment, then that man was Oliver Peel. he alone, with his Victorian ideas of how to bring up daughters, was responsible for the mess Carrie seemed to be in. Treat a woman like a child and she would behave like one. Deprive her of parental affection, and she would seek that affection elsewhere. And Libby . . . Harry gripped the wheel hard. He would never know what had caused her to try to break off the engagement a month or so back. All he knew was that, though quieter of late and less prone to dramatic outbursts, she was now anticipating their wedding day with a quiet serenity that made him love her more that ever — if that were possible. Taking one hand from the wheel he placed it on her knee, and was rewarded when she covered it with her own hand, answering his pressure with a loving response that made his blood rise until his farmer's face was suffused with a ruddy glow.

'Nearly home,' he said.

Less than ten minutes later Harry was again at the wheel of the car with Libby beside him and Carrie seated in the back.

'I'm sure I know where to find Mungo,' Carrie was saying. 'It's not far. Turn left here, Harry. Now right. Here! This is the place.'

Stopping the car, he saw that they were beside a high hedge, and all at once he was remembering the old manor house, drooping into decay even when he was a boy. Now he supposed it was no more than a derelict ruin, cloaked in trailing ivy, with no future for it but the trundling rumble of bulldozers when the town council decided the time was ripe for development. Hardly the place for . . . He raised a resigned eyebrow as Carrie, getting out of the car, asked them to stay where they were, promising she would be as quick as possible.

'Let her go,' he told an indignant Libby. 'She knows what she's doing, and as far as I can remember there's a little summer house just inside that hedge. She won't be going all the way to the house, not on a night as dark as this.'

'So that's where they met.' Libby sounded smug. 'I often wondered where Carrie met him when she was late home from school. Talk about a dark horse! Fancy that,' she added.

'Let's forget Carrie for a little while.' Harry put his arm across the back of the seat and drew Libby to him. 'Oh, love. I'm just counting the days now, aren't you?'

'I hope she knows what she's doing.' Libby returned his kiss absent-mindedly. 'If she's not back in ten minutes I'm going in there after her. I am!'

Mungo was there, inside the summer house, in the dark, sitting on the edge of the chaise longue and smoking, flicking the ash on to the pile of spent cigarettes at his feet.

'It's all right, it's only me.' Carrie closed the door behind her and, guided by the red glow from what must have been his umpteenth cigarette, went to sit beside him, keeping her distance and speaking slowly and firmly.

'You have to go home, Mungo. You have to go home now, and face her . . . face Beatrice. I've had to face my father, and you must face her. This is something you can't run away from, Mungo, but . . . ' Her voice faltered. 'You have to keep away from my father, for the time being. He will find out who

162

you are, and where you live. Not from me. Never from me. But he *will* find out, and when he does he'll come for you.'

She started to put out a hand towards the silent cringing figure sitting beside her on the rickety sofa, then drew it back. 'What we did — what we were doing last summer was wrong, and this is our punishment. But running away won't help. It's not like running away from the war, Mungo, because the war was far away, but this is here. You have to be a man.' She sighed. 'Mungo! Are you listening to me? Are you?'

When he began to cry she felt the pity drain out of her, leaving her mind crystal clear. Her sympathy wilted away, so that she had a sudden desire to get up and go, leaving him to wallow in his grief. She asked herself how she had ever imagined she loved this man. How *could* she have loved him, and dreamed of him every waking moment? Ached for his touch, and felt a day wasted when they had not been together? Run out to meet him, climbing through the hedge all those warm summer days to lie with him in this musty place. Lied to Libby . . .

'Libby and Harry are waiting for me outside on the road in the car.' She stood up. 'They went to your house tonight and saw — saw your wife.' She fought down a desire to slap him as he moaned like a wounded animal. 'Oh, you needen't worry, they didn't say anything. They were only trying to warn you.' She opened the door slightly, letting in the damp night air. 'It's going to be foggy, Mungo. If you come now I'll ask Harry to run you home. We can drop you at the end of your street.'

'I'm not going.' The first words he spoke sounded thick in his smoke-rasped throat. 'I'm never going back there, ever!'

Carrie was achingly tired. It had been, she was sure, the worst day of her whole life, and now she could take no more. 'If you don't get up and come with me, I'll go and fetch Harry. He's big and strong, and his evening has been ruined already through my fault and yours. He's also a very patient man, but he's a doctor and I know he will never leave you sitting there, rotting like the leaves.' She kicked out with her foot. 'You'll catch pneumonia if you stay here all night; you must be frozen stiff now, so are you coming of your own free will or shall I go and fetch Harry?'

Carrie waited as he stumbled past her out into the darkness, through the gap in the hedge and over to the waiting car.

'Will you take him home, Harry?' Carrie made the request humbly, only to step back in surprise as Harry leaned over the back of his seat to open the rear door.

'Is he ill?' It was the doctor in him speaking now. 'Unable to walk?'

Carrie turned to where Mungo cowered against the hedge, lighting yet another cigarette, the flame from the match trembling in his shaking hand.

'No he's not ill. Just very frightened,' she said slowly.

'Then get in.' Harry turned back again. 'He can walk. I'm damned if I'll take him home. He's not a naughty schoolboy. Anyway, I've had enough. I need a drink.'

'Harry is right.' Libby's voice rang with pride at the unexpected limits to her fiancé's benevolence. 'Enough is enough.'

As they drove away, Carrie, rubbing at the window and peering out into the darkness, saw Mungo take his first stumbling steps in the direction of the town.

A faint lingering pity welling up inside her died, leaving in it's place a healing sense of relief, and the comforting knowledge that from now on the man called Mungo McDermot would in time be no more than an unpleasant memory.

From now on, the forgetting could begin.

CHAPTER EIGHT

'One thousand four hundred looms stopped mainly as a result of the strike; valuable orders lost while our continental rivals collected the orders. *We* taught them to weave, and now the foreign buggers are taking *our* trade!'

Bleary-eyed, Oliver Peel looked up from his desk and waved the tackler Jimmy Earnshaw away with a dismissive gesture.

But the little man stood his ground. 'That faulty loom's still banging up, maister. The weft's not leaving the shuttle right. I can stop on and feckle it if you want me to.'

Oliver knew the worth of Jimmy Earnshaw. The small man with the bushy moustache and deeply lined face had a hundred and fifty looms in his charge. He was better than a qualified engineer at improvising with a weight or a wedge when the tension of a machine needed keeping up. He also knew that Jimmy had the sensitive feel necessary to maintain the correct delivery of the cloth, and without him the weavers would be all at sea. But at that moment a banging loom seemed of little importance.

'Get on home, Jimmy,' he said, keeping his right hand on the whisky bottle in the half-open drawer of his desk. 'It'll keep till morning.'

The little man chewed hard on the plug of tobacco wedged in the side of his mouth, and turned reluctantly to go. He didn't hold much cop for the

166

man slumped behind the big desk, but there were times, and this was one, when he felt heart sorry for him. Oliver Peel looked dreadful, all red-necked and bloated, with his eyes sunk deep into pads of swollen flesh. Aye, he were a sick man if ever there were one; it would be a hard man what couldn't feel pity.

'Goodnight then, maister.' The tackler opened the door, and turned, adjusting his soiled mercerized cotton scarf. 'It's a terrible night out yon.'

'Goodnight, Jimmy.' Oliver took the bottle out of the drawer and tipped it into the glass hidden behind the files on his desk. It had taken him three days to find out the address of the man who had brought shame and humiliation to his house, and now he was ready for revenge.

The whisky bottle was empty when he pushed himself unsteadily to his feet. He took his bowler hat and thick melton overcoat from the stand in the corner, and putting the hat on first struggled awkwardly into the heavy overcoat. Normally his drinking did not begin in earnest until he had eaten his evening meal and retired to the billiard room with his accounts. Now the drink was inflaming his empty stomach and firing his muddled brain. He turned out the light and walked unsteadily to the door, remembering to lock it behind him before dropping the keys into his pocket.

Mr Crankshaw, the mill manager, had left at the same time as the weavers streaming out into the mill yard when the hooter blew. Curling his lip at the man's uncluttered desk, Oliver walked through the outer office and into the yard. For a moment it was as though he was blinded. He swayed, stretched out a hand and touched a cold damp wall. Then, as he shook his massive head from side to side like a wounded animal trying to clear its vision, he saw dimly in front of him the outline of the mill gates.

Some warning told him that tonight was not the night; that to take the short cut along the canal bank to the street where Mungo McDermot lived was foolhardy in the extreme. But the whisky urged him on. Lurching in a reeling walk, he turned down the short street and made his perilous way down the stone steps leading to the murky waters of the canal.

It was a stretch of rough bank often used by colliers as a training ground for their whippets, where boys dangled twine in a vain attempt at fishing, carrying their pathetic catches home in glass jamjars tied with string. Certainly not the place to be on a dark night, with fog swirling up from the dirty water, concealing the dusty grass verge and merging it with the uneven path. Two hundred yards, that was all, before Oliver came to the steps leading to the house whose number was burned into his brain.

He had no clear idea in his mind as to what he was actually going to do to the apology of a man who had, so his informant had told him, sat out the war on his backside. Oliver groaned aloud. Willie had given *his* life for his country — that bright shining young life holding such promise. But of one thing Oliver was sure; Mungo McDermot wasn't going to get away with it. He, Oliver Peel, would see to it that he never worked again, even if he personally had to confront every bloody board of governors to blacken a character that already stank to high heaven.

Carrie — well, she was a woman, and could always find plenty to do around the house. He had never held with his daughters working, anyway. Women should stop at home where they belonged — where God intended them to be. Besides, with Libby gone, her sister would be a comfort for her mother.

Mumbling to himself, Oliver caught his foot on a loose stone, lost his balance and staggered to the right, one arm flailing to save himself. The stunted grass bordering the canal was slippery, and as he fought to regain his balance his feet slid from under him. The splash his heavy body made as he fell into the water seemed to be swallowed up by the fog which closed round him, and as he sank the evil-smelling water rushed into his open mouth, choking him.

The silk-lined heavy overcoat soaked up the water like a sponge, dragging him down again as he surfaced. He opened his mouth to shout for help, flung out an arm to grasp the stunted grass at the side of the bank, then sank back into the water.

His bowler hat, its sleekness polished by Carrie that morning, floated away like the hump of a wet black seal. The water was in his ears, his mouth, filling his lungs as his frantic struggling took him further away from the bank into the middle of the fog-shrouded canal. Kicking out he tried to get rid of his shoes, but sodden with water they only helped to drag him down again.

The realization that he was dying penetrated his drink-fuddled brain, and as he choked and struggled the name screaming through his head was that of his son.

'Willie! Willie!'

Then the dark waters closed over him for the last time.

When the fog lifted early the next morning, wafted away by a cold wind, they found him, every tissue in his massive body sodden with water. When Harry identified him in the mortuary he turned his head away and ordered that the coffin be immediately sealed. When Libby and Carrie, stunned and

169

disbelieving, stood in the newly opened Chapel of Rest they saw no more than a plain oak coffin surrounded by high-banked chrysanthemums behind an alcove lined with purple velvet curtains.

Carrie was weeping silently, but Libby, dry-eyed, stared at the box which held the remains of the man she had tried in vain to love and had finally hated.

'It's my fault.' Carrie repeated the words she had been saying ever since the police had called to report the finding of the body. 'He was going to find Mungo,' she had wailed. 'That's the only reason he was where he was, and now I have to live with that for the rest of my life.'

'He was drunk,' Libby said. 'He could have stepped out in the road under the wheels of a car. It was the drink killed him, so stop it! Carrie! I won't hear you torturing yourself with remorse. Our father was sick in his mine, and if he *had* been on his way to find Mungo, who knows what might have happened?' She turned to Harry for reassurance. 'If he hadn't been drinking he could have got out of the canal, and if he *had* found Mungo he might have killed him.' She lifted her chin. 'Better to have drowned than have committed a murder.'

With his arms round both girls, Harry led them out of the darkened alcove, past the curtained partitions and down the steps, nodding to the undertaker who watched them go with clasped hands and a suitably doleful expression.

'We should have had him brought back to the house. It seems dreadful leaving him there all alone.' Carrie got into the back of the car and buried her face in her hands.

Libby, with two high spots of colour burning on her cheekbones, turned round from the passenger seat.

'And have Mother upset more than she is already? With him lying there in the billiard room with a lily in his hand, and Mother lying upstairs in bed having a heart attack at the thought of it? Father is *dead*, Carrie. There is nothing you can say or do that will bring him back again. He's dead, and Mother is alive. She's the one we have to be thinking about. I am right, aren't I, Harry?'

'You never loved him.' Carrie's voice from the back seat was no more than a whisper, but on hearing it Libby whipped round again.

'Did *you* love him, Carrie?' Her voice rose. 'Did any one of us love him, if the truth were told?' She beat with a clenched hand on the back of the seat. 'Father was impossible to love and dying hasn't suddenly changed him into a plaster saint. So stop being a hypocrite, Carrie, because that's what you are!'

Harry, driving with his usual caution, raised both eyebrows as he decided to let them get on with it. It was an uncanny experience listening to the sisters quarrelling. It was as though Libby was talking to her own conscience and it was answering back through Carrie.

'You're so hard!' Carrie was moaning through her sobs. 'You'll be telling me next you're glad he's dead!'

'I am not glad he's dead.' Libby, the voice of reason, spoke again. 'But I can't *feel* anything. I can't at this moment think of one kind thing he ever did or one kind word he said. I wish I could, but I can't.'

'He was our father . . .'

'Oh yes, he was our father. He got Mother pregnant, then when there were two of us and girls at that he turned away from Mother and from us, to Willie.' Libby's head drooped. 'It was Willie, always Willie . . .'

'Do you think he'll be with Willie now?' Carrie's

voice was calmer and through the driving mirror Harry could see her dabbing at her eyes with a screwed-up handkerchief. Silently he willed Libby to say what her sister wanted to hear, then gave a resigned sigh when the answer came.

'I doubt it. Unless Willie went straight down to hell. Because that's where Father will be, make no mistake about that.'

So why, Harry asked himself as he stopped the car outside the big house with every one of its windows curtained out of respect, why in the name of all that made sense was it Libby who with her sister's arm round her, was crying her eyes out as they went up the steps together?

'The wedding must go on. Exactly as planned.'

Ettie Peel, dressed in the morning for once, was sitting in the high-winged chair by the fire, the day before the funeral. Harry stared at her as if he doubted the evidence of his own eyes. It couldn't be, and yet the small, timid woman seemed to have grown physically since hearing the news of her husband's death. Gone was the hang-dog expression and the nervous habit she had of rolling finger and thumb together. It was as though with the dominance of Oliver's presence removed from the house she had come into her own, found that she could make decisions, and with the discovery grown in stature. For hours she had been closeted in the billiard room with Mr Crankshaw, the mill manager, listening, accepting advice, and agreeing that for the time being the mill would carry on as before.

'We owe it to the weavers,' she had said. 'You must engage an under-manager, Mr Crankshaw. That will be possible, I suppose?'

Then, assured that with the recent closure of two

mills in the town there was likely to be a queue for the position, Ettie had nodded, satisfied, and thanked the bewildered little man for his cooperation.

Harry, entering the house as Oliver's mill manager was leaving, had thought that he too had grown in stature, running down the steps and heading in the direction of town like a man who had just had a purpose in life handed to him on a plate.

'You can trust me, Mrs Peel,' Mr Crankshaw had said. 'I will try and see you don't have to worry. I promise you that.'

But Ettie looked far from worried as she talked about the wedding, now only four weeks away.

'People will talk,' she said, 'but let them. Your parents had planned to move to their retirement bungalow before Christmas, and your new assistant starts the first week in January, Harry, so if we postpone the wedding there are going to be a lot of people with their plans upset. And besides, the concept of a whole year of mourning is going out of fashion. We saw enough of that with the old Queen.' She nodded at her two daughters sitting side by side on the chesterfield. '*I* will wear black, of course, perhaps with a touch of white at the throat, but you must wear the outfits you had planned to wear.' A suspicion of a smile lifted the corners of her mouth. 'You are carrying lilies, Libby, and your dress is mauve georgette, Carrie, so the niceties are being adhered to, in a way.'

'That is very noble of you, Mrs Peel.' Harry was ashamed of his overwhelming relief. Not even to himself had he admitted his despair at the thought of the postponement of the wedding. He glanced over to where Libby sat, staring into the fire as if they were discussing a matter which had nothing to do with her. A far from imaginative man, he had wakened in the night a lot lately from a dream where he waited at the altar in vain for his bride to walk towards him. Once he had gone through the whole of the wedding ceremony only to lift the veil from his wife's face and see that it was Carrie smiling up at him. Then turning round in horror he had seen Libby in a bridesmaid's dress laughing at him, tossing her head back and laughing, with all the astonished guests in their pews gazing at them in open-mouthed dismay.

'I don't know what we would do without you, Harry.' Ettie groped for a handkerchief and dabbed at her dry eyes. 'We're a pretty helpless lot without a man. You think everything is in order for tomorrow? I hope we haven't left anybody out, but poor Oliver, he hadn't many friends . . .' She sighed. 'Even the collection at the mill for a wreath was pitifully small. I suspect Mr Crankshaw put most of it in himself. I would have liked to have thought that the weavers were saddened by Oliver's passing. It would have been nice to have seen some of them walking behind the hearse . . . As it is, there will only be three cars.'

Libby opened her mouth to say something, only to be gently kicked into silence by a sideways movement of Carrie's foot.

'It will soon be over, Mother.' Carrie's eyes filled with tears. 'We are the only ones who matter really. Father never gave a damn about what other people thought about him, and if he knows, I don't suppose he's caring now.'

'I just wish he could have died in his own bed.' Etties next sentence caused an amused exchange of glances between Libby and her fiancé. 'It would have made the whole thing more decent somehow.'

* * *

174

Oliver Peel was buried in the windswept cemetery on the very day the coal owners' terms were agreed in Lancashire.

'How Father would have gloried in the miners' defeat.' Libby, ready before Carrie, walked without knocking into her sister's bedroom. 'But I'm not sure it *is* defeat. The trade unions will go from strength to strength now, and a lot of the pits will go bankrupt. Nothing will ever be the same.'

Carrie, pulling on a pair of black kid gloves, widened her eyes in protest. 'How can you talk politics at a time like this? Sometimes I think you have no feelings.'

Libby gave a twitch to the back pleat in her twin's coat. 'It's because I have feelings that I worry, can't you see? All that suffering and all that hunger, all for nothing. I'm not sure what we should be mourning today, Carrie. Our father, who if he were still alive would be storming up the stairs waving the newspaper and shouting that the coal owners will have the whip hand from now on, or for the whole futile army of tired and defeated men going back for less than they were getting before. I'm sorry, but it's all mixed up in my head, and I can't decide who or what to cry for. Does that make sense?'

'It's time to go now.' Carrie walked over and opened the door. If Libby could keep from crying, then she would too. But thinking about the miners did seem out of place that day. It wasn't right, somehow. Then, as they went down into the hall and she saw Harry Brandwood, subdued in a dark suit with a black tie, come forward with his hands outstretched to her sister, Carrie felt the tears spring to her eyes.

Libby had Harry, while she had no one. Then as she blinked the tears back she realized that she too was crying for entirely the wrong reasons on that sad and doleful day.

Poor father, she thought, as with Sarah Batt beside her Ettie came down the stairs to ride into town for the first time in years, her head tilted as if it were a celebratory outing she was going to and not her husband's funeral.

Poor, poor Father . . . Carrie walked out to the sleekly polished black funeral car, her throat tight with the tears she swore she would not shed.

Although by northern standards it was a very quiet funeral, Westerley opened its doors that day to more people than Carrie could remember. There was the vicar and his wife, Harry's parents, Mr Crankshaw from the mill, the family solicitor, two of Ettie's cousins from Manchester visiting the big house for the first time, and even little Jimmy Earnshaw, the tackler from the mill. Ettie had seen him standing on his own, well back from the funeral party at the graveside, and had gone over to him to whisper a few words as he stood there, twisting his flat cap into an unrecognizable shape. And now there he was in the lounge, holding a glass of sherry carefully by the stem, an embarrassed captive audience as Libby chattered non-stop beside him on the chesterfield.

Mrs Edwards had done them proud, and the dining table, with two extra leaves slotted into position, groaned with a spread that was more like a banquet than a funeral tea. There was a side of ham, a pressed tongue, bowls of salad, a huge fruit cake, plates of scones, fairy cakes and a fresh fruit salad flanked by a jug of thick yellow egg custard.

It was just like a party, Carrie decided, a party that would never have taken place if the master of the house had been present. She watched carefully as Martha Cardwell jerked nervously from sideboard to table, handing round cups of tea from the Rockingham tea service. To Carrie's knowledge the cups and saucers had only been taken out of the display cabinet before to be washed and replaced.

There was no sign of grief on Martha's flat expressionless face, and yet surely she was feeling *something* ? Carrie shuddered, then turned her head swiftly as a burst of laughter came from the window seat where two of her father's old Rotarian friends shared a joke together. Why had they come? What was the point in paying respect to the dead, when during his life Oliver Peel had earned far more dislike than respect?

And look at her mother — talking animatedly to the vicar's wife about the Christmas Bazaar and promising to help with the handicrafts stall. It was years since Ettie had been to church. Only the week before she had explained to Libby that it would be impossible for her to go and hear the banns for the wedding read out.

'I can't kneel, and I would only have to go out halfway through the service. You know what being shut in with a crowd of people does to me.'

And yet here she was, excited at having her two cousins to visit, plying them with food, and being the perfect hostess.

It was as though, with Oliver's death, the whole house had suddenly come to life.

Leaving unnoticed, Carrie walked across the hall, curled her fingers round the brass doorknob of the billiard room, opened the door and slipped quietly inside.

Although the blinds had been lifted and the long plush curtains drawn back in the other rooms of the house, this room, her father's special bolt hole, had been left shrouded in funereal gloom. Carrie walked over to the window and slid the heavy dark green curtains back, hearing the brass rings clink together as the room was flooded by the grey diffused light of a winter's afternoon.

Bolt hole. Yes, that was the word for it. This was where Oliver had escaped night after night to sit at his desk, the whisky decanter to hand, working on his papers, a lonely man unable to delegate even the smallest part of his worries to his workforce. His own fault, oh, certainly his own fault. Carrie sat down in the chair with its hand-carved, curved back and arms, and ran her fingers round the leather-bound blotter. And as she sat there she became for one moment her father, sitting alone, hearing the sounds of footsteps on the stairs, the telephone ringing in the hall and Libby's voice or her own answering. Seeing Martha coming in to make up the fire, and swivelling round in his chair as she bent over the coal scuttle, her small rump outlined in the too-short skirt. Simple, unlessoned Martha, to whose arms he had crept for comfort.

Carrie shivered, crossing her arms and trying to rub away the chill seeping into her bones. Now she was seeing him grope his way in the fog down on to the canal bank, bent on revenge. Why else had they found the slip of paper in his pocket with Mungo's name and address written on it in his decisive hand? And no matter how many times Carrie had told herself there was no love behind Oliver's intentions, she still felt it was her fault.

Pushing the chair back and jumping up so quickly that it spun round of its own accord, Carrie almost ran from the room, wrenching open the door and stepping into the hall to meet a burst of chatter, the clatter of crockery and the sight of Mrs Edwards, flushed with the excitement of it all, bustling into the dining room with yet another loaded tray of food.

'I'm going out for a walk.' Running down the stairs with her black coat flying open and a scarf tied round her hair, Carrie bumped into an astonished Libby who was busily chivvying Jimmy Earnshaw into the lounge for a final cup of tea.

'You can't go out! Not now!' Libby gripped her arm. 'What will people think?' She stepped back as Carrie pushed her none too gently aside. 'And anyway it'll be dark soon.' She followed her sister to the door and into the vestibule. 'Are you all right? You look terrible. What's wrong, Carrie?'

As Carrie opened the big front door the late afternoon dampness wrapped her round like a soggy blanket.

'What *could* be wrong? It's only Father's funeral, isn't it? Why don't you go back in there and put a record on the gramophone? Then maybe you can all have a bit of a dance.'

She was running away from the house, dodging round the parked cars, down the drive, out into the lane, taking in great gulps of cold air as if it were the first proper drink she had had that day.

The tears were there, a solid wedge of grief, an overwhelming pity for the father she could not love. Turning left at the end of the lane she walked away from the direction of the town, past the detached houses set high up from the road and fronted by flights of stone steps. As the smart black coat had no pockets she wrapped her cold hands in the ends of the woollen scarf, and walked on with head bent, letting the tears flow, feeling them running down her cheeks.

She saw the man's shoes first, black lace-up boots like her father's weavers wore, but different in that they were polished until the toecaps gleamed. He was walking quickly, and when she expected him to pass he stopped and spoke, so that she raised her tear-drenched face in startled surprise.

'Libby Peel! Why are you crying? What are you doing out all alone in the dark like this?'

The voice was unrefined, but not unpleasant. Even in her distress Carrie noticed that. He was staring at her in amazement, his dark eyes puzzled, stretching out a hand to her, then letting it drop back to his side.

'But you're not Libby, are you?' He shook his head from side to side, taking in the face he thought he knew — same nose, same mouth, same high cheekbones, but with one startling difference. The eyes. These eyes, brown and long-lashed, wet with tears, were gentle and kind, not bold and challenging. He frowned. He had kept that face in his memory not for any sentimental reasons, but because Libby Peel's face was one not easily forgotten. And yet . . .

Carrie took a hand from the enveloping scarf and dashed the tears from her cheeks. 'I'm Libby's twin sister,' she said softly. 'Did she not tell you about me?'

The man shook his head again. He seemed unable to take his gaze from the tear-drenched face staring up at him, and again he felt the overwhelming urge to take this girl into his arms and comfort her. Not as once he had trailed a finger down her sister's face in teasing fashion — nothing like that.

'She said she had a sister, but not a twin.' He smiled, 'But now I see you are not really alike, not really, not at all . . .' His voice trailed away, but he made no move, just stood there, looking hard in disbelief.

'My name is Tom Silver,' he said at last, and held out his hand.

Putting her own into it, Carrie felt in the strong, firm clasp the first sensation of peace that had come over her that day.

CHAPTER NINE

'And he thought you were me?' Libby threw down the almost finished pair of pink crêpe-de-Chine camiknickers into which she was stitching a lace insert. Her face was suddenly as rosy as the material. 'Well, go on. Tell me what else he said.'

Carrie stared with surprise at her sister's flushed face. For a reason she couldn't quite fathom she had put off telling Libby about her meeting with Tom Silver until the week after the funeral, and now her twin was demanding to know why.

'Why didn't you tell me about this before?' Libby lowered her head. 'Did he ask you about the wedding?'

Carrie was sweetly reasonable. 'Love, it was the day of Father's funeral. If you must know, we talked about funerals, not weddings.' She smiled gently, remembering. 'He agreed with me that there is something pagan about burying a person with a ham and tongue spread, and relatives you haven't seen for years appearing as mourners. I was surprised how understanding he was.'

Libby picked up the sewing and stabbed her needle into the lace. Her voice was sharp. 'Well I hope he didn't say he was sorry to hear that Father had died. Our father was one of the bloated capitalists Tom Silver despises. He has real Bolshie ideas, that man.

He was sacked from his job on the *Weekly Times* because of them, and he was going to work at a jobbing printer's out Hoghton way. Did he tell you how he was getting on there?'

'He only stayed three weeks.' Carrie bent her head over her own sewing, a pale blue trousseau nightgown for Libby, with fine feather stitching down the bodice. 'He starts work on the evening paper in the New Year. He said the other place was soul-destroying.'

Libby sniffed. 'Not enough scope in small business for bother-making, I expect. I'm surprised the evening paper is taking him on. I would have thought that after being victimized he would automatically have been blacklisted. The two weeks the paper was out of print during the strike must still rankle with the management. Maybe Mr Silver is learning to keep his mouth shut.'

'It's obvious you don't like him very much.' Carrie winced as she noticed the size of the stitches in Libby's sewing. 'You've never talked about him. I would have thought you would have to know someone pretty well to dislike them so much.'

'I know his *sort*!' Libby pricked her finger, sucked at it furiously, then hurled the half-finished cami-knickers to the far corner of the chesterfield. 'Oh God, how I hate sewing!' She ran her hand through her fringe until the calf-lick at the hairline pushed the hair up on end. 'So he thinks there's something pagan about funeral teas, does he? Well, *I* think there's something even more pagan about a bride tarting herself up in pink camiknickers just because she's getting married. Are you *sure* he never mentioned the bloody wedding?'

Calmly Carrie went on with her sewing. When Libby swore it was a sure sign something had upset her badly, something far more important than the sewing she detested so much.

'He never said a word about the wedding,' she said gently. 'Why? Should he have?'

'No!' Libby shouted the denial. 'Are you seeing him again?'

This time it was Carrie's turn to put down her sewing and push it to one side. 'Seeing him again? Good heavens, no. I met him accidentally, we talked for a while and that was that. What are you so agitated about?'

'I am not agitated.' Libby spoke through clenched teeth. 'It's just that Mr Silver is not a man I would like to see you getting friendly with. He's only one step up from one of Father's weavers, even if he does fancy himself as an equal.'

'Libby Peel!' Carrie's voice was teasing. 'Listen to who's talking! I thought you were the one who always said all men were equal in the sight of God.' She wagged a finger. 'That used to be one of your favourite sayings, and anyway Tom Silver doesn't wear clogs and a greasy muffler. He even sounds his aitches, and blows his nose into a handkerchief instead of through his fingers.'

'That's not funny!' Jumping to her feet, Libby made for the door. 'That was *crude*, not funny. And don't you go thinking that just because you talked to him for a few minutes means you know him better than I do. Because you don't! Tom Silver is a jumped-up, arrogant man. It amuses him to pretend to be friendly with people out of his class. He mocks all the time, yes he does, *and* envies those who live in better houses and don't go on strike just to get their own way. He's got a chip on his shoulder as big as a whole forest of trees. He should have been working in Moscow, not Hoghton! He probably prays to

Lenin instead of God!' She turned, her face contorted with an anger bordering on terrible despair. 'So don't go mentioning his name to me ever again. Not ever! Do you hear?'

When the door slammed to, Carrie sat with a hand to her mouth for a moment, staring out through the big bay window at the scudding clouds. So her mother had been right last night when she had said that Libby was suffering prewedding nerves. 'Just let's keep our fingers crossed that she doesn't change her mind in the next few weeks,' she had said. 'Libby will never meet another man more right for her than Harry. He has the patience of a saint with her, and he's going to need all that patience in the years to come. But Harry is strong underneath all that apparently easy-going nature. He can handle our Libby, and my guess is he's waiting until he gets married to show a bit of stick.'

'Mother!' Carrie had laughed her surprise.

'And not before its needed,' Ettie had added, softening her words with the smile that came more often to her lips lately.

Carrie picked up her sister's sewing from where it had been thrown in a heap, shook it out and, and with her tongue protruding slightly from between her lips, began unpicking Libby's tortured stitches.

On some occasion, most likely at one of the Labour meetings Libby used to attend, Tom Silver had annoyed her . . . Carrie frowned as she threaded her needle, holding it up and squinting at the light. But the man she had met and talked to that dark afternoon had no unkindness in him, she could swear to that. Why, she could never remember seeing such warm eyes in a man's face. There had been an almost feminine understanding in them as she had choked

185

back her sobs and told him how the funeral party had upset her. She had felt no sense of shame in talking to a stranger like that. Then look how he had insisted on walking her home, shaking his head when she had said with truth that the dark lane leading to Westerley held no terrors for her.

'May God go with you, Miss Peel,' he had said before walking away, and somehow, going back into the house with all the lights glowing and overhearing one of Ettie's cousins thanking her hostess for a 'nice' time, she had been able to see the funny side. The whole thing had got into perspective somehow.

Martha Cardwell had been sent packing by Ettie the day after the funeral. 'So Mother knew,' Carrie had said. 'She must have known all the time. So why didn't she assert herself when Father was alive?'

'Because she would never have won, that's why. Because Mother wasn't born a fighter. She's only coming into her own now because there is no one actively opposing her,' Libby had declared.

'The oracle has spoken!' Carrie had teased, and their eyes had met in shared laughter.

'These things will never be ready in time for the wedding,' Carrie now muttered to herself as she put the camiknickers down and started on a row of French knots round the neck of the nightgown. 'Not that Libby will care. She's only tried her wedding dress on once since it was finished, and if georgette doesn't hang properly it looks awful. At least her veil is long enough to cover the back, and oh, please God, let it be fine on the day. It's quite a long walk from the car to the church door, and what could look worse than white stockings and satin shoes all splashed with mud?'

Still muttering to herself Carrie bent her head and got on with what had to be done, as nervous and worried as if she herself were the bride-to-be,

And upstairs Libby lay on her bed staring at the wall, seeing nothing.

'Tom Silver *is* rude and arrogant! No matter what Carrie says. I know him, and she doesn't. He isn't worth even the nail on Harry's little finger. He isn't!'

Turning her head into the pillow, Libby bit her lips hard. 'Oh, why did he have to come into my life again just when I thought he had gone away? Why did he have to come back?'

There was a most terrible moment when, coming down the aisle on Harry's arm with the ivory georgette dress hanging beautifully and the embroidered net veil caught up in a cap with pearls and orange blossom flowing out behind her, Libby thought she saw Tom Silver disappearing out of the church door.

There was the same tilt to the dark head, the same set to the thin shoulders, but when the man turned round and she saw how mistaken she had been, the colour drained from Libby's cheeks and her hand on Harry's arm trembled.

This was the man she loved, she told herself, and later that night, at Southport, when he took her gently in the big bedroom at the hotel overlooking tree-lined Lord Street, Libby clung to Harry fiercely with a passion that delighted and touched him.

'Oh, Harry . . . Harry . . . I do love you so much, so very much.'

Over and over again she whispered the words, lying in his arms, with the pale blue nightdress lying in a heap at the foot of the bed, and the pink crêpe-de-Chine camiknickers lying across a chair where Harry had dropped them as he undressed her, his brown eyes shining with adoration.

Then, when he was sleeping deeply with his head against her shoulders, Libby stared up into the darkness, vowing that she would be a good wife to this man.

'I was a good teacher, and now I'm going to be a good doctor's wife,' she told him when they came back to the red-brick house on the other side of the park to Westerley. 'You'll wonder how you ever managed without me.'

Harry, bursting with pride and love, took her face in his hands and gazed deep into her eyes as he left on his rounds that first morning after the honeymoon. 'I'll make short shrift of this morning's patients,' he promised. 'All the time I'll be longing to be back here with you. Around one o'clock, darling. Will that be all right?'

Waving him off from the porch, Libby told herself how lucky she was to be married to such a man. To walk straight into a house like this, furnished with the antiques his parents had left behind, saying they were too big and too dark for their new bungalow at the seaside. To be mistress of her own house, to arrange things exactly as she wanted them arranged, to go into the kitchen and tell the cook-general — another legacy from Harry's parents — what they would like for lunch, and to leave the daily help, a pleasant woman, to her brushes, dusters and mops.

And to have nothing to do . . .

Slowly she walked back into the house, into the lounge where a coal fire glowed, with the brass fire irons and the brass fender giving off sparks of reflected light. Glancing at the Westminster-chime clock on the mantlepiece she saw the time. Eleven o'clock. At school the children would be in from their mid-morning break, sitting at their desks, hands on heads, waiting for permission to open their desks and get out their English grammar exercise books. She wrinkled her nose at the rembered smell of urine emanating from boys and girls who slept three, four and sometimes five to a bed. Sleeping in rooms where the sickly stench of bugs came from the walls, and where fathers lolled unshaven in front of empty grates. A side of the coin that even Harry, for all his goodness, refused to recognize.

She had loved those children. In spite of their nit-infested heads and the dirt ingrained underneath their fingernails, she had loved them. And now here she was, an idle woman with nothing to do.

When the telephone rang she ran to answer it. Perhaps it was Carrie? Oh, yes, please, let it be Carrie! She would invite her over that afternoon, and together they would go through the house and decide what changes were to be made. The curtains in this room, for instance. Libby thought they were hideous, absolutely revolting.

'Yes?' She frowned as a high-pitched voice crackled in her ear.

'Is the doctor there? I would like to speak to the doctor. It is urgent, very urgent.'

Libby sat down, holding the receiver against her ear, picking up the pencil lying at the side of the notepad on the polished mahogany table.

'If you will give me a message I will let the doctor know as soon as he comes in. He is out on his rounds at the moment, I'm afraid.'

The voice at the other end of the wires was high with indignation. 'But surely you are able to get in touch with him? I have to see him right away. *Now!* I am in such pain . . . such pain.'

'Who is that speaking, please?' For someone in agony the voice was very strong and peevish, Libby thought. She licked the point of the pencil and waited.

'This is Mrs Morgan. Mrs Morgan of Bramwell House. Who is that? You don't sound like Dr Brandwood's girl. What has happened to Phyllis?'

'Phyllis went when Dr Brandwood retired. I am Doctor Harry's wife.' Unconsciously Libby was adopting her school-marmish voice. 'If you will tell me your symptoms I will see that my husband gets your message when he comes in at one o'clock.'

'My *symptoms?*' The loud voice rose an octave. 'Since when was it necessary to describe one's symptoms over the telephone? Dr Brandwood knew all about my migraines, and he always came round straight away. To give me an *injection*. I can't possibly wait until one o'clock. Surely your husband left you a list of the people he was visiting? All you have to do is ring round until you find him. That's what Phyllis always did.'

'I am not Phyllis.' Libby gripped the telephone hard, raising her eyes ceilingwards. 'And I suggest you go and lie down and wait until the doctor returns. If you are a sufferer from migraine, then surely you know that is the best thing to do anyway.'

'How dare you!' The voice crackled with such ferocity that Libby held the receiver away from her ear. 'I have been a patient of Dr Brandwood's for over ten years and never, never have I been spoken to like this! You can tell your husband when he comes in not to bother coming to see me. I will find a doctor who knows how to get his priorities right. Someone with a little more sympathy. Goodbye!'

When the line went dead, Libby sat quite still for a moment before hooking the telephone back on to its stand. It was silly, she told herself, but the exchange of words had left her quite shattered.'

When Harry came in at half past one for a lunch already drying in the oven Libby told him about the call. 'Mrs Morgan from Bramwell House?' Harry frowned. 'I'll have to go round there straight away.' He shrugged his shoulders when Libby reminded him that he hadn't eaten since half past seven that morning. 'Look, love, Mrs Morgan and her husband are two of my best patients. They pay promptly, and migraine isn't exactly what you would class as an imaginative illness. It can be completely demoralizing when it strikes.'

'Well, it hadn't struck this morning!' Libby followed him to the door, still protesting. 'You should have heard the way she shouted at me. A person with migraine can hardly lift a head from the pillow. She was rude, Harry, rude and arrogant!'

He turned and drew her to him for a moment. 'Well, real or imaginary, love, Mrs Morgan is my patient and besides, she exerts quite an influence in this town. Insult Mrs Morgan and you insult half the country. I must go and at least try to pour oil on troubled waters. I can't afford to lose that account. It's a bad start, Libby, a bad start.'

'And I'm to blame?' Libby drew away from him to glare into his anxious face. 'Oh, Harry. Women like that aren't worth bothering about. You'll most likely find she is finishing a good lunch when you get there.'

She went back into the house, closing the door none too gently behind her. But within the hour Harry was back, obviously fighting hard to keep his normally controlled temper.

191

'Mrs Morgan had left orders not to let me into the house.' He threw down his bag. 'And there was a car I thought I recognized outside in the drive. So that's one account closed.' He shot her a guarded glance. 'School-marm tactics don't work when you are talking to patients, Libby. I must ask you to be more tolerant in future, even if you feel in your mind that the caller could be malingering.'

'I know children,' Libby said, with a calmness belied by the anger sparking from her brown eyes, 'children who come to school with a fever or worse because their mothers realize they can be kept warmer at school than in an unheated house. Mothers who turn mangles with their insides dropping out. I've *seen* them, Harry, and yet you expect me to have patience with a pampered woman who imagines she has a headache? A spoilt woman who only needs to crook her little finger for you to go running? Is that smarmy bedside manner of yours what you trained seven years for?' She waved a hand at the telephone. 'And am I expected to kowtow and jump to attention when a woman like Mrs Morgan calls the tune? Well, I can't do it! It's degrading.'

She looked very beautiful in her anger, but this time Harry was not impressed. This time he ignored her.

'I see you have a lot to learn, Libby. If you will have a sandwich sent through into the surgery, I'll eat there. I have some paperwork to do before I go out again.

'He was as bad as Mrs Morgan.'

Libby sat opposite Carrie in the lounge at Westerley the same afternoon. 'Oh, Carrie, we've quarrelled already, and I thought when we got married the bickering between us would stop. I thought we disagreed so much because the wedding and everything was getting on my nerves, but I was wrong. I looked at him this morning, Carrie, and I didn't *like* him, let alone love him. What am I going to do?'

Carrie hid a smile as she listened. Her twin was talking quickly, waving a hand to emphasize a point, eyes flashing, cheeks flushed. And, oh, it was good to have Libby in the house again, even for a short time. With Libby around the whole world seemed different. Even her more outrageous statements had a touch of comic drama about them. Privately she was glad Harry had stood up to his wife. He was learning already, and the time would come when Libby would settle down in her role as doctor's wife, playing it with as much dedicated intensity as she played every other part. At least it made a change from politics. Carrie sighed. Only yesterday Mr Crankshaw had been up from the mill, explaining to her mother that the cotton trade was so seriously hampered by heavy rates and taxations that the coming year was going to be a testing time.

'It's all on account of the tremendous cost to the state of the coal strike,' he had said. 'Did you read in the paper that the miners' secretary on a visit to Moscow has prophesied a revolution in England? Inevitable, he says. He believes that the government and the mine owners between them beat the working man down in his demand for a living wage. But he says their victory will be the dearest victory that British capitalism ever won.'

Oh yes, it was a good job Libby wasn't on *that* hobbyhorse. At least her marriage to Harry seemed to have dampened her ardour for the Labour movement. Now it only remained to be seen which soapbox she was about to leap on.

Carrie had not long to wait.

A month later, when the February snow lay dirty and trodden in the streets of the town, Libby announced that she was giving a small dinner party for the express purpose of introducing Carrie to a Burnley friend of Harry's, a divorced man by the name of Roger Fish, son of a mine owner. Since his wife's desertion he had been fending for himself, leaving his small girl in the charge of a series of unsuitable housekeepers.

'He's looking for a wife.' Libby, making no attempt to be circumspect, filled Carrie in with the details. 'There's a house, neglected of course, but you could soon set that to rights. Not good-looking, but then, what do looks matter? I don't mean repulsive,' she added, 'just a bit bald, and with a laugh that grates, but once you get past that he's nice. You'll take to each other at once. I'm sure of it.'

'What shall I wear?' Carrie asked the question with pretended innocence, and wasn't in the least surprised when Libby took her quite seriously.

'Your rose-coloured overblouse with the black velvet tie, and your velvet skirt. I'll wear my black velvet. You should stand out nicely against that.'

'Libby!' Carrie's eyes brimmed with ready laughter, but her sister failed to see anything remotely amusing. So Carrie sat back, in the way she had always sat back when Libby started on her 'steam-roller tactics', and allowed herself to be taken over. Conditioned by closeness, Carrie nodded and agreed.

To tell the truth she was glad of the opportunity to get out of the big house for a while. Ettie, actively fearing Sarah Batt's imminent departure now that her mother was becoming too frail too look after her grandson, had already lost some of the euphoria which had sustained her since Oliver's death. She was in danger of sinking into semi-invalidism again, and when she did so Carrie knew her role would be that of the unmarried daughter, a slave to the house and her mother's whims.

This Roger Fish — well, he didn't come into it. She wasn't a slab of meat to be sold to the highest bidder and besides, a bald head and a laugh that grated . . . oh Lordy! The corners of Carrie's mouth twitched with laughter again, but with great effort she managed to keep her face straight as Libby went on planning the dinner party.

'A week next Friday, then?' Having arranged everything to her satisfaction Libby rose to her feet and started upstairs to say goodbye to her mother.

'I'll be there,' Carrie promised. 'Bois-de-rose, overblouse and all.'

'Harry will fetch you,' said Libby, over a disappearing shoulder. 'At seven o'clock sharp. And if he's called out to a patient, then I won't be responsible. I just won't!'

'How can a man be so stupid as to keep mixing us up when we're dressed in completely different frocks?'

Libby beckoned Carrie out of the room as the two men settled down with their afterdinner cigars and the decanter of port.

'Roger Fish isn't even *trying* to get us right, in my opinion. Something tells me he thinks we're funny. A couple of freaks in a circus tent. The next time he calls me Carrie, then apologizes, I shall say something very rude.'

Carrie followed her down the hall and into the

drawing room. 'So you don't think he fancies me as the next Mrs Fish, do you?'

'Or me,' Libby said promptly, and as their laughter exploded they clapped hands to their mouths and sank down together on the overstuffed sofa, leaning on each other, rocking together in shared merriment.

'He's not all that bald.' Carrie sat up, wiping her eyes. 'And his laugh isn't that bad, either. A bit squeaky, but you could get used to it if you were hard pressed enough.'

Libby, with one of her abrupt and bewildering changes of mood, suddenly gripped her sister's hand. 'You're not still pining for that awful Mungo man?'

'No, I'm not.' Carrie tucked her handkerchief back up her sleeve. 'I never think about him. Mr Eccles took him back, apparently, and I'm glad. Mungo was the breadwinner. He needed his job more than I did. I wouldn't be surprised if he hadn't convinced the headmaster that *I* was the one who did the grabbing that day down in the cloakroom.' She shuddered. 'Not that it matters now. It's all water under the bridge.'

Then at the mention of water they both stared at each other, their dark eyes wide.

'And yet *he* was the one directly responsible for Father drowning.' Carrie sighed. 'I wake in the night sometimes and wonder how I could ever have imagined that I was in love with him.' She shuddered. 'I must have been out of my mind.'

'Have you seen Tom Silver since that day?' Libby turned her face away, trying to keep her voice light.

'No, never,' Carrie said, the sudden blush warming her cheeks surprising her. Then, as the two men came in from the dining room, they were confronted

196

by two identical faces, wearing two identically guilty expressions.

Now what's been cooking, Harry thought, coming forward with a smile on his ruddy face, and taking care to leave the place next to Carrie free for Roger Fish.

'I will drive you home, if I may.' The bald head inclined itself towards Carrie solicitously. 'And I must thank *you*, Libby, for a most enjoyable evening.' The high-pitched laugh wobbled nervously. 'Perhaps before too long you will all come and have dinner with me? My present housekeeper is a splendid cook. She'll be glad of the opportunity to display her skills.'

'That would be lovely.' Libby's brown eyes were wide and innocent as she exchanged a glance with her twin. 'Wouldn't that be lovely, Carrie?'

'Delightful.' Carrie narrowed her eyes at her sister's treachery, but outside in the drive she allowed herself to be helped into the passenger seat of the car.

'You must show me the way.' The nervous laugh twittered again. Carrie explained that it was only five minutes' drive to Westerley, her conscience pricking slightly. It had been unforgivable of Libby to throw them together like this so obviously, but Roger Fish was, she felt, a lonely man, covering up his loneliness by a too-ready laugh, and the heavy-handed joke of not being able to tell them apart.

'It must be difficult bringing up a little girl without her mother.' Carrie's voice was gentle with sympathy, filled with a genuine remorse at her off-hand manner all the evening.

The man by her side shot her a quick glance from beneath surprisingly bushy eyebrows. She was very beautiful, this girl who was the image of her sister.

More beautiful than the other one in an indefinable way. Following her instructions, he drove the car round the drive and up to the steps leading to Westerley. Then thoughtfully he turned off the engine. She was tender-hearted, too. The wine with the meal and Harry's generous pouring of the port afterwards had blurred his vision as he looked at Carrie's oval face above the high collar of her velvet coat. She drooped her head and fiddled with the clasp of her silk purse.

'I hope I haven't offended you. Libby told me that your . . . that your wife . . . ' The gentle voice faltered.

'My wife went off with someone else.' Roger Fish felt his own voice deepen dramatically. 'She never wanted the child, and when Claire was born it seemed to take Elaine farther away from me.' He sighed, his face so close that his breath made the marabou trimming flutter enticingly. I will never understand how a woman can leave her baby, but there it was, and now, well, I just do the best I can.'

'Oh, I'm so sorry.' Carrie put out a hand and touched his sleeve. 'Would you have her back, your wife, if she came?' The brown eyes were filled with compassion, causing him to draw in his breath sharply. 'It could be that she was depressed after the baby came. It happens sometimes, and maybe this — this other man — maybe she was just infatuated. There can't have been much about him to take a wife away from her husband and child, but women sometimes fall in love with the most unlikely men.'

It was an intimate moment there in the car with the doors and windows closed, and the scent she was wearing made his senses reel. This Carrie Peel, with her quiet ways, gentle voice and dark eyes, was a dark horse if he was any judge of women. And since his wife's desertion Roger Fish prided himself very much on being a judge of women.

'There are times,' he whispered unforgivably, 'when my life is as dark as the lives of the ponies down my father's mine.' He thought Carrie swayed towards him; he could have sworn it — women always fell for a bit of the old sob stuff. With a swift movement he pulled her close to him and then, as he felt the scented warmth of her, his mouth found her soft lips.

As the kiss deepened and his hand slid down Carrie's back to draw her even closer, he felt himself thrust away with a strength he would never have believed the small girl possessed. When he reached for her again, telling himself that all women played hard to get at first, the stinging slap to his right cheek made him reel back in astonishment. What he did not know, what he could have never have been expected to know, was that to Carrie Peel he was not, in that moment, a maudlin man who had had too much to drink, but a wild man with angry frustration, holding her captive against the wall of a basement cloakroom.

In the next moment Carrie had reached for the door handle, wrenched the door open and almost fallen out of the car, frantic in her desire to get away from him. As he sat there, dazed, a hand to his burning cheek, he saw her run wildly up the steps to the big front door, then disappear inside without a backward glance.

'Well, bugger me!' Roger sat there, leaning on the wheel for a moment, then pulling the door closed started the car and drove away down the drive, muttering to himself at the vagaries of women, and in particular of the girl who had been thrown into a blind panic by one harmless kiss.

He was on the main road, heading for home, when the sight of the silk purse on the seat beside him made him curse aloud again. There was no way he was going to turn back and knock at the door of the big house set at the end of the winding lane. He sighed, and took the turning leading to the doctor's house. A quick explanation and a handing-in of the purse at the door, and he could be away. Back to Burnley and the housekeeper would be waiting up for him, her housecoat tantalizingly open and her willing body ready for his caresses.

He drew up at the front of Harry Brandwood's house just in time to see Harry getting into his car and driving swiftly away, leaving Libby standing on the doorstep with her figure in its black dress etched against the light streaming from the hall.

'Are you coming in?' Libby took Carrie's purse from him. 'Harry has gone out on a case.' She held the door invitingly open. 'Another panic that could easily have waited until tomorrow; another case of the one who pays the piper calling the tune.'

There were two spots of bright colour high on her cheekbones. She was gloriously, beautifully angry, and Roger did not hesitate. He might have summed one of the sisters up wrongly, but this one, well, she was a completely different kettle of fish. Snatching the trilby hat from his bald head he followed her into the lounge and accepted the drink she offered him, telling himself that as rum goes went, this beat the best of them.

When, twenty minutes later, he staggered out once again to his car, a hand to a burning cheek — the left one this time — he was laughing silently, accepting the fact that he was too drunk to drive, then reminding himself that he had driven in a far worse condition than this.

'God Almighty!' he muttered as he clung to the wheel, his head spinning. 'Two of them! Two identical faces, and two identical reactions. All in the space of half an hour. By the time he was well on the road to Burnley the two faces had merged and become one, and he was laughing uproariously, slapping the wheel with the flat of his hand, his high-pitched laugh filling the interior of the little car.

'Roger Fish is not the man for Carrie!' Libby was sitting up in bed when Harry came up the stairs, so tired that the normal ruddy colour of his face had faded to a patchy grey. 'I never want to see him again. How you could have possibly thought he was her type I don't know.'

Too tired to demand an explanation, Harry began to undress. 'I thought the evening went off rather well,' he said mildly, then went out and across the landing to wash his hands and clean his teeth. When he climbed into bed, a solid, comfortable figure in his striped pyjamas, with his hair brushed flat against his head and a clean handkerchief in the pocket of his jacket, Libby settled herself in his arms, laying her head on his shoulder, her hair tickling his chin.

'I wasn't going to say anything yet, but I should have . . . is it too soon to think I might be having a baby?'

Harry's thoughts as he sank into a sleep from which the telephone bell was to propel him out of bed and into his trousers at five o'clock the next morning were a mixture of pride and satisfaction. Now his Libby would have something more to occupy her mind than a jealous monitoring of the restricted time he was able to spend with her.

It was as well he could not see the expression

on his beloved's face as she stared up into the darkness, her palm still itching from the slap she had administered to Roger Fish's leering face, a heavy depression settling on her as she realized that now she would be more a prisoner to the house than ever, that her craving for excitement and freedom was to be thwarted for a long, long time to come.

CHAPTER TEN

'It will be a boy. I know it will be a boy. I *order* it to be a boy!'

It was the end of March before Libby told her mother about the coming baby, wanting to be, as she confided in Carrie, quite sure first.

Ettie's heart was playing her up again now that she was realizing that even without Oliver's brooding presence Westerley was still a house where the most frequent comings and goings were by the tradesmen to the back door.

Carrie seemed, to her mother's eyes, to be drifting more obviously into spinsterhood with every passing month. Without her twin she was only half a person, a shadow, and since the dinner party in January Libby seemed to have abandoned the idea of finding a husband for her sister.

But a baby . . . well, that was what they all needed. Ettie smiled at Sarah Batt busy in the corner with her sewing. 'We *order* a boy, don't we Sarah? And more than that — I have a feeling he will be just like Willie.' Her blue eyes grew dreamy. 'The Lord works in a mysterious way, and somehow I know He is going to give me back my Willie in my grandson. I have never felt that Willie was really dead. I always felt that one day the door would open and he would walk in with his fair hair shining and his blue eyes teasing, the way they always did. And now I know.

Libby is going to give him back to me, aren't you, love?'

'Mother!' Libby exchanged a glance with Carrie. 'That's a fanciful notion. It could be a girl. There's a fifty-fifty chance of it being a girl. You know that.'

'No!' Ettie rose from her chair in her excitement. 'Sarah! Give me a length of cotton from the workbasket there. And Libby, give me your wedding ring.'

'What on earth for?' Libby, pleased at seeing her mother's face crease into lines of animation, decided not to argue but to humour her. Holding up her left hand she slipped the heavy gold band from her third finger. 'Now what?'

'Lie down. Put your feet up on the chesterfield. Sarah thread the cotton through the ring. Now, hold it in your fingers over Miss Libby's stomach. Like this, Sarah. No, don't put any pressure on it.' She clapped her hands together. 'If it swings round and round then it will be a girl, but if it swings backwards and forwards, then it's a boy.'

'I don't like to, Mrs Peel.' Sarah, her round face troubled, held out the ring and the length of cotton. 'I don't think we are meant to tamper with fate like this. The Lord will send Miss Libby whatever he thinks fit, and I'd rather not . . . It's wrong, that's what it is. Wrong!'

Ettie's face fell, but Libby, lying flat with her toes upturned, spoke sharply. 'Sarah! Don't be so silly! It's only a game! C'mon now, this is even better that reading *Old Moore's Almanac*. Let's see if it really is Willie's reincarnation I've got in here!'

'I won't do it!' Flushing bright scarlet, her round eyes starting from her head, Sarah threw the ring from her. 'You've no cause to speak like that, Miss Libby! You're upsetting your mother. Just look at her. If she has an attack it will be all your fault!'

'But it was Mother who began it.' Bewildered, Libby sat up, and as she bent down to pick up the ring from the carpet she saw Sarah Batt's feet in their sensible lace-up shoes scurry away. Then, as she raised her head, she saw the door bang closed behind the hurrying figure.

'*Now* what have we said?' Libby stared at the door, then sighed as she saw the way her mother lowered herself back into her chair, steadying herself on the arms, then dropping suddenly as if she had an arthritic hip. 'What's got into Sarah lately? *I'm* supposed to be the one who makes scenes and goes off in huffs. Pregnant women have a free licence to do that!'

'She's a Catholic,' Ettie said sadly, as if that explained a lot, then looked hurt as her daughters burst out laughing. 'Perhaps it was a silly thing to do. It's just that I want it to be a boy so very much . . . so very, very much.'

'I'll do my best, Mother.' Libby stood up and went over to the window. 'By the time those green leaves have turned to brown you'll know one way or the other.'

She turned round, snatching up her coat from the chair where she had thrown it when she came in, thrusting her arms into the sleeves in her old restless way. 'Oh God! I'll never have the patience to wait until then. I'm tired of being pregnant already. Harry's quite disgusted with me because I haven't even felt sick yet. Most of his patients go into a decline from the minute they conceive. Still, it's early days yet. I may start eating coal and fancying beetroot with custard any day now!'

* * *

But at the end of a disappointing August, when rain fell almost daily from bleak skies, Libby was still disgustingly healthy and so bored she felt there were days when she could throw herself on the carpet and scream aloud.

Reading the local papers from cover to cover she saw that Tom Silver had been made a councillor. There was a photograph of him staring into the cameras with a dedicated expression in his dark eyes, and a report which said that for a new boy Mr Silver was already making his presence felt. On one occasion he had stood up and berated his fellow councillors for taking plants from the conservatory in the park for their own gardens. And on another occasion he had brought to the notice of the meeting the state of the market place when the stalls were taken down on Wednesdays and Saturdays.

'Hordes of ragged children scrambling about for cut oranges and bruised apples,' he had said. 'We know the high incidence of unemployment in this town, but must we revert to Dickensian times? Are our children so undernourished that they have to forage in overflowing dustbins?'

He had gone down personally, the report stated, and talked to the children, taking the names of some of them and visiting them in their houses. What he had seen had appalled him.

'Houses so poorly furnished that there weren't enough chairs to go round. Bugs in the walls, and bare flag floors. Mothers with nothing to give their children but great doorsteps of bread sprinkled with margarine and sugar, and everywhere the smell of poverty . . .'

Libby put the newspaper down and stared into the coal fire burning high in the wide tiled fireplace. It was as though Tom Silver was there in the room with her, talking, pointing with a thin finger, black hair falling forward over his forehead, reminding her that there was one law for the rich and another for the poor, and always would be if something wasn't done. He was reminding her of the children, the bright pupils who, having missed their chances of a grammar school education, were now thrown out of work by the closing of the mills, and forced to queue at the labour exchange. For what? Three shillings a week at the most,

Libby shivered. She had been in danger of forgetting all that.

She was like a big fat cow, waddling around, feet splayed, back arched, stomach sticking out. With characteristic dramatic honesty Libby berated herself. Complacent wasn't the word. No, the word was unfeeling, uncaring. Her pregnancy had slipped by and in those long waiting months she had slipped quietly into the category of those who had, and to hell with those who had not.

She would write to Tom Silver. She would sink her pride, because after all she was a married woman now, and the humiliation of that September night when he had called her bluff was a thing of the past. She would write to him and congratulate him on speaking out, and more than that, she would pledge herself to join the fight after the birth of her baby.

Heavily she got up from the chair and went over to the writing table, but when she bent her head over the thick notepaper and wrote the date at the top in her flowing hand, the headache that had been threatening all day erupted into a thousand hammers beating her skull. Her throat ached and suddenly the room took on the dimensions of an overheated prison cell. Pushing the paper away, she walked flat-footed into the hall.

For Libby to think was to act, and within a few minutes she was outside, a long cardigan hanging loose over her smocklike summer dress, her head bare as she breathed deeply of the humid air blanketing the street like a shroud.

She had meant to walk down the park gates and wander up the Broad Walk towards the duck pond, her usual afternoon walk, but the main shopping centre of the town was only five minutes' walk away and beyond that was the market place. Libby walked on, ignoring the stares of passers-by. With characteristic defiance she had made little attempt to disguise her condition, refusing to stay in during daylight hours, as was deemed to be right and proper by her contemporaries. To be pregnant was normal. To be large and ungainly was normal also, and if people wanted to stare, let them stare.

She plodded on, past the Town Hall and over the road to the market, where at the end of that Wednesday market day the stallholders were packing their goods away into crates before beginning the task of taking down the stalls. By now her head was throbbing and her face burning as if she had been sitting in the sun too long. She had brought no basket, no purse, and if she had done so she would have handed out the money to the children she saw diving underneath the stalls, waiting with hands outstretched for the display oranges cut into two pieces to show their juiciness.

Horrified, Libby watched the children, some of them wearing clogs and some boots several sizes too big for them. Waiflike children, with white faces and straggly hair. Dirty-legged, cheeky mites, more ragged than any she remembered teaching in her church school before she had married and forgotten how poor the poor could be.

The cobblestones seemed to be pushing their way up through her thin summer shoes with their pointed toes and bar-straps. Now Libby left the fruit and vegetable stalls to cross to the secondhand clothes stalls, with their hanging rows of musty-smelling coats and frocks, and their rows of shabby shoes and tangled piles of stockings.

'Are you all right, love?'

Libby blinked as a woman dismantling a stall spoke kindly to her.

'You look all in.' She came round the front of the stall and touched Libby's arm. 'Don't you think you'd better be getting home, love? It's starting to rain, and from the look of that sky we're in for a real wetting. Would you like to sit down for a bit? There's a box behind here, and I think there might be a drop of tea left in the can.' The woman turned to call out to her neighbour on the next stall. 'This lass is all in, but I can't get her to say nowt. I think she's sickening for something. Her time's not up yet, though. She hasn't dropped. She's carrying too high to be going into labour just yet awhile.'

Libby walked away, hearing them talking about her as if they were referring to someone else. She could not understand it. She had come down here to find Tom Silver. She hadn't known it before, but it was quite clear now. What wasn't clear was the fact that now there were stalls where she had thought to see an empty market place, with Tom standing on a makeshift platform telling a mysteriously disappearing crowd that he was on their side.

'That's right love. Get back home.' The woman's voice spiralled after her as, stolidly placing one foot in front of the other, Libby forced herself to walk on. She was muddled, with the heat pricking all over her body. She welcomed the rain, she really welcomed it. In fact, she would lift her face and feel the cool drops wetting her skin.

'It's a long way to Westerley.' She said that aloud, then smiled at the absurdity of it. 'It's a long way to Tipperary.' That was how it should go. Tipperary, not Westerley. She would laugh at such a silly mistake, if only her throat hadn't closed up in that painful way.

She was trudging past the park gates when she remembered suddenly that she no longer lived at Westerley. That was good. Where she lived wasn't so far as Westerley; where she lived was only a few turnings farther on. And when she got inside out of the rain Tom Silver would be there, setting a match to the fire and ordering her to take her stockings off. He would be bossy but kind, his thin face set into lines of mocking humour. He would give her a mug of tea, not a cup, because folks in the street where Tom Silver lived never drank from cups. Cups with fluted rims edged with gold were for the sort of woman she had become. The woman whose babies were put into treasure-cots with organdie drapings, not into an empty drawer lined with newspapers and old blankets.

The red-brick house with the surgery built on to the side was there, just a few more steps, and it was here she lived, and she was glad, because she could go no further. . . .

'You have looked after scarlet fever patients before, nurse?' Harry took the shabby Gladstone bag from the little woman and led the way upstairs. He failed to see the glint of indignation in Nurse Tomkin's grey eyes behind the whirlpool lenses of her round spectacles.

'Yes, doctor.' The answer was mild and deferential,

but what Nurse Tomkin was saying underneath her breath was that she had nursed more scarlet fever patients than what he'd had hot dinners. With her sixtieth birthday farther behind her than she was prepared to admit, Nurse Tomkin had done her training in a Manchester teaching hospital and been filled with righteous indignation when the powers-that-be had refused to accept her application to go to France during the war. Properly trained she might be, but she still believed that a hot bread poultice slapped on to a wheezy chest worked wonders. Aye, and a good suck at a whole bag of acid drops, with the spit shot into a bowl, was the only method guaranteed to cure bleeding of the gums. Scarlet fever! She had her remedies for that, too. She'd soon have it sweated out of this young doctor's wife.

But even Nurse Tomkin, trained not to show her feelings, drew in a sharp breath of dismay when she saw her patient propped up on the pillows, eyes glazed, mouth dry and cracked, rasping from the tortured throat.

'How far gone is she?' The short-sighted eyes took in Libby's swollen stomach, rising like half a barrel beneath the sheets. 'Near her time?'

'First week in October.' Harry stood by the bed, an unprofessional anguish creasing his face into lines. 'I didn't want to have her moved to the isolation hospital. I want her nursed here, at home.' He laid his hand on his wife's burning forehead, then bent his head closer as Libby muttered feverishly in a high garbled voice, her eyes filled with terror as if she were living out some unbearable nightmare. 'I couldn't bear to see her taken away.'

'Quite right, doctor.' Nurse Tomkin glanced round the room with approval. 'It's understood that there's no one to come in here but me and you?'

Harry nodded. 'Anything you want — anything . . .' He backed towards the door. 'Just ask.' He tried to smile. 'Since this epidemic began they are sleeping two to a bed in the hospital.'

'You go down to your surgery.' Nurse Tomkin rolled up her sleeves, baring arms as red and mottled as if she had sat in a hot bath for far too long. 'What I would like is a camp bed, or even a sofa over there by the wall.' She dismissed a mahogany tallboy with a wave of her hand. 'That can go out for a start. I would like to sleep in here. There's no call for a night nurse, though that was mentioned.' She bent down and rolled up a rug laid by the side of the bed. 'I'll put what I don't want out on the landing, then I'll want a tray with my own things. Own cup, own knife and fork. You have help in the kitchen?'

Well, that was a daft question, she muttered to herself as the doctor left the room at last. Of course they would have help in a house like this. She stared round the bedroom at the highly polished furniture, the silver hair brush on the dressing table, the dark green satin eiderdown and the pillows edged with hand-crotcheted lace. Still muttering, she stood with her neat head cocked to one side, mentally making a list of the things she needed. Those china ornaments off the mantlepiece could go, and all that clutter on the dressing table. This room would be as near to a hospital ward as she could get it, or her name wasn't Nellie Tomkin.

She was picking up a silver-framed photograph when surprise made her hold still for a moment. 'Now what?' she asked herself out loud. 'What was a photograph of old Mrs Batt's grandson doing here in this room?'

She stared down at the laughing face of a fair-haired boy, squinting into the camera as if the light was too much for him. Well, well . . . She glanced over to the girl in the bed. She had been told that her patient was one of the Peel twins, and yes, the Peel house was where Sarah Batt worked for a Mrs Peel whose husband had been drowned last year.

Nurse Tomkin's small mouth pursed itself up, as if anticipating a kiss. No wonder Sarah Batt was so devoted to the Peel family when the married daughter kept a photograph of Sarah's illegitimate son Patrick on her dressing table. She sniffed. The Peels must be an unusually broad-minded family.

Carrying a side table out on to the landing, Nurse Tomkin followed it by the photographs, and a lot of what she called unnecessary clutter. There would be no harbouring of dust whilst she was in charge or she would know the reason why. Then, mentally armed with a list of what she considered *was* necessary, she went downstairs to worry the life out of the cook in the kitchen.

On the way back upstairs she stopped on the landing long enough to pick up the photograph again. Holding it close to her near-sighted eyes she stroked her chin thoughtfully, her mind ticking over as she worked out dates.

For two days Libby hovered between life and death. Sponged down with vinegar and water, fed from a feeding cup filled with boiled water and sugar, her every breath monitored by the stalwart little figure in the dark blue dress and white starched apron, Libby rambled, tossed, protested feverishly. Now and again she opened her eyes to see a pinched dedicated face leaning over her. At times she suffered the indignity of an ear pressed to her bare stomach, and when at last the fever broke and the sweat poured down her sides, she felt the soothing touch of a sponge washing her all over her hot sticky body. She felt strong arms lifting her against high-piled pillows, and when she protested feebly a voice cajoled her into submission. If she moaned at night, the wrinkled face was there, hands lifting her head to spoon sweetened water into her mouth. If she wanted to pass water, the bedpan, warmed to comfort, was slipped underneath her bottom and left there for just long enough and not a minute longer.

Whilst Libby was sick Nurse Tomkin loved her with a fierceness that would have put the most devoted of mothers to shame. It was as simple as that. For a long time now all Nellie Tomkin's compassion had been lavished on the ailing, the dying, only to be withdrawn when they recovered. And recover they usually did under her round-the-clock ministrations. For the healthy, Nellie Tomkin had very little time. Her acid tongue and biting sarcasm, nurtured on a life embittered by disappointments, meant that in the village where she lived alone in a tiny cottage she was thought by some to be a witch.

So when at the end of September she saw Sarah Batt walking down the lane after attending Mass in the old priory, she planted herself in front of her with her broad feet in their usual ten-to-two position.

'This your weekend off?' She stared at Sarah's red hair, peeping untidily from the ugly cloche hat pulled low down over the narrow forehead. It was said that Sarah Batt had never looked at a man since her downfall of roughly nine years ago, but with her country-fresh complexion and her round blue eyes she was a comely enough lass. This alone was enough to sharpen Nellie's tongue. 'It's a small world, wouldn't you say, Sarah?'

'Aye.' The only way Sarah could have walked on was to have pushed the determined little figure aside, but her eyes narrowed nervously as she waited for what was to come next. Gossipy Nurse Tomkin never so much as passed the time of day with the folks of the village unless she had something unpleasant to impart. Sarah waited with a premonition of dread seeping through her.

'I've been nursing somebody you know very well.' The eyes glittered behind their thick lenses. 'One of the Peel twins. The married one, Miss Libby, married to Dr Brandwood.'

Sarah's expression was now the resigned stonelike passivity of someone waiting for the axe to fall. 'Oh, yes?'

'She's better now, but whether she'll survive her confinement is another question altogether. It's a good job she was far on in her pregnancy because they are coming round to thinking that scarlet fever contracted early on can damage the unborn child. They are sending for me again when she's due. Dr Brandwood was mighty pleased with me. I thought for a while I was going to have two patients to nurse. He's besotted with that wife of his.' The uneven teeth showed in the semblance of a smile. 'But she'll survive, that lass. Plenty of spunk there. I only had to turn my back during that last week and she was out of bed. Strong as an ox with spirit to match, that one.'

Sarah stared down at the ground, her eyes following the progress of a flurry of red-gold leaves from the trees bordering the lane. Why didn't the old witch come to what she was determined to say? 'I must go, Nurse Tomkin.' Sarah took a step forward, then sighed as the plumply solid little figure stood her ground. 'My mother is far from well and I'd like to do a batch-bake before I get the train back this evening.'

'Your mother has a hard life looking after that lad

of yours at her age.' The greying head nodded twice. 'How old is he now? Nine? Ten?'

'Patrick will be ten in November.' Sarah lowered the ugly felt hat, wishing she had the nerve to push the old woman out of the way. 'I have to go. Excuse me, Nurse Tomkin. Me mother will be wondering where I am I stopped to make my confession, and I'm late already.'

Nellie Tomkin, a lapsed Methodist herself, sniffed her disapproval at such heathen ways. Then she dealt her stomach punch.

'A funny thing, Sarah. Well, at least it was a bit of an eye-opener to me not knowing the Peels like you do.' She paused, savouring the moment. 'I saw a photograph of your Patrick in my patient's bedroom.' The eyes, magnified to nightmare intensity by the thick lenses, picked holes in Sarah's suddenly quivering face.

'But you couldn't have. They — the Peels — they've never seen Patrick. Never set eyes on him.' The healthy colour drained from Sarah's face, leaving the freckles standing out like brown measles. 'You must have made a mistake.'

'No mistake, lass, though when I asked Mrs Brandwood who the little ladd was, she said it was her brother Willie who had been killed in the war. Naturally I kept my mouth shut, but it's a funny do all right. What do you make of it, Sarah?'

What Sarah made of it caused the ground to come up and hit her smack between her eyes. As the blood left her head, she crumpled at the knees, the grey sky with its scudding clouds dipping and wheeling around her.

And now the face bending over her, slapping her cheeks, loosening the top button of her coat, was filled with compassion, the evil glint in the eyes quite gone.

With Sarah Batt's sudden and unexpected metamorphosis into a patient, Nurse Tomkin was all solicitude.

'It was only a little faint, lass. Come on now! Up's-a-daisy!'

Trembling and sick, Sarah felt the small woman pull her to a standing position, with arms as strong as steel ropes.

'Shock does that sometimes. Drains the blood from the brain. See, I'll walk home with you lass.'

Nurse Tomkin was all sympathy now, but Sarah's refusal was immediate. 'Thank you. But I am all right.' She forced a wan smile. 'I don't know what came over me. It was likely going to Mass without a bite of breakfast.'

Pulling her hat down even further over her face, she walked away without another word. She could not have thought of anything to say if she had tried.

When she got back to the cottage her mother was sitting in her chair by the fire, her head back and her eyes closed. Seeing her like that, defenceless, with the yellow tinge to her skin and so thin that her clothes hung loose, Sarah made up her mind. Now that Nurse Tomkin had guessed the secret so carefully guarded all these years, Westerley was as out of bounds as if it were a hundred miles away. Because when Miss Libby's baby came and Nurse Tomkin was in charge, the interfering busybody wouldn't be able to keep her mouth shut. Sarah knew it in her very bones, and she moaned despairingly. Because when Nurse Tomkin remarked on the uncanny likeness between Patrick and the dead Willie, then Miss Libby would know straight away. Miss Libby hadn't been in the back row when brains were dished out, and she would know . . . oh, dear sweet Mother of Jesus, she would know all right. She would remember Sarah's reluctance ever to speak about her son; she would remember the panic whenever she had tried to probe; she would ask that nice Doctor Harry to describe Patrick. And, worst of all, she would tell Mrs Peel.

When the dinner was over and Patrick had gone scrumping with his pals in the fields beyond the village, Sarah unburdened herself to her mother. 'I *know* Miss Libby, and when her suspicions get warmed up she'll ask the doctor to drive her out here to see for herself.' Sarah's broad face crumpled. 'Oh, Mam, when they see Patrick there won't be no turning back. Mrs Peel has never really cottoned on to the fact that her Willie is dead. She even prays that Libby will have a boy to take his place, never dreaming that her grandson is here, growing up so like his father that it *is* him born again.' Her mouth tightened. 'Oh, why couldn't Patrick have had red hair? Or black? Why couldn't he have looked like you or me dad? Why did he have to be the dead spittin' image?'

'They can't take him from us.' Mrs Batt winced and without thinking laid a hand over the pain in her back. 'There's no law. Is there?'

Sarah found she was having to look away from the suffering on her mother's face. It was time she came home to stay. Nurse Tomkin had been right. Bringing up a rough, highly strung boy was no task for an ailing, elderly woman. Sarah felt the tears spring to her eyes and blinked them quickly away. She knew what was wrong with her mother. Grandma Batt had gone the same way, wasting to the size of a little bird, with her skin that strange pale yellow colour. And her mother knew it too.

'Why don't you have the doctor, Mam?' Carefully she tried to keep her voice light. 'He could perhaps give you a rubbing bottle for your back . . . or something.'

'There's nowt wrong with me that a rubbing bottle can cure.' Mrs Batt straightened up in her chair, but the pain lay like a dark shadow on her face even as she tried to smile. 'You mustn't let nobody take that lad from you, Sarah. We've fetched him up and he's ours. And Miss Williams at the school says he will likely pass the scholarship to the grammar school.' The faded eyes shone with pride as she got up and pushed the kettle over the flames. 'I keep thinking how proud your dad would have been of him. He would have been so chuffed with a grandson at a grammar school.'

'Then it's all settled.' Sarah got two pots down from the dresser. 'I have to go back after tea, but I'm going to tell them that after next week I'm coming back. For good. I'll tell them a lie,' she said, keeping her back turned. 'I'll say that you aren't well enough to look after Patrick no more.'

'And no more I am.'

When Sarah turned and saw the resigned dulled expression on her mother's face she felt terror grip her tight, as if a hand had suddenly squeezed her heart. And when she left to catch the train back to Westerley in the late afternoon she knew she was making the journey for the very last time.

CHAPTER ELEVEN

'But it's ridiculous, Mother! Two of us living in a house this size. Eight bedrooms and only three of them slept in. Mrs Edwards has the whole of the top floor to herself, and now that Libby has gone, and Sarah . . .' Carrie's voice tailed away as she saw the ready tears spring to Ettie's eyes at the mention of Sarah's name.

'All these years,' Eddie mourned. 'After us taking her back when she had disgraced herself, then her leaving just when it suited her. Young girls don't know the meaning of the word loyalty these days.'

'But Sarah's first loyalty was to her own mother, and her son.' Carrie knew she was wasting her time, but went on just the same. 'And besides, Sarah wasn't exactly a young girl. She was twenty-seven, Mother. It was time she tried to make a life of her own.'

'But she doesn't seem to want even to *remember* us.' Ettie touched her eyes with her handkerchief. 'All these weeks and never a line.'

'Sarah never was much of a scholar,' Carrie reminded her. I doubt whether she could put a letter together. And she was proud. You know that. Anyway, what has Sarah leaving got to do with us staying on here?' Her normally serene expression was clouded with concern. 'If we lived in a smaller house I might be able to find another teaching position. At least I could *try*.'

She was still young, Carrie reminded herself. She

could feel herself daily settling deeper into the role of unmarried daughter, fetching her mother's reading spectacles, going into town to change her mother's library books from Boots. Not bothering to wear her skirts at the fashionable length; playing the piano in the evenings, and getting on with her self-imposed task of covering the dining chairs with tapestry seats. Nothing ever seemed to happen, and yet, when she lay in bed, staring up into the darkness, it was as though she was holding herself still, expecting something to happen. Some exciting turn of events that would fill her days with more than the humdrum everyday running of a house. Not for the first time she wished she were more like Libby. What Libby wanted, Libby got. Not a vestige of martyrdom lingered in Libby's bones. Carrie frowned at the delicate stitching stretched over the frame on her lap. Was that what *she* was becoming? A martyr, sacrificing herself on the altar of her mother's possessiveness?

In a louder voice than she had intended she said, 'Well, I think we *should* look around for a smaller house. Perhaps one of the detached houses by the park. Nearer to town so that you could walk to the shops.'

Ettie held up a hand, a surprisingly strong hand as Carrie had so often realized when, helping her mother up to bed, the grip had tightened on her arm.

'The Peels have lived here for well over a hundred years. Westerley is part of your heritage, Carrie, and some day you will marry,' Ettie added vaguely, 'and your son will go on living here. When I'm gone', she finished sadly.

'To have a son I need a man first.' Carrie ignored the wounded expression on her mother's face. 'I am nearly twenty-four, Mother. All my friends are married, with homes of their own. I'm the odd one

221

out, Mother. My life is passing me by. I won't go on spending my days keeping this place going. It's too much.'

When Ettie's lower lip began its customary trembling, Carrie forced herself to look away, but she accepted the fact that for the time being anyway the question of the house must be shelved. There was something about the small quivering figure sitting opposite her that made her insides melt with love. Oliver Peel had made his wife what she was, and it was too late to change her now. Carrie turned her head as the telephone rang in the hall.

'That will be Libby,' she said. 'Are you coming to speak to her?' As she turned with a hand on the brass doorknob, she saw the way her mother was already levering herself up from her chair, an anticipatory expression in her dulled eyes. 'Oh, God help us,' Carrie whispered as she took the receiver from its hook, 'When a telephone call makes our day.'

'I waited until it was over.' Harry's voice, ringing with triumph, came passionately alive over the wires. 'Libby went into labour last night, and it's a girl, a beautiful girl, weighing six pounds four ounces, with ten toes and ten fingers.' There was the break of emotion in his voice as he went on, 'A straightforward birth with no complications. Libby sends her love.'

'A girl,' Ettie said, coming into the hall and leaning against the wall as if for support. 'That is so strange. I was sure it would be a boy.'

'But aren't you *glad*?' Carrie, guiding her mother back to her chair by the fire, felt as deflated as a pricked balloon. 'Aren't you pleased you have a granddaughter, and that Libby's all right.' Going over to the sidetable she lifted the sherry decanter. 'We must celebrate, Mother! You are a grandmother, and

I'm an aunt. Surely a little drink won't upset you? Oh, Mother, *please*! Please be glad. For Libby's sake let's be happy together. Please?'

'You know sherry always upsets my liver.' Ettie smoothed her skirt down over her knees. 'But *you* have one, dear.' She saw the expression in Carrie's eyes and added, 'Well, of course I'm glad that Libby has had her baby safely, especially after her being so ill with scarlet fever. But they can't very well call a girl Willie, can they?'

Carrie closed her eyes for a moment. 'I have to be more forceful. I have to be more firm. I have to get out of the house for at least part of the day.' She was muttering to herself as she poured a far larger sherry than the time of day warranted, tilting her head back and half draining the glass before she took it back to her chair. Her needlework waited for her, its soft colours as muted as the atmosphere in the large, chilly room.

Nurse Tomkin was in her element with a new-born baby to care for, especially one that resembled a skinned rabbit with twig-thin legs and a mauve tint to its mottled skin. Bustling round the bedroom with her flat-footed walk, she felt a sensation of gloating power as she nurtured the secret beneath the white starched bib of her apron — the secret that could, at a word from her, throw the Peel family into a proper flummox.

The week after Sarah Batt had slid in a faint at her feet, Nurse Tomkin had answered a knock at the door of her cottage to find the red-haired young woman standing there, her face reflecting a terrible anxiety.

'It's about that photograph, Nurse Tomkin.' Sarah had blurted out the words, then followed her into the cottage, refusing to sit down, just standing there red and troubled, so troubled that even Nurse Tomkin's spiteful curiosity had taken second place to her genuine concern.

'You *knew* that photograph wasn't my Patrick. You knew that when you stopped me that day coming home from Mass.' Sarah's hands, chapped and swollen by a lifetime of service, twisted together as if she was working up an invisible lather. 'So what are you going to do about it, Nurse Tomkin? Are you going to tell them that I have a boy who is his father born again?' Sarah's voice rang with passionate pleading. 'Because if you do, then they'll come for him. And when they see him they'll try to make me realize how much they can do for him They'll tell me they can send him to a good school. Then they'll give him their name.' The round eyes swam with tears. 'Mrs Peel has never believed that her son was dead. Never, not to this day. And when she realizes that Patrick was born on the very day that Willie died . . .' Sarah took a step forward and for a moment Nurse Tomkin thought she was going to go down on her knees.

It was the Irish Catholic in her, she decided. That red hair and her mother's maiden name of Mary O'Leary — no wonder this sturdy daughter of hers had let a man have his way with her, with all that superstitious passion smouldering behind those blue eyes.

'If you give me away then I will kill myself.' Sarah repeated this in a harsh whisper. 'If you tell the Peels what you have found out then I'll do away with meself. I swear by our Lady. I will cut me throat with the bread knife. I will! I mean it!'

'Then who would bring your Patrick up?' Nurse Tomkin's voice was brisk. She didn't hold with histrionics. 'Don't get so worked up, Sarah. See here now. Come and sit down. I'll make us a pot of tea, then we can talk about this in a sensible fashion.'

'I don't want your tea, an' I don't feel like being sensible!' Sarah Batt had gone as white as on the day she fainted. 'I just want your promise that you won't say nothing. I want you to swear it on the Bible, Nurse Tomkin.' She lowered her voice a fraction. 'Me mother won't live all that much longer. I know what ails her as well as you do, and when she's gone then there will be just me and Patrick. For the first time just the two of us.' Sarah's blue eyes glared defiance. 'I'll work me fingers to the bone to keep him. I'll get up afore it's light and go and scrub out the shippens over at the farm, then work in the sculleries or the *fields*, if they will take me on.' Her body was shaking as violently as if she had St Vitus's Dance. 'I will catch the train into Preston and go on the streets if need be. But they will never have him, the Peels won't. Never! Never! Never!'

And now, as she faced Libby sitting up in bed. Nurse Tomkin felt the sensation of gloating power again. With a few words she could set ripples widening that would have repercussions far more exciting than any of the little hoohas she had managed to stir up in the whole of her long and industrious life.

Libby spoke fretfully. 'But you don't understand, Nurse! I don't *want* to feed my baby. My husband agrees with me that she will come on just as well on Cow and Gate. The very idea of breast-feeding disgusts me.'

Nurse Tomkin could scarcely believe it. Mentally she compared the lovely face with Sarah Batt's homely features suffused with anguish on the day she had come to the cottage. That had been real mother-love, a word this little madam didn't know the meaning of.

One who had, and one who had not.

In that moment of revelation, Nurse Tomkin made up her mind. Sarah Batt's secret would be safe with her. Not for anything was she going to hand the Peel family their grandson on a plate. They had enough. They didn't deserve that little lad with his corn yellow hair and his bright eyes that charmed one even when he was at his most impossible.

'Then if you won't give the baby her ten o'clock feed, you'd be better off without your cup of coffee, Mrs Brandwood. Your liquid intake will have to be curtailed for the next few days at least.'

Nurse Tomkin nodded decisively, then with her starched apron crackling as if it had a life of its own she stalked out of the bedroom and down the stairs in search of her own morning cuppa and two or three Marie biscuits.

Carrie politely nibbled the sugar-coated biscuit held out for her approval by the dignified elderly assistant in the shop in the town's main shopping street.

'Yes, you can include a tin of those in our order,' she agreed, handing over the neatly written list. 'They are rather nice.'

Then, with a wicker basket over her arm containing nothing more than four library books, she walked down the street and turned the corner, making her way to the offices of the evening newspaper to hand in the announcement of the birth of Libby's and Harry's daughter.

It was a golden day, an autumn day with the trees in the cathedral grounds scattering brown and yellow leaves and the wind for once no more than a soft sigh. She was wearing a beige costume with a little Peter Pan fur collar and a small cloche hat to match pulled down over her forehead, hiding her fringe and leaving the side pieces of her dark hair framing her face.

The little outer office was crowded, and the young man behind the counter seemed to be taking a long time to pacify a flat-capped Irishman who was arguing loudly. Carrie heard the glass-fronted door open, then felt an embarrassing blush stain her cheeks as a delighted voice hailed her.

'Miss Peel! Carrie! Yes, definitely Carrie! How are you? You remember me?'

It had been a long time but, oh yes, she remembered Tom Silver. She had followed his career in the papers, smiling at some of his more outrageous remarks in the reports of council meetings, and now that he was actually there, standing by her side, smiling, she realized that she had never forgotten him for a single moment.

There was a genuine note of pleasure in his voice as, after waiting for her to hand in the notice, he took her by the elbow and walked with her down the steps and into the sun-warmed street. Then, with the trams and the buses streaming out from the Boulevard, he told her that he could well be spared for half an hour at least and that she must come and have a drink with him in the big hotel on the corner.

When they were seated in an alcove with their drinks on the little round table in front of them, he turned towards her so that he could look full into her face. 'Now, Carrie Peel! Hello!'

She looked down at her hands, only shakily composed. There was something so intimately gentle in his look and his voice that for a wild uncontrolled moment she thought she was going to cry. She had been crying the last time they had met, the only time they had met, she remembered, and with an effort she pulled herself together.

'Libby has had a baby. I was putting the announcement in your paper.' She busied herself taking off her

227

gloves and then stroked them into position on her lap. 'A girl. They are going to call her Isobel.'

'So that's Libby settled.' Tom smiled at her. 'And you? What are you doing with your life now, Carrie?'

There were shadows on her face, and he felt an illogical desire to stretch out a finger and smooth them away. When he had thought about Libby it had been with a sort of compassionate affection that filled him with remorse for treating her so cruelly that September evening in the lane outside the big house. Now *this* one — this one with Libby's face but with that difference in the eyes — had been put from his mind with conscious deliberation.

'There's nothing to tell about me,' she was saying softly. 'But you? *You* are a celebrity. I read about you in the paper. You're still fighting battles, aren't you, Mr Silver?'

'Tom,' he said, then nodded towards the group of men shaking hands as they met at the bar, pot-bellied men with florid complexions, drinking their beers before moving through into the dining room for expense-account lunches. 'I haven't joined *their* ranks, if that's what you mean. Carrie.'

'But the strike is over and forgotten,' she said guilelessly. 'The miners are back at work and my father's mill is flourishing, even in spite of foreign competition. What does a man like you *do* when the town is sliding back into prosperity?'

To her surprise he threw back his head and laughed out loud. 'Carrie! What have you been doing with yourself? Oh, aye, things might have been looking up for the likes of them.' He jerked his head towards the bar. 'Masons, Rotarians, pit and factory owners. They never need to worry where their next meal's coming from. Everything they do is put down to expenses, like those drinks they're enjoying now.'

228

He shook his head at Carrie, then flicked the fur collar on her coat with an impatient finger. 'No, the hope for the future doesn't lie with the likes of them. The only hope for better working conditions is through the Labour movement, though I've been disappointed in the way some of the Labour councillors seem to lose contact with the very people they are put there to serve. We've a long way to go yet before we reach an ideal society. And if you do say too much in defence of the needy you're accused of having Bolshie leanings.'

'I do hope you don't lose your job again.' Carrie noticed how the green pullover underneath his dark jacket had been badly washed so that the wool had erupted into little bobbles. Hardly knowing what she was doing, she put out a hand and touched his sleeve. 'You've been victimised once. I know that because Libby told me. So isn't once enough? You can't fight the way things are, Tom.' She said his name shyly. 'There will always be those who have and those who have not.' She paused. 'Libby went through a stage of not wanting to accept that; she wanted everyone to have the same advantages she had, but she seems reconciled to the idea that a system like that could never be.'

'And you?'

'I have thought about it.' She was very serious as she tried hard to be honest. 'It's just that I can't see how it would *help* for me to become poor overnight. My father and grandfather worked hard, you know. So — I get on with what I have to do, and what I have to do at this moment is take care of Mother and Westerley. And I feel the same resentment as if we sat by an empty grate all day and I went out to the corner shop to get things on tick. Oh, I know I must be shocking you, because you'll be thinking one can't

229

compare, but that's the way I am. I would never have chained myself to railings for the vote. I could never stand on a platform shouting the odds. I'm not one of the intellectual elite. I wasn't even a very good teacher, nowhere as good as Libby.' She smiled. 'I go to church to evensong, and half the time I can't believe what I'm praying about. My ideas are half formed; they must be. All I want is to be happy, and to make the people I love happy too.' Her hand shook as she lifted the tall sherry glass and drained it. 'And now I must go, or Mother will work herself into a state wondering where I am.'

Tom stood with her on the pavement outside the newspaper office, and when she raised her face to the sun he thought her dark-fringed eyes had a bruised look about them, as though she had not been sleeping well. He realized he did not want to let her go.

He shuffled his feet. 'I'd like to see you again. Soon.' To his surprise his thinking was too confused to mention a definite date. 'May I telephone you?' Suddenly he took her hand in his 'Oh, Carrie. I'm putting myself across badly, but there's so much I'd like to show you.' He was looking deep into her eyes as the tooting of a car horn made him turn quickly.

And afterwards Harry Brandwood was to tell Libby that Carrie had stared at him as if he were a complete and utter stranger.

'I took Carrie home,' he told Libby, eating his lunch with her in the overheated bedroom from a tray on his lap. 'It saved her catching the tram, but I don't think she was glad of the lift.' He chuckled. 'The way she was holding hands with that man — a man I don't recollect ever meeting, by the way — I got the feeling she would have preferred to ride on the tram just to be alone. She certainly hadn't much to say to me.'

'What was he like?' Libby put her knife and fork

down, her face suddenly peaky above the pale blue bedjacket 'Did she tell you his name?'

'No.' Harry went on eating, oblivious of the tension in the air. 'But he worked in the compositors' room of the evening paper. She told me that.' He chewed happily. 'A tall, thin chap with long hair. No hat. Not a man your father would have approved of, I can tell you that much.'

'Not a gentleman?' Libby's voice dripped ice.

'Well, hardly. Not at first glance.' Harry speared a piece of sliced carrot on his fork. 'I wasn't holding up the traffic, nothing like that, but Carrie didn't bring him over to introduce us. If you ask me, she was sorry I appeared like that.' Innocently he rubbed salt in the wound. 'She was looking very pretty. More animated than I've seen her for a long time. I've been worried about Carrie lately. She allows herself to be manipulated, and with all due respect, love, your mother can be a bit overpowering. In a helpless way, if you know what I mean.'

Libby, taking a tight hold on herself, controlled the urge to lean over and tip what was left of her husband's lunch on to his lap. The thought of Carrie holding hands with Tom Silver was making her feel sick. The binder round her swollen breasts was suddenly like a tourniquet, cutting off her life's blood, so that she found it hard to breathe. And there was nothing she could say. She was stuck here in bed for another ten days at least, with that bossy woman glaring at her through her thick spectacles, with the baby crying in that high plaintive wail. And now her sister was betraying her by meeting Tom Silver on the sly and being intimate enough with him to hold hands in the street.

The euphoria she had felt just after the birth had drained away, and now her immediate desire was to strike out at whoever was nearest — Harry, munching stolidly through his lunch, his face ruddy and contented.

'I've told Nurse Tomkin that you agree with me about stopping breast-feeding,' she said casually.

Harry, forgetting his natural good manners, spoke with his mouth full of food. 'You have *what*?'

'I sent her out for bottles and a tin of Cow and Gate. She's downstairs now mixing it up, or whatever you do with it.' She picked up her own fork and began to eat.

'But why?' Harry stared at her in amazement. 'Why did you tell her that? It isn't true, damn it. You have enough milk there to feed half a dozen babies.' Bewildered and angry he pointed to the corner where the baby whimpered in her frilly cot, making smacking noises with her tiny mouth. 'She needs your milk, Libby. Breast-feeding is your *duty*, it gives the baby an immunity to certain diseases, besides being easy and natural.' He touched the bolster case pinned round his wife's swollen breasts. 'Besides, your stomach will go flatter quicker if you breast-feed. It's your *duty*!' he said again. 'As a doctor I forbid you to send all that good milk back.'

'I'm not a cow, Harry.' Libby, assuaging the hurt he had inflicted on her by telling her about Carrie and Tom Silver, set her face into lines of determination. 'Besides, I refuse to be tied to feeding times. I refuse to be cajoled into the barbarity of it.'

'The barbarity of it?' Harry rose to his feet, holding the tray in front of him and looking round wildly for somewhere to put it. 'Good God, woman! What kind of talk is that? I look at you sometimes, Libby Brandwood, and I wonder what I see. There are women in this town who are having to feed their babies on pobs, bread soaked in milk, half diluted with water;

women who have no milk in their breasts because they are undernourished. And you, fed on nothing but the best . . .' He jerked his head towards the beefsteak on his wife's plate. 'You deny your child what is hers by right!'

'I thought you had no time for undernourished women,' Libby said sweetly, seeing in her mind's eye Tom Silver holding Carrie's hand. 'I thought that women who couldn't pay your fees didn't even exist for you, Harry.'

He left the room angrily, hurt and bewildered. Libby pushed her own tray from her and turning her head into the lace-edged pillows, wept like a child.

When, all unsuspecting, Carrie called that afternoon, still wearing the becoming costume with her hair curling over the brim of the tiny hat and her eyes shining as if a candle had been lit behind them, Libby, without preamble, said what she was bursting to say.

'Harry told me you were with Tom Silver this morning.'

Carrie blushed a deep rosy red. 'Yes. I told him about the baby, Libby, and he sent his kind regards.' She was so full of a strange sweet feeling that in her innocence she said entirely the wrong thing. 'He wants to see me again, Libby, and I think he means it. He's such a strange man, isn't he? He doesn't seem to have a thought in his head for himself. He's the sort of man who will kill himself worrying about other people. And he's had such a sad life. Did you know his wife was killed during the war, when he was in France at the front.'

Libby's breasts were throbbing, making her want to tear off the tight binder. She could feel the wetness as the milk soaked through the layers of material, and she could still see Nurse Tomkin's look of disgust as the baby had refused to suck at the rubber teat of the bottle.

'Did he tell you he once asked me to go away with him?' Libby's voice was high through her physical discomfort. 'Did he tell you how he asked me to go into the house and pack my things? "I'll wait ten minutes," he said. Has he asked you to do the same?'

Carrie's head drooped low as all the bright promise of the morning disappeared. 'I didn't realize you had known him that well,' she said slowly. 'You never told me. Why didn't you, Libby?'

'I did try to warn you.' Libby winced and slid farther down in the bed. 'Tom Silver is an ambitious man, Carrie. He has proved that by getting himself on to the council so quickly. And that's only the first step. Westminster is where Mr Silver has set his sights, and if to get there means climbing on the shoulders of one of the town's most prominent families, then he will do just that.'

'But he — he didn't strike me as . . . I thought he . . .' Carrie's voice was a whisper.

'You or me. What does it matter?' Libby reached for a grape from the bunch at the side of her bed. 'To a man with his sights set high, one twin is as good as the other. He even mistook you for me the first time you met.'

Carrie's head drooped even farther, and Libby saw a single tear drop on to the folded gloves on her sister's lap.

'It's funny really, if you think about it,' she said spitting a grape pip neatly into a cupped hand. 'I thought after your Mungo episode you'd be more worldly-wise.' Then, the damage done, her dark eyes softened as she looked with genuine fondness at her twin's bowed head. 'Have some grapes, love,' she said.

'And don't look so distressed; there are plenty more fish in the sea.'

'Like Roger Fish?' Carrie's expression was hard and un-Carrie-like as she made the feeble joke.

And as they laughed together, as they had always laughed together, Libby refused to see that her sister's eyes were now as bleak as moorland stones.

CHAPTER TWELVE

The middle classes, Tom remembered wryly, as he rang the door bell set high in the big front door at Westerley, did not call uninvited. They telephoned or wrote a letter first to make sure it was convenient. He smoothed his wet hair away from his forehead and waited, surprised to find that his heartbeats had quickened. All he needed was a nosegay in one hand and a box of chocolates in the other, and the poem he had been struggling to write in his pocket.

It was a dark November evening, with the fields surrounding Westerley wreathed in damp, clinging mist. His jacket was beaded with droplets as if he had walked through a shower of rain. He must be mad, he told himself. He rang the bell again, then wished he hadn't as the door opened. Carrie was standing there, dressed in something long, blue and flowing, looking even more beautiful than he remembered.

'Mr Silver! Tom!' Her voice was high as she stared at him in amazement. 'Come in! Oh, what a dreadful night! You look so cold.'

Leading the way into the big lounge, she told him to sit down in a wing chair at right angles to the fire roaring up the wide chimney and throwing out a heat that made his face burn. 'Mother is upstairs, and Mrs Edwards has gone to the pictures, but I'll get you a hot drink. Or would you perhaps like something stronger?'

'A cup of tea would be very welcome.' Tom's eyes took in the large room, the thick carpet, the heavy mahogany furniture, the chintz-covered chesterfield and the long velvet curtains shutting out the winter.

'You were going to bed.' He nodded at Carrie's housecoat and beaded slippers. 'I've come at an inconvenient time. You haven't been ill, have you?'

'I often wear this thing after dinner,' Carrie explained gently, realizing with a pang of tenderness that he thought she was wearing her dressing gown. 'You just sit there and get warm. I won't be a minute.'

Then, with flushed face and hands that surprised her by their trembling, she stood in the kitchen willing the kettle to boil.

When Tom was balancing a fluted cup and saucer on a bony knee, he suddenly said, 'My late wife's mother died last week?'

Carrie, confused, mumbled regrets and wondered what he was leading up to.

He took a sip of the tea, then put the cup carefully back in its saucer. 'No, don't say anything. She was old and tired and her time had come. But one of the last things she did was to ask the owner of her house if I might be allowed to take it on. The rent is five shillings a week, but it has two up and two down, and an outside lavatory in a tiny yard. A palace compared to the place I've been living in.' He grinned. 'So you see sitting before you a man with his own house. Would you say that makes me into a man worth knowing, Carrie?'

'Where is it?' Carrie looked away from the unspoken message in his dark eyes.

He told her and she saw, in her mind's eye, the district with its warren of short streets, and endless

237

rows of chimney pots, the doors opening straight on to the pavement. She nodded. 'It's up by the infirmary, isn't it?'

'It's nearly a hundred years old.' Tom sat forward in his chair, the cup and saucer tilting so precariously that she got up and brought a small table and placed it in front of him.

'There. I should have done that before. Won't you mind living alone?'

She thought he was going to take her hand so she moved quickly back to her own chair, picked up her cup and then set it down again when she saw that it trembled in her grasp. The dark eyes never left her face.

'I've lived alone for many years and never minded till now.'

There was no mistaking the expression in his eyes, and even as her body responded Carrie was filled with resentment and anger. She felt like weeping, and if she wept this would be the third time she had met this man and felt her insides dissolve into tears.

'I think I have fallen in love with you,' he said slowly. 'It's unbelievable, and yet it's true. I think I loved you from the time I found you walking down the road on the afternoon of your father's funeral.' His voice was so low she could barely catch what he was saying. 'You need a man to take care of you, Carrie. You're so lonely it makes me want to put my arms round you and hold you safe.' His glance swept the room. 'You have all this, and yet you need so much more. Am I right?'

He made no move towards her, and yet when she shrank back on to the cushions it was as if she were warding off a physical attack. When she spoke her voice startled him with its harshness.

'Are you asking me to go away with you, Tom

Silver? Are you saying that you'll give me ten minutes to go upstairs and pack my things?' She lifted her chin. 'Like you asked my sister? Only, according to Libby, you waited outside in the cold for her. Now you've moved on a step and can wait by the fire.' She gave a short laugh. 'You made a mistake when you decided that one sister was as good as the other. Libby and I are twins, Mr Silver, and twins tell each other everything. Libby warned me what to expect, but even so I'm surprised at your temerity and your haste.'

Her heart was knocking wildly against her ribs. It wasn't really in her to hurt and to shock, but her feelings were no longer her own. She had thought he had just come to *see* her — that would have been enough — but now, by his impetuous talk of love, he had brought Libby's words to mind as clearly as if she were there in the room laughing at him.

'We're two people, though, Libby and I. You can't just take up with one where you left off with the other. You'll have to find some other way to further your political ambitions.'

Tom stared at her and then with a sudden movement he jumped to his feet, knocking over the little table and crashing the delicate cup and saucer on to the tiled hearth so that they smashed into smithereens. He came over to her quickly and knelt beside her.

'I'm not a gentleman, Carrie, so there's nothing to stop me from telling you the truth. I won't imitate Douglas Fairbanks and rush from the house in a welter of misunderstandings. I want you, and I'm going to fight for you, and you must listen to me. Carrie! Look at me!'

But she found she could not lift her head. She could only stare down at the carpet, until she felt his fingers wrenching her chin round so that she was forced to look up into his face.

'What I did to Libby was cruel and despicable, I admit it. But I didn't do it because of her money or connections. In fact, I don't really know why I did it, except that when I saw this house and remembered my own wretched room — when I thought of her doctor friend waiting for her and remembered how alone I was — I wanted to hurt her. I saw she had a thing about me, and just then I wanted to put her into an impossible position. And later I was too ashamed to get in touch with her and apologise — I was afraid of making things worse.' He paused for a moment, then went on urgently. 'Carrie, I like Libby a lot, but you must believe me when I say I never loved her, and I never seriously wanted her to come away with me — for ambition or any other reason. Please believe me, Carrie!'

He sat down beside Carrie and drew her stiff, resisting body into his arms. He could feel her gradually relaxing as he held her close. Then his hand was on her neck beneath the soft weight of her hair, and his mouth, delicate at first, trailed its sweetness down her cheeks lingering at the corners of her mouth until with a groan he pulled her close, into a kiss which deepened as her lips parted and they clung together, their bodies fusing as if they were one person.

When at last he raised his head he was seeing, not the cosy overfurnished room with its heavy drapings, the high-banked fire striking sparks off the brasses, and the silver photograph frames on the side tables, but the little back living room of the house he had just left. A room with a black fireplace with a cut steel fender, a slopstone beneath the window, in a street where women gossiped on doorsteps and children

240

played their chanting games with a rope stretched across the cobbles.

He could never . . . he must never . . . he had so little to give, and yet as he bent his head to kiss her again and felt her response, he whispered, 'Carrie . . . oh, Carrie, my love. I love you so much. I can't let you go.'

'You must *never* let me go.' The wide sleeves of the silken wrap fell away from her bare arms as they crept round his neck, holding him even closer. 'I won't *let* you let me go.' She was half smiling, half weeping. 'I don't know you, and yet I think I'm in love too. How can that be?' Her voice came muffled from his shoulder. 'But don't put me on a pedestal, Tom. I — oh, what would you say if I told you I lost my teaching job because I was found in the arms of a fellow teacher? That he's married, and for the whole of last summer I used to meet him. In a deserted summer house.' She raised her head and he saw that her face was scarlet. 'But we didn't — that is, we never —'

'Made love properly?' He was smiling a teasing smile. 'Oh, Carrie, love. I'm not one of those men who think they have always the right to be the first. What will happen between you and me isn't written yet, but when it is it'll be on a blank page with no ghosts to look over our shoulders.'

Then he closed his eyes. What was he doing? What was he promising when he had nothing to promise? He had wanted to *see* her, that was all. The urgency of his need to see her had wiped out any practicalities; he had never intended to touch her. But holding her close he knew that he was committed to loving this lovely, lovely girl for ever.

He was so thin that Carrie could feel his bones through the tweed jacket. His lips when he kissed her were firm, not soft and fleshy as Mungo's had been. She was filled with such tenderness, such compassion for his need of her that she thought she would die of it. Carrie stirred in his arms, wanting nothing more than that the clock on the mantelpiece would stop its ticking, that time would stand still, with nothing of the outside world intruding. She was not Libby, working out ways and means. Her waiting time was over, and somehow they would find a way to be together.

Neither of them heard the door click open. At Ettie's voice Carrie looked up, staring at her mother with dream-dazed eyes.

'Mother!' Moving from the circle of Tom's arms but still holding on to his hand, Carrie looked neither guilty nor surprised. 'This is Tom Silver.'

As Tom got to his feet Ettie came forward into the room, ignoring his outstretched hand. 'I thought I heard voices . . .' She walked unsteadily to the winged chair and lowered herself into it, pulling the folds of her wrap round her knees, her face a study of disbelief and dismay. 'I don't think we have met before Mr — Mr Silver?'

His face, Carrie saw, looked younger, more vulnerable. Gone was the teasing mockery. It was as though the past half hour had transformed him, leaving a dignity she had never seen before.

'I wish we hadn't met like this, Mrs Peel.' Gently he disengaged Carrie's clinging hand. 'I wanted to court your daughter properly, to meet her with your approval. It must seem — it must be a shock —' He broke off as the small woman watching him clutched her heart, starting to breathe quickly so that he saw the rise and fall of the lace cascading in frills down her bodice.

'Will you please go, Mr Silver?' Ettie leaned back

and closed her eyes. 'And Carrie. My tablets. They are on my bedside table. Will you fetch them, please?'

'I'm sorry,' he said again, but Ettie's face wore its shut-in waxen look, the ploy she always used when anything unpleasant occurred, the defence she had always put up when Oliver had made one of his scenes.

Carrie shook her head at Tom, moving towards the door, her eyes pleading with him to follow her.

In the hall he reached for her again. 'Is she ill?' He jerked his head towards the closed door. 'What is it? Her heart?'

Carrie put a hand to his cheek and answered him sadly. 'Mother will not face up to things.' Her voice hardened. 'My father made her like this. When she is scared she moves into illness. Oh, why did she have to come downstairs just now?'

'Will it make any difference?'

'To us? I don't know,' she said dully.

'Carrie?' Ettie's voice floated through the closed door in a long, plaintive wail. 'Are you there?'

'Coming, Mother.'

Resolutely she put him from her. 'You must go now. I have to see to her.'

Fiercely he pulled her close for a last embrace, so close that she could feel his ribs pressing against her. 'When will I see you again?'

'Soon.'

'Tomorrow? Can I come again tomorrow?'

Then, even as he let himself out of the house, she was running upstairs. And when Tom stepped outside into the cold seeping fog of the November evening it felt as if the heavy clang of the big front door had shut out all that was warm and comfortable in his life.

Pulling up the collar of his jacket and shoving his

hands deep in his pockets, Tom walked back down the winding lane with the trees on either side pointing winter-bare branches to the dark sky. He would catch the tram into town, and maybe even another tram out to the street where he now lived. Back to a house that had seemed like a palace but was now only a place to live. And he had thought . . . he had even dared to dream . . . but in that long, disquieting stare, Oliver Peel's widow had crumbled his dreams to dust.

He started to run, swinging himself aboard the tram with a recklessness that brought a shouted warning to the conductor's lips.

The tablets were washed down with a tumbler of water held in Ettie's shaking hand. Her lips had a strange blue tinge to them, and Carrie watched her anxiously.

Was she genuinely ill? She certainly looked dreadful, with her nose all pinched, and a hectic spot of scarlet burning on her cheeks. Or was that the fire? Carrie glanced at the leaping flames suspiciously. Before she left the room the fire had been deadened to a red glow, and yet now it was as though someone had put the poker to it, loosening the banked slack and the huge slab of coal, so that the flames roared upward again. Could her mother, in the middle of what appeared to be a genuine attack, have leaned forward, picked up the heavy brass-handled poker and tended the fire?

'Mother?' She took the tumbler from Ettie's hand. 'Don't you think you ought to go back upstairs? I'll follow you when I've done this.' Kneeling down she swept the shattered cup and saucer on to the brass fire shovel.

'*He* did that.' It was more of a statement than a

question. The pupils of Ettie's eyes seemed to have grown, almost obliterating the blue, as she stared with pointed emphasis at Carrie's housecoat. 'Did you know he was coming? Was that why you helped me upstairs to my room straight after dinner, Carrie?'

'Oh, Mother!' Carrie felt her happiness dissolve. 'How can you think that?'

'How can I *not* think that?' Ettie's mouth worked itself into an ugly shape. 'It seems to me that even losing your job through — through carrying on with a man in school hours has not taught you a lesson. But I never thought you were so hard up for a man that you would allow someone of his type to make love to you. Have you no shame? No pride?'

'What do you mean, someone of his *type*?' Carrie's voice was dangerously quiet. She pulled at the tied belt of the housecoat, feeling as if her mother had caught her stark naked. 'Tom Silver is a good man. He is a councillor. He has a house of his own, and a job.' She heard herself justifying Tom's status and despised herself.

'He is common.' Ettie's face was a mask of bitterness. 'He talks in a common voice, and he wears a common suit. His hair needs cutting, and his shirt reminded me of a pyjama jacket. And he wants to *court* you. Oh, my God! What sort of an expression is that?' She glanced at the broken pieces of china on the small brass shovel still held in Carrie's hands. 'No wonder he broke them. Did he pour his tea into the saucer and blow on it first before drinking it?'

Putting down the shovel on the hearth Carrie went to the far end of the tiled fireplace and laid her head against the mantelpiece. 'Don't humiliate me, Mother. Why are you trying to hurt me?'

Ettie did not answer. Her throat was choked with fear, the fear that had caught at it when she had opened the door and seen the two lovers in each other's arms. For they *were* lovers, in the purest sense of the word. When their faces had turned towards her the surprise had been there right enough, but that was all — no guilt or shame. When he had stood up, still holding on to Carrie's hand, there had been a dignity about the tall, thin man, a steadiness in the dark eyes — and in that one moment she had known. This was the man who would take Carrie away from her. He was a working man; not a weaver with cotton fluff in his hair, nor a miner with dirt on his face, but a working man all the same. He would, to use his own working-class phraseology, *court* Carrie and then take her away.

Then there would be no one in the big house but herself. No husband, no daughters, no Sarah, just herself growing older alone. The sudden pain as Ettie made the familiar gesture of clutching her heart was real this time. It was like a knife being slowly twisted beneath her ribs.

Carrie raised her head, staring down into the fire. 'I am going to marry him, Mother. He hasn't asked me yet, but when he does I am going to say yes. And no one is going to talk me out of it. Not you, not Libby. Nobody!'

The pain was doubling Ettie over, she was gasping for breath — it was filling her chest with fire, and the sound she made brought Carrie to her knees, her face a mask of shock as she saw the beads of perspiration standing out on her mother's forehead.

'I'll get Harry! Mother! Stay still. Oh, please, Mother! Don't die!'

She ran from the room, tripping over her long silken skirts in her haste. Unhooking the telephone receiver, she prayed he would be there.

'It's real!' she told the reassuring voice of her

brother-in-law. 'Oh, Harry, come quickly. This time it's real!'

'She has what Harry calls a dry pleurisy.'

When Carrie went to meet Tom four days later after pleading with him on the telephone to stay away from Westerley, her heart was wrenched with a pain she had never thought she would be able to bear.

'Libby is with her now, but I can't stay. She won't have a day nurse, Tom, and she has only agreed to a night nurse because Harry insisted.' She took his arm as naturally as if they were husband and wife, and he steered her towards the same restaurant where once Libby had jumped up from the table by the window and rushed out into the street.

'It's too cold to stand talking outside, love.' He looked round at the crowded upstairs room filled with chattering women, and smiled. 'I never thought the day would come when I would join this lot on a Saturday afternoon. Do they always make this much noise?'

There were no gaps to fill, no explanations of how they knew that their relationship had progressed from a shy awareness of each other to this sweet intimacy. He felt his chest rise in a great sigh of relief as he saw his own love mirrored in her eyes. He stared down through the window to a crowded street where an early snow powdered the pavement, only to be blown away in an instant by the piercing wind.

'I can't see you for a while. Not until Mother is a lot better.' Their eyes were clinging, their hands entwined across the white tablecloth. 'And you mustn't come to the house. Harry says she must be kept calm.' Carrie closed her eyes for a moment as she felt his fingers caressing the throbbing pulse at her wrist. 'She has to sleep propped up on pillows, and she hears everything. There is no way I could ask you to the house without her knowing.'

'Was I so much of a shock to her, then?' The fingers stopped their caressing as the waitress, balancing the tray on a jutting hip, placed a teapot, milk jug, sugar bowl and two cups and saucers on the table in front of Carrie. 'Was it the shock of meeting me that made your mother ill?'

Busying herself with the tea she turned an unhappy face towards him. 'It didn't help,' she said with characteristic truthfulness. 'But she had been feeling ill for a long time, and this coughing doesn't help her heart. Mother has always been delicate.'

'And when she is better?' Tom was stirring sugar into his tea with a face set and cold. 'Will she welcome me into the family *then*, Carrie?' His dark eyes twinkled. 'You know we'll be getting married?'

Not 'Will you marry me?' Just 'We'll be getting married.' Carrie pressed her lips together in a gesture that even as a child had always meant she was hugging her happiness to herself. Conditioned by her twin's stronger personality she was content to be led, and here for the first time in her life was a man who was prepared to do the leading.

'And the next time you can get away we'll go and see the house.' Tom looked at her with love. 'Shall we say tomorrow afternoon?'

Carrie remembered that Libby and Harry were bringing the baby to show Ettie, and she smiled. 'Tomorrow afternoon,' she agreed, 'but you'll have to meet me at the end of the lane. It's too soon yet to upset Mother again. You don't mind, do you, Tom?'

But he had minded. Carrie knew that. This wasn't a man prepared to do his courting on the sly, as if they were both in their teens and avoiding the hostile reaction of a possessive parent. This wasn't Mungo willing to meet her in a secret place, their love a furtive thing to be hidden from the world.

As she hurried home, preparing herself for the inevitable questions and petulant suspicions, Carrie sent up a silent prayer of thanks that the telephone calls, the harassment from Mungo had stopped. Now she could wipe the memory of that long hot summer off her mind as if it had never existed. What lay in front of her was a future so full of shining promise that as she walked from the tram it seemed that her feet scarcely touched the ground.

Oh, by the way, Beatrice McDermot came to see me last week.' Libby, very smart in a small fur toque matching the coat thrown casually over a chair, smiled at her sister.

Carrie turned pale. 'Mungo's wife came to see *you*? For heaven's sake, why?'

The baby was upstairs being shown off to her grandmother by a doting Harry, and the two girls were alone in the lounge, Carrie feverishly trying to get away and Libby sitting complacently in the middle of the massive chesterfield, her fingers twisting a long rope of amber beads into a knot.

'Why shouldn't she come and see me? We had met, remember? That day Harry took me to Mungo's house on an errand of mercy. To warn him that Father was on the warpath.'

Libby felt a pang of guilt as she saw the way the happiness had faded from Carrie's face. Harry had said that of course Carrie must go out, that something must be done to give his sister-in-law more freedom, and Libby had agreed. Until she had guessed where Carrie was going, whom she was meeting, and then the urge to hurt, to wound and destroy had taken over.

'There's nothing sinister about it. Heavens, Carrie, to look at your face anyone would think the woman had come to make trouble.' Libby stopped fiddling with the beads and smiled. 'It was about the boy. Edwin. His mother feels now that the time has come for him to have more schooling than she is able to give him, and she remembered that I had suggested the same. So — I've talked it over with Harry, and Mungo will drop the boy off at my house three mornings a week, then his wife will pick him up at lunchtime. I'll try to teach him to read.' She spread her hands wide. 'I *had* to find something to do, and this was a heaven-sent opportunity. I'm a trained teacher, Carrie. A *good* teacher. I'm not content merely to stay at home, like you. I'd go stark raving mad!'

Carrie let that pass. Closing the door, and closing her mind to the image of Tom waiting in the drifting winter rain outside, she tried to keep her voice low and reasonable.

'But why Mungo's son? Just when I'd thought all that was behind me, why him?' Her brown eyes clouded with anxiety. 'You must have known it was an insensitive thing to do at the very least. You must have, Libby.'

'Mrs McDermot doesn't know about you and her husband, does she?'

Carrie moved her body as if trying to avoid something. 'I pray she never knows. I don't know what Mungo told her when he lost his job, but for all his faults he wouldn't involve me. He wasn't that bad.'

'Well then?' Libby's tone considered the matter settled. 'Now you had better go if you don't want to keep him waiting. Where is it Mother thinks you're going this time?'

They stared at each other in an agony of

bewildered frustration. Two identical faces; two minds with conflicting desires. Far more than ordinary sisters, the twins had power to hurt one another, but not without sharing the pain. Now, each striving for her independence, they faced each other like jousting knights, their faces full of what, to the uninitiated, would have seemed like mutual dislike.

They met, Carrie and Tom, whenever they could snatch a few precious moments together during that long, hard winter. The unemployment figures were rising daily, the outlying factories and mines were closing down one after the other, and some of Tom's own union members were working a three-day week. His evenings were spent at one committee meeting after another, his weekends sitting at the roll-top desk in the tiny living room of his new house. He became accustomed to the regular knock at his door, heralding a neighbour with a form for him to fill in, or a query about where to apply when the rent man threatened a family with eviction. He went to a house where he saw a table spread with newspapers, and six children standing round it dipping crusts of bread into a tin of condensed milk set in the middle. He heard a widow sob on his doorstep after queueing for two hours down at the labour exchange, only to be told there was no work for her, no work of any kind. He fought with his own management to keep his men on full-time, even when he realized that short-time would soon be inevitable. Clever boys won scholarships to the grammar school and he pleaded with their parents to let them go somehow, only to discover they were forced to leave after one term to work in stop-gap jobs which brought in the few shillings needed to keep the rest of the family in bare necessities.

At one time he was almost persuaded to seek Labour nomination, but his common sense came to his rescue. He was not educated enough to put the workers' case across in a dispassionate manner, and he knew it. His temper was too short, and his reasoning too emotional.

'My place is here,' he told Carrie. 'Up here in the north we are going into the worst depression the country has ever known.'

One February evening Carrie was helping him to strip the wallpaper from the tiny front bedroom of the terraced house.

'Your mother must be well enough by now to accept the truth about us,' Tom urged her. His dark eyes twinkled. 'Why don't I come and present myself as a suitor? I'll wear my best suit and tell her that I have a job which is as permanent as any job can be at this time. I'll explain to her that I have a house, and that — most important — I intend to spend the rest of my life caring for you.'

He threw down the knife he was holding so that it dropped with a clatter on the bare boards, took away the brush she was using to paint the old wallpaper with water, then kissed her.

'Carrie! I love you so much, and I want you so much. We are neither of us children playing at getting to know each other. You must know we can't go on like this. The neighbours must see you coming and going; even they would never believe that our relationship hasn't progressed much beyond a sweet companionship.'

He steered her towards the bed. 'Carrie — I want to marry you now. Tomorrow. Today. Not at some distant time when your mother has decided to come to terms with the thought of me. Pulling her down beside him, he began to kiss the soft hollow of her

252

neck, his lips tracing the pulse beating there, so that her whole body curved into his, and she sighed with pleasure.

They had been stripping the paper by the light of two candles, one set in a holder on the small cane bedside table, and the other flickering from a saucer on top of the rickety stepladder. Tom put out a hand and snuffed the nearest candle at exactly the same time as the second one died, leaving the room bathed in the soft light from the lamp standard outside in the street.

'I love you . . . love you . . .' His voice was very gentle as he began to unbutton the front of the heavy coat she had kept on in the damp chill of the little bedroom.

Carrie's voice was a whisper. 'Oh, Tom . . . this is the first time for me.' Her voice grew stronger. 'But I want to belong to you — even if — even if we can't be married for a long time. I want you to, but I can't help feeling it's wrong . . . I'm not — not a prude or anything, but suppose. . . ? Oh, Tom, I'm afraid that this might — that something — that —'

'I'll take care of you.' His hands were unfastening the buttons of her dress. 'Pull this blanket over us. I don't want you to catch cold. See, you're shivering.'

And now she was helping him, sitting up so that he could pull the dress over her head, and he was whispering as he caressed her. When he took her slowly and carefully she felt tears on her face.

After it was over they lay for a long time, entwined in a silence so deep it felt as if the world had stopped turning. Then at last Carrie tangled her fingers in his hair and he lifted his head to stare deeply into her eyes.

'That really surprised me.' she told him, and he laughed softly.

'Oh, but that was just a practice run,' he answered solemnly, and in the yellow light she saw his own eyes were bright with tears.

He insisted on helping her to dress, grinning as his fingers fumbled with the suspenders anchoring her silk stockings.

'You won't wake in the night and wish this had never happened, will you, love?' His voice was suddenly serious. 'You won't hate me for this, will you sweetheart?'

Her answer was to take his face in her hands and kiss him with small soft wifely kisses. 'Never. I won't be afraid again. And we *will* be married, but that'll be just a formality, because I feel married to you now.'

When they went out into the street the lamps were like oranges floating in a sea of fog. He insisted on coming with her on the tram, where they sat together, fingers closely entwined, both of them lost and floundering in a haze of love.

CHAPTER THIRTEEN

Mungo McDermot was late dropping the boy off at Libby's house that morning. Harry was already in his surgery, Nurse Tomkin was settling the baby upstairs, and Libby, fretting behind the lace curtains, frowned as she saw the drop-shouldered man turn into the gate a full twenty minutes past his usual time.

The bitterly cold February had been followed by a March beset with gale-force winds, and as a wind-blown Mungo handed over his charge, Libby's annoyance at his unpunctuality sharpened her voice. 'You're going to be late for school, Mr McDermot.'

Then, as she drew the small peak-faced boy into the hall she gave a gasp of dismay. 'Oh, your face! What have you done to your face, Mr McDermot? Your eye looks terrible. Would you like me to ask the doctor to take a look at it! You can't go to school with a swelling like that. It needs attention.'

But Mungo was already turning away. 'I'm not going to school this morning.' He took a few wavering steps back down the path. 'I got up in the night in the dark and bumped into a door. It's nothing.'

'Well then.' Libby closed the door reluctantly and held out her hand for her pupil's overcoat, her heart aching with pity as she stared down at the small, pinched face, the eyes which she knew saw and understood everything but gave nothing away.

'She hits him,' she remembered Carrie saying.

255

'Mungo's wife drinks, and when she drinks too much she hits him, knowing that the boy can't hear. Sometimes he comes to school with his face all bruised.'

'We'll start where we left off yesterday,' she said, speaking slowly, almost miming the words. Leading the boy into the dining room she positioned herself opposite him so that he could see every slight movement of her lips. 'What is that?' With a finger she pointed to a picture of a cat. 'C . . . cat.' Edwin's lips pouted in an exaggerated fashion, as he struggled to speak the simple word which came out as an expressionless croak.

'Well done!' Libby took his small hand in her own, holding it against her mouth as she repeated the word. 'Cat. Cat.'

Usually this procedure made the boys intelligent eyes crinkle into amusement, but this morning his face remained solemn and set, as if part of him was walking away with his father down the path, as if somewhere in his silent world he suffered in a completely adult way for the man who allowed his wife to scream and rage and smash out at him with whatever came to hand.

Libby shuddered. How much did he know, this little boy, whose mind, she was discovering, was a prisoner in a brain never stimulated by sound! There was an adult awareness in his eyes that made her want to put her arms round him in comfort. But at the moment she was his teacher, and he was her pupil, and what mattered was the unlocking of his mind.

'Now this.' She pointed at the picture of a house, a difficult one this time, and taking his small hand in her own opened her lips to the rounded vowel, then pursed them to the consonant. 'House . . . house . . . house.'

At twelve o'clock, the time when Beatrice should have called to pick up her son, the hour came and went. Edwin lunched with Harry and Libby, sitting at the table between them, silent and stolid, picking at his food, pathetically oblivious to the conversation going on above his bowed head.

'There's something wrong.' Libby crumbled the bread on her sideplate, her appetite gone. 'I'll take him home myself. It's Nurse Tomkin's afternoon off, but she'll see to the baby if I ask her.'

'It's time Nurse went back to her own village, anyway.' Harry's red face gave nothing of his true feelings away. If the boy couldn't hear, he could see, and from the look of him he'd had his fill of grown-up battles for a while. 'You know how I feel.'

'I'll take him now.' Ignoring her husband's remark, Libby got up from the table and touching Edwin's arm propelled him towards the door.

'I'll run him back,' Harry offered, but she shook her head.

'I need to get out of the house,' she said, leaving Harry sitting at the table with a troubled expression darkening his pleasant face.

Used to silence, the small boy trotted along at her side, down the wide road, past the park, his cap pulled low over his forehead and his hands thrust deep into the pockets of his tweed overcoat. Libby's coat with its high fur collar kept her neck warm, but left her legs prey to the cold, blustery wind. The curling feather on her cloche hat blew across her face, gently stroking her lipstick, and now and again she pushed it back with an impatient hand.

When they reached the house she saw that the big front door was open. As Edwin turned the knob on the vestibule door and stepped inside, she stood irresolute, wanting to hand him over properly before leaving.

Feeling embarrassed and a little silly, she called out, 'Mrs McDermot? It's me, Mrs Brandwood. I've brought Edwin back. Is anyone there?'

Edwin turned a questioning face up to her as Libby, making up her mind, pushed him in front of her down the narrow lobby and into the living room at the back of the house. 'Mrs McDermot?' she called out again, then the words tailed away into an awful silence as she stared down at the man lying face downwards on the carpet, a pool of blood seeping from a gash on his head and running down his white starched collar.

The silence was broken horribly by the low gutteral sounds coming from Edwin's mouth. Harsh, animal-like noises, all his careful tuition forgotten as he communicated in the only way he knew.

Before Libby could move he was down on his knees, his fingers bloodied as they touched his father's hair, his face a mask of horror as he stared over to where his mother crouched in a corner, her fat face working convulsively, a breadknife clutched in her hand.

Beatrice McDermot was drunk. As the woman pulled herself up slowly by the edge of a chair, Libby moved to pull the boy away from the still figure on the floor. 'Upstairs!' She mouthed the word, her face on a level with Edwin's staring eyes. 'Go upstairs! Now!'

Then as he obeyed, Libby ran back down the lobby, her legs turned to water, to throw herself into the surprised arms of a sober-coated man letting himself out of the house next door.

'Have you got a telephone?' She gripped the lapels of his coat, staring wildly into the astonished face beneath the bowler hat. 'Yes? Oh, thank God! Telephone for the police! Quickly! There's been a murder next door.'

She wanted to run. All she wanted to do was to run as fast as she could, away from the street, to put as much distance as possible between her and the scene she had left. But there was the boy . . . With her hands held to her trembling mouth Libby recalled the sodden, drunken expression on Beatrice McDermot's bloated face, the insane gloating in the small eyes as she had advanced towards her son with the knife held in her hand.

With her heart beating like a tomtom, choking her throat with its pounding, Libby forced herself to turn and go back into the house, hearing the ruby-red panels of glass in the vestibule door shiver in protest as it swung to behind her.

With a small sigh of thankfulness she saw that Beatrice was still in the living room, too stupefied by drink to climb the stairs after her son.

'Give that knife to me!' Libby advanced towards her, her teachers voice ringing out so clear that even in her terror its calmness surprised her. 'Mrs McDermot! Give that knife to me Now! At once!'

The fat jowls quivered, and the small eyes, sunk into cushions of fat, narrowed into evil slits, but the knife dropped to the floor.

Keeping her eyes on the swaying, whimpering woman, Libby picked up the knife and put it on the sideboard. 'Now we will wait for the police to come,' she said. Beatrice slid to the floor again, wailing and weeping, rocking herself backwards and forwards, her short arms folded round her body. Libby stood quite still, willing away the next ten minutes, the longest minutes she had ever experienced.

When Libby heard a car draw up outside she

closed her eyes for a moment in a fervent prayer of thanks. Now it was all over. The police would take the wailing woman away; they would take the man that had been her husband away, and Libby could go home. And she would take the boy with her. Harry would know what to do next. Oh, Harry . . . At that moment she knew she would have given anything to see his square-set body coming through the door, his face full of concern as he held out his arms to her.

'*She* did it! Libby's eyes flew wide as Beatrice struggled to her feet and faced the two policemen coming in through the door, one in uniform and the other in plain clothes. 'She's been carrying on with my husband, and when I threatened to tell *her* husband she went for me with a knife.' She pointed to the knife on the sideboard. 'There it is!' She took an unsteady step forwards. 'It was me she went for, but he got in the way.'

Libby shook her head from side to side. It wasn't possible that the drunken woman could be saying such things. Beatrice was paralytic with drink. For the past fifteen minutes she had been moaning incoherently to herself, crouched on the floor, and yet now her voice held the ring of truth as she pointed to Mungo's body.

Then, before anyone could move, Beatrice lurched across and with the toe of her shoe turned her husband's dead body over so that his face, the eyes wide open, the skin a dirty grey, presented itself to them in all its horror.'

'See ! Beatrice pounced. 'Here's her photograh! She was trying to snatch it from him when I found them together. See! See for yourself !'

And as Libby looked, she saw Carrie's face staring at her from the photograph held in Beatrice's outstretched hand. Carrie, before her hair had been cut, smiling into the camera, wearing the white blouse she had pin-tucked herself, her dark eyes steady in the sweet serenity of her face

'See for yourself!' Beatrice said, then was sick on the carpet.

When they put her into a cell down at the police station Libby couldn't believe it was happening to her. When she heard Beatrice shouting obscenely she asked about the boy and was told that he was being taken care of. When she was told that they were trying to contact her husband but without success, she put her head down in her hands and wept, imagining Harry going about his business, making his prolonged afternoon calls in blissful ignorance of what was happening.

When they brought her into an interview room an hour later and she saw Carrie standing there, Libby went straight into her sister's arms, all antagonism forgotten as they clung together. Two halves of one, as united as if the shadow of Tom Silver had never come between them.

'It's all right, love. Everything will be all right.' Carrie smoothed Libby's hair away from her forehead. 'When Nurse Tomkin couldn't find Harry she telephoned me. There's nothing to be afraid of. Hush, hush . . . don't cry.'

When the plain clothes man coughed discreetly by the door and they moved apart, he asked Carrie to go through into the next room. 'I'll call you in when I'm ready,' he said. 'Just wait till you're told, lass. Right?'

Libby stood with bowed head as they brought Beatrice in. A cleaned-up though still sour-smelling Beatrice, defiance flaring from her eyes, and only the quivering of her chins betraying her agitation.

'Are you sure that this is the woman who you say was having an affair with your husband, the deceased?' The policeman placed the photograph in the middle of the table. 'This woman?' He pointed to Libby. 'This same woman as on this photograph?'

Beatrice nodded firmly. 'See for yourself. What can't speak can't lie, can it? It's her all right.'

The detective constable made a sign to the uniformed man standing by the door, then as Carrie came in he motioned her to stand beside Libby.

'Now.' He spoke firmly. 'Now, Mrs McDermot. Are you still sure that the lady you accused is the one in the photograph? That *she* was the one who went for your husband with the knife this morning?' His voice whispered, silken soft. 'Because this lady here,' he pointed to Carrie, 'has told me that *she* was the one friendly with your husband and *her* alibi this morning is as tight as a sealed drum.' He motioned to the sisters to stand even closer. 'Now, make up your mind, Mrs McDermot. Do you still stick to your statement?'

Beatrice's mouth stayed open in a wide startled 'O' of amazement. Blinking, she stared as if she could not believe the evidence of her eyes. Identical faces, identical hair, noses, eyes . . . She stared first at the photograph, then at the two faces staring at her silently. She staggered, the sickness rising thick in her throat again, then before her fuddled brain could react coherently, the detective barked at her, '*You* killed your husband, Mrs McDermot! You found him looking at the photograph, and in a frenzy of jealousy you went for the knife and you killed him. You've been attacking him for years. Isn't that true! Isn't it? Well?'

Before Beatrice could reach the sisters, her arms were pinioned behind her by the policeman standing

262

by the door, but he was too late to stop the spit shooting from her mouth straight into Libby's face.

'Yes, I killed him!' she screamed. 'He was a *nothing!* A weak bundle of nowt! He wasn't a man! He wasn't even man enough to fight for his country. I *hated* him. He wasn't even man to give me a proper son. He deserved to die! I wished he'd died more slowly, but oh no, one slash and he went.' She fought like a maniac as the policeman dragged her away. 'He didn't even put up a fight for himself! He just stood there and let me do it — just stood there, egging me on!'

It was a long time before her cries died away, and even when they had stopped both Libby and Carrie knew that they would be hearing them for a long time to come.

When the detective said they could go, they walked away together as if they were one person, leaving him scratching his head and staring after them, scarcely believing the evidence of his own eyes.

CHAPTER FOURTEEN

'There's a man at the door says he wants to see Miss Carrie.'

Mrs Edwards, wearing a flour-spattered apron, looked flustered. It wasn't her place to answer the door but what with the new girl being off with the flu, the morning help having gone home and something serious going on in the lounge, she didn't know whether she was coming or going. Added to which, her deafness had stopped her from hearing the caller's name properly.

Harry jumped to his feet at the sight of her anxious face. 'I'll see to it, Mrs Edwards.' He turned and nodded at the three worried faces. 'If it's a reporter I'll send him packing. We have nothing to say to the papers, not now or ever.'

He was back in less than a minute with Tom Silver, a grim-faced Tom who, going straight to Carrie, took both her hands in his own.

'They gave me the brief details to set up at work.' His eyes searched hers. 'It merely said that Mungo McDermot had been murdered and his wife is helping the police with their inquiries. But there are rumours, and when I heard them I just put my coat on and came straight out.' He shook her hands gently. 'Carrie, love, you mustn't set foot out of the house. I know what the press can be like when they scent a mystery.'

Then for the first time he seemed to be aware that there were others in the room. 'Mrs Peel.' He nodded politely in Ettie's direction, still keeping hold of Carrie. 'I apologize for barging in like this, but I couldn't stay away.' He gave Libby a cursory glance and a brief nod. 'Libby . . .' Then he held out a hand to Harry. 'You must be Dr Brandwood? My name is Silver, Tom Silver.'

'Glad to know you.'

Harry shook the outstretched hand, pumping it up and down, his innate good manners not quite good enough to conceal the flash of interest in his eyes. So *this* was the man Libby had been so scornful about. The man she was convinced was after the Peel money. Well, well . . . Tom Silver might not be old-school-tie material, but neither was he a flat-capped moron. Quite presentable really, Harry decided.

'Oh, Tom.' Carrie drew him down to sit beside her on the chesterfield. 'I'm so glad you've come. Everything has been so dreadful.' She caught hold of his jacket sleeve. 'It was Libby who found the body, not me.' Then in a low voice, never taking her eyes from his face, she told Tom the whole story. 'We were going to have the boy brought here but the police told Harry that one of Mungo's wife's sisters had already been and taken him away. Libby thinks this will have undone all the progress she was making with his speech. She wouldn't be surprised if he never tried to speak again. For a child to see his father . . . oh, Tom, Mungo's wife is *insane*. He used to tell me she was, but I thought he was exaggerating, and now Libby is involved, and it's all my fault — oh, Tom . . .'

As though they were entirely alone, Tom took her in his arms, holding her head, stroking her hair, whispering, groping in his pocket for a handkerchief, and then drying her eyes as tenderly as if she were a child.

Libby watched them closely, seeing, with a painful sense of loss, the love of two people belonging together as if they were indeed one person.

'Harry!' Her voice was harsh and abrupt. 'Now that Mr Silver is here I think we can go.' She reached for the fur-trimmed coat lying across the back of a chair, holding it out for Harry to help her on with it. *You* will have patients waiting and I have the baby to see to. Mother? You are sure you don't want to come back with us? Mr Silver will see that Carrie is all right, I'm sure of that.'

'I think I'll go upstairs and lie down for a while.' Ettie, too, got up from her seat by the fire and held out a wavering hand to Harry. 'Perhaps you will see me to my room, Harry? My head is aching and my back hurts.' She took a few tottering steps towards the door, sliding out as usual from a situation she found intolerable. 'Ask Mrs Edwards to have something sent up to me on a tray, will you, Carrie?'

Embarrassed but obedient, Harry took her arm. Libby drew on her gloves. 'You know where I am if you need me, Carrie.' The door closed behind them.

'Ah, well . . .' Tom's dark eyes held for a moment their customary twinkle. 'No one could exactly say that I'm welcome round here, but what does that matter?' He traced the outline of Carrie's mouth with a finger. 'This will blow over, love. Whatever comes out in the paper, the public have short memories.' He smiled at her with love. 'Today's news is tomorrow's fish-and-chip wrapping. Always has been and always will be. Right?' He tightened his arms round her. 'And when your mother's settled in her bed I'm going up to talk to her. No, don't say anything. I'm not going to slink from the house this time like an intruder. Your mother can't collapse on me twice on the trot. Even your brother-in-law might suspect that she might be malingering this time.'

Suddenly he was very serious. 'You have to make up your mind, love. You should have come for me before you went along down to the police station. My office is only a minute away, for heaven's sake. You must understand that from now on we face things together.' He hugged her tightly. 'Even murders, love. You're never going to need to face any kind of trouble alone. Never. You understand?'

'But it was Libby who suffered, not me.' Carrie shook her head. 'Not me. She might have been killed, Tom. She want back into that house alone to protect the boy, and never even said that the photograph wasn't of her. She was so brave. Far braver than I would have been.'

'Rubbish!' Tom held her away from him, looking deep into her troubled eyes. 'Your sister will always be able to stand on her own two feet; she's made that way. She might *look* like you . . .' He grinned. 'And seeing you together for the first time gave *me* a bit of a turn, I might tell you. But I know how completely different you are.' He took a deep breath. 'Now! Do you think your mother will be decently in bed and ready for me tó go and see her? Because that's exactly what I'm going to do, and if she faints I'll just wait till she comes round, then tell her we're getting married all the same. Ready?'

'Alone!' he whispered, as Carrie let him into the big front bedroom where Ettie lay against her pillows, a handkerchief soaked in eau de Cologne pressed to her forehead. 'You go back downstairs, and leave this to me. Right?'

He walked to the foot of the bed and stood there, his chin up in a gesture that, had the frail woman in the bed known it, spoke more of shyness and reserve than defiance.

'I would like a word, Mrs Peel,' he said.

Ettie's eyes were closed behind the scented handkerchief, but her mind was working feverishly. Like Libby, she had seen the love that shimmered between this man and her daughter, and seeing it had known for certain this time that she had lost.

'I am not very well, Mr Silver.' There was a plaintive pleading in her voice. 'This terrible business has upset me dreadfully. And now I would like to sleep.'

Tom stood his ground. He felt completely out of place in a room like this, with its thick carpet and billowing satin eiderdown on the bed. There was a fire burning in the grate, and he wondered what this tiny woman would say if she knew that it was the first time he had ever *seen* a fire in a bedroom? Down his street babies were born in unheated bedrooms, put to sleep in drawers lined with newspaper and tatty blankets. There were chamber pots underneath the beds instead of a bathroom down the landing, candles set in saucers, and coats on the bed in the middle of winter when ice formed on the inside of the windows.

He cleared his throat. 'Mrs Peel, I want to marry your Carrie.' He found he was gripping the mahogany bed-end. 'I know I might not seem much cop to you, but I have a job, I have a house, and I will cherish Carrie for the rest of my life.' He raised his voice without meaning to. 'As long as I'm there I won't let the wind blow too hard on her, Mrs Peel.

She will only have to ask, and if it's in my power then I will give her whatever she wants. I'll be faithful to her; when she's sick then I'll nurse her, and when she's happy then I'll be happy too. I haven't known much joy in my life, Mrs Peel; I was left without mother or father when I was sixteen, but I managed somehow, fending for myself and serving my time to get myself a steady job. I've been married before, Mrs Peel, to a young lass who got blown to bits in an explosion at the munitions factory out Darwen way. I was in France at the time, at the front line, Mrs Peel — I didn't even get home for the funeral. She was a nice young lass, my wife, and her mother and me, we liked each other a lot.' He coughed. 'I would like to think that you and me might get on fine, Mrs Peel. We have a lot in common, after all, you loving Carrie and me loving her as well. I would like it fine if you came to see us a lot. Not that our house would be anything like this, but you'd be right welcome, Mrs Peel.'

He took a necessary breath. 'I know you can hear me, Mrs Peel, underneath that hankie, and I haven't finished yet. Not by a long chalk. I want you to know that my politics come in a different colour from what yours do, and although I haven't been to church for a long time, if I *did* go it would be Chapel where the prayers aren't all set out in a book, but spoken from the heart, in the way I'm speaking to you. And another thing. When we're married, Carrie and me, I'm not that proud that I won't let her buy some of her own clothes, if that's what she wants, but everything else, Mrs Peel, *everything else*, I provide. I promise you this — as God's my judge, and oh aye, I believe in Him all right — I'll make her a good husband, and what's more I'll look after you. You being Carrie's mother makes you my responsibility as well. When Carrie's babies come they won't have a nurse to see to them, but they'll be *your* grandchildren and if any of them take after you then I'll be well satisfied. You're a bonny woman, Mrs Peel.' He came round the bed and gently lifted the handkerchief from Ettie's face. 'So you can come out from under there and stop that play-acting. All right then, Mrs Peel?'

The tablets administered by Harry were taking effect. Ettie felt drowsy and warm, and the earnest face bending over the bed seemed to have fuzzy features, and a smile that was lop-sided in its gentleness. Her eyelids were as heavy as if pennies had been laid on them, and when she spoke her voice came muffled on the very edge of sleep.

'I heard you all right, Mr Silver,' she said. 'And what you said sounded like poetry. Do you know that?' Her smile wavered. 'Do you know how long it is since anyone told me I was a bonny woman?' Her hand came up and Tom clasped it in his firm grasp. 'My husband wasn't a man for pretty speeches . . .' Her head moved from side to side slowly. 'And though I'll regret it in the morning when I wake up, I feel, right this minute, that you might be just the man Carrie needs.' She tried to lift herself up on an elbow but fell back. 'You're a nice young man, Mr Silver. A very nice young man, *and* kind. And do you know something?' The drug was making her as maudlin as if she had drunk half a bottle of whisky, and realizing this, Tom smiled.

'Yes, Mrs. Peel?'

'I think you and I might be friends some day . . . I do. I really do. But I wish you'd have your hair trimmed a bit. You can talk like a poet, but you don't have to *look* like one. Do you, Mr Silver?'

* * *

270

'She was *flirting* with you!' Carrie, coming into the room and overhearing the last few words, turned to Tom in amazement as they went back down the wide staircase together. 'It's no wonder women fall in love with you.' When they were back in the sitting room, she reached up and pulled his face down to hers, holding him still between the palms of her hands. 'Oh, Tom. If you and Mother are going to get on so well, why don't you come and live at Westerley after we're married? She'll be so lonely when I'm gone, and the house is so big. We wouldn't be in each other's pockets all the time.'

'You don't mean that?' Gently Tom disengaged her hands and put her from him. 'You said that without thinking, didn't you?'

'No, I mean it.' Carrie's face was flushed. 'When I thought that you and Mother were going to be — well, not exactly seeing eye to eye, there was no question of it. But now . . . oh, Tom, think what it would mean to Mother having a man about the house, and think what it would mean to me to be able to keep an eye on her all the time. She'll take to her bed permanently when she's all alone. She will I *know* her, remember.'

'Carrie!' Walking over to the fire, Tom pushed a piece of coal into position with his shoe. 'How old is your mother, love?'

'What has that got to do with it?'

'How old is she?'

'Fifty-nine. No, fifty-eight. She'll be fifty-nine in September. She was thiry-four when we — Libby and I were born. Why?'

'Then she isn't an old woman. Not by a long chalk.' Tom put out a hand to draw Carrie to him, but at the look in her eyes he drew it back.

'She's a sick woman, Tom.' Indignation flushed

271

Carrie's face to pink. 'She's been an invalid ever since I can remember. It was having us — twins — and then later Willie being killed. It's understandable.'

Rubbish!' Tom kicked at the coals again. 'I know women who lost their sons in the war and kept straight on standing at their looms. I know women who have babies, one after the other, and still go out scrubbing right to the moment of birth. There's nothing wrong with your mother but what goes on in her mind, and that's unhappiness. She wants to be needed, love. Can't you see?'

'And me asking you to live here doesn't mean I'm thinking about her?' Carrie stood erect, both hands clenched by her sides. 'Isn't that caring?'

'Caring for someone isn't the same as letting them think you need them.' He dismissed her last words with a wave of his hand. 'That mother of yours hasn't been needed for a long long time. Not by your father, nor by you and Libby. It's staring at you from her face, love. The blank loneliness of never being needed. I know!'

'You seem to know a lot about her in a short time.'

'Yes, as a matter of fact I do.'

'And you won't even consider coming to live here?'

'Not for a minute.' He grinned, then saw at once the grin was a mistake. 'Carrie, love. Can you see me being waited on by a maid in a pinny? Can you see me letting that woman who let me in call me "sir"? If she came in now to see to the fire I'd snatch the coal shovel from her. I'd be ashamed to let a servant do for me.'

'So you think Mrs Edwards is downtrodden, do you?' Carrie felt the sting of tears behind her eyelids. The events of the morning were making her edgy and prickly. Tom was being unreasonable.

They were quarrelling for the first time, at least *she* was quarrelling. *He* was merely stating what he thought to be the facts, and expecting her to agree. She waited with eyes narrowed for what he would say next, and when he said nothing she burst out childishly, 'All right then! Go into the kitchen! Go right now and ask Mrs Edwards if she feels in any way like a slave. Ask her where she would be if it wasn't for us. And if she won't tell you, then I will. In the workhouse, that's where! She hasn't got any family or any money, and she's practically stone deaf. So where would people like her be if it wasn't for people like me and my kind, Tom Silver? You think the whole population should be equal. But they will never be equal, because that's the way it has always been. Ask Mrs Edwards to take my mother's place and she would die of boredom in a week. Ask my mother to take Mrs Edwards's place and she'd be dead of overwork in a week.'

'And yet I'm expecting you to make that transition?' At last Tom felt his own temper rise. He glanced at the clock. 'I have to go to a meeting tonight so I must go now. Maybe rushing here wasn't such a good idea after all.'

Watching him go Carrie frowned and bit her lip. Tom would spend the rest of his life fiercely upholding what he felt to be right. She reminded herself that his sometimes unbending attitude had lost him his job once. Was it possible that the same attitude could help him to walk away from his love? She had a sudden picture in her mind of her life as it had been before he came into it, and she took a step forward, ready to throw herself into his arms and tell him that she would live with him in a tent if need be. Anywhere, as long as they were together.

But, as if warding her off, Tom put the width of the door between them and spoke to her through the opening. 'Think well on it, Carrie. Go upstairs when your mother has had her sleep and talk to her. *She* knows and understands how I feel. She'll tell you that happiness doesn't always come wrapped up in expensive paper. You think deeply about it all, Carrie. Then let me know.'

His fear was as great as hers, if she had only realized it. When he left the house, taking the steps down to the drive two at a time, Tom was already doubting some of the things he had said to her. Was he being fair? He was speaking that very evening on the subject of class privilege, but here he was proposing to step over it with no regard for the implications. Oh, Carrie . . . Carrie, love. Tom swung himself on to the tram platform just as the conductor rang the bell, his face a mask of worry above his high starched collar.

'Mother seems almost resigned to the idea of me marrying Tom.'

Carrie sat with Libby in the nursery watching Nurse Tomkin feeding the baby. It never occurred to her not to talk family business in front of the little woman carefully holding the feeding bottle at the right angle. Besides, Nurse Tomkin wasn't exactly a servant, more like one of the family now. Those strange, short-sighted eyes behind the whirlpool lenses seemed to miss nothing.

Carrie smiled at her sister. 'I don't know what Tom said to Mother, but he obviously charmed her yesterday. You were wrong about him wanting to move into Westerley, Libby. He wouldn't hear of it.'

Libby was feeling very fragile that morning. Harry, in spite of his obvious concern for her, had berated her soundly on her rudeness to Tom Silver.

'Those two will marry,' he had said, 'in spite of whatever you or your mother might say. I thought it was very touching the way the chap went straight to Carrie when he came in. It was as though no one else existed. He won't be intimidated, that one.'

There was a great weight of misery in Libby's chest. Last night she had wanted Harry to make love to her. She had wanted him to take her fiercely, even cruelly, but ever considerate he had kissed her a chaste goodnight and actually tucked her in before going down to write a letter to the *Lancet* on the high incidence of heart attacks in the town. He had a theory that it might have something to do with the lack of lime in the drinking water, and though he was only skirting round the idea he hoped his tentative probings might interest someone able to follow them up in a more practical way.

Oh, Harry . . .' Libby had cried into her pillow. 'Why don't you *make* me love you?' Then she had stared wide-eyed at the ceiling. 'And what will I do now that Edwin will no longer be coming to the house for lessons?'

Now she stared at her baby, bald except for a fringe of hair straggling down into the nape of its fat neck. Maybe Harry was right and she should send Nurse Tomkin back to her village. She moved in her chair with the old restlessness, her dark eyes looking for something that wasn't there, searching for the stimulation, the excitement so necessary to her existence.

'Mother could come and live here.' She spoke without thinking, then shook her head. 'But Mother will never leave Westerley. She'll grow old quickly and die soon, and there's nothing we can do about it.' She sighed. 'Oh, why did Willie have to go and get himself killed? He would be married now and the natural heir to Westerley and the mill, and Mother would live the rest of her life surrounded by Willie's children.' She pushed at her fringe so that the calf-lick stood up in an untidy spike. 'That bloody awful war. Its consequences never end for some, do they?'

Nurse Tomkin sat the baby up and started to wind her. The small eyes were narrowed into slits as she wrestled with what passed for her conscience. The promise she had made to Sarah Batt she had kept, but now . . . well, all things being equal, maybe she could . . . Settling the baby back on her other arm she thrust the rubber teat into its wildly groping mouth.

'Sarah Batt's mother died a month or so back,' she said, as if telling the news to the baby.

Immediately two faces, identical in their expressions of concern, turned towards her.

'Oh, poor Sarah!' Carrie spoke first. 'What will happen to her? The cottage was only rented to them as long as Mrs Batt lived. Isn't that right?'

Nurse Tomkin nodded. 'Yes, that's right.' She prized the teat from the baby's mouth to stop the milk from being gulped too quickly. 'I saw Sarah when I went back last weekend. She's in a right mess. She was going out scrubbing at one of the big houses, but now they are cutting down on staff she's got the sack.' She sniffed. 'It's all these mills closing, and the mines paying the miners next to nothing. The women come out from the town and take our jobs. For less money,' she added bitterly.

'So Sarah is without a job?' Libby exchanged a glance with Carrie, a glance which the little woman noted with satisfaction — so far so good.

'Yes. Before long she'll be without a roof to her head, and she can't go for a living-in job because of the boy.' The grey head dropped over the tilted bottle. 'He's a right larnt-up one, that lad. Too big for his boots, if you ask me, but a clever scholar, they say.' She waited, holding her breath. Well, she hadn't broken no promise yet, had she?

'So there would be nothing to stop Sarah coming back to Westerley?' Libby's voice was eager, her lethargy forgotten now that there was something she could organize.

'There's still her son.' Carrie sat forward, clasping her hands round her knees. 'But Mother wouldn't mind having Sarah's son living with her. Not if it meant getting Sarah back. Would she?'

'But why hasn't Sarah got in touch?' Libby frowned. 'She knows how upset Mother was when she left. I used to think that Sarah meant more to her than we did.'

'Pride.' Carrie nodded. 'You know what Sarah was like, how she would flare up if we tried to talk about her boy.'

'Hiding her shame,' Libby broke in quickly. 'As if that mattered now, after all this time.'

'So we'll write. Now. Today.'

'Can she read?'

'Oh, heavens, Libby, her son will read the letter to her.'

So fascinated was Nurse Tomkin at the turn of the conversation that she was allowing the baby to suck at an empty bottle. Listening to those two was like listening to one person speaking. Two minds perfectly attuned, and she had said practically nothing, given nothing away.'

'Sarah is past thinking straight, if you don't mind me interrupting,' she said. 'That lad of hers grows out of his britches faster than a stick of rhubarb growing from a muck heap. His mother is going without, if you ask me.'

'Without food?' Carrie was horrified.

Nurse Tomkin nodded. 'If I was you, Mrs Brandwood,' she focussed her myopic gaze on Libby. 'I would get the doctor to drive you out there this Sunday.' She hoisted the baby on to her shoulder and rubbed its back in a circular motion. *I'll* be here to see to the baby.'

'But it's your weekend off,' Libby protested, not too vehemently.

'I don't mind.' Nurse Tomkin closed her eyes to hide the glitter of triumph at the way she had managed things. 'Why not take your mother with you, Mrs Brandwood? The country is lovely just now. It would do her good to get out of the house; this business yesterday must have upset her a lot.'

She smiled to herself as the two sisters immediately got up and clammed their mouths tight shut. Their reticence didn't bother Nurse Tomkin. She had been the one to answer the telephone when the police rang, hadn't she? And she had already found out enough to be going on with. She would ferret out the whole truth one way or another, and for the time being she had done her good deed.

It rained hard on Sunday, but they still drove out to the country. From the car window Ettie watched the rain falling on the fields and the little gardens fronting the stone cottages.

'Are you sure we ought to be interfering like this?'

She asked the question to Libby's back, but Libby was, as Carrie would have said, 'on the warpath'.

'We are doing the *right* thing,' she said firmly.

But when Sarah, painfully thin and tired-looking,

opened the door to them, Ettie forgot her misgivings immediately.

'Sarah? May we come in? I have something I want to ask you. It's a favour, a very great favour.' She glanced up at the grey sky. 'We are getting wet, dear. It won't take a minute. May we come in?'

The little back room of the cottage was so small, the ceiling so low, that when they all sat down Ettie had the feeling that the walls were closing in on them. She smiled at Sarah. 'Don't look so scared, dear. We heard about your mother, and we are sorry, so very sorry.'

Sarah nodded. Her mouth was hanging half open, giving her a look of utter stupidity. It was all far worse than Libby had expected it would be. The whole atmosphere smelled of poverty, and Harry was shifting in his chair, obviously wishing he was miles away. So with her usual lack of finesse, Libby came straight to the point.

'Carrie is getting married, so Mother needs you, Sarah. It would make us all very happy if you came back. With your son, of course,' she added. 'Westerley is more than big enough, and we all feel it would be a very suitable arrangement, especially as Nurse Tomkin told us you are under notice to leave this cottage.'

'Well, Sarah?' Ettie leaned forward. 'What do you say? Will you at least think it over, dear?' Then, getting no response from the still figure, she added, 'We don't want to upset you, Sarah. What's troubling you so much, my dear? You must at least try to tell us. We have come because we want to help.'

For a long moment no one moved or spoke. Suddenly the back door opened and a young boy hurtled into the room, socks slipping down over muddy boots, thin jacket black with rain, blue eyes sparkling with mischief. As he hesitated, snatching his cap from his head, a shaft of sunlight broke through the clouds, transforming his barley-pale hair to a halo of gold.

Libby gasped in astonishment. Ettie jumped to her feet, clutching both hands together in front of her chest, swaying as the colour drained from her cheeks to leave her face a strange chalky white.

'Go upstairs to your room, son!' Sarah's voice shattered the uncanny silence, rough with despair so terrible that it might have been a voice speaking from the grave.

'But Mam. . . ?'

Bewildered by the ring of faces, most of all by the sight of the small elderly lady rocking herself backwards and forwards as if she was barmy, Patrick stood his ground. 'I was just going to . . .'

'Upstairs!' Sarah was on her feet advancing towards him. 'These — these people will be going soon . . .'

Patrick stepped back as the moaning woman held out both her arms. With his blue eyes searching first one strange face then another, he said, 'Are you all right, Mam? What's happened? I'd rather stop down here with you.'

'Patrick!' Sarah's voice was as sharp as the crack of a whip. 'Upstairs! You and me will talk later. Do as you're told!'

Stumbling in his muddy boots, half defiant and more than a little afraid, Patrick did as he was told, running up the uncarpeted stairs then closing the door of his room with a loud crash.

The sound coincided with Ettie's release from her half-paralysed state of shock. Going over to Sarah, she took her by the shoulders and shook her with a force one would hardly have believed she was capable of.

'That boy is Willie! Oh, dear God in heaven, that child is Willie's son! He is my Willie as a little boy. Sarah! Your son is my grandson. *Isn't* he?'

'No! No, Mrs Peel! He's not. He's not!'

Sarah's pathetic, almost hysterical denial was sliced away by a downward sweep of Libby's hand as the teacher in her took over. In a firm, no-nonsense voice, she stated briskly, 'Of course he is Willie's son, Sarah. He's the living image of the brother I once had. It was like seeing Willie come to life again. So let's sit down and talk about it calmly.'

'Yes. Calm down, Sarah, and you too, Mother. This isn't doing you any good.'

At the sound of Harry's quiet tones, Sarah dropped down into her chair, setting it rocking furiously. When she spoke her voice was still full of despair.

'I knew there'd be no keeping it from you once you set eyes on him. That's why I kept him away from you all these years!'

With her face wrenched out of shape, she turned to Ettie. 'Oh, Mrs Peel, forgive me.' Tears rolled from the blue eyes. 'Willie never loved me, never really *loved* me, but it happened when he came home on that last leave. I was too frightened to tell you. Mr Peel would have killed me for being a bad girl with his son in his house, an' it wasn't like that. It wasn't!' She took a deep breath. 'Willie never told you how it was out there in the trenches in France, Mrs Peel, because he knew you couldn't have borne to listen. But he told *me*. An' it was terrible! Willie wanted to spare you, but *I* listened, an' I comforted him, as best I could, Mrs Peel.'

'My grandson . . .' Ettie began to speak as if she were quite alone, as if not a single word of Sarah's pathetic confession had penetrated her understanding.

'All this time, and I didn't know. That lovely, lovely boy, my Willie's son, and I never knew?'

'But you can't have 'im! He's *mine*!' Sarah gave a shout of anguish. 'Since me mother died, he's all I've got!' She was looking directly at Libby now. 'You think because you've a lot of money you can just come here and — and —'

'Sarah!' Ettie, all pretence at pride gone, went to kneel down on the cut-rug by the rocking chair. Libby opened her mouth to say something, but Harry silenced her with a look.

'It's all Nurse Tomkin's fault,' Sarah muttered. 'She went back on her word. After she'd promised she went back on her word.'

'Nurse Tomkin said *nothing*.' Ettie's normally soft voice rang with conviction. 'Until that boy came through the door not one of us here today even guessed. Oh, Sarah! Listen to me, dear. Mr Peel is *dead*. It's me, Mrs Peel, you are dealing with now, not my husband.'

Kneeling up straight she tried to pull the stiff unyielding young woman into her arms. 'Think, Sarah. You would be coming to me as the daughter-in-law I never had, and Patrick . . . oh, my dear, I could give him so much. The best schools, the finest education money could buy.'

Sarah's face peaked into lines of obstinacy. 'But he'll pass his scholarship, Mrs Peel. My son is clever. He won't need no money to pay for his education. He'll win his own way.'

'But what about his clothes, his shoes, and his books?' Libby could contain herself no longer. 'It takes more than brains to keep a boy at a grammar school, Sarah.'

'You'll take him from me, Miss Libby!' Sarah was shouting now. 'I know you! Once you get a hold of him he won't be mine no longer.'

'Don't be silly,' Libby said, then opened her eyes wide as Harry pulled her to her feet.

'This is between Sarah and your mother,' he said firmly. 'We'll go outside and wait in the car. Coming, Libby?'

When they had gone Sarah looked into Ettie's upturned face and saw that the older woman had scarcely noted their departure. Her whole soul was in her pleading eyes. It was no longer mistress and servant; now they were merely two women meeting on common ground.

Taking both of Sarah's hands in her own, Ettie said gently. '*You* are Patrick's mother, dear. You would have first say in everything concerning him.' Tenderly she shook the work-worn hands. 'You trust *me*, don't you?'

Sarah nodded, biting hard at her bottom lip. 'Oh, yes. You was always good to me, Mrs Peel.'

'Well then, dear?'

It was as though Ettie had stopped breathing as she waited for Sarah's answer. She knelt there, small and dignified, her face still a chalky white and her eyes never leaving Sarah's face. Sarah wavered.

'And you wouldn't change his name or nothing? There wouldn't be no solicitor's papers making him over to the Peels or anything?'

Ettie shook her head. 'My house would be home for both of you, for as long as you wanted to stay — that's all,' she promised. 'This I swear to you.'

For a long moment the only sound in the tiny room was the sudden shifting of a log on the leaping fire. Then getting up from her chair and going to the foot of the stairs. Sarah called out, 'Patrick? Come down here. That's a good boy.'

When Ettie joined Libby and Harry in the car her

face was transfigured by a blinding joy that was almost tangible.

'Let's go home. I have a lot to do,' Ettie said, her smile like a blessing.

CHAPTER FIFTEEN

'Now we can all be happy,' Carrie said, holding hands with Tom. Her eyes filled with mischief. 'Oh, Tom, it's just like the ending of a book where everyone walks off into the sunset.'

Tom grinned down at her, humouring her, loving her with such transparent devotion that Libby had to turn away. She ached to be tinged with the same kind of happiness, but there was always this feeling of restlessness, this disappointment, this certainty that somehow her life had taken a wrong turning.

She watched Harry talking to Tom Silver, easily, freely, and it came to her that if only Tom could have stayed as a dream-like shadowy lover in the background of her life, then her feelings for Harry would have been intensified. Fidgeting with the long rope of beads hanging down the front of her waistless dress, Libby frowned at the irrationality of this idea even as she accepted its truth.

She ached for Harry to look at her in the way Tom was staring at Carrie, and yet, if he had, she knew she would have met the look with indifference.

What was *wrong* with her?

The wedding took place at four o'clock on a Saturday afternoon in May. There were no church bells ringing, no choirboys in red surplices singing 'O Perfect Love'.

Carrie's dress was Macclesfield silk, Libby's Chinese shantung, and they both wore hats shaped like the bells on a sprig of lily of the valley. Sarah's straw hat was decorated by what looked like a field of poppies, daisies and cornflowers, and accompanied by Patrick in a neat grey suit, she was almost as radiant as the bride.

Back at Westerley for the quiet family reception, Patrick was placed by Ettie's side at the big table in the dining room, a table set with cold ham, salads and a huge joint of underdone beef.

Carrie managed to have a quiet word with Sarah. 'We're lucky to have such a good Catholic college in the town, aren't we? Mother tells me Patrick has settled in so well his masters are already talking about his future. Has *he* any ideas of his own about what he wants to be?'

'An officer in the army,' Sarah said at once, then her round face went pink with pleasure. 'Oh, Miss Carrie, Patrick can't hear enough about his father, and Mrs Peel is only too happy to oblige. They spend hours, the two of them, poring over old photographs.' She bit her lip. 'I did wrong not telling him the truth, but then you see, I never realized how . . .' she struggled to find the right word, 'how uncomplete he felt not knowing.'

Carrie patted her arm. 'Well, one thing is certain, Sarah. There'll never be another war in Patrick's lifetime. Not after the last one.'

'Yes, that's a blessing.' Sarah crossed herself furtively over the bodice of her crêpe-de-Chine two-piece. 'That would be something I couldn't bear.' Then she sat up straight as Harry began his well-rehearsed speech. 'Ssh,' she said to no one in particular.

The telephone rang just as the speech ended and

Ettie's new maid, a young weaver from the mill, beckoned importantly from the doorway.

'It's for you. Doctor,' she announced, and with an apologetic glance in his wife's direction Harry walked quickly into the hall.

'Oh, no!' Libby gave a deep sigh. 'You'd think his patients would leave him alone, just for today.'

But when Harry came back into the room his expression was grim.

'There's been an accident at Crowhead colliery, a roof fall a long way out with ten men trapped.' He looked straight at Libby. 'I have to go, love.'

Then he turned to Ettie. 'I'm truly sorry, but I'll have to leave right this minute. I have things to collect from the surgery.

'I'm coming with you.' Libby moved towards him. 'We have put upon Nurse Tomkin's good nature long enough as it is.' Her smile was brilliant. 'I was going to say "be happy", but I don't think either Carrie or Tom needs that advice.'

Before Harry had turned the car out of the drive, she turned to him in exasperation.

'Why you, Harry? That colliery is five miles away. Why pick on you, for heaven's sake?'

Harry pressed his foot down hard on the accelerator. 'They are going to need all the help they can get, by the sound of it. It's two hours' walking to this particular coal face, apparently, and with so many trapped men who might need medical attention on the spot, and me being on call —' He glanced sideways at Libby. 'You could have stayed on at the party, though.'

'They didn't need me.' Beneath the flower-pot hat her face was set and bleak. 'Mother has Patrick, and Carrie has Tom. I almost felt it was a double celebration, didn't you?'

Harry collected what he needed and rushed out of the house with his bag. She followed him to the door. Smiling at her, he turned to wave, and as he slid behind the wheel she saw that his wedding posy, a white carnation, was still fixed in his buttonhole. A sudden premonition caught at her breath.

'Take care!' Libby's words were lost in the sound of the car's engine, leaving her to go slowly into the house and close the door behind her.

At nine o'clock, when he had been away for over three hours, she went up to the nursery to tell Nurse Tomkin that she would see to the baby, should she wake up and demand a bottle. Like her mother before her, Libby's baby slept in snatches, ignoring set rules and going her own way.

Libby looked down at the small sleeping face. 'I must have something to do,' she explained.

Nurse Tomkin's eyes glittered behind her spectacles. 'I once saw a man hurt real bad. He was a fitter though, not a miner. There was a valve needed opening so they put a plank over the cage to the shaft wall. He fell off it, and they brought what was left of him up in a bag.' She sniffed. 'Nobody knows the conditions those men have to work under. It's no wonder they came out on strike, and for what? I've heard it rains like the clappers down some pits, and do you know what they pay them extra for getting soaked? A shilling a day! I ask you!'

Listening to her, Libby felt the blood drain from her face. She shook her head. 'But the doctor won't have to go down. The rescue party will have their own doctor. If my husband is needed at all it will be at the surface.'

At eleven o'clock, with the baby content after an extra bottle, Libby went to the window of the front

288

bedroom, lifted the curtain and stared down into the quiet road.

She had not heard the rain, but now the pavements were shining black and a soft wind sighed in the trees. Too uneasy to undress, she wandered downstairs, moved the guard away from the dying fire, then built it up again with coal from the brass scuttle in the hearth.

Harry had said it was almost two hours' walk to the coal face where the men lay trapped . . . Libby shuddered as she watched the flames begin to lick round the shiny nuggets. At the time of the strike she had read how the miners worked on their knees, and sometimes lying flat on their stomachs, with sixty tubs to fill before they reached anything approaching a living wage. At the time she had been horrified; now it came back to her with a fresh shock.

No wonder Tom Silver felt as he did . . . and yet . . . it was *Harry* who was actually risking his life for the miners, not Tom. Libby looked at the clock on the mantelpiece ticking the slow minutes away. Leaning her head back she closed her eyes. Her thoughts were leading her down avenues she had never explored before. Unlike Tom Silver, Harry had no platform on which to stand and shout the odds. All Harry did was go about his daily routine, soothing the sick and closing the eyes of the dead.

She slept for a while, then started up when she thought she heard a car outside. But there was nothing but the silent avenue with its trees waving dark branches against the night sky. Back by the fire she sat motionless for another hour, then went to sit in the darkened nursery, falling asleep, waking, then falling asleep again until a grey finger of light touched the window.

'Is the doctor not back yet?' Even as the baby gave

289

her first experimental cry, Nurse Tomkin came through the door with her grey hair straggling round her shoulders, a brown woollen dressing gown hugged tightly to her squat figure.

'Something has happened to him.' Libby's eyes were bleak with a feverish worry. 'I knew something terrible was going to happen at the wedding tea when everyone was so happy. When the telephone rang I knew I was right. It doesn't pay to be too happy. Being too happy is asking for trouble.'

If Nurse Tomkin had known Libby as a child, then as a young unmarried woman, she would have known this was the old dramatic, fanciful Libby talking, but even so, the nurse knew there was no point in arguing with her when she was in this mood. So when Libby said she was going to ring for a taxi and go out to the colliery, she merely nodded. But when she was alone once again with the baby, Nurse Tomkin voiced her thoughts out loud to herself.

'She's feared for him now she thinks she might be losing him. There's some who need a bit of a shake-up before they realize which side their bread's buttered on.'

They let Libby through the gate and into the colliery yard when she told them who she was. Walking over to the pit head she joined a small knot of women standing quietly in the falling rain.

'They've got nine of them up, love.' A woman with a hard face gentled into resignation moved her hand from beneath a grey fringed shawl and laid it for a moment on Libby's arm. 'The one left down there has a pick through his body. It had to come out, and when the doctor went down there was a second fall, and now they're trapped good and proper. Three of them — the poor bugger with the steel inside him, the doctor and the manager.' She nodded. 'Oh, aye, the manager's down there for all he's supposed to be a hard nut.'

Libby felt sick; she could have been sick right there. She knew the doctor was Harry. She had known even before she came, but she went to ask just the same, and as she ran across the yard to the office she saw, lying on the cobblestones, the white carnation, muddied and flattened, trampled by rushing feet. She saw herself in her bell-shaped wedding hat slotting it into Harry's lapel, and she remembered how she had turned her face away so that his kiss had landed on her cheek instead of her lips.

'Oh, Harry . . .' She wanted to scream out her terror. She wanted to demand that the rescue party, still in their sweat and pit clothes, take her down with them. But knowing that would be impossible, she stumbled away to stand with the women, her beige coat with its ermine collar a sharp contrast to their sombre clothing.

'Usually it's the single men they send down.' The woman who had touched Libby's arm began to speak as if their conversation had never been interrupted. 'But they're all family men, all three of them.'

'The doctor is my husband. We have a baby, a little girl.' Libby felt the bile rise in her throat again.

'It's my son-in-law down there,' the woman confided. 'My daughter is near her time, so I made her stop at home.' She stared straight ahead, seeing nothing. 'There's nowt we can do, anyroad.' Suddenly her voice rose to a startling angry wail. 'Why couldn't they have fetched him up with the pick still in him? Why?'

A woman standing behind spoke up, her voice roughed with compassion. 'There's nowt you can do but wait, Mrs Parker. She's had it all before,' she whispered to Libby. 'Her husband was killed on the job three years back.'

'Oh, dear God. Oh, no!' Libby moved closer and touched the grey shawl. 'There's a car waiting for me. Would you like to go and sit inside it? You are wet through, Mrs Parker. Please let me take you to the car.'

'I'm stopping where I am.' The woman spoke without moving her head. 'I want to see him when they bring him out. For my daughter's sake it's the least I can do.'

Libby nodded, understanding at once. It had been a cold wet night for May, and now it was a cold wet morning. The fur at her neck was already uncomfortably sodden, and she could feel droplets running down her back. She glanced down at the women's feet sturdily clad in clogs, then at her own shoes with their thin soles, the soft cream leather patched with damp. There was no more talking, no weeping, just a quiet standing there, keeping out of the way of the men rushing backwards and forwards. The ambulance was waiting, doors open, red blankets piled on stretchers, the driver's face impassive beneath his peaked cap.

'Are you by yourself, Mrs Brandwood?' A man in a trilby hat came and spoke softly to her. 'Will you come into the office and wait there?'

'I'm stopping where I am.' Unconsciously Libby echoed the words of the woman by her side. 'But thank you. Thank you just the same.'

'The cage is coming up!' It was a great sigh, and as Libby felt herself urged forward, she saw them coming out. Black-faced men with eyes picked out in the coal dust on their faces. As they trailed away dejectedly towards the office, she felt her own shoulders slump in sympathy.

She could taste the wine in her mouth, sour and nasty, the wine she had drunk at Carrie's wedding. She wanted to be sick, but knew she couldn't give way with the women crowding her in. If they could stand it, then so could she.

Like an echo from the past, she heard Tom Silver's teasing voice: 'Finding out for yourself how the peasants think and feel?'

Libby frowned and bit hard at her lip. She had been so sure she was in the right, that time down on the market place at the beginning of the strike. She remembered how she had seen Harry striding towards her, his face set into lines of uncharacteristic anger, and she remembered how she had taunted him for his lack of feeling.

'Oh, Harry . . .' Even as she went on standing there, her face set into a stony mask, she was screaming his name aloud somewhere deep inside her.

When the sky lightened and the rain softened to a raw drizzle, she saw the cage descend yet again, and found she was praying as she had never prayed before. 'Oh, God! Let Harry be alive. Even if he's hurt, let him live long enough for me to tell him I'm sorry. Don't let this be my punishment for not loving him enough.' If Harry died, she told herself fiercely, the one thing she would never be able to put from her mind would be the memory of his hurt face as she had turned away from his kiss. She stared across the yard to where the carnation still lay, a dirty white mark on the greasy cobblestones.

Loneliness swamped her.

At seven o'clock she sensed that Carrie was there. Turning round she saw her twin coming across the yard with Tom Silver, and the next minute she was being held in Carrie's arms.

Now at last she could give way, but not until Carrie

had led her away with Tom following close behind. Sobbing, Libby told them, sparing them nothing.

'Harry is trapped down there. It's a long way out, and there was a second fall. They are trying to get through, but I think I heard one of the men say something about *gas.*' She stared straight at Tom and saw her own despair mirrored in his dark eyes. 'Oh, Tom . . . what will they do if they can't get them out? Harry won't be left buried deep in the dark, will he? Not Harry. He was — he is always so *clean.*'

She was close to hysteria now. 'I can't bear to think about him all black and cold and wet. Oh, Carrie, he's still wearing his wedding suit.'

Over her head Carrie and Tom exchanged meaning glances.

'Come home with us, lass. It may be a long time yet, and there's nothing to be gained by you staying. Come home with us.'

Libby's refusal was immediate. 'No! No! I have to wait. I have to be here when they bring him out. Even if it takes for ever, and even if he — if he's dead, I have to be here, waiting for him.'

She looked at Carrie and her new husband as if seeing them properly for the first time. 'This is your honeymoon. Today is your first day together in your new house. You must go back.' She nodded towards the women standing solidly together waiting impassively, silently for what must be. 'I'm with *them*. I'll be all right.'

'Do you think I'd leave you?' Carrie's voice was a passionate cry. 'How can you think for one minute that I would leave you to bear this alone? Oh, Libby . . . Libby, love . . .'

Tom followed more slowly as they moved back towards the group of women. 'Two halves of one,' he told himself wryly. The thought touched him deeply so that when he looked up at the grey clouds, moving swiftly now, he found he was blinking tears from his eyes. It had been a strange wedding night, his bride tossing and turning beside him, waking suddenly to sit up and call her twin's name aloud.

Now, as the watery sun tried to break through the clouds, he took his place by the two sisters, accepting their closeness and somehow glorying in it.

It was after another two long hours of waiting that the second rescue party came up from the mine.

'They've got through to them!' The murmur spread like a sigh through the knot of watching women. 'Thank God. They will have them up soon. You can always tell by the way they look.'

'Aye, it's something on their faces.'

Another hour went by, then the first stretcher came out, with the unconscious pit manager lying on it.

'He's lost a leg.'

The women pressed forward, one of them shaking the arm of a rescuer. 'Is it true?'

The news was conveyed in a low voice. 'He says the doctor took the leg off down there. It was the only way they could get him free.'

Carrie felt her sister stiffen. 'That means Harry could be alive! Oh, Carrie, he *has* to be alive. Please, please God, let him be alive!'

But the face of the man on the next stretcher was covered with a blanket, and his body lay twisted into a grotesque shape.

'That's Jack.'

The little woman in the grey shawl buried her face in her hands. 'Them's his boots. Oh, God, how I can tell me daughter I don't rightly know!' Her eyes hardened. 'I could tell her that the Lord giveth and the Lord taketh away, but I doubt that will give her much comfort. She'll know the baby will just be another mouth to feed with no man bringing in his wage of a Friday. So I won't say it . . .'

She was led away by a neighbour just as the third stretcher was brought out. With a great cry Libby broke free from Carrie's restraining arm and rushed forward.

'Stand clear, missus!'

The ambulance men moved into action but ignoring them, Libby bent over the stretcher to kiss the dirt-ingrained face above the swaddling blanket. The thick brown hair was matted with coal dust, and an ugly gash clotted with dried blood gave Harry's face a strange twisted expression.

Harry!' Libby whispered his name at first, then her voice rose to a scream. 'Harry! Open your eyes Oh, Harry, darling, darling love, open your eyes and speak to me! It's me, Libby. Harry? I love you!' She raised a piteous face to one of the rescue party standing close by. 'He won't die, will he! He's not hurt badly enough to die, is he!'

Hands pulled at her, trying to drag her away, but with the strength of a madwoman she resisted. With all semblance of control gone, Libby tried to pull the unconscious man up into her arms.

'Now then, love.' A rescue worker moved Libby round to face him. 'The doctor is alive, lass. He's a bloody hero. His foot's broken with us having to drag him out at the last, but he'll live.'

The miner's exhausted face was touched with grief for the loss of his workmate, but with infinite patience he appealed to Tom. 'Get her away, lad. The sooner the doctor's seen to at the hospital the better.' He lowered his voice. 'His foot needs looking at right away.'

But it was Carrie who led Libby gently away, and

Tom who told the driver of the waiting car to follow the ambulance to the hospital. Tenderly he helped the sisters into the back of the car, his heart aching at the sight of the two identical faces, both tear-streaked, pale and drawn in their shared anguish.

'When I thought he might have been killed I wanted to die. Oh, Carrie . . . if Harry had died then I would have wanted to die with him. Oh, how could I have loved him so much, and never known it? How?'

'Harry never doubted that you loved him.' Carrie's voice was soft with understanding. 'You are the joy of his life. You must know that.'

'Oh, yes, I do.'

Tom found he was having to blink back the tears from his own eyes as Libby whispered, 'Oh, Carrie. I thought I wanted — oh, I didn't know *what* it was I wanted. I had Harry and the baby, and yet . . . And now God has given me another chance. I don't deserve it, but He has given me another chance.'

Then, as the car swung out of the pit yard in the wake of the speeding ambulance, Tom turned round and saw the sisters clinging together, comforting and soothing as they would always comfort and soothe each other.

'See, girls. The sun is beginning to shine,' he said softly.

Footsteps in the Park

MARIE JOSEPH

For Brian and Mike

One

Stanley was late, and it wasn't like him. Usually he was there before her.

'Same time, same place,' he'd said the day before after they'd said their lingering goodbyes at the Corporation Park gates, and Dorothy had watched him walk away from her, dark head bent, as if his addiction to study had weakened his neck muscles, planting his undeniably big feet awkwardly as if he were counting the cracks in the pavement.

Although it was nearly May, and supposed to be spring, there was a sad soft drizzle in the air, and a sighing wind shivered the branches of the surrounding trees into nebulous shapes. Dorothy shivered and pulled the collar of her navy-blue gaberdine raincoat up round her neck, sinking herself further down into it and moving to the far end of the park bench.

She met Stanley Armstrong every day, after school finished at four o'clock, to sit close to him in innocent proximity, partially hidden from passers-by by rhododendron bushes and a weeping willow tree, oblivious to anything but their all-consuming and fascinated interest in each other.

At that time of day, little groups of men, some of whom had been on the dole for long periods since coming home from France in 1918, were making their way home. Shuffling along the paths of the town's Corporation Park in twos and threes, smoking their Woodbines down to the last fraction of an inch, making their way back to their terraced houses in the narrow winding streets. Flat-capped and morose, with scarves knotted carelessly over collarless shirts made of striped union flannel.

The Lancashire town, in the depths of the early thirties depression, was a standing on corners, holding its breath kind of place, with the ache of idleness stamped on the faces of its menfolk. The disparity between those who had and those who had not as great as at any time in history.

Dorothy Bolton, for ever guiltily and romantically conscious of the fact that she was one of those who *had*, waited impatiently, hugging her leather case with her initials stamped in gold on its lid close to her, glancing down the path and wondering what on earth was keeping Stanley.

At seventeen and a half, in the sixth form of the local High School for Girls, she filled out her white blouse with high, well-rounded breasts. Breasts that, restrained only by a liberty-bodice, bobbed embarrassingly up and down as she walked with the rest of her form into assembly, causing some of the younger girls to nudge each other and giggle. Her blue and green striped tie was pinned down to the blouse with her prefect's enamelled badge, and her hat, a much pummelled into shape version of a district nurse's cap, was tucked away out of sight inside the leather case.

If she closed her eyes, she told herself, and counted to a hundred, Stanley would be coming towards her when she opened them. He would come along the path from the nearby Grammar School for Boys, his shabby satchel underneath his arm in the only acceptable way of carrying it, his blue prefect's cap protruding from it, ready to be thrust hastily on his head should he meet a fellow pupil. He would smile at her and sit down beside her, laying one arm across the back of the bench, resting his hand on her shoulder. Ready, if anyone walked past, to lift the hand and pretend to be scratching his head, so as not to compromise her in any way.

'I shall probably join the B.U.F. when I go up to Oxford

8

at the end of the summer,' he had told her grandly the day before. 'I've given it a lot of thought, and I can't bring myself to believe that the only way of being radical is to be a Commie. In spite of what Stephen Spender says, Russia's social set-up doesn't appeal to me over-much, though they do seem to be escaping the worst of these depressive years.'

Dorothy sighed, opened her eyes, sighed once more, and closed them again. She knew that she was far from stupid, but she was often completely out of her depth when Stanley talked in that way. Politics were rarely mentioned in the red-brick house called Appleroyd in which she lived, except when her father blamed the bloody Government for his shares going down, or her mother wrinkled her nose at the very mention of the word Socialism.

Dorothy did have a dream, however, where she was a woman undergraduate up at Oxford, with a little study all her own. Where she would smoke cigarettes in a long holder, and have brilliant conversations with friends sitting on cushions, putting the world to rights, and listening to Benny Goodman's records. . . .

'I'm sorry I'm late, Dorothy.'

And Stanley was there, standing in front of her, breathing quickly as if he'd run all the way, and wearing, not his school blazer with Cardinal Wolsey emblazoned on its top pocket, but a tweed jacket and dark-grey flannels which fell in folds over the tops of his shoes. His thin face drooped naturally into lines of perpetual anxiety, but as he stood before her on the asphalt path, Dorothy thought his face held the stunned look of the suddenly bereaved.

'You haven't been to school, have you? What's wrong? Have you been ill?' she asked all in one breath.

He came and sat down beside her, looked round furtively, then kissed her cheek before taking a stub of a half-smoked cigarette from the top pocket of his jacket.

'Any objection?' he asked, as he always did.

Dorothy shook her head, feeling tender towards him because of his gentlemanly concern, then waited patiently

9

until he'd used four matches and disappeared behind the turned-up collar of his jacket before getting the cigarette to light.

Then at last, as the tip glowed brightly, he said: 'I can only stop for a minute. I've got to get back home. Something awful has happened, something I can't believe myself.' He turned dark anguished eyes towards her. 'My sister's missing. Our Ruby. We've had the police round to our house, asking questions and everything. My mum's going frantic.'

He dragged heavily at the cigarette stub, holding it as if it were speared on to the end of a pin; glanced at it as if wondering what it might be, then flicked it over the spiked iron railings bordering the duck pond in front of the bench.

Immediately three brown ducks appeared from behind a sheltering bush, and fell on it with angry, frustrated beaks, and Dorothy put her hand on his sleeve in a comforting gesture.

'You mean she's left home? Run off, or something?'

Stanley shook her hand away as if impatient at her lack of understanding. 'No, not run off. *Missing*. You know, like you read in the paper. Missing from home. Disappeared.'

Again the anguish in his eyes dismayed her, and she saw with alarm that he looked as if he'd been crying, as if he might burst into tears there and then. He took her hand and patted it gently between his own. 'She came home as usual from the mill last night, then she had her tea and got ready to go out. With a friend, she said, but I've been telling you for ages how mad she's got lately when Mum's tried to ask her where she goes. "I'm sixteen," she'd say, "and I don't have to account for my every movement. I'm not a kid at school. I bring good money home." You know how she is. I've told you.'

Dorothy put her leather case down beside the bench, suddenly feeling its weight on her knees.

'Yes, I know you told me, and we agreed that she was bound to feel resentful working in the mill while you were still at school, especially with you being two years older than her. Maybe she felt it more than you thought, and she's just gone off to show how unfair she thinks it is.'

Dorothy warmed to her explanation. 'Or perhaps she's had a row with the boy next door she used to go out with. Perhaps she's been secretly fretting for him ever since they finished?'

Stanley's face took on a 'you haven't been listening to me' look, and Dorothy said she was sorry but that she'd only been trying to help.

His mouth actually quivered. 'She took *nothing*. Not her warm coat, not anything. And besides, she's never been that mad at me or at Eddie Marsden from next door. The police asked Mum to search her room to see what was missing, and it's all there, even her Post Office book with three pounds in it. She was saving up for the holiday week at the end of July.' He felt in his pocket for the cigarette stub, and seemed genuinely surprised to find that it was no longer there. 'They're saying that foul play can't be ruled out. You know how they talk . . . I spent most of last night looking for her, going round to her mates' houses and everything, then this morning, before it came light, I went down to the station.'

Dorothy felt his worry transfer itself to her, as if a sudden damp weight was holding her still. Silly phrases such as 'oh well, I expect she'll turn up' or 'she's probably trying to give you and your mother a fright' trembled on her lips, but she didn't say them. How could she, with Stanley sitting beside her on the bench, frozen into anxious silence, pulling at a thread on the sleeve of his jacket, his whole attitude one of such hopelessness that she wanted to put her arms round him and stroke the fear from his thin suffering face?

Sometimes his long dark face reminded her of pictures of Jesus on the Cross, but she had shied away from the thought, feeling it was more than faintly blasphemous.

'Was Ruby worried about anything? Did she *seem* worried

11

at all?' she asked at last, and he muttered that was what the police kept harping on.

'Mum told them that she has three looms in your father's mill, and that she seems to be popular with the other weavers – that everybody likes her.'

'She's very pretty,' he went on, seeing, in his mind's eye, a picture of his young sister, a girl with his own colouring, a gentle girl with black curly hair falling in wispy tendrils over her forehead, soft-eyed, like a misty portrait of a country maid.

'Some of the questions that chap asked,' he said, beating one fist into the other. 'Like was she fond of the lads? Over-fond they meant. Making out that she was a bit of a wrong 'un.' He swallowed hard so that the Adam's apple in his throat moved up and down. 'Mum told him straight that the only boy she's ever been out with is Eddie Marsden next door, and when they checked with him down at the Co-op where he works they found that he'd been in the house all last night.'

Dorothy at last began to see the seriousness of it all. 'How awful!' she said, shaking her head from side to side. 'Is there anything I can do? I have a shorthand and typing lesson in an hour's time, but I can go home now and tell my mother I'm going down to your house . . .'

'Oh, she'd like that all right,' Stanley said with bitterness. 'No, there's nothing anyone can do really, and I'd best be getting back.' He got to his feet, pushing himself up from the bench like an old man with an arthritic hip. 'I won't be going back to school till this lot's sorted out, but I'll try and come here again tomorrow.' He rubbed at his forehead with a clenched fist, then without saying goodbye, started to walk away from her, his head bent as usual, his elbows tucked close into his sides like a long-distance runner.

Dorothy watched him go, then picked up her case. She had a suspicion that his mother cut his hair, as the back always had a kind of torn and ragged look about it. She often thought poetically that it gave him an added vulner-

12

ability. Then she started off in the opposite direction, walking as quickly as she could without drawing attention to herself by actually running, because she was late. . . .

'Your Dorothy's late home from school,' Ethel Rostron remarked in a conversational tone to her sister, Phyllis Bolton. Then she rubbed a satisfactory pinch of salt in the wound. 'Is she still friendly with that boy called Stanley Armstrong, out of Inkerman Street?'

'She has netball practice,' Phyllis said quickly, family loyalty decreeing that she didn't let the side down, even if she did happen to be worried out of her mind. Why her younger daughter had to be so different from her sister Margaret, she couldn't think. But then they'd always been like chalk and cheese, the one conforming, and the other always thinking the opposite of what her mother felt she should be thinking.

She patted her hair, but only gingerly as it had been set that morning at the new salon in King Edward Street. An urge to confide her worries to her sister struggled with the desire to keep up her end at all costs. Though it was all very well, she thought privately, for Ethel to be smug, just because her daughter Beryl hadn't even looked at a boy as yet.

'Chance is a fine thing,' she pondered nastily, mentally comparing her own two daughters' fair-haired prettiness with Beryl's own sallow, straight-haired plainness.

'I believe his sister has three looms in Matthew's mill?'

Ethel was all set to get her own back, her jealousy over Margaret's recent engagement to the highly eligible Gerald Tomlin getting the better of her. Gerald, who had come up from London to work as an accountant in Matthew Bolton's mill, was staying with her until the wedding, and his suave manners, plus his undisputed charm, made her sick to her very stomach with envy at times. Beryl was to be brides-maid along with her cousin Dorothy at the wedding in

13

June, and even a mother's love couldn't gloss over the fact that the pale-green taffeta chosen for the dresses would enhance Dorothy's pink and white complexion, whilst making Beryl look as if she were just getting over one of her frequent bilious attacks.

'I've heard tell his mother, Mrs Armstrong I mean, takes in washing, and has done ever since her husband died two years ago. Poor soul,' Ethel added with insincerity.

She was eating afternoon tea at her sister's house, Appleroyd, the biggest of the big red-brick houses overlooking the Corporation Park. Eating with her coat off whilst keeping her hat on.

Keeping one's hat on in the afternoon went with wearing white gloves in Summer, with a spare pair in one's handbag, and with pulling the lavatory chain before one actually sat down so that no one within earshot would know what one was doing. Although Ethel could be earthy and explicit in her language when she chose, she was a great one for inserting ones and whoms into her speech, and usually managed to get them in the right place. The hat toned with her grey tweed dress, and had ear-flaps to show it had been modelled on Amy Johnson's flying helmet.

'They say the poor woman had three "misses" before she managed this boy and his sister,' she said, adjusting the hat with one hand, and reaching for a scone with the other. 'Why their sort always goes in for big families beats me. Goodness knows, French letters are cheap enough.' She pretended not to see Phyllis's expression of disgust. 'Goodness knows, me and Raymond managed without much trouble, though after what I went through with bringing our Beryl into the world I do admit he's always been extra careful, if you know what I mean?' Phyllis obviously did but wasn't prepared to acknowledge it, so she went on, lowering her voice to avoid being overheard by her sister's daily help, a Mrs Wilkinson, working in the kitchen across the hallway. 'Are the Armstrongs *Catholics*?'

'The boy would be at St. Teresa's College if they were,'

14

Phyllis said, trying not to look as irritated as she felt. 'He's at the Grammar School, and they're Chapel, or so I believe.'

'Well, as long as they're *something* that's the main thing,' Ethel said, 'and I've known some quite nice Methodists,' she went on. She bit into the scone, and a shower of crumbs lodged on her massive shelf of a bosom, made bolster-shaped by the insertion of strategically placed darts in her bust bodice.

They stared at each other for a while with sisterly appraisal, their mouths munching rhythmically.

'Your Mrs Wilkinson has a light hand with scones,' Ethel said, reaching for her third. 'You've been lucky to hang on to her all these years, Phyl. My Mrs Greenhalgh has no more idea of how to bottom a room than fly. It takes her a full half hour to clean my front bay. More interested in what's going on in the road than in what she's doing. You'd think with all this unemployment about she'd want to impress, knowing how many women there are queueing up to earn a few extra shillings a week.'

Phyllis nodded. 'Yes, I know. But they take it from their dole money, Ethel, since this Means Test came in, so it hardly makes it worth their while working.' She lowered her voice to a whisper. 'Mrs Wilkinson is lucky because her husband has a steady job, even though he is on short time at the moment.'

'Hard times,' Ethel said sadly, standing up and showering crumbs on to the carpet. 'Well, I'd best be off. Our Beryl has a piano lesson at five, and I like to be there. He seems a nice enough young man, but you never know. It's the quiet ones one has to keep one's eye on.'

'That's true.'

Phyllis tried not to smile as she agreed through a fleeting vision of her niece Beryl, sitting on the piano stool in the hideously furnished lounge of Tall Trees, her sister's house. Beryl, her ample bottom overflowing the stool, her podgy hands moving laboriously up and down the piano keys, her lank brown hair escaping from its tortoise-shell slide and

15

falling round her plump cheeks. All this whilst her music teacher, the young assistant organist from St. Hilda's Church, struggled with his rising passion.

'No, you can't be too careful,' she said, going with her sister into the hall, and handing her a grey flecked tweed coat from the tall cupboard with hand-carving down its panels.

'Who would be a mother?' Ethel asked as she walked down the drive with her feet at a quarter to three.

'Who indeed?' said Phyllis, closing the vestibule door with a bang so that its red glass panels shivered in protest. A couple of hours of Ethel was quite long enough these days. She'd have to talk to Dorothy about the boy from down Inkerman Street. Perhaps suggest a little musical evening with records on the gramophone, or a light supper with that nice young crowd from the tennis club. She might even get her to invite the Armstrong boy so that she could see him set against boys of her own class. She picked up the tea-tray and carried it through into the kitchen.

Mrs Wilkinson, small, and so thin that her body moved skeleton-like beneath the cross-over pinafore she wore, was taking a satisfied peep at the hot-pot simmering slowly on the middle shelf of the gas oven. Her hair, which should have been grey, was a strange prune colour, due to the cold tea which she combed through it every day, and her bird-bright eyes glittered behind the whirlpool lenses of her spectacles.

'Coming on nicely, Mrs Bolton,' she said. 'I've turned it down as low as it will go; it's the only way to cook hot-pot. Long and low. Same with rice pudding. Sure you wouldn't like me to put one in? Seems a waste of a shelf.'

'Cheese and fruit,' Phyllis said firmly. 'Mr Tomlin's coming tonight, then he's taking Margaret to the cinema. We mustn't make it too heavy a meal.'

She used to say pictures before he came up here, and before she started trying to talk London-posh like he does, Mrs Wilkinson thought, then aloud she said: 'I bet Mr

16

Tomlin's never tasted hot-pot like this in all his natural. They don't know how to cook, Londoners don't. Cucumber sandwiches is all they know about, and he looks as if he could do with a lining on his stomach. If you don't mind me saying so, Mrs Bolton.'

Phyllis wrinkled her nose appreciatively, the conversation with her sister having made her temporarily mindful of her help's undoubted qualities. She leaned forward, a string of amber beads swinging outwards from her chest, noticing the way the potatoes were already taking on the required brown crispness whilst, beneath them, the neck-end chops and the mushrooms cooked themselves into a succulent simmering mash of goodness.

'Mr Tomlin will leave his usual compliments for the chef,' she said with a smile, 'the way he always does when he eats here.'

Mrs Wilkinson beamed, showing a flash of sparkling white false teeth, and a glimpse of artificial gum the shade of a ripe orange.

'That Mrs Greenhalgh, who works for your sister, thinks she's it. Just because her husband's a butter-slapper at the Maypole. And that's all he is, even though he does try to make out that he's the manager. What he brings home in that case he carries is nobody's business, but live and let live, that's what I always say, and always have said.'

She was astute enough to know that Mrs Bolton was shoving up with her, but why should she bother? As long as her pound a week was forthcoming every Friday afternoon, there was no need for her to go moithering herself. It was a nice enough job, with no scrubbing apart from the lino in the kitchen and bathroom, and no windows to clean on account of Philips, the handyman and chauffeur, seeing to them.

And there were plenty of perks. It wasn't for nothing she carried her cross-over pinafore and fur-trimmed bedroom slippers up the hill to Appleroyd every morning bar Sundays in an empty basket. Twelve years she'd worked for

Mrs Bolton now, and hardly a day when she didn't walk back down the hill with a little something in the basket. It might be merely one of Mr Bolton's shirts with slight fray to the cuffs, or it might be a bag of windfalls from the back garden, or even one of her ladyship's cast-off nighties. She always referred to Mrs Bolton as 'her ladyship' when she talked about her to her husband Ned, a porter on the railway.

'What's 'er ladyship come up with today?' he'd ask, having a look in the basket for himself. 'No wonder the country's in the mess it's in when some folks can afford to give good stuff like this away. Better watch yourself if you put that nightie on tonight, lass. See you in that, and I won't be responsible.'

Then he'd twiddle his non-existent moustache and slap his wife on her non-existent behind. A proper caution Ned was, as she was always telling Mrs Bolton.

They had a comfortable relationship as long as she was careful not to overdo the familiarity. Mrs Bolton liked to hear a bit of gossip, in spite of her prim and proper swanky ways, and Mrs Wilkinson had genuinely felt she was doing her employer a good turn when she'd told her about the way Dorothy walked home from school hand in hand with Stanley Armstrong out of Inkerman Street. You couldn't be too careful with girls, and she should know, with both her daughters having to be married. And what went on in the pavilion overlooking the Garden of Remembrance between the High School girls and the Grammar School boys would make your hair curl, even if it was as straight as a drink of water.

'Not that it's any of my business of course,' she'd said, down on her knees in front of the wide tiled fireplace in the lounge, newspapers spread all around her as she cleaned the fire-irons and the brass ornaments off the mantelpiece.

She'd dipped a piece of an old vest recently worn by Mr Bolton into the Brasso. 'The Armstrongs are a clean-living family from what I hear, and it must have been hard going for her since her husband was taken two years back. He worked at the Gas Works, and some say it were the smell what got on his chest.'

Phyllis had tried hard to look as if she thought this possibility was likely. She wanted to find out as much as she could without actually asking questions, but she did wish Mrs Wilkinson would go easy on the Brasso. 'The more you put on the more you will have to rub off,' she had once said mildly, only to have to suffer two days of injured silence as Mrs Wilkinson sulked around the house, sighing into her mid-morning pot of tea. So, despising herself for her weakness, Phyllis merely averted her eyes.

Mrs Wilkinson had then told how poor Mrs Armstrong was forced to take in washing.

'And how she manages with just a living-room with a tiny back scullery leading off it, I don't rightly know. A friend told me that the poor soul has the rollers on her mangle so tight that she's in constant pain with straining over the wheel. With half her insides hanging out I shouldn't wonder.' She reached over for the three brass monkeys in their hear, speak, and see no evil attitudes. 'Their Stanley takes the washing out for her after he finishes school, so it shows he's not got above himself even though he does go to the Grammar School. He's going to the university, you know.'

'A state scholarship,' Phyllis said in some desperation.

Mrs Wilkinson breathed hard on the trio of monkeys. 'All found I believe through a grant or trust or summat. There's no doubt about him being clever, no doubt at all. I've heard his mother goes on about him as if he might be Prime Minister some day.'

'Socialist, of course,' Phyllis had said bitterly.

Two

When Dorothy came in she called out to her mother, then ran straight upstairs to change out of the despised school uniform and to have a good think about Stanley and the way he had looked when he'd told her about his sister.

She couldn't take it seriously somehow. Girls who went missing from home were headlines in newspapers, not girls one knew, and although she had seen Ruby Armstrong in the distance once or twice down at the mill, her impression had been that the girl possessed Stanley's quiet dignity. Certainly not the type to deliberately frighten her mother out of her wits by staying out all night.

No, there would be some explanation . . . perhaps she'd missed a last tram and been afraid to go home. If Mrs Armstrong's determination to see her son through university was anything to go by, she was a strong-willed woman.

She'd had an interesting conversation with Stanley about their respective mothers only the day before, sitting close together on the secluded bench by the duck pond.

'It's a wicked thing to say, but there are times when I'm ashamed and embarrassed by my mother,' she'd said.

She could still recall Stanley's understanding nod.

'It's a perfectly normal part of your growth development, Dorothy. Don't you see? There's often an element of hate in the relationship between a mother and a daughter. Ruby's going through that phase at the moment with our mum. It's a striving for independence, a growing desire to sever the umbilical chord.'

Dorothy unbuttoned her navy-blue serge skirt and stepped out of it. Surely the word hate was a bit much when used in connection with one's mother? It was just that her mother was so . . . so insular-minded. Her horizons were set no further than her own ornately iron-wrought front gate. She wasn't interested in the least about what was going on in Europe, or at the Disarmament Conference, or in the fact that a man called Hitler, a man who loathed the Jews, had recently become the German chancellor. Phyllis didn't want to talk about it. All she wanted to talk about was Margaret's engagement to Gerald Tomlin from London, and the approaching date of the wedding.

'What we need in this country is a leader with fire in his belly,' Dorothy had told her, quoting Stanley, and Phyllis had said. 'Fire in his *stomach*, dear. Belly isn't a nice word for a young girl to use.'

'Thy belly is like an heap of wheat set about with lilies. Thy two breasts are like two young roses that are twins,' Dorothy had replied, just to be difficult. 'You'll be saying that the Song of Solomon isn't nice next.'

'Parts of it are extremely vulgar,' Phyllis had retorted, unabashed.

One thing was certain, Dorothy told herself as she started to roll down her black woollen stockings, her sister Margaret would never want to sever the umbilical chord. It was as if she had obediently fallen in love with Gerald Tomlin just to please her mother. Because, as a continuation of the good little girl she had always been, she could be happy only if her parents were happy.

Muttering to herself as she rummaged in the untidiness of her dressing-table drawer for a pair of lisle stockings, Dorothy asked herself how any girl of twenty-one, as pretty as Margaret, could be smitten with a man in his middle thirties with sandy hair, freckles, and wet lips? Personally she found him utterly repulsive with his charm laid on with a trowel, and his yellow spotted cravats, not to mention the hideous Max Baer pouched sports jackets he chose to wear.

21

To love a man like that . . . ugh! It was enough to make one feel sick, she told herself, turning round and checking that the seams of her stockings were straight. Then she wondered vaguely whether to tell her father about the lecture they'd had that day at school about careers in the Civil Service. The prospect of going to work in the mill office appalled her, even though the draughty little building was situated down a long flagged slope, well away from the deafening clatter of the looms in the weaving shed.

Which brought her thoughts back full circle to Ruby Armstrong. No wonder she'd run away. What chance had *she* had to improve her station by learning shorthand and typing privately? What chance of anything with a brother as brilliantly clever as Stanley, and with a mother who washed other people's clothes all day so that her son could stay on at school and pass one exam after another?

Dorothy opened her wardrobe door and took out her favourite dress of the moment, blue crêpe with white spots and a white floppy organdie bow at the neckline.

It was certainly funny that Ruby hadn't taken any of her clothes with her, but then she'd probably had this wild romantic notion of walking out of the house into the arms of her lover – because surely there was a lover somewhere? – with nothing but the clothes she stood up in. It was like a story out of a magazine. Like the beginning of a serial in one of the *Woman Pictorials* Mrs Wilkinson brought to the house.

Leaving everything behind, everything she had held most dear, she walked away to a fresh beginning, a new life with the man who loved her from the depths of his very soul. . . .

'Are you there, Dorothy?' Margaret Bolton put her head round the door then came in and walked straight over to the mirror.

'Just look at my hair,' she said without preamble. 'Gerald's coming to dinner, and I haven't time to wash it and get it dry. It's been one hell of a day at the office. Mr

Martin gave me four letters to type at the last minute, then he made me do one over again. He might be the Education Officer, but he's hopeless at putting words together.' She held out a strand of her fair hair. 'Do you think if I wet the ends with sugared water and put a few curlers in, it would curl up in time?'

'It looks all right to me,' Dorothy said, easing her feet into black court shoes without glancing in her sister's direction. 'Anyway, when you marry your Gerald, he'll have to see you looking a mess sometimes. Will you be sleeping in curlers like you do now, with Ponds cold cream on your face?'

'Of course not. I'll wait until he's gone to the mill, then I'll put my curlers in underneath a turban.'

Margaret was answering quite seriously, having thought this out only the week before. 'Gerald doesn't even like me putting my lipstick on or powdering my nose in front of him. He likes his women to look as if they make no effort at all to look pretty.'

'His *women*?' Dorothy raised an eyebrow.

'A joke,' Margaret, who never made them, said. Then leaning closer to the mirror she pulled at her half-fringe, tram-lines of anxiety furrowing her broad forehead. 'I wish you'd try to be nicer to Gerald, our Dorothy. He's not all that happy at the moment having to stay with Auntie Ethel and Uncle Raymond until the wedding. Uncle Raymond is always talking about what it was like in the trenches in Flanders Fields all those years ago, and Beryl stares at him.'

'Stares at him? Whatever for?'

'Gerald thinks it's because she has a crush on him. She does it when they're having a meal, and he says he can't chew his food properly because every time he looks up from his plate, there she is. Staring at him.'

'Well, at least he can't accuse me of that,' Dorothy said, running a comb through her thick curly hair and being glad it curled naturally and didn't have to be helped along with

23

hot water with sugar melted into it.

'Stanley Armstrong's sister's missing,' she said all at once.

Margaret turned round from the mirror looking so much like her mother that Dorothy flinched.

'You mean that boy out of Inkerman Street? His sister?'

'You know very well who I mean. You must have heard Mother telling me how I'm lowering myself being friendly with a boy like that.'

'There's no need to get so uppity for heaven's sake.'

Dorothy jerked at the narrow belt on her frock. 'She's for ever reminding me how lovely the boys at the tennis club are, and urging me to join the Young Conservatives. And why I have to learn shorthand and typing privately when I could leave school in July and go to the Technical College in September, I don't know. Is there some virtue in paying for education? I have to mingle with the scholarship girls at school after all.'

'You've got Bolshie ideas, our Dorothy. And I knew something was wrong when I telephoned Gerald at the mill. He sounded quite upset and he said the police were there. Something to do with one of the girl weavers, he said.'

Dorothy tweaked the organdie bow into position, and leaning round her sister at the dressing-table, outlined her lips with purple lipstick then wiped it off again.

So Stanley had been right. They were treating it as foul play. Mrs Armstrong must have convinced the police that her daughter would never have stayed out all night without letting her know. She felt the gloom of unease settle around her as if someone had suddenly draped a damp blanket over her shoulders. She wanted for some inexplicable reason to take her feelings out on Margaret who was watching her now with a martyred expression on her face. The shorthand lesson loomed ahead in her mind like the promise of some medieval torture, and she wanted her sister to retaliate to her mood by shouting at her, or at least by walking out of

24

the room and slamming the door. There were times when she could hear herself being nasty, and the feeling was strangely exhilarating.

'A demonstration of one's baser feelings is common,' her mother had told her once. 'Anyone would think you were a mill girl at times, Dorothy. In clogs and shawl.'

Dorothy hadn't bothered to remind her mother that the girls at her father's mill never wore clogs and shawls; that it was Grandma Lipton, Phyllis's mother, who had gone to work dressed like that, being knocked up by a man called Daft Jack who walked the early morning streets, rattling on the windows of the terraced houses with a stick with umbrella spokes on the end of it. To mention this would have tightened Phyllis's mouth into a grim line, and frozen her neat features into a mask of distaste.

It was for this reason that Grandma Lipton had never been brought from the Nursing Home to be there when Gerald Tomlin was visiting.

'She does it on purpose,' Phyllis had said. 'She's proud of the way we've got on in one way, and yet in another she resents it.'

'Look, Dorothy,' Margaret was saying, her interest in the missing Armstrong girl having evaporated, 'I wish you'd just try and be nicer to Gerald. He'll be Father's partner in the mill one day; he's taken the financial side over altogether now, and when we're married he'll be your brother-in-law, remember. We'll be living not all that far away, and you'll be coming to see us often I hope.' She opened her blue eyes wide in accusation. 'He knows you don't like him, you know.'

'He probably thinks it's because I've fallen for him and am madly jealous that you're the one he's chosen, him being God's gift to women,' Dorothy said, biting her lip and turning away.

She knew she could never tell Margaret the main reason for her active dislike of the elegant young man from London. Just how, for heaven's sake, did you tell someone

25

with their wedding coming up in June that you wouldn't trust their precious fiancé any further than you could throw him?

Her real aversion to Gerald Tomlin had started the day she had seen him flirting with one of the mill girls as they streamed out of the yard on their way home late one afternoon. He was leaning against his red MG sports car, a fawn raincoat tightly belted round his waist, a cigarette held casually in his long fingers, and what he was saying was making the young girl giggle in a familiar way that would have made Phyllis's blood run cold. She was a big girl, with the front piece of her hair peroxided to a white candy-floss, and as Dorothy watched unseen from the office window, Gerald had suddenly turned her round and fondled her plump behind before giving it a resounding slap.

She wasn't a prude, heavens, not that, and she wasn't a snob, heavens not that either, but it wasn't quite in keeping with the gentlemanly behaviour he displayed when he came to Appleroyd. Perhaps there was more of her mother in her than she realized. . . .

No, she could never tell Margaret, nor could she tell her that the New Year's kiss she had received from Gerald had disgusted her and almost made her feel sick.

It was what the girls at school would have described as a French kiss, with his slack mouth opening over her own, and his tongue probing wetly and rhythmically.

It had been almost a case of incest, she had told herself dramatically afterwards, and had wondered how Margaret, her fastidious, prim, and reserved sister could possibly put up with it? Compared with that nauseating kiss, Stanley's kisses were hard and fierce. And very much to be preferred, she decided.

'Are you very much in love with Gerald?' she asked, trying to imagine Margaret responding to such a sickly embrace. And failing.

'What a thing to ask!'

Margaret fiddled with the silver-backed brush on the

dressing-table, the back of her neck going slightly pink. 'You've been reading Mrs Wilkinson's *Woman Pictorials* again, haven't you?' She gazed up at the ceiling as if searching for the right words. 'Life isn't a bit like it's set up to be in those stories you know.'

'No, you're right. Life is like Gerald Tomlin,' Dorothy said, not quite underneath her breath. Then feeling ashamed of herself, left the room and went downstairs to set the seal on her nasty mood by lying to her mother about the mythical netball practice. Getting so carried away that she even described the way she had hurled the ball into the net from a distance of at least ten yards. . . .

She was back from the typing lesson just in time to sit down at the dinner table with the family. She had been driven back by Philips, and he'd told her there had been a police car in the mill yard all the afternoon.

'Right excitement there were in the weaving sheds,' he'd said with some satisfaction. 'Tongues clacking almost as loud as the looms. They say they're thinking of dragging the duck pond in the Corporation Park.'

'Why?'

'Because that's where all the courting couples go, isn't it?'

She blushed and hoped Philips hadn't noticed, but he had changed the subject, and anyway he wasn't interested in what she did, only at the moment in telling her about his lady friend's mother, who apparently was on her death-bed, which meant he could marry Vera at last.

He was a neat man, with tiny hands and a bald head which he concealed beneath his peaked cap. What bit of hair he had was plastered to his scalp with solidified brilliantine, and he had a habit of smacking his lips at the end of each sentence, which must, Dorothy had often thought, drive his fiancée mad.

'The problem is that Vera wants us to live in her house in

Charlotte Street, but I don't want to give my little place up,' he said, with a loud expressive smack of the lips. 'I've just got it to my liking with a back-boiler in the living-room that heats the water a treat. But Vera's adamant.'

He pronounced it as 'adayment', and Dorothy, over the blush now, thought of Vera, who could have been any age between forty and sixty, and who wore her black hair in pin-wheel plaits over each ear, and sported white ankle socks over her stockings. Vera ran the Church Guide Troop at St. Hilda's as if the patrols were training for military manoeuvres, and the very idea of her lying by Philip's side in a double bed filled Dorothy with a kind of hysterical horror. Gerald Tomlin had said that Philips was a pansy and would never marry, and that Vera was a natural spinster, clinging to her invalid mother and making her an excuse not to marry.

'They're born virgins, the two of them,' he had said, making sure that Mrs Bolton was well out of earshot before using a word that she would have considered indelicate. 'Any couple who court for over twenty years have no intention of marrying. I've seen the inside of Philips's house, and no woman could keep it as clean and tidy as that.'

Dorothy had felt bound to agree, having seen with her own eyes a potted plant on a doyley on the draining board in the kitchen, and covers covering the covers on the three-piece suite in the front parlour.

'I bet he goes to bed with his vest on underneath his pyjama jacket,' Gerald went on, and Dorothy's father, who did exactly that, had merely grunted as he'd come into the room and caught the tail-end of the conversation.

Matthew Bolton's big face settled into lines of content-ment as his younger daughter took her place at the dinner table.

'Hallo, chuck,' he said, winking at her, and thinking what a corker she looked in that blue spotted dress. By the heck but she were a bonny lass, even though from the expression on her face she looked as if she might be spoiling for a fight as usual. Always asking questions there weren't no answers to, and not knowing what it was she wanted to do when she left school. Wondering what life was all about, and worriting about things far beyond her control, things she could do nowt about. Not like Margaret there, who took it all for granted. He beamed again at Dorothy who wrinkled her nose at him affectionately.

He'd been doing a bit of wondering about life himself lately, come to that. What with the worry of them bloody Japs modernizing more and more of their cotton mills, and supplying the British markets at a price he couldn't hope to compete with. Not with the overheads he'd got. Already he'd scrapped a third of his looms, and a good job it was he'd stuck to his father's maxim of not spending a penny unless he could put his hand in his back pocket and cover it with another. And still seeing his family went short of nowt into the bargain.

At the other end of the long mahogany table, his wife was presiding over the brown dish of hot-pot, as regally as if it were a gold-plated dish, her hands daintily occupied as she passed the plates round.

'Typed any good letters, Dorothy?'

Gerald Tomlin was smiling at her with his freckled pouchy face, his wet eyes glistening with anticipation as he took a plate of food from his prospective mother-in-law.

Everything about him is wet, Dorothy thought, with the familiar feeling of distaste. His hair shines too much, and his lips look as if he'd just licked them ready to give one of his awful sloppy kisses.

'I'll never be as good a secretary as Margaret,' she told him, being polite and rather humble for her sister's sake. 'This evening we had to type in time to a military two-step on the gramophone, and the keys on my typewriter kept on coming up all jammed together. I think I'd have been better off with a funeral dirge.'

Gerald threw back his sandy head and laughed as if she'd said something unbearably witty. He laughed so much that there was almost a touch of hysteria in it, and he really was pathetic, Dorothy thought with distaste. Then saw the expression on her sister's face, and seeing, got the answer to the question she had asked earlier.

Margaret was in love. Really in love. The head-over-heels kind so strongly advocated in Mrs Wilkinson's magazines. She must have been at her hair with the sugar and water, Dorothy decided, for now it curved softly on to her flushed cheeks; her eyes shone blue, and when she smiled her mouth was a soft and dreamy curve of contentment. She studied her sister's face with a morbid fascination. Margaret seemed to be smiling affectionately at the hot-pot on her plate, pushing it gently from side to side, almost as if she found its beauty too much to bear.

'The time I start smiling at hot-pot I'll know I'm really sunk,' Dorothy told herself, and made up her mind to go on trying to be nice to Gerald.

'I like your tie,' she told him, knowing this remark was sure to please as Gerald was a snazzy dresser. And at once he beamed round the table and told them all that it was hand-made silk from Harrods in London, and that with the matching crêpe silk handkerchief peeping from his top pocket, it had set him back all of twelve and sixpence.

'But worth every penny, Gerald,' Phyllis said, and Dorothy tried not to raise her eyebrows as she remembered the times her mother had reminded her that to mention the cost of anything was extremely common.

'I even put Mrs Wilkinson's wages in an envelope so that I don't have the embarrassment of handing her the actual money,' she'd once said.

It was no good, Dorothy told herself, she couldn't bring herself to like the bland young man sitting by her sister's side. She would try, just as she was trying now not to mention the intruding worry in her mind of Ruby Armstrong's disappearance. She knew how much her mother hated controversial and serious subjects being aired at the table. And Phyllis had gone to a lot of trouble, ladling the hot-pot into her best Wedgwood dinner plates, and using the silver knives and forks from the polished mahogany case on the sideboard.

'Unpleasant subjects should always be kept from the table,' was another of her sayings, and Dorothy knew she wouldn't be able to bear it if the missing girl was mentioned and her mother said, as she was bound to say, that she had got what she was probably asking for.

'If she said that I would just walk out,' Dorothy told herself silently, and watched Gerald being pressed, obviously against his will, to accept a second helping.

'My compliments to the chef,' he said, just as she had known he would say.

It was no good. She couldn't keep silent after all. She had to ask. She could still see Stanley's thin face, noble with suffering, and the police might have told her father something? Perhaps even now Ruby was weeping on her mother's shoulder, saying that she didn't know what had made her do such a dreadful thing; swearing that she didn't mind working at the mill, that she fully understood that anyone as brilliant as her brother had to have his chance.

'I heard today . . .' she began.

'Margaret and I . . .' Gerald said at the same time.

'Sorry,' Dorothy said. And the moment was gone.

Gerald smiled, showing white teeth as small as a child's first milk teeth. 'I'm taking Margaret to the Rialto, to the Second House. Would you like to come with us, Dorothy? I could sit between you; a thorn between two roses, what?'

Dorothy thanked him, and explained quite truthfully that she had piles of homework to do. Then, as Gerald started talking about the film, she decided that being nice wasn't a virtue at all. It was merely the way one wanted to be at a given time. A form of self indulgence, in fact.

What hypocrites we are, she thought, every one of us.

'I saw the film in London at the beginning of the year,' Gerald was saying. 'Charles Laughton makes a topping Henry the Eighth, and Merle Oberon as Anne Boleyn is

31

simply superb.' He waved his fork about to add emphasis to his words. 'She is that marvellous and rare thing, a stunning woman with intelligence as well as beauty.' He patted Margaret's face to show he meant no offence. 'And Robert Donat . . . well . . .' Words seemed to fail him. 'He takes the part of Catherine Howard's lover, and his voice is superb, sort of hoarse with a marvellous sense of feeling in it, if you know what I mean. Superb,' he said again.

Dorothy leaned forward, forgetting it was Gerald she was talking to, and not Stanley.

'I read that they show the jovial side of the King's nature, not his selfish cruelty. Surely that's all wrong?'

Gerald smiled his shiny smile. 'People go to the cinema to be entertained, not to witness the unsavoury details of history, my dear.'

Dorothy gave up trying to be agreeable. 'That's just silly. If the film people want to show actual characters who lived and breathed, then they should show them as they were, warts and all. So why can't we be shown Henry as he was, with all his unsavoury habits, and his . . .'

Gerald's smile dimmed a little. 'Perhaps until you see the film for yourself . . . ?'

Ignoring the warning glances her mother was sending her from across the table, Dorothy said that she was in all probability going to see it with a friend on Saturday.

'Which friend?' her mother asked, forcing her to lie, and realizing from the knowing look on Gerald's face that he knew that she was lying.

Oh God, she thought miserably, why did her family hang on to his every word as if he were Moses? Couldn't they see that he would break Margaret's heart? Why, oh why, couldn't her sweet and kind sister have fallen in love with Edwin Birtwistle, the captain of the tennis club for three consecutive seasons, a director in his father's firm at twenty-five? Edwin Birtwistle would have loved Margaret for ever more, and never ever kissed her sister with his mouth wide open, or fondled another girl's bottom in broad daylight.

'I had been thinking that perhaps you and I could go to the First House tomorrow night, dear,' her mother was saying, her beads making little clattering noises on the edge of the table as she stacked the plates together. 'Your father has a Rotary meeting, and we could have high tea in the Emporium Café first.'

'I am going with a friend on Saturday,' Dorothy said in some despair, wishing she could say the friend was Stanley. Wishing he could come to the house like Gerald Tomlin, and be accepted and listened to. Wishing they could hear the marvellous way he talked, his dark eyes eager, his voice going gruff when he talked about a subject dear to his heart.

Wishing he wasn't going away. . . .

Three

After Stanley had left Dorothy in the park, he ran all the way down West Road with a long loping stride, his elbows tucked into his sides and his grasshopper legs covering the ground at an incredible rate, like a long-distance runner.

The houses, set well back from the road, were ivy-covered, solid and secluded in their respectability, a different world away from the mean street in which he lived. A group of girls in scarlet blazers and peaked caps were coming out of the private school on the corner, and a girl with a bold face called something out to him, but hearing nothing, he ran on.

At the bottom of the road, on the main trunk thorough-fare were the tram-lines, running parallel all the way into the town. For a moment he hesitated as he heard the rattle and whine of an approaching tram, calculating whether it would be quicker to catch it or take a short cut back to the house.

Already his breath was catching in his throat, and there was a stabbing, pricking pain in his left side, but he didn't slacken his pace, running along for a while at the side of the tram, then turning into a street of Victorian houses which had been turned into solicitors' offices.

He'd had no right to leave his mother alone, he knew that now, but it had seemed important that Dorothy shouldn't be kept waiting; that he told her what had happened before she heard it from her father. And his mother had under-stood. Or at least she had seemed to understand.

34

'It's the waiting,' she'd kept saying all the long day, 'The waiting, and feeling so helpless like.'

He had left her ironing a pile of shirts heaped high in her ironing basket. Standing at the living-room table with the familiar folded blanket in place. Slipping the heated flat-iron into its polished slipper while the second iron hotted up at the blazing coal fire.

'How can you work at a time like this?' he'd asked her, and she'd gone on working without looking up.

'If I stopped doing something I'd go out of my mind. It's the waiting, you see,' she'd said again.

On he ran, along a wide street lined with shops, a third of them closed and shuttered, with slogans written on their empty windows. UP THE BOLSHIES. DOWN WITH THE MEANS TEST. Past a massive poster proclaiming that EVERYWHERE YOU CAN BE SURE OF SHELL. Past a tripe shop with the white honeycombed offal laid out in the window on a marble slab, flanked by pigs' trotters, and a pig's head with an orange in its mouth.

Past a chip shop, almost knocking over a woman coming out with a basin of fish and chips covered with a white cloth . . . reminding him that he was hungry.

Into the labyrinth now of steep streets with terraced houses opening straight on to the pavements, with house-wives standing on their doorsteps, gossiping, arms folded over the flowered cross-over pinafores they wore like a uniform, keeping watchful eyes on their children as they played hopscotch, using the flagged pavements as their marking grounds.

On through a back passage, slipping on the greasy cobblestones, ducking under lines of washing, past a small boy walking with legs wide apart, sobbing loudly because he'd wet himself. Seeing it all. And seeing nothing.

And as he turned into Inkerman Street, they were there, the vultures, pretending to be stoning their window-bottoms, some of them mopping their front steps and the surrounding flags for the third time that day. Turning eager eyes towards him as he ran panting to number twenty-seven.

'Is there any news, love?'

That was Mrs Crawley from across the street, a neighbour who spent all day wearing her husband's flat cap and an apron made out of sacking, and went out each night wearing a tight black suit and a pillar-box hat with an eye veil. Rouged to kill and up to no good, as everyone said. She *would* be the only one with the nerve to ask outright, Stanley thought, and shook his head. Not because he wished to snub her, but because there wasn't the breath left to speak.

And besides, Mrs Crawley had the right to ask if anyone had. The street's official benefactor, she was the first one called on when a laying-out became necessary. Propped against her back-yard wall was a spare lavatory door, kept for such a purpose.

'Keeps 'em nice and straight,' she would say, laying the corpse out flat on its unyielding surface, closing the eyes for the last time with pennies weighting down the lids, arranging the lifeless hands in a neatly folded praying position over the newly washed chests. No point in paying the undertaker when Mrs Crawley would do it for no more than a cup of tea or a glass of throat-stinging ginger wine.

Mrs Crawley it was who had scrubbed the oilcloth in Ruby's room till the pattern had almost vanished when Ruby had been taken off in the ambulance to the fever hospital burning with diphtheria two years before. Making the entire house reek to the rooftops of Jeyes Fluid for days to come.

Mrs Crawley who had sat up with the three-year-old Ruby when the pneumonia had almost finished her. Sitting up all night so that her mother could get some rest. Keeping the steam kettle going, changing the sheets from under her when the fever broke and she lay bathed in sweat. Searching the town on a Sunday afternoon when Ruby, over the crisis, fancied a bit of ice-cream.

Oh, yes. Mrs Crawley had the right to ask. . . .

'Mum! I'm back!' Stanley called out as he closed the front door behind him. 'I wasn't long, was I? I told you I wouldn't be.'

But the woman who turned her face towards him as he walked down the passage, past the front parlour, and into the living-room, was a woman for whom time had lost all meaning. One hour, or two, or three, what did it matter? All she was waiting for was the knock on the door to say that Ruby had been found safe and well. The other supposition she would not countenance. So she did what she had to do, as if she'd been wound up inside, all her being concentrating on the shirt she was ironing on the table in front of her.

Otherwise she'd crack, and she knew it.

Double bits first. Cuffs, neck-band, button-trim, wrong side first. Spitting on the iron first to see if it was the right heat. She could tell that by the way the spit bounced off and slid along the gleaming slipper. Stiff collars, damp dry from the big basin of starch with a dab of dolly-blue in it. Collars ironed to a polished smoothness with the iron running over a piece of fent from the mill. The mill . . . Oh God, that's where her Ruby should be at that moment, standing at her looms on the wet flagged floor with her flowered overall over her dress, and her dark curly hair wisping softly round her bonny face. Back to the collars. Curving them round her hand, then layering them one inside the other, making sure the fold was in the right place.

When she saw Stanley she straightened up for a moment and stared at him through dark eyes sunk deep into their sockets with worry and exhaustion. She laid the iron on its rest for a moment.

'They came again while you were gone. He said they were going to drag the duck pond in the Corporation Park at first light tomorrow. Seems one of her work-mates was standing by the side gate in West Road last night about ten o'clock with a boy, and thought she saw Ruby go in with a boy. Or a man. She couldn't see either of them; didn't look really, but she thought it might have been our Ruby's voice.'

'Oh, Mum. . . .'

Stanley went to her and gently brushed the hair away from her hot forehead. It was unbelievable how in one short day his mother's looks had changed to what he imagined they might be when she was an old, old woman. Surely flesh could not sag in the space of twenty-four hours? Less than that. Deep wrinkles appearing where wrinkles had never been before?

In spite of her long hours at the dolly-tub, fishing clothes out of the boiler with the rounded stick, and her back-breaking stretches at the mangle with its wide wooden rollers, Ada Armstrong was a handsome woman. The country freshness of her Cumberland upbringing had never quite left her cheeks, and her hair, black and coarse as wire, without a single strand of silver in it, sprang away from her forehead, refusing to lie smooth.

Stanley gave her a push towards the rocking chair set by the fire. 'Sit down, Mum. Just for a few minutes. I'll get you a cup of tea.' His mind shied away from what she had just told him. They couldn't think . . . not the duck pond in the park? Not the very place he'd just left with the wind rippling its dark green surface? Ruby with her hair, her pretty hair caught up in the long grasses, her body bloated and swollen . . . 'They don't know anything; it's only that they have to follow up any kind of lead they get. Please sit down, Mum. To please me. You'll be ill.'

So to please him Ada sat down for a second on the very edge of the chair, then got up and followed him through into the scullery.

'She wouldn't be going in the park with a boy at that time, not our Ruby. She was always in by ten. Besides she always told me where she was going, and last night she was going with a mate from work to the Bulb Show in town then back to this girl's house.'

'Which girl, Mum?' Stanley filled the kettle and found a

match for the gas. 'They haven't found her yet, have they?' He had to make her *think* however cruel it might seem to be. His logical mind couldn't accept that there was nothing, not a single clue. In spite of her recent secretiveness, Ruby was an honest girl, with every expression on her face there for all to read. He had to try again.

'Did she ever even hint to you that she had found herself another boy? Even give you the slightest suspicion that she was doing something she had no right to be doing?'

Ada followed him to the cupboard as he reached for two cups and put them side by side on the draining board. Her usually clear voice was low. 'What I've been thinking I don't rightly like to say.'

Stanley went back to the kettle and she followed him there. 'You must say it, Mum. Even if it doesn't seem important. You must say it.'

Ada sighed a deep sigh. 'Ever since she packed it in with Eddie Marsden next door, she's been different. Keeping herself to herself, and snapping at me when I've tried to talk to her.'

The kettle came to the boil and Stanley carried it over to the teapot, his mother no more than a step behind him.

'I think she's been going out with a married man. Oh yes, I do, and you don't need to look like that, son, because them what's never come up against temptation don't know what they're saying.'

Carefully Stanley poured the hot water out in a steady stream. 'There's a Spanish proverb that says "He who avoids the temptation avoids the sin." I wasn't shocked, Mum.'

'It all fits in somehow. She's been telling me lies, that's obvious. The sergeant told me she hasn't been seeing the girls at the mill, not if they were telling the truth, that is. But they couldn't tell him anything. Not a word, so she's been just as secretive with them as she has with me. I know my girl and she was probably too ashamed to tell anyone what was going on, don't you see?'

39

Without waiting for the tea to brew Stanley poured it into the cups, laced them both liberally with sugar, and went out to the small meat safe in the yard where they kept the milk.

'You mean you think she's gone off with this . . . this married chap?'

'Aye, I do.'

'Without taking her warm coat, or her nightdress, or anything?'

He carried the cups into the living-room and set them down on the table next to the pile of ironing. Then, although the room was hot to the point of suffocation, he lifted a square slab of coal from the scuttle and put it on the fire. At that moment warmth spelt comfort somehow . . . Guiding his mother to the rocking chair he put the cup of tea in her hands.

'Look, Mum, you could be right. I hope you are right, but I can't think, I can't believe . . .' He sat down opposite to her in the big armchair that had been his father's. 'Anyway if you are right, all the police have to do is to check on some poor woman whose husband didn't come home last night. She'd be bound to report him missing to the police, wouldn't she, just as we did our Ruby?'

'Perhaps he doesn't come from this town? Perhaps he's just in digs here?'

'Then his landlady would report it. Mum, that still doesn't explain why she didn't smuggle some of her clothes out of the house. You know what she's like about her things. She creates every time anybody touches anything. No, I can't believe she would leave the lot behind.'

'Are you trying to prepare me for the fact that she's dead?'

Stanley quickly denied this. 'No, of course I'm not. I just feel that by talking round it we may dig up some reason. It's making us *think*, Mum, the way the sergeant asked us to do.'

Ada still hadn't put the cup to her lips. She was staring

into the fire now, wrinkling her brow as she tried to concentrate.

'She didn't take anything out with her because it was *unpremeditated*. That's why. She met this chap and they decided to go away on the spur of the moment, and when they think the dust's settled a bit Ruby will write to us. She always did get carried away. Look how she thought she was madly in love with Eddie next door.' Ada turned towards Stanley eagerly, willing him, willing herself to believe she had stumbled on a rational explanation. 'And why did she finish with Eddie? There were never a proper reason for that now, were there?'

'She was . . . is only sixteen,' Stanley corrected himself quickly, horrified at his slip of the tongue. 'She told me herself that she thought the girls at the mill were daft, drifting into marriage with the first boy they went out with. She told me a lot of them are back at their looms now, with their mothers looking after their babies.'

'She wanted better than Eddie,' his mother said as if he had never spoken. 'His mother came in for a minute while you were out, and she says that when Eddie came home for his dinner he told her the police had been to the shop asking him questions. She said the manager was quite upset and insisted on shutting them in the store room at the back to talk.'

Stanley watched her with love, ready to take the cup from her hands.

She was so tired, he realized, she scarcely knew what she was saying. But she was drinking the tea now, taking great gulps of it, and the glow from the fire was bringing back the colour to her cheeks. Perhaps he could persuade her to eat something? A boiled egg? Stanley felt he could manage that without too much difficulty.

'Are there any eggs, Mum?' he was saying when the knock came to the door, a knock followed by Mrs Crawley's voice calling out 'Can I come in, Mrs Armstrong?'

She was already in, a bright yellow headscarf covering

41

the curlers in her hair, holding a basin covered with a tea cloth out before her. 'Now I don't want no refusals,' she said, putting the basin down on the table next to the basket of unironed shirts. 'And you can call me an interfering old bugger if you've a mind to, but I reckoned you wouldn't be feeling like cooking for your teas, not just now. So I've been down to the chip shop, and there's two two's and a pennorth of dabs each, all salted and vinegared, ready to eat, and I wouldn't bother with plates if I was you. Just get 'em down as they are. Fingers was made before forks, as Shakespeare said.'

To his dismay Stanley saw the way his mother's face crumpled, and the way she looked down at the cup in her hands, biting hard on her lips. That was his mum all over . . . worry she could take, poverty she could cope with, heartbreak too, but kindness – that was another thing altogether. Kindness demoralized her. It seemed as if she was at a loss to know how to deal with it; so over the years she had armoured herself against it. Built a dirty great wall up around herself, making it plain that independence was all, that a kindness could only be accepted on her own terms.

'I'll get me purse,' she said and walked over to the top drawer in the sideboard.

'That'll be eightpence then, Mrs Armstrong,' Mrs Crawley added, knowing her neighbour too well to protest, and holding out her hand for the money. 'By gum, but there's been more steps mopped in this street today than I've seen in all the years I've lived here,' she told Stanley as he walked with her down the lobby to the front door. 'Any more news yet, love?'

He shook his head. 'Thanks for the chips, Mrs Crawley.' He hesitated. 'And thanks for not asking her any questions.' He jerked his head backwards.

Nellie Crawley's usually gruff voice was soft. 'How's she bearing up then, lad?'

'She'll have to get some sleep tonight or she'll crack. I'm

wondering if I ought to go down to the chemist's and ask him for something to give her before he closes.'

Nellie gave him a none too gentle punch in the shoulder. 'Don't waste your time, love. She wouldn't take it, and I wouldn't blame her. She'll want to know the minute there's any news, not be sound asleep under the influence of old Brandwood's herbal concoctions.'

'You're right, Mrs Crawley.'

She started to walk away. 'I'm *always* right, love. That's what gets me old man down, the fact that I'm always right. Now you go back in and see she eats them chips while they're hot.'

But when Stanley walked back into the living-room, his mother was weeping silently into the covered basin, holding it in her arms and rocking it backwards and forwards as if it were a child.

A child she had lost and never thought to see again.

Four

After Margaret and Gerald had left for the second-house pictures, holding hands and smiling at each other, Dorothy helped her mother with the dishes.

'Why don't you just stack them and leave them for Mrs Wilkinson to do in the morning?' Dorothy asked, and her mother said it wasn't in her nature to leave the kitchen a mess.

'You can always tell a woman's character by the tidiness or otherwise of her kitchen,' she said, and looking round at the gleaming surfaces and the hanging cups all facing the same way, Dorothy could see that this was true.

Phyllis's character was unblemished by a single idiosyncrasy; her thoughts faced all the same way like the blue and white cups; she spoke in clichés, and even they were polished to grammatical perfection before she uttered them. She seemed to have forgotten what she would have called the argument, and what Dorothy would have called the discussion about the film at the dinner table. She wore an apron with a frill round it, tied in an immaculate bow over her high-necked woollen dress, and she washed the dishes, using both rubber gloves and a little mop at the end of a stick, and talked about the hat she couldn't find for the wedding.

'It's no use. I'll have to decide on navy blue and get gloves and shoes to match. It's the done thing to have all one's accessories to tone,' she said, handing Dorothy a plate, 'in a darker shade than one's outfit. I think I'll get

44

that obliging little Mrs Pearson in the hat market to put a piece of ribbon in the same turquoise as my suit round the brim of my hat. What do you think?' She pushed a strand of hair away from her forehead with a rubber encased hand. 'I can't make up my mind whether it will give my outfit a put-together look, or make it appear a bit on the home-made side.'

Dorothy dragged her thoughts back from Inkerman Street and what might be going on there. 'It's a good job Gerald hasn't got any parents, or you'd be having to consult with his mother to make sure you didn't clash.'

Phyllis held up a fork to the light, considered it done, and slotted it into the big white jug on the draining board. 'The bride's mother always has first choice as to colours,' she said, very seriously. 'Poor Gerald. He's bound to feel it on the day, not having any relatives on his side. I've told him I'm arranging for some of ours to sit in the right hand pews to even things up a bit.'

Escaping with relief, Dorothy found her father upstairs in the big front bedroom exchanging his dark grey office jacket for the woollen cardigan he would have worn if Gerald hadn't been to dinner. Caught off-guard he looked tired almost to the point of exhaustion, with purple sagging pouches underneath his eyes, and a too hectic flush on his cheeks.

Dorothy came straight to the point.

'Dad. I was talking to Stanley Armstrong after school, and he told me that his sister Ruby, one of your weavers, is missing from home. He said the police had been to the mill. What do you make of it?'

Matthew Bolton yanked off his tie and gave her a shrewd glance from beneath his thick wildly curling eyebrows. No use trying to fob off this younger daughter of his with soothing words. Ask her dad a question and she got the answer straight, the way he knew she wanted it.

'Aye, it's a bad business, love. The police seem to be convinced in their minds that it isn't the usual case of a young girl leaving home and catching the train down to London to the bright lights, to show her folks something or other. They're tying it up with those two murders out Barnoldswick way last winter. They never caught whoever did them, and this case has all the hallmarks.' He fought a losing battle with his back collar stud. 'Pretty young girl with a recent history of secretiveness at home, telling lies where she goes of nights. But they can't prove a thing till they find . . .'

'A body,' Dorothy finished for him. 'Oh, Dad, it doesn't bear thinking about. Did you know Ruby Armstrong? I mean did you know her well enough to sum up what she was like as a person? Did she strike you as the sort of girl who would just clear off without saying a word? Her mother's a widow, you know.'

Matthew sat down heavily on the side of the double bed, so heavily that the box-spring mattress creaked in protest. Then he eased his feet out of his black shoes and into a pair of tartan house slippers. 'That's better, by heck. I try, lass. I try to keep tabs on all my weavers, but it's not like it were when your grandad ran the mill. He had time to take a fatherly interest in all of them, but it's as much as I can do to keep up with the administration side these days. As much as I can do to keep the looms running full time.' He stroked his chin. 'Aye, things have changed, and not for the better.' He put up a warning finger, then smiled. 'Thought I heard your mother coming up, but she's on the telephone. To your Auntie Ethel I shouldn't wonder. About this 'ere wedding.'

'The hat,' Dorothy said, and they smiled and nodded at each other.

'About this Ruby Armstrong girl, chuck. I can tell you one thing, and that is she's a good and quick worker. A bit of a different cup of tea from some of the other weavers. Not always shouting and shrieking to her mates all day.' He undid the top button of his trousers for further comfort. 'I remember like it were yesterday her mother bringing her to see me about two years ago when she first started in the weaving shed. Aye, she'd be about fourteen, just left school. I can see her now, standing there in the office in her navy-blue school mac, all big-eyed and shy, with her mother doing all the talking. More or less telling me that if I didn't look after her daughter she'd give me what for. Nice woman though. Just lost her husband. But a bit of a tiger. Wanting the best for her kids all along the line.'

'Stanley's won a state scholarship to Oxford,' Dorothy said, the pride in her voice giving her away. 'He's really clever, Dad. Special clever. You know?'

Matthew patted a place beside him on the bed.

'Special to *you*, love?'

Dorothy swallowed, hoping to avoid the hated blush. It worked sometimes, but not this time. 'I think so, Dad. We can talk, you know? Really say things that matter to each other, though we argue a lot of the time. He's always on the side of the under-dog.' She smiled. 'He says you're a bloated capitalist.'

Matthew roared with laughter. 'Does he now? Doesn't he know that's what he'll be when he's finished at yon university, and got himself a good job? There's nowt like a bit of education and a few letters behind a man's name for turning a Bolshie into one of us. You ask him if he'll be prepared to work along o' the masses when he can put them letters behind his name? I've seen many a man join the ranks of what he had considered to be the privileged, when education lifts him up amongst them.'

'He's not a Bolshie,' Dorothy said quickly. 'He just wants a better deal for everybody, regardless of creed, colour or class.'

'There were a chap called Jesus who wanted that,' Matthew said with a grim smile. 'But it don't work in practice, love. There'll always be them what comes out of the top drawer, and them what stays in the bottom. I'd like to meet this lad of yours sometime, but your mother worries about you, love. Some day, when you have kids of your own, you'll understand. That Mrs Armstrong and your mother, they're both tarred with the same brush, you know, if you think about it. Both wanting the best for their children, be it three looms in a weaving shed, or a place at university, or a husband who's passed his accountancy exams and talks posh.'

'You like Gerald, don't you, Dad?'

Dorothy's voice was no more than a whisper as she heard the telephone being replaced on its hook downstairs.

'Aye, I like him. He knows his job, I'll say that for him, though I've always felt that chaps who work with figures and the balancing of them are bound to be double dealers in a certain kind of way. All them accounts to make come out right, they're bound to push them one way or t'other if you think about it. He makes our Margaret happy, and he makes your mother happy, and that's all that matters it seems to me.'

Dorothy leaned up against him. 'You're a right softie, did you know that, Dad?'

He dropped a kiss on her hair. 'Get away with you, love. But think on what I've said now, and don't go getting yourself all involved before you've had time to grow up and see what other fish there might be in the sea first. All right?'

She smiled into his cardigan. 'And how many times has Mother told me that you and her were childhood sweethearts? That neither of you had ever known anyone else?'

'There were a war on, love, and I was sent to France right at the beginning. Things were different.'

'Of course,' said Dorothy.

'Matthew?' Phyllis's voice spiralled upstairs with more than a touch of hysteria in it. 'Can you come down a minute? I've just been talking to the man at The Pied Bull about the reception, and he says the room we've booked can't take more than seventy-five.'

Matthew got to his feet and shrugged his shoulders. 'Coming love. I'll nobbut be more than a minute.'

Then he put a hand on Dorothy's shoulder. 'Try and be

happy, love. That's all I want for you in the long run, and your mother too, if you could but realize it. This Ruby girl – she'll turn up, you'll see. Things have a way of turning out right, and this boy . . . remember he's got years of study in front of him, and you don't want to be missing out on all the fun you could be having by waiting for him or anything daft like that. Take my word for it, he'll change, and you'll change.' He walked towards the door. 'Let it slide, love. Just let it be till you're both old enough to know your own minds. You won't believe me now, but there's no hurry. No hurry at all.'

'Matthew!'

'Seems like there is!' he said, winking broadly at his daughter before he left the room.

Dorothy, alone in her room, with the sound of rain spattering the tall windows, and a wind sighing in the tall elm tree at the bottom of the back garden, tried to care whether Cromwell had been a good leader, and failed. What was the point in swotting for a Higher School Certificate she wasn't going to take anyway? And how could she possibly concentrate on events that had happened three hundred years ago when what was happening now filled every corner of her mind? If only Stanley was on the telephone, she could ring him and find out. If only she'd asked him to slip out somehow and ring *her*. '*Oliver Cromwell was a man of the people*,' she wrote then chewed the end of her pen and stared at the wallpaper until the triangles filled with baskets of flowers went out of focus.

At twenty past nine she went downstairs and joined her parents in the lounge.

Matthew turned to her with the smile that always lit his face whenever she came into a room. 'Want me to keep the wireless on, love? The talk's finished but it's Jack Hylton's band on next. You like him, don't you?'

'I don't mind,' she said, in such a dispirited way that her

mother laid her knitting down in her lap for a moment, and raised her eyes ceilingwards as if searching for patience.

Dorothy flopped down in a corner of the huge chintz-covered chesterfield. 'I am an awful worry to her,' she thought, with a sudden flash of perception. 'There's no communication between us at all. I can't play the part she wants me to play therefore we have nothing of consequence to say to each other. I am driving her mad tonight because I can't stop wondering what's going on in Inkerman Street, and I can't tell her the reason for my restlessness because I couldn't bear the things she'd say.'

Matthew hadn't told his wife about the missing weaver either. He shifted in his chair . . . Was he frightened of his own wife, or summat? Nay, never say that. But what he didn't want, after the long and tiring day at the mill, was a long discussion on Dorothy's friendship with yon poor lass's brother. He knew his Phyllis, and the mystery of the lost girl would be as nothing compared with the fact that Dorothy was involved, even indirectly.

'Love is the sweetest thing,' the band on the wireless was playing, and he couldn't resist giving his daughter a wink. Nay, dammit, what was more normal than thinking you were in love at seventeen? Maybe he was an abnormal father or something? He'd read somewhere that fathers were supposed to be jealous of their daughters' sweethearts. Well, all he could say was that he would be right glad to see both of them nicely married off. In white, of course, to please Phyllis, with him all dressed up in a top hat and tails like Sunny Jim on a packet of Force cereal, if that was the way she wanted it. . . .

'Sitting like that, slid down in your chair, is giving you a big stomach, Matthew,' she was saying now, so pretending he hadn't heard her, he closed his eyes and crossed his hands over the offending part of his anatomy. Dashed if he'd let a woman tell him how to sit in his own chair, his closed and shuttered expression said.

'I think I'll go up and have a bath,' Dorothy said, jumping up quickly and leaving the room before her mother could ask her please not to take all the hot water, as she never failed to do.

'What's the matter with her tonight?' she heard Phyllis ask before she got to the foot of the wide oak staircase.

Followed by her father's answering murmur, 'Leave her be, love. Just leave her be. . . .'

And she was lying back in the warm scented water when she heard the telephone ringing in the hall, and her father's measured tread as he went to answer it. She tried to hear what he was saying, and it was impossible, but he wasn't on long, and as she climbed out of the bath and started to dry herself, she heard a tap on the bathroom door.

'It's me, love,' her father said, and something in the sound of his voice made her wind the big pink towel round her body, tucking it in above her breasts. She opened the door and knew even as she saw his face that what she had been dreading had happened.

'It was the station, love,' Matthew told her, his red face redder than ever with concern for her. 'Now I don't want you going and upsetting yoursen, but I did promise to tell you the minute I heard owt.'

'They've found her, haven't they?' Dorothy bowed her head and stared down at her bare feet.

'It was Sergeant Bates, chuck. He promised to let me know.'

'Tell me, Dad.'

Matthew sighed, wanting to spare her, but knowing that he couldn't. 'Aye, they've found her body, love.' Then he reached for her and held her close, just as if she were a child again and he'd come up the stairs to rub her dry.

'She were in the Corporation Park. Strangled by the looks of her, the sergeant said. They've sent a man round to tell her mother . . . Aye, it's a bad business all right.'

Dorothy's voice came muffled from his shoulder.

51

'Where in the park, Father?'

Matthew turned his head and saw his wife coming along the landing. He shook his head at her. 'Keep out of this, please,' his expression said.

'By the duck pond, chuck. Hidden beneath a rhododendron bush. Seems a courting couple trying to shelter from the rain stumbled over something . . . Now then, hold up, love. Come on now, let's get you to your room and into bed.' He patted her shoulder with small comforting gestures.

But Dorothy was past comfort, past noticing or even caring that the pink towel was slipping down exposing one rounded breast. Her heart was pounding so loudly she felt she would suffocate with the sound of it.

'Oh, no! Oh no . . . I was talking to Stanley this afternoon in the park. We were sitting on the bench where we always sit, one of the benches near to the duck pond. We could have been sitting right where . . .' She raised an anguished face. 'Stanley was late, and then when he came he told me that Ruby hadn't come home all night. And all the time we were talking she could have been lying not far away. Perhaps not more than a few yards from us. He was actually telling me that she was missing, and all the time . . . Oh God! She might even have been alive. And we just sat there . . .'

Her voice rose high, wavering on the verge of lost control. Matthew shook her gently.

'She wasn't alive, lovey. Now stop torturing yourself with thoughts like that. You're letting that imagination of yours run away with itself again.' He was guiding her slowly along the wide landing as he talked to her in his flat voice, his northern accent becoming more pronounced as his concern for her increased.

'She were *dead*, chuck. There were nowt you could have done even if you'd found her. Now, come on, be a good girl and get into bed.'

Dorothy started to whimper, 'I've got to go to Stanley.

I'm his friend, and he'll want to see me. I can't just go to bed, I can't. Oh, Dad, how could anyone do that to a girl like Ruby Armstrong? She was so pretty. I've seen Gerald and Mr Sowerbutts talking to her down at the mill. Everyone liked her. They did, didn't they? She was a *good* girl. She didn't mess about with boys, Stanley told me. She'd only been out with the boy next door . . . oh . . . her poor mother . . .'

'Into bed, love.' Matthew motioned to his wife and nodded at the blue nightdress lying over the foot of the bed.

'Help her into that, lass, then go down and make a pot of tea. Strong and with plenty of sugar in it. I'll stay here.'

And for once in her life, Phyllis Bolton didn't argue. . . .

Matthew tucked his daughter into her bed, and pulled the satin eiderdown up round her shoulders. Her face was the colour of putty, and her eyes were staring at him, trying to make him understand.

'Take me down to Stanley's house, Dad. Please.'

He shook his head firmly. 'It wouldn't be right, love. Now listen to me. It's not the time for anyone else to be there, not tonight. This is a private time, both for Stanley and his mother. The police will be as kind as they know how to be, but there'll be things, unpleasant things to be done.' He hesitated, then went on: 'Someone will have to identify the . . . the body, and there'll be more questions. I doubt if anyone down there will see their beds tonight.' He knelt down awkwardly and took her hands in his own, squeezing them gently, trying to soothe, at a loss to know what to say, wondering just how far things had gone between his Dorothy and this boy, this *special* boy who would have to be more than a son to his mother this night.

'I'll take you in the morning,' he said, unable to bear the pleading in her eyes. 'First thing. I'll want to let Mrs Armstrong know that I'll help her in any way I can, and you can come with me. First thing.'

From downstairs came the sound of light voices in the hall, and the sound of Margaret's laughter, suddenly switched off as Phyllis told them what had happened.

Dorothy raised herself on one elbow, her blue eyes wide with distress. 'Don't let them come upstairs, Dad. Don't let them come near me. I couldn't bear to talk to them just now.'

'There'll nobody come near you, love,' Matthew said, rising stiffly from his knees and taking a cup of tea from Margaret as she started to walk into the room.

'Gerald wants to know if there's anything . . .' she began, and the look on her face turned to one of astonishment as her father turned her round and pushed her none too gently from the room.

'Tell Gerald . . . oh tell him to push off,' he said firmly and closed the door.

Five

The policeman stopped under a street lamp half way up Inkerman Street. Its yellow beam showed the serious set of his pointed features and the rain glistening on the folds of his cape. 'No use in stopping, Albert,' he told himself. 'What has to be done has to be done.' Then he walked with a heavy tread further up the street and knocked three times on the door of number twenty-seven.

By God, did it never do owt else but rain in this damned town? And what was he doing standing here? He ought to be going to bed like all the other occupants of the street. He glanced at the lighted upstairs windows and saw a face appear from behind the drawn curtains of the house directly opposite. Aye, the happenings of the day had given them something to talk about right enough. Something to take their minds off the dole queues and the worry for some of them as to where the next meal was coming from. He knocked again. . . .

When he heard the footsteps coming down the passage towards the door, he wished he could just turn and walk away. Run away, he meant really. Back down the sloping street with its flagstones glistening with rain, back to his own little semi-detached house out on the Manchester side of the town, where his wife would be waiting with a pint pot of cocoa, and the fire burning in the grate, and his new-born son asleep upstairs in his cot. Back to sanity, and back to normality.

The door opened, and the young man who stood back to

let him pass looked as if he hadn't slept for days. His eyes were bloodshot and sunk deep in his face – two dark holes that looked as if they'd been chiselled out of his flesh. He didn't speak, just preceded him down the darkened passage into the light of a living-room, where a woman sat by the fire, so still she might have been growing there.

The policeman took his helmet off and held it underneath his arm. 'Mrs Armstrong?'

'Aye.' Her voice was no more than a whisper.

He had to say it. Quickly too, there being no way of softening a blow like this. No way of leading up to it nicely. . . .

'Mrs Armstrong. I'm afraid I've brought bad news. We've found your daughter's body in the Corporation Park. At least her clothes and her description fit.' He turned to Stanley, the poor woman obviously having failed to take in what he was saying. 'I'd like you to come with me, lad, to make the necessary indentification.'

There, it was said, and oh, dear God, who in hell's name would want to be a policeman? This was a far cry from taking down details of lost cats and dogs, picking up Friday night drunks out of the gutter. They were both staring at him as if they hated his guts, as if it were his fault or something. If one of them didn't speak he'd have to say it all over again. He put the helmet down on the table. 'Mrs Armstrong?'

Then, to his horror, the still brooding statue of the little woman came to life. Making a sound like a kicked-in-the-belly animal, she put a hand over her mouth, got to her feet and ran out of the over-heated room.

He heard her retching and vomiting out in the back scullery, an abandoned sound, terrible in its lack of dignity, awesome in its total despair.

The boy standing by the table turned to follow her.

'I'll just go . . .' he said over his shoulder, and the policeman took a handkerchief from his pocket and wiped the rain and perspiration from his face.

'If she wants . . .' he began, but Stanley was already by his mother's side, watching helplessly as she vomited, then in between the bouts of vomiting, banged her head again and again on the stone slopstone.

To the end of his days he was never to forget the terrible sound of her forehead being dashed over and over on the unyielding stone. Banging, banging away in a frenzy of disbelief, as if she would knock the truth out of her mind, her active brain a riot of confusion.

'Mum . . .' he said, and tried to put his arms round her, but she knocked him away with a force that made him stagger back and clutch at the gas-stove to keep his balance.

'Mum! You'll hurt yourself.'

'No!' she was shouting. 'I'll not believe it. I'll not. Tell him to go away with his lies. Ruby's not dead. She'll come back home. I'll not listen to him. I'll not listen.'

Then she straightened up, turned around, and put both hands over her face, and as Stanley reached for her, he saw the blood running down between her fingers.

Dazed, moaning with a dreadful whimpering sound, his mother swayed, temporarily out of her mind with grief. Making no further protest when the policeman came and led her gently back to her chair by the fire. Kneeling by her side and wiping the blood from her head with his white handkerchief.

'Is there a neighbour, lad? A woman who could come in and be with her?' He spoke softly over his shoulder to Stanley.

'Mrs Crawley. I'll go and fetch her . . . It's only across the street, only a minute. I'll not be a minute . . .'

And reaching the front door, Stanley almost pulled it off its hinges with the force he used to get it open quickly enough.

'What can Mrs Crawley do?' a voice in his head seemed to be screaming over and over. He was not and never had been a swearer, his father having instilled in him the belief that there were enough words in the English language

57

without needing to curse, but now the voice was shouting: 'What can bloody Mrs Crawley do? What can *anyone* do?'

And they'd gone to bed. He could see the light on up-stairs. What right had they being in bed when his mother needed, when his mother. . . ? Stanley banged on the door as if the very hounds of hell were hard on his heels.

'Mrs Crawley! Mrs Crawley . . .'

But it was Mr Crawley who answered the door. Under-sized, shrivelled little Mr Crawley, with his indefinite features set anonymously in his forgettable face; a man so dominated by his wife that he hardly seemed to exist. He blinked at Stanley, and screwed up his face as if trying to place him. Half way through undressing for bed, he was trying to pull his dangling braces back over his shoulders, making ineffectual little grabs at them.

''Old on, lad. There's no call for thee to try to break door down.' Then he saw Stanley's face. 'Eh, lad, I didn't know it were thee. Come in with ee. I'll get 'er.' He went to the foot of the stairs, and shouted with surprising strength in his voice. 'Nellie! It's yon lad from across street.' He turned back to Stanley. 'Nay, lad. Come in out of the wet. It's a nasty neet all right.'

And moving like a machine, Stanley stepped inside.

Within minutes Mrs Crawley was there, the saviour of Inkerman Street, clattering her way down the uncarpeted stairs, with a coat thrown over a grey and trailing night-dress, her hair a-bristle with curling pins, and her sunken mouth proclaiming that her teeth were reposing elsewhere for the night.

'They've found her,' Stanley heard himself say. 'In the park. Me mum . . . oh, Mrs Crawley, can you come? I've got to go with the policeman, and she can't be left by herself.'

'Aye,' Nellie Crawley said, and started off down the lobby just as she was, leaving her husband hovering silently and uncertainly in the background.

'She might do herself an injury,' Stanley told her, as they

58

crossed the darkened street together. He looked up in apparent surprise to feel the rain on his face. 'But it's Ruby all right. They had a description of the clothes she was wearing.'

Mrs Crawley tripped over the kerb, and as Stanley put out an arm to support her he caught the smell of spirits on her breath.

'Poor bloody little sod,' she said, and he felt that his father would have understood.

'Aye, there's some bad buggers, there are 'n all,' Nellie said, pushing open the door of number twenty-seven, and stepping inside.

Apart from the deep purple bruises on her throat, Ruby Armstrong might have been sleeping. Her face had a waxen quality about it, and there was a leaf caught up in her dark curly hair.

Still moving as if in a dream, Stanley gently picked it out and let it fall to the ground.

'This is your sister? Ruby Armstrong?' The police sergeant's voice was quiet and filled with compassion. Nay, God damn it, he had a daughter at home about the same age as this poor lass. His fingers trembled as he held the sheet aloft. It didn't bear thinking about.

Stanley nodded. 'It's her all right.' Then, before the sheet fell into place over that still face, he touched the pale face gently.

'Goodbye, Ruby,' he said foolishly, and turned away.

And when it was over the police sergeant said they would see him home, but Stanley shook his head.

'It's not far.'

And the trams were still running, lumbering and rocking along the lines, dropping passengers in the middle of the road beneath their spider's web of wires. People were going home from the second-house pictures, peering through the steamed-up windows, rubbing at the glass with their hands.

The same people who would read of Ruby's death in the papers the next morning, gloat over the details, shudder when they thought for a tingling moment that it might have been them; might have been their daughter.

Stanley walked on, shoulders hunched, hands thrust deep in his pockets, slouching along, like one of the great army of unemployed, with all hope gone. But now his despair was even more terrible than theirs. Heedless of the rain soaking his dark hair, flattening it to his skull, thinking of his father, and remembering how Ruby had run down the street to meet him when he came home from work every evening at half-past five.

Thinking what his dad would have done to the man who had done this unbelievable, terrible thing.

Harry Armstrong had been a quiet man, not given to rages or violent turn of speech, but it seemed to Stanley as if he was there, walking beside him now, his thin face blazing with murderous anger.

'I'll swing for him that did it, so help me God,' he was saying, and his words found an ache in his son's heart and mind.

'Mum,' he promised, muttering to himself as he turned the corner into Inkerman Street, 'I'll not rest until they find him. I'll give up the scholarship, and work and stay with you. I'll find work somewhere. Anywhere. Just so long as I'm with you. It was all a bit too much like a dream anyway, me going to Oxford. You'll have to forget it, Mum. It just wasn't meant to be . . . that's all.'

Matthew stayed with Dorothy until she slept, a twitching sleep induced by weeping, and a subconscious desire, he guessed, to escape from the realization of what had happened. Tomorrow she would be as calm as a canal on a summer's day. That had always been Dorothy's way. Flying into storms of crying, getting it all over and done with, then settling down to the inevitable. He sighed and

60

made his way downstairs to where his wife and Margaret were sitting over a dying fire, the sherry decanter on the coffee table between them.

'Gerald's gone,' Margaret said, looking at her father with a hurt look on her face, remembering what he'd said upstairs, but making allowances for him.

'He talked very sensibly,' Phyllis said, 'and he's coming to pick Margaret up in the morning, because he thought you would most likely be wanting to go down and see that poor girl's mother. He can't get over it,' she added, staring down at the glass in her hands. 'We were going to make a pot of tea, but we felt like something stronger, didn't we, Margaret?'

'You never think a thing like this could happen in your own circle.'

Phyllis gave her elder daughter a swift glance. 'Well, not exactly in our own circle, dear, but I know what you mean. I expect you *will* have to go down there in the morning, Matthew?'

Matthew sat down in his chair, and rubbed his receding forehead wearily with the back of his hand. 'Aye, I'll be going down first thing. It's the least I can do.' He looked his wife straight in the eye. 'And I'll be taking Dorothy with me. Seems she's been seeing a lot more of that lad than we realized, and telling us lies all along the line.' Like that poor dead lass was telling *her* mother lies, he thought, shaking his head. 'From what she's told me I gather she's pretty fond of him – they met and talked this afternoon, not more than a few yards away from where they found the body. Now you know why she was so upset.' He sighed. 'Our Dorothy's a bit too young and a sight too vulnerable to cope with a situation like that. She's going to need all our understanding for the next few days; you know how she takes things too much to heart, always has.'

Phyllis exchanged a glance with Margaret, but before she could say anything, Matthew went on: 'Now lass, this isn't the time to quibble. The right or wrongs of whether she should have been meeting him on the sly don't seem to matter. Quibble now, make an issue out of it now and she's not likely to forgive us. Ever.'

His wife took a dainty sip from the sherry glass. 'All I was going to say, Matthew, *when* you give me a chance to speak, was that I feel sure you don't want Dorothy *involved* in this dreadful affair any more than I do.' She took another sip. 'I agree with you that she takes things very much to heart, coupled with this intense loyalty she has towards her friends, but I feel strongly that this time she needs protecting against herself.'

Margaret nodded, and Matthew knew that they had been discussing ways and means of making him see what they thought was sound sense. 'I never meant it that way,' he thought, 'but here we are, here we've always been, two sides. Me and Dorothy on the one side, and Margaret and her mother on the other.'

'There'll be reporters, Father, and you know what they can be like. You're involved already with the poor girl working at the mill, but once they find out that Dorothy is friendly with the brother, can't you imagine what they'll make out of it? There hasn't been a murder case they could get their teeth into for ages, apart from the two unsolved ones out Barnoldswick way.'

'Four years ago,' Phyllis said, 'there was a woman in Agincourt Street who killed her husband with the coal shovel when he came home from the public house one night. Too drunk to defend himself, they said.' She sniffed. 'Agincourt Street's round the corner from Inkerman Street, isn't it?'

The inference was deliberate, and Matthew felt his throat contract with a kind of pain. All right then, he was allowing himself to get emotionally involved already; he was caring too much, but if the alternative was to sit there sipping sherry and calmly thinking out ways and means of disconnecting yourself from what had happened – well, he knew the way he'd choose to be. God damn it, people were *people*, weren't they, regardless of whether they come from Agincourt Street or Buckingham Palace? He found he was clenching his fists so that the nails dug into the palms of his hands. . . .

'This is a young and decent girl who has been brutally murdered,' he said, trying to control the pitch of his voice. Phyllis was always accusing him of talking too loud. 'It could have been you, Margaret. Or Dorothy. Aye, it might well have been our Dorothy as it seems she's been meeting this lad in the park every day after school.' He gave up the attempt to speak quietly. 'And do you know why she's been meeting him in the park, in a secluded place, on the sly, then? Because she knew she couldn't bring him back to this house. Because every time she tried to mention his name her mother's nose wrinkled as if there were a bad smell under it. Because she wasn't prepared to face the schemozzle of bringing her friendship out into the open. That's why.'

Phyllis put her glass down on the low table, saw that it had left a ring, and took it up again to wipe the rounded base with her handkerchief. 'I expect, Matthew,' she said, obviously determined to keep her own voice low to show the difference, 'I expect you have conveniently forgotten that if this poor young girl's mother had been more concerned about the company her daughter had been keeping, this ghastly thing might never have happened? At least Dorothy knows that we disapprove of her meeting this young man, and this, this dreadful thing that's happened, may show her that we could have been right.'

'You mean that murders don't happen in the best of circles?'

'I mean, Matthew, that the young girl in question probably had a far different set of values from the ones we've set our two girls. They think differently, and you know that's true. They live in these hard times by a system of a communal pooling of their wages, no planning, no system. Why, during the General Strike a friend of mine told me that the miner's wives were dressed like middle-class women.'

Now Matthew really lost his temper. 'What in the name of thunder are you talking about woman? No wonder there's bloody revolutions! What the hell have the miners' wives in the Strike got to do with what we're talking about?'

Phyllis was quite unruffled. 'Then there's the wedding to think about.' She smiled a small tight smile. 'It wouldn't look good now, would it, if the chief bridesmaid was pointed out as the girl who was friendly with that boy whose sister was murdered in the Corporation Park? You have a certain position to keep in the town, Matthew, and things get twisted. People *exaggerate*.'

Matthew could take no more. Going over to the sideboard, he took out a bottle of whisky. He got to the door and came back for a glass. 'I'm going to bed, lass. Otherwise I might be tempted to say something I might be sorry for.' He turned, the bottle swinging from his podgy fingers. 'And in the morning, Dorothy's coming with me when I go to see that poor widow woman.' More telling words failed him . . . 'So put that in your pipe and smoke it,' he said, closing the door none too gently behind him.

But when Phyllis came up to bed ten minutes later, the whisky he'd drunk had done no more than soften his mood. Made him see both sides of the pictures, the way he always did when confronted with a problem at the mill. It had been this quality, recognized by his influential friends years ago, that had made them try to persuade him to let his name go forward as a potential magistrate, and perhaps paradoxically it had been this very quality that had made him refuse.

'Nay, but I'd be no good at playing God,' he'd said. 'And besides I haven't the time to spend sitting on my backside on the Bench. Nay, leave that to them what've got themselves sorted out better than what I have.'

And in somebody's book, Phyllis was a good woman, a marvellous hostess and a conscientious mother. No doubt about that. So, seeing her set face, and sensing her air of injured martyrdom, he put his arm round her when she got into bed beside him. 'I know you mean well, lass. You always do, especially when it comes to thinking what's best for the girls. But this is something far more important than worrying what folks might think. And even a local murder's a nine days' wonder, don't forget. Come June and the wedding, and it will all be a thing of the past. The police will catch the man who did it, and that will be that. But our Dorothy will find it hard to forgive you if you try to stop her standing by a friend at a time like this. Other folks might forget the murder, but she'll never forget your attitude.' He tried to pull her closer to him, and kissed her clumsily on her cheek.

'The smell of whisky makes me feel sick,' Phyllis said, but she didn't turn over, and he knew that for the time being he had won. For the time being at least. . . .

There was only a tiny mention of the murder in the *Manchester Guardian* when he picked it up off the mat early the next morning, but the *Daily Mail* had spent a hectic night scrapping its first page, and had printed the details in banner headlines.

YOUNG MILL GIRL BRUTALLY MURDERED, it said, and Matthew sighed. This would put the cat among the pigeons all right. Heavens knew what the *News of the World* would make of it on Sunday when more details had been released by the police. He could see it now, with a photograph of Ruby Armstrong's three looms in the weaving shed, and on-the-spot interviews with her mates. He imagined the excitement it would bring into *their* drab lives, with every one of them claiming to be the dead girl's best pal.

He took the papers up into the bathroom with him whilst he shaved, in what he knew was a vain attempt to prevent Phyllis seeing them. He wished, not for the first time since he had married, that his wife was the kind of woman who stayed in bed till he'd got off to work. But that wasn't Phyllis's way at all.

The routine never varied. He had the use of the bathroom first, whilst she washed at the wash-stand in the bathroom. Then Margaret and Dorothy took turns in the bathroom, and by the time they got downstairs, Phyllis was there, fully dressed in tweed skirt and jumper, pearl earrings screwed into the lobes of her ears, and her immaculate hair and the red mark across her forehead proclaiming to the discerning that she had slept the night securely enmeshed in a hair-net.

It was orderly, organized, and calculated to send a man off to his work with the feeling that, whatever the day in front of him might bring, the start to his day had been as devoid of stress as a paddle in the sea at Blackpool.

But this was no ordinary day. He winced as the razor slipped and nicked a piece out of his chin, then with a strip of lavatory paper sticking to the small cut, he walked back along the wide landing to his room, with the bed already turned down ready for Mrs Wilkinson's ministrations, and the bottle of whisky, and the glass he'd used, taken away, so that it could never be said that Mr Bolton drank in bed. . . .

And Dorothy was pale, but composed, just as he had prophesied she would be, and Margaret was late sitting down at the table, having spent longer on her face and her hair than usual. Phyllis was determinedly saying nothing.

'Two strong wills out to please themselves,' she had told the bacon as she flipped it over in the frying-pan. Two rashers each, with the eggs broken into a cup first. 'So what is the point of *me* saying anything?' Besides, Gerald was coming round to pick Margaret up, and heaven forbid that he would think they were the sort of family who made bother over the breakfast table. He had hinted vaguely about having had a nanny when he was a small boy.

'I can just imagine him as a dear little red-haired Christopher Robin, can't you?' she had asked her sister Ethel, who had gone home and told her husband Raymond that she thought Phyllis was getting carried away.

'You'd think their Margaret was marrying into royalty,' she'd sniffed.

He rang the bell just as Phyllis was carrying the plates through into the dining-room.

'That smells good, Mrs Bolton,' he said, smiling.

He was wearing a suit she hadn't seen before in a dark blue cloth, with a matching waistcoat, and his hair, flattened to his head with brilliantine, shone a darker red in the sunshine streaming through the high window in the hall. Margaret, who had let him in, kissed him on his closely shaven cheek, and thought he looked and smelled delicious.

'Don't tease Dorothy this morning,' she whispered to him. 'You've seen it in the paper about the beastly park murder? You remember I told you she was friendly with the girl's brother? Well, Father is taking her with him when he goes to the house. Mother and him had words about it last night.'

'Beastly business all right,' Gerald said, and followed her into the dining-room.

'Cup of tea, Gerald?'

Phyllis raised the pot and smiled at him. 'I do believe we might be getting some warmer weather at last. It says on the wireless that it's going to rain later, but I refuse to believe it.'

Gerald shook his head. 'No tea for me, thank you, Mrs Bolton. I'll just sit here and look at the papers if you don't mind.' And he took them from the sideboard where Matthew had hoped they might lie until he'd left the house.

'Aye, it's in,' he said, in answer to his wife's raised eyebrows. 'Trust the *Mail* to be quickest off the mark.'

'Beastly business,' Gerald said, reading the account avidly as they ate. 'Don't feel you have to hurry back to the mill, Mr Bolton. I can cope with anything that might crop up, and fob the police off if they try to disrupt things too much.'

Matthew smiled wryly, wondering what old Tom Sowerbutts, who had worked at the mill as under-manager since his father's time, would have to say to that. Wondered, not for the first time, if Tom's decision to retire at the end of the year had anything to with the arrival of the young accountant from London.

'New brooms sweep clean, Mr Bolton,' he'd said when Gerald's method had clashed with his own well-tried schemes. 'And never let it be said that I clung on when my time came to go. Besides, the wife and me have set our minds on a bungalow at St. Annes. It'll be nice for the grandchildren to come and spend their school holidays with us – all them sand-dunes to play hide-and-seek in, and Blackpool not more than a tram ride away.'

'We won't be stopping down Inkerman Street, just calling there,' Matthew told Gerald. 'It's just the least I can do to offer to help in any way I can.' He folded his white starched napkin up and rolled it into the right shape for the silver ring. 'Finished, Dorothy, love?'

And in spite of his warning glances, Phyllis followed them to the door, handing her husband his trilby, and telling Dorothy to come straight back with Philips in the car.

'I won't feel safe with you out on the streets till they've caught that man,' she said, and flushed as Dorothy gave her an unexpected kiss on the cheek.

'Thanks a lot, Mother, for not going on about it. If I . . . if I can see that I'm in the way, I won't even go in . . . it's just that I want Stanley to know that I'm . . . that I . . .'

Phyllis counted ten to stop herself from saying that surely a nicely worded letter would have done just as well, but in any case Mrs Wilkinson was coming up the path clutching the inevitable basket, and whatever Phyllis might have said was certainly not for *her* ears.

And to anyone walking down the tree-lined road that spring morning, with the sunshine lying dappled on the wide pavement, and with Philips holding the door of the car open as his employer and his daughter climbed in, there was nothing to suggest that life in the big house wasn't going on in its usual serene way.

'Good morning, Mrs Bolton,' Mrs Wilkinson said as she made her way round the back of the house to the side door.

'Good morning, Mrs Wilkinson,' Phyllis answered, waving as the car reversed into the road.

Then she closed the door and walked into the kitchen where Mrs Wilkinson was tying the strings of her flowered apron behind her back, and saw the *Daily Express* reposing in the basket on top of the fur-trimmed bedroom slippers.

'That poor little lass,' Mrs Wilkinson said, sitting down on a kitchen chair to ease her feet out of her bunion-shaped black lace-ups. 'To think that your Dorothy is so friendly with her brother! It brings it home don't it? – when you actually know the family what's involved. I could see how pale she was, poor lass, she must be right cut up about it. Did she know the sister – the one what's been murdered – as well?'

Phyllis closed her eyes for a moment. It was beginning already. . . .

Six

'You've been to Stanley's house before, have you, love?' Matthew Bolton's voice was gentle. This was not the time for recriminations, or even for questions, and the way he phrased it made it sound more like a statement of fact.

Dorothy shook her head. She looked scared half way to death, as if what she was doing was a tactless embarrassment, but had to be done all the same. Like strangers gatecrashing somebody's funeral, Matthew thought grimly. He patted her knee.

'I'm not trying to pry, chuck.'

She forced a smile. 'I know that, Father, but Stanley's mother knows about me. She's told him off many a time for not being more open about being friendly with me. She asked him was he ashamed of me, or something?'

Matthew's mouth turned up at the corner. Aye, he could just imagine Mrs Armstrong saying that. She would see nowt wrong with her son being friendly with, or courting, a mill owner's daughter. She'd reckon her Stanley was doing Dorothy a favour . . . he'd come up against that fierce kind of pride many a time in his dealings with his workers at the mill. He didn't suppose Ada Armstrong would turn a hair of her black head if her Stanley took the King's daughter back for tea. And that was something Phyllis would *never* understand. Pride to her was based on possessions – what a man had, not what he was. Change a man's accent and his mode of dress and his status in life matched. Nay, Phyllis would never understand. He breathed deeply, staring

70

straight forward, transfixed, at nothing. What was it his father used to say?

'Do what's right, lad, and there's no one in the whole world better than thee. Allus remember that.'

They were turning now into Marston Road, a long road with the houses, though terraced, of Victorian respectability. Each with its own flight of steps, some of them made of dark red and yellow tiles, adding a note of almost Continental cheerfulness. Here lived the white-collar workers of the town. The clerks, the shop managers, the printers and compositors, with unleafing bushes in the tiny iron-railed front gardens, and if they were lucky, the box-room plumbed in as a bathroom. Matthew was pleased to see that Dorothy was leaning forward, staring out of the car window with interest. Seeing how the other half live, Phyllis would have said.

'Do you know, I've never been along here before? Isn't that awful? I've lived here all my life and I've never even been this way.'

The part of her that was all Phyllis was deciding privately that these houses weren't bad at all. One of them had a striped awning over the front door, almost a replica of the one Philips would be fitting over their own polished front door, should the sun shine for more than two days running.

But Philips was signalling right now and turning the car into a much narrower street, and therè, far below them, was a panoramic view of the town, its thousands of chimney pots on thousands of roofs lit to a mellow softness by the early morning sun, its tall mill chimneys pointing black fingers into the blue sky.

Here, as the car moved slowly down the steep slope, the houses huddled closely together, front doors opening straight on to flagged pavements. Women, down on their knees on pieces of matting, were mopping doorsteps, edging them with a thick line of yellow-stone, wiping over a semi-circle of flags directly in front of their own door. Throwing pails of water over the entire frontage, then

71

sweeping the water into the gutter with long-handled brushes. Standing on straight-backed chairs to clean the windows with wash-leather bundles, the more daring sitting out of the top windows, clinging on with one hand and feverishly rubbing away with the other.

'It's the next street, Mr Bolton.'

The back of Philips's neck betrayed his ill-concealed excitement at what was going on, by taking on the hue of a ripe tomato. After all, as he was to tell Vera that evening, going to the house of a murder victim was not the sort of thing everybody did every day. It had upset him, of course it had, but all the same, there was a sense of importance and even of excitement at being involved, even if only indirectly. Like all the people who had claimed to be patients of Dr Crippen. . . . He shuddered pleasurably.

But if Philips had been expecting to have to beat off crowds of reporters, or avid sightseers round the door of 27 Inkerman Street, he was doomed to disappointment. Death was respected and given its fair due in streets like Inkerman Street. Now that it was common knowledge that Ruby Armstrong was dead, the flag-moppers and step-stoners were at the backs of their houses, doing their gossiping over the yard walls, or standing in little groups beneath the lines of flapping washing in the cobbled backs. Front doors were closed, and some of the neighbours, in a gesture of sympathy, had drawn their long curtains, giving the short steep street a closed and shuttered appearance.

Philips parked the black car at the kerb, and before he could get out to open the rear door, was told to stay where he was.

'We'll not be long,' Matthew said, holding out his hand to Dorothy. Then, crossing the pavement, he raised the iron knocker set high in the door of twenty-seven, and gave three short raps.

'I won't know what to say . . .'

Dorothy turned a worried face towards him, looking, at that moment, far younger than her seventeen years. 'To say

72

we're sorry seems so . . . so inadequate.'

'Just coming's enough, love,' Matthew whispered, hearing the sound of footsteps down the uncarpeted passage behind the door. 'It's you coming what he'll appreciate.'

And when Stanley opened the door, and she saw his thin, suffering face, there was no need for words. To her dismay, tears sprang to his eyes as he opened the door wide for them to pass, and Matthew left them there, staring at each other with a mute and touching obvious affection. By God, but they're really smitten with each other, he thought as he found his own way through into the living-room.

Ada Armstrong was sitting by the inevitable fire, wearing a black cardigan over a navy-blue dress, her face as white as a corpse's, her hands for once idle in her lap. Her lack of surprise at seeing him standing there by the big square table, covered now with a maroon velour cloth, told him that she was in a state of complete and utter shock.

Matthew put his hat on the table. 'Good morning, Mrs Armstrong,' he said. 'I've come to tell you that, if there's owt I can do, tha's only to speak.' He went over to her and touched her gently on her shoulder. 'Tha remembers me? Matthew Bolton, from the mill?'

She nodded, but didn't speak. It was going to be harder than he'd imagined. He put an envelope on the table next to his hat.

'Tha'll be needing this, Mrs Armstrong.' He tapped it with a finger. 'There's folks might think I'm being tactless at a time like this, but I've never been one for keeping me mouth shut when to open it might help. And I don't suppose tha's much put by.'

'Put by?' she said, and the pale lips in the dead-white face lifted just a fraction at the corners.

Matthew moved over to a chair, and lifting the tails of his black overcoat, he sat down. By the gum, but it was hot. What with the sun slanting in through the window and that great fire roaring away up the chimney, already he could feel the beads of perspiration standing out on his

73

forehead. She read his thoughts.

'Three buckets of coal, all left outside 'back door. Folks is very kind.'

'Aye, you find your friends. . . .' Matthew nodded. 'And I'm going to tell that lad of yours to come to me for owt you might need . . .'

She looked him straight in the eye, then glanced at the envelope on the table. 'I'll not insult you by refusing, Mr Bolton. You're a good man, but our Stanley will see to things. He's finished all his exams so he'll be stopping off school till after the . . . the funeral.' She tilted her head bravely. 'He might only be a lad, but he's doing what has to be done.'

'This is Dorothy, Mum.'

Stanley came into the room with Dorothy following, and led her over to his mother's chair. 'She's come to see if there's anything she can do.'

'Like running errands, Mrs Armstrong,' Dorothy said, the words she had been rehearsing deserting her completely. 'There must be food you need . . . and I'll know better what to get than Stanley. Or writing letters for you . . .' She faltered. Gosh, that was a silly thing to say. Now this little woman who was staring steadily into that enor-rious fire would think *she* thought that she couldn't write. 'Or ironing,' she added desperately, causing Matthew, even in spite of the circumstances, to raise an eyebrow in surprise, as never, to his knowledge, had he seen his younger daughter wielding an iron.

Ada Armstrong nodded, still without looking at Dorothy. She didn't want to look at her, if the truth were known. This was a young girl, not much older than her Ruby had been, a pretty girl with a soft and tender voice, and hair as fair as Ruby's had been dark, curling sweetly round her bonny face.

And she was alive.

And Ruby was dead. . . .

'We have a good neighbour,' Stanley said quickly, step-

74

ping in for his mother. 'She's out doing a bit of shopping now. She says she'll take over me mother's commitments till . . . till . . .' He stopped talking and stared at the floor.

'There's to be a post-mortem. At two o'clock this afternoon,' Ada said then, speaking directly to Matthew. 'He's going down . . . I wanted them to bring her home, but it's not . . . it's just not possible.'

'They'll get him, Mrs Armstrong,' Matthew said. 'They're clever, the police are. They'll leave no stone unturned. Aye . . . Aye,' he said again, standing up and reaching for his hat.

'That won't bring our Ruby back though, will it?' She was rocking the chair gently, backwards and forwards, her face as expressionless as the poker resting in its stand in the hearth.

Again Matthew pressed her shoulder, then he turned to Dorothy. 'I'll be waiting in the car,' he said, and walked out of the room, down the brown-painted passage and out into the street, conscious of twitching curtains as Philips scrambled out and held the door open for him to climb inside. He was conscious of a dismaying sense of anticlimax. He'd said it all wrong. Whatever he'd come to say, he'd said it all wrong. It was all very well feeling sorry from a distance, *sincerely* feeling sorry and wanting to help. But it wasn't brought home to you that what had happened had happened to real people; could have happened to Dorothy. Or Margaret. Damn it, it could have been Phyllis sitting there in a chair having to listen to what was practically a stranger mouthing stupid offers of help. He should have sent the money round from the mill with a messenger . . . and it weren't enough, nowhere near enough. The way she'd looked when he'd said that bit about having a bit put by. Phyllis was right in some ways. There was a big gap, a bloody big gap, and nowt could bridge it. Matthew sat there, brooding into the top of his hat which he'd laid across his knees.

'I'll come again if I may, Mrs Armstrong,' Dorothy was

saying. 'May I come again?'

Ada nodded. 'If you want to, lass. Our Stanley'll be glad to see you.'

'Even if I couldn't care less' her expression said, and overcoming with difficulty a sudden urge to bend and kiss the pale cheek, Dorothy turned away and, choking back tears, walked out of the room.

Behind the front door Stanley put his arms round her. 'I'll not forget you coming,' he whispered. 'It's not that she doesn't like you; it's just that . . .'

'I'm not Ruby,' Dorothy finished for him. Then, as her heart seemed to be physically swelling with emotion inside her, she looked up and gently touched his hair. 'I love you,' she said. 'If it helps to know that, I love you, Stanley.'

Then she was outside in the street, running round the car to get in beside her father, the tears streaming down her cheeks.

The car broke down two streets away from the mill, the engine dying with a splutter as Philips changed into bottom gear. So leaving it standing black and square at the side of the road, they walked the rest of the way, three abreast, Matthew muttering that he'd give that garage what for when he telephoned. 'You can't trust nobody to do a proper job these days,' he said, then turned to Philips. 'It might be better if you went there, now, in person. If I get through it'll only be that bit of a lad in the office. Come back and tell me what they say, and tell them I want that car on the road by this afternoon. And don't take no for an answer,' he shouted as Philips touched the neb of his cap and crossed over the street.

'From the looks of that sky it's going to rain,' he said. 'Shines before seven, rain by eleven. It never fails.'

He glanced sideways at his daughter. Her eyes and the tip of her nose were red, but she seemed to have regained some of her composure. He said impulsively, wanting to comfort, 'He seems a nice lad, that Stanley. I'll talk it out with your mother, chuck . . . we . . . we've been playing it all wrong it seems to me. From now on he can come to the house whenever he wants to. I don't want you hanging about in the park on your own waiting for him, and besides, things is different from when I was a lad. Then, if a young man came to call, it meant but one thing, that wedding bells were in the offing. There were no such thing as having a member of the opposite sex as a *friend*.' He looked at her hopefully, but she said nothing. 'Aye, we've got to move with the times.'

'Mother will never see it that way.' Dorothy's tone was bitter. 'And it had to take his sister's murder before *you* could feel that way.' She knew she was being more than unfair, but she couldn't help it. It was a dramatic statement, and high drama seemed to be the order of the day.

Gerald Tomlin came to the door of the office to greet them. *Shining* with importance, Dorothy told herself.

He fingered his tie as he spoke. 'They've only just left – the police that is, Mr Bolton. I told them you'd be back within the hour, but they couldn't wait.' He raised a hand and smoothed back his already smooth hair. 'They've got a chappie over, a detective sergeant, and he says they're going to start a door-to-door enquiry, checking on every single man in the town. Wanting to know his whereabouts on the night in question.'

Matthew was already shrugging himself out of his overcoat. 'Good. That shows they mean business then. I reckon they'll have him within the week.' Then he sat down at his desk and pulled a sheaf of papers towards him, his mind on the busy day ahead. 'That rain? Aye, I thought as much; tha'll have to get used to the sun being a bit shy up here, Gerald, it doesn't hang about for long.' He read the first letter on top of the pile. 'Seen this one, Gerald? Is this all they can say in answer to the stinker we sent them last week?' He pinched the bridge of his nose between thumb and forefinger. 'Bless my soul, we've got to get you home some way, love. I promised your mother I'd send you back with Philips.'

Dorothy walked over to the window, and watched the rain as it bounced up from the greasy cobbles. She could hear the noise of the looms from the weaving sheds. A sort of muffled banging and clattering. Tolerable at that distance, but to the weavers standing at their looms? A hissing jet of steam came from the side of one of the tall chimneys. At twelve o'clock the loud hoarse hooter would go, and the mill workers would stream out, going home for their dinner, the girl weavers arm in arm, the cotton fluff thick in their hair and on their clothes, and the men walking quickly, avoiding the little groups of men standing idle on the street corners. To have a job was to set a man apart. Stanley had said that. She wrote her initial on the dirty window pane. How filthy everything was, filthy and noisy, the grime was in the very air. No wonder the women, at the first sign of sunshine, had feverishly tried to clean the outside of their houses. No wonder Ruby Armstrong had deceived her mother to meet a man who had perhaps told her that he loved her, promised her he would take her away from all this . . . She'd never had a holiday, Stanley had said. Never, as Dorothy did once a year, in the July wakes week, travelled first class down to Eastbourne and walked across the springy turf of Beachy Head, feeling the wind whipping the colour into her cheeks as she stared down at the sea pounding the rocks far below. And now, at sixteen, Ruby was dead . . . Dorothy crossed out her initial with a fierce and steady cross, the unfairness, the bitter injustice of it choking her throat again with tears.

'It's only a cloudburst,' she said without turning round. 'There's a patch of blue in the sky over there. I'll wait a while, then walk.' She bent her head, unconscious of her father's pitying glance, and the way he shook his head at Gerald Tomlin. 'I'd go straight to school if I'd thought to put my uniform on, but I'd rather wait till Monday really before I go back. They . . . the girls in my form will be talking about it, and asking me things, and I couldn't bear it. I wouldn't know what to say.'

'I'll run her home, Mr Bolton.'

Gerald was behind her, his hand on her shoulder; she could smell the lavender tang of the brilliantine on his hair. 'I can be back in half an hour,' he said.

There wouldn't have been any point in arguing, Dorothy told herself, as she lowered herself into the passenger seat of the red sports car, keeping a tight hold on her skirt. It would have been impossible to explain that she would have liked nothing better than to have walked all the way home alone in the rain. Feeling it beating down on her head, soaking through her blazer, and ruining her new patent-leather shoes. The last thing in the world she wanted was Gerald Tomlin's company; being shut in like this with him, in close and intimate proximity was making her flesh crawl. I must be *allergic* to him, she thought hysterically.

No, if she'd refused, her father would have thought she was mad, as well as rude, and Gerald, sitting beside her, hands resting lightly on the steering wheel, would have interpreted it as another snub. Before starting the car he had lit a cigarette, holding it lightly between his fingers. Without asking her did she mind, as Stanley would have done.

And Mother thinks he's perfect, she thought childishly.

There was one thing you had to admit, and that was his expertise in driving his car. Even with the cigarette in his hand he drove swiftly and smoothly, almost as if the car was an extension of himself. Already the rain was slackening off; umbrellas were being lowered, headscarves untied, and women on their way back from the shops were telling each other that they never knew what to wear these days, what with the weather being the way it was.

'See, the rain's stopped. I could have walked after all,' Dorothy said, and was slightly ashamed at the reproachful look Gerald gave her.

'*Be honest now, you don't give him a chance,*' she told herself silently, then felt even more ashamed as a woman holding a small child by the hand stepped off the pavement without looking. Jamming on the brakes, Gerald put out his left arm in an instinctive gesture of protection to prevent her from being thrown forward against the windscreen.

'You have to be prepared for that,' he told her. 'Sorry if it startled you, love.'

The unexpected endearment, coupled with his genuine concern for her made her feel more ashamed than ever, and his next words made her actually squirm in the low seat with embarrassment.

'You and me seem to have got off on the wrong foot somehow, Dorothy. I wish there was something I could do about it.' Stopping to allow a small group of women board a tram, he turned to her and smiled. 'Am I such a terrible fellow?'

There was nothing she could say to that, and when, turning off the main road, he stopped the car, pulling into the kerb and switching off the engine, she found she could not meet his eyes.

'Perhaps it's time we had a little talk,' he said, winding down the window and throwing the cigarette stub into the road. He put a hand lightly over her own. 'Maybe this is the wrong time . . .' He squeezed her hand gently. 'It must have been simply ghastly for you this morning. It was a very brave thing to do, going to see Stanley and his mother.' Another pat on the hand. 'Have the police come up with anything fresh? They seem to be baffled by the total absence of clues.'

'There's to be a post-mortem this afternoon,' she said in a low voice.

Letting go of her hand he reached for another cigarette. 'Ah, well, I suppose that was inevitable.' He busied himself with his lighter. 'Did you know the . . . the dead girl personally, Dorothy? What I mean is, would you have said she

80

was the confiding type? Likely to tell her brother anything that might help the police?'

She shook her head. 'I can't remember ever having *spoken* to her, and no, that's the awful thing, she must have kept her meetings with whoever did this dreadful thing quite private.'

He blew out a stream of smoke, then wafted it away from her face, apologizing. 'But you know the brother *very* well?'

There was a teasing quality in his voice now, and she blushed. 'Margaret must have told you.'

'Margaret tells me everything. That's how it should be.' He smiled at her. 'I love your sister very much, you know that, don't you? And I intend to love and cherish her for ever. You know that too, don't you?'

Dorothy nodded, wishing that he would start the car again and drive on.

'And because I feel that way, I find the fact that her little sister doesn't like me, *very* hard to bear.'

'But I don't . . .'

'I know what you're thinking. You're surprised that a bloke like me who comes from south of the Wash should be so outspoken. You think that you and your fellow Lancastrians have the monopoly in calling a spade a spade. That I, because of my public school background, should be all stiff upper lip. But you could be wrong, Dorothy Bolton, with your bright gold hair, and those blue eyes that look at me and find me wanting.'

She stretched out her legs and studied her shoes. He had the most beautiful voice, she would say that for him, and perhaps, maybe she hadn't really been fair to him? But he was holding her hand again, and she wished he would take it away. There were little tufts of ginger hair sprouting from between the knuckles, and something about his touch that repelled her. How *could* Margaret find him so fascinating? She forced herself to meet his eyes, and was immediately thrown into confusion by the wealth of sadness she saw reflected there.

This man, this red-haired stranger who had come into their lives, was unsure of himself. He was pleading with her to like him, as if it mattered a great deal, as if he couldn't bear her rejection of him. She began to pleat her skirt with her free hand.

'Has it ever occurred to you that I am not the over-confident type you obviously think I am, Dorothy? That coming up here and finding Margaret, and being accepted into your family gives me such happiness that I am afraid? Yes. Afraid, positively scared.' Dorothy smoothed out the pleats she had made, then started again.

'My father was a colonel in the Indian Army, and when I was a small child, I was left in the care of an aunt and uncle who gave me everything but love. Then, as soon as I was old enough, I was sent away to school, and because my aunt was by then an invalid – nerves mostly, which didn't help – I spent the shorter hols in the charge of school matrons.' His eyes, surely the palest of blue she had ever seen, twinkled at her. 'Why do all school matrons have busts like upholstered shelves and fierce moustaches, I wonder?' He closed his eyes for a moment, then went on: 'When my parents were killed I was told of their deaths so casually that the person who told me might have been passing the time of day. And from then on it was nothing but a lonely determination to pass my accountancy exams; a constant fight against the temptation to give it all up and get a job which would help me to live at a decent standard.' He puffed vigorously at the cigarette. 'I don't want to bore you with a description of what the past ten years have been like, but all I can say is that coming up here and falling in love with Margaret, and being accepted as part of your family has shown me that my own personal barometer is rising at last.' He touched the tip of her nose lightly with his finger.

'And the only fly in the ointment is me?' Dorothy whispered, but she was half smiling, and did not cringe away as he leaned forward and kissed her cheek.

'You *frightened* me,' he said, 'with your way of looking at me with those lovely eyes narrowed into suspicious slits, as if you were determined to think the worst of me. And I've been a bit of a bounder in my time, I admit. Girls and booze you know, but nothing serious . . .'

He knows that I saw him flirting in the mill yard, Dorothy thought, and he's trying to tell me that all that's past. . . .

'But as soon as I fell in love with Margaret and she with me, the slate was wiped clean,' he was saying now. 'So do you think we could start again, Dorothy, so soon to be my sister? From this very moment?'

Then, without waiting for a reply he switched on the engine and pulled swiftly and smoothly away from the kerb.

And then they were driving up the road which ran at the side of the park, and he was putting his foot down hard on the accelerator.

And for some unknown unearthly reason Dorothy found that she was thinking about her much loved Grandfather Bolton, with his waxed moustache and the wrapped sweet in his top pocket waiting there for her childish fingers to find. At his death she had been desolate, but her father had taken her on his knee, big as she was.

'Grandpa hasn't gone, lovey,' he'd said. 'The ones we love never die, not really. The things they've said come back to us, at the right times, to comfort us, and to guide us . . . tha'll see.'

And what Grandpa Bolton was saying was as clear as if he'd been there beside her. He was twiddling with the pointed ends of his glorious moustache and smiling.

'A man what touts for sympathy never deserves it,' she remembered him saying. 'It's the chap what says nowt that we come to admire.'

Now when and where had the old man said that, and why should she remember it just at this moment? Of one thing she was quite sure. Gerald Tomlin wouldn't have been Grandpa Bolton's cup of tea either.

Seven

Dorothy was no more surprised to find that her Auntie Ethel had called round than her mother had been when the door-bell rang before ten o'clock that morning. What was in the papers was far too interesting to discuss over the telephone. And a murder almost in the family so to speak! The sister of the boy her niece Dorothy was supposed to be so friendly with! Well, that would be one in the eye, however kindly meant of course, for her sister who had always got the biggest plums since they were little girls. There'd been no doing with her since Margaret had got herself engaged. Ethel could just see her at the wedding. Perfectly dressed as usual, Phyllis always seemed to get the right thing, whereas she, Ethel, no matter how much she paid, never seemed to add up all of a piece somehow. She wasn't jealous, of course she wasn't, but it wouldn't do Phyllis any harm to be taken down a peg or two, and she'd said as much to Raymond that morning after Gerald had left the house, driving his car out of the drive as if he were on his way to his own funeral, and late at that.

'But there's nothing serious between Dorothy and that boy,' Raymond had said, looking at her over the top of his spectacles. 'They're still at school, the both of them. It's only a boy and girl friendship, and what can you expect when they're still at school at their age?'

'Ha, ha,' Ethel had said, signifying that she knew a lot more than she was prepared to say, and regretting from the bottom of her heart that she didn't.

No, Dorothy wasn't in the least surprised to see her Auntie Ethel sitting there, with the inevitable hat skewered to her greying hair. But she was surprised to see her cousin Beryl sitting dead centre of the big chintz-covered chesterfield, the red blazer and skirt of the private school at the bottom of West Road doing less than nothing for her sallow complexion.

'Seems like you're both playing truant this morning,' Ethel said, munching on a Marie biscuit. 'Beryl's got a bad period, haven't you, love? What she goes through every month is nobody's business, though it was just the same with me at her age. Do you rememer, Phyllis? Worse than labour pains my cramps were.'

Dorothy saw her mother flinch, and accepting a cup of coffee gratefully, wondered, not for the first time, how two sisters could have had the same mother and father, been brought up in the same house, and yet turn out so entirely different? Periods at Appleroyd were things to be endured, never spoken of, a feminine nuisance, along with childbirth, and what her mother called *that* side of marriage.

'I well remember the agonies I went through on the day I was confirmed,' Auntie Ethel was saying. 'Mother had had our white dresses made at Madge Gardener's little place round the back of the Emporium, do you remember? Nice little woman who skenned like a basket of whelks, never knew which eye to talk to. Anyway, what was I saying? Oh yes. There I was in that white dress, sure that when I walked up the aisle there'd be a patch . . .'

Phyllis could take no more. She actually put up a hand as if to stop the traffic, and turned to Dorothy. 'That sounded like Gerald's car turning round in the drive, dear? What happened to Philips? I wanted him to get the blind down from the attic for the front door. We don't want the new paint coming up in blisters.'

Dorothy sat down next to Beryl and smiled at her. 'The car broke down,' she explained, 'and Father sent Philips to the garage to see if they could send someone out to it straight away. We weren't far from the mill, so we walked, then Gerald offered to bring me home.'

'Lovely manners,' Ethel said, reaching for another biscuit. 'A public school gives a boy something you can't get anywhere else. Raymond says it's because they train them to be leaders. Do you know that, even though he's been staying with us all this time, he still stands up when I go out of the room? And he won't touch a thing on his plate till I've picked my spoon up – or my fork. Lovely.'

Then, as if suddenly remembering what she'd come for, she turned to Dorothy. 'I hope it wasn't too harrowing for you this morning, love, going down Inkerman Street. Your mother told me how you felt you had to go, and I will say this for you, Dorothy, you've always stuck by your friends, no matter what they've done.'

Dorothy bowed her head. *Oh, God, it was awful. They were all sitting there like vultures, waiting to pounce. Waiting for her to tell them something that the papers hadn't managed to get hold of. Even her mother, sitting there with her knees pressed close together, hoping she wouldn't say too much, but fascinated just the same. And Auntie Ethel with her round eyes starting from her head like chapel hat pegs, as Grandpa Bolton would have said . . . Why did he keep coming into her mind. Why?*

'Well?' the three pairs of eyes queried.

'I don't suppose you stayed more than a minute,' Phyllis said, giving her the cue.

Dorothy shook her head. 'There's to be a post-mortem this afternoon,' she told them reluctantly. 'At two o'clock.'

Ethel nodded with satisfaction. 'To see if she was interfered with; there's some men should have it chopped off and that's a fact.'

Phyllis's thick eyelids lowered themselves like defensive shutters. 'Why don't you and Beryl go upstairs, dear? You can show her the drawings Margaret made for the head-dresses, and see what she thinks.' She drew a circle in the air with her forefinger. 'It's a round wreath, Ethel. Tiny rosebuds, we thought, and I've booked the three girls in for early appointments at Pierre's. You wouldn't consider having Beryl's hair permed? Say, just the ends?'

Firmly Ethel shook her head. 'It takes the nature out,' she said, 'all that baking. It stands to reason.'

Phyllis sighed. 'Ah well. I'm having mine done the day before of course. I'll be far too busy to go into town on *the* morning. If I pin it well and keep my net on it should be quite all right.'

'Your mother only sent us upstairs so that you wouldn't say anything else about the murder,' Beryl said, sitting down gingerly on the edge of Dorothy's bed. 'I think it's awful the way everybody's going on about it. I'm not going to ask you anything about it, so don't think I am. I saw Stanley Armstrong the other day when I was coming out of school. He was running down West Road, and he looked awful.'

'I didn't know you knew him?'

'I've seen you together lots of times, coming out of the side park gates. But you never saw me.' Her glance was sly, and Dorothy turned away to hide the hated blush.

'Gosh, I do wish I'd been born a boy,' Beryl went on. 'It was awful in the night. I was rolling about in bed with pain. Mother says she'd take me to a specialist in Manchester if she wasn't sure I'd grow out of it. I can never be in the netball team or anything because if it comes on the day I'd be there sitting on a deck-chair in the cloakroom with a hot-water bottle on my stomach and Miss Haydock giving me hot water with Indian brandy in it.'

'Is that what you have to do when you're ill? Sit on a deck-chair in the cloakroom?'

'There's nowhere else.' Beryl rubbed hard at her stomach. 'Yes, I do wish I'd been a boy.'

Dorothy sat down on the padded stool at her dressing-table, and privately agreed that life would have been easier for Cousin Beryl if she had been a boy. An only child, she would, if she'd been a he, have gone straight into her

87

father's timber business, needing neither Matriculation nor Higher School Certificate, nor indeed any of the social graces Auntie Ethel seemed determined to drum into Beryl. Music lessons, elocution, extra coaching in French, and dresses made by Ethel's own dressmaker, a Miss Randle, whose idea of chic was to have enough material left over for a matching belt and a push-back beret style hat. She looked in the mirror and saw her cousin's reflection. She really did look rotten. The round face had a greenish tinge to it, and as she drooped forward, her greasy hair fell over her face, not quite concealing two angry red spots on her chin.

'What sort of a mood was Gerald in when he brought you home just now?' she asked unexpectedly.

Dorothy pulled a face at herself in the mirror. 'Oh, oozing charm as usual. He told me his life story, wanting me to feel sorry for him for some reason. Why do you ask?'

Beryl jerked her head upwards, presenting a suffering face to the ceiling. 'Because he was really snotty at breakfast, that's why. I thought perhaps he and Margaret had had a lovers' tiff. They went to the pictures last night, didn't they?'

'How did you know that?'

'Because I asked him where he was going, that's why. Usually he just says "out" when I ask him. Mother says I shouldn't ask him so many questions, but I worked it out when he first came to stay with us that it would be the only way of getting him to talk to me. He ignores me. I could be a stick of furniture for all he knows or cares, he certainly doesn't use his charm on me. That's because I'm not pretty like you, and I'm not, so you don't need to say I am. Oh, I do wish I'd been a boy, 'cos looks wouldn't have mattered then. I mean to say, look at your Stanley. Nobody could say he's good-looking, now could they? He's too thin for one thing, and pale. Not like Gerald. He's got lovely colour, hasn't he? Do you know who I think he'd be the spit image of if he had dark hair? Ronald Colman. His voice is exactly the same . . . Gosh, fancy being married to someone like that! Your Margaret doesn't know how lucky she is.'

What was it Margaret had said? Dorothy shook her head sadly as she remembered: '*Beryl stares at him when he's eating. And follows him about asking him personal questions. If we weren't getting married soon Gerald says he'd have to find somewhere else to stay. She's driving him bonkers.*'

Oh poor Cousin Beryl. It had been the same for as long as Dorothy could remember. Always in love with someone; for ever nursing an unrequited passion for the most unlikely people. The biology mistress. Taking little posies of flowers to school and leaving them with anonymous little notes on her desk. That tall boy in the choir, the golden-haired one who snuffed out the candles before the sermon with the air of knowing how beautiful he looked doing it. Before his voice had broken Beryl had gone to every service on Sundays, sitting where she could feast her eyes on him, and once drawing his profile in the flyleaf of her hymn book. Once, a long time ago, she had put her arm round Dorothy's waist and said, '*Let's be best friends for ever, you and me, and tell each other everything, shall we?*'

With a feeling akin to shame Dorothy remembered the way she had stiffened and moved away, muttering that she didn't want to be best friends with anyone, that best friends weren't her line at all. She looked at the bowed figure, the drooping head, and with a flash of intuition realized that this was the way it would always be for Beryl. Always swooning with love for someone unattainable. Perhaps deliberately unattainable . . . The issues were too complex for her to unravel at the moment; her mind was still reeling with the shock of seeing Stanley and his mother trapped in their inconsolable grief. In more normal times she would have discussed it with Stanley in the way they sometimes would spend hours discussing other people's idiosyncrasies.

'*You'd think there was only thee and me normal,*' he had said once after they had spent a satisfactory half-hour analysing her mother's motivations. Yes, Stanley would have had a very satisfactory theory about Beryl. . . .

And now she had fixed on Gerald. Driving him mad with questions; watching him, *prying*, just so he would have to talk to her.

'He hasn't gone out in the evenings as much lately,' Beryl was saying gloomily. 'Before he got engaged to Margaret he used to go out almost every night in his car.' She fingered one of the spots on her chin sadly. 'When I asked him where he was going, he laughed and said he just liked driving alone. Fast, in the dark all on his own. Out as far as the moors. It made me think of Heathcliff wandering alone over the moors looking for someone to love.'

'Heathcliff?' Dorothy's reaction was more disparaging than she had intended it to be. 'I can't think of anyone less like Heathcliff than Gerald Tomlin. For one thing Heathcliff didn't drive over the moors in a red MG sports car. He *strode*.'

'I'm glad he's found happiness at last. He's got such a lovely accent.'

'He talks like an ha'penny book,' Dorothy said, getting up from the stool. 'Let's have a look at the sketches, shall we? I've had just about enough of Gerald for one morning.'

'I simply love weddings, don't you?' Beryl trailed along the landing, walking carefully. 'Gosh, wouldn't it be awful if Margaret had her you know what on her wedding day? Won't it be beady if they have a baby straight away?'

Eight

'You can talk about inquests and post mortems till the cows come home,' Ada Armstrong said, her face set in stubborn lines of disbelief. 'But if our Ruby had been expecting I'd have known.' She glanced at Stanley, then away and at Mrs Crawley. 'Tha's only a lad and not supposed to know about such things, but you can't live in a house like this with the only privacy being if tha goes out and bolts theself in the outside lavatory. And anyway, our Ruby weren't that sort of girl. If she'd thought she was like that and her not wed she'd have been half out of her mind. She couldn't have kept a thing like that from me.'

Mrs Crawley's face, beneath the inevitable halo of day-time curlers, was soft with compassion. No gleam of fas-cinated interest, Stanley noted, no shocked surprise even, certainly no wait-till-I-tell-the-neighbours attitude. Just honest-to-goodness sympathy, and a desire to help.

'They said she was almost three months gone,' Stanley said, turning to Nellie Crawley. 'So if it was the same man who killed her – and they're sure it must have been now there's a motive, so to speak – that would mean she was meeting him around Christmas time.' He turned back to his mother. 'Mum, we've got to *think*. What did she do about Christmas time? Did she go to any parties? I know some of the girls from the mill had parties . . .'

'She weren't like that,' Ada said, shaking her head as if she would shake the words away. 'I would stake my life that Ruby weren't like that. She was a good girl . . . a good girl.'

91

'It's the good ones what get caught,' Mrs Crawley said. 'The poor little sod. She must have been well nigh out of her mind, keeping that to herself.' She shook a finger at Ada. 'And it's not the worst sin now, Mrs Armstrong, not by a long chalk. I've always thought that. There's bloody-mindedness, and coldness, and meanness, and lust. Aye, lust, Mrs Armstrong. And I'll swear by our Holy Mother that your Ruby weren't guilty of none of them.' She jerked her head in the direction of the scullery and winked at Stanley. 'Put the kettle on, there's a good lad, and you sit you down, Mrs Armstrong. You've had more than you can take, and that's a bloody fact.'

Ada looked at her piteously. 'How could I not know? What's been happening in this house, for the love of God? Me only daughter meeting some man on the sly all these past weeks, and having his baby, and I didn't suspect? What sort of a mother have I been? Why couldn't I see there was something sadly wrong with her?' She looked for a confirmation that could not be given. 'How long did she think she could keep it from me? I'd have tried to under-stand. Even if she wouldn't tell me who it was – and he was a married man, I'm more convinced of it than ever now – I would have stood by her.'

'Of course you would, love.' Mrs Crawley was guiding her gently towards the rocking chair. 'You're not the sort of mother to throw her daughter out on the streets because she makes a slip. You'd have looked after her and then you'd have brought up the baby yourself while she went back to work.' The curlers glistened in a sudden shaft of sunlight as she got carried away. 'You'd have put him in yon basket where them shirts are, you would, and if any of the neigh-bours 'ad said anything, you'd have spit in their eye.' She patted Ada's arm. 'And I'd have spit in t'other one for you, love, that I would.'

'It was an older man,' Ada said, picking up her pressing cloth from the table and twisting it round and round in her hands as she talked. 'I've thought so all along, and I'm

92

saying it again. Ruby went out with Eddie next door for a good twelve-month, and I'll swear there was nothing going on. She had her head screwed on all right, and she'd have known how to handle Eddie Marsden if he'd started anything.' The piece of fent tore down the middle and she flung it from her. 'So it must have been an older man, one with a smooth tongue, a *persuasive* sort of man who could undo in one minute all that I've been telling her since she grew up. "Never sell yourself cheap" I used to tell her. "If a man wants to marry you enough, he'll wait."'

'Not like my bugger,' Mrs Crawley said, lowering her voice in the vain hope that Stanley out in the scullery wouldn't hear. 'I were four-month gone when we got wed, then just two weeks to the day after the wedding I lost it. And that were it.' She gave her cackle of a laugh. 'Maybe it were all that jumping down steps and sitting in a tin bath swiggin' gin what did it. Any road I never had another chance.' She winked at Ada. 'And it weren't for t'want of trying, not in them early days it weren't.'

It was no use deciding not to listen. Not a bit of use closing the scullery door that was never closed anyway. Mrs Crawley's voice carried like a clarion call. She was talking about the funeral now.

'How much did you have on 'er, love?'

'Nothing. Harry didn't believe in insurance.'

'Well, I've never heard nowt like that before. I've had twopence on me husband and threepence on me mother-in-law for years. If she doesn't die quick I'll have bought all t'bloody cemetery.'

Stanley waited for the kettle to come to the boil. They seemed to have forgotten that he was there . . . He could feel a sickening sensation churning away in his bowels. He kicked absent-mindedly at the frayed piece of coconut-matting laid over the flagged floor.

Not Ruby. Not his sister, the quiet, gentle, dark-haired

girl who had had to go in the mill so that he, Stanley, could study and swot to his heart's content in a room of his own. Had her pride in his scholastic achievements been more mixed with envy than he had guessed? Had she sought comfort in the arms of some unknown man because the conditions at home had become intolerable to her? Had she resented more bitterly than he could hope to have guessed the fact that she had had to work in some weaving shed whilst he stayed on at school? Had she given herself – he used the phrase without a trace of self-consciousness – to this man with a silver tongue who had promised her an escape and ended up with his hands round her throat, squeezing the life out of her?

The sick feeling in his stomach was growing worse. He opened the back door and took a few deep breaths, then he turned off the gas underneath the kettle, closed the back door softly behind him and went outside. Down the three stone steps, past the meat safe, down the sloping backyard with the low soot-blackened walls separating it from its neighbours, out to the lavatory, where he bolted himself inside.

It was what Mrs Crawley had said. Meant kindly but bringing home to him as nothing else had that Ruby was dead. DEAD. 'How much did you have on her, love?' Oh, God, the man from the Prudential knocking at the door on Friday nights, early, before the tea-things were cleared away in the street, catching folks before they went out to spend their wages if they'd been lucky enough to have a week's work behind them. Twopence on our Edie, threepence on me dad. No wonder his father had thought the whole system barbaric . . . and yet. . . .

Now they would have to plan the funeral, or at least *he* would have to plan the funeral. There'd be people they hardly knew in shiny black, and his mother leaning on his arm, with the neighbours in the street watching with compassion. With compassion, aye, but watching just the same.

94

Shut away in the tiny enclosed space, he stared round him at the white-washed walls, the squares of newspaper hanging by a string from a nail, shut away, he scuffed with his feet the tattered rag rug on the flagged floor. Over the outside wall, out in the back he could hear the children from the house three doors up shouting to each other as they came home from school. Old Mrs Preston was calling her cat in, banging on a tin plate, crying its name. The man next door, out of work now for eighteen months, pulled the lavatory chain and shuffled his way back into the house, and streets away the rag-and-bone man called out his unintelligible cry. Life was going on, would go on just the same after Ruby was forgotten. He, Stanley Armstrong, would get up in the mornings and go to work, if he'd been lucky enough to find a job. His mother would wash more shirts, Dorothy would leave school and start as a typist in her father's office, and in a few years' time she would marry a young fellow who was a director in his father's firm. They'd have the reception at The Pied Bull over on the edge of the moors, and their photographs would be in the weekly paper, laughing into each other's eyes, with a description of the bridesmaids' dresses underneath. And all this would be a million years away.

And if you'd asked him, he couldn't have told you why he suddenly felt an aching, terrible despair, so that the sobs tore at his throat with a rasping noise that made him stuff his fist into his mouth. He knew that he was crying for his sister, for what seemed to be the death, too, of all his hopes, but there was more. There was something else his tormented brain was weeping for. His ideals, his unexpressed emotions about love and tenderness. And lust. Mrs Crawley had been right to use that word. He, Stanley Armstrong, had lusted after Dorothy Bolton. He'd dreamed of her, but in his dreams his love for her had been no more than a stroking of her yellow hair, a holding her close, a kissing of her eyelids.

The tears ran down over his hand and he groaned aloud.

95

But that wasn't love. Not the reality of love. Love was Mrs Crawley sitting in a tin bath and drinking gin, and love was Ruby lying on the grass with the weight of some unknown man above her. And love was Ruby dead with a leaf caught up in her hair.

Mrs Crawley's voice could be heard calling out from the open back door.

'Are you all right, love? Your mum wants to know. Are you all right out there?'

But he made he reply, just stayed there with the agony of disillusionment growing inside him as if it were a living thing.

Nine

'Where was he ringing from, dear? I shouldn't think Mrs Armstrong is on the telephone, is she?'

Phyllis's voice breathed a tolerance she was obviously far from feeling. It had been a most trying day again, with Dorothy mooning round the house with a cold that didn't seem all that much in evidence, and Mrs Wilkinson going on and on asking questions.

'My heart grieves for that poor dead girl and her family, but I have never met any of them, so I can't tell you *anything*, Mrs Wilkinson,' she had said. 'Our only connection is in that she worked in the weaving shed, and that Dorothy has been walking home from school with her brother.'

'And that hardly makes us *relatives*,' she'd added under her breath.

Even Gerald had rung and tried to wriggle out of taking Margaret to the Police Ball that night. She'd heard only one side of the conversation of course, but she could tell that Margaret had been quite put out about it. And quite rightly when they'd had the tickets for weeks. Phyllis was reduced to playing patience, a ploy she always used when under stress, just as some women scrubbed floors or others went out and bought themselves a new hat. She laid a black jack over a red queen.

The last straw had been when Ethel called round and asked if she would be going to the funeral.

'As a token of respect merely,' she'd added quickly, seeing the look on her sister's face. 'On account of the girl

97

working for Matthew, and with Dorothy being her brother's little friend.'

And now Dorothy was refusing to answer what was surely a perfectly straightforward question. Phyllis repeated it: 'Where was Stanley ringing from, dear? I don't suppose anyone in Inkerman Street is on the telephone, are they?'

Her younger daughter came and drooped in the doorway, her face pale, and her blue eyes shadowed as if she hadn't slept for a week.

'No, Mother, they use tom-toms to communicate with each other down that end of the town,' she said. Then as if she knew she had gone too far she went on: 'Stanley was ringing me from a house at the top end of the street. The man living there is a Trade Union Secretary, and in cases of emergency he lets the neighbours pay to use his telephone. He's a kind man apparently. Stanley says he even went out of his own living-room so that he could be private.' She hesitated for a moment, then sighed. 'Ruby was going to have a baby.'

Phyllis's small face seemed to set itself neatly into lines of smug satisfaction. She tapped with the edge of a playing card on the polished table.

'There you are, then. I'm not surprised, not in the least.'

'Stanley and his mother were *very* surprised,' Dorothy said quietly.

Phyllis turned up an ace and laid it down in triumph. 'Well, of course they would be. A mother is always the last person to believe that sort of thing of her own daughter, not that she wouldn't have stood by her, I'm quite sure she would. But at least it gives the police more to work on.' She frowned at the eight of spades.

'What do you mean by that, Mother?'

'Well, now the police know the kind of girl she was, they will know the kind of man to look for.' She shuffled the cards together in exasperation. 'I knew it wasn't going to come out. Yes, he was probably one of many, and when the girl told him that she was going to say he was the father of her child, he lost his temper and killed her. It won't be the first murder to happen that way, and it won't be the last. Especially if he happened to be a married man. Oh yes, it puts a different complexion on the whole thing now. Dorothy! Where are you going? Must you always walk away when I try to talk to you?'

Dorothy was walking slowly upstairs, wondering vaguely if she was in any way psychic. Or just plain fanciful? Watching her mother's small mouth as she talked, the playing cards held neatly in her well-manicured hands, she had felt again that strange sense of evil, of impending horror. In her own house, the house she had been born in, solid, red-bricked, its dark mahogany furniture gleaming from Mrs Wilkinson's ministrations. Something terrible was going to happen, she knew it. The knowledge of it was a crawling in her scalp, a feeling in her very bones. She stood on the landing, quite still, rubbing the tops of her arms as if she felt a sudden draught.

She could still hear the heartbreak in Stanley's voice when he spoke to her, using the clipped exaggerated emphasis of words as people did when they were unaccustomed to using a telephone.

'Ruby wasn't promiscuous. She was a very reserved, private sort of girl . . . you know?'

'You don't have to be promiscuous to start a baby.' Whispering in the hope that her mother wouldn't be able to hear. 'It must have been someone she thought she was in love with. Someone she *was* in love with, I mean.'

'I agree, but it's shaken my mother up. She feels it must have been all her fault somehow. Her not guessing and everything, then Ruby not wanting to tell her. She wouldn't have been turned out of the house or anything. My mother has strong principles but she's not a hard person. She would have understood and tried to help.'

'Of course she would.'

They had never talked on the telephone before, and there

was an awkward breathing silence between them, the shyness that came down like a barrier at times, made worse by the proximity of others.

'I'd best be going then, Dorothy.'

She had lowered her voice, her glance going towards the sitting-room door, open a fraction, imagining her mother with the pack of playing cards in her hand, the neat head on one side in a listening attitude.

'Will I be seeing you after school next week?'

Stanley coughed, forgetting he was holding the receiver, and she jumped. 'I'm not going back till after the funeral . . . I have a lot of things to sort out in my mind. About Oxford. I may have to get a job, as a clerk, anything. I want to talk to you, but it isn't easy at the moment . . .'

'Is it very awful, love?'

'If I wasn't there to tell her to come to the table, to go to bed, and to get up, I think she would just sit there without moving. Mrs Crawley says it's the shock. The minister's been from the chapel, but he said all the wrong things . . .'

Dorothy started to go into her own room, then changed her mind. She didn't feel like being alone, and Margaret was there next door getting ready for the Police Ball. She would listen. She would tell her that Stanley *couldn't* give up his chance of going to university, not after winning a state scholarship. Against overwhelming odds he'd *won* his right to go. . . .

'Is that you, Dorothy?'

Margaret sounded gay and happy. 'Come in and talk to me, I'm almost ready.'

And as usual Margaret was bewailing the fact that she looked a positive mess whilst looking as pretty as a picture on the lid of a box of chocolates. Dorothy could see it . . . a garlanded swing with Margaret laughing at a blue sky with her pink and blue net skirts billowing round her. She was busily applying vaseline to her eyelids, rubbing it in with the tip of her little finger, then closing her eyes and squinting in the mirror from underneath lowered eyelashes to get

100

the effect. She spoke without turning round, carefully, so as not to disturb the petunia-shaded lipstick on her wide mouth.

'For a minute I thought when the phone rang that it might be Gerald. He didn't want to go to the dance tonight for some reason, but I did what Mother does when she persuades Father into changing his mind . . .' Margaret smeared the vaseline over the top of her lipstick. 'I told him it didn't matter in the least; that I couldn't care less whether we went or not, and he was so taken aback it ended with him persuading *me* to go!' She peered anxiously down the front of her dress. 'You don't think this dress is a wee bit low in front, do you? I'd pin my pearl brooch across it, if I could find it. I've looked in my jewel-case and it's not there.'

Dorothy walked across to the wardrobe. 'The last time you wore it you had it pinned to the neckline of your green and brown dress.' She produced the dress with a flourish. 'There you are! You must have forgotten to take it off when you put the dress away.'

Tongue protruding slightly, Margaret pinned the brooch at the middle point of the sweetheart neckline of her dress. She pouted. 'It's a bit scratchy, but nothing shows, that's the main thing.'

She looked so seriously worried that Dorothy, in spite of her mood of depression, laughed out loud. 'Doesn't Gerald know that you've got bosoms, then?'

Margaret answered her quite literally, unaware as usual that she was being teased. 'Well, of course he does, silly. We *are* engaged, remember. No, it's not that, it's just that he can't bear other men staring at me.'

Dorothy fidgeted round the room, picking up the small gilt clock from the bedside table, holding it to her ear, then putting it down again, picking up the white fur jacket from the bed and holding it to her cheek for a moment. 'Is he very passionate, your Gerald?'

Margaret wasn't offended. At eighteen Dorothy was

bound to be becoming curious about such things. She felt quite matronly as she answered her. 'He's had a past, of course,' she confided with more than a touch of pride. 'One couldn't expect anything else with him being a man of the world and living on his own in London for so long. But he *respects* me.' She patted the brooch with a satisfied hand. 'Mother says it's far better for a bride if the man is experienced when they get married.'

Dorothy dabbed behind her ears with Margaret's scent, a woody perfume she decided she didn't much care for. 'But wrong for the girl to be?'

'Well, of *course*, Dorothy. No man wants shop-soiled goods now, does he?'

Dorothy started to answer. Actually opened her mouth to answer, then closed it again. How can we be sisters? she asked herself, silently and dramatically, searching the ceiling as if looking for the answer. Sisters, flesh of the same flesh, blood of the same blood, brought up together in the same house, of the same environment exactly? How can we be so close when we think so differently? She felt suddenly very, very old; at least twice as old as Margaret, and ten times as wise. Rather wistfully she unfolded a pink chiffon hankie lying on the dressing-table and sniffed the pink powder-puff nestling inside, leaving a smear of rose rachel powder on the tip of her nose.

'I only wish Gerald could find his cuff-links as easily as you found my brooch,' she heard Margaret saying.

Dorothy saw the reflection of her eyes widening in surprise in the mirror. She had been with Margaret to choose the cuff-links as an engagement present for Gerald, and the memory of the time it had taken to decide on a suitable gift was still sharp in her memory. For over half an hour she had stood at the counter of Adamson's, the jewellers in King Edward Street, hopping from one foot to the other with impatience as Mr Adamson himself had spread the counter with a piece of black velvet, laying out tie-pins, wristlet watches and cuff-links in a shining display. Margaret's final choice had been the cuff-links because they were shaped like flattened hearts.

'Symbolic,' Margaret had sighed.

'Most unusual,' Mr Adamson had said, winking slyly at Dorothy.

'But how *could* he have lost them?' she said sharply, then she saw Margaret's face flush with loyalty.

'People do lose things, you know, Dorothy, and Gerald's terribly upset about it. In fact, he made me promise not to tell anyone he'd lost them. They're sure to turn up, he says, so for heaven's sake don't tell Mother, or you can imagine . . .' Her voice tailed off in mid-sentence as the unmistakable sound of Gerald's car was heard in the drive outside.

'He's here!' she cried, and Dorothy thought she looked as if a candle had been lit inside her head, so that her mouth and eyes radiated light. Like a turnip on Hallowe'en night, she thought, not very poetically.

But even she had to admit that they made a beautiful couple as they left for the dance, and whilst Phyllis twittered round Gerald, pressing him to a sherry to 'put them in the right mood for a lovely evening together' she intercepted the look he gave his fiancée as surreptitiously he raised one arm slightly to show her that the cuff-links were safely restored to their rightful place in the starched turn-back cuffs of his dress shirt.

'I could have sworn they were smaller than that,' Dorothy muttered to herself as she stood with her mother and waved them off from the door.

'What did you say, dear?' Phyllis asked.

'Oh, nothing,' Dorothy said. 'Just thinking aloud, that's all.'

'I think I'll go mad and have another sherry,' Phyllis said, with the air of one who felt that she deserved some kind of solace.

Ten

'I can't expect Mrs Crawley to go to the market for me; she's doing far more than enough already, and I've never been one for putting on kindness,' Ada Armstrong said. 'But what she pays for her greengrocery at the new shop down on the bottom doesn't bear thinking about. Mr Crawley's in work of course, so she doesn't have to count her pennies like we do.' She pushed at her hair until it stood up straight away from her forehead as if she'd been startled by a headless ghost. 'No, I can't expect her to go down the market late this afternoon when they're selling some things off cheap, and it wouldn't do for me to be seen out till after the funeral – wouldn't be decent.'

Stanley closed his eyes, sending up a silent prayer that at last his mother was showing what the doctor would have called an *interest*. 'I'll go down if you like, Mum.'

'Life must go on,' the minister from the chapel had said, and he supposed that an interest in cut oranges and bruised tomatoes could be interpreted as a beginning. Besides, the claustrophobic atmosphere of the tiny living-room with its banked-up fire, its steaming clothes and continual coming and going of neighbours with offerings of seed-cakes and batches of soda scones was beginning to get on his nerves. He knew he was being selfish and that his place was by his mother's side, but he wanted to feel the wind on his face, wanted to run and run until his heart pounded in his ears, wanted to see Dorothy and talk to her about his decision to leave school and forego his place at university – wanted to

104

forget, just for a little while, what had happened.

Once or twice, whilst Mrs Crawley talked with his mother, helping to fold the washing brought in from the backyard, he had escaped upstairs to his bedroom, and sitting down at the card-table by the window had opened a book, had even taken his pen and dipped it into the bottle of blue-black ink, putting himself out of reach of Mrs Crawley's darting tongue and the closed-in misery of his mother's face.

Through the net curtains he could see the walled-in backyards of the houses opposite in Balaclava Street, drenched in brilliant sunshine, the tin baths hanging on the walls, the coal-sheds and the outside lavatories — even sometimes a glimpse of their white-washed interiors. One particularly sunny afternoon a woman had appeared from her back door carrying a battered deck-chair, and there, just as if she were setting it up on the sand facing the sea at Blackpool in wakes week, she had positioned it next to the dustbin. Then lying back in it she had lifted her skirt to expose fat white thighs, and closed her eyes. A sleek grey cat had joined her, curling itself up on the flagstones, and after a while the woman had unbuttoned her blouse, turning the revers in so that the top curves of her enormous breasts were revealed, offering herself to the sun like a sacrifice.

He had watched her fascinated and repelled at one and the same time, staring until his eyes ached at the corners, then jerking himself back to reality as he heard footsteps on the stairs and the sound of Mrs Crawley's voice coming through the thin plywood his father had erected to separate the two rooms.

'I'm being honest, Mrs Armstrong, I'm your friend and I wouldn't let you go to your own daughter's funeral looking a sight now, would I? And navy blue's every bit as respectable as black. Go on, try your 'at on. No, not like that, Pull if forward a bit. Sailors went out two years ago. That's better. It only needs dusting off a bit, that fur-felt catches every speck, and I'll tell you what, love, I'll lend you me bit of fox to put round your neck. I've never been up 'cemetery yet but what it wasn't blowing fit to freeze your bits and pieces.'

Then his mother's murmur, so low that it was impossible to catch what she was saying. Stanley strained to catch the words without being in the least interested, then stared through the window again.

The sun had gone in and the woman sunbathing folded her deck-chair and carried it inside the house, followed by the cat with its tail erect. A lowering cloud appeared to be so thick that he felt if pressed it would drip apple juice, like the muslin bag his mother sometimes suspended over the big blue bowl in the kitchen when she made apple jelly. His head felt as if someone were adding little sums up in it, pressing with the point of a pencil on every single figure. The thought of life going on, just as the minister had predicted it would, in that house, with the door of Ruby's room closed, her narrow bed stripped of its covers, the wire behind its cretonne curtain bare of her dresses, filled him with a terrible, blank despair. He dipped the pen in the blue-black ink and tried to write a poem about the awful-ness of everything. Wrote three lines then tore it up and dropped the pieces into the empty biscuit tin he used as a waste bin.

'You just write me a list of what you want me to get, and I'll go down the market,' he told his mother. 'I won't take the basket, I'll fold a carrier-bag and carry it underneath my arm,' he said, and was touched almost to the point of tears to see how what could have passed for a smile crossed her face.

'Your dad will never be dead as long as you're alive, Stanley,' she said. 'He wouldn't carry a basket neither, not for love nor money he wouldn't. I remember once he brought me a bunch of violets home on a Saturday when

106

he'd been to watch the Rovers, and he stuffed them into his mac pocket rather than carry them through the street.' She licked the point of her pencil and thought for a moment. 'It didn't do them no good neither, but I put them in water with an aspirin and they come up just as good as new.' She sighed. 'It's no good. I can't get my mind on food. It doesn't seem right that we have to eat somehow. I'll give you three shillings and you can get just what you think fit, There'll be cut oranges and bruised tomatoes if you go now . . . oh love, it's all wrong that we should be feeling hungry or bothering about anything when Ruby's . . . when she's not coming through that door no more. I still can't believe it somehow.'

'You'll start feeling better after the funeral on Monday,' Stanley said, then immediately wondered what had made him say such a damn fool thing?

'If anyone else tells me once more that time will heal I'll be like Nellie Crawley and spit in their eye,' his mother had said only the day before. But what else was there to say but platitudes and trite remarks? What *did* one say to the newly bereaved? Stanley folded the carrier-bag into acceptable masculine folds and tucked it beneath his arm.

'You'll be all right till I get back, then?'

Then, as she nodded, he bent his head and kissed her awkwardly on her cheek, knowing that had been quite the wrong thing to do as he saw the rush of tears to her eyes.

'Grief should bring closeness,' he told himself as he walked quickly with head bent forward as usual down the street.

'Everyone can master a grief but he that has it,' he muttered, then as he crossed the street: 'Old Shakespeare had the right words for everything – the old rascal didn't miss a trick.'

'Everyone can master a grief but he that has it,' he said again, causing two women who knew him to turn to each other and say how sad it was that what had happened in the Corporation Park to that poor boy's sister had obviously turned his mind.

'Talking to *himself*,' they told their respective husbands over their Saturday tea of a quarter of tripe – off the seam.

'I'll go down town and pick the brooch up for you if you'd like me to,' Dorothy told her mother. 'Then you won't need to worry about me not getting enough exercise. I'll run all the way down Steep Brow,' she added with the air of one who is dispensing a great favour.

As usual Phyllis tried hard not to sigh at her younger daughter. They were in the front garden and she was down on her knees on a small cushion kept specially for the purpose. She wore her gardening outfit, an old tweed skirt, a long cardigan and a shady hat, although the sun was no more than a watery trickle of light through low-slung clouds. With hands encased in a pair of leather gauntlet gloves she was planting pansy clumps in a neat and well-ordered row, planting them at equal distances from each other, pulling at their foliage until she felt they were roughly the same size, and patting the earth down around them with neat, precise, little pats. Like the contents of the house itself, her garden was the epitome of order and neatness. As one blue vase on one side of the mantelpiece was flanked by its twin on the other, so the shrubs and flowers in Phyllis's garden bloomed in matching identical pairs. If a rose bush came into flower at one side of the velvet lawn, then its counterpart came into matching bloom on the other. In their due seasons the tulips marched down the border like well-drilled soldiers, the daffodils grew in evenly spaced precision to uniform heights, and the privet hedge looked as if it had been manufactured and not grown.

'If she didn't think it was common she'd have got Philips to clip out a couple of ducks at each side of the gate,' Dorothy had told Stanley once when they were playing their favourite game of analysing her parents.

'With identical twin gnomes fishing in matching ponds in the middle of the lawn,' Stanley had said. 'It's a sign of insecurity, you see, Dorothy. Two means more, double means twice the normal.'

'I see,' Dorothy had said, not seeing at all.

Sitting back on her heels Phyllis eyed her with resignation.

'Why you couldn't have gone with Margaret to the tennis club I don't know. Gerald's picking her up there later because he doesn't want her to walk back through the field way alone.' She shook her head as if in sorrow. 'When I was your age I spent every single minute of every single Saturday at the tennis club. I never mooned about doing nothing the way you do.' She got up from her knees and stared with something akin to distaste at the soil on the tips of her gloved fingers. 'Well, I suppose you *could* pick my brooch up for me. Mr Adamson did promise to have it ready today, and I want to wear my grey striped blouse for bridge this evening. It looks nothing without my cameo at the neck.' She looked down at her arm as if expecting to see one of her leather handbags looped neatly into position. 'Never mind the money, just tell Mr Adamson to charge it to us. Goodness knows we've spent enough money there lately with the engagement presents and the silver knife for cutting the cake, not to mention the crucifixes for the bridesmaids.' She knelt down again and trimmed off a leaf which had grown out of proportion to the others. 'It was only the safety chain that needed mending.' Then, trying hard to sound casual, she said: 'Where are you going this evening, dear?'

'I *was* going to the pictures with Stanley,' Dorothy told her, feeling that, under the tragic circumstances, lies in that direction would be in bad taste. 'But he doesn't feel he should go anywhere until after the funeral.' She raised her voice in an attempt at bravado. 'I was going to say that I was going with Mavis and Edna, two girls in my form, but I've promised Father I'll stop telling lies about meeting Stanley.'

Phyllis allowed herself an upwards sideway glance. Her daughter looked very virtuous standing there in her pleated skirt, with the Peter-Pan collar of her white blouse turned down over the collar of her school blazer. Almost as if she were blaming them for her former deceit, Phyllis thought, stabbing furiously into the soil with her index finger.

'Your father's going to the funeral on Monday to represent the *mill*,' Phyllis said, with the emphasis on the word that counted. 'Gerald was going with him but he's stood down to let Mr Sowerbutts go in his place. Margaret says he can't bear to discuss it. He's a sensitive young man, you've only to look at his face to see that he suffers inwardly. Probably because of his sad beginnings.'

'My heart bleeds,' Dorothy said underneath her breath as she walked away down the path, leaving her mother muttering feverishly into a seedling. . . .

She wasn't, Phyllis decided, going to raise the issue at the moment about this dreadful boy from Inkerman Street. Let them get his poor sister decently buried first, then she'd make Matthew listen. Knowing Dorothy as she was sure she did, it was more than likely that the whole sordid business had tinged the friendship with an aura of glamour. Dramatized it into something brave and wonderful. Made Dorothy feel she must stick by him no matter what. She stood up, dragged the cushion a few feet to the right and knelt down again. Now it seemed that he was refusing to go back to school and talking about giving up his place at university. Mrs Wilkinson had heard it from a friend of a friend. And if he left school, what then?

She probed daintily in the cuttings box as if she were selecting a chocolate cream and being careful not to take a hard one by mistake. At eighteen he was too old to take up an apprenticeship that might give him a trade in his fingers, even if there were any openings at the present time. And with nothing but book learning to offer, academic qualifications not backed up by a degree or any training for one of the professions, he would probably end up signing on at the Labour Exchange. Hanging about outside with his hands in his pockets, just one more statistic in what the papers called the economic graveyard of lost hopes. She knelt back on her heels, proud of herself for remembering the phrase: Matthew would in all probability offer him a job at the mill, knowing Matthew. But it would have to be a job created especially, with a hundred men standing by for every job available.

The town was full of boys who had never worked, the occasional packet of cigarettes and a daily meeting at the billiard halls being the only pleasure in their drab lives. Oh, she read the papers all right, and listened to Matthew when he was up on his soap-box. The very street in which that boy lived – she could not bring herself even to *think* his name – existed merely because it had been built originally as cottages, well, terraced houses for the mill workers. She stood up and rubbed at an aching knee.

And if this grisly thing hadn't happened, he would have gone off to university at the end of the summer, and out of sight would surely have meant out of mind. She walked stiff-legged into the house, seeing, in her mind's eye, a clear picture of herself having to tell Mrs Wilkinson that Mrs Armstrong was coming to tea. She saw Dorothy helping that boy to carry a basket of washing through the streets; saw her bridge friends sniggering behind their cards. Saw it all, and was depressed beyond measure.

Dorothy was thinking about Stanley so thoroughly that she didn't see her cousin until they were almost nose to nose.

'I've been playing tennis in the park,' Beryl told her unnecessarily, swinging her racket with three tennis balls in a green net wound round the handle. 'Talk about being lovesick. You're as bad as Gerald. you are.' She lowered her voice, although the tree-lined road was completely deserted. 'I swore I wouldn't tell a living soul, but he's lost one of the cuff-links Margaret bought him. I was on the landing after lunch, and I saw him searching his room. He was opening drawers and then banging them shut. He was even looking underneath the carpet and feeling with his hand to see if they'd rolled there somehow. I asked him what he was looking for, and he jumped a mile. Then he told me how terrible he felt about losing them with Margaret buying them for him and everything. He said it made him quite sick just thinking about it as they were more precious to him than the King's crown.' She sighed. 'Isn't that romantic? You won't tell a living soul about it, will you? I've only told you because I think it's so beautiful.'

'As if I would,' Dorothy said, backing away. If she didn't hurry up the shops would be closed.

But Beryl hadn't finished. 'As a matter of fact I saw him in the park just now, walking along a path with his nose nearly touching the ground. But I didn't let on. He thinks I spy on him, for some reason.' Her plain face shone with perspiration beneath the wide brim of her school panama. 'It's real spooky in the park. There's a piece of tarpaulin over the place where you know what. Me and Connie – she's the girl I've been playing tennis with, and she beat me again, you might know – we went to look. Isn't it awful about that girl who got killed having a baby? Mother says . . .'

'I can't stop,' Dorothy said quickly. 'I've got to catch the shops before they shut. See you in church tomorrow morning?'

'Suppose so,' Beryl said. 'And you won't split about what I've just told you? I think you're beastly rotten about Gerald, if you want to know. He says he trusts me and that when they're married I can go and stay the night with them sometimes.' She walked away, the tennis racket banging disconsolately against her fat legs sprouting from white ankle socks, leaving Dorothy feeling, as usual, vaguely ashamed, and with the feeling that she could have been kinder. Cousin Beryl will be making people feel guilty all her life, she reasoned, with a sudden flash of perception.

She blushed and turned her head away as three boys standing on a street corner whistled after her. She could

112

almost bring herself to feel sorry for Gerald Tomlin having to live under Beryl's constant vigilance.

She was half way down Steep Brow when she suddenly remembered that Gerald had *found* the cuff-links; that he had been wearing them the night before. At least they had looked like the same. But had they? She remembered standing at the door and waving them off to the dance, Margaret in her garden-swing dress, and Gerald in what her father always called his penguin trappings. She had thought then that the cuff-links appeared to be smaller than the original ones. She stepped off a kerb and stumbled, causing a man at the tram-stop to say 'whoops-a-daisy'. And if he had found them why was he still searching? And why was he searching in the *park*?

Her mind raced ahead so that she walked along, seeing nothing of the busy Saturday afternoon crowds, hearing nothing as the trams rumbled by. *If* Gerald had lost the cuff-links he could have replaced them. He could have gone back to the jeweller's shop and bought a similar pair. He could have done it to spare Margaret the knowledge that he had lost her present to him. He could have. Of course he could have. She bumped into a pram and was loudly told to look where she was going by the baby's mother.

But if he'd done that, why was he still searching his room? Lifting the carpet, according to Beryl. And why was he in the park walking along with his head bent? Gerald Tomlin didn't go for walks in the park. Gerald Tomlin didn't walk anywhere, the red sports car being almost an extension of himself. Someone called out a 'hallo', but she glanced through them, showing no recognition. Yes, the searching beneath the carpet in Gerald's room could mean that he couldn't bear to think he had misplaced the original pair on account of their sentimental value. Mother was always saying what a lovely romantic streak Gerald had in him. 'Not like a northern man with his mind filled with

113

nothing else but beer and football,' she'd said more than once.

And Margaret herself had said how upset he was at losing the cuff-links. So upset that he wanted it kept a secret. But Gerald had what Mrs Wilkinson's magazines called 'charm'. He would, or at least he *could* have said that he'd lost them and elicited sympathy, not irritation. Gerald Tomlin always managed to come out the hero, usually the suave Ronald Colman type hero, in every story he told against himself. And charming people did tell stories against themselves just to make themselves appear all the more charming. That was another truth about people she had found out for herself, and one she must tell to Stanley when next they met.

'Tolstoy is the only writer who can hold up a mirror to a man's soul,' Stanley had said, and gone on to say that was the kind of writer he would be one day when he was qualified to earn money, to take time off to write.

Dorothy turned into King Edward Street without the faintest recollection of having got there, was surprised to find herself standing outside Mr Adamson's jeweller's shop, and stood for a moment staring at the rows of diamond rings in the side window, each one mounted on a velvet pad with the price neatly tabulated underneath. One ring costing a hundred and fifty pounds had diamonds as big as peas, and even in her state of mental agitation she found that she was pursing up her lips in a gesture of disbelief.

The door-bell pinged as she went inside, and Mr Adamson's Saturday lady, a plump treble-chinned girl of about thirty with a black dress stretched tightly over her pouter-pigeon bosom, came forward.

'Can I help you?'

Dorothy bit her lip and glanced over to the side counter where Mr Adamson was setting out rings on a mat of black velvet, showing them off to an obviously embarrassed young man and an obviously triumphant girl who was insisting on trying on each ring and holding up her hand to the light to check them for sparkle. The jeweller, one of Matthew Bolton's Rotary friends, was leaning forward, explaining about built-up shoulders and claw settings, smiling like a benevolent Father Christmas on the young couple, and telling them to take their time.

'Take your time about it,' he was saying at that very moment. 'It's only once.' Then he laughed and stroked his mutton-chop whiskers. 'Or at least we hope it's only once.'

The couple giggled and leaned on each other, and Dorothy spoke, softly to the assistant.

'I'll wait for Mr Adamson, if you don't mind. It's personal.'

'As you wish, miss.'

The Saturday lady sniffed with a sideways twitch of nostrils and walked with a rather offended tripping step into a room at the back, where through a small window Dorothy saw her light a cigarette and blow a thin stream of smoke up to the ceiling as if to disconnect herself from the whole matter.

Yes, if Gerald Tomlin *had* replaced the lost cuff-links for a new pair, it would have still been quite feasible that he would go on searching for the originals. And the normal place, the most *likely* place, would be his bedroom. Nothing was more annoying than losing something and having no idea where one has lost it. Father was always losing a cuff-link or a collar stud.

'A place for everything,' Mother would say, 'and everything in its place, and no, Matthew, Mrs Wilkinson has not moved them. She dusts round everything, even the lace covers on your tall-boy, as well I know.'

Dorothy stood on one leg and sighed deeply. But if her father couldn't find what he was looking for in his room, would he be likely to go searching for it in the *park*? Walking along the paths with his head bent, searching, pretending he was just out for an afternoon stroll, but in reality searching? Along the side paths, the long, winding paths leading to the duck pond, the place where. . . .

Yes, it had been Beryl's mention of seeing Gerald in the park that had made the warning bells ring.

Dorothy sat down with a sudden thump on the horse-hair-covered chair placed there for customers with weak legs or hearts. Her own legs felt as if they had started to melt, and her heart was beating with loud and heavy thuds somewhere it had no right to be.

She was getting carried away, as her mother would say. She was as usual allowing her imagination to run off with itself. Even her last school report under General Comments had said that she should try to hold her imagination on a tighter rein.

She took a handkerchief with a bunch of flowers embroidered on one corner out of her blazer pocket and blew her nose on an uncomfortable French knot, and when Mr Adamson spoke to her she jumped as if someone had shot a poisoned arrow into her back.

'By the left, Dorothy, but you were far away,' she heard Mr Adamson say. 'That's three times I've spoken to you, chuck, and you haven't heard a word.' His large face beamed concern. 'Would you like a drink of water, love? You've gone right pale and no mistake.'

Dorothy tried a shaky smile.

'Just thinking, Mr Adamson, that's all. Honestly, I'm fine.'

The jeweller wasn't convinced. 'Hope you're not sickening for this flu, chuck. There's a lot of it about. Your auntie was in only a few days back and we had to sit your cousin out at the back on a chair. Green as grass she were. It's a treacherous month May is; one minute you think it's springlike, and then the next it's as parky as the middle of winter.'

'My cousin Beryl is always sitting outside shops on chairs,' Dorothy said, and he laughed a surprisingly thin laugh for so big a man.

'Come in for your mother's brooch, have you then,

116

chuck? It's all ready wrapped up for her, and you can tell her it's on the house. It were nobbut the pin at the back needed replacing.' He reached underneath the counter and produced a small parcel. 'Soon be the wedding, won't it? My wife's nearly driving me mad talking about what she's going to wear. Who's going to look at *you*, I keep saying, but it makes no difference. She's out now with a piece of stuff in her handbag trying to find a pair of shoes what matches.'

Dorothy picked up the parcel and put it in her blazer pocket. Her fingers tightened round it as she tried to make her voice sound casual.

'Nobody at our house talks about anything else but the wedding.' She hesitated, then plunged on. 'You've met our Margaret's fiancé, haven't you, Mr Adamson? He's a very nice person, isn't he?'

'Out of the top drawer right enough, chuck.'

Dorothy glanced around her in desperation. The door-bell tinkled and as a woman with a loaded shopping basket came into the shop the Saturday assistant came out from the back with her little tripping step.

'The cuff-links,' Dorothy said feverishly. 'The ones Margaret bought him for their engagement present. . . ?' Her voice tailed away as she realized her chance was almost gone. Already the woman customer was glancing over in their direction, making it quite clear that she, too, wished to be served by Mr Adamson, and the assistant's nostrils were dilating in disgust.

Then, as Dorothy was to tell Stanley afterwards, fate intervened.

The jeweller leaned forward confidentially.

'So you're in on the secret, are you then, chuck?'

Dorothy nodded, holding her breath.

'Lovely thought to come in here and buy a replacement for the ones he'd misplaced. Long before he'd had a proper chance to look for them, really. "She mustn't know," he kept saying, and I was only too happy to find him a pair almost the same but a bit bigger.' He winked. 'Good business for me and a perfect solution for him, though I have said of course that should the others turn up I'll take them back. Knowing your father so well and everything.'

The assistant came over, and with her black-clad bosom a mere few inches away from the jeweller's gaze, whispered to him.

'You'll have to excuse me, Dorothy love,' he said, then placed a podgy finger over his mouth. 'Mum's the word now. All right?'

'All right,' Dorothy said, and walked from the shop, her smile as false as the string of pearls Mr Adamson kept draped over the silver-framed photograph of himself in his mayoral robes of three years before.

It was as if something she had always known but never admitted had suddenly taken shape in her mind. As if the reason for her instinctive and unexplained aversion to Gerald Tomlin had suddenly been justified. As if Grandpa Bolton had suddenly materialized, telling her that first impressions were usually the right ones. She could still recall the feeling of distaste when she had first met Gerald's shiny blue gaze.

She walked slowly away from the shop, past the Home and Colonial Store with its smell of freshly ground coffee, at that very moment being poured into little dark brown bags by the counter assistants in their clerical grey cotton coats. Past Blake's café with its tray of cream fancies displayed downstairs, and its winding staircase leading to the upper floor, where the well-to-do matrons of the town met on market days for a pot of tea and a well-buttered sultana scone.

On across the road to the market place, with the stall-holders already packing their unsold wares; past the open entrance to the fish market, with its overpowering smell assailing her senses.

Walking slowly, seeing nothing, thoughts too complex for understanding zooming round and round in her mind like a moth caught in a basin-type light fitting. Actually muttering aloud, halting and giving a small cry of alarm as she felt a sudden light touch on her arm.

And seeing Stanley standing before her, tall and pale, with a carrier-bag held shamefacedly in his hand, a head of celery and sticks of rhubarb protruding from it.

Eleven

There was something essentially sensual, primitive and wanton about all the mounds of fruit and vegetables so lavishly displayed on the market stalls, Stanley had always thought. Especially as he had calculated that only roughly a quarter of the town's population could actually afford to spend with any kind of freedom. There was a family up at the top of his street with a father who had been out of work for eight years. His mother had told him once that they ate meat (a shilling's worth of stewing beef) only once a week, and drank out of condensed milk tins.

'Tea, tinned milk, margarine, bread and potatoes,' his mother had said was all they ate. 'Six children and another on the way, and bugs crawling over the bedroom walls. She's stopped even *trying* to keep the place clean.'

Food as luscious as locusts, he thought bitterly as he waited in a small queue at the salad stall, watching the quarters of shiny dark green watercress and tender spiked lettuce leaves being lowered on to the wide scales. Pale firm tomatoes, blood-red radishes, green-tufted spring onions, and beetroots steaming from a recent boiling. And right behind him the fruit and vegetable stalls. Oranges piled in tempting pyramids, red Delicious apples, with the ones at the front polished to a shining brightness. Potpourris of root vegetables ready bunched together for the stock-pot, and tiny new potatoes needing only a rub of the thumb to rid them of their thin skins.

Food for the gods; food to enjoy, to sink your teeth into a

juicy pear, to taste the soft white flesh . . . He remembered the way Ruby would bite into an apple when his mother came back from the market on Wednesdays and Saturdays. Wiping it first, then biting with her sharp little teeth, eating it right to the core, pips and all. To his dismay he felt the sting of tears behind his eyes.

Then to control himself he fingered the money in his pocket, doing little sums in his mind, as carefully as any conscientious housewife.

Past the fruit stalls, at the very edge of the market, with their little tables set out on the pavement, he could see the shrimp women from Southport in their flowered pinafores and their poke-bonnets, with the tiny pots of buttered shrimps set in rows. He nodded to himself . . . He must somehow work out his budget so that there was enough money left to buy a pot for his mother. Funny the way he kept on thinking about his father since it happened. With force of habit he tuned into his subconscious. Maybe it was because he was trying, in his own way, to stand in for his father in an attempt to help his mother? Trying to think what the quiet man would have said, would have done.

Every Saturday dinner-time, on his way home from work, his father had stopped at the shrimp women's tables and bought his wife a pot of the pink tiny shrimps crowded together beneath their solidified lid of butter. And on a good week he would add a carton of rum butter, gritty with sugar, warm tasting, a reminder of her Cumberland up-bringing.

Oat-cakes drying on the rack, shrimps in a pot, and rum butter spread thickly on the toast. Saturday evening round the inevitable coal fire, with Ruby sitting on the rug between her father's knees as he rubbed her newly washed hair dry. Dark, springy, curly hair, that he would never recall without seeing that leaf caught up in it as she lay on a slab at the mortuary with a sheet over her naked body. He swallowed hard on the lump in his throat, a lump as big as a hard-boiled egg.

'A quarter of loose lettuce leaves and one medium-sized beetroot,' he told the white-coated woman behind the stall, then counted his change carefully before passing on to the fruit and vegetable stalls, where, after concentrated comparisons, he bought a cauliflower, and noted with satisfaction that the rhubarb was reduced in price in deference to the lateness of the afternoon.

And there was enough, just enough money left for a pot of shrimps. He fingered the coin in his pocket, exchanging it already in his mind for the tiny white pot, noting with relief that the shrimp women were still sitting at their tables, poke-bonnets nodding as they counted out their day's takings.

Then turning swiftly in the right direction he came face to face with Dorothy.

'Well, hallo,' they said together, then said it again, blushing to the roots of their respective hair-lines, staring at each other in delighted amazement, as if their meeting was unexpected enough to qualify as a miracle.

'I've been shopping for me mum, for me mother,' Stanley said, explaining away the shame-making carrier-bag.

'Me too,' Dorothy told him, patting her pocket, then she put out a hand and gripped his arm tightly. 'Stanley, seeing you like this was meant to be. Honestly.' She glanced quickly from him to the milling crowds of late shoppers thronging the narrow alley-way between the stalls. 'I've got to talk to you. It's about your – it's about your Ruby. I've found something out, but we can't talk about it here.' She lowered her voice dramatically. 'It's awfully serious. Honestly.'

Stanley fingered the single coin in his jacket pocket, and without a moment's hesitation suggested that they went into the nearby Market Place and had a cup of tea at the railed-off cafeteria set amidst the stalls. Well, his mum would never know that she had nearly had a pot of shrimps for her tea, would she? And the rhubarb had been a decided bargain. What he'd lost on the roundabout he had gained

122

on the swings, so to speak. It was all relative, he told himself as they walked side by side into the covered Market Place, past the stalls laden with Miss Muffet prints, sixpence a yard, the bales of unbleached calico, the edge-whipped flannelette sheets, the pink and blue directoire knickers, the winceyette nightgowns, the combinations displayed with embarrassing showmanship.

And the small cafeteria was deserted, the two girls behind the counter busily wiping down the wide surface with damp cloths.

'You sit here,' Stanley said, hiding the carrier-bag beneath a table, and going over to the counter.

'We're just shutting,' a girl with dolly-rouged cheeks told him, and he blushed and laid the coin on the damp counter.

'Two teas, please,' he said firmly.

'I said we're just shutting,' the girl told him again.

He looked her straight in the eye. 'It's not half-past five yet, and we won't be long. You don't have to brew a fresh pot. All right?'

Sighing, she picked up the huge brown tea-pot and slopped tea into two thick white cups.

'Does your mam know you're out then?' she said, and her friend said, 'Shut your gob, Mavis. Never let it be said that we stood in the way of love's young dream, eh?'

Blushing so that his ears glowed pink, Stanley looked round to see whether Dorothy had heard, but she was sitting hunched over the table with a look of such misery etched on her face, that when he sat down opposite to her, he stretched out a hand and gently stroked her cheek. The girl with rouged circles on her round cheeks grinned and drew a heart in the air with an arrow through it for her friend.

'Juliet and her bloody Romeo,' she said, and they giggled together as if it were the joke of the year.

'What is it then that's so important?' Stanley said, pushing a big glass bowl of sugar in Dorothy's direction.

She shook her head. 'I don't take it. Oh, Stanley, it's so awful I don't know how to begin.'

He ladled three spoonfuls into his own cup. 'Well, try, then. Come on.'

She lowered her voice to a soft whisper. 'I've found out that Gerald Tomlin, you know, the chap our Margaret's going to marry next month – oh God, I've found out that he could have been somehow involved with your sister. With your Ruby.'

Stanley stopped stirring the sugar round in the thick dark tea and let the spoon clatter back into the saucer. 'Say that again.'

'He . . . well, he lost a pair of cuff-links, and made a great to-do of swearing our Margaret to secrecy, and then he said he'd found them, but I've just been in Adamson's jeweller's, and I tricked Mr Adamson into telling me that Gerald hadn't found them at all; that he went into the shop and bought another pair almost the same. As much like the first pair to fool Margaret anyway.'

Stanley blinked, picked up his cup, drank from it, discovered it was only lukewarm and put it down again. Always quick to see the point of any statement immediately, he would have smiled had it not been for the look of intense misery on Dorothy's face. He answered her with caution.

'But how does that tie in with our Ruby? What I mean to say is, how does the fact that he lost a pair of cuff-links, and if he lost them from his shirt he would only lose *one*, surely? And wouldn't it be a quite natural thing to do to try to replace them rather than upset your Margaret? I suppose she bought them for him in the first place, then?'

Dorothy nodded. 'They were her engagement present to him.'

'Then where's the mystery?'

She bit her lip and spoke so quietly that he had to lean towards her, almost to lip-read to decipher what she said next.

'But he's *still* looking for them. Desperately searching for them – or one of them – as if he wasn't sure where he'd lost them, or it, and as if it was vitally important that he found out. He was lifting the carpet in his bedroom. My cousin Beryl spies on him because she has a crush on him, and she saw him, and as far as I can make out he got flustered and told her not to tell anyone. But she couldn't resist telling me not half an hour ago because Beryl doesn't get secrets told to her you see.'

Stanley tried to see. 'Well, I can understand him lifting the carpet. Maybe he's the kind of person who can't bear to lose things. I'm a bit like that myself. If they'd rolled off the bed or off his tall-boy, then under the carpet is a perfectly normal place to look. I honestly don't follow . . .'

Dorothy's blue eyes narrowed to slits. 'Ah, but listen to this. Beryl also saw him later this afternoon. After she'd finished a game of tennis. Stanley . . . he was in the park, walking along with his head bent, obviously still searching. He's just not the kind of bloke who goes for walks in the park. For walks anywhere. He takes that car of his even if he's only going a hundred yards down the road.' She ran a finger round the rim of her cup. 'And that's not all. I think I've known all along that he was seeing, well . . . taking some of the girl weavers out from father's mill. Before he got engaged to our Margaret, I'll give him that. And he tells lies. He's a pathological liar if you want my opinion. He told me he only knew your Ruby to nod to, but I remembered in bed last night that once when I went down to the mill – oh, months ago, I saw him talking to her. It was probably about work. I never thought any more about it, till last night, and even then it didn't seem to matter. But now . . .' she lifted her eyes.

'Go on.'

'Well, he talked to me one day when he ran me home in his car, and he was trying to tell me something.' She frowned in concentration. 'He was trying to win me over to his side, to tell me that whatever he'd done before, none of it was of any importance now that he'd fallen in love with Margaret, and was going to marry her. Real sob stuff. No, don't say anything. I'm talking it out in my mind. It's more a *feeling* I have about him, a something I've sensed ever since he came. He's a *cad*, that's the right word. Or at least he was. Now . . . well, I don't know . . . And since the murder he's changed. He's badly frightened, I know he is. He didn't want to go to the Police Ball, and he's got out of going to the funeral on Monday. Mother would say I'm letting my imagination run away with me as usual, but it's a creepy sort of premonition I have when he's around, and when Beryl said she'd seen him in the park this afternoon, well it all clicked into place.'

She fell silent, and Stanley stared at her, feeling the same way he had when an over-enthusiastic team-mate in the school football team had kicked the ball straight at him and winded him. He didn't know what to say, and yet his mind, the part of his brain that was being trained academically to deduce, to pick out the salient points in a discussion and discard the rest, was working overtime. For a long moment they sat there, opposite to each other, with the thick white cups on the smeared table in front of them, knees touching, looking into each other's faces, marooned there in the busy Market Hall as if they had been marooned on a secluded and secret island.

'So we'll have to go to the police,' she said at last.

'No!' Stanley's voice was husky as if he was recovering from a cold. 'No, Dorothy.' He reached for her hands and then stared down at them joined together with his own. 'It's too soon. There's not enough. It's not even what they would call circumstantial evidence.' He held on and she tried to break away. 'Listen! You can't do that to your family. Think what it would mean. He may have met Ruby, he may well have been seeing her, but apart from the bit about Beryl seeing him in the park . . .'

'Walking along with his head bent.'

He nodded. 'But I always walk with *my* head bent. My mother's always telling me off about it. Apart from that, there isn't a thing really to pin on him, not a thing.'

126

She managed to pull away from him this time, her cheeks flushing with anger.

'But it all fits. Can't you see? It's like a jigsaw puzzle in my head, with every piece fitting into place.' She actually beat at her forehead with a clenched fist. 'You told me yourself that Ruby had been unnaturally secretive, and of course she would be. A girl like Ruby would be, well . . . like putty in his hands. He's what they call a charmer, Stanley, you don't know him like I do. You don't know him at all.' Her voice rose. 'He's devious, that's what he is. Devious and slimy and shiny and a *liar*. But I'll say this for him, I really do believe that when he got engaged to Margaret he stopped seeing other girls. I really believe he intended to be faithful to her, and it might have been like that, but when Ruby found she was having a baby, found out for sure, she had to see him to tell him, and she persuaded him to see her just once, and when she told him he panicked and . . . and killed her!'

Stanley shook his head from side to side. Like a stupid tortoise, she thought wildly. Sitting there with that stupid carrier-bag at his feet, with that stupid stick of rhubarb sticking out of it, and his head shaking from side to side. As if he hadn't taken in a word she was saying. As if it wasn't his sister lying dead in the Chapel of Rest waiting to be buried in the windy cemetery in two days' time.

'I'm going,' she said, getting up and walking quickly away from him, leaving him sitting there as if he'd been struck dumb, with the two girls behind the counter watching her go with fascinated interest.

And there they were, as Mrs Wilkinson was to tell her husband that tea-time, Mrs Bolton's younger daughter, Dorothy, and that Stanley Armstrong out of Inkerman Street. Chasing one another out of the Market Place, him calling her name out loud, and her crying if she hadn't been mistaken. Just like a couple of kids out of Foundry Street, who wouldn't be expected to behave any better.

'You could have knocked me down with a feather,' she

was to say. 'I saw them with my own two eyes as I was taking the short cut down the back steps to the tram stop. "Dorothy! Don't go. Wait for me!" he was shouting at the very top of his voice, and her running and crying. Her mother would have had a pink fit if she could have seen her daughter showing herself up in public. And you'd have thought he would have had more respect for the dead, carrying on like that with his sister not even decently buried.'

'Nowt but a lovers' tiff,' Ned said, more interested in what was for his tea.

And Stanley would have overtaken Dorothy's flying figure easily, but at the entrance to the Market Place he had to pull himself up sharp to prevent knocking over a small boy with an ice-cream cornet in his hand.

'Where's the fire?' a tall man said, scooping the child up out of his way. 'It'll be over afore tha gets there if tha's not quick about it.'

Calling an apology over his shoulder, Stanley ran on, catching up with Dorothy at the foot of the wide flight of stone steps leading into the Town Hall building.

With his free hand he grabbed at her wrist, but she jerked away from him and hurried on, walking quickly, talking to him out of the corner of her mouth.

'You want to know what I feel like, Stanley Armstrong?' she said as if he had asked her. 'I feel as if you've just thrown a bucket of cold water over me, if you want to know.'

He saw a stick of rhubarb about to fall to the ground and shoved it back into the carrier-bag, and seeing him do it was illogically, to Dorothy, the last straw.

'You care more about that stick of rhubarb than what I've just told you. You don't believe a single word of it, do you?' When he didn't answer, she said loudly. 'I don't swear, but bloody hell. Hell's bloody bells.'

He put out his hand towards her again, but she knocked it away with a fierce little swipe.

'Dorothy listen!'

'You listen to me and I'll listen to you. It's your own sister we're talking about, remember?'

She was walking so quickly she was almost tripping over her feet, refusing to look at him, almost beside herself with exasperation. He had never seen her other than passively what Mrs Crawley would have called 'lady-like', and her excitement was catching. They were approaching the bottom of Steep Brow now, and suddenly, heedless of the stares of passers-by, he caught her arm in a grip so firm she was forced to stop. He swung her round to face him, and the expression in his dark eyes was so intense, so pleading, that her angry words died away.

'I've got to go back now, Dorothy. I can't walk home with you shouting at me like this, even if I wanted to. I promised I wouldn't be out long, and me mother's in such a state I have to watch out for her all the time. But after tea tonight, Mrs Crawley's coming in to sit with her, and I'll come round. I'll come up to your house about half-past seven. I'll stand at the corner of your road, and I'll wait for you, and we'll find somewhere to go and talk about it. All right?'

His voice was quiet and controlled, but his manner was as aggressive as if he were shouting at the top of his voice. 'And in the meantime you keep it to yourself.' He went on in that deceptively calm voice; 'My God, Dorothy, how do you think I feel? If there's even a scrap of truth in what you say, I won't be able to keep my hands off him. But it's dangerous talk. It's worse than dangerous.' He shook her arm none too gently. 'If we can prove that he was seeing our Ruby, then I'll be off to the police station so quick you won't see me for dust. That satisfy you?'

Dorothy sighed deeply. She felt tired and beaten, bewildered and lost. She drew in a great intake of breath. 'All right then, but you don't need to wait at the corner of the road. Leave it till eight o'clock, and I'll be alone in the house. I'm tired of standing on corners, Stanley, and I

129

never want to sit on a bench with you in the park again.' She shuddered. 'I might tell them you're coming round and I might not. It all depends.' She turned to walk away from him, and before he set off in the opposite direction, he stood and watched her go.

But she didn't turn round, just walked away, her hands deep in the pockets of her blazer, her feet trailing as if she was in no hurry to go home, in no hurry to go anywhere at all.

Twelve

'I've been down to the selling-out shop and fetched four bottles of stout,' Mrs Crawley said, almost before her head came round the door. 'So get the poker in quick, Mrs Armstrong, and we'll waste no time in giving it a bit of bite.'

Ada did as she was told. She thrust the long poker with its brass handle into the glowing fire, positioning it between the bars of the grate, and watched as Nellie Crawley took off her headscarf and coat, draping them over the back of a chair. She moves about this house as if she's lived here all her life, she thought, not unkindly. It was queer how things turned out. She didn't even have to get up from her chair to get two pots from the scullery. Nellie Crawley knew where they were.

'Don't move, love,' she was saying. 'I'll see to it. By heck but it's cold out. Him as said "Ne'er cast a clout till May is out" knew what he were saying. I didn't cast me vest all last summer, and I doubt if I'll be doing it this. Best place to be is round the fire on a night like this. I've got goose-pimples on me goose-pimples if tha wants to know.'

Ada smiled briefly. If anyone had told her that in such a short time she would have come to know, and aye, – why not say it? – come to *love* the loud-mouthed blowsy woman from across the street, she would have said they were daft. Coarse Nellie Crawley might be, as 'common as muck' folks in the street said, but she didn't know what she'd have done without her these past few days.

'Here we are then, love, one for thee and t'other for me.'

131

Nellie set two pint mugs down on the hearth, and smiled. 'That'll put some lead in tha' pencil, cock.'

Ada nodded. She knew that all things being different, Nellie Crawley would be spending her Saturday evening goodness knows where. Setting off down the street in her black costume, and her pill-box hat with the eye-veil pulled down over her thickly powdered face. Setting off to meet a man? A lover? Or merely to sit in the corner of some public house with a couple of blowsy friends, drinking the hours away till closing-time, leaving her little husband nodding over the fire, listening to the wireless. So they said. It had long been a matter of conjecture in the street as to where Nellie went or what she did on her nights out. But it was none of their business. And none of hers, Ada reminded herself, feeling a twinge of shame as she remembered her own theories as to the kind of woman Nellie Crawley was. 'No better than she should be, and as brazen as brass with it,' she had said herself, on more than one occasion.

Nellie leaned forward, took the poker out of the fire, spat on it and returned it. 'Your Stanley upstairs?'

Ada shook her head. 'He's gone out, Mrs Crawley. I might as well tell you, I'm a bit bothered.' She twisted a corner of her apron round in her fingers. 'He's gone up the park end to see his girl. Matthew Bolton's daughter, our Ruby's boss at the mill.' She gave the poker an extra riddle, turning it round and round in the red embers. 'What her mother thinks about it, I don't rightly know.'

Nellie's voice rose on a squeak of indignation. 'Your Stanley's as good as any of them toffee-nosed sods any old day.'

'I know. Don't get me wrong. I just don't want him to get hurt more than he has been, that's all. It doesn't do. Not that I think owt will come of it; it never works when the money's on the wrong side, and if our Stanley sticks to what he says about not going to the university . . .' She sighed. 'I've persuaded him to bide his time in that direction; there's neither of us thinking straight just now. He were upset about something at tea-time, something more than our Ruby I mean. He'd met that lass down on the market and I think they'd had words. She's bonny enough, but I bet she can be a bit of a tartar. But our Stanley's a sensible lad.'

'And as good as them any old day, Mrs Armstrong. I don't know the lass, not moving in such exalted circles like, but she could do a lot worse for herself than your Stanley, whether he's been to Oxford University or not. If he does leave school he'll not be on the dole for long won't your Stanley, you mark my words.'

'She's only seventeen.'

'Aye, reet enough, but at her age I'd been working for four years and courting strong. More bloody fool me.'

'She's still at school, Mrs Crawley.'

Nellie took the poker out of the fire, nodded with approval at its red and glowing tip, and thrust it into one of the mugs of stout, beaming all over her thin face with satisfaction as the dark brown liquid frothed and hissed over the rim.

'Get that down tha gob, Mrs Armstrong. That'll warm the cockles reet enough, and stop fretting about your Stanley. He'll likely know half a dozen more girls afore he decides to settle down.' She passed over the flowing mug and put the poker back in the fire. 'Don't seem right to me keeping a lass at school when she's a grown woman.' She put her feet on the fender and pulled up her skirt. 'Nowt like warming your bits and pieces in front of a good fire. Aye, I've seen them High School girls, titties bursting out of their gym-slips, making eyes at the boys from the Grammar School. I'll tell you straight, Mrs Armstrong, I don't hold with too much of this education for girls. For boys it's all right, I suppose, if they're clever like your Stanley, but what happens to them girls wagging their behinds in their gym-slips? I'll tell thee. They gets married straight from school, knowing nowt. What good is Shakespeare and that algebra stuff when the babies come along? Tha doesn't need to pass an exam to know how to change a mucky nappy. Come on, get tha feet up aside mine on the fender, and later I'll nip down to the chip shop and fetch us a three and a fourpenny. And no arguing about the money, either. I got me divi last week, and it's burning a hole in me pocket. What's money for if tha can't spend it, I'd like to know.'

Ada's eyes swam with the ever ready tears, and she groped in her apron pocket for a handkerchief. 'I'll never be able to pay you back for what you've done for me these past few days, Mrs Crawley.' She blew her nose hard. 'I had a letter from my brother up in Maryport this morning, and he finds now he won't be able to get down for the funeral Monday morning. It would mean him coming tomorrow, see, and he's frightened to take the time off his work. He says they're looking for excuses to lay men off at the mine, and he has four children still at school.' She sighed deeply. 'We were very close when we were young, but well . . . tha knows how it is. There never seemed the money for the train fare, and over the years we stopped going, and when me husband was alive we didn't seem to need no one else. And since then it's been work and more work. We were such a happy family, the four of us, not always quarrelling and bickering like some folks. And now there's only Stanley and me left. I can't credit it somehow.'

Nellie thrust the poker into the second mug of stout. 'Aye, this fear of coming out o' work makes cowards of us all. I've seen men lie and cheat and do their own kith and kin down to keep a job. My old man's as soft as they come, but he'd make a bargain with owd Nick himself to stay in work. It's getting to the stage when them that has a job feels ashamed. You know summat? I don't get me groceries all at once from the Co-op now. I gets them a few at a time so I don't have to walk up the street with a laden basket.' She tilted her head back and drank deeply, then wiped her mouth with the back of her hand. 'I'll bet they're short of nowt where your Stanley is tonight. I'll bet that Matthew Bolton has never had to want for a bob or two.'

'All the same, I'd have liked our Jim to be at the funeral

Monday,' Ada said, starting to cry again. 'Our Stanley's only a boy; it's too much for him, he's been so wrapped up in his books he hasn't left enough time over for just living, and now it seems all that learning is going to waste.' She choked on a sob.

Nellie patted her knee. 'Have a proper cry if tha feels like it, love. Don't mind me, far better that tha gets it out of tha system now than bottles it up. Worst thing anyone can do is to bottle it all up. I knew a woman once who never cried once when her old man passed over while watching a football match, and six months later to the day she were riddled from head to foot with the arthritis. Couldn't move nowt but her eyeballs. And I'm not going to tell thee that time heals, because it bloody doesn't. All time does is stop it bleeding a bit, that's all.'

'I wish our Stanley had worn his suit to go up there,' Ada said five minutes later. 'But he's gone out in his pullover and a sports jacket that doesn't fit him no more. I'd like him to have looked his best. But they won't listen.'

Then, remembering how Ruby hadn't listened either, she started to cry again, softly, as if there was a well inside her that would never dry up.

'I like your jacket,' Dorothy said insincerely when she opened the front door to Stanley's ring. 'I've never seen it before, have I? Here, give it to me, and I'll hang it up.'

She took it from him, noticing the frayed edges to the cuffs, feeling the rough texture of the cheap material, and, turning round to face him, thought how pale and ill at ease he looked in the green sweater with its V neck showing off a quite hideous red spotted tie. She much preferred him in his school blazer and striped tie, she decided, despising herself even as she thought it.

And as she stared at him, in the few seconds it took for her to see how different, how out of place, he looked against her home background, it came to her that she didn't love him.

135

Not really *love* him. She liked him, and she wasn't a snob like her mother, heaven forbid, but in that flash of a moment, Dorothy's infatuation, her seventeen-year-old's infatuation for the gangling boy standing beside her, died. And if Phyllis had been able to read her daughter's mind, she would have been silently applauding.

Dorothy was appalled, horrified and bewildered, and to cover her confusion she took him by the hand, and led him down the oak-panelled hall and into the sitting-room.

How was it possible? she was asking herself silently; how was it possible to love someone one minute and then look at him and know that you had been wrong? Was this what her father had meant when he had advised her to take her time? She squeezed Stanley's hand in contrition, pleading with him in her mind for forgiveness.

Stanley stared round him, trying hard not to stare and failing completely. His eyes took in the size of the room, more than twice the size of the living-room at home, the height of the ceiling, the depth of the cushions on the three-piece suite. He blinked at the brightness of the cream-tiled fireplace with its raised hearth and its twinkling brasses. His toe traced the pattern of the thick carpet, and he boggled at the bookshelves let into wide niches at each side of the fireplace. Leather-bound books, in sets, arranged in rows of equal sizes, their bindings matching, looking as if the only time they were taken down was for dusting. He pulled at the knot of the hideous tie as if it were strangling him.

'Well, sit down then,' Dorothy said, and he obeyed, sitting on the very edge of a chair, hitching up his trouser legs, and speaking in a low voice as if he were in chapel.

'Did you tell them I was coming?'

Dorothy sat down opposite to him on the massive chester-field, curling her legs up beneath her. 'Well, I daren't after what you said this afternoon, dare I? But in any case, Gerald was here, and I went up to my room.' Her eyes clouded. 'Honestly, he gives me the willies. I know I won't be able to talk naturally to him till this thing's sorted out. I've got a feeling he knows I suspect something.' She twisted a strand of hair round her finger. 'He's like a slimy snake, except that snakes are really dry.'

Stanley stared at the cut-glass sherry decanter on the low table by the side of his chair, flanked by four glasses arranged in pairs. Just for a moment he forgot the seriousness of what he had come for as he thought of the contrast between those sparkling glasses and the amber-coloured liquid, and the mugs of stout he guessed his mother would be drinking with Nellie Crawley.

'You haven't said anything to your mother and father? You kept it to yourself like I said?'

Dorothy narrowed blue eyes at him. 'I daren't say a word about anything, I told you. I'm scared of you, you were so fierce this afternoon. No, I'll keep it to myself for the time being,' she said calmly. 'I had a long think about what you said, and you're right. I'm too impulsive, always have been, and he's not likely to run away, is he? Not when he's decided to brazen it out.'

'Aw, Dorothy.' Stanley's tone was rueful. 'All right then, just suppose there is something in what you say? No, he won't run away, just as long as he doesn't suspect that we suspect.'

'We? I thought you rejected everything I said? That's how it seemed to me this afternoon.'

Stanley's thin face took on what she thought of as his suffering look. Its holier-than-thou look, she thought with a twinge of irritation. Funny how different he looked sitting there in her own familiar surroundings. Uncomfortable, wary, frightened almost. As if he were perched there on the edge of the chair ready to get up and run from the room at any given moment. Poised for flight. Out of place. He didn't match, she thought sadly. Everything else in the room matched, but Stanley Armstrong didn't. Suddenly she felt scared.

'Come over and sit next to me,' she invited, patting the

moquette cover with her hand. 'It's quite safe, they'll not be back for ages yet.'

And then, as he took her in his arms and held her close, as his lips searched for hers and closed over them with the familiar hard closed-mouth kiss, it was all right again.

'Oh, Dorothy, you're so beautiful, you're the most beautiful girl in the world,' he whispered. Then he kissed her again, and this time the kiss was deeper, and as they clung together she could feel his heart thudding like a sledge-hammer against his ribs. How thin he was! She ran her hands over his shoulders. And how young he was, how very young! And vulnerable. She held him closer still and felt him tremble.

This wasn't the same as kissing in the park, or on the back row of the pictures, or in a darkened shop doorway. Then she hadn't experienced this overwhelming sense of power, this knowing that in spite of his cleverness, his practical theories, she was the one in charge. It was wonderful and it was terrible. Terrible and sort of disappointing. She buried her head in his green woollen chest and caught the unmistakable whiff of moth-balls. How awful if she started to giggle! So far she was quite unmoved. Pleasured, but quite unmoved. She stretched her body out on the wide cushions and felt his body adapt itself to hers. Felt his chest, his loins, and a hardness that made her catch her breath with surprise.

His face was hot against her own, burning as if he had a fever. She made no move to stop him when his hand fumbled with the buttons of her blouse, caught her breath again then as she felt the feather-light touch of his fingers on her nipples, she felt them grow hard and whimpered as the heat rose in her own body.

'Oh, Dorothy,' he moaned, and she tangled her fingers in the springiness of his hair, and pulled his head down, and as his mouth closed over her breast, she jerked her head back with a low sound of delight.

Then, with a suddenness that left her limp and disbelieving, he sat up away from her, pulled the front of her blouse together, and in a voice that shook, begged her to forgive him.

'I'm sorry,' he muttered, looking away from her into the fire. 'I shouldn't have done that. Can you ever forgive me?'

Buttoning up her blouse, Dorothy refused to look at him.

'I respect you,' he insisted.

'I know you do,' she comforted.

Then he covered his face with his hands and groaned aloud.

What he could never tell her was that he might have gone further, might even have tried to . . . . but that even as he caressed her he had suddenly been reminded of what had happened to Ruby. In another moment his self-control might have snapped and then he would have been no better, tarred with the same brush as that man, that unknown man who had forced himself on his sister and taken away her virginity. For she had been a virgin until then, just as Dorothy was a virgin. He knew it, and the knowledge of what he might have done filled him with a revulsion against his own sex.

'I'll never spoil thee, Dorothy,' he said quietly, using the Lancashire dialect as he always did when moved.

Dorothy got up and going over to the mantelpiece, took down a silver cigarette box. Her face was flushed and her eyes as heavy as if she'd been crying. He thought she had never looked lovelier.

She held the box out to him. 'Have a smoke. Go on, I can wash the ashtray before they come back.'

He stretched out his hand to the neatly layered cigarettes, marvelling at the length, their firmness. Already he could feel the tang of the smoke curling round his tongue, the steadying of his nerves as he inhaled. 'They'll smell it, won't they?' he said.

'The whole house reeks of my father's pipe, hadn't you noticed? My mother's tried everything, from a cut onion in a saucer to spraying the air with her precious lavender water.' Then as he took one she placed a heavy cut-glass ashtray on the little table by his side.

'I've decided to let Beryl in on it,' she said.

He stopped in the act of lighting up. 'Beryl?' he repeated, his face a study in disbelief.

Dorothy sighed. 'My cousin down the road. You know. I told you this afternoon. I told you that Gerald had sworn her to secrecy about losing the cuff-links, remember? He wants her on his side too. In case any awkward questions are asked, don't you see?' She took the spent match from his fingers and threw it impatiently into the fire. 'Don't look so . . . so affronted! We won't mention your Ruby, we'll just say that we suspect that Gerald is being unfaithful to Margaret, and we want her to help us to catch him out. She's so romantic that if she thinks it's all in the cause of true love, or untrue love, she'll do anything she can to help. After Gerald confiding in her, then us, she'll feel like a double agent, can't you see? So when you've finished that cigarette we'll go down to her house. It's only down the road, and I know she's in on her own because her mother and father have gone out with my parents, to the same place. Yes, that's what we'll do. We'll talk to Beryl, then we'll have a dekko in Gerald's room.'

'Now look, Dorothy.' Stanley shook his head from side to side as if he couldn't believe that the girl planning and scheming so coolly could possibly be the same girl who, not five minutes before, had lain in his arms, as carried away as he had been. He could have sworn it. Now she was tapping with her foot on the floor, waiting for him to pull himself together and finish his cigarette. He was learning about women, he was, aye by heck, he was learning fast.

He saw that his hand still trembled as he held the cigarette to his lips, and scorned his own weakness. 'Now look, Dorothy,' he said more firmly. 'I've been thinking about what you said ever since you said it, and there's nothing – not one shred of evidence that would stand up in any court in the land. I don't know what's come over you, and that's a fact.' He drew deeply on the cigarette. 'He couldn't have been meeting our Ruby on the sly and not told the police when this happened. He'd be bound to know they'll find out. Somebody would have seen them together. Somebody always does. Look how many people have told your mother about seeing *us*.'

'He has a car,' Dorothy said slowly, emphasizing each word as if she were talking to a backward five-year-old. 'And it was the winter when he was meeting Ruby, remember? Dark, Stanley Armstrong. Dark.'

She sat down and clasped her hands round her knees. 'All right then, maybe I did get carried away this afternoon, but he *knew* her, Stanley. I've seen his eyes when it's come up, and oh, he knew her all right. And if he knew her and had been seeing her then he could perhaps help the police to find out who murdered her.' She lifted a knee with her clasped hands and rocked herself backwards and forwards. 'Oh, my God, I feel it so strongly, can't you see? I've never hated anyone in my life before, but I hate Gerald Tomlin so much I can actually feel my skin crawl when he's near to me. Do you believe in spiritual perception, Stanley?'

'Perception yes, but not necessarily spiritual.'

'Well then. He's scared half out of his wits, Stanley. He is. Honestly. And next month he's going to marry my sister, who is about as perceptive as that standard lamp over there, and that doesn't mean I don't love her dearly because I do. And if you won't come with me to Beryl's, then I'll go myself, and you can go home.'

'Dorothy! Stop it. I don't know you when you're like this.' His voice was filled with reproach.

She held her head high. 'You know me a bit better after tonight though, don't you, Stanley Armstrong?'

'Come here,' he said softly, crushing the cigarette out in the ashtray. 'I promise I'll be good this time.' Then as he wrapped her in his arms, he whispered into her hair. 'I need you so much. I just want to hold you like this, and close my eyes and pretend nothing awful has happened. I want to pretend this is our house, and you are my wife, and I want to forget I've left me mum crying by the fire waiting till Monday when they'll be burying our Ruby on top of me dad in the cemetery.' He stroked her cheek gently. 'There's so much that's good in the world, Dorothy, so much of it right here in this room, and I want a part of it . . . I'm selfish and cruel because I don't want to go back down the hill to Inkerman Street. I'm dreading Monday, and having to be brave for me mum's sake. I want it all to go away, Dorothy. I want to pretend just for a little while that it never happened. You don't know how awful it is in that house. I feel I'm breathing now for the first time since it happened.'

She held his hand to her cheek and turned her lips to it, then froze into instant watchful silence as she heard the grating of a key in the lock of the big front door.

'Oh, my God, they've come back! Pretend you've come about the funeral. Just act normal. They can't *do* anything.'

She was moving with the speed of light, emptying the ashtray into the fire, tucking her blouse into her skirt, moving to sit as far away from him as she could, so that when the door opened they were sitting there stiffly as if arranged, like dummies in a shop window.

And it wasn't, as she had thought it would be, her mother and father returning early from their bridge party, but Margaret, radiant with happiness, followed into the room by Gerald Tomlin.

142

Thirteen

'Well? What did I tell you?' Dorothy said as soon as the big front door closed behind them. She was pulling at Stanley's hand urging him on, and he felt he'd had enough, more than enough. His mind, still dazed with grief, his *academic* mind, geared to study, to the assimilation of facts, to the light relief of what he realized now had been merely surface conversations with the girl at his side, reeled dizzily from what had just happened.

He hardly recognized the determined set of Dorothy's face, saw nothing of the former quiet acceptance of her devotion. She was *obsessed*, he told himself, totally obsessed.

'Did you see the way his face changed when he saw you?' she demanded. 'What did you think about him? Don't you think his eyes are strange? Could you even bear to look at them knowing . . . ?'

'We know nothing,' Stanley said. 'You must be crazy. Do you realize what you're saying?' He shook his head wearily from side to side. 'Folks have been hung for less.'

He took her by the elbows and forced her to stand still. 'Give me a chance to think, to *breathe* for heaven's sake.' She was dancing with impatience, but still he held her fast. 'Dorothy. Dorothy. Calm down, please. What they must think of us rushing out like that, I don't know. You should have stayed and let me talk to him, given me a chance to weigh him up. I felt a fool, an utter fool.' He looked back over his shoulder to the house. 'I should have stood my ground, not allowed you to rush me out of the room; they're probably laughing their heads off at us now. And if there is anything in what you say, if he did know Ruby, then by our very behaviour he's bound to know that we suspect.'

A man walking his dog went by and glanced at them with curiosity, and Stanley waited until he was well out of ear-shot.

'And as for saying that Gerald's face changed, well, of course it changed. He came into that room and saw us sitting there, both looking as guilty as hell, then without a hallo or a goodbye, you grab me by the hand and drag me out of the room, as if I were a naughty child, snatching up our coats in the hall and banging the front door behind us. Of course his face changed. He'll think we're mad, completely out of our minds. That's what he'll think and that's all.'

Dorothy wriggled impatiently out of his grasp and started to walk quickly ahead of him, so that even with his long loping stride he had difficulty in keeping up with her. She talked furiously to him over her shoulder.

'Gerald Tomlin *knew* who you were. There was no need to say anything, because he knew.' She pulled savagely at a privet hedge, then scattered the leaves on the ground as if leaving a paper-chase for Stanley to follow. 'He knew who you were because you look like your sister. You told me how alike you were.' Her voice rang with triumph. 'If he hadn't known that I was friendly with you, he would have known who you were. And it was a shock. A terrible shock. I saw his face go white. His face went white and those funny wet eyes of his dilated; I wouldn't have been surprised if he'd dropped down on the floor in a dead faint.'

She turned into the wide driveway of a detached house, the gates and the garage door left open for a returning car. 'This is where my cousin Beryl lives. You can come in with me, Stanley, or you can go home. You can go back down Inkerman Street, and you can tell your mother that you've met the man who I believe got your Ruby into trouble, even if he didn't kill her. You can tell her that and you can say

144

that you quite liked the look of him, actually.'

'Dorothy!' Stanley's voice was more of a groan. 'What did you expect me to do, then? Knock him down when I can't think of a single reason for doing so? Dorothy. Please listen to me. I'm listening to *you*, honestly I am. I'm listening and I'm thinking, and as soon as you tell me one single fact that makes me even slightly suspicious, then I'll tell the police, whether he's your future brother-in-law, or not. But it's dangerous talk. Can't you see? Do you ever stop to think that you could be turning your dislike of Gerald into a reason for all this wild talk? Do you mean that you expected me to accuse him, then and there?'

As Dorothy put her finger on the door-bell, a chime of bells ding-donged up and down the scale, and Stanley leant against the door-post, feeling in need of its solid support.

Dorothy pressed the bell again. 'Surely Beryl's not in bed at this time? She's probably been told not to answer the door. I'll shout through the letter-box if she doesn't come in a minute.'

Stanley kicked at a loose piece of gravel. 'I suppose they'll tell your mother and father that I was there? I'd much rather have come openly the first time and met them properly, like a civilized being.'

Just for a fleeting moment Dorothy was caught off guard. The thought that her mother did not regard this tall troubled boy as a civilized being flashed through her mind. His mother took in washing, and his sister worked in a cotton mill and had been ill-bred enough to get herself pregnant, and murdered. And yet his code of honour, his innate sense of what was right and proper was far greater than her own . . . There was something wrong somewhere.

'They won't tell,' she said, 'that's the last thing they'll do. Sisters don't sneak on each other, and Gerald certainly won't mention meeting you.'

'Seeing me, not meeting me.'

'Well, seeing you then. Oh no, Gerald won't want to start a discussion about you or anything to do with you. He can't

145

bear your family to be mentioned, Margaret told me. Something to do with his sensitive disposition. He makes me sick. Can't you see?'

'There's someone coming,' Stanley said miserably. He felt ill, and the hammering in his head was starting up again. The tension of the past few days was taking its inevitable toll, and the cool logic he prided himself on was deserting him with every passing minute. He was behaving totally out of character, and Dorothy had changed out of all recognition from the girl he thought he knew. The Dorothy he knew had been content to listen to his views for hours at a time, her pretty face aglow with admiration as he expounded his views on life in general, and Stanley Armstrong and his ambitions in particular.

Ruby was dead, gone for ever, and something in him had died with her. What had happened to her that night in the park so filled his mind with animal loathing that in some strange inexplicable way he had transferred some of that emotion to the girl now tapping her foot impatiently as she waited for the door to open. And if he had done what he'd wanted to do he would have been no better than that unknown man who had squeezed Ruby's breath out of her, then left her with her black hair tangled with mud and leaves. The enormity of what had almost happened caught at his own throat as surely as if fingers pressed on his windpipe.

And all he really wanted to do was to mourn. To scream and yell his grief aloud; to stop trying to be a man with a stiff upper lip, as stiff as the collars his mother dipped into her bowl of starch. All he wanted to do was to put his head down somewhere and cleanse himself with tears.

But somebody was calling out from the other side of the big ornate front door.

'Yes? Who is it, please?'

Dorothy raised exasperated blue eyes skywards. 'It's Dorothy. Open the door, Beryl. It's not Jack the Ripper.'

And if Cousin Beryl had not been already tucked up in

bed, it was obvious that she was on her way there. The dark brown woollen dressing-gown, its cord pulled tightly round her thick waist, did less than nothing for her sallow complexion, and the side pieces of her lank brown hair were rolled up in steel curlers. As she saw Stanley standing beside Dorothy, her hands went straight to them, pulling at them in an attempt to wrench them out. Two spots, chalky with calamine lotion, disfigured her rounded chin.

'Oh, Dorothy.' Her eyebrows were sending a message to her cousin, and Stanley read it correctly.

'How could you come and bring him without letting me know? Now he's seen me looking like this, and I'll feel awful every time I see him.'

Once, a long time ago, he had let Eddie Marsden in when Ruby was sitting by the fire with a towel round her newly washed hair, and she had given him what for afterwards. 'You could have left him on the door-step till I'd had time to run upstairs,' she'd stormed. And Ruby had been exactly the same age as this fat girl, stiff with embarrassment, dithering in the porch, tearing at the steel curlers in her hair.

'You'd better come in then,' she said ungraciously, and miserably Stanley stepped behind Dorothy into a square hall, an almost exact replica of the one he'd recently stepped out of, apart from the fact that the walls were papered in a bottle-green geometric design instead of being wood-panelled.

'You know Stanley by sight, don't you?' Dorothy made the introduction casually, walking before them into the room on the right and leaving Stanley shaking hands with a totally demoralized Beryl who was trying to wipe off the calamine lotion and take out the one remaining curler at the same time.

'I'm sorry,' he whispered, meaning it even as he realized how stupid it sounded.

'And I'm sorry about . . .' Beryl said, blushing so red that her eyes seemed to sparkle with unshed tears.

147

'It's all right,' Stanley said inadequately.

They walked into a large room papered with a design as glumly oppressive as that in the hall. In spite of his misery Stanley looked around him with curiosity, and his mind registered the fact that never in his life had he seen so ugly a room. The cosy little living-room at home with its black fireplace and the firelight flickering on the cream distempered walls seemed almost luxurious by comparison. Here the paper-frieze, following the lines of the picture-rail, was a design of bright yellow hanging blossoms, and the doors and window-frames were painted in an only slightly subdued shade of the same colour. The vast tiled fireplace had a ziggurat motif which was faithfully reflected in the carpet, and the chairs and sofa were upholstered in cold, unyielding leather.

'Sit down then,' Beryl told him, and smiled for the first time.

She sat down opposite to him and fixed an unwinking gaze on him.

'Have you been to the pictures?' Her hand flew to her mouth, like a naughty child caught out saying something she shouldn't. 'Oh, golly, I'm sorry. Of course you won't have been to the pictures, not with . . . with everything. Oh, gosh.'

'It's all right,' Stanley said again.

Dorothy stood between them, her hands in her blazer pocket. 'Beryl? Can we trust you?'

Stanley winced. 'Look, I don't really think . . .'

'Can we, Beryl?'

The round brown eyes almost popped out with the vehemence of Beryl's nod.

'Cut my throat and hope to die.'

'We want more than that.' Dorothy walked purposefully over to a glass-fronted bookcase and opening the door with a small key already in the lock, took out a large, leather-bound Bible. 'Right, now come over here, Beryl.'

Stanley wished himself anywhere but where he was. He

148

wished he had stayed at home. He wished he was dead. . . .

Dorothy opened the Bible with a flourish, and put it down on a chromium and glass-topped table. 'Place your hand there then.'

And obeying at once, striped pyjama legs flapping beneath the boy's-style dressing-gown, Beryl walked over to her cousin and laid a podgy hand on the open page.

'I swear to keep my mouth shut about what I am about to hear. For the time being,' Dorothy prompted.

'I swear to keep my mouth shut. For the time being,' Beryl repeated in tones of awe.

'Right.' Dorothy slammed the Bible shut and returned it to its place in the bookcase. 'Now listen. We've found out . . .' She glanced briefly in Stanley's direction and sighed. 'At least, we *think* we've found out that Gerald Tomlin is being unfaithful to Margaret.' She refused to look at Stanley. 'We think he may even have got a girl into trouble, and we want you to help us to prove it.'

'But they're getting married . . .' Beryl sat down with an ungainly thump on the nearest brown leather chair. 'Oh, how awful! I can't believe it. They're madly in love. Passionately,' she added, blushing again in deference to Stanley's presence.

'Maybe. That's as maybe,' Dorothy said, 'and we think there may be evidence, proof, rather, in his bedroom.' She turned her back on Stanley. 'So I'm going up there to have a look round, and you're going to stay down here with Stanley, and on my way up I'm going to bolt the door, so that should anyone come back, they won't be able to get in, and I'll have time to get back downstairs.'

Beryl looked as if she might be going to burst into tears. 'And what will I say then if they do come back? What will I tell my mother when she asks why the door was bolted? That's what I want to know.'

Dorothy glanced at Stanley for sympathy, and found none.

'You'll think of something. Anyway, if they do come back

they'll be more concerned about you having a boy in the house than about the door being bolted. And you can blame that on me.'

Beryl took a large handkerchief from her pocket and screwed it up into a ball. 'It's all right for you, Dorothy Bolton. I'll be the one who gets into trouble, not you. My mother will kill me if she finds out. She made me promise not to open the door to anyone.'

'Gerald excepted of course.' Dorothy was already on her way to the door. 'Oh, the irony of it.'

'I'm coming with you,' Stanley stood up, not knowing, as Mrs Crawley would have said, whether he was bloody coming or bloody going.

'No, you stay here with Beryl, then if I get found out you won't be involved. I won't be long.'

And Dorothy disappeared; they heard her running light-footed up the stairs.

Stanley and Beryl stared at each other, transfixed.

'My mother would kill me,' Beryl said. 'I'm not brave like Dorothy. She – my mother I mean – she stopped me playing with Dorothy when we were little girls because she was always getting me into trouble.' She started to fringe the end of her dressing-gown cord. 'She thinks it's awful, Auntie Phyllis – that's Dorothy's mother – allowing Dorothy to go out with you.' She was far too upset to weigh her words. 'And if she knew that you'd both been in here whilst they were out, she'd blame me.' She bit her lip. 'And as for her going up to Gerald's room. Oh, it's awful. I've looked in the doorway many a time, but I've never been in. My conscience wouldn't let me.'

'She's thinking about her sister's happiness,' Stanley said with some desperation, feeling loyalty of some kind was called for.

Footsteps walked up and down on the other side of the high ceiling, and for a moment it seemed that the big glass light fitting shivered. Stanley shivered with it. Since Dorothy had left the room her cousin's raisin brown eyes

150

had never left his face.

'She stares at Gerald,' he remembered Dorothy saying, and for a moment felt a twinge of sympathy.

'Dorothy's got this bee in her bonnet,' he said. 'I think I'll go up and fetch her down. You're right, Beryl, it's not fair to you.'

'No!' Her voice rang with the beginnings of hysteria. 'Oh, it's awful! If anyone was to come back, and you were upstairs with Dorothy, they'd think you were . . .' She closed her eyes in horror. 'They'd think you were . . . well, upstairs and everything, both of you, and me downstairs.' Her voice tailed off as she blushed scarlet, overcome with an embarrassment she would live through for days just remembering. 'My mother's very strict with me. She doesn't allow me to go out with boys. Oh gosh!' She plucked at the dressing-gown cord with frantic fingers. Now what had she gone and said? This boy's sister, sixteen like herself, had been allowed to go out with boys, had actually done *it*. Oh, gosh, how awful! It wasn't his fault. He was nice, far too nice for her bossy cousin rooting around in Gerald's room upstairs. She stared at him straight in the eye.

'What's your favourite subject at school, Stanley?' she asked with a kindly but stunned kind of desperation.

Dorothy found what she was looking for within minutes of entering Gerald's room. On top of the walnut tall-boy was a round leather stud-box, and inside was an assortment of studs and cuff-links. She took it over to the bed and turned it upside down on the quilted satin bedspread. The back-studs she pushed aside and concentrated on sorting out the cuff-links. Eight pairs in all, including the pair she had seen Gerald wearing the night of the Police Ball, the second bigger pair he had bought secretly at Adamson's the jewellers.

With one link spare. The slightly smaller type she had seen Margaret buy as an engagement present weeks before.

Her heart-beat quickened as she tossed it from one hand to the other. So she was right. He had come in that terrible night with one link missing, and in his agitation had not know where he had lost it, had even dared to hope that he had dropped it in his room as he tore frantically at his clothes before getting into bed and burying his face in the pillow to shut out the sound of Ruby's dying gasps. Her imagination soared. Then, with the cuff-link in her hand, she got up from the bed and began to pace the room. Backwards and forwards, forwards and backwards, taking in the contents of the room with the surface of her mind.

The blue silk dressing-gown hanging in disciplined folds from a hook behind the door, the tortoise-shell brushes laid out side by side on the dressing-table with its three mirrors reflecting her worried face in triplicate. The row of books on the shelf behind the bed. Auntie Ethel's hideous taste in furnishings, the olive-green of the bedspread at shiny shouting variance with the electric-blue curtains hanging at the tall windows. And the all pervading smell of Gerald's lavender-scented brilliantine. She wrinkled her nose in distaste.

Then suddenly the sound of a car, the revving of an engine pulled her up sharp. Gerald was coming back! Frantically, as she shuffled the studs and cuff-links back into the leather box, she tried to remember if the red sports car had been in the garage as she came up the drive with Stanley. Had she seen it, or had she been too preoccupied with trying to make Beryl answer the door that she hadn't noticed? Pulling the door behind her she flew down the stairs, and went into the sitting-room where two pairs of startled eyebrows raised themselves in urgent enquiry.

'I thought I heard Gerald's car,' she said, but Beryl shook her head. 'It's in the garage. He left it there and walked to your house with Margaret. I watched them from the landing window.'

Dorothy collapsed rather than sat down in the nearest chair. 'My God, but it was spooky up there. I thought I'd have heart failure when I heard that car.' Her laugh had more than a touch of hysteria in it. 'I was out of that room quicker than a drink of water.'

Stanley stood up. 'Well, I hope you're satisfied. What you hoped to find I don't know, but I'm going home. Right now, Dorothy.' He turned to Beryl. 'You've been a sport.' Doubling his hand into a fist he touched her lightly on the shoulder. 'Now you'll know me the next time you see me.'

'I won't tell,' Beryl said, her face as solemn and her eyes as round as a night owl's.

'She won't, you know,' Dorothy said in the hall, bending down and unbolting the front door.

'She's a good kid,' Stanley said. 'Come on, I'll see you home.'

Dorothy shook her head. 'I'll just go back and have another word with Beryl.'

'Then I'll wait for you.'

'No, there's no need, honestly. It's only a hop skip and jump.' His face in the darkness was tense-looking and sad, and she laid her cheek briefly against the sleeve of the shabby jacket.

'Don't look so worried, please, Stanley. I won't do anything stupid, honestly. And Beryl won't say anything. I know her, she'll think it's all too romantic for words.'

'What? About Gerald being what you said he was?'

'No, about meeting you, I mean.'

'And Gerald?'

She turned her face into his shoulder so that her voice came muffled, 'Oh, forget that for now. I was so scared up there in his room I don't want to think about it . . . you'd best go now. And Stanley?'

'Hmm?'

'I'll be thinking about you on Monday. I'll be at school, but I'll be thinking about you every single minute.'

Suddenly she wanted to put her arms round him and cry and cry, and the feeling was as overwhelming as the fear that had caught her by the throat in the upstairs room not five minutes before. 'Go now. And God bless.'

She didn't ever remember saying that before. It was what the vicar always said when they took their leave of him in the church porch every Sunday morning. It was what her father used to say when he tucked her up in bed when she was a child and she would have no one but him to bid her good night. And it was what Grandpa Bolton had always said. 'God bless, lovey. God bless.'

Then Stanley walked away from her, and she watched him go as she always seemed to be watching him go. Head bent, with the long, loping careless stride, wrists protruding from the awful jacket. Sighing, she went back into the sitting-room.

Beryl was standing in front of a large bean-shaped mirror, busy with the curlers again.

'You might have rung up and said you were bringing Stanley round,' she grumbled, licking her thumb and forefinger and sliding a piece of hair between them. 'How do you think I felt with him seeing me in my dressing-gown and with my hair all pinned up?' Her eyes were suddenly sly. 'You'd been snogging, hadn't you? I can see a love-bite on your neck. He's nice, and I felt ever so sorry for him. He didn't like you going up to Gerald's room one little bit. He didn't say anything, but I knew. And anyway, what does it matter if Gerald has been unfaithful to your Margaret? Men always have a past, and it will be awful if you go and spoil the wedding now. And if some silly girl has got herself into trouble then it's her fault. It's always the girl who eggs the boy on; a boy gets worked up quicker than a girl. And anyway, it's only that sort of girl who gets worked up anyway.'

Dorothy closed her eyes. 'You've sworn on the Holy Bible not to tell, remember?'

'I know, and I'll be damned to eternal hell-fire if I tell. I *know*. That's two secrets I'm keeping now. I wish I had one of my jolly own to keep.' She rubbed her stomach. 'I think I'll go and have a biscuit.'

'And I'm going.' Dorothy hesitated. 'Do you *like* Gerald, Beryl? As a person I mean?'

Beryl was already en route for the biscuit barrel. 'I've never really thought about it. He's a bit of a dark horse, I suppose.'

'How is he a dark horse?'

Beryl pulled at her bottom lip. 'Well, like I told you, before he fell in love with your Margaret, he used to go off in his car and just say he was going out. That was a bit rude, wasn't it?'

'Unless he had something to hide?'

Dorothy followed her cousin into the kitchen, and shook her head when the biscuit barrel was held out to her.

'I'll tell you one thing.' Beryl spoke through a mouthful of Marie biscuit. 'We had a policeman round just before tea.'

Dorothy held her breath. 'Go on.'

Beryl took another biscuit. 'Well, you know they're asking all the men in the whole town where they were on the night Stanley's sister was killed.'

'Yes, I know.'

'Gosh, I'm hungry. Well, when they went to the mill Gerald was out, so they came here. They were coming here, anyway, to ask my father. He was at the Masons.'

'And Gerald?' The clock was ticking so loudly that Dorothy glanced towards it. 'And *Gerald*?'

'Well, he said that he'd gone for one of his drives in his car. You know, I told you, he was always going for drives.'

'Yes. Yes?'

'I'll just have one more biscuit. Well, he said he had been for a drive that night, but he hadn't. He went out, but he didn't take his car. He walked.'

'How do you know?'

'Because I watched him from the landing window. He left the car in the garage that night.'

Dorothy sat down on a kitchen chair.

'And you told the police that?'

Beryl sniffed. 'As if I would. He only forgot, didn't he? As if everybody will remember exactly what they were doing that night, and anyway, I would have to have said I was watching, wouldn't I? And Gerald would have known I watch him, wouldn't he? And he would have got cross, and I don't like him being cross, do I?'

She reluctantly placed the lid on the biscuit barrel. 'Anyway, what does it matter whether he went out in the car or walked? He had nothing to do with that horrible murder, had he?'

'Of course he hadn't.' Dorothy spoke quickly. 'So he's been cross with you before, has he, Beryl?'

But even as she opened her mouth to answer, there was the sound of a key grating in the lock, and for the second time that night Dorothy froze.

'He's back. I'm going. Out the back way. Better he doesn't know I've been here. All right?'

'It's all right, he's going straight upstairs, he often does that. He doesn't have any supper.' Beryl's voice was hoarse with biscuit crumbs.

But putting her finger to her lips, Dorothy turned the key in the back door and slipped outside, leaving Beryl with her own finger to her lips in rather mystified understanding.

'See you at church tomorrow.'

'Suppose so.'

Then she was outside in the narrow passage-way between the house and the garage, outside in the road, running, with her heart pounding and her thoughts so chaotic that her mind was a formless blank.

And it wasn't until she was walking up her own drive that Dorothy put her hand in her blazer pocket and felt the cuff-link, hard and round . . . and the knowledge that she had, in her headlong flight from Gerald's room forgotten to replace it, filled her with terror.

If she was right. If there was anything in what she suspected, then her safe little world was safe no longer.

From now on Gerald Tomlin would know that someone knew. And knowing would turn him from a merely frightened man to a man of desperation.

Fourteen

Before Dorothy had closed the door behind her, even before she had gone swiftly upstairs, knowing she could not, at that moment, face Margaret, she had decided what to do with the cuff-link, weighing now as heavy as lead in her blazer pocket.

She would have to take a chance on Gerald discovering its loss that night, and the next morning, in church, she would pass it over to Beryl, saying she had slipped it in her pocket, accidentally, when she thought she'd heard Gerald's car outside, reminding the luckless Beryl of her sworn promise and the threat of hell-fire if she went back on it.

And if Beryl refused she would go back with her cousin to the house and somehow, some way, she would put it back herself.

Of one thing she was absolutely certain. The cuff-link had to be replaced. Because, in a strange paradoxical way, now that she held what could have been evidence of Gerald's involvement in her hand, she was convinced of his innocence.

Thinking he was guilty was one thing; actually proving it, she was finding already, was another.

And if Gerald was a typical man, if he was anything like her own father, he would wriggle out of the shirt he had been wearing that day with the links still in place. How often had she heard her mother reprimanding her father for doing just that?

158

'One of these days, Matthew, Mrs Wilkinson will put them out still fastened to your shirt for the laundry-man, and that will be that. Surely it's only a small thing to ask. Quite honestly I don't understand you, Matthew.'

But Gerald didn't have a wife who nagged. Not yet. Gerald Tomlin might not be a murderer, but he was the kind of man to whom neatness and order were the equivalent of a second skin. The kind of man who would pull his shirt over his shiny red head, sit down on the shiny bedspread in that meticulously tidy room, then take the cuff-links out of his cuffs and put them in the leather box on the tall-boy.

Dorothy tiptoed across the landing, and closing her bedroom door behind her, leant against it, shutting her eyes as if she would shut out the terrifying supposition. For if he found the odd one missing when he lifted the round lid, if he checked . . . oh dear God, what would he do? Especially if there was any truth in what she had been convincing herself was not the truth? Her vivid imagination soared on black wings, into a nightmare situation where the smooth-tongued Gerald, smooth-tongued no longer, confronted a quaking Beryl, forcing her to admit that she had been in his room.

'I swear I haven't,' Beryl would say, shaking with terror inside the brown woollen dressing-gown.'

And Gerald would think that the police had been, searching his room, searching for the cuff-link that was the twin to the one they had found buried by leaves beside Ruby's dead body.

Now Dorothy's imagination had run away with her, completely and terrifyingly out of even a semblance of control. How could she have thought a moment ago that Gerald was innocent?

'I tell you, Gerald. I swear that no one has been in your room. How could they have been when I've been alone all evening?'

That was Beryl, thinking of the hell-fire awaiting her if she broke her vow of silence.

'The truth, or I'll . . . or I'll . . .'

That was Gerald Tomlin, narrow-set eyes blazing, who having killed once, had nothing to lose.

His hands, those sinewy hands, with the ginger hairs sprouting sickeningly from between his knuckles, were reaching out for Beryl's plump throat. Her poor, silly little cousin, whose death would lie irrevocably at Dorothy's door. . . .

Dorothy screamed aloud as the door was pushed open, sending her almost sprawling on the carpet. Beryl had proved no heroine and Gerald was here, to demand an explanation! Dorothy felt the hair on her head gently raise itself away from her crawling scalp.

'For goodness sakes! It's only me. What on earth's the matter with you, Dorothy? First you rush out of the house, dragging that poor boy with you, and now you behave as though I've just walked in with my head tucked underneath my arm.'

Margaret was smiling, very much the elder sister, teasing, patronizing, serene in her own cocoon of happiness, generously tolerant because of it. Her golden hair was sweetly disarranged, and at the corner of her smiling mouth her plum coloured lipstick was tellingly smudged. She walked over to the dressing-table and smiled at her reflection, well pleased with herself, and spoke soothingly over her shoulder.

'I'm not going to split on you, our Dorothy. Surely you don't think for one moment that I would? It's not a crime having a boy in when Mother and Father go out.' She went pink. 'Though I do hope you know what you're doing. Some boys would take advantage, you know. They're not all as nice as Gerald, or as your Stanley. I wouldn't have minded having a chat with him, the poor boy, shown him how sorry we all are. He must be going through a dreadful time just now.'

Dorothy said nothing. Her heart was still pounding as, carefully wriggling both arms out of the blazer sleeve, she

160

took it off, holding it straight in case the cuff-link did the unthinkable and rolled out of the pocket and on to the floor. Then, with measured movements, she took a hanger from her wardrobe and put the coat away, closing the door, and turning the key in the lock.

'What did you say?' she asked.

Margaret twisted round on the dressing-table stool, still smiling.

'Oh, never mind. But there's no need for you to be in such a tiz-woz, honestly, love. We won't talk about it if you don't want to.' She put her head on one side and spoke slowly, like a kindergarten teacher calming down a naughty child. 'Now then. Tomorrow morning after church, Gerald and I are going over to the house to do some measuring in the kitchen. Why don't you come with us? We can help Mother with the vegetables for the dinner before we go if we get up early enough.'

Dorothy sat down on the bed, and stared at the pointed toes of her black court shoes. 'Is Gerald going to church with us then? I thought he was a non-believer?'

Margaret frowned. 'Well, actually, he's meeting me outside with the car, but he did go when the banns were being read, remember? And it isn't that he doesn't believe really, you know. It's just that organized religion doesn't appeal to him. He thinks that one can be as close to God in the middle of a field, or out on the moors.'

'Or in the park?' Dorothy heard herself say.

'Well, yes, in the park if you wish.' Margaret leaned forward, clasping her hands earnestly between her knees. 'Look, Dorothy. That mention of the park came right up out of your subconscious, didn't it? I've been reading a book about that sort of thing. From the library. You'll have to try to forget that terrible happening in the park, you know.'

'How?' Dorothy glanced towards the wardrobe door, then quickly away again.

Margaret shook her head, more in sorrow than anger. 'I

161

know it must be difficult you being so friendly with that poor girl's brother and everything. But terrible things do happen in life, and if we took them all to heart, then we'd never know a single moment's peace.' She looked lovingly at Dorothy sitting with shoulders hunched almost up to her ears. Genuine sympathy filled her heart and her voice, and even as she went on she heard herself modulating her voice in deference to her sister's sadness. 'You're sensitive, like me. We're a sensitive family. All the Boltons are sensitive. Even Father, though he does appear to be a bit gruff and outspoken on the surface.'

Dorothy lifted her head for a moment and stared at her sister in surprise. 'But Father is the most sensitive of us all,' she wanted to say, then saw it was no use. Margaret was blinking her eyes as if trying to remember a verse from a poem to illustrate her meaning. '*Oh, God, please let her get up and go, and let her not read the evil thoughts that beset me,*' she prayed silently, but Margaret was obviously determined to have her well-intentioned say.

'I've never told you this before, Dorothy, but reading that library book showed me how wrong it is to dwell on the sordid.' She put up a finger and stroked a smooth cheek. 'And, anyway, you get wrinkles if you think negative thoughts for any length of time. But once, a long time ago, when I was about seven years old, a girl who was in the same Brownie Pack as me died of diphtheria. She was called Elsie. Or was it Enid? No, it was definitely Elsie. Well, although Mother would have had a pink fit, me and another girl went to the house and took a bunch of flowers, and for some reason Elsie's mother asked us in and took us into the parlour where the coffin was.' Margaret's placid face grew crumpled lines with the effort of making herself clear. 'She, the dead girl, was dressed in her Brownie uniform, with her Pixie badge sewn above the pocket, and all the badges she'd earned sewn down her sleeve. There was a great big mirror on the wall, and the whole terrible thing was reflected in it. There were two little curtains pulled to over her face, but her hands were white and crossed over her chest, and the coffin was flanked by two huge vases of carnations. It was awful. Can you imagine? The smell was something I'll never forget, sort of sickly sweet, and now you know why I insisted on no carnations in my wedding bouquet. The very sight of them brings the whole thing back, and all because I kept it to myself and *dwelled*. So you see I do know how you feel, but unless you put it out of your mind, or at least talk about it, it's going to leave a nasty blot on your subconscious. Don't you see?'

Dorothy nodded, clenching her hands until the nails bit into the palms.

'I see,' she said, 'and I'll try. Honestly I'll try.'

Margaret smiled on her with sisterly affection. 'And you don't need to worry about Mother finding out that Stanley came round tonight when she was out. I won't dream of telling, and Gerald won't mention it. He's more understanding than you think, you know. When we discussed it after you'd rushed out like that, do you know what he said?'

'What did he say?'

'"Forget it," he said. "They're only kids. As far as I'm concerned," he said, "there was no one in when we came back."' Margaret's voice held more than a touch of pride. 'Just think. He even smoked three cigarettes, one after the other, so that if Mother came back and smelt smoke, she wouldn't get suspicious. That's how considerate he is.'

She came over to where Dorothy sat dejectedly on the edge of the bed and touched her sister's hair in a fleeting caress. 'So stop looking so solemn, love. Just think of the nice things that are happening to us all, and about all the nice things to come. At the end of the summer I'll be married and living in my own home; you'll have left school, and although you won't believe it now, you'll go out with simply lots of boys before you decide on the right one.' She walked over to the door and turned. 'And somewhere there's someone just as super as Gerald waiting for you, you'll see.'

163

Dorothy nodded. If Margaret didn't go away and leave her alone she felt that her head would drop clean off with the nodding of it. She stretched her mouth into what she hoped would pass for a smile. 'All right, I'll remember, Margaret. Good night.'

Then listening intently until she heard the bathroom door open and close, Dorothy unlocked the wardrobe and took the cuff-link out of her blazer pocket. Stared down at it with distaste and subdued a sudden urge to open the window and hurl it away, out of sight. What had she done? Oh, dear God, what had she done? Then, thinking she heard a noise, she quickly replaced it, and locking the wardrobe again took the key out and put it underneath her pillow. A quick and necessary dash to the toilet whilst Margaret was closeted in the bathroom, and then a swift undressing and a dive into bed, without washing or cleaning her teeth.

When her mother called out to her from the landing half an hour later, she pulled the sheet over her head and pretended to be asleep. But she knew that if it had been her father's voice the temptation to talk to him would have overwhelmed her. Seeing his kindly face bending over her with concern she would have surely blurted out the whole mixed-up and unbelievable story from start to finish. Because then he would have sorted it out for her, the way he had always sorted things out for her since she was a child.

And when at long last she slept, it was to dream of Gerald, down on his knees in the middle of a field, praying to his own particular God, with his hands clasped in supplication, the red hairs sprouting sickeningly from between his knuckles. . . .

It was Church Parade the next morning, and when they arrived at the weathered stone church, the Guides and Brownies were already in their allotted pews at the front, with Philip's Vera in her Guide Captain's uniform at the end of a row, the navy-blue felt hat with its brim turned up at one side, squashed down over the whirls of plaits covering her ears.

Under her stern vigilance, the Guides sat straight and unsmiling in three solemn rows, but in front of them the Brownies held little whispered and giggling conversations together, their brown knitted caps bobbing animatedly.

Margaret, wearing a powder-blue coat with a matching hat shaped like a shallow dish with a feather going straight up at the side, glanced over at the Brownies and smiled at Dorothy. The smile said, 'Aren't they sweet?' and was calculated to show that no grim memories were troubling her that lovely spring morning. She lowered her head over her hands for a brief moment, then turned and smiled at the pew behind. Even the large urn of well-spaced-out carnations and greenery by the altar steps did nothing to dim the brightness of her smile, Dorothy noted.

Margaret was happy and wanted everyone to share in her happiness. Gerald would be waiting outside the church for her in his red car after the service, and in six weeks' time she would stand by his side and become his wife. Till death did them part.

Dorothy, reading her sister's mind with accuracy, bowed her head in prayer.

'Oh, God,' she prayed. 'Let me pass the cuff-link over to Beryl without anyone noticing. Give me a chance to persuade her how important it is that she puts it back. And please, God, forgive me for meddling. Forgive me for letting this awful imagination of mine run away with me, and let them find the man who killed Ruby quickly, so that Margaret's Gerald will be shown to be innocent, and forgive me for thinking that he had anything to do with it. Let it be that I turned him into a murderer in my mind because I don't want him to marry my sister. Like something out of Margaret's library book, as she explained. And tell Grandpa Bolton, if he's up there with you, to stop nudging me and putting thoughts in my head, and words in my mouth. For the sake of your son, Jesus Christ, amen.'

And watching her younger daughter's apparent devotion,

Phyllis smiled to herself, well satisfied.

The child was merely going through a phase, that was all. Adolescence was a difficult time, she mused, twiddling with a pearl ear-ring that was in danger of coming adrift. Like the menopause, adolescence affected some worse than others. She stole a sideways glance at her elder daughter. Margaret, bless her, now she had never been adolescent. Not a moment's worry since she was born. Phyllis looked up at the stained-glass window above the altar, depicting the Good Shepherd with the lost lamb in his arms. The colours were beautiful, especially with the sun slanting through them like that. Yes, it would be a worthy setting for the wedding ceremony. Margaret's train would look lovely as it fanned out behind her as she walked with Gerald to be prayed over after they'd been pronounced man and wife. That would be the moment when the choir in their red surplices sang *Love Divine* in charming descant. And how beautifully the red roses in Margaret's bouquet would tone in with the surplices, and how wise Gerald was to have decided on pale grey for his morning suit. With his red hair it would be just perfect. Phyllis sighed with contentment, then narrowed her eyes as her sister Ethel walked past the end of the pew accompanied by her husband. . . .

What was Ethel thinking about, wearing a purple hat to a dusty-pink coat? Really, she had no idea of what went with what, no idea of style at all. Goodness knows what she'd look like at the wedding, and goodness knows, Phyllis thought with pleasant smugness, what Beryl would look like in her bridesmaid's dress, even though she had given strict instructions to the dressmaker to go easy on the gathers round the second bridesmaid's dress.

She started as she felt Dorothy plucking at her sleeve.

'Where's Beryl?' she was whispering. 'Why isn't she with Auntie Ethel and Uncle Raymond? I saw her yesterday and she said she'd be at church this morning. Why isn't she . . . ?'

The row of worshippers in the pew in front stood up, and as the processional came slowly from the vestry, the rest of the congregation scrambled to their feet, searching for the right place in their prayer books.

And with anguish eating into her heart, and a mist of fear clouding her eyes, Dorothy stared down at the familiar words, her imagination taking wings again, soaring to the high dome of the ancient church.

'Oh, God,' she prayed as the congregation sank to their knees, 'don't let Gerald find that the cuff-link is missing. Let him decide to wear one of his sports shirts with buttons on the cuffs today. And, dear Lord, if he should discover that it's gone, make him think that he's forgotten where he put it. And let him be innocent of any involvement with Stanley's poor dead sister. Let him be hateful and slimy, and a liar with a sordid past, but don't let him have been Ruby Armstrong's lover. And let this be a lesson to me for allowing this terrible imagination of mine to run away with me. And if Grandpa Bolton's up there with you, tell him to stop prompting me about Gerald. Tell him that our Margaret loves him, and that he'll make her a good husband. Amen . . .'

The child is getting religious, Phyllis told herself, noticing the way Dorothy sank to her knees for the prayers, holding her hands piously over her face, and the way her lips moved during the reading from the Old Testament. She saw the way her younger daughter's eyes fixed themselves on the gold crucifix above the high altar, and the way her eyes filled with tears during the intoning of the Creed.

She wouldn't, she told herself bitterly, put it past Dorothy to do something absolutely beyond the pale, like wanting to turn Catholic. It would be just like her. And during the sermon she debated with herself which would be the worst, having a daughter who owed allegiance to the Pope, or one who boasted a mother-in-law who took in washing. She rose to her feet without having heard a single word of the vicar's short sermon, and sighed deeply. One thing she knew for sure, and that was that Dorothy would bring trouble. She felt in her bones that some way, somehow, this wilful child of hers would bring disgrace to them all.

'But let Margaret get married first,' was her final prayer. As the service ended, she collected gloves and handbag, and walked straight-backed from the church.

Fifteen

'The minute,' Phyllis said, 'the very minute we get into the house, Matthew, you must have a good talk to Dorothy. No wonder she's walking on in front of us like that. Just look at her slouching along and scuffing her best shoes. You'd think she was seven and not seventeen.'

They crossed the road from the church, and automatically Matthew did a little skip behind his wife to place himself on the kerb side of the pavement. Manners, he knew, mattered to Phyllis even when she was in the highest of dudgeons. And something had upset her good and proper this time. Her face was set into seething lines of anger, her mouth a thin grim line, and yet when the curate's wife rushed past en route for her kitchen and the Sunday dinner, Phyllis gave her a dazzling smile and even agreed that it was indeed a lovely day.

By heck, but she knew how to play to the gallery, Matthew thought wryly. There were times when he'd back his missus against Greta Garbo any old day.

'First she argues with our Ethel. Telling her she wants to see their Beryl, when all the time Ethel was explaining that Beryl would have gone over to Laurel Road to Raymond's sister's for their dinner. "She promised me she'd be at church this morning," she kept saying, as if Beryl could help waking up with one of her funny turns.'

'But if Beryl's well enough to go out for her dinner, surely she was well enough to go to church,' Matthew said mildly, feeling in his bones that he was missing the point, as usual.

'You're missing the point, as usual. Where Beryl had gone didn't come into it. The thing was that Dorothy should have accepted it, not gone on and on. I never thought she was all that close to Beryl, anyway.'

A woman in a yellow dress, holding a child by the hand, came out of a gate as they walked past, and Phyllis gave her a dazzling smile. 'She'll be our next president of the Inner Wheel,' she said in her normal voice, then resumed in a careful whisper. 'And then when our Margaret tried to persuade her to get into Gerald's car to go with them to the house, she actually knocked her hand away. Don't tell me you didn't see that.'

'I was talking to Raymond. Things are bad down at the yard. He says there's no orders coming in at all.'

'I don't blame Gerald entirely for saying what he did, though I must say I was surprised. The worst thing was that our Ethel heard him, and that was bad enough. Her eyebrows almost disappeared underneath that atrocious hat.'

'What *did* he say?' Matthew felt obliged to ask. 'Raymond says he had to lay off four more men last week.'

Phyllis sniffed. 'Raymond exaggerates, always has. Gerald, for your information, looked at Dorothy and said, "Either get in the bloody car, or stay out; either way makes no difference to me."'

'And what did our Dorothy say to that?'

'She told him to go to hell.'

'Are you sure it's not you who's exaggerating now, love?'

'I only wish I was.' Phyllis increased her pace to keep up with her rising anger. 'I've never been so humiliated in my whole life. And outside church too. Fancy coming straight out of church and using language like that.'

'Well, Gerald hadn't been to church,' Matthew said mildly, 'though I admit there's no love lost between him and Dorothy. Still, he's a lot older than she is, and he shouldn't have spoken to her like that.'

'She *provoked* him. She's always provoking him. She's one

170

on her own is our Dorothy. I can't think who she takes after
. . . If she didn't look so much like Margaret I'd wonder
sometimes if they gave me the wrong baby in the Nursing
Home. I can't think of anybody on either side who she takes
after. Did you see her in church? Down on her knees
praying as if she was half way to a nunnery, then behaving
like someone not in their right mind outside.'

They turned the corner into their own tree-lined road,
and Matthew did his little sideways skip again as they
crossed to the other side.

'And I wish you'd stop twiddling about like that,' Phyllis
said ungratefully. 'It gets on my nerves. First I'm talking to
you, then you're gone. No, it's the company our Dorothy's
been keeping . . . and before you remind me about that boy
out of Inkerman Street having won a scholarship to Oxford,
let me remind you that breeding can't be learnt from books.
It's inborn. And if she thinks I'm going to have him up to
the house, she's another think coming. And if all she wants
to do with her life is to mix with the working class, snogging
on the back row of the pictures on a Saturday night, and
standing in shop doorways, doing goodness knows what –
oh yes, I wasn't born yesterday, Matthew – well, all I can
say is that we've failed. We've given her everything, and all
she wants to do is to throw it all back in our faces.'

Matthew sighed. 'Surely things aren't as bad as that,
love? I admit she's been behaving a bit strangely these past
few days, but what can you expect? Ruby Armstrong's
murder came too near for comfort. Can't you see? Dorothy,
in spite of all your wishful thinking, was *involved*. She was
actually talking to the brother a few yards away from where
they found the body, tha knows.' His wife's eyebrows rose
at the slip into dialect, but he took no notice. More was at
stake, he felt, than him minding his ps and qs. 'It wasn't
just a sordid crime she read about in the paper; it happened
to the sister of someone she knew very well. She's about
the same age as that poor lass, give or take a year or two,
and it isn't easy to take a thing like that in your stride,

171

love. Not at seventeen.'

He clicked open the gate, and held it wide for his wife to pass through, raising his trilby hat to the man next door who was cutting his hedge. Then, lowering his voice, he said, 'I haven't managed to fathom it out yet, but I feel that our Dorothy's contrasting the fuss about the wedding with that poor lass's fate. Perhaps for the first time in her life she's finding out that life isn't fair, that it never was and never will be.' He stood back to let Phyllis go before him into the house. 'Leave her be, love, and it'll all blow over, you'll see.'

'She's gone straight upstairs,' Phyllis said, after a quick peep into the downstairs rooms. 'If I hadn't to see to the joint I'd have a word with her myself, but what I have to say will keep.' She took off her hat and patted her hair back into shape. 'You go up and see if you can talk some sense into her.' She handed her coat over to him. 'And make sure you hang this on a padded hanger, please.' Her eyes met his in honest bewilderment. 'And why that poor girl getting herself murdered should have anything whatsoever to do with our Margaret getting married, beats me. Margaret didn't even know her.' She walked with her quick light step towards the kitchen. 'And if Dorothy doesn't behave herself at the table I'll send her upstairs, whether she's seventeen or not.'

Hauling himself up by the bannister as if it were a ropeladder on a ship and not a wide polished piece of oak, Matthew went heavily upstairs. Trying to talk sense into Phyllis when she was in this mood was nigh impossible. He'd be glad when this wedding was over, by heck he would. He'd offered Margaret all the money the reception at The Pied Bull was going to cost, plus another two hundred for the fancy clothes and what not, and suggested that she eloped with Gerald.

'Don't be funny, Father,' she'd said, but he hadn't been trying to be funny. At the moment he'd meant it, from the bottom of his heart. He paused at the bend of the stairs, feeling the familiar tightness in his chest, as if there were an elastic band squeezing the breath out of him. By heck but he were out of condition, right enough. He unbuttoned his waistcoat. In a way he could side with Dorothy, if that was the reason for her behaving so strangely these past few days. It did seem all wrong to be spending money as if it were water on a fancy wedding, when the dole queues were stretching half way round the Labour Exchange and right down Queen Street. Men with brown paper tacked inside their vests, and pieces of cardboard shoved inside their shoes to keep out the cold, working on their allotments and their hen-pens all day long to try and eke out their meagre intake of food with vegetables, and a chicken at Christmas if they were lucky. And the way things were going, it looked as if Raymond might have to close down in the not too distant future. He sighed as he continued his way upstairs. He'd be all right, Raymond would; he'd more than a bob or two put by, but some of his men had been with the firm since leaving school, and had felt secure enough to start buying their own houses. By the heck, it didn't bear thinking about. . . .

Wearily he went into the bedroom and sitting down on the edge of the double bed, crossed one leg awkwardly over the other and began to pick at the knot in his shoe-laces. He supposed he'd better have a word with Dorothy, partly to pacify Phyllis, and partly because he was a bit worried about her himself. He hadn't wanted to add fuel to the fire by admitting that he had seen a bit of what had gone on outside the church out of the corner of his eye when he'd been talking to Raymond. But it were right enough that there were no love lost between his younger daughter and Margaret's intended. For one startled moment he'd thought they were going to come to blows, matching up to one another on the pavement, for all the world like two fighting cocks. He eased his feet into his slippers. There was a lot of his father in Dorothy, and that was a fact. If the old man had taken it into his head to dislike someone, then that was it. No compromise; no being pleasant just for the sake of appearances.

'He don't like me, and I don't like him,' he remembered his father saying once about a completely inoffensive little tackler at the mill. 'And that's bloody that.'

'But there's such a thing as tolerance, and live and let live,' Matthew muttered to himself as he went out on to the landing and knocked on the door of Dorothy's room. And the sooner this lass of his grew up a bit and realized it, the better for all of them. . . .

And, so preoccupied that he forgot to wait for Dorothy's voice telling him to come in, Matthew opened the door and walked straight into the bedroom.

Dorothy was lying flat on her bed still wearing her shoes and her blazer, her toes pointing up to the ceiling, and her face drained of colour. She didn't turn her head, and Matthew doubted if she'd even heard him come in. Just for a moment the elastic band tightened itself round his heart again as he looked at her. By the heck, but there was summat wrong all right. Summat serious too. This was more than one of her Bolshie moods. More than an idealistic aversion to wedding preparations taking precedence over Ruby Armstrong's murder. His lass' was in real trouble, and if that lad from down Inkerman Street had been up to owt with her, he'd tear him limb from limb, and he wouldn't even wait till 'funeral were over tomorrow either. Matthew walked towards the bed. But she weren't like that, not his Dorothy. She were nobbut a child, and as pure as the driven snow; he'd stake his life on that.

Sitting down on the bed, which creaked in protest, he patted her hand. 'Now then, chuck, let's have it. However bad it is, let's have it straight. There's nowt so terrible that can't be put right. Not now your old dad's here. Come on now, tell me all about it.'

Dorothy's other hand, the one in her pocket, curled round the cuff-link. Slowly, as if she was dreaming, she turned her head and stared at her father. And the terrible anxiety on his red face broke down her defences, so that she sat up and threw herself against him, burying her head in the tobacco-smelling comfort of his old cardigan, at the same time as his arms came round her and held her tight.

'I can't tell you,' she sobbed when the first bout of crying was over. 'It's so awful. I can't begin.'

Matthew rocked her gently, backwards and forwards, knowing from experience that she would have to get her cry over and done with first. It had always been the same, ever since she was a little lass. First the explosive torrent of tears, the passionate unburdening of whatever was troubling her, then the whispered expression of her feelings. And half an hour afterwards, he reminded himself, the swift return to normality, with her pinched smile at variance with the swollen eyelids and little tear-blotched face.

Dear God, he asked himself silently, why did this one of his chicks have to be so vulnerable? Why did she have to get herself so *involved*? By heck, but life was going to hurt her badly. If it hadn't hurt her already . . . He held her away from him, trying to get her to look at him, but her head dropped down to her chest.

'Is it anything to do with that lad? That Stanley?' he said, dreading what she might be going to tell him, but knowing that there'd be no peace for either of them till it was said.

'In a way.' She gulped. 'In a way it has.'

Matthew patted her head. 'Take your time, love, come on now, get it over with, and whatever it is we'll have it put right. There's nowt so bad as can't be mended, you know that.'

'It's . . . it's about Gerald. Gerald Tomlin . . .'

'Aye?' Matthew's voice soothed and encouraged, showing nothing of the surprise he felt, and into his shoulder Dorothy made her confession.

'I think I've always known that he was meeting girls from the mill – oh, before he got engaged to our Margaret. He used to take them for drives in his car; he almost admitted it to me himself, but that wouldn't have mattered, because he

175

loves our Margaret, I'm sure of that, but I think that one of the weavers he was meeting was Ruby Armstrong.'

'Go on.' Matthew's voice held a grim note now.

'I think he was meeting her secretly, right up to getting engaged three months ago, then, give him his due, he stopped seeing her, but then I think . . . I've worked it out that when Ruby found out for sure that she was pregnant, she persuaded him to see her. Just once.'

Matthew stopped the rocking motion, and held her very still.

'I even think it may have been the night she died, because Beryl told me he lied to the police. Not a big lie, just saying he went for a drive when really he went for a walk. She watches him go out, you know, from the landing window.'

'Carry on.'

'Stanley told me that a weaver from the mill was standing at the West Road gate of the park that night with a boy, and she thought she saw someone like Ruby going into the park, with a boy. Or a man.'

'And does Stanley know all this, then?'

'Not about Gerald lying to the police. I only found that out after he'd . . . afterwards.' She paused for a moment. 'And he, Gerald, he lost a cuff-link, one of the pair Margaret bought him for their engagement present.' Her hand crept into her pocket again. 'And he went down to Mr Adamson's shop and replaced it. But he's still searching for it, because I've figured out that he can't think where he lost it. So he's still searching in his room.'

'And how do you know that, love?'

'Beryl. She watches him.'

'Why?'

'Because she has a crush on him. She's like that. And yesterday she saw him in the park, after she'd been playing tennis, and she said he was walking along a path with his head bent. Near the duck pond.'

'Bit of a long shot, chuck?'

'Not when you're desperate.'

176

'And Beryl knows what you think?'

Dorothy shook her head. 'I'm not that daft, am I?'

Matthew took a deep breath. 'It's dangerous thinking, lovey. You know that, don't you?'

Dorothy nodded into his shoulder. 'I know, and I haven't finished yet.' She let out a shuddering sigh. 'Last night I went round to Beryl's house when Auntie Ethel and Uncle Raymond were out, and I stole the odd cuff-link from his room.'

'You what?'

'I did. I didn't mean to take it, but I thought I heard someone coming and I panicked and put it in my pocket, and I meant to give it back to Beryl this morning after church and get her to put it back, but she wasn't there, and then when I saw Gerald he looked at me as if he hated my guts and swore at me, and I think he may have found out what I did.' She moved against him. 'I think Beryl might have told him, even though I got her to swear on the Bible that she wouldn't.'

Matthew closed his eyes.

'And now you're not sure? Is that what you're trying to tell me, then?'

She nodded. 'I prayed and prayed in church that I'm wrong, and if I am, and if he's found out that I was in his room last night, I still have to explain how I came to take the cuff-link, and I can't. And I'm so mixed up I don't know what I am, or whether what I think is real or just in my imagination any more. And don't tell Mother, but Stanley came round last night when you were out, and he says that even accusing Gerald in my mind is dangerous. But Gerald Tomlin knew Stanley's sister all right. Even if he didn't meet her that night, he knew her. And he could be the father of Ruby's baby. I know it inside me. It all fits.'

Then at last she lifted her head, and over her father's shoulder saw her mother standing in the doorway.

Phyllis was wearing the frilly apron, tied in a neat bow at the back, looking so ordinary, so much her meticulously organized self that, when she spoke, the voice that came as a low growl from her throat startled Matthew so much that he stood up, unable to utter a word himself, moving his big head from side to side in a desperate fashion.

How long had she been there? Had she heard what had been said? And if she had, then heaven help them.

He moved towards her, holding out his hand, but she ignored him as if he wasn't in the room at all.

Dorothy slid from the bed and faced her mother, her head up, not as much in defiance as in fear. Her mother's face was contorted almost out of recognition with a rage so terrible it seemed to leap from her throat like a living thing.

'You wicked, wicked little devil! You brazen, interfering little sod! How dare you suggest that Gerald had anything to do with that young whore from down Inkerman Street?' She put up a hand as if to ward off anything Dorothy or her father might say. 'Who, I ask you, but the devil himself could have put such thoughts into your head? You . . . you little bugger.'

'Don't swear, Mother.'

It was a foolish thing to say, but Dorothy never remembered her prunes and prism mother uttering so much as a 'damn'. It was as though Phyllis was possessed. And if the devil was in that room at that moment, he was in her mother's heart, not her own. She swayed where she stood. 'But, listen, Mother. I don't know for sure . . . I said I didn't know. But I had to find out. For Margaret's sake, I had to . . .'

'Shut up!' Phyllis took a menacing step forwards. 'How dare you even mention your sister's name after what you've just said? Don't you know, or have you forgotten, that her wedding-dress is hanging there in the spare room? And even at this very minute she's with that decent young man looking over the house they're going to live in together?' She narrowed her eyes. 'I knew this morning, even as you knelt by my side in church, that you were up to something. Muttering your mealy-mouthed prayers, you little sod.

And I'll tell you what's wrong with you, what's always been wrong with you. You're jealous of your sister. Jealous as hell. Jealous because she's going to marry a fine man, and jealous because as far as disposition goes you're not fit to grovel at her feet and lick her big toe. You've been against this wedding right from the start, and now you think you've found a way to bugger it all up.' Her voice rose. 'Aye, and bugger us all up too. Not content with mixing with the scum of the earth yourself, you want the rest of your family to be dragged down with you. And I suppose you've told Beryl all this cock-and-bull story? That's what you were saying, wasn't it?'

'I haven't. I only said I thought that Gerald . . .'

'I said shut up!' Phyllis's face was as frightening as her voice now, all pretence at refinement gone. 'Aye, you'd like that,' she went on. 'You'd like your Auntie Ethel to think we were mixed up in a bit of muckiness, wouldn't you? You'd like them to think we've been taken down a peg, wouldn't you?'

'Oh, Mother, please . . .'

'Don't you try to come the little innocent with me now, Dorothy Bolton. Only somebody with a sick mind could have dreamed up the story I heard you tell your father just now. Inferring that Gerald had something to do with that sordid murder . . . and when they come back from the house I want you gone. Go where you bloody well like, but I'm not having you sitting at my dinner table with thoughts like that in your head.'

Matthew put out his hand to touch her, but she knocked it away with a fierce slicing motion.

He tried again. 'Come now, lass. It were a shock hearing it like that. It's been a shock to me, and I'm sure that Gerald's done nothing very terrible. But it needs sorting out . . .'

'Not this time, Matthew. This time you can't sort anything out. Because the only one that needs sorting out is her.'

And as Dorothy took a step forward Phyllis's fist shot out and caught her full on the mouth, and as she cried aloud and tried to shield herself with her arms, Phyllis took hold of her by the shoulders and shook her so that her teeth rattled and the blood spun in her head.

It was like a drunken street brawl, a Saturday night punch-up down in the main streets of the town, with Matthew, galvanized into action at last, pinning his wife's arms behind her back. With Dorothy rushing headlong from the room, stumbling down the stairs, wrenching at the big front door, and running out into the bright spring sunshine, with no thought in her head but that she must get away. . . .

Sixteen

For what seemed like an eternity, but could in reality have been only a few seconds, Matthew felt as if he was being split into two people. One half of him was running down the stairs after Dorothy, and the other half was ministering to his wife, trying to calm her into some sort of normality.

And staying where he was in the bedroom he could still see himself, in his mind's eye, calling Dorothy's name, with the neighbours looking up from their hedge-trimming, and coming from their Sunday dinners, to see who was making all that commotion in the normally quiet, respectable road.

'I'd never have caught up with her,' he muttered to himself as he tried to draw Phyllis into the circle of his arms, straining at her as she stiffened against him.

'I blame you for this,' she said, quieter now, but still speaking in that rough, alien voice. 'You've spoilt her since the day she was born. Giving in to her whims and making excuses for her.' She started to whimper. 'We were too old; we're too old to cope, there's too much of your father in her. There's bad blood somewhere there.'

'Rubbish.' Matthew wished he could sit down, but it didn't seem the right time, even though his legs felt as if they were weighted with lead. 'You'd no right to hit her,' he said sadly. 'She's not a child. You'd no right to land out at her like that.'

Phyllis turned her back on him and walked her straight-backed walk to the door. To his amazement he could see that already her normal self-control was asserting itself,

181

and the immediate transition from a shouting virago to her customary prim refinement seemed so shocking that he felt a physical churning of disgust in his stomach.

Groping for the bannister he followed her down the stairs, fumbling with his feet for each step like a blind man as she talked at him over her shoulder.

'Margaret and Gerald will be back at any minute, and they mustn't suspect that anything's been happening. Not by any sign at all must they suspect that we've had words.' She turned at the bottom of the stairs, and her face was as smooth as if they'd had a slight difference of opinion about whether to open a tin of peaches or a tin of pineapple for pudding. 'We'll tell them that Dorothy had a telephone call from a friend, and has gone there for dinner.'

'Just like that?' Matthew followed her into the kitchen.

'Yes, just like that,' Phyllis said, taking the oven gloves down from the hook by the gas-oven and thrusting her hands inside them. Then before bending down to open the oven door she stared straight at him with a direct look that started the churning sensation in his middle once again.

'What our Dorothy said was never said. It's gone. Done with, and never to be referred to again. Not ever. And when she comes back you can tell her that yourself because it will be a long time before I can trust myself to speak to her . . .'

Matthew took his handkerchief from his trouser pocket and wiped his forehead, and if anything at all had been registering in his wife's mind at that moment she would have seen the way he sank down on to a kitchen chair, and seen the greyness of his usually ruddy cheeks, and the way his mouth had fallen slack and strangely blue.

'And Dorothy?' he asked. 'Don't you even care where she's gone?'

Phyllis took a ladle and started to baste the sizzling joint of beef, spooning the hot fat over it with a hand as steady as a rock.

'You know as well as I do where she'll have gone to. Down Inkerman Street. To that boy. To where she belongs.

And as far as I'm concerned she can stay there.'

Matthew blinked hard as if to get her into focus. This was his wife, the mother of his two daughters. The mother of Dorothy as well as of Margaret. He blinked his eyes again.

'And if she repeats what she said?'

'She said nothing!'

Matthew spoke slowly but clearly as if trying to make himself understood to a backward five-year-old child. 'Dorothy is headstrong, and foolish at times, we both know that, but however terrible the consequences might be, lass, we've got to talk about what she said. We've got to talk it out between the three of us even if it's just the means of setting it right between her and Gerald. She'll be coming back.' He turned his head as if already he heard his daughter's returning footsteps. 'She always comes back, after all she's run down the road in a flaming temper more times than Gerald's had hot dinners. I know, I know. This time she's gone too far, this time that imagination of hers has really gone off the rails, and she's been foolish and impulsive, but it's got to be thrashed out. If Gerald . . .' He licked his dry lips. 'If Gerald had been seeing that poor lass – and what he did before he started courting our Margaret seriously is his own concern; he's not a mere slip of a lad you know, and I wasn't born yesterday either, I've seen the way he stares at a pretty girl.' Matthew recoiled from his wife's glare. 'Nay, lass, there's no need to look like that. The man what doesn't look twice at a pretty lass might as well go into a corner and roll up then stiffen himself. But if Gerald *did* meet the Armstrong lass, well, he's got to be a man and own up. He's got to tell the police because – don't you see, chuck? – it could give them a lead as to who she was seeing – who she saw that night.'

'Gerald is not the type of young man to associate with your weavers,' Phyllis stressed each word. 'And Dorothy said *nothing*. And if she opens her mouth outside this house then my door will never open to her again. Never.'

Matthew sighed. He'd read somewhere once that under

great stress people could blank out a part of their minds, refusing to believe, or unable to believe that which they refused to acknowledge to be truth. But this was Phyllis. His wife. A woman with predictable reactions to any given situation. Narrow-minded and bigoted maybe, but predictable.

'You don't mean that, love,' he said, shaking his big head from side to side. Then, as the sound of the front door opening and closing cut short another spate of angry words, he saw the way Phyllis arranged her face into a smile of welcome, a smile which made him recoil and put up a hand to his mouth as if she had hit out at him also.

Margaret came straight through the hall into the kitchen, swinging her Sunday hat in her hand, her coat unbuttoned, glowing with the special kind of happiness that Gerald seemed to be able to instil in her. Her voice held a teasing quality. 'Here you both are, then, looking as guilty as a pair of old Nicks. What's been going on?'

'Going on, dear?' Phyllis's smile cracked a little at the corners. 'What do you mean? There's nothing been going on, has there, Father?'

Margaret sniffed the air with appreciation. 'Gosh, but that smells good. We were driving up Steep Brow just now when we saw our Dorothy walking down the other side, and though I swear she saw us, she turned her head away and started to run.' She turned to Phyllis. 'You've found out, I suppose?'

'Found out what?' Phyllis's smile disappeared as if someone had stepped forward and wiped it from her face with a damp flannel.

'About that Stanley boy coming round to the house last night when you were out. Good heavens, there's no need to look like that, the pair of you. Dorothy isn't the first girl to have a boy in when she's alone, and she won't be the last. He looks harmless enough, honestly.' She laughed and ran her fingers through her hair. 'Can't you see that if you ignore him he'll disappear? He isn't Dorothy's type, I can tell you that. Gerald and I are always saying that she'll have to find a boy who can dominate her before she can respect him, and this boy definitely isn't the domineering type. It was funny really, the way they scuttled out when we came in. Like two frightened rabbits.'

Matthew found his voice at last. 'Where's Gerald then? Making sure the car's all right? I didn't hear you drive in.'

Margaret turned to go upstairs. 'Gone after Dorothy, of course. He'll calm her down if anyone can. He dropped me off at the end of the road, then he reversed round the corner and went after her. Want to bet that by the time I've set the table she's back, pleading to be forgiven?' She put her head on one side and glanced at them mischievously from beneath her eyelashes. 'You are a fuddy-duddy pair. Can't you see that she's a bit upset with that awful thing happening in the park? There's nothing for you to look so worried about. Honestly.'

And as the soft click of her bedroom door closed behind her the door-bell rang. Apologetically, as if someone had merely brushed the bell with a finger, then regretted it immediately.

'He's found her already.' Matthew closed both eyes with the enormity of his relief.'

'I tell you, Matthew. If she says as much as a word . . .'

'You get on with the dinner.' He walked heavily out of the kitchen and down the hall, his step faltering as he opened the door and saw the bulky form of his friend Arnold Bates, standing there on the step, as obviously a policeman as if he was wearing full uniform and not the tweed suit with the canary-yellow waistcoat and the watch-chain draped across his ample middle. Profusely apologetic, he stood there in the Sunday sunshine, twisting the brim of a brown trilby hat round and round in his hands.

'Morning, Matthew.'

Almost without volition, Matthew pulled the big door partially closed behind him. 'Morning, Arnold.'

'Looks like summer's come at last.'

'Aye. Not before time though.'

'But there's still a nip in the air if tha' moves out of the sun.'

'Aye, that's right.'

'Missus well?'

'Aye. And Gertie?'

'Fair to middlin'. Still has her usual rheumatism about this time of the year. Always at its worst when 'weather perks up.'

Then Sergeant Bates looked his old friend in the eye. 'I've come on a tricky errand, Matthew. Just come from your brother-in-law's house. Tha knows. Raymond Rostron,' he added unnecessarily.

Matthew found he was holding his breath. 'They've gone out for their dinner, but they'll be back about three no doubt. Hope there's nowt wrong down at the yard. Raymond's worried enough without any trouble in that direction.'

The sergeant shook his head. 'Aye, well.' Then he studied a loose piece of gravel on the path with intense concentration. 'Well, it were really their lodger I wanted to see. Mr Gerald Tomlin.' He kicked the gravel furiously with the toe of a well-polished shoe. 'Your lass's intended. Tha' knows?'

Matthew glanced over his shoulder. There was no need for him to be holding his breath now. It was holding itself, or so it seemed. 'He's not here,' he whispered. His voice sounded as if it was coming from a long way. 'But he'll be here soon. Aye, that's right. He'll be coming soon. He's coming here for his dinner.'

'Good.' Sergeant Bates avoided his eyes, staring now with interest at the tip of a thumb-nail. 'Then I'll come inside and wait if tha' doesn't mind. There's just one or two questions I'd like to ask him. Routine tha' knows, purely routine.'

'In connection with Ruby Armstrong's murder?'

The words were out before Matthew could stop them,

186

before he even knew his mind had formed them, and completely oblivious to the sudden narrowing of the sergeant's eyes, he stepped round him and strode quickly to the gate. Straining his eyes against the sun, he stared down the road, anticipating the roar of the engine in Gerald's red car, praying that it might turn the corner, *willing* it to appear.

And seeing and hearing nothing . . .

Seventeen

Although Dorothy was walking in the direction of Inker-man Street, she was doing so without intent. Walking aimlessly as the despairing do, putting one foot in front of the other, her mind at times a blank and at times seething with resentment.

In the last hour, since coming out of church, the wind had dropped, and the midday sun, high in the sky, was warm on her shoulders.

'Don't like it when it comes too soon,' a woman was telling her next-door neighbour as she stood, arms folded, squinting at the clear blue sky.

'Aye, we're bound to suffer for it later,' her neighbour said, going inside and closing the door on the sunshine.

Dorothy, hands deep in her blazer pocket, turned into Balaclava Street, walking with head bent so that she almost stumbled over a chair placed in front of a bay window. A woman, shelling peas into a white basin, grinned at her. 'If this is going to be summer, then I'm making sure I'm on 'front row for it.'

Dorothy smiled back at her automatically . . . Mother would have been horrified. In Phyllis's code, to sit out at the back of the house was in order if one was decently screened from one's neighbours. But to sit out at the *front* of the house put one entirely beyond the pale.

'Oh, Mother . . .' she muttered, walking straight into the chalked-in squares of a hopscotch game, causing a tiny girl, balancing on one foot in a numbered flagstone, to shout out in indignant protest: 'Left yer glasses at home, then?'

'Sorry.' Dorothy walked on. 'Sorry . . . sorry.'

Sorry she'd made such a mess of things, sorry she'd upset her mother so much, sorry for herself, sorry for Stanley. Sorry for the whole terrible, terrible mess.

'But she shouldn't have hit me . . .' Her mouth hurt and she could feel the swelling where her top teeth had caught her lip at the unexpected violence of the blow. People didn't hit people. Not Phyllis's kind. A woman like Phyllis was always in control; even a flash of temper showing merely as a tightening of the lips, a narrowing of the eyes.

It wasn't dignified . . . she had known exactly where she stood with her mother, knew exactly how far she could go. Now she felt as if she had never really known her mother, and as if she would never really know her again.

And she'd have to go back. She had known she would have to go back, even before she'd reached the end of her road. The white-hot flame of her own anger was dying down, the grand dramatic gesture of flinging herself out of the house was being superseded by a feeling of embarrassment. Embarrassment and a slow acknowledgement of her own sound common sense.

If she didn't go back, then where *could* she go?

Certainly not to Stanley's house, even though her footsteps had instinctively led her in that direction. They had enough to worry them with the funeral tomorrow. Not to Cousin Beryl's house because they had gone out to dinner. To Mrs Wilkinson's?

'Please, Mrs Wilkinson, may I come in? My mother's hit me across the mouth and told me to bugger off.'

No, Phyllis ought not to have hit her. It wasn't right. They weren't supposed to do things like that in the red-brick houses up by the park. Without realizing it, Dorothy began to whimper.

'Anything wrong, chuck?' A man with a narrow grey face, with a flat cap pulled low down over his eyes, leaned back against a window-bottom, smoking a Woodbine tucked neatly into the curved palm of his hand.

Shaking her head, Dorothy walked on quickly.

Oh no, there was nothing wrong. She'd only put the cat amongst the pigeons, as Grandpa Bolton would have said. Oh no, nothing wrong. Just that she'd done it this time, done it right and proper. Her fingers curled over the cuff-link down in the patch pocket of her blazer as she walked over to the edge of the pavement, staring down at a grate.

All she had to do was to drop the cuff-link between the grids, watch it disappear, and the evidence, if evidence it was, would be gone for ever. She teetered on the kerb, swaying slowly backwards and forwards.

Then she lifted her head and saw Gerald's red car cruising leisurely down the street towards her.

'Tha'd best come in here, Arnold.'

Matthew led the way into the lounge, the cosy, chintzy room bright with sunshine, the brasses round the massive cream tiled fireplace a-twinkle with the three monkeys on the mantelpiece shining in three-fold splendour.

Sergeant Bates, trilby hat still clutched in his hand, sat down on the very edge of the chesterfield, and refused a drink.

'Not when I'm on duty, Matthew, thanks all the same.'

'But surely . . .? Matthew took up his normal stance in front of the fireplace, hands clenched deep inside the cardigan pockets. Pulling it out of shape, as Phyllis would have said.

The sergeant coughed. 'The missus?' he asked.

'In the kitchen.' Matthew nodded towards the Westminster chime clock. 'It's nearly dinner-time.'

'Aye. Well . . .' Sergeant Bates started to spin his hat round at a feverish rate. 'This is a helluva spot for us both to be in, Matthew. I'd have given anything, anything, but with you being a pal and everything . . .' He looked up and sighed. 'I've left the car outside Raymond's house.'

Matthew walked over to one of the easy chairs and perched himself awkwardly on the well-padded arm. He couldn't bring himself to sit down in it properly, not with part of him still straining after Dorothy. Not with part of him picturing Gerald searching the streets at the wheel of his red car. Gerald who . . . oh God!

'Say what tha's come to say, Arnold.' Then he forced himself to continue. 'Tha's taking him in. I'm right, aren't I?'

His solid homely face suffused with colour, the sergeant nodded. 'Aye, I'm afraid I am, lad.' He placed the trilby down on the cushion beside him, found he couldn't manage without it, and picked it up again, examining the brim with a look of intense concentration. 'I'm sorry, Matthew. Heart sorry I am. This is the hardest thing I've had to do ever since I were a bobby on the beat, but we've had our eye on him for a bit. Seems he had a bit of a field-day with some of the lasses at the mill when he first came up here.'

'But that doesn't make him a . . .' Matthew couldn't bring himself to say the word.

'No, it doesn't, but one or two of the things he told us didn't match up, then this morning, one of your weavers, a big blonde lass, came into the station with her father. Wouldn't talk to no one but me, so they sent for me. He'd made her come. Practically had to drag her through the streets, he said.'

'Mabel Earnshaw?'

'Aye. How did you know that, then?'

Matthew put one hand inside his cardigan, and rubbed his chest bone. 'She was a mate of Ruby Armstrong's, though I could never see what they saw in one another. One were as brash as t'other were reserved.'

'Aye. Well, it seems that Ruby had confided in the lass, this Mabel. Sworn her to secrecy 'bout three months back. Told her she was meeting Mr Tomlin on the sly. Said her mother would kill her if she found out.'

191

'She would 'n all.'

'Told her she was meeting him on the night.' The sergeant coughed and cleared his throat. 'On the night in question.'

Matthew got up from the arm of the chair and began to pace backwards and forwards. 'And she's kept quiet? It doesn't seem feasible. I can't believe that somehow. Can you?'

Sergeant Bates nodded. 'Seems Mr Tomlin saw her down at the mill the morning after, and managed to convince her that whilst he had indeed met Ruby, he had left her in the park. Swore it with tears in his eyes apparently, and convinced her that he had nothing to do with that poor lass's death.'

He twisted round to face Matthew, who was staring out of the window at the sun-drenched garden. 'Told her that if she said anything she would lose her job.'

'Oh, my God!' Matthew raised his voice. 'They know they only have to come to me.' Then he paused. 'She's not very bright, Mabel Earnshaw, but she's the only one working out of a big family. There have been times when I'd have sacked her, but knowing that . . .'

'Exactly. Seems her father's been out of work for three years, and the only money going into that house is what Mabel earns.'

'Bloody Means Test.' Matthew shook his head. 'But I still can't see how she could have kept quiet.' He lowered his head. 'She could have come to me. They allus know they can come to me.'

Sergeant Bates rubbed the finger and thumb of his right hand together, and Matthew interpreted the gesture at once.

'Blackmail? Oh, dear God in heaven!'

'Empty bellies have a special code of their own, Matthew. Seems one of the children has had consumption and needs proper food and milk. So there were no questions asked at home.'

192

'The mother. Don't know what she's like now, but she used to be a wrong 'un, Arnold. She'd ask no questions.'

The sergeant sniffed. 'Aye, they didn't call her tanner-a-time for nowt. But all the same I believe that lass when she said she doesn't believe that Mr Tomlin had anything to do with young Ruby Armstrong's death. "He's a proper gentleman," she kept saying over and over again.'

'But you think he did it?'

It seemed as though his world stood still, as though even the brasses round the fireplace stopped their twinkling as Matthew waited for the sergeant's reply.

'Arnold! How very nice.'

Phyllis's right hand was extended in a smiling welcome, her apron whisked off and held behind her back in deference to her unexpected visitor. Only an extra sharp brittleness in her speech giving away her agitation to her husband. She moved forward into the room. 'I thought I heard Matthew bringing someone in, but I was busy with the dinner. Just look at you sitting there without a drink in your hand, and this the cocktail hour.' She laughed nervously. 'Matthew, what can you be thinking about? And how's Gertrude? We're looking forward to seeing you at the wedding . . .'

'Sit down, love.'

Matthew spoke softly, but in a strange way his voice rang out like a pistol shot.

'I can't sit down now.' Phyllis flashed a brilliant smile at the sergeant. 'You men are all the same. You think a Sunday dinner appears on the table all by itself.' She walked towards the door, and something in the set of her shoulders told Matthew that she knew. Knew, and didn't wish to hear. Thought that, by walking away into the shining neatness of her kitchen, the terrible thing that was happening would be restored to pristine oblivion also. He felt behind him for the edge of a chair and sat down. Oh God, in Thy infinite mercy, have pity on her. What she had to hear would kill her, as stone-dead as if someone had fired a bullet straight at her heart.

He exchanged a glance and a quick nod with the sergeant.

'Phyllis. Come back here, love. There's something you have to know. Arnold isn't paying a social call, not this time.' He ran his tongue over his dry lips. 'It's about Gerald, love. Arnold's come about Gerald.'

'No!' Phyllis swung round. 'It's not true. She's made it all up, the little sod. She didn't waste much time running to you, did she? She must have well nigh burst her lungs running to the nearest telephone to spread that muck.' She stared wild-eyed at the astonished sergeant. 'And you believe her? You'd take notice of a little lying runt like that?'

Matthew reached for his wife, and although he could have sworn he was shouting, the words he spoke were no more than a whisper:

'It's got nothing to do with Dorothy, nothing. Listen, for God's sake. We've got to find her, because it looks like Gerald's gone after her. He suspects that she knows something, and he's gone after her.'

Sergeant Bates was at the door in two single strides. 'You tell me that now, Matthew! For God's sake, man, let's get going. Fast.'

With a tormented backwards glance at his wife, Matthew followed the burly figure of the sergeant out of the house, leaving Phyllis running upstairs, the adrenalin pumping so fast that it seemed her feet scarce touched the stairs. The one thought in her head was to get to Margaret, to hold her, to comfort her, to promise they'd go away, far away, and never come back. Never. Never.

And as she opened the bedroom door, she saw Margaret sitting serenely in front of her dressing-table, staring calmly at her reflection in the mirror, blue eyes smiling back in tranquil oblivion.

'Mother! I'm sorry. Is dinner ready? I was day-dreaming. Is Gerald back?'

Phyllis stumbled forward, holding out her arms. Then,

as her daughter turned round, she ran back along the wide landing, into the spare room where the white satin wedding-dress hung from the picture-rail, wrapped in its covering sheet. And pulling it down, she tore at the neckline with a strength that was more than human, felt the stitches give, and tore and tore, ripping, scrabbling at the fragile lace.

Then suddenly, as if pole-axed, she fell backwards on to the floor, eyes and mouth agape, the terrible turn of events for ever obliterated from her mind as she stared unseeing at the ceiling.

And it was Margaret who telephoned for the ambulance, dialling with trembling fingers, calling in vain for her father, sobbing for Gerald, for Dorothy – for anyone to come quickly. Seeing her whole world turned upside down, her happiness in jeopardy, as she knelt by her mother's still form and felt for a pulse that seemed to be non-existent.

'Get in!' Gerald Tomlin held the door of the red sports car open. 'Come on, you little ninny, I'll run you home.' He glanced at his wrist watch, pushing back a cuff to check the time, and Dorothy sighed with relief. Cuffs with buttons, she noticed thankfully.

He smiled at her. 'Five past one, and you know what your mother is about meals being on time. Come on. You don't want me to have to get out and lift you into the car, do you? We're getting some funny looks from across the street as it is, and it wouldn't look nice now on a Sunday, would it?'

Dorothy hesitated. She felt drained, as if someone had inserted a tap in her head and siphoned all her blood away. The anger had gone, evaporated away somehow into the clear blue sky, floating over the tall mill chimneys, and all that was left was a tired and sad bewilderment, and a numbness that the sun could do nothing to alleviate.

Gerald gave the door of the car an extra push. 'Well? Are you coming back of your own accord, or do I have to drag you by that golden hair of yours?' He grinned. 'Whatever's troubling you sweetie, don't let it spoil your dear mother's Sunday joint. It wouldn't be cricket now, would it?'

There was a woman standing at the door across the street eyeing them curiously, her arms folded across her flowered pinafore. Dorothy lifted her head. And the sun was shining, and Gerald Tomlin was the man her sister was going to marry and he might well have been a philanderer, but he couldn't have done that terrible thing. He was . . . he was a gentleman.

Sighing, as if somehow it had all been resolved without her having to do anything about it, Dorothy got into the car. It wouldn't be the first time she'd returned to the house with her tail between her legs. Flouncing out after a difference of opinion with her mother had come to be looked upon as a family joke. Once as a child, she remembered now, half smiling to herself, she had packed a case, squashing her teddy-bear in on top of her favourite book and her pyjamas and a frilly party dress. Then half way down the road she'd turned back again, taking her place at the table as if nothing had happened.

'That's better.' Gerald patted her knee, let in the clutch and drove away from the kerb. 'Sensible girl. Now why don't you tell Uncle Gerald what it's all about? Confession's good for the soul.' He laughed shortly. 'Or so they say.'

Dorothy glanced at him quickly, but his eyes were on the road, his hands steady on the wheel. He was driving with his usual expertise, concentrating as if he were in a stream of traffic in Regent Street instead of driving down a narrow street with no other cars in sight. Signalling right, he turned into the wide street of Victorian houses, the odd one here and there with striped sun-blinds flapping over closed front doors.

'We're going the wrong way.' Dorothy sat up straight in the low seat, the aftermath of shock at her mother's behaviour leaving her . . . Leaving her with every single nerve in her body alive and quivering. 'This isn't the way home, Gerald. You should have turned left, not right.'

But he made no sign of having heard her, just drove on, away from the west side of the park, away from the wide avenues of red-brick houses, along the almost deserted street. Past a piece of spare land with a group of boys kicking a tin can around, dribbling it from one to another, calling out to each other in high excited voices.

'Get tha skates on, slowcoach!'

'Give us a chance!'

Dorothy stared at them, wondering what would happen if she called out and screamed for help, then she glanced quickly at the set profile of the man at the wheel. Oh, God, but she was the chump to end all chumps . . . She was the character in the play, who, alone and undefended, went off quite willingly with the prime suspect in a murder case. The stupid character at the end of a novel, who, in the last chapter, took a calculated risk, putting herself in the hands of the villain, as if she alone could solve the mystery. How many times had she groaned and put her library book aside, or switched off the wireless, snorting with disgust? And now, she, of her own volition, had got into a car with a man who, she was sure, knew that she knew far more than was good for her. . . .

She shivered and clung on to the sides of her seat as the car, coming to the end of the made-up road, bumped and jerked along a rutted path, with a patchwork of allotments stretching away upwards to the left, and a stubbled field on the right sloping down to the deserted playground of a council school.

And beyond the school, the sprawling panorama of the town: row upon row of terraced houses, with pepper-pot chimneys, curling in curving lines to the cluster of tall mill chimneys pointing sooty fingers up into the clear blue sky. Dorothy turned her head and saw, across the allotments, a long way ahead, the spiral of yellow smoke from a lone bonfire.

'Where do you think you're going?' Her voice trembled

on the verge of lost control. 'There's nothing at the end of here but an old quarry – Bill Foot's Delph . . .' Her hand covered her mouth to stifle a scream as she visualized the derelict place, supposed to be haunted, the place where, years ago, a tormented man had hurled himself to oblivion.

'Well, Dorothy?' Gerald suddenly, with a squeal of brakes, brought the red car to a halt by the side of a hen-run, where a cluster of white and scrawny hens, separated from them by a tall wire-mesh fence, bobbed and scratched feverishly at the brown and dusty earth.

'Well, Dorothy?' Gerald took his hands from the wheel as slowly and lovingly as a concert pianist finishing a concerto. 'Don't you think it's time you told me what this is all about?'

Already the sun had deepened his fair skin to pink, and the wind had tossed the red quiff of hair from its sculptured perfection so that it lay untidily across his wide forehead. He turned his wet and enquiring gaze full upon her, wide-eyed and questioning, and even in that moment of apprehension she wondered how her sister Margaret could possibly find this man attractive? To her he was repulsive, both in looks and manner, nauseatingly repulsive, and never more than at that minute.

He was staring bulging eyed at her, holding her glance with his own, willing her to speak out, daring her to keep silent, their mutual dislike flaring like a living flame between them.

And suddenly Dorothy's fear left her, and rage rose up in her throat, almost choking her. Suddenly, with a flash of intuition, she knew that this man was the one afraid, not her . . . this man who had come unbidden into their lives, wheedling his way into her father's respect, flattering her foolish, snobbish mother into total subjection, and stealing Margaret's heart. Placid, trusting Margaret, who would have believed that black was white, if someone said it firmly enough.

Their eyes were holding hard. It was a moment of recognition, of putting their cards face down on the ruddy table, as Grandpa Bolton would surely have said. And Dorothy knew what she must do.

Putting her hand into her blazer pocket, she took out the cuff-link and held it out to him on the palm of her hand, not speaking, just holding it out to him, her eyes still steady on his face.

He shook his head, bowed it low, then lifted it sharply, the pale eyes narrowing into threatening slits. 'Where in the name of God did you find it? Tell me, you little interfering sod. Tell me where you found it?'

And as he snatched it from her, hurling it away from him, so that it cleared the wire-mesh fence, falling amongst the hens who fell upon it with a wild flapping of wings, Dorothy knew that he thought it was the *other* one. The cuff-link he had lost that rainswept night in the park, and had been searching for ever since. . . .

And with the realization came the knowledge that she was looking on the panic-stricken face of Ruby Armstrong's killer.

There was a fierce heat welling up inside her, coursing through her body and showing itself in tiny beads of sweat on her upper lip. Her teeth were clenched as she said, 'You did it! You killed that poor girl, and then you dragged her underneath the rhododendron bush and left her lying there. And you went back home, and you went to bed, and you came to our house and you sat at the table and you ate, and you took Margaret to the pictures, and you smiled and smiled . . .' She was shaking now, clenching her fists to stop herself from raking her finger-nails down his shiny pink cheeks. 'And you thought you'd have got away with it. Oh, my God!' She shook her head slowly from side to side. 'And you'd have married Margaret. Married her with that on your mind . . .'

She was so consumed with the power of her anger that even when he stretched out a hand towards her, she felt no fear, merely drew back from him with a look of such loathing

199

on her face that he was the one to recoil.

For the space of a few seconds they stared at each other, then his hand shot out and gripped her round the wrist, in an iron grip that made her cry aloud. 'Right,' he said, snapping out the word. 'Right. Now the cards are on the table, Dorothy. And I suppose you told her big brother what you found out? I suppose you told your precious dad? Was that why you were walking down Steep Brow with a face like an accident going somewhere to happen?'

'No! You're wrong! I told no one.' She tried to wriggle free, but his grip tightened. 'I was running away . . .' Her mind was working frantically. 'I was running away because my mother had found out that Stanley came to the house last night when they were out. She said some dreadful things, and I just walked out. I've done that before when my mother and me have rowed,' she added with desperation.

'Right!' he said again, then before she could move to scramble from the car he had started the engine. Driving on, caring nothing once again for the springs of his beloved car, driving over the rutted road, his foot pressed down hard on the accelerator.

There was murder in his eyes, murder in the way he wrenched at the wheel. This man had killed once, and Dorothy knew that he would have no compunction in killing again. She screamed, and the sound was torn from her throat and tossed away in the slip-stream of onrushing wind.

She fumbled for the door handle, but his hand came out and held her fast.

'No!' she shouted. 'I haven't told anyone! No one, Gerald. Believe me . . .'

But Gerald Tomlin was past believing anything. The temper that had got him into one serious scrape after another all his life, the temper that had caused him to reach out and choke the life out of Ruby Armstrong, was burning him with its all-consuming fire. And this girl, this slip of a girl by his side had taken his shining future in her hands and destroyed it . . . as he would destroy her.

On two wheels the red car turned the corner and roared up the unmade road to Bill Foot's Delph. And in front of them a grassy bank sloped down to the quarry. Stopping with a squeal of brakes, Gerald reached over Dorothy, opened the door and pushed her out, sure that in her state of terror she would be an easy victim for what he planned to do.

But fear had made Dorothy strong, and instead of paralysing her, it lent wings to her feet as she ran towards the quarry, and not away from it as he had expected her to do. Her mind working feverishly she calculated that, if she could crawl beneath the flimsy railing erected not ten yards away from the edge of the sheer drop, she could make her way round to the other side, and if she could climb the grassy bank there, reach the houses seen as a row of chimneys deep in the hollow.

Then she heard a sound behind her that seemed to freeze the very marrow in her bones. The revving of an engine as Gerald drove the car straight for her. . . .

Sure of his undoubted expertise in driving the red car, Gerald was confident enough to take a calculated risk. Sure that after he had run her down he could swerve away from the brink. . . .

With all the strength at her command, Dorothy took a flying leap to land face downwards in the long grass, as Gerald missed her by a fraction of an inch, careering on, for once in his life, the *last* time in his life, misjudging his distance, so that the car, skidding out of control, plunged over the edge of the quarry, turning over and over, bouncing down to the bottom, where it burst into flames.

And it was Mr Crawley who found her, stumbling along the pitted road at the side of the allotments, her face dirty and streaked with tears, her yellow hair falling round her face. Mr Crawley, going home quietly after damping down his fire, to his Sunday dinner after a blissful morning with his pigeons, holding them tenderly in his hands, like the child he had never had, soothing, ringing, spreading their wings wide as he talked to them.

'Nay, lass,' he said. 'Nowt's worth crying like that for, nowt in this silly old world . . .'

And it was Mr Crawley's arms that came round her as she gasped out what had happened, incoherent, pointing back up the hill, shaking, sobbing, trying to make him understand.

And when she had finished he took off his old tweed cap, scratched his head, then put it back again.

'Now tell me where tha' lives, lass, and I'll take thee home,' he said.

Before the afternoon was over, the clouds had formed, the sun had gone, and it was raining hard. As though the bright sunshine of the morning had never been.

Dorothy sat with her father and Margaret in a side room off the women's surgical ward in the infirmary, staring at her mother who lay unmoving and unseeing in the high white bed.

There was nothing they could do. Nothing it seemed that they would ever be able to do ever again for Phyllis Bolton – the Phyllis Bolton they'd always known.

'I want it straight,' Matthew had told the Senior Consultant, a greying man with tired eyes. 'I can cope with the truth, tha knows, so none of tha soft soap, if tha doesn't mind.'

'She's suffered a massive stroke,' the doctor had said, pulling no punches as the broad-shouldered man standing squarely before him had requested. 'She'll never walk again, or speak again. The most you can hope for is some slight movement in her right foot . . . unless there's a miracle.'

'Don't believe in them,' Matthew said, and thanked the

202

doctor for his frankness, before going back to join his daughters in their bedside vigil.

'I'll stay at home and help to look after her,' Dorothy promised, and what could have passed for a smile crossed Matthew's face. He leaned over and patted her hand.

'I know tha will, chuck,' he said, and knowing this younger child of his even better than he knew himself, he realized that at that very moment she meant it. She were made of good stuff, his Dorothy. He shuddered when he thought how nearly he might have lost her. Felt again the upsurge of relief when, with Arnold driving his car like a maniac, they had found that funny little chap walking along Marston Road with his arm round Dorothy.

'She's had a bit of a shock, gaffer,' Mr Crawley had said, and Matthew, even as he clasped her in his arms, had felt that must surely be the understatement of the year.

Aye, his Dorothy would be all right, and now weren't the time to tell her that he would never allow her to sacrifice herself for the left-over life that this speechless, vegetable of a woman had in front of her. . . .

Poor Phyllis. And poor Margaret. Matthew saw that she was still crying softly into a screwed-up handkerchief, her eyes swollen to narrow slits, and her face puffy and red.

'I want to die!' she had screamed when the ambulance had taken her mother away and he'd had to break the news to her about Gerald. 'I want to die. Oh, Daddy, let me die . . .'

She hadn't called him Daddy for a long time, this uncomplicated daughter of his, and somehow it touched him more than her flowing tears and anguished cries. She wouldn't forget this day, not for the rest of her life, but he knew, he knew as sure as the sun would rise on the morrow that, given time, his Margaret would survive. It were the other one . . . Matthew patted Dorothy's hand again. Aye, things went deep with her. . . .

'We'd best be going,' he said. 'There's nowt we can do here.'

And with a backward glance at the still figure on the bed, they walked together down the long stone corridor with its garden-fence-green walls, out of the infirmary to where the black car was parked.

And as they drove into the circular drive and saw Stanley Armstrong waiting patiently in the porch, sheltering from the rain, Matthew whispered to Dorothy to get her sister up to bed.

'I'll have a word with the lad,' he said.

Margaret, still weeping, allowed Dorothy to help her to undress, protesting that she didn't want to live, turning a ravaged face into her pillow, and holding out a wavering hand for another handkerchief.

'How can I ever go out again?' she wailed. 'I'll never go out again. I'll stay in the house and never face people again.'

Dorothy tucked her in, saw that already her poor swollen eyelids were drooping and, closing the door softly behind her, ran downstairs.

The telephone was ringing as she reached the hall, and she told a stuttering Edwin Birtwistle, the captain of the local tennis club for three consecutive seasons, that his kindness in ringing was appreciated. That she quite understood he felt he must get in touch, and that Margaret was taking it all as well as could be expected.

'Tell her that all her friends are standing by her,' he said, and as Matthew came out of the sitting-room Dorothy put a finger to her lips and glanced back upstairs.

Matthew nodded, then pulled a wry face. 'Bad news travels fast, chuck,' he said. 'Go and have a word with him – he's waiting in there.'

'I had to get in touch,' Stanley said, just as Edwin Birtwistle had said. 'Mr Crawley came over with Mrs Crawley. Oh, Dorothy . . .' He stretched out a hand and drew her to him. 'What can I say? I'll never be able to forgive myself for not . . . for not . . .'

Dorothy was so tired that even the effort of forming her mouth round the words was too much of an effort for her. She leaned against him, feeling her legs grow weak beneath her.

'You know about my mother?' she whispered.

He stroked her hair. 'Your father's just told me. It's awful . . . oh God, can anything else happen? It's all so awful!'

Then, as they sat together on the chesterfield, he told her that Matthew had told him that he was making his mother an allowance so that he could take up his scholarship to Oxford.

'In the middle of all this he told me that,' he said, shaking his head. 'He's a wonderful man, your father.'

And strangely enough there was nothing more to say . . . and so they just sat there, with the rain pouring down the window panes, and when he got up to go Dorothy walked with him to the door, and stood there until he had walked away, turning the corner out of sight. Tall, falling over his feet, head bent, the rain beating down on his thin shoulders.

She found her father sitting at the kitchen table, his hands clasped together on its scrubbed surface, sitting there as if he was wondering what to do.

Dorothy went to him and leaned her cheek against his thinning hair. 'That was a nice thing you told Stanley,' she said softly. 'Now he won't go making any dramatic statements after the funeral tomorrow about giving up his scholarship. That's what he intended to do, you know.'

Matthew nodded. 'I guessed as much. In fact he told me as much. He's a grand lad, chuck.'

Dorothy moved round and went to sit opposite to her father at the big table. And the house was quiet around them, with only the steady drip of the rain outside to break the silence.

'Aye, a grand lad,' Matthew said again.

Dorothy saw the way his features were blurred into unfamiliar lines with exhaustion and the sadness of the day. Some day she'd tell him that what had been between her and Stanley was all over. Perhaps she'd even try to explain how her love for him had died at the moment she had taken his jacket from him and hung it up in the hall.

'Love can die at the most unexpected moment, the most mundane moment,' she would say. 'How can that be? Tell me how that can be?'

And even her beloved father, in his infinite wisdom, wouldn't be expected to understand. . . .

But she was wrong. For Matthew Bolton, aged at least five years in the space of an afternoon, and tired beyond sleep, would have understood perfectly.

How could the love of so many years have died in a single second, he was asking himself silently at that very moment? How could he have looked at Phyllis as she lashed out with her fist at Dorothy and known that never, for as long as he lived, would he feel the same way about her again?

Look after her he would. Cherish what was left of her for always, without question, but something in him had died and would never be restored.

'Thank God there'll be no trial and all the muck-raking that would have entailed,' he said at last, as if they were continuing a conversation, and as if at an unspoken command they reached across the table and clasped hands.

'It'll be reet, lass,' Matthew Bolton said. 'Things usually turn out reet in the end.'

'You sound just like Grandpa Bolton,' Dorothy said, and as she saw the way the tears sprang to his eyes, she got up quickly and, moving over to the gas-stove, put the kettle on.

'A cup of tea?' she asked, being careful not to turn round.

Maggie Craig

MARIE JOSEPH

For
Marilyn and Kate

I

Maggie Craig was just six years old when she took on Miss Hepinstall, Infant teacher at her father's village school. She challenged that strict disciplinarian with such fury that the children, sitting upright in their scarred desks, felt their mouths drop open, and their eyes stand out like chapel hat-pegs.

Teddy, the youngest of Maggie's three brothers, an incurable chatter-box, had been told to stop talking twice. Twice when once should have been quite enough, and when Miss Hepinstall caught him bobbing his brown head towards a boy across the narrow aisle, her beetle brows drew together, and her mouth set into a tight, thin, angry line.

So angry was she at having her authority flouted that it seemed to her startled class that the little top-knot skewered to the top of her head quivered as if it had a life of its own.

'Come out to me, Teddy Craig!' she shouted. 'I warned you, and I will not warn you again. Out here! This very minute!'

The children shuffled their feet, holding their respective breaths, some with fear, and some with a kind of shamed excitement, because once Miss had drawn blood. Last year, which was even better, Millie Hargreaves had fainted dead away, only coming to when her face had been fanned with the register. And the next day her mother had come to the school and had shaken her fist at Miss and threatened to report her to the School Board, but nothing had come of it.

7

On the not infrequent occasions when Miss wielded the thin and flexible cane, it swished down through the air with a terrifying sound then landed with a thwack that felt its echo in the palms of the watchers, causing the more sensitive amongst them to close their eyes. Some were actually in tears at the remembrance of the stinging agony.

Thomas Craig, Maggie's father, in charge of the older children on the other side of the sliding doors dividing the two classrooms, also possessed a cane, but his was laid harmlessly across his desk next to the Bible. No one could ever remember it being used.

'A good man, but too soft by half,' Miss Hepinstall often told her mother, a hopeless cripple, gradually seizing up with the arthritis; an old woman with a tongue on her that would make a whiplash seem like a whisper of silk.

'Me daughter makes a good teacher because she's frustrated at never having had a man. It has to come out somewhere, even if it's only on the childer's hands at school,' she had told the embarrassed minister from the Mission Hall one day. 'It's not natural for a woman not to have a man to boss her about, tha knows, Vicar.'

In her daughter's class the children sat at their desks as straight as if they'd been born with pokers for backbones, sometimes for half an hour at a time, with their hands on top of their heads. Miss's word was law, and the fact that the eight-year-old boy approaching her desk now with dragging feet was the son of the schoolmaster, mattered less than nothing to Miss Hepinstall.

Disobedience would not be tolerated, and must be punished with something far more telling than a reprimand.

'Hold out your hand, Teddy Craig!' she ordered. 'Your *hand*, if you please!'

Her arm was actually upraised to administer the first of the three strokes, when Maggie shot out from her desk in the front row with the force of a stone shot from a catapult.

Pink cheeks reddened to fury, long hair flying free from its restraining ribbon, feet in boots too big for them,

8

tripping over a crack in the floorboards, Maggie went into action.

Throwing herself dramatically in front of her brother, she spread her arms wide, and glared into the face of the astonished teacher.

'Don't you *dare* hit our Teddy! He's got a gathering on his thumb he has. Yes he has! It would have a bandage on it if me mother hadn't said it had to have the air get to it. Don't you dare hit him! Don't you dare!'

The shocked surprise on Miss's face was so immense that it was comical to see. The fact that anyone so small would dare to question her methods stunned her into immobility at the child's undoubted courage. For a moment she actually did not know what to do.

'You will sit down at your desk, Maggie Craig,' she said quietly, 'and you will hold out your *other* hand, Teddy Craig,' she said, even more quietly.

But although the cane was raised three times, to swish down with venomous power on the boy's left hand, Miss Hepinstall knew, and the class knew, that Maggie was the winner of that particular battle.

'I told Miss she couldn't hit our Teddy on his sore hand. I told her good and proper,' Maggie announced to her mother after school was over for the day.

She was sitting round the big scrubbed table in the living-room of the School House, eating her second slice of bread, still warm from the fire-oven and spread thinly with rum butter as a special treat.

Hannah Craig looked at her four children eating stolidly; Teddy signalling to Maggie to keep quiet, with Benjamin and Jonathan, unidentical ten year-old-twins, nodding at their little sister with approval.

Maggie's brown eyes, the left one flecked with green, shone and sparkled with the triumph of the afternoon as she basked in the attention she was getting from her brothers.

'As good as a boy any old day,' they often said.

9

'Trust our Maggie to stand up to old Miss,' Jonathan said, and Maggie glowed.

Hannah tried hard not to smile as she watched her little daughter showing off as she played to the appreciative audience. How bonny and sturdy she was, smiling round the table through a milk moustache, glorying in their obvious adulation.

'She's going to be the strongest lad in the family,' Doctor Bates had said when she was born.

'And the cheekiest,' Thomas, her father, had said with an indulgent smile.

But enough was enough.

'Stop that, and get on with your tea,' Hannah said, as carried away with her success, Maggie was brandishing a knife to give a near perfect imitation of Miss Hepinstall's grim expression as she wielded the cane.

'You *naughty* boy, Teddy Craig!' Maggie said, and able to keep her face straight no longer, Hannah joined in the laughter.

As the mother of three rough sons, boys with permanently scarred knees, black finger-nails, and hair that grew straight up no matter how hard she tried to smooth it down, Hannah had been overjoyed when Maggie was born.

Here at last was the girl child she had prayed for, the dainty little mite who would follow her around the house, lisping prettily in spotless white pinafores, sitting on a footstool at her mother's knee, learning to knit and to sew.

Instead of that Maggie preferred to be out with her brothers in the long summer evenings, fishing with a piece of string in the stream, climbing the low stone walls, working the pump at the well for the pails of clear cool water for the next day's washing, cooking and cleaning.

Only the summer before when Maggie was just five years old and the well was not full enough to keep the pump going, Hannah had caught her lying flat on the ground with her bloomers showing, dangling a bucket on a rope down into the murky depths, the great iron lid moved to one side.

Maggie it was who collected the yard-sticks for the fire-oven, and Maggie who had been caught peering through the filthy window of the derelict cottage at the end of the village, trying to catch a glimpse of the two hermit bachelors who lived there in squalor. One of them had come out to chase her, brandishing an old violin above his head.

'I'll scalp thee alive if I catches thee again tha little varmint,' he'd shouted, and Maggie had run home, skirts flying, tam-o'-shanter falling from her head, not to throw herself in her mother's arms as she sobbed out her fright, but to ask exactly what a varmint happened to be.

There was something *fierce* about her only daughter, Hannah often thought. Then she would think what a funny word fierce was to use in describing a little girl as pretty as Maggie. It was just that she was so protective of everyone, afraid of nothing, certainly not of Miss Hepinstall who in the weeks following the caning episode, picked on her unmercifully.

'Every time I go through into the other classroom our Maggie seems to be standing in a corner facing the wall,' Thomas told his wife. 'There's not much I can do about it either without being accused of favouritism.' He rubbed the left side of his nose with his forefinger, the way he always did when worried. 'It's a tricky business having my own children in my own school.'

Hannah smiled on him with love. 'It'll do our Maggie good to have some of the spots rubbed off her. She's spoilt enough at home without being kowtowed to at school.'

And you would not relish having to stand up to Miss Hepinstall, Hannah told herself, but silently, shaking her head at her husband as he stood before her, dark eyes anxious, neat well-formed head on one side as he waited to see what she thought about it all.

She smiled on him with such love, this man of hers, this scholarly gentle man who had met and married her when she was in service, keeping house for three middle-aged unmarried sisters over at Todmorden.

He had been on a walking trip, carrying his belongings around in a parcel looped over his shoulder with string, sleeping in barns, and meeting her one bright summer's day as she carried a pail of warm frothy milk down the lane from the farm to the house where she worked.

The ten years' difference in their ages hadn't seemed to matter at all, nor the fact that at seventeen she could barely read.

'I will teach you,' he said, and so he had, sitting with her in the downstairs living-room of the School House, holding her hand, and running her fingers over the words: kissing her when she stumbled over a long word.

The village he taught in was spread over the outskirts of a cotton mill town, a part of the Pennines flanked to the east by the Yorkshire wool towns, and by the Lancashire cotton towns to the west.

It was a straggling stark place, with grey stone houses set against sombre skies in winter, which even in summer still retained their greyness as if not even the sun could warm their stones to light. Originally a hamlet, the village was built across a tributary of a river, a river whose valleys were filled with factories, mills and sloping streets, the terraced houses packed close together, sometimes back to back and interlocking into each other.

Thomas Craig did not visit the towns unless he had to, and even then he hurried back to his village as quickly as he could. He loved his village, and the moors behind it. With more money to spare for his education, he would have been a botanist, but as an amateur he walked for miles, bringing weeds home in his pockets and laying them on the kitchen table. Then he would search in his books of reference to find the names, and point out his treasure to Maggie.

She was the child of his heart, and he would take her to a hill he knew, and they would lie in a hollow until the silence was broken by the song of a lark, or the call of a grouse. He would show her the shifting peat bogs, formless and menacing, and he would point out a hunk of tree-knot, and explain that once, many thousands of years ago, there had been a forest growing there.

Thomas Craig was a small man, no more than five feet six inches tall, but the way he held himself gave the impression of height. It was from her father that Maggie inherited her direct glance, and her way of walking with her head held high. But it was from her mother she got her thick brown hair, and her practical way of assessing a problem, making a quick decision, then getting on with it.

An ardent and practising Methodist was Thomas Craig, but although the doctrine of THOU SHALT NOT had been instilled in him from his childhood, Thomas wanted no truck with a being who could condemn any of his congregation to eternal damnation. When the paid minister was sent away from the Mission House for lack of funds, it was Thomas who led the prayers and read to the dwindling congregation of the gentle love of Jesus.

When someone died in the village, it was Thomas who prayed over them, and Hannah who helped with the laying-out, washing them for the last time, and crossing pale hands over nice clean chests.

She was called to help with a laying-out very early one morning, just a month after Maggie had stood up to Miss Hepinstall. . . .

Little Amos Smith, a sickly child, the youngest in a family of eleven, had died of inflammation of the throat the night before, choking to death on a membrane his mother said was like a piece of tight muslin across the back of his throat.

'It was the quinsies, Mrs Craig,' she sobbed. 'No matter how many vinegar poultices I put on him I could not bring the fever down.' She lifted her apron and wiped her eyes. 'Every spring regular as clockwork he got the quinsies. It was pitiful to see him, but this time he didn't seem to have the strength to fight.'

'For a shilling a week paid regular she could have brought Doctor Bates to that child,' Hannah fretted to Thomas when she got back to the house. 'Moses Smith works in the Quarries, so it's not as if there's no money coming in.'

She unpinned her hat from her shining hair. 'For one shilling a week the whole family could have benefited, with free medicine as well. Some folks don't seem to have the sense they were born with.'

Thomas hovered about, trying to help with the rushed breakfast, but doing no more than getting in the way.

'That's all right, love,' he reminded her gently, 'but a shilling a week is a shilling a week when there are eleven mouths to feed. It's a fortune to Maria Smith, remember.'

'Misplaced thriftiness,' Hannah fumed, bustling round the room, long skirts swishing as she moved from fire to table, then from table to fire. 'There's some as never get their priorities right,' she grumbled, setting a pan of milk to warm.

The three boys, boot-laces trailing, shirts hanging out of their trousers, hair standing on end, got on with the impor- tant task of spreading honey as thickly as they dared on great wedges of bread. Maggie sat with knife poised, more interested in what was being said.

'Who's dead then?' she asked, in a light conversational tone.

Hannah snatched the pan of milk from the fire, just catching it in time.

'Little Amos Smith has gone to live with Jesus,' she said.

'Will he like it then? Living with Jesus? Amos Smith always had a candle coming down his nose. Will he not have one now that he's gone to . . . ?'

Hannah's voice, more stern than Maggie had heard it for a long time, stopped her saying what she had intended to say.

'Maggie Craig! If you don't get down from that table and come here this minute, you'll be late, and then what will Miss Hepinstall say?'

'Late again, Maggie Craig!'

Her little daughter's pursed-up mouth was so like her teacher's that Hannah smiled for the first time since coming into the house.

'Come here then and have your rag pinned on,' she said, and tweaked at the wings of the white pinafore in a vain effort to stop them slipping down the sleeves of Maggie's dark green dress.

The ritual of nose blowing insisted on by Miss Hepinstall before morning prayers meant that a clean rag had to be found every day, plus another for wiping the children's slates.

'That rag smells awful when I've been spitting on it all day,' Maggie grumbled as she twitched away from her mother.

'Then stop sniffing at it,' Hannah said, standing at the door and waving as the four of them walked down the short lane to the school, waiting as usual until she had seen them turn into the playground: Maggie, first as always, tammy slipping to the side of her head, the thick weight of her hair already coming loose from its ribbon fastening, calling over her shoulder to her brothers, telling them to hurry up. Benjamin walking pigeon-toed and tripping over his own feet; Jonathan whistling and trailing a hand along the low stone wall, and Teddy bending down to pick up a stone and hurl it hopefully at a bird rising suddenly out of the hedge.

Four of them, and each one as different as chalk from cheese, Hannah thought as she went inside. Then putting the memory of the small dead face she had washed so carefully not an hour before, out of her mind, Hannah built up the fire with sticks, turning the room into a furnace. Wednesday was baking day, just as Monday was washing day even if the moors were awash with rain.

Little Amos Smith was buried in the churchyard a few days later with all the village in attendance. Mr Jarvis, the undertaker, could always be relied upon to give a dignified performance, and the sight of his long thin face set into lines of professional suffering, held Maggie spellbound. Funerals fascinated her, and she often wondered who would bury Mr Jarvis when *his* turn came to die? Who would arrange for six men of equal height to carry the coffins, sometimes for miles, over rough unmade roads, over moorland and across streams, to the little churchyard? It never occurred to her that Mr Jarvis was merely doing a job; to Maggie he was the sole instrument of God, the middle-man between this world and the next.

Hannah saw nothing wrong in having her four children lined up at the edge of the newly dug grave, heads suitably bowed, bunches of wild flowers in their hands. Thomas was not quite so sure, but his wife told him firmly that death was a part of living.

'No good pretending it doesn't happen. That's what makes folks grow up frightened of it.'

Thomas was to remember her words, when just two weeks later Hannah died of the undiagnosed diphtheria that had killed little Amos Smith.

Hannah *was* afraid of dying. It showed in her eyes, and it showed in the desperate way she clung to his hands, and in the rasp of her tortured throat as she made him promise to keep the family together.

'I promise,' Thomas said, but he had no idea what it was she had asked him to promise. He was stunned. He was numbed. He could not and would not believe that his Hannah would leave him.

She was his joy and his strength; he had the intelligence to realize that. He might be the one with the book-learning, but she was the one with the commonsense, the one with her feet on the ground. Without her he was nothing, nothing at all.

Doctor Bates had been angry and amazed, when called

to the School House. He had found Hannah already too far gone for him to do much more than demand to know why he had not been called out before?

A choleric gentleman, with a nose that looked as if it might burst like a ripe plum at any minute, he shook his big head sadly when Thomas told how his wife had gone on working in the house, keeping to her rigid day-to-day timetable, even pretending to eat with them at table.

'She swore she was just coming on with a cold, then when she was forced to take to her bed, I found a hunk of bread crumbled in her apron pocket. She must have dropped it in there so we would not notice. . . . Oh, God! What am I going to do?'

'Why should God want to punish us like this?' he cried, when Teddy followed his mother to the grave a week later, choked with his own spittle.

'You've still got me, Dada,' Maggie said, standing by his chair, solemn-eyed with the awfulness of it all.

'And us,' the twins added in unison.

Thomas looked at them as if he did not know them; almost as if he had never seen them in his life before.

For the rest of that summer, into the mists of autumn, on into the freezing winds of winter, Thomas Craig turned his back on life, teaching with automatic practice during the day, and leaving his three children to the kindly but intermittent care of the village women.

The nights he read away, refusing to go up to the room he had shared with Hannah; dozing in his chair by the fire.

At times Maggie would be awakened by the sound of wood being thrown on to the fire, and creeping downstairs, a matronly little figure in her long nightgown, she would find her father asleep, his arm trailing to the floor where a book had slipped from a listless hand. At seven years old, she accepted the fact that she would never see her mother again; an acceptance that Thomas, it seemed, would never acknowledge.

The house grew dirty, with a layer of kitchen grease adhering to the pans that were seldom used; the children climbed in and out of unmade beds, and when one day Miss Hepinstall held her tongue from telling Maggie that potatoes could be grown in the tidemark round her neck, she decided the time had come to act.

Leaving her mother settled down for the night, as comfortable as the old woman's aching joints would ever let her be, she rammed her hat down over the black bun on top of her small head, skewered it into place with a pearl-handled hat-pin, buttoned her coat over her one-piece bosom, and heedless of the biting wind, set off for the School House.

The door was on the latch, and after two brisk raps with the knocker, and getting no reply, she marched inside. From his customary seat by the fire, Thomas raised his head from his book and glared at her.

Expecting the look and ignoring it, Miss Hepinstall wrinkled her nose at the smell of neglect, averted her spinsterly eyes from a pile of intimate washing spilling out from a tub in the corner, and sat herself down. Because she had come on an errand of mercy, she did so without wiping the seat of her chair first with her handkerchief. It would never do, she decided, to antagonize Thomas before she had even opened her mouth.

He closed his eyes rudely, and willed her to go away. Since Hannah's death he had as little to do with women as possible, hating them because they were alive and his wife was not. Besides, Miss Hepinstall was sitting in Hannah's chair, as angular, dark and hard, as Hannah had been curved, brown of hair, and soft. Even the mask of kindness sat on the teacher's face like a grimace. She leaned forward, resting gloved hands on her tall umbrella.

'What I've come to say won't take a minute, Mr Craig, but it's got to be said; there's nothing more certain than that.'

The lift of Thomas's eyebrows was an insult that a lesser woman would have flinched from, but used to her mother's black looks and bitter tongue, Miss Hepinstall said in her loud penetrating voice:

'How long are you going to sit there feeling sorry for yourself, Mr Craig? Your wife is not coming back, you know.'

The words, as sudden as they were unexpected, hit Thomas like a blast of hot air from the carelessly opened door of a furnace. He actually rose from his seat, and for a moment Miss Hepinstall thought he was going to step forward and strike her. Then, with his fingers gripping the arms of his chair, he sank back again.

The long umbrella was pointed directly at his face, as she went on with the saying of her piece:

'If you carry on like this, the children will be taken from you, and you will end up in the Union Poorhouse. I've held my tongue for long enough, Mr Craig, and what I'm saying is only for your own good. I've never been one to mince my words, you know that.' She took a necessary breath. 'I've seen you standing up in front of your class with half your dinner spilt down your front, and I don't mean just one day's dinner neither. The discipline in the school has gone to pot, and your Maggie's neck is that mucky I've a job to tell whether she's taken her scarf off or not. Why, when your wife was alive, that child's hair shone like the sun on a copper warming-pan. I would not be surprised to find that it's alive with nits.'

It was, it must have been, the mention of Maggie's hair that did it. Shining like the sun on a copper warming-pan . . . like Hannah's own hair, thick, long, clean-smelling hair, washed every week without fail with green soft soap.

Thomas opened his mouth as if gasping for air. How often had she sat on the floor between his knees whilst he dried it for her? Hair that cascaded over his hands when he sometimes took the pins out for her at night, a tender

19

prelude to their love-making. Upswept hair, with tiny curling tendrils wisping down into the soft hollow at the back of her neck. . . .

Miss Hepinstall watched his mouth working with a kind of detached sympathy, already forming in her mind the wording of the suggestions of practical help she had in mind. She was totally unprepared for what happened next, and embarrassed to the point of panic when it did.

With a great shout of anguish, an animal howl of grief, Thomas abandoned himself to the agony of loss multiplying silently inside him. With mouth wide open, and tears streaming down his face, he sobbed his torment, quite oblivious to the fact that Miss Hepinstall had crept away.

Shocked and dismayed she walked back down the lane in the rain, the umbrella held over her head but unopened and unfurled.

And although neither of them made any reference to the visit, from that day onwards, things began to improve a little. Thomas took on a woman from the village, a forty-year-old widow, with faded hair drawn back so tightly that her expression was one of perpetual surprise.

He would not have her about the house when he was there, so the minute he came in from school in the afternoon, she knew that was her signal to go. With no more than a nod in Thomas's direction, she would fold up her print apron, lift the kettle from the fire and fill the teapot already warming in the hearth.

'There's your teas ready,' she'd say, and Maggie would sit in Hannah's old place at the table, pouring the tea into blue-edged cups. With two cushions on the chair to raise her up, she would slice a loaf into man-sized wedges for the boys, her pink tongue protruding from the corner of her mouth.

'She'll cut her fingers off one of these fine days,' Jonathan said.

'Why does she have to do everything so fast?' Benjamin wondered.

'Because I'll never get through if I don't,' said Maggie, crimson with importance.

Thomas noticed nothing, and at the end of another drifting year, with only a token resistance from their father, the boys started work at the Quarries.

They walked the five miles there and back, working mornings one week, and afternoons the next. Their job was to wheel the drilled-out stony rubbish away on four-wheeled bogies to the tip.

'Hannah Craig would come back and haunt that husband of hers if she knew them two lads had gone as muck-chuckers,' the village women said. 'You'd have thought their father would have wanted something better for them.'

But Jonathan and Benjamin grew tall and strong. They sang as they walked up the fell together, happy to be released for half a day from the tedium of book learning, and the closed-in boredom of their father's classroom.

In the mid-nineties, when Maggie was twelve years old, and there was talk of the Quarry being shut down, the two boys walked off together to the nearest recruiting centre and joined the army.

They were jubilant from the moment of entering the Barracks, excited at the prospect of what promised to be a life of adventure, weaned completely and at once from the travesty of what had been a happy home.

At the end of their first year of soldiery, with merely a handful of letters to remind Thomas that once he had two sons, the still heart-broken man had a stroke.

Barely aware that anything had happened, he tried to talk to Maggie when she came downstairs, but the words he spoke were a meaningless jumble.

Maggie was petrified.

'Sit there, Dada,' she said, trying to smile. 'You're poorly. Sit there and I'll go and tell Doctor Bates.' Fear made her heart flutter in her breast, and running helter-skelter down the lane she stopped first at Miss Hepinstall's cottage.

'Me father can't talk,' she said. 'And his face looks funny.'

'Daisy?' Miss Hepinstall's mother's voice spiralled downstairs, and even in the middle of her bewildering anxiety, Maggie felt a twinge of surprise. Whoever would have thought that anyone as unflower-like as Miss could possibly be called Daisy?

There was a short cut to the doctor's house, and Maggie knew she would have to take it, in spite of the bull that had a nasty habit of running down the hill with its tail stuck up in the air, trying to jump the wall when anyone passed by in the lane; in spite of the fact that the lane itself was supposed to be haunted by a coach driven by a headless driver, she knew she had to go that way.

She was solely responsible for her father now, just as Miss was responsible for her awful mother, and bulls with their tails stuck up in the air, and headless drivers of ghostly coaches were as nothing compared to the importance of that.

With her face set into a determined mask, Maggie ran on, praying that God would save her if anything untoward happened.

Thomas Craig never taught again after that day. Believing that he might find a mundane job in a factory, Doctor Bates somehow made the time to find them a terraced house to let in a cobbled street in the nearby cotton town, and another teacher and his family moved into the School House.

The mill was no more than a stone's throw from the back door of the little house at the bottom end of Foundry Street, and on the day after they moved in Maggie walked across the bridge over the canal to see the overlooker.

He was a man with small eyes as hard as moorland stones, and he took Maggie on as a doffer. She started work at six o'clock in the morning, and spent her day running round the weaving shed with the bobbins. Her task was to fill the big basket skips, then, standing on a piece of wood because she was too small to reach the looms, she would put the bobbins on the machines, climb down, wheel the skip along the damp floor, and start all over again.

Working without a break she ran home at dinner-time to make sure her father had a bite to eat, and if she was late back the overlooker would swear at her.

'The old skinflint's docked me money again,' she would tell Thomas, and he would look at her as if it was her own fault.

In the evenings there was the food for the following day to be seen to. There was the washing, the baking, the ironing, everything done to a set routine, just the way her mother had done it.

Thomas, shrivelled into a tiny gnome of a man, followed her around, mumbling in the strange language that had got only minimally better since his stroke. 'To think we should come to this,' was what he was trying to say. 'Oh why should the good Lord punish us like this?' he would ask, but Maggie was usually too busy to listen.

Because she was young and strong, the work got done somehow, but she was only twelve and a half years old, and after a long day in the mill, followed by an evening spent cleaning and cooking, she would fall into bed and feel as if she was dropping sheer away, down through the feather mattress into a sleep so deep it was a kind of dying.

Her father's face seemed to alter in bone structure as he complained in his hesitant speech of one cause of discontent after another. His eyes and cheeks sank into hollows, and he developed a nervous habit of rubbing his thumb and forefinger together, as if he were rolling a piece of bread into crumbs.

At the end of a sultry July afternoon, Maggie came home from the mill with her cotton blouse sticking to her back with sweat. It ran uncomfortably down her sides, and stood out in glistening beads on her rounded forehead.

There was nowhere to wash at the mill, and as she stood at the slopstone and splashed cold water over her face and arms, Thomas sat with his back decently turned, grumbling in his stuttering monotone:

'I left the back door open today to catch what bit of air I could. I swear the noise of the looms shivered the ornaments on the mantelpiece. How you stick it I don't know. Your mother would turn in her grave if she knew that you'd gone in the mill. You know she was set on you being a teacher, don't you?'

'Now how could I have gone to be a teacher and left you? Perhaps when you're better and I'm older,' Maggie said vaguely, soothing him, as she wiped herself dry on the coarse roller towel hanging behind the back door.

The soap she had washed herself with was the same mottled soap she used for scrubbing the floor and the washing, but her skin was as petal soft as the wild roses in the hedges bisecting the fields of her country home. Smoothing her hair down with still damp hands she went to stand in front of Thomas, challenging him to meet her eyes.

But her father never looked anyone straight in the face nowadays.

'Look at me, Father!' Maggie ordered. 'Come on! I'm going to give you a bit of a telling off.'

Thomas's eyes slid away, indicating that he was not interested in anything she might have to say, but Maggie persevered.

'There's nothing to stop you walking up to the park now, is there? I know you walk slow, but you've all day to get there and back. I'll make you a bite to take with you if you like.' Exasperated, she put both hands on her hips.

'Father! Listen to me! It's not doing you any good just sitting here in the house. You're going to start *growing* into that chair if you're not careful.'

Thomas's eyes were dreamy. 'How like your mother you are when you get your paddy up. You grow more like her every day.'

'The *park*,' Maggie repeated.

Thomas nodded, as if the meaning of the word had just become clear to him.

'Oh, yes, the park.' His words became jumbled as he

24

went on. 'Well, I admit I did like going there once or twice, when we came here at first.' He sighed heavily. 'Just to see a glimpse of green, but it's not the green we used to know, Maggie. That green is mucky green. The grime in the air has filtered down and coated the grass with a film of soot. It has, Maggie.' He held both hands idle on his lap and began to roll the fingers and thumbs together. 'I picked a blade and pulled it through my fingers, and do you know what? They were coated with filth. No, I'm better off staying in.'

'But you can't stay in for the rest of your life!'

Maggie pulled a clean blouse over her head. 'You can turn round now, Father.'

But he had said his say, and was gone from her again, staring at nothing, wishing back a life that would never be again.

At the end of that year, he walked no further than the row of shops at the top of the street, making his laborious way, shuffling his feet, his eyes downcast, like an old man searching for his last halfpenny.

'I can't seem to cheer him up at all,' Maggie wrote to her brothers, posting it off to their regimental address with the feeling that she might as well be posting it into a tree.

Doctor Bates surprised her one Saturday afternoon, riding out from the village in a hill farmer's high trap which was delivering eggs to the market stalls.

'I've to be back there to meet him in under the hour,' he said. 'Is your father upstairs, Maggie?'

She was down on her knees polishing the fire-brasses when he came down again, wrapping them in an old sheet to keep them clean and shining for Sunday, the way her mother had always done. But as soon as she saw the doctor she stood up and stared at him, anxiety creasing her forehead like a roll of corrugated cardboard.

'He's no worse, is he, Doctor?'

Doctor Bates fiddled with his watch-chain. She was very bonny, this girl, this *child* standing before him. She had the bold solid look he'd noticed in so many East Lancashire girls. Soft in colouring, but with a fierce determination about her. Aye, fierce. That was the word to describe young Maggie Craig. With her childhood gone before she had savoured it, solemn-eyed, hands folded in front of her over the sacking pinny covering her flowered cotton overall. Brown hair looped back from a centre parting and pinned high at the back of her head in a tight bun.

How much simpler things would have been if the good Lord had issued a double ticket when Hannah Craig had died of the diphtheria. One for her and the other for her husband.

The twins were as self-centred as their father, and they could have got on with their soldiering, and this little lass could have come to live with him and his wife in their three-storeyed house set into the hill.

Maggie was bright and pretty, and would have filled their declining years with joy. He touched the end of his violet nose with his finger, and Maggie looked quickly away.

The doctor was going to tell her something serious; she could tell that by his expression. She was worried sick about her father, but that nose! Jonathan had once said that if you set a match to it there would be an explosion.

'The doctor would disappear in a cloud of blue smoke. Pouff!' he'd said.

Maggie gulped the giggle back in her throat, a little girl again with her brothers teasing her straight face away, then raising their eyes in mock despair as her laughter bubbled out.

Just for a moment she could hear Miss Hepinstall's piercing voice:

'Out here at once, Maggie Craig! You'll be laughing the other side of your face before the day's out. Hold out your hand!'

Miss *Daisy* Hepinstall. 'Oh, flippin' heck,' as the girls at

26

the mill were always saying. 'Maggie Craig thinks sum-mat's funny again.'

'Your father,' the doctor was saying carefully, 'has some-thing wrong with him. A sort of nervous complaint which is making him grow old – senile – before his time has come to grow old.'

He fingered the nose again, but for Maggie the urge to giggle had gone, and her face flushed red with a terrible anxiety.

'That's it,' she agreed. 'He does look like an old man. His hair is turning proper white, and he won't walk anywhere if he can help it. But there's no pain because I keep asking him, and anyway I'd know. My father is not a very good sufferer.'

Doctor Bates permitted himself a fleeting smile, but oh, dear God, it was all wrong that this lovely child should have full responsibility for the failing man upstairs. He tapped the nose, then his head. 'There's a *fault* in your father's brain, and this fault is preventing the messages getting through to his limbs – telling them to move. Do you see? That is why he shuffles instead of lifting his feet up when he tries to take a step, and that is why he spends so long in his chair, and lying on his bed. His reactions are those of some-one much older.'

'Is he going to die, then?'

Maggie's voice was low and pleading, but her eyes demanded that she be told the truth, no matter what.

'No, he's not going to die, love. He could live for a very long time, but he's never going to do a day's work again. Certainly not teaching. There might be something in the mill. . . .'

'Never!' Maggie's tilted chin emphasized her defiance. 'Me father's not going in the mill, not sweeping or some-thing like that, and that's what it would be because his fingers aren't quick enough for him to be a weaver.'

She spoke with quiet determination. 'Me father was a teacher, Doctor, and he wouldn't be like he is if me mother

27

were still alive. It's his heart what's stopped those messages getting through to his legs, isn't it? It nearly killed him when me mother died.'

Doctor Bates took his watch out of his pocket, and raised bushy eyebrows as he saw the time.

Out of the mouths of babes, right enough. But he did not go the whole way with that theory. No, Thomas Craig was a sick man, but a weak man also, and more than a bit of a coward come to that. He should have pulled himself together, smartened himself up a bit, and looked around for a woman to marry.

Not to put in his wife's place, or even in his bed for that matter, but a woman who would have taken the burden from this little lass's shoulders.

He walked towards the curtain that separated the living-room from the front parlour, and parted its folds with an impatient gesture. He had come to help, and what had he achieved? Nothing.

'Heard from the boys?' he asked as he stepped out on to the pavement.

'No, not for a long time, but they're not much at writing letters. They'll just turn up one day, the both of them brazen as brass.'

Doctor Bates hesitated before walking away up the street. There was something in the way Maggie held her head . . . by the gum, but she was going to be a bonny woman. She was smiling at him as graciously as if she was showing him out of a grand house, and she wasn't a child at all. The blue stuff of her cotton blouse atop the awful sacking pinny was pulling in creases underneath her arms, and the buttons down the front looked ready to pop at any minute. He tried to work out exactly how old she was, and wondered vaguely if there was someone, another woman, to explain certain things.

As if she had been conjured up out of his thoughts, a short stout woman came out of the house next door, a cup held in an outstretched hand.

28

'Have you such a thing as a cup of sugar, love? I've got me scones half mixed and I'm that much short.'

Then she saw the doctor, and whipped the cup out of sight beneath her pinafore. 'Ee, I didn't know you'd got company, love. I'll come back when it's more convenient like.'

The doctor raised his hat, his mind registering the twinkle in Maggie's eyes. Either the borrowing was a regular occurrence, or the neighbour had seen him through her front window and come to see what was going on. And Maggie knew it. She'd all her chairs at home had young Maggie Craig.

He continued on his way, his mind more at ease. Yes, that neighbour looked like the salt of the earth type. She would keep a motherly eye on Maggie, and her father, he felt sure of that. Closer than Siamese twins the folks in some of these little streets. In and out of each other's houses with basins of nourishing broth, and running for the doctor if one of them looked like dying. Yes, he'd done his duty by the Craig family, more than his duty come to that. His own widespread practice was as much as he could manage, and he wasn't getting any younger. His wife was always reminding him of that.

Stepping out briskly, his mind at ease, Doctor Bates turned into the main street leading to the market square, and mentally crossed the Craig family from his list of worries.

'Who was that, then?' Clara Preston asked the question without preamble. If she wanted to ask anything she asked it straight out, and why not? If folks did not want to tell they could always keep their mouths shut. She would not take offence. She'd find out in her own good time, anyroad.

'He'd got a right conk on him, and no mistake. Bet you wouldn't have to tell *him* what to do with a bottle of beer.'

Maggie smiled, busy at the dresser filling the cup with

29

sugar. She knew that Clara had timed her appearance deliberately, wanting to know who the visitor was, and why she had not been told of his coming.

She had weighed Clara up from the first week in Foundry Street. Keep your own counsel and Clara would find out somehow. Tell her everything and she would be your friend for life.

And this wasn't the time to turn your nose up at a friend, even one as unlikely as Clara Preston, with the glide in one eye, and a mother next door who kept her as close as if she had never left the womb.

'You don't want to speak to *her*,' Clara would say of a neighbour. 'She's no better than what she should be, me mother says.'

'I wouldn't get your meat from that butcher's. They say he's got another woman,' Clara would say.

Maggie hesitated, but not for long. The urge to talk about her father was overwhelming.

'He's not really ill in his body, Clara. It's just his mind forgetting to tell his body what to do. That's why he never wants to walk far.'

Clara's left eye glided into the corner.

'He didn't say your dad would have to go in the looney-bin, did he?' She sat down obviously relishing the prospect.

'Of course not. It's just that he never really picked up after me mother died. It was the shock brought this on, you see.'

Clara brightened up. 'Aye, shock's a terrible thing. I once knew a girl who set stiff as a board when a man showed her his johnwilly down by the canal. They had to carry her home like a plank.'

Maggie's laughter rang out, then she glanced towards the foot of the stairs and clamped a hand over her mouth.

'You are a one, Clara Preston. Sometimes you say worse things than the girls at the mill. Me Grandma Butterworth would have made you wash your mouth out with soap and water if she had heard you say that.'

30

She picked up the poker from its stand, and moved the kettle-grid over the fire.

'Let's have a cup of tea, eh?'

'Thought you was never going to ask,' Clara said with a fat smile that almost disappeared into the folds of her neck.

'Aye, you're right, love. Compared to you I'm as common as muck, and don't deny it, for it's the gospel truth. When you first moved in and I heard the way you speak I told Arnie, I said: "Them next door is out of a higher drawer than what we are".' She set the rocking chair into motion with a movement of her foot. 'Not that it bothers me. Folks is folks, and if you do what's right, me mother says, you won't go far wrong.'

Maggie sat down in the chair opposite to Clara, and listened to her talk with amused affection. It was hard to believe that Clara was only twenty-four, a married woman for only three years. There was a middle-aged look about her flat features, and a matronly shelving of her drooping bust. There was nothing *glad* about Clara's mournful pudding of a face, but it was a kindly face just the same. She would have been surprised if she could have overheard Clara reporting to her mother:

'She knows nowt that little Maggie Craig doesn't. She might read poetry books and newspapers, but she needs telling a few things, she does that 'n all.'

So Clara had explained to Maggie what she could expect to happen now that her chest had started 'sprouting', leaving her feeling that her whole body had suddenly become dirty, with one place in particular singled out for unbelievable nastiness.

'And that's only the beginning of what women have to put up with,' Clara said, fat jowls wobbling earnestly. 'If men had to put up with what women do they wouldn't go around looking so chuffed with themselves. It's nothing to get upset about, love. Just remember never to put your hands in cold water when you're like that, and as for the other thing, well you don't need to know owt about that for

31

years yet. Just never allow a boy any liberties, that's all. All men have a nasty side to them. It's best to remember that.'

'*What* liberties?' Maggie had wanted to know, but Clara, her duty done, had pretended not to hear.

Maggie handed a cup of tea to Clara, then passed over the sugar basin.

'My father used to be able to recognize the call of birds, and he used to take me for walks and go so far that he had to carry me back on his shoulders. You wouldn't have known him in those days, Clara. I can only just remember him when he was different, but I know he was a lovely man.'

Maggie unhooked the wool-stitched holder from its nail on the wall, and bending down to the hearth, filled up the tea-pot. When she straightened up her face was flushed from the heat of the fire, and silky brown wisps of hair curled down her neck from the tight bun on top of her head.

Suddenly Clara felt inexplicable anger rise up sour in her throat, and without knowing why she was cross, said in a loud voice:

'If you'd rub your hands on the soap, then smooth them down over your hair, you'd find it wouldn't come down like that. And you need a new blouse, Maggie Craig. You're all busting out of that one, and it doesn't look nice.'

Then, as Maggie clutched at the offending button-trim of her blue blouse, Clara relented.

'If you like I'll show you how to make a tuck across your bust-bodices, so that your front won't show as *two*. It's showing two what makes it disgusting.' She patted her own bolster-shaped one-piece bosom.

'If you bring me one of your bodices down and find me a bit of thread and a needle, I'll do it now while your dad is out of the way.'

Maggie nodded. 'It is good of you, Clara.'

'I shall pass through this world but once,' said Clara surprisingly as her face creased into its squashed and joyless smile.

'Fancy Clara knowing that,' Maggie thought as she ran

quickly up the steep dark stairs, then she peeped into her father's room and saw that he was lying on his bed facing the wall.

In her own room she sat down on her bed for a moment and worried about him, then she worried about her shape. She wished she wasn't growing into such a rude shape. But *why* was it rude?

Of one thing she was certain. She could never ask Clara to explain some of the things the girls talked about at the mill. Not with Clara's father being the Sunday School Superintendent at the Chapel, and with her mother having wanted to be a missionary before she got married.

She took a clean white bust-bodice from the top drawer, and stared at it, then lifting her eyes, she saw her reflection in the swing mirror, and the way she was indeed busting out of her blouse.

Suddenly, without warning, she felt an almost paralysing wave of longing for her mother. For Hannah, the mother she vaguely remembered swishing her round the School House kitchen, skirts billowing out as she moved with quick decisive movements from fire to table, then table to fire.

'Feeling sorry for yourself will get you nowhere fast, Maggie Craig!' she said, putting her tongue out at her reflection. Then she ran downstairs to find that Clara was pouring herself yet another cup of tea.

2

'Oh for a man . . . oh for a man . . . oh for a mansion in the sky,' Maggie sang at the top of her clear tuneful voice.

It was the week before her seventeenth birthday, and although her father had deteriorated over the past three years, he was still alive. And the sun was shining outside the mill, even if its rays were filtered down through a maze of tall mill chimneys. Maggie had three looms to tend now, and well, if her father wasn't any better, she told herself that he could certainly have been a lot worse.

'Being happy is a state of mind, not a matter of circumstance,' she had explained seriously to one of the loom sweepers only that morning as they waited in line to brew up their breakfast mug of tea.

Then they had both burst out laughing, the nineteen-year-old boy, and the girl who was giving him what he called her 'bossy teacher's lecture'.

Joe Barton reckoned he was the only person in the tall grey cotton mill who could tumble Maggie Craig down off her high horse. Joe thought she was the most beautiful girl he had ever seen, and in the six months since he had come to know her, she had brought a colour and a gaiety into his life he had never known before.

They weren't courting, heaven's sakes not that, as Maggie said herself, but she did concede that they were a little bit more than friends. She caught Joe's eye as he walked past her looms, and when he winked at her she winked back. There was no trace of shyness in the cheeky wink. Being brought up with three older brothers had knocked that sort of daftness out of her early on, and privately she thought the other girl weavers were stupid the way they blushed and giggled if a boy as much as spoke to them.

But oh no, she certainly wasn't courting. Keeping company with a boy meant you were thinking of getting married, then either living with his family or yours till you could find a house with a rent you could afford, and enough furniture to start you off. Then it was him coming home for his tea, then off to the pub every night with his mates, and you stopping at home and having babies one after the other. It was him going to the football match every Saturday afternoon, and continual arguments about money and the lack of it. An' all the fun in your life finished before you'd had any.

Maggie's fingers moved busily as she sang at the top of her voice. She was enjoying the freedom of singing her heart out against the deafening clatter of the machinery in the weaving shed. Although the stone floor ran damp beneath her feet she could sing and she could work and let her thoughts run free. As free as the birds her father used to love to watch. But by the gum it was hot! She ran a finger round the band at the throat of her striped blouse, then undid the top two buttons.

Life was strange. Look at the packet she'd had for the past three years. Solely responsible for a man aged into near senility by self-pity, no time for girl friends her own age, because let's face it, they were still having their hair-ribbons tied on by their mothers when she was chief cook and bottle-washer.

Maggie started on another rousing chorus: Oh aye, life was strange all right, and until she had met Joe Barton and walked in the park with him of a summer and laughed at nowt with him as they snuggled close together in a doorway of a dark night, there hadn't been much to laugh at really. But then you accepted what happened day by day if you had any gumption. She'd tried to tell Joe Barton that when he'd grumbled about the way the overlooker kept constant tabs on them.

'If you argue with the likes of him, you only come the worst off.'

Joe had grinned and put up his fists in a mock fight.

'If he docks any more of me money off I'll knock his block off,' he'd said. 'His *bloody* block off,' he had added, just to show Maggie that she hadn't bossed him out of swearing, not quite.

Maggie shook her head. No, Joe was wrong. You accepted what happened day by day because you knew, you were *certain* that something good was bound to happen. If not the next day then the day after. You just kept on in the meantime. You ran home at dinner-time to give your father his dinner, then you ran back, and when the hooter went at half past five, you ran home again to cook tea for a man so shelled in his own solitude that there were times she imagined he was looking at her and wondering who she could be.

And at that very moment, Joe Barton, father unknown, mostly of no fixed abode, was asking himself the very same question:

Just who the hell did he think he was? For over six months now he'd told his lies to Maggie Craig, making her believe his father was dead, letting her think he lived like she did, in a decent house in a decent street.

Foundry Street? God Almighty, compared to the two rooms he was sharing at the moment with his mother and his sister Belle, Foundry Street was bloody West End Road, up by the park where all the town's toffs lived. It hadn't mattered up to now because Maggie was nobbut a young lass, and their friendship had not been the kind where a young couple sat together on the sofa holding hands. What had there been apart from long conversations as they sat on the grass in the park together, a Sunday School ramble into the Ribble valley? But now Maggie was hinting that she would like to take him to her house to meet her invalid father.

'Perhaps if you see him, Joe, you'll understand why I can't get out all that often.' She'd blushed and dimpled. 'I'm not being forward. I'm not forcing you into *declaring* yourself or nothing like that. You won't have to state your intentions and swear that you can keep me in the manner to which I have become accustomed.'

'Maggie Craig!' Joe had pinched her cheek, laughing into her eyes. 'How is it you can say the things other people only think and get away with it?' They had ended up running down the long grass slope from the Conservatory in the park, with Maggie tripping over a trailing bootlace and falling, and Joe throwing himself down beside her.

'Joe!' she'd screamed as he tickled her. 'If any of the Chapel folk come by and see us I'll be condemned to hell-fire, and you with me. Stop it! Stop it, Joe!'

Working steadily when he felt the overlooker's hard eyes on his back, Joe made up his mind. He was going to do what he should have done a long time ago. 'Come out for a bit after tea,' he told Maggie as they joined the stream of weavers thronging the street outside the mill after the hooter had gone. 'I want to take you to meet my mother.' His dark eyes were bleak. 'I think you should meet her before I meet your father.'

'Why? She got two heads or something?'

'Half past six. At the top of your street, when you've had your tea,' Joe said, then walked away.

Montague Court was only ten minutes' walk away from Foundry Street, but Maggie had never been round that way before. She'd heard about it of course, and Clara had said it was what she called the red light district.

'Red lights above the doors,' she'd said, her left eye gliding into its corner. 'There's a woman lives down there what has no nose.'

Now Joe was telling her that *he* lived there, that when he'd said vaguely that he lived round Queen Street way, he had not been telling exactly the truth.

'Montague Court. The bottom half of number fourteen,' he said as they walked along the canal bank. He swaggered and whistled, telling Maggie that he was upset about something. 'Two rooms with an outside tap and a lavvy we share with three other families. Dirty buggers too,' he stressed.

There was a jauntiness in his step and his voice that almost broke Maggie's heart. She knew he was poor, but then most folks seemed to be poor, and poverty was no disgrace. She knew he was doing this *before* she took him to her own home to give her a chance to change her mind.

In his own way he was saying: 'See, this is how I live, Maggie Craig. Now do you still want to be my friend and introduce me to your father who was once a schoolmaster?'

He was walking so quickly that she had to do a little skip now and again to keep up with him, and though she wanted to put out a hand and touch his arm to show that she understood, and it didn't make no difference, there was something about the expression on his face that stilled her hand. Grim was the word for it, and scared. Yes, scared to death.

'Not far now,' he said, and turned sharply left away from a main road so that they climbed upwards into a maze of streets with houses not much different from Maggie's own.

True the semi-circle of flagged pavements were mostly unmopped, and the window bottoms were without a neat line of yellow stone marking out their edges, but they were not that much different.

'Just like Foundry Street,' she said kindly, but Joe made no sign that he had even heard.

'Down here. And never let me catch you coming down here on your own, especially after dark. Ever! Do you hear me?'

Maggie felt a strange ripple of fear in her stomach as they turned abruptly into a narrow street, with the houses

38

clustered so close together that it seemed as if one minute they were in the soft yellow light of an early summer evening, and the next in the murky gloom of a February winter's night.

There were no pavements, just an extension of the cobble-stones right up to the front doors. A bare-bottomed child crawled at the feet of a woman who was sitting out on her front step, suckling a baby from a breast as heavy and pendulous as a bladder of lard. Maggie averted her eyes, and lifted her skirts away from the greasy and slimy cobbles.

Number fourteen had a front door so scarred that it gave the impression of having been kicked in more than it had been opened. A strange sweet stench met them as they stepped inside, and Maggie had to fight down an urge not to cover her nose with her hand. They were in a room with very little furniture, apart from a horse-hair sofa with the stuffing hanging out, a table made from two orange boxes pushed together, and a mattress in one corner with a couple of brown blankets thrown over it.

Maggie blinked, and when her eyes became used to the darkness, she saw that a small fair-haired girl was sitting on the sofa, a girl who hung her head in shyness, then turned away.

'Belle.' Joe spoke quietly and urgently to his sister. 'Where is she? Through there?'

The girl nodded.

'With him?'

Another nod. Joe glanced at the door leading into the back room and raised his eyes ceilingwards. Then as if remembering that Maggie was there he led her forward.

'Belle, love. This is Maggie. You remember I told you I was bringing her?'

Belle looked up and Maggie saw that the pale eyes were filling with tears which spilled over and ran slowly down her cheeks. She stared at Joe with a pleading expression as if begging to be forgiven.

'She was ready, Joe. Honest she was. All waiting like you said. Dressed, with a frock on and everything.' The fair head dropped again. 'Then *he* came.'

'The big one that says he's a sailor from Liverpool?'

'Aye, an' he had a bottle with him, Joe, and he started laughing and he tried to make me have some.' Belle turned her head from side to side in distaste. 'But I wouldn't open me mouth, then they went through there.'

Joe went to sit beside his sister and put his arms round her, pulling her to him. 'He didn't try to, you know . . . to touch you? Like last time?'

'No, he didn't. I think you frightened him with what you said you would do to him, Joe. I think he thought you meant it, Joe.'

Maggie stood a little to one side, watching, listening to Joe speak to Belle in a low resigned sort of voice.

But what Belle had just said made him shout in sudden anger. 'I should think I bloody did mean it. If he tries to touch you again I'll swing for him.'

Maggie glanced round her. Oh, dear God in heaven, she knew what it was to be poor. Sometimes of a Thursday there was nothing left in her purse but her key, and Clara was poor because Arnie's wages did not amount to much. And she could remember the poverty of the women in the farm labourers' cottages, women who when their boots were worn out had to stay indoors until the money could be found for another pair, and them usually handed down from somebody else. But this poverty was a different kind. This place was a slum, a *hovel*, and now she had placed that strange sweet sickening smell.

Once as a small child, her mother had taken her into a cottage where an old woman had recently died. Hannah had gone to rescue a terrified cat, and in reply to Maggie's outspoken query about the 'horrible' smell had explained:

'That smell is bugs, love. Once they've got in the walls you can't shift them without a stoving.'

And Joe lived here. He had laughed with her, and kissed

her, then come back to this place. Maggie was staring at him with pity when a burst of loud laughter came from behind the closed door.

'I'm sorry, Joe,' Belle said again.

When the door was banged back almost to the plaster, the man framed in the opening was the biggest man Maggie ever remembered seeing. Heavy-jowled and unshaven, he was buckling a wide leather belt round the top of his trousers and laughing with his head thrown back, showing brown uneven teeth. Behind him was a young-old woman, so like Joe in the set of her features and the way her dark hair sprang back from her forehead that Maggie blinked.

For a moment, as Joe stood up from the sofa and faced her, Annie Barton knew a moment of sheer panic. Her glance went to the girl standing there beside her son, a fresh-faced bonny girl with country pink cheeks, wearing a clean print dress.

That was the way she used to look. That was the way Belle should look now, not shriven up like an old woman before her fourteenth birthday. Anger suddenly took the place of fear.

'Wait for me outside, Ned,' she told the big man. 'I'll not be long.'

'You heard what she said.' Joe's voice was low but firm.

Maggie held her breath as the big man's darting glance went from Joe to his mother then back again. Then she let it out in a sigh of relief as with a shrug of massive shoulders the man went to the front door, opened it and stepped outside.

'Now!' Annie Barton said before Joe could speak. 'Let's get it over with, our Joe.' She jerked her head in Maggie's direction. 'All right, so I shouldn't have gone in there when I knew she was coming, should I? But Ned came unexpected like, and afore you jump on your soap box, just you go through there and see what he's brought this time. Enough food to last us a month.'

41

'I provide for that.' Joe's hand shot out as he gripped his mother's wrist. 'We could manage if you'd try.'

With a twist of her thin body she broke loose from his grasp, rushed over to the cluttered mantelpiece and snatched a piece of paper, thrusting it in front of Maggie's horrified face.

'See, lass! See here what he makes me do! Every mouldy penny he expects me to write down afore he'll hand over another. See! Have a sken at that. Rent half a crown. Gas fivepence. Two candles a halfpenny. Soap a penny and a tin of milk twopence. Go on, tek it, and see for thyself what a skinflint tha's courting!'

The sound that came from Belle frightened Maggie more than the loud shouting of the dishevelled woman. It was the cry of a small, wounded animal, ashamed to the point of collapse.

'Oh, Mam, stop it,' she moaned softly. 'You know if it wasn't for our Joe there'd be days when we didn't eat at all. Stop showing him up, our mam. Just go!'

Then as the front door slammed behind her mother, Belle lifted her head and smiled a tremulous smile at her brother.

'Soon I'll be living in at me new job, then you can stop fretting about me, our Joe.' She turned to Maggie. 'He has to try to make her write it down or else she spends every penny on drink.' The watery smile widened. 'And if you hadn't been here he'd have clouted her one. He's not always as quiet as this. If you hadn't been here I don't know what would have happened.'

'I do. I'd have thrown that big lout outside for a start off,' Joe muttered.

'You and who else?'

And incredibly they were laughing, the pair of them, pulling Maggie down to sit beside them on the moulting sofa, the three of them shaking with a laughter bordering on hysteria.

'And I'd got the best tea-set out,' Joe grinned, pointing to four saucerless cups set out on the rickety makeshift table.

'And Mam was going to crook her little finger when she drank, like this.'

Joe's eyes met Maggie's with an expression that cut straight through to her heart.

'It doesn't matter,' she whispered. 'It doesn't matter, truly.'

'Wait till you meet my father,' she kept saying in the weeks that followed when Joe refused to even consider a return visit. 'He won't shout at me, I admit, but he'll probably close his eyes and carry on rocking himself in his chair when I take you in.' She touched Joe's arm. 'Neither of us come from what anyone could call a *stable* background, Joe. My father won't make any friends, and your mother makes too many, that's all.'

She clamped a hand over her mouth. 'Oh, I'm sorry, I really am. I didn't mean it like that.'

'But it's true,' Joe told her, his young face dark and anguished. 'My mother's a whore, a drunken whore. If just one of Mam's men even tries to touch Belle, I'll kill him. Stone dead.'

Maggie nipped his wrist as they walked along, so that he had to turn and look at her.

'Stop talking like that, Joe Barton. You're not going to kill anybody, and one of these days you're going to come to tea, and Belle too. See?'

'You're the boss,' Joe said, but he was smiling again, and that was enough for Maggie.

'Jesus wants me for a sunbeam,' she sang at the top of her voice on the afternoon of the following Sunday. The sun was still shining, and she had managed to push Thomas out through the front door, making him promise to walk to the top of Foundry Street and back.

She was happy, because unless things were terrible, she felt she owed it to herself to be happy.

She knew, of course, that Sunday was supposed to be a day of rest, and that if she disobeyed the rules of her Chapel she might end up in hell-fire, but surely, she argued, cleaning the little house and stopping in with her father, her *earthly* father, was doing more good than going with Clara to Chapel in the morning and the evening? Surely her heavenly Father would understand?

And Joe was coming to tea soon. He'd promised.

Sometimes, on the very rare occasions when Thomas was out of the house, she had this overwhelming urge to shout and sing, to climb on the table set squarely in the middle of the room and dance on it.

'Jesus wants me for a sunbeam, and a flippin' fine sunbeam I'd be,' she sang, standing on tiptoe and staring at herself in the large mahogany-framed mirror over the mantelpiece. She stuck out her tongue, and all at once she was little Maggie Craig, six years old, pulling faces in class and goading Miss Hepinstall to fury. Once, too impatient to reach for her cane, the teacher had grabbed Maggie's slate from her hands and clouted her over the head with it.

She wasn't fed up, not really. It was just that her father was always *there*, following her around the house, lurking behind her like a doleful shadow, a shadow with more substance than himself. He was so *negative*. Maggie was sure that the messages Doctor Bates had said could not reach his brain would be all the wrong ones even if they got there.

'Go and have your rest, Father,' she would say.

'The only rest I want is my eternal one,' he would answer back.

If it wasn't for all the larking about that went on at the mill, and Joe's return to good humour, she bet her face would have forgotten how to smile. She stretched her

44

mouth into a wide grin, then still watching herself, she said:

'You are not a very nice person, Maggie Craig. Carrying on like a mad woman just because your father's gone out of the house for a bit. He's ill and he can't help being as miserable as sin, and one day you'll be old and I bet you'll be a miserable old faggot.'

She sucked in her lips as if over toothless gums, chewing wildly on nothing, then burst out laughing, feeling the laugh catch in her throat as the front door opened with such force that it banged right back to the plaster wall.

Clara's voice rang out like a clarion call.

'It's all right, love. Don't worry now. We're fetching your dad back. He fell off the kerb and couldn't get up, that's all.'

Carried into the house between two men – Arnie and Mr Isherwood, a blacksmith-striker from number fifteen, Thomas lolled like a filleted corpse, his eyes closed, and his face the colour of putty.

'Put him on the sofa,' Clara ordered, her eye swivelling into the corner. 'You'd best run for the doctor, Arnie.'

'Or the undertaker,' she amended, not quite underneath her breath.

Maggie stared at her father's closed face, too shocked to move or speak. She had pushed him out into the street, and if he was dead it was all her fault.

Arnie stood, poised for flight, small and insignificant, neat head on one side, whilst Mr Isherwood, his part in the drama played out, moved towards the door.

'If there's owt . . . ?' he said vaguely.

'Thank you,' Maggie said, going down on her knees by the sofa, and Mr Isherwood went back to his own house to tell his wife that in his opinion Mr Craig was already knocking on the pearly gates.

Clara thought so too, and decided that she would make the funeral spread for Maggie. Ham and tongue, with a batch of her scones to follow. She felt heart sorry for Mr

Craig, of course she did, but he was a miserable old fella, older at fifty than her grandpa had been at eighty-two. She jumped at the sound of Maggie's voice.

'I'm going to make a pot of tea. Would you like a cup?'

Her voice as she got to her feet was bright and cheerful. Clara stared at her as if she had not heard aright. Then she saw the way her eyes twinkled as she exchanged a glance with Arnie, and her bewilderment increased.

They were tickled about something, those two, laughing while Mr Craig was on his way out, lying there with his eyes closed, and his jaw hanging loose and slack.

'Father? Would you like a cup of tea?'

Maggie repeated the question, and this time there was no doubt about it. She *was* winking at Arnie, and he was winking back at her. Clara sniffed. Well, all she could say was she wished they would let her in on the joke, that was all.

'I think you will have to fetch the doctor, Arnie,' Maggie was saying now, her voice low and mournful. 'There'll be nothing for it but the Infirmary.'

'Or the Workhouse,' agreed Arnie.

'Ah, the Workhouse,' said Maggie with a deep sigh.

Clara stepped back a pace as the recumbent figure on the horse-hair sofa raised a languid hand up to his forehead, opened his eyes, and said in a weak but clear voice:

'Where am I?'

'In your own house,' Maggie told him briskly, swinging the kettle-stand over the flames with a deft flick of her wrist. 'And now I'll make that cup of tea. I could do with one meself.'

'You mean the old devil was shamming?' Clara's face was a study as she faced Arnie in the living-room of the house next door. 'Upsetting Maggie like that, and letting you and Mr Isherwood carry him in. I can't believe it. He looked as if he was at death's door, you can't deny that.'

46

Arnie nodded and stroked his sparse moustache.

'Oh, aye, he looked a right gonner, I'll grant you that, but he'd made up his mind he wasn't going to walk up the street no more, and now he's won. Well, hasn't he?'

'Well, I suppose he can't keep having to be fetched back.' Clara still sounded doubtful.

'He's a crafty old sod,' Arnie said, and Clara winced as a look of pain ran like a reproachful shadow over her flat features.

'I wish you wouldn't swear like that, Arnie. I know you get it from some of those Irishmen you work with, but it doesn't sound nice. Me mother was only saying yesterday that she's seen some of them rolling drunk down by the market. Rolling about and cursing and swearing. They should have stopped where they were, me dad said.'

She gave the oilcloth on the table an unnecessary wipe with the edge of her apron.

'I'll just go next door for a minute. There's plenty of time before we start getting ready for Chapel.'

'Don't know why you don't have a door cut through the wall,' Arnie muttered as the front door closed behind his wife. 'Save you going out in the wet, that would.'

Still muttering he went out into the backyard, and stood for a while, his thumbs tucked into his waistcoat pockets, staring with a blank expression at the soot-blackened walls flanking his tiny garden. Over the wall to his right he could hear his wife's voice as she talked to her mother. Their voices were loud, strident, as if they were rowing, shouting a normal conversation to each other. Arnie bowed his head. Mother and daughter, thicker than the thickest of thieves, thinking alike, two minds as one, with Clara's father chipping in just now and again like a forgotten echo. Agreeing with them because he daren't do nowt else.

'They only tolerate me because I married their Clara,' Arnie told himself out loud. 'They knew that mugs like me didn't grow on trees. . . .'

He jumped as if suddenly prodded in the back as the

knocker on the front door rapped three times, and immediately his expression changed.

'It's Maggie,' he told himself, and hurried back into the house to ask her in.

He knew it was Maggie because everyone else in the street just lifted the latch, called out 'yoo-hoo', and walked in. But not Maggie. Clara had been right when she had said that the Craigs were out of a different drawer, and it was funny but even when Mr Craig had been lying on the sofa with his mouth agape, he had still looked like a gentleman. Arnie stood back to allow Maggie to walk past him, through the parlour and into the living-room. He jerked his head.

'She's next door. Gone to tell her mother what she missed by not being out on the flags when your dad fell down.'

Maggie smiled and gave Arnie a look that said she was not going to take sides, then or ever. She looked so pale that Arnie pulled a chair forward and told her to sit down, then stood in front of her stroking his moustache and trying to think what to say.

If he told her she looked tired she'd deny it; if he told her what he really thought about that miserable old father of hers, she would be up in arms. If he offered to make her a cup of tea she'd say she'd just had one, and if he told her he was sorry, she would ask him what for.

But he was sorry for her, and it was a sorrow that went far deeper than pity. It was, all at once, a terrible anger, taking him unawares, and making him sweat. He ran his finger round his starched Sunday collar.

By the left but she was growing up into a bonny lass. Her brown hair was so tightly raked back that it might have been scragged into position by a garden fork, but there were little curly tendrils escaping round her forehead, and more wisping down behind her ears. From where he stood he could see the sweat standing out on her upper lip, in the tiny soft groove, the sweet hollow from her nose to her mouth. Funny him noticing that. . . . And she wasn't as innocent as she looked. She had a boy, Clara said so, and a rough sort from Montague Court at that.

'I've persuaded me father to go upstairs and lie down on his bed,' Maggie was telling him now, then she leaned forward, and the bit of unbuttoned blouse at her throat fell away to reveal the suspicion of soft curves. Arnie swallowed hard.

'You knew it wasn't a proper faint out there in the street, didn't you, Arnie? He looked awful though.' She sighed, pressing her lips together in a childish gesture. 'I wish you could have known him before we came to live here, Arnie. He was such a *clever* man. He had over fifty children in his class and he could put his arms on his desk and recite poetry to them, and they would just sit listening, not a fidget between them.' She shook her head. 'It's such a *waste* him being like this. I sometimes wonder if I'm treating him right, you know? If I ought to be a bit firmer with him? Then when I have been, like this afternoon, he makes me feel guilty, and a bit ashamed.' Her head drooped. 'It was a bit cruel mentioning the Workhouse, because he's always going on about ending up there, as if I would let him.'

She got up from the chair, and smiled. 'I'd better go. You'll be wanting to get ready for Chapel, and I've got me ironing to do.' A rounded dimple deepened at the corner of her mouth. 'I'll never go to Heaven like you, Arnie. You'll be playing your harp up there, and I'll be fetching the coal in down there.'

'Nay, that you won't.'

Arnie's normally quiet voice was loud and assertive, and Maggie looked at him in surprise. He was staring at her with his eyes sort of glittering, and he hadn't said much come to think of it. She'd done all the talking. Maggie turned towards the door. Well, there was nothing unusual in that. He often sat there listening to Clara talking without saying a single word. Arnie was one on his own, as her father often said.

49

'Don't go yet!' he said abruptly.

She smiled at him. 'But I have to go, Arnie. I didn't tell me father I was going out, and if he wakes up and finds himself alone . . . besides you're going to Chapel.'

'I'm fond of you,' Arnie said, blurting the words out. 'Right fond.'

Maggie felt an embarrassment so acute it was a pricking sensation in her stomach. She had no idea what to say back. . . .

'Well, I'm fond of *you*,' she said at last, her face hot, 'and of Clara. You've been good friends to me since we came to live next door. It's been like having someone of me own.' She took a step backwards and found she was up against the hard edge of the table. She steadied herself with her hands.

'I'll have to go now, Arnie.'

Arnie was breathing heavily with his mouth slightly open. He looked so funny she wanted to laugh, even as she knew this was no laughing matter. Then he came right up to her, and putting both hands on her shoulders, brought his face close to hers. His breath had a musty smell about it, and she could see the way the hairs of his small moustache were stained yellow with the smoke from his pipe.

Maggie brought her hands up and tried to push him away, and as if he had been wanting her to do that, he slid his hands down to her waist and jerked her towards him so his body was pressed close to her own.

'Let me kiss you, Maggie! *Please*! You've got to let me!'

His mouth was over hers, open and wet, and with a strength she wouldn't have given him credit for, he held her clamped against him as his tongue probed determinedly against her clenched teeth.

'Let me, Maggie . . . oh let me, I bet you let that boy of yours do it,' he moaned, and to her horror, she felt one of his hands leave her waist and grip her breast hard. He began to rub himself up and down against her, forcing her legs apart with his knee, then the hand squeezing her left breast crept down and started to hitch up her skirt.

In a wild anger, torn between humiliation and fear, Maggie acted instinctively. Bringing her knee up to his groin as hard as she could, she raked her nails down the side of his face, causing him to stagger back.

Then to her horror, he slid down to his knees, sobbing incoherently into the folds of her long skirt.

'I'm sorry . . . oh I'm sorry, Maggie, love. I don't know what made me. . . . Oh, Maggie. She won't let me near her, and if I try anything on she tells her mother, I know she does, and they look at me as if I was dirt what the cat brought in. Oh, don't tell her, Maggie. Promise me you won't . . . promise. . . .'

Shaking with hurt pride, and almost retching with disgust, Maggie prized the clinging hands from her skirt.

'I won't tell anyone,' she promised, 'not anyone. Ever.'

Then she ran out, through the parlour, wrenching open the front door, clutching the edges of her blouse together, and praying that no one in the street was watching.

In her own house, she ran straight up the stairs to her bedroom, and sitting on the edge of her bed, rocked herself backwards and forwards, holding the tears inside her as she stared down at her bared breast and saw the imprint of Arnie's fingers on her flesh.

With a shudder she remembered the terrifying hardness pressing itself against her stomach, then she unbuttoned the torn blouse with fingers that shook, and rolled it up to hide it away at the back of a drawer.

She poured a little water out of the jug into the bowl on the marbled top of her wash-stand, and making a lather with the soft water and the cake of mottled soap, she washed the top part of her all over, pulled on a clean bust-bodice, and buttoned a fresh blouse over the top.

Then she lay back on her bed, and stared at the ceiling, trying to hold back the tears which spilled out at the corners and ran sideways down her cheeks. 'Oh, Joe,' she whispered. 'You'd kill him if you knew, wouldn't you? Oh, Joe. . . .'

Then Maggie's vivid imagination took flight as she pictured Arnie, divested of his trousers, clutching the stout reluctant Clara to him in bed, slavering over her, with the yellow-stained moustache pricking her face, one hand squeezing her enormous breasts, whilst the other . . . here Maggie gave up with a shudder. Swinging her legs from the bed she leaned close to the mirror and wiped away all trace of tears. Then with her back straight she opened the door, stepped across the tiny square landing and went into her father's room.

'Feeling better now?' she asked him.

Thomas turned a face violin-shaped with self-pity towards her, and failed to see the recent torment on his daughter's face.

With the selfishness of a man for whom the problems of others had ceased to exist, a man who would grumble that he hadn't finished his dinner if the world came to a sudden end, Thomas noticed nothing.

Indeed, if he had noticed any trace of tears on Maggie's face he would have assumed that they had been on his behalf.

She had made him go out when he did not want to go out, because what was there to go out for in these mean streets? There was no chance of a bird rising suddenly from a hedgerow, or seeing a clump of primroses, their petals wet from a shower of spring rain. Here there was nothing but grey streets, and people with faces as grey as the washing perpetually hung across the backs, flapping wetly against sooty walls.

'I've got you some tea in the oven. Would you like it, Father?'

Maggie's usually clear young voice was subdued as she stood at the foot of his bed. Just for second Thomas felt the tiniest twinge of conscience.

It must have upset her seeing him brought back like that. She was only a young lass after all. About the same age his Hannah had been that day long ago when he had seen her coming towards him down a country lane, wearing a blue frock with the sleeves rolled up above rounded elbows.

'What was that you said, Hannah, love?' he said.

Maggie clenched both hands on the rail at the foot of the bed.

'Father, it's me, and you know it's me. You can't go on living in the past. Nobody can.' She shook her head in tired resignation as Thomas stared at her with the bewilderment of a little boy chastised for something he had not done.

'There's a dish of finnan-haddy in the oven, Father. I've done it in milk, just the way you like it.'

'With an egg cracked into it?' The dark eyes narrowed with greed.

'With an egg cracked into it.'

Thomas spoke with stumbling hesitation. 'Well, I suppose I'll have to eat it if you've gone to the trouble, though it will likely lie like a lump of dough on my stomach, the way I feel.'

'I'll bring it up.' Maggie turned towards the door, then as she groped for the rail bracketed to the wall at the top of the dark stairway, she heard Clara's voice calling out from downstairs.

'Yoo-hoo! It's only me, love.'

Entirely without volition Maggie's hand crept to the breast that Arnie had kneaded with hard fingers not half an hour before, then running quickly down the stairs, she parted the curtain and faced Clara with her head held high.

Anger was taking the place of distress now, and if Arnie had given the game away, and if Clara had come to say anything, well she was ready for her.

But Clara's voice was as stridently normal as usual.

'You've changed your blouse, love. Does that mean you're going to Chapel tonight?'

Keeping her face averted, not quite ready to stare Clara

straight in the eye, Maggie skirted the table and taking the oven-cloth down from its hook, opened the door of the fire-oven.

'No. I just felt a bit hot in the other one. I always get hot when I'm ironing.' She took out the steaming dish of fish. If she was blushing now then it would not matter – not with the afternoon sun still streaming through the window, and the fire blazing away in the grate. The room was like a furnace anyway.

'What I've come for,' Clara said suddenly, her voice brisk and full of purpose. . . .

'Excuse me,' Maggie said, apprehension tightening itself into a knot in the pit of her stomach. 'I've got to take this upstairs to me father. He's much better, but he still looks awful. Could you pass me that plate warming in the hearth, Clara, please?'

Why should she feel guilty when she had no cause for feeling guilty? Maggie asked herself. But Clara was obviously leading up to something.

'That looks good.' Clara peered into the dish. 'You've been busy this afternoon, haven't you, love?'

Maggie held her breath, but continued with what she was doing.

'Whoops!' Clara said. 'The way you're slapping that there fish on the plate, there will be more on the floor than in the dish. Nay, what I came in for was to ask if you would like to come to Chapel tonight with me and me mother and dad? Arnie says he will listen next door, and your father only has to knock on the wall if he wants owt.' She sniffed and jerked her head towards the dividing wall. 'He's in one of his moods, Arnie is. Tripped over a loose edging stone round that flamin' garden of his and scratched his face on his flamin' rose bush. Serve him right if you ask me for messing about with them of a Sunday.'

Maggie pulled open the knife drawer set into the front of the table.

'Yes, serve him right,' she smiled, weak with relief. 'And

yes, I think I will come with you to Chapel. It'll get me out of the house for a bit.'

'Then you can come with us to the prayer meeting after,' Clara said over a plump disappearing shoulder. 'It's a Mrs Carmichael what lives with her son up Hodder Street. She's bad with her legs and her chest, and can't get to Chapel. They say she served her time to millinery in the Hat Market.'

'Then I'd best put me new hat on,' Maggie said, with a flash of her usual smile. 'We don't want her thinking we don't know what's what down Foundry Street, do we?'

Kit Carmichael reminded Maggie of an elephant. Big and soft and grey-suited, the skin of his neck hung in flabby folds over his high starched collar, and he shook hands with her in the flabby gesture of an extended waving trunk.

'It's good of you to come, Miss Craig,' he told her in a strangely high-pitched voice, a light voice at variance with his size. 'Mother will be right glad to see a fresh face.' He inclined his big head in a conspiratorial whisper. 'She's never had her foot over the doorstep for the past year. This half-hour is the highlight of her week.'

He led the way through the front parlour, its glory reflected in a large round wooden-framed mirror tilted slightly forward from the wall above the high mantelpiece. Like every front room in the street, it smelt of cold soot and years of being unused, and the delft rail was lined with blue china plates.

'This is Miss Craig, Mother,' he said, leading them into the back room. 'She lives next door to Mrs Preston. You know Mr and Mrs Hobkirk, Mrs Preston's mother and father, don't you?'

The woman sitting up in bed was as small and intense looking as her son was large and mild of manner. She threw

55

Maggie a darting glance from beneath well defined dark eyebrows.

'I thought Mr and Mrs Hobkirk lived next door to Mrs Preston. Nobody told me they'd flitted.'

Her voice was deep and throaty, and at least an octave lower than her son's. Maggie averted her eyes from the invalid's flourishing moustache.

'No, Mother. They haven't moved. Miss Craig lives the *other side* of Mrs Preston, dear.'

Mr Marsden, the minister, cleared his throat, and in a determined voice, because he had four other visits to make, said:

'Let us pray.'

The little group round the bed lowered their heads obediently, and folded their hands together.

From beneath downcast eyelashes Maggie studied them with interest.

The Reverend Marsden and his wife, small, grey-haired, almost a mirror image of each other, devout and pious as befitted their standing in the Chapel community. Clara's parents, Mr and Mrs Hobkirk, eyes squeezed so tightly together with heavenly fervour they appeared to be suffering the most exquisite torture. Mr Elphick, the tiny dwarf man who pumped air into the newly installed organ behind the choir stalls, and Miss Birtwistle, crossed in love, so it was rumoured. Clara, with her clasped hands almost hidden beneath the shelf of her matronly bosom.

And Mrs Carmichael's large son, Kit.

Studying him carefully, Maggie decided that he was 'nice'. In spite of the fact that only a little while before she had decided that all men apart from Joe were less than the beast of the field, she knew, without being told, that Kit Carmichael was different. A mother's boy, no doubt about that. Head on one side, and tongue protruding slightly, Maggie set about calculating his possible age – difficult because of his bulk – but around thirty-five she thought. Yes that would be about right.

Maggie blushed and lowered her head as he opened his eyes and stared straight at her, but not before she had seen the kindly gleam of amusement in his eyes.

Yes, she wasn't mistaken. He *was* nice. . . . Not as nice as Joe, but *nice*. . . .

The Reverend Marsden threw his head back so that his face was parallel to the ceiling.

'Save this our sister from the ravages of the flesh,' he intoned. 'Lift her up so that she shall see Thy face and know that Thou art beside her. Comfort her in the dark watches of the night, and sustain her in her cruel affliction, until the day she comes into her glory, when she shall know pain no more.'

'Amen.'

'Amen,' Maggie said, stealing a glance at the small woman with the dark gypsy colouring, her high-necked nightgown decently covered by a high-necked bedjacket, topped with a three-cornered shawl.

Then as if to justify the prayers on her behalf, Mrs Carmichael began to cough, a great bark of a cough, so shattering to her thin frame that her face turned purple, and the deep-set eyes bulged forth. Maggie started forward with outstretched hands as she flung herself backwards on her pillows, tiny hands clutching the air as if she clawed for breath.

But Kit was there before her, taking his mother's scrabbling hands into his own, talking softly to her, calming her, smoothing the black wiry hair back from her forehead.

'You're all right, Mother,' he told her firmly. 'I'm here, and there's nothing to be afraid of. These are your friends come to pray for you. . . .'

Mrs Carmichael stopped coughing with dramatic suddenness. Her contorted features relaxed, and the Reverend Marsden resumed his praying.

'Hear our prayer, oh Lord,' he commanded.

'And let our cry come unto thee,' answered the Hobkirks, whilst Kit Carmichael patted his mother's face with one hand, and plumped up her high-piled pillows with the other.

'Amen,' said Miss Birtwistle with such deep feeling that Maggie had to swallow hard to rid herself of the giggle rising up in her throat.

'No, you're not a nice person, Maggie Craig,' she told herself for the second time that day, as in the wrong key, and with Mr Hobkirk raising his tenor voice in a shaky descant, the short service was ended by the singing of the twenty-third Psalm.

It was no good. More than one person singing without accompaniment always made her want to laugh. She stared fixedly at the wall, not risking a glance either to the right or the left as she joined in the singing.

What was she doing in that overheated room anyway? Standing there with her best Sunday hat on round a complete stranger's bed. A woman who in spite of her recent coughing fit was now singing in a husky baritone?

Mrs Carmichael and her father. Trying it on the both of them. Touting for sympathy, even though some, she supposed, would call it a cry for help. Maggie stood on one foot then eased herself on to the other. There was tomorrow's dinner to prepare, and her father to make comfortable, and Arnie to avoid . . . she stole a sideways glance at Clara singing away at the top of her voice.

Arnie had made her feel *diminished*, yes that was the word, he had spoilt an easy undemanding friendship, and if he ever tried anything like that again . . .

Maggie's expression grew so fierce that Kit Carmichael, watching her, decided that she was making up her mind never to come again. He sighed, head bowed as the Reverend Marsden pronounced the Blessing. . . .

'Seems funny,' Maggie told Clara, as they hurried back down the street, with Mr and Mrs Hobkirk following at a more leisurely pace. 'Him seeing to his mother, and me seeing to me father.' She laughed. 'She came round from her coughing fit almost as quick as me father came round from his fainting do.' She steadied her hat with one hand as a sudden gust of wind threatened to blow it away. 'Did you notice how *gentle* he was, Clara? More like a woman than a man. You'd never expect such a big man to have such a high voice, would you?'

'They say he does *everything* for her,' Clara said darkly. 'It seems all wrong to me somehow to think of a man seeing to his mother. I mean she is a woman after all.' She sniffed. 'Arnie's never seen me properly undressed, but they say Kit Carmichael washes his mother down twice a week.'

'Can't she get out of bed at all?'

'On her good days she sits out in a chair. Her son does all the housework, and the cooking and what not, as well as working as a day servant to an old man in a house up North Park Road. I've heard the old man thinks the world of him, and won't let a woman come near him, not for love nor money.'

'He's a good man,' Maggie said, her interest in Kit Carmichael completely evaporated. They turned into the row of shops leading to Foundry Street. 'But not my cup of tea somehow.'

'They say he doesn't bother with girls, and never has,' Clara volunteered, wondering if Maggie would understand what she only vaguely understood herself, but Maggie was walking quickly now, twitching her long skirt up as they crossed an uneven place in the road.

Her conscience was troubling her as she told herself her father ought not to have been left alone for so long, even though she had left him comfortable in bed, with a warm fish tea settling in his stomach.

He hated her going out at the weekends, even though she had told him all about Joe, about how nice he was and how she was bringing him to tea one day.

'I'm on my own so much during the week,' he'd say.

'Steady on, love. Where's the fire?'

Clara was panting along at her side, but Maggie walked even more quickly. She ought not to have left him, but when she got in she would make him laugh, describing the prayer meeting to him. As deeply religious as he was – as he *used* to be – Maggie corrected herself, her father could always find the over-sanctimonious amusing.

'I'm sure God Himself has a good laugh sometimes,' he'd once said.

Clara said goodnight to her and pushed open the door of number four.

'That you?' Arnie called, as she stopped to unpin her wide hat and tidy it away neatly in the sideboard cupboard.

Then as Arnie turned a vacant face towards her, and as Clara opened her mouth to ask him what he thought he was doing sitting there and watching the fire go out, through the thin walls dividing the house from number two, they heard the scream.

'It's Maggie!' Arnie said, and moving more quickly than Clara had ever seen him move before, he started for the door.

Maggie kept her best coat and hat upstairs in the walnut cupboard in her room, so she went up just as she was, deciding against calling out in case her father was asleep. Sleep was all he seemed to want to do these days, she told herself as she ran lightly up the uncarpeted stairs. Sleep and eat, and grumble in a voice which had no light or shade. Almost like the voice of a deaf-mute, she told herself.

The door of his room was closed, properly closed, not just left ajar as it normally was. Maggie frowned, feeling a small trickle of fear in her stomach as she turned the knob, pushed at the door, and felt something holding it from the inside.

'Father? Let me in! It's me, Maggie,' she added absurdly, heaving and straining at the door, then with heart pounding, putting her shoulder against it, leaning on it till it gave so suddenly she almost fell inside.

For a moment she lost the power to move, to make a

sound, to even breathe as she looked on what was left of Thomas Craig. For a moment it seemed as if the man lying on the floor by the side of his bed had two mouths. Both of them spilling blood and grinning at her.

So great was her shock that at first it did not register what had happened. Blood was everywhere, staining the cotton bedspread and spreading in a sticky shiny pool by her father's head, down on the cold linoleum.

Then she saw the open razor by one outstretched hand, and knew that he had slit his throat, slashing it from ear to ear.

She knelt down beside him, and screamed. And screamed. . . .

For just that one night, and then only because the shock seemed to have driven her willpower away, Maggie slept next door in Clara's spare room. If it would not have shocked people and been an insult to her father's memory, Maggie would have gone straight back to the mill.

Back in the house she made herself walk upstairs. She was going to sleep alone that night, no matter what anyone said. So she forced herself to open the door of Thomas's room, to see for herself that there was nothing to be afraid of.

Immediately her glance went towards the empty bed, but she walked over to the bedside table, and there was her father's leather-bound copy of Wordsworth, a book he had once carried around with him on his country walks as if it were his second skin.

Maggie picked it up and held it against her cheek for a moment, feeling the rush of tears to her eyes. A slip of paper, concealed in the leaves, fell to the floor, and as she picked it up she saw he had written a sentence in his neat schoolmaster's print:

'A power is gone, which *nothing* can restore.'

The word 'nothing' was underlined, then underlined again, as if he was trying to tell her something.

She backed towards the door, trying not to see the stain on the mattress, stripped by Clara and her mother the night before. Downstairs the fire was giving off little sluggish puffs of smoke, as if it needed and missed Thomas's constant attention with the brass-handled poker. As she knelt down to see to it, Maggie's foot caught in the rocker of his chair and set it into silent motion.

'Oh, Father,' she sobbed, catching the chair and holding it still. 'You would not even *try* to let me make you happy. And now you'll never see Joe, and I wanted you to like him. I thought he might have made you laugh. . . .'

'Our father started to die the very day our mother left us,' she wrote to her brothers, sitting at the table, with a new Waverley nib in her pen. Then she pushed the writing pad to one side and covered her face with her hands. . . .

And in the days that followed, she saw to the things that had to be seen to. She failed to convince herself that what her father had done was a sin in the eyes of the Lord, and she went to his funeral against all advice, holding on to her hat in a corner of the windswept cemetery, with Clara lending a solid arm of support.

When Doctor Bates came over to see her, a little older and a lot more stooped, but with the nose still in glorious bloom, she listened to him gravely.

'You have no cause to feel remorse,' he said, as everyone else had said. 'Your father had a mental condition that meant he could not even try to overcome his depression.'

Maggie nodded.

'But on the day he died he had collapsed in the street, Doctor, and I mentioned the Workhouse to make him come to.'

'And I bet as soon as you said that, he *did* come to?'

'But I ought not to have said it.'

Her head drooped, then she lifted her eyes and gave him her straight and candid gaze.

'I looked after me father, Doctor Bates, and I . . .' She hesitated, finding it impossible to talk openly about love to the nose. 'I was right fond of him, but till I die I'll wish I'd made more fuss of him when he was brought in from the street. I knew he was trying it on to force me to stop talking about fresh air.' Just for a moment her voice wavered on the verge of lost control. 'He said he *hated* fresh air! Me father, who knew the call of every birdsong.' She blinked the unshed tears rapidly away.

'He wanted sympathy. . . .' She spread her hands wide. 'Oh, Doctor Bates, me father wanted sympathy every day; he wanted to talk every day about how unfair it was me mother dying. And there were some days when I just hadn't any more sympathy to give.'

The doctor moved his big head up and down in a motion that said he had heard it all before.

'Maggie, love. Listen to me. If you had talked to as many bereaved folks as I, then you would believe me when I tell you that we always, yes *always*, wish we had said this, or not done that.' He wound his heavy gold watch-chain round his fingers. 'What we have to think about is your future. . . .'

He looked genuinely worried, so worried that Maggie put out a hand and touched his arm.

'I can take care of myself, Doctor. As long as I keep in work, my wages cover the rent of this house and give me enough to eat. I've got three looms now.' She smiled to cheer the doctor up. 'And I could always take in a lodger or two. Arnie Preston next door works at the bottle factory, and he says there's always Irishmen looking for a good place to live.'

It was terrible, the doctor told his wife that evening, terrible seeing that young girl, pink-cheeked and dry-eyed, calmly telling him that she would manage.

'Talking about having Irish navvies living in, and her no more than seventeen and as bonny as a morning in spring. I remember her mother as a bonny woman, but young

Maggie Craig is a real beauty, and as innocent as a new-born babe. I'd stake my life on that.'

His wife shook her grey head. 'It's to be hoped she doesn't take up with the wrong one now that she is entirely alone. That girl has got to find love and affection from somewhere, it stands to reason.'

Doctor Bates fingered his watch-chain.

'There was a whisper about a boy at the mill, but I don't think there can be anything in it. Maggie's only a child.'

'That's something she has never had a chance to be,' Mrs Bates said sadly.

Joe Barton walked down Foundry Street and knocked at Maggie's door the day after the funeral.

When he saw her white face and the way her eyes filled with tears when she saw him standing there, he walked straight in, kicked the door closed behind him, and took her into his arms.

It was the first time they had been alone, in a house, by a leaping fire; the first time he had seen Maggie cry, and the sight of her tears moved him so deeply that he drew her down beside him on the sofa, tangling his fingers in the soft weight of her hair, loosening it from its little high-pinned bun so that it fell clean and sweet smelling round her face.

'I love you,' he whispered, almost in tears himself. 'I love you . . . love you . . . love you.' Then to try to still the trembling of his own body, he held her closer, listened as she told him in jerky halting sentences how it had been.

'There was blood everywhere,' she sobbed, and Joe covered her mouth with his own, kissing the words away.

When they slid down on to the rug together, Maggie's arms were round his neck, and as their bodies fitted closely together as they lay side by side, Joe told her he was going away.

'Tonight,' he whispered, then as her arms clutched him tighter he told her why.

'Belle had to have dresses and aprons and caps for her new job, and I'd earned a bit more by staying on late at the mill, you know that.' He lifted his head and looked down at Maggie's flushed and tear-stained face. 'I hid it away in a place where I thought me mam couldn't find it. But she'd had it, Maggie. She'd got her thieving hands on it, and spent the lot on drink. It was for Belle, and she still took it, knowing.'

'Oh, Joe. . . .'

Maggie raised a hand and stroked the thin and earnest face bending over her. 'Poor, poor Belle. What will she do? She was looking forward to that living-in job so much. What will she do now?'

Joe grinned. 'Oh, Belle got her things all right, love. Me mam's big man stopped the night and left his money in his back trouser pocket, so I took it and gave it to Belle, and now she's safe, and I'm off, because when that loud-mouthed sod finds out he'll have the police on me. As sure as my name's Joe Barton he'll have me put away.'

They kissed again, a slow lingering kiss, and when Maggie spoke her voice was slow and dreamy as though what she was saying bore no relation to the meaning of the words.

'Where will you go, Joe? I can't bear it if you go away. . . .'

Joe was going away and she didn't want to believe it. He was kissing her and swearing he would come back, that he would marry her when he had a decent job.

'And we'll live in a house like this,' he was saying.

He was whispering into her cheek and turning her mouth into his, and his teeth were hard against her lips so that she opened her mouth, and his hands were moving gently over her.

Not like Arnie's, nothing like Arnie's. Joe was moving with a fierce protective urgency, lifting her clothes, murmuring to her, broken words, moaning sighing whispers of love.

There was one sharp swift pain, when for a moment, she

saw her father's dead face and cried out, then it was all rushing comfort, soothing, straining movements of love.

'Maggie . . . Maggie. . . .'

Joe's voice lingered in her ears, even long after it was over and he had gone, leaving her alone in the empty house with what she was sure was her father's sad little ghost waiting for her at the top of the stairs.

3

Kit Carmichael read the short piece in the *Weekly Times*. It was flanked on one side by a full column advertisement of Carter's Little Liver Pills, and on the other side by a report of a meeting at the Teetotal Mission.

'You remember Miss Craig coming to our prayer meeting, don't you, Mother?'

Mrs Carmichael's small black eyes filled with dislike.

'Navy blue hat with dog daisies on it. Aye I remember her.'

Kit leaned over the bed rail and read the piece aloud in his high-pitched voice, then tapped the paper with a podgy forefinger.

'It must have happened the very night she came here. Perhaps at the very time she was joined with us in prayer.' He smoothed back his tightly curled hair. 'I think it would be the right thing for me to call and express our sympathy, Mother.'

'They wouldn't be able to take his coffin into the Chapel, not with him having done away with himself.' Mrs Carmichael spoke with some satisfaction.

'He was *insane*, Mother. He wouldn't be responsible for his actions.'

'They always say that.'

Kit saw the way her right hand crept to her throat, but before she could begin to cough, he was beside her, holding on to her hands and talking quickly.

'Mother. Miss Craig will be all alone now. I believe she has looked after her father ever since she was a tiny girl.

Now surely there's no harm in me going to see her and telling her how sorry I am? How sorry we both are?' He stroked her face. 'You won't be by yourself because it's the Sewing Ladies' Class.' He gave her chin a little tweak. 'See, there's one of them at the door now. I'll let her in on my way out.'

All the way down the street, he muttered to himself, as he had been muttering to himself for many years now. . . .

It was ridiculous that a grown man of thirty-five should have to be beholden to his mother for his every movement. He had started all wrong when his father went off to live in Liverpool with that soprano he'd met in the town's Operatic Society during the rehearsals of one of Messrs Gilbert and Sullivan's pieces. He hoped she had not seen that the same company were doing *Sorcerer* at the Theatre Royal that very week. It would bring it all back to her. And every time it was brought back to her, she had an attack.

Kit stepped off the kerb without seeing it, and twisted over on his ankle. He was too soft, that was his trouble; too inclined to let his sympathy run away with him.

Turning into Foundry Street, he walked with his short tripping steps down to the house at the bottom. A curtain twitched as he went past a house, and for a moment he wondered if he had perhaps been a bit hasty in coming to call on Miss Craig.

Not for a moment would he dream of besmirching her reputation. But it was too late to turn back now. . . .

When Maggie opened the door to him, dressed from chin to ankles in mourning black, her face a pale oval above the frilled neck-line of her blouse, Kit hardly recognized her as the girl with the twinkling eyes who had stood round his mother's bed so short a time ago.

Quite without volition, his innate kindness overcoming his shyness, he held out both his hands.

'You poor little thing,' he said. 'You poor poor little girl.'

'You'd better come in, Mr Carmichael,' Maggie said, and stood aside to let him pass.

Kit Carmichael was well aware that there were those who found him an object of amusement, considered him to be a mother's boy, but he did not care.

His not caring was in no way derived from apathy, but rather from the fact that his complete lack of conceit made the sly jibes at his lack of masculinity of no importance whatsoever.

'Our Kit hasn't got a mean bone in his body,' his mother was fond of boasting, and she spoke the truth. Kit poured affection and generosity on to everyone he met, so that even those who laughed behind their hands at his high squeak of a voice and his girlish complexion, laughed with tolerance rather than with spite.

'Has your Kit never walked out with a young lady?'

Mrs Earnshaw lived next door, and often came in to keep his mother company, and her voice carried through into the front parlour where Kit was taking the willow pattern plates down from the rack and giving them a bit of a dust.

He stiffened, the duster held still in his hands.

'As a matter of fact, Mrs Earnshaw, he's got a lady friend coming for her tea on Saturday. Miss Craig from the Chapel. Lives by herself since her father came to a sad end.'

'Not the Mr Craig what . . .?'

Kit saw in his imagination the first finger of Mrs Earnshaw's hand drawn across her turkey throat in a revealing gesture.

'Aye, that one.'

'Serious then, are they?'

Not wanting to hear any more, Kit walked over to the dividing door and closed it none too gently.

It wasn't that he was annoyed at his mother discussing him like that with the neighbours, he was used to that, but he had to smile the way she had made out it had been her idea about Maggie coming to tea. Kit put a plate back and took down the one next to it. It was surprising the dirt on these plates, especially as there had not been a fire in the parlour grate since last Christmas. . . .

It had taken him almost two months to get his mother to agree to meet Maggie again. Two whole months, two attacks, and countless arguments about the foolishness of giving a 'girl like that' ideas.

'I knew the minute I set eyes on her what she was after.'

'Now, Mother, don't talk daft. I bet you can't even remember what she looks like.'

'Cheeky face and a hat with too much trimming on it.'

It was no good. He would never get his mother to think any different. Kit breathed on a plate and rubbed it hard, smiling with tolerance. You could never blame his mother for being afraid he might leave her one day. Not after what his father had done to her.

Kit sat down for a minute, taking his weight off feet too small for his bulk. Then he leaned his curly head back against the antimacassar, and closed his eyes.

There had been a girl once. He shuddered with the remembering of it.

He would be perhaps eighteen, nineteen, something like that. He had gone with a lad called Harry Burton to the Theatre Royal to see Billy Thomson's Concert Party.

He would never have gone if Harry had not taunted him about being tied to his mother's apron strings, backed up by the other lads from down the street.

'Go on, Kit. Be a devil.'

'Tell her you're going to the Mission to sign the bloody pledge.'

They were jeering at him; caps pulled down over laughing faces, and so he had gone with Harry Burton, a grinning Harry with larded-down sideboards gleaming, and his Prince Albert moustache combed into neatness.

And the Concert Party had been enjoyable, and the

70

inside of the theatre not quite the den of vice his mother had made it out to be. The second half was in the form of a Nigger Minstrel Show, with the men's faces blacked, and Bones asking Sambo:

'Who was that lady ah seen you walkin' with las' night?'

And Harry had loudly joined in the reply, much to Kit's embarrassment:

'That was no lady. That's ma wife.'

Then at the end Harry had actually put three fingers in his mouth and whistled his satisfaction.

'I'd have a pennorth of hot potatoes if I wasn't dressed up like a bloody toff,' he said as they walked back along the Boulevard. 'Just look at that poor little donkey. It's fast asleep between the shafts, and don't look round,' he continued in exactly the same tone of voice, 'but there's two girls I know behind us. Want an introduction, Kit?'

His eyes were sly, and as they stopped beside the cart, he turned round, pretended to be overcome with surprise, beamed all over his whiskered face, and made the introductions with great aplomb.

'Agnes. Florrie. This is Kit, a mate of mine, and if you smile at him nicely he'll buy you a paper of spuds. Won't you, Kit?'

Kit winced as he remembered the way they had paired off. Harry with Agnes, and Florrie taking his arm and swaying along beside him, teetering on the tiny heels of her high-buttoned boots.

At first they kept more or less together, then as they turned off the main street down an alleyway leading to the canal, Harry, with his arm round Agnes's waist, dropped behind.

'We'd better wait for them, I think,' Kit said.

Florrie laughed, taking his arm. 'Don't be daft. They'll be glad to be shot of us.'

Kit persisted. 'What have they gone round that corner for? Does your friend live down there?'

Florrie pressed his arm into her side, leaning so close that he caught a whiff of strong scent mixed with sweat. She grinned up at him showing small uneven teeth.

'You are a caution, honest you are. I've never met a lad like you before. Why have I never seen you before? I know most of Harry's mates, but I don't know you.'

Kit tried to pull his arm away, but realized the only way he could do that would be to wrench it from her grasp, and he could not face the indignity of that. He was sweating slightly, and ran his free hand round his collar.

'I'll see you home, Florrie, then I must leave you.' He said her name with difficulty, stuttering a little. 'I told my mother I was going . . . well, I told her I was going somewhere else than where she thinks I've been. She gets herself worked up if I don't come home when she expects me to.'

At this Florrie did exactly what he had been praying she would do. She moved away from him, swinging round to face him.

'Your *mother*? Did you say your mother?'

Utterly without guile, more naive than a cosseted girl of seven, Kit explained with serious politeness that his mother was all alone; that she was not at all well. And that he normally stayed in with her of an evening because she had been on her own all day.

'She would be really upset if she found out that I had been to the theatre.' He wrinkled his forehead earnestly as he tried to explain. 'My father used to go to places like that, and it led him into bad ways, so she's a bit biased, you see.'

Florrie stared at him as if she could not believe he was quite real, her head on one side, and a tip of pink tongue protruding between her lips.

'How old are you, Kit?'

'Nearly nineteen.'

'Where do you work?'

'For a man up North Park Road. I keep house for him, but only on a daytime basis.'

'So you can be with your mam at nights?'

'Yes.'

'And you always tell her where you are going when you go out?'

'I've told you, she gets worked up when she doesn't know where I am. There's only me can quieten her down.'

'Well, stone the flamin' crows. . . .'

Florrie was walking towards him now, and the only way he could try to avoid her bumping into him was to step backwards. And behind him was a wall, a dirty wall that would make marks on his jacket if he leant against it.

She came forward relentlessly, and Kit forgot about getting marks on his checked jacket, his neatly patterned, nipped in at the waist jacket, as her arms slid round his neck.

'How many girls have you been out with, Kit?'

He clamped his mouth tight shut, waves of horror washing over him and making him feel sick.

'How many girls have you kissed, Kit?'

The smell of her was in his nostrils, turning his stomach right over as Florrie peered up into his face, laughing at him with her mouth wide open, showing her tongue.

'I don't think you know nowt about owt, do you, Kit what's your name? I think you're still a great big baby.'

Then, before he could stop her, she had clamped her mouth over his own, and he could taste her spit, and feel the whole length of her body pressed up against his own. She was wriggling like a little eel, and suddenly Kit forgot to be polite. Forgot that he was 'Sonny' Carmichael, the apple of his mother's eye, a boy who never forgot his manners, especially when there were ladies present.

'You dirty little . . . you dirty little *bitch*,' he shouted, using a word he had never used before. Then gripping her by the arms he thrust her from him so violently that she almost fell.

Her hat, a silly flat purple straw, one his mother would not have given house-room to, came off in the struggle, and in the frenzy of his humiliation Kit kicked it away from him, then as she bent to pick it up he pushed her so hard that she

73

fell sprawling on the greasy cobbles with her hair coming down.

Kit moved his head from side to side on the antimacassar as he remembered the way he had waited for her to get up without stretching out a hand to help.

'You great soft 'aporth!' she had shouted, actually dancing up and down with rage. 'Go on. Run home and tell your mam. Most likely she'll kiss you better, and you'll like that, won't you, you great sissy!'

Mrs Earnshaw opened the door and stood there, pulling her shawl into position round her shoulders, and watching him with her foxy pointed face.

'Your mother's waiting for you, Kit,' she said, and it seemed to him that her eyes were sly.

Sly in exactly the same way Florrie's eyes had been.

4

When Maggie missed the first month she was not unduly worried. There could be many reasons why nothing had come on the day it should. She told herself the shock of finding her father lying there, his white hair all matted with blood, could be the cause, or it could even be she was inwardly horrified at what had happened between her and Joe lying by the fire.

The more she went over that in her mind the more impossible it seemed to be. She wasn't like that. She wasn't like some of the girls at the mill who talked about what they did with boys. She had more sense.

And more than once she had suspected that the girl weavers were just showing off, because look what happened when Elsie Arkwright suddenly went to live with her auntie down in Sussex. Everybody had been shocked out of their minds. They had talked about it for days in whispering and horrified disbelief.

'I have this friend,' Maggie told Essie Platt, a big girl with her hair fluffed up into a frizz at the front. 'She's a bit scared she might be going to have a baby.' Then she hung her head and felt the blush creep up from her throat, making her eyes water. 'But she . . . it was only the once.'

Essie nodded firmly. 'Then it's all right. Nothing can happen the first time, especially if she's never been with anyone before.'

'Oh, she hasn't!' Maggie was shocked at the idea. 'She's not like that. It was . . . this friend says it was the first time in her whole life.'

'Then tell her to stop worrying.' Essie smiled a sly smile. 'Worry's the worst thing out for upsetting the system.'

Maggie saw the way that from that day onwards Essie's circle of friends eyed her up and down then looked quickly away. For another few weeks she deliberately lulled herself into a sense of false security, repeating to herself what Essie had said during the times when the worry almost paralysed her with its implications.

Every day she looked for a letter from Joe, telling herself that maybe he could not write well enough to compose a letter.

'I was off school more than what I was there,' he'd said.

She remembered Thomas saying that the proportion of children leaving school unable to read or write was a disgrace.

'Half-timers in the main. Children who somehow, through no fault of their own, get left behind in a big class of brighter pupils. Children who move from one place to another and slip through the educational net somehow.'

'We're always doing moonlight flits,' Joe had grinned. 'Once we escaped through a top window and over the roofs.'

Maggie, oblivious to the deafening clatter of the weaving shed machinery, bit her lip and nodded. Yes, that would be it. Joe was proud, above all else he was proud. He would never have admitted that he could not write. Somehow he would have covered up. Her father had explained that too:

'They master the ability to print their own name and that's all.'

Then with a sinking of her heart Maggie remembered Alice Barton taking the slip of paper down from the mantelpiece and thrusting it in front of her face. All written in Joe's neat handwriting . . . Rent, tea, candles, tins of milk.

That night she took down one of her father's books from the shelf in his room, running her fingers over the leather binding. Always, even towards the end, Thomas had tried to find solace in poetry, but when she tried to read the print blurred before her eyes.

'Oh, God,' she prayed, down on her knees, holding the book close to her chest. 'Don't let it be true. Please don't let it be true. If it is I don't know what I'll do. I keep thinking about what I *could* do, and there's nothing to show, nothing wrong with me really but the worry going round and round in me head till it feels it might burst open. And Kit Carmichael's asked me to tea, and oh God I have no interest in going anywhere or doing anything. I can't seem to talk to anyone with this great black cloud on me. An' I know that worrying like this is the very worst thing, so just for a week I'll stop fretting to give it a chance. I'll put my trust in Thee,' she ended. 'For Jesus Christ's sake, amen.'

'If Kit Carmichael has asked you there for your tea, then he's serious. He hasn't bothered with girls before, you know, love.'

Clara's eyes were sly. 'You keep quiet, I notice. Not been upsetting you has he, love, this Kit Carmichael?'

'He's kind,' Maggie said, moving the lamp so that it shone directly on to the sewing in her lap. 'I can't ever remember meeting anyone so kind. I think if I asked him for the moon he'd climb up and get it down.'

'His mother looks like something what's dropped off a flitting.'

Maggie lowered her head over the blouse she was feather-stitching without smiling, and Clara sat forward.

'You feel all right, don't you, love? You've been acting different lately. Are you sweet on him?'

Maggie wished Clara would just get up and go. She could not talk naturally, it was no good. Oh, dear God. . . . Apart from the one thing there were no signs. No being sick in the mornings, nothing. Oh if only Clara would go back next door. . . . She was better left alone, like they were

77

leaving her alone at the mill now. She merely stood at her looms, willed herself into a state of numbness, even as her fingers busied themselves with the cotton threads and the intricate machinery. She ran home when the hooter went and half the time did not even bother to make herself any tea. She made herself go to Chapel because there in God's house she could pray to Him with all her heart and mind not to let it be true. She was anaemic, she was imagining the worst, and one day, perhaps tomorrow, it would come right and this terrible anguish would all be over.

'*Are* you sweet on Kit Carmichael, love? He walked you home from Chapel again, didn't he?'

Maggie pricked her finger and sucked at it furiously.

'If you don't mind, Clara, I think I'll go upstairs and have a bit of a lie down. I keep having these headaches coming on.'

'Doctor Williams's pink pills,' Clara said at once, but getting up and going just the same.

The room where the sick woman lay was smaller than Maggie remembered; smaller and more oppressive, with the inevitable coal fire burning high in the grate.

'Do I look all right?' she had asked Kit nervously when he called for her, and he had nodded without really looking at her, muttering that they must hurry.

'Mother is having one of her off days,' he explained. 'I ought not to have left her alone, but I knew you would be waiting for me.'

Maggie sighed. She had willed herself to make the effort, even told herself that getting out a bit might take the worry off for a while, but it was still there, tightening her chest, smudging dark shadows underneath her eyes, and pinching her face into lines.

'It might be better if we waited for another time then?'

Kit licked his lips. 'No. She says she wants you to come. She's like that, is Mother. One minute you would think she was dying, but she never gives in. I could hear her panting for breath when I was upstairs getting ready.'

And hating me with every panting breath, Maggie thought, as after a silent walk through the streets, silent because she was feeling the worry starting up again, and because Kit was urging her on so quickly there would not have been breath to talk anyway.

'We're here, Mother!' he called out the minute the door was open, and for the second time Maggie stood to attention at the foot of Mrs Carmichael's bed.

The old woman lay, propped high with pillows, dark eyes sending out shafts of stabbing dislike, busy fingers smoothing and pleating the turned-down sheet.

'I'll take your hat and coat,' Kit told her, and as Maggie obediently unpinned her hat, divested now of its daisies, and unbuttoned the long coat, she was conscious of the unwinking stare from the bed.

'Take them upstairs, Kit. I don't like the front room being untidy. Then stop up in your room for a bit. I want to have a few words with Miss Craig on my own.'

He hesitated, but only for a moment, then with an apologetic glance at Maggie, he did exactly as he was told.

Mrs Carmichael pointed to a chair. 'Sit down, Miss Craig.'

Her beady eyes were on Maggie's blouse, and perching on the very edge of the chair Maggie wondered for a wild moment if she had guessed something was wrong and was looking to see if her shape was any different.

She told herself not to be so silly and glanced surreptitiously round the room when Mrs Carmichael closed her eyes.

Hardly a touch of colour brightened the drabness of the heavy, suffocating furnishings. Brown fringed mantelborder, maroon bobbled tablecloth, oilcloth the colour of beef tea, covered with two rag rugs pegged from pieces of black cloth. Sepia pictures framed in black, two ebonized vases each corner of the mantelpiece, and a marbled clock

79

dead centre. Flat iron resting on the range and a dark mahogany chest of drawers covered with a brown runner, and overall the powerful smell of camphor.

Maggie noticed a tray set on top of the chest, with three flowered cups and saucers, a milk jug covered with a net weighted down with beads, and a plate covered with a tea cloth.

Everywhere signs of a woman's touch, and yet she realized that the thin spare little woman in the bed had had no part in it. Her heart warmed to the gentle man waiting upstairs.

The minutes grew and lengthened.

Mrs Carmichael took note of the way this girl sat with her back ramrod straight and her head held high. The black eyes narrowed into calculating slits. No milk-pobs mill girl this. Not one she could send packing with a flea in her ear.

A beauty too, with a complexion that looked as if her cheeks had been newly scrubbed, and heavily fringed eyes that met hers with unwavering frankness. Just for a fleeting moment the old woman was back in time, seeing herself as she had once been. A young woman, with cloudy dark hair, breasts high and proud. Entirely without volition she put a claw-like hand over her own wasted, stringy breasts, and felt a stab of jealousy so acute it felt as if a dagger had been thrust into her chest.

'Kit tells me you live on your own,' she said suddenly in a hoarse growl of a voice, startling Maggie into a nervous betrayal of her feelings by the quivering of her long eyelashes.

'Yes, that's right, Mrs Carmichael.'

The dagger in her chest gave an extra twist as the old woman pushed herself higher on her pillows. This girl had a refinement in her speech that had never been learnt down Foundry Street. The flat vowels were there all right, but there was breeding there somewhere, she would swear to it.

'How old did you say you were?'

'Just seventeen, Mrs Carmichael.'

So this young madam thought she was going to give as good as she got, did she? Well, she would see about that.

'Have you nobody of your own? No family?'

'Two brothers. Twins. They joined the army years ago. I don't hear from them often.'

Mrs Carmichael digested this for a moment, then she pulled at the high neck-frill of her calico nightdress before saying:

'And your father cut his own throat?'

Maggie's head drooped. 'Yes, that's right.'

'What drove him to that, do you suppose?'

'Nothing *drove* him to it, Mrs Carmichael. He was ill. He had been ill ever since my mother died of the diphtheria years ago. He wasn't himself when he did it.'

'Not himself? Do you mean he was mental?'

Maggie's eyes met her own with a directness that would have made a lesser woman flinch, but the old woman was fighting for what she considered to be her very existence, and only the constant pleating and re-pleating of the turned-down sheet betrayed her agitation.

'My father had a stroke, then he developed an illness of the nerves that affected his brain. The doctor explained it to me. It was a kind of depression he had no control over.'

'Doctors know nothing.'

'No, Mrs Carmichael.'

This was getting them nowhere fast, and any minute Kit would be coming back down the stairs, and brewing the tea, and passing round the potted-meat sandwiches he'd taken such a time over, slicing off the crusts and cutting them into triangles, just as if the Queen herself was coming for her tea.

'And you think you're going to get my son, do you, Miss Craig?'

Maggie drew in a sharp breath.

'I don't think nothing of the sort, Mrs Carmichael. But

Kit is a good and kind man. I've never met a kinder man in the whole of my life. You must feel very lucky to have a son like that.'

With an abruptness that brought Maggie swiftly to her feet, the old woman slumped back on to her pillows, her eyes wide open, her fingers clutching the air as she gasped for breath. It was like the time of the prayer meeting, but worse. There was a loud rasping sound as Mrs Carmichael fought for breath. Her face turned blue, and the deep-set eyes seemed to fall back in their sockets, rolling right back with the whites gleaming like milk jelly.

'Kit. . . .'

The cry was a strangled groan, and even as Maggie moved, she heard his running footsteps down the stairs.

Pushing her to one side, he lifted his mother, held her hands, reached for a piece of cloth and sprinkled something on it.

Even in the middle of her distress Maggie found she was reading the lable on the bottle with complete detachment.

'Mr Himrod's cure for even the most distressing cases of asthma.'

Kit held the cloth to her nose. 'It's all right, Mother. I'm here.'

She pushed the cloth away, and pointed an accusing finger at Maggie.

'She . . . she. . . .'

Horrified, Maggie stepped back a pace, then another, her eyes wide and startled. 'I didn't say anything,' she gasped. 'I said nothing to upset her, Kit. Nothing.' She felt the blood drain from her face, as for the first time in weeks she forgot her own frantic worrying.

Mrs Carmichael was dying; she was going to peg out right there before her eyes, and it would be all her fault.

She ought not to have stood up to her and said that about her being lucky to have Kit. She was too outspoken and always had been. Anxious to make amends she forced herself to approach the bed again, but even as she stretched out a hand Mrs Carmichael knocked it away with a slicing motion of her own.

'Go through there, Maggie,' Kit whispered, jerking his head towards the dividing door, and willing to do *anything* that might help, Maggie walked through into the parlour, and stood trembling by the net-shrouded window, looking on to the quiet afternoon street, placing her hand over the pin-tucks to still the fluttering of her heart.

There was an aspidistra plant in a pot standing on a bamboo table in the window, and without knowing what she was doing, Maggie stroked a shiny dark green leaf, then drew her hand back as its coldness gave her no comfort.

The room was very damp and smelt of chilled soot and beeswax polish, and as the laboured breathing coming from the living-room showed no signs of easing, she faced the truth.

Kit would never marry her nor anyone whilst his mother was alive. He was more than a son to his mother; he was the husband who had deserted her, the daughter she had never had, the lover she needed to ease her sense of rejection. It was dreadful and it was also terrible, but it was true. . . .

Maggie rubbed her arms and shivered as the minutes ticked by. She wondered if she dare creep upstairs and retrieve her hat and coat, and quietly let herself out of the front door? It would be the best thing all round, she thought, with resignation.

When at last, Kit came to her, closing the door behind him, she looked at his face and saw that there was a man who could take no more.

Not a weak man, nor even a dominated man, but a man bowed down with responsibility, with a kindness and a compassion he could not and never would deny.

He came straight to her, and put his arms round her, holding her up against him, so that she felt the warmth and the gentleness of him, the *softness* of his undeclared love for her.

'I've got her off to sleep,' he said. 'Oh, Maggie. I'm that sorry. I can't begin to tell you how sorry I am.'

His hand was on her neck, beneath the heavy weight of her hair, stroking gently, caressing. . . .

'Oh, Maggie, what am I going to do? Tell me what I ought to do?'

Because she pulled away from him at that moment and saw the suffering in his eyes, the words she had meant to say were stilled.

What she had wanted to say was:

'Stand up to her, Kit. Make her see that she can't have an attack just when it suits her. Harden yourself! Tell her if you want to go out with me then you will go out with me. . . .'

But it was no good, and she knew it. The ailing woman in the next room had bound the big kindly son to her as surely as if she had tied him to her with steel ropes. And he was too kind to do anything about it. . . .

Wearily Maggie put up her hand and tucked in a stray wisp of hair.

'Fetch my things from upstairs, love. I'm going home, and I'm going on my own, because I know now that your mother needs you far more than I could ever do.' She half smiled. 'And it might be better if you stopped coming down to see me, Kit. After all, it's not as if we were courting seriously or anything, is it? Anyway, you don't know me, not really.' Her voice rose as she fought for self-control. 'One of these days you might be ashamed of me. You might wish you'd never walked me home from Chapel, or brought me to see your mother.'

'Oh, Maggie,' he whispered, not understanding. 'Oh, Maggie. . . .'

And the cry that came from him was more like a groan, and it was a sound that filled Maggie with anguish and exasperation. In her own agony she was not sure which. . . .

At the end of three months Maggie gave up hope and gave up looking every day for a letter from Joe. Although she wasn't sick in the mornings, there were signs now that she was definitely pregnant. Her breasts were rounder and fuller, and she had to lace her stays tighter to hide her slowly thickening waistline. Her cheeks were so pale that she had to pinch and pinch at them to make them glow rosy again, but the warm colour faded in a matter of minutes.

Even as she stared at herself in the mirror it went, leaving her as pale as a little frightened ghost.

Clara came in one day, without knocking as usual, and after watching Maggie drag herself listlessly from her chair to swing the heavy kettle on its stand over the coals, she said straight out:

'There *is* summat up, isn't there, Maggie?'

The tone of her voice was kind and caring, but there was something in the way Clara's left eye glided into its socket that told Maggie she knew.

'There's nothing wrong! Nothing!'

She was shouting without meaning to, and it felt as if her heart had moved up from her chest and was beating wildly in her throat.

'I'm tired, that's all, Clara,' she said more softly. 'It's been that warm lately I've been off me food, and since Father went I haven't felt like cooking much, not for one, it doesn't seem worth it.'

Clara wasn't listening. What she said next proved that.

'What about that black-haired boy who was always hanging about at the top of the street? Standing there whistling with his hands in his pockets? I was always seeing you running up to meet him at one time.'

Maggie was sure now that Clara would be able to *hear* her heart beating, or even *see* it pounding away, boom, boom in her ears, rushing and thumping as if it would burst her head wide open.

'He's gone away. He went away a while ago. To get a job, a better job. I thought I had told you.'

Clara leaned forward, podgy hands on podgy knees.

'You told me nowt. But you're going to tell me now, aren't you, lass? That Joe's gone away because he did something dirty to you, and he's not going to stand by you. I'm right, aren't I?'

Maggie jumped up so quickly that her chair fell over with a clatter. Standing sideways on to Clara, twisting her hands she presented a perfect view of her gently swelling stomach, no bigger than the soft curve of a throat but enough to convince her of the truth.

'You're going to have a baby, Maggie Craig.'

'No, it's not true!' Maggie's cry of anguish was torn from her trembling lips. 'Yes it is true, but Joe went away because if he'd stopped the police would have been on to him. He doesn't know . . . oh, Clara, he doesn't even know.'

And just for a moment, a wild impossible moment, it seemed to Maggie that it was her mother sitting there in the rocking chair. Hannah was holding out her arms, and enfolding Maggie in them, telling her to have a good cry and get it over with.

'There, there, l'al lass,' she was saying in her Cumberland accent, as soft as the water trickling down from the hills. 'It will be right, you'll see.'

Maggie bowed her head and let the tears roll down her cheeks, feeling the salt taste of them as they trickled into the corners of her open mouth.

'Don't tell anyone, Clara,' she sobbed. 'Promise me you won't tell anyone. Joe will come back any day now. He said he was coming back when he got a good job, and we'll get married and then it won't matter. *Promise* me, Clara.'

'As if I would tell,' Clara said, 'I can't think of what to say. I'm flabbergasted, that's what I am.' She got up heavily from the chair and nodded towards the kettle. 'I won't stop for a cup of tea, now, love, but I'll tell you something for nothing. If I got my hands on that Joe I'd throttle him till his tonsils burst out of his collar stud. Nay, I can't credit it, no way I can't. As if you didn't have enough trouble, but

86

then they say trouble always comes in a three, so you've one more to go yet.'

Her flat plain face working with an emotion and a sympathy quite genuine, Clara walked splay-footed to the front door, closing it quietly, almost reverently, behind her.

Passing her own door without a glance, she went into her mother's house, walked through the front parlour and into the living-room.

Ignoring her father she spoke directly to Mrs Hobkirk.

'Aye, it's true, Mam, but I've promised not to tell, so think on you keep your mouth shut at the Sewing Class tonight.'

'As if I would tell. That poor little lass. That's what comes of having no mother to guide her.'

Mrs Hobkirk was already pinning her hat on to her wiry hair, her mouth a grim line of satisfaction at having her suspicions verified.

'But that's one secret no woman can keep for long, and to think Maggie Craig looks like butter wouldn't melt in her mouth. Thank God her father is no longer alive to see his daughter's shame.'

'Think on what I said,' Clara reminded her.

Mrs Hobkirk sniffed, then meeting one of the sewing ladies on her way to the meeting she had the pleasure of passing on the news without even having had to wait till she got there.

They were all at Chapel that Sunday evening. All the sewing ladies grouped together, with Clara and Arnie in their usual place at the back. Mrs Hobkirk darted a sidelong glance at Maggie, turned round and whispered something to the pew behind, and Maggie lowered her head over her folded hands.

'Oh, God, dear loving Father of Jesus, Clara's mother knows, and if she knows then everyone else will know. And I'm asking you what to do, oh my loving Father, because I don't know where to turn. Help me, please, and show me what to do. Help me to go on working at the mill for a long time yet, and help me to try somehow to put a bit by, because when there's no money coming in, what will I do? Will I have to go to the workhouse or to one of those places for fallen women?'

The tears gathered in her eyes and splashed down on her cotton gloves.

'Am I a fallen woman, God? I don't feel like one . . . oh, Joe. . . .'

Maggie lifted her head then quickly lowered it again. It felt as if every eye in the Chapel was upon her, and when a woman carrying a bible started to edge her way along the pew and saw it was Maggie, she turned swiftly away, going to sit three rows in front.

But not before she had hissed a single word.

'Jezebel!'

Maggie felt a cold shiver trickle down her back. Her hands trembled so much she could not find the place in her hymn book, and though she held her head high and tried to sing, no sound came from her lips. Though the Chapel was full she was alone in the long pew, and when the hymn was over and they sat for prayers, bending heads over folded hands, a woman's voice behind her said distinctly:

'Praying won't get thee nowhere, Maggie Craig. You being here is an insult to God. Make no mistake about that!'

Maggie wanted to put her hands over her ears. She wanted to rock herself in her misery, but most of all she wanted to get up and walk out. Back down the aisle with the steel tips on her boots ringing on the metal grids, back to the house in Foundry Street where she could pull down the blinds and shut herself away.

When Mr Marsden went to stand behind the pulpit to give his sermon he banged with his fist and called on God to punish the wicked, and Maggie was sure he was speaking directly to her.

Frozen, with tears like slivers of ice inside her, she told herself that Mr Marsden knew too. He had been so kind to her when her father died, and now he would think she had been wicked even as Thomas lay scarcely cold in his grave.

The sermon was over, and Mr Marsden bowed his head.

'Let us pray for those who fall from grace,' he intoned, casting his closed gaze to the high ceiling, speaking slowly because he was, as usual, making up the words as he went along. 'Let them repent of their evil ways. Let them hide their shame from the godly, and walk from henceforward in the paths of righteousness.'

Completely carried away by the flow of the high-sounding phrases, Mr Marsden's beautiful voice droned on. Maggie bowed her head even lower, the tears inside hardening into a tight knot in her throat. The minister's prayer was bouncing back at her from the walls; she knew that if she lifted her head and looked around, every eye in the Chapel would be upon her. Now all desire to get up and walk out had gone. She merely wanted to slide down from the hard seat and lie on the wooden floorboards, hidden from sight.

When it was over Mr Marsden announced the last hymn, and there was a rustling of pages as the congregation found their places. It was one of Maggie's favourite hymns, but as the voices swelled to the rafters, she heard nothing. Mr Elphick might be pumping the organ till the sweat ran down his little wrinkled face, and the tenors in the back row of the choir stalls were giving of their best in the soaring descant, but still Maggie sat there.

All through the first verse she sat huddled in her seat, conspicuous now as she had never meant to be, tittered at from the row behind, and stared at from either side.

'We thank Thee that Thy Church unsleeping, while earth tolls onward into light. . . .'

The congregation, led by the choir, started on the second verse, and suddenly Maggie felt a light, a feather-light, touch on her arm.

89

'Stand up, Maggie,' a familiar voice whispered, and looking up she stared straight into the kind brown eyes of Mrs Carmichael's big son Kit.

Some courage he had not known he possessed had moved him to do this thing. Some well of pity deep inside him had made him leave his own pew, and go to stand by her side.

'Is it yours?' his mother had demanded when Mrs Earnshaw had departed in triumph after imparting the shocking news.

Then she had nodded with satisfaction, the blank amazement on her son's face telling her what she knew already.

'I could have told you what she was,' she went on. 'I tried to tell you, but you wouldn't listen. I knew from that first time Maggie Craig stood round my bed what sort of a girl she was. *Now* will you listen to me? I bet she doesn't rightly know which lad it is herself.'

She had raised herself up on her pillows and pointed a finger at him. 'Keep right away from her, sonny. She'll be looking for some mug to pin the blame on, you mark my words.'

'Poor little Maggie.' Kit had left her sitting up in bed, the three-cornered shawl round her shoulders. He had climbed the stairs and sat on his own bed, staring at the wall.

'Why?' he asked himself. Not who, but why? Because he knew who it was. He had seen them together once in the park, and their joined hands and their mingled laughter had filled him with inexplicable anger.

When Kit walked by Maggie's side out of the Chapel there was a little knot of people already gathered on the pavement outside. Clara Preston, red-faced and looking as if she was giving her mother a piece of her mind, and Arnie, turning his cloth cap round and round in his hands. Then four or five of the sewing ladies, staring at Maggie with a terrifying stillness that made Kit's blood run cold in his veins.

He held tightly to Maggie's elbow, feeling sure she would

fall down if he let go. His heart was thudding madly, and he knew that when his mother heard about this, as hear she surely would, there would be the very devil to pay.

One of the women drew her long skirt aside as they passed, and another – no, he must have imagined it – turned her head and spat on the cobbles.

'You ought to be ashamed of yourself, Kit Carmichael!' a woman shouted.

'Have you no shame?' another called out, and suddenly Kit could bear no more.

'Let them cast the first stone!' he cried in his shrill voice, knowing he was identifying himself with their vulgarity, but unable to stop himself.

'You shouldn't have done this, Kit.'

Maggie's voice was low as he led her away, and she was so small, so desolate that her concern for him made him feel at least ten feet tall.

'You mustn't come in,' she said when they stood at the door of the bottom house in Foundry Street. 'You've stuck your neck out for me enough tonight, and I won't have you talked about, not when you've done nothing to deserve it.'

Kit coughed, shuffled his feet, ran a finger round his stiff white collar and blushed like a young girl.

'Will he see you right, Maggie? I know it's none of my business, but will he do right by you?'

She was fitting the key into the door so that he did not see her face as she answered.

'He's gone away, but I'm expecting him back. And thank you, Kit Carmichael. I'll never forget what you did for me, not till the day I die.'

Then, with a swift glance up and down the deserted Sunday evening street, she stood on tiptoe and kissed him gently on his smooth cheek. 'God bless you, Kit. Always.'

She opened the door, turned briefly, smiled at him with her mouth, but with despair clouding her eyes, and stepped inside.

Kit walked slowly back up the street, his heart already

in his boots at the thought of the scene with his mother. He saw her, in his mind's eye, ranting and raving, and he told himself that as this seemed to be his night for sticking up for people then he would have a go at sticking up for himself.

But his resolution wavered even as he reached the top of the street, and turning right instead of left, he decided to take the long way home.

5

'Is what I did the worst sin of all?' Maggie asked Clara in the weeks that followed. 'Is nagging and meanness and vindictiveness not just as bad? What do you think, Clara?'

But Clara, who had never been taught to think, just shook her head.

'I don't rightly know, love,' she said.

Now the pattern of Maggie's days was set. It was getting up when the knocker-up rattled his wire-tipped pole against the window. It was raking last night's ashes from the fire, laying it ready for the evening, then running to the mill with her tea and sugar screwed up in a piece of paper for the brew-up at eight o'clock.

Lacing her stays as tightly as she could and letting out the fasteners on her skirt, the signs of the baby were only there if they were looked for. True her breasts were fuller, but then she had never been lacking up there, she told herself, and by moving the buttons on her blouses she managed.

At dinner time she ran home, always alone, forced herself to eat a slice of bread and jam, then it was back to the mill and standing in the damp atmosphere by her looms all through the long noisy afternoon until the hooter went and she was free.

Free to go back to the house, light the fire and force herself again to eat something a bit more substantial, an egg or a slice of ham. Freedom to Maggie meant isolation, a shutting herself away from other people, the way Thomas had done. But she refused to think about that.

One evening when she was just over four months pregnant she waited until it was dark, then she took her coat down from its peg behind the back door, pushed her hair up into a tammy, and walked out of the house, round the corner on to the canal bank.

She had promised Joe she would never go down that part of the town alone, but he had gone away and she had to see for herself.

It was a night of shifting clouds and pale glancing moonlight, turning the canal into a glistening ribbon of silver.

'One in the family's enough,' Maggie muttered, looking away from it. 'That's the easy way out, and besides, I'm not done yet, not by a long chalk. Joe will write when he's found a good job. He will . . . he will. If he knew he would be back for me like a flash, police or no police. An' if we had no money then I'd take in sewing. I could if I set me mind to it. . . .'

She walked even more quickly as she entered the maze of streets leading to Montague Court. In the middle of one narrow street a small crowd had gathered round two drunken men who were fist fighting with the ferocity of a pair of hungry tigers. One man had blood streaming down his face, and his opponent, a man twice his size, was ramming his fist repeatedly into the battered face.

One of the watching men shouted at the top of his voice:

'Police! The bloody rozzers are coming!'

Maggie watched, holding a horrified hand to her mouth as the small crowd disappeared, dragging the victor with them and leaving the bleeding man lying in the middle of the street being loudly sick. The awful retching sound made her clutch her own throat, and when the policeman puffed and lumbered round the corner, she walked away.

When she reached Montague Court she was panting for breath and there was a stitch in her side like the thrust of a sword. To catch her breath for a moment she clutched at a lamp-post, and as the wavering light shone down on her upturned face, two women crossed the street and stood in front of her with arms folded.

One of them put out a finger and poked Maggie in the chest.

'We've been watching you, we have. We saw you trying to speak to them men at the fight. This is our beat so bugger off!'

Maggie straightened up, holding her hand to her side, as the second woman, well into middle-age, gave her a push that almost sent her sprawling.

'Bugger off then, or we'll have your guts for garters. See?'

Trembling in every limb Maggie walked on and knocked at the door of number four, seeing, out of the corner of her eye, the two night women watching her. She knocked again.

From the dim yellow light coming from behind the blind she knew there was someone in, and just for a moment she imagined the big unshaven man opening the door, reaching out a hand and pulling her in. She glanced down the street to where the women still stood, and as the sweat broke out on her skin she raised her hand and knocked for a third time.

'Who is it?'

The voice was a woman's voice, thin and wavery, threaded with fear, and as the two night women began to walk towards her, nudging each other and laughing loudly, Maggie called out:

'I've come to see Mrs Barton. It's Maggie Craig.'

There was the sound of a bolt being drawn back before the door opened for about six inches. Maggie smiled, then the smile faded as she saw that the woman standing there bore no resemblance to Joe's mother. This was a woman who looked as if she was dying where she stood, with sparse grey hair pulled back from a face as yellow as the buttercups Maggie remembered from her childhood.

'I thowt it were the rent man,' she said. 'Come on in, lass, and tek your coat off. Did you say as 'ow you wanted Mrs Barton?'

The sweet smell in the tiny room was even worse than Maggie remembered, but the bits and pieces of makeshift furniture were the same. The wooden boxes still stood in the middle of the floor, and from the way a brown blanket was pushed back on a single bed Maggie realized that the woman had been lying down.

Her face seemed no bigger than the perimeter of a teacup, and the flesh had dropped away from her face so that it resembled a skull, with forehead, nose and chin jutting out. The effort of getting up to open the door had proved too much for her, and now she sank back on to the bed, staring at Maggie from sunken eyes.

'Mrs Barton's dead, love,' she said. 'They came and took her off to the Infirmary, but it were too late. She had choked on her vomit, they said, drunk as a lord.'

'And Belle? Can you give me the address where she works now?'

Maggie wondered why the stitch in her side wouldn't go. She'd stopped running, and what the woman was telling her wasn't exactly a surprise. She would have been more surprised to see Joe's mother sitting there, staring at her with Joe's eyes.

It all fitted in somehow. Joe had never existed, Belle and the big rough man had never existed, and what she was left with now was a dream-like memory of coming here. And what she was left with now was Joe's baby inside her.

'She was a bad lot that Mrs Barton,' the sick woman was saying. 'I hope I'm not treading on any toes, but she was a real wrong 'un.' She shook her head wearily from side to side. 'I'm not much help, love. I'm sorry. I'm not much help to nobody because I'm on me way out.' She smiled, and it was as though the skull parted its lips in a hideous grimace. 'We was lucky to get this place to rent.'

'We?' Maggie wished she could say something to comfort the bird-like woman lying back against her pillows, but she was struggling against a desire to give way and slide down on to the floor in a faint. She forced herself to stand upright, though the pain in her back drained the blood from her face.

'Me husband. He'll be back soon, and then we'll have a nice drop of stout. He's a good man. One of the best, and good men don't grow on trees, not round these parts.'

Maggie backed towards the door, trying to smile. She heard her own voice as if it came from a far-off place.

'I hope you soon feel better, then,' she whispered.

She saw a man turning into the Court as she closed the door gently behind her. He was walking quite steadily, carrying a jug held in front of him. She hoped the stout would help, because the part of her that was all her mother made her want to go back, to see to things, to fill a bucket from the tap out at the yard, and scrub the filth from the floor.

'Maybe I'll go back tomorrow with some gruel,' she told herself aloud, but even as she said it she knew she wouldn't.

'When we're in trouble we behave like animals,' Thomas had often said, and he was right. 'We just curl up in a corner and let the rest of the world get on with it.'

Maggie walked as quickly as she could without actually running. Out of the Court, out into the dark labyrinth of streets, past a corner pub with the clinking sound of glasses and the smell of beer and sawdust coming from an open window. The stitch had come back, but not as bad; the night women were nowhere to be seen, and down on the canal bank the silver water still shimmered and rippled as though beckoning her in.

She stood for a moment, swaying, her eyes fixed on the gleaming width of water. Oh, it was true . . . Joe had behaved like an animal. He had been threatened so he had run away. He had made love to her because she was warm and soft, and just for a while he needed softness and warmth badly.

Now she would just have to settle her mind to what had

to be and get on with it. And getting on with it did not include jumping into that deceptively attractive stretch of water. Once she was in she would feel the dirt and smell the stench, and down at the bottom there would be dead dogs and cats, and she was young. She was Maggie Craig who had defied Miss Hepinstall, and given her brothers back as good as she had got.

For the first time since the terrible thing had happened, Maggie knew real blazing anger. Not the wild tempers of her childhood when she had snatched her tammy from her head and stamped up and down it, but a deep revulsion at the way she had allowed this thing to happen.

She remembered a book she had once read, where the heroine, faced with the same situation, had actually banged her head against a stone wall.

'You fool! You fool! You fool!' she had cried.

'An' if I thought it would do any good I'd do the same,' Maggie muttered, turning away from the water and climbing the bank up to the bridge.

When she woke in the night and discovered the first signs that she might be going to miscarry, Maggie got up, the white-hot anger somehow sustaining her. Some instinct, maybe some far-off memory of the village women, worn out with constant child-bearing, made her get down on her knees and start scrubbing the living-room floor. By the time she had finished, the pain in her back had moved round to the front and was a dragging agony, but she emptied the bucket, re-filled it at the slopstone, and without bothering to heat the water from the kettle, she pulled down the blind in the parlour, carried a single candle through and began to scrub again.

She knew exactly what she was doing. She knew that if the baby was meant to be then no harm would come to it, but she knew equally that the sign she had been given was going to be interpreted by her as a definite nudge.

Every pore in her body was pouring sweat when she had finished the front room floor. Her hair was sticking to her head, ends wisping down her neck, and when she held the candle up to the mirror, it was the face of a woman well into middle-age staring back at her.

When she crawled into bed again she knew she was not going to keep the baby, so she faced the truth fair and square.

One part of her had wanted Joe's baby, oh yes, no doubt about that. There were moments when she had put her hand over her stomach and imagined how it would be when the baby started to kick. She had wondered whether it would be a boy or a girl, and she had imagined Joe coming back and marrying her, and the three of them living together in the house. She would keep on with her sewing and Joe would learn to weave, and she would set a good dinner before him every single day.

But life wasn't like that. Life did not tie up knots neatly and manufacture happy endings. Joe had gone, and she would have had the baby all alone, with the Chapel folk looking down their noses at her, and the neighbours eyeing her up when she went out with her stomach all sticking out.

Where would the money have come from when she had to stop work at the mill? She would have had to put the baby out to mind, and its milk would come out of a two-penny tin, and she wouldn't have liked to see her baby bowed with rickets or catching the cough because it wasn't nourished enough.

No, her baby wasn't going to be bearing the stigma of illegitimacy for the whole of its life . . . not now. Thank God, not now.

'Oh, Joe. . . .' Maggie felt the anger drain from her, and at last knew the relief of tears. When the knocker-up came down the street she was moaning to herself, turned on her side with her legs drawn up.

But when he came the morning after, she got up, washed herself all over, dressed herself, and went to the mill.

6

When the telegram came from the War Office Maggie folded it neatly back into its envelope, placed it behind the clock on the mantelpiece and told no one.

The official wording informed her with deep regret that the troopship *Himalaya* had left Cape Town for Natal with drafts of the York and Lancaster Regiment, and had run into heavy weather. The captain had hove to with the intention of dropping anchor in Durban, when Private Jonathan Craig had been swept overboard. Private Benjamin Craig, his brother, had immediately gone to his rescue and had perished when a life-line thrown to them had snapped in two.

A week now since it came and Maggie had come home from the mill, gone upstairs without bothering about the fire, and was sitting on the edge of her bed studying her face intently in the swing mirror atop her chest of drawers.

It was strange, but her face looked just the same as ever. A bit peaky since she lost the baby, and still pale, but that was all. Now that the nights were drawing in she went to work in the dark then came home in the dark, so pale cheeks were only to be expected. No, the trouble was in trying not to think, trying not to *realize*.

So if she went on mapping out each day, planning every hour in detail, it was possible that the time would go on till the pain in her chest would dissolve away. At least she slept . . . oh God, how she slept!

'Sleep has always been Maggie's salvation when she's ill,'

Hannah used to say, but oh no, she must not think about her mother, or her father, or Joe, or the night she lost the baby, or the message from the War Office. She must not think of *anything*. She had to go to the mill and she had to buy enough food to keep her from starving, and she had to remember to order enough coal to keep the lean-to shed in the yard filled. Apart from this there was nothing else she needed to do.

And today in particular she must ignore the stabbing pain in her chest and the way her head throbbed, because it was all in her imagination.

But what were the boys doing sailing out to Natal? She had thought they were safe from the war over in Canada. How could they go to fight in a war and never even let her know?

'Now they are dead,' Maggie told her reflection, 'and you must go up to the shops before they close. You know that, don't you?' So, quietly and thoughtfully she went downstairs and put on her coat and hat.

Clara always wore a shawl when she bobbed out to the shops, but she wasn't Clara Preston. She was Maggie Craig, and her father was the schoolmaster at the village school. Her mother wore a blue dress with the sleeves rolled up, and she baked apple-pies with shiny brown crusts, and fatty-cakes, stiff with currants, and oatcakes she laid over the rack to dry.

Miss Hepinstall was cross, but she wasn't afraid of her. Little Maggie Craig was not afraid of anything. Of owt, as Clara would say. Her hat was slipping, so lifting her arms up with difficulty – what was wrong with them? – she pinned it on more firmly, then whimpered as a strand of hair refused to be tucked back out of sight.

Then with back erect, and head held high, she set off up the street, and as she walked the cobbles seemed to blur together and become one.

She was not ill. She could not afford the *time* to be ill. There was no buzzing in her ears, and the little hammer tapping away in her skull was all in her imagination. No, she was just a bit dizzy, that was all.

What she had to concentrate on was how lucky she was to have the house with the rent book all paid up to date. No hiding in the stairs when the rent man came on Friday nights like some of the women in the street.

'Never spend a penny unless you can cover it with another,' her father had always said.

No, she would never get into debt. Never.

See, she was doing all right telling herself about the good things and not dwelling on the bad. It was just a matter of concentrating.

Conditions at the mill were good compared to what they were at some of the others. Yes, that was something to be glad about. Why, only a while ago she had read one of Thomas's books telling what it was like in some of the Manchester mills. She had never been there, but the book told of workers living in narrow alleys, in one up and one down houses, with next to no sanitation. Irish workers in the main, and it was no good Clara telling her that they had been brought up like pigs, and lived like pigs, blaspheming with every other sentence. Owing allegiance to the Pope, and using Jesus and his mother Mary as swear words.

Clara's horizons were indeed set no further than her own front doorstep. Dear Clara. Kind Clara. Salt of the earth Clara.

I love her, Maggie thought. In spite of the fact she couldn't keep a secret longer than two minutes. She is my one true friend.

It was funny how heavy her basket was, especially as there was nothing in it yet.

No, that book had been written by a writer who had never experienced the aching grind of poverty, never slept ten to a room, never sent his children out to play bare-bottomed, to paddle in their own dirt. He was reporting, not identifying.

Maggie opened the door of the shop, and the pinging of the bell set the hammering up behind her eyes again.

She could not think what it was she had come for, so she asked for some sugar, and watched through a swirling mist as it was weighed into a three-cornered poke. Then she asked for some Monkey Brand for the simple reason that she could see it there on the shelf. She pointed to the tall butter-pat with a design of a girl in a summer dress stroking a cow on it, and finished off by asking for a slice of cheese. She swayed as the shopkeeper pulled a piece of wire through it and thought how clever he was.

When she came out of the shop, it had started to rain, heavy drenching rain. Nothing like the rain she remembered from her childhood. Surely the rain then had been sweet and gentle, falling like a soft mist, not bouncing up like this from the cobbles and blinding her when she turned her face up to the sky?

Here was where she turned to go back down Foundry Street. There was where she lived, right at the bottom, in the house exactly like all the others, and inside it was cold because she had forgotten to bring the coal in from the yard.

She stopped, puzzled, and put a hand up to her forehead, and was even more puzzled to feel that her skin was dry and burning as if on fire.

No, she had been quite wrong. She could not possibly live down that mean little street, with the tall mill chimneys standing sentinel over it. She was little Maggie Craig, and she lived in the School House, and there were fields, and hedgerows thick with hawthorn, and her father was the schoolmaster. She had three brothers, and they teased her and pulled off her beret, and threw it over the low stone wall, and she climbed over to get it back, showing her bloomers.

It had landed in a cow-clap, and she had taken it into the house, holding it at arm's length, holding her nose. Her mother had rinsed it out, then washed it, but it had never again been quite the right shape. Maggie put up a hand to her head and was surprised to find a hat pinned to the slippery bulk of her hair.

What was she doing wearing a hat? Oh, yes, now she remembered. She had been dressing up in her mother's clothes, and she had walked to the gate to meet her father with her mother's weekday coat trailing behind her, and her mother's shopping hat balanced on top of her cloud of unruly hair.

Her father had carried her inside perched on his shoulders, and her mother had only pretended to be cross when she saw the mud-trimmed hem of her coat.

'Maggie Craig, you'll be the death of me!' she'd said, and when her father had kissed her, Maggie had put her arms round them both and squeezed and squeezed, and they had all finished up laughing . . . and laughing.

Oh, no, she did not live down there, not down there. Maggie put the basket down, and lifting her aching arms, unpinned the hat, then dropped it into the streaming gutter.

'I'm coming!' she cried, then picking up the basket again, she turned her back on Foundry Street, and walked away with little stumbling steps, in the opposite direction.

When Arnie knocked at the door of Kit Carmichael's house and saw the big man standing there on the step, waiting patiently to hear what he had to say, the breath caught in his throat, and he had to swallow twice before he could get the words out.

The fact that the bloke was wearing an apron over his trousers did nothing to help either.

'Oh, my God, what are we coming to?' Arnie thought.

It was all very well Clara and her mother making him come out in the pouring rain on what he was sure was a fool's errand. He knew this was the last place Maggie would be. Full of pride Maggie was, and anyroad Clara would have been the first to know if she had taken it into her head to call on Kit Carmichael. Wasn't Clara capable of wheedling the truth out of anybody? Aye, she were that. There were no secrets kept from Clara.

'Why, Mr Preston!' Kit's voice was higher than usual with surprise. He smiled and whipped off the apron. 'I was just setting things to rights before I locked up for the night. There's a lot to do with having to leave my mother alone during the day.' He looked up at the dark sky. 'And what a night it is! Come in . . . come in.'

'I'd rather not.'

Arnie's diffidence was like torture to him at times, and now the enormity of what he was doing overwhelmed him. He stepped back a pace.

'It's Clara. Mrs Preston. You know? Me wife. She and her mother went next door to Miss Craig's house – she's been locking herself in lately, and sitting in the dark they think, and well, she hasn't been looking well you see, so they went to try to persuade her to go to the doctor's. The last few nights we've heard her coughing through the wall.' Arnie coughed himself, and stuck his hands deeper into his pockets.

'Maggie's ill?'

Kit asked the question quietly, but his words rang out like a pistol shot. He opened the door wide. 'Come in, Mr Preston. I'll get my coat, right this minute. Come on in.'

'No, it's more than that. At least she is ill we think, but . . .'

Arnie gave up, and remembering to pull his dripping flat cap from his head, stepped inside, and guided by the light from the back room, followed Kit with reluctance, telling himself that once again Clara and her mother had stuck their noses in where they'd no business to.

To further his acute embarrassment, there was a bed in the small and cluttered room, and in it an old woman with the face of a tired monkey. Arnie held his cap in front of him, twisting it round and round in his hands.

Eyes as black as two lumps of shiny coal looked from him to Kit, then back again.

'Mother.' Kit's voice held the kindly tolerance Arnie felt would have been more in keeping when speaking to a backward child.

'Mother, this is Mr Preston from down Foundry Street, and I am going out with him for a little while.' He raised his voice. 'Miss Craig has been taken ill and I am going to see if there is anything I can do. I will leave the lamp turned up like this, so you will be all right, and I'll get back as soon as I can.'

The old woman plucked at the bedclothes, eyeing Arnie with narrowed eyes.

'I know who he is. You don't need to tell me who he is. He's married to that stout woman what skens, the one who sometimes comes to the Meetings. Wears a brown coat and a hat like a chamber-pot, and sings out of tune.'

'Mother!' Kit looked across at Arnie apologetically, then as he took his coat down from a peg behind the door, Mrs Carmichael put a hand to her throat and began to cough.

Kit hesitated, but only for a moment. Giving Arnie a little push he followed him out of the room, calling out as he went.

'You'll be all right, Mother, as long as you stop in bed.'

Then before Arnie knew what was happening they were out in the street with the front door pulled to behind them.

'It may have seemed cruel,' Kit explained, starting off down the street with such long strides that Arnie had to take little running skips to keep up with him. 'But my mother just did not want me to come out. You could see that. She *plays* on me, Mr Preston. Oh, she is very sick, I grant you that, and of late her mind wanders, and her memory is shocking, but if I had not got you out quick she would have seen to it that I never got away.'

He slackened his pace a little. 'I am so grateful that you thought to come to me, Mr Preston. But I must ask you this. Is it Maggie herself who has asked to see me, or is it your wife's idea? You see the last time I saw Maggie she gave me the impression that she did not want to see me again. Not that I blame her, mind. Not with things as they were then.'

Then, without waiting for an answer, he set off again.

Arnie tried to talk and to run at the same time, without much success.

'Mr Carmichael! I never said she was ill in bed or anything. It was you what jumped to that conclusion. Nay, the missus sent me to see if Maggie was at your house, because they went in and she wasn't there. In her own house, I mean. There's no fire or nothing, and not much food . . . Mr Carmichael! You'll get yourself locked up for running like that at this time of night.'

Arnie gave up trying to keep up with Kit's flying, lumbering figure. It was no good anyroad. He dug his fingers further down into his coat pockets, and bent his head against the sweeping driving rain.

He still felt guilty whenever he remembered that summer afternoon when he had tried it on with Maggie. He had scared the living daylights out of her, and to the day he died he would never know what had come over him. He trudged on. But he wasn't responsible for this carry-on. Not by a long chalk he wasn't. And it were more than likely that Maggie would be there when he got back, and they would feel right fools then. . . .

He turned into Foundry Street and saw something lying in the gutter, and bending over it, recognized Maggie's hat because of the way she had tied the black ribbon in a whacking great bow at the back.

'Cheers it up a bit,' she'd said.

'Oh, my sainted aunt!'

Arnie picked it up, his slow mind working out the possibilities, each one more terrifying than the last.

She had been set upon and carried off. She had gone to drown herself in the canal. She had taken after her father. Clara always said that sort of thing ran in families. . . .

Bearing the ruined hat aloft like a morbid trophy, Arnie lifted the latch of his own house and walked through into the living-room. To see his father-in-law sitting by the fire, in *his* chair, drinking tea out of *his* favourite pot.

'They've gone in next door, lad,' Mr Hobkirk said, jerking his head towards the dividing wall. 'By the gum, but tha's wet. It's a nasty neet all right.'

'How long has she been missing?' Kit stood on the rag rug in front of the grate with its heap of dead ashes, and asked the question calmly, only the urgency in his high voice betraying his distress.

'We don't know but what she *is* missing, Mr Carmichael,' Clara said, exchanging a significant glance with her mother. 'It's just that I didn't hear her moving about since she came home from the mill tonight. You know, raking the fire out or anything. So I came in to see if she was all right.

'She doesn't *look* herself,' Clara added. 'And she doesn't do enough cooking for herself. When her father was alive she was always taking something tasty out of the oven to tempt his appetite, finicky fella that he was.'

'Never a smile for nobody *he* hadn't,' Mrs Hobkirk said.

Feeling nervously impatient, but too polite to show it, Kit said:

'Have you been upstairs, Mrs Preston?' He coughed discreetly. 'And out to the back? She might have gone out there then been taken ill.'

'We've checked,' then after exchanging another glance with her mother, held out the telegram.

'I know it might seem like noseying, but we found this.'

'And after . . .' Clara's eye flickered. 'After what her father did, and with her well, having that other trouble in the summer, and now looking so poorly we thought we ought to read it.'

With obvious reluctance, Kit took the telegram from the

envelope and read it. Then, with hands that had been stiff with cold, and were now suddenly clammy, he muttered. 'And you thought she might have come to tell me?'

'With you having been friendly like,' Clara said, and was nudged into silence by her mother.

'So we sent Arnie.'

When the front door opened and closed, the three faces turned eagerly towards it.

Arnie held the hat in front of him.

'I found this,' he announced.

'Oh, that poor child.' Mrs Hobkirk took it from him and handed it to Clara. 'See, the pin's still in it.'

'As though it had been snatched from her hand.' Clara stared at it, her mouth working with emotion.

'Where did you find it? Where, Mr Preston?' Kit picked it up and turning it round and round in his hands, walked over to the window.

Out there, in the dark and rain, over there was the canal. He turned swiftly and threw the hat down on the table so that it covered the telegram completely. His teeth dug into his bottom lip.

'*Where* did you find it?' he asked again. Curse the man. Did he have to think before he could answer even a straight question like that?

'Lying in the gutter. At the top of the street,' Arnie told him, moving his head in that direction.

Kit nodded to them.

'Try to get the fire going. And put the kettle on,' he ordered, then leaving them standing there, an open-mouthed trio, gazing helplessly at the bedraggled hat, he ran from the house. Banging the front door behind him so that the little house shook to its very foundations.

Maggie had no thought in her feverish mind of walking to her death when she left Foundry Street behind her. No melodramatic desire to end it all. Just a feeling of need. A

109

terrible hurting need to be back in the country once again, to get away from the dirt and the meanness of the streets, from the terraced houses that grew in rows like a regiment lined up on parade. To forget that she ever knew Joe Barton – just to be back in the lanes where the hedges grew, where cottages were fronted by gardens overgrown with moon-daisies, marigolds, and night-scented stock. Where fields were thickly carpeted with yellow buttercups, and her brothers ran in from the pump, their brown hair flattened and wet against their heads.

If only her chest did not hurt so much, she could walk more quickly. And she needed to hurry because Hannah, her mother, was waiting for the jug of blue milk from the farm to make into a pudding stiff with rice.

And oh she loved going to the farm, in spite of the wild cats that sometimes streaked across her path from the barn. There were great hams curing in the rafters, and inside the dairy it was cool with its scrubbed stone table with the groove in the middle filled with water. There were milk dishes and wooden pails neatly arranged in rows, and everything smelt clean and sweet.

She had to go slowly now in case the milk spilt, but one day she had put it down carefully on the grass to lie on her stomach as she watched an army of ants going methodically about their daily task. And Benjamin had come up quietly on tiptoe behind her, and tickled her neck with a piece of grass so that she had jumped up and knocked the jug over.

No, this was not the right place. Even the sky was wrong. This sky was dark and heavy, and there were puddles in the road with the gas lamps reflected in them. She must hurry, and yet she could not hurry, and in spite of her slowness there was a trickle of sweat running down her face, and down her back. She was panting as though she had been running for a long long time.

Her hair had come loose when she wrenched her hat off. It hung in heavy wet strands down over her shoulders into her eyes, and it was a basket she was carrying, not a jug of milk.

She put it down because it was heavy and the heaviness was making the pain burn harder in her chest, so she left the basket there and tried to cough the pain away.

She stopped trying to run after that. She just put one foot in front of the other and stumbled and fell, then picked herself up and stumbled on again. She turned into yet another street filled with the darkened windows of unused front parlours, and for a moment she knew who she was and why she was out there in the dark, wandering aimlessly in the rain.

A door opened and a woman stood on the step, straining her eyes into the blackness, her body etched against the dim light coming from the back room. A child clung to her skirts, and two more children clustered behind her.

'Is me dad coming yet, then?'

'Nay I can't see no sign of him yet.'

'Can I have a sugar butty, Mam?'

'You can have nowt if you don't stop that moithering.'

Maggie stood quite still in the shadow of the wall, her coat and the darkness of the night rendering her invisible. Then the woman went inside the house, pulling the children after her and closing the door with a slam. For a moment they were silhouetted there in the dividing doorway, then that too was closed, and the house fell into darkness again.

Maggie remembered how her mother had always kept the lamp burning in the front window of the School House, sending out rays of welcome to whoever walked up the path. A sob caught up in her throat, then more sobs crept up, till her whole body was shaking, then she was crying with her mouth wide open, the tears pouring down and mingling with the rain on her face.

She was crying, not because she was lost and could not find the School House. She knew now that it was miles away with someone else living in it.

What she was crying for was the fact that it had come to her that she was alone, entirely alone in the world, the only one left, without even the right to think of the boys marching down a foreign road, climbing a foreign hill, or sailing on a foreign sea.

For the space of a terrible second, she saw with vivid clarity a towering wave carrying Jonathan away; she saw his face as he cried for help, and she saw Benjamin trying to reach him, stretching out a hand before they disappeared for ever.

'Oh, God!' she moaned, feeling her way along the wall because her legs no longer seemed able to support her. She turned into a back alleyway, and sliding slowly to the ground, closed her eyes.

'I'll manage,' she muttered. 'I've managed before on me own, and even if I'd had the baby I would have found a way. It's just that I feel so ill, and I daren't be ill. I can't *afford* to be ill.'

She craved a drink. More than anything else in the world she wanted a drink. Her throat was parched and burning, and if she lay there with the rain-wet cobblestones underneath her, she knew she would die.

And she did not want to die. In spite of everything she did not want to lie here and die. . . .

Painfully, slowly, working herself up the wall with hands gripping the sooty uneven stones, she managed to stand upright, and now her mind was clear. She had to get into the warm. She had to get where it was dry.

With the unerring instinct of a sick animal she stumbled forward in search of warmth and shelter, and help.

The street lamps were out now, but all at once she knew where she was. She recognized the tall houses on her left, each with its own little paved front garden. Here the better-off lived, the men with a trade in their fingers, and two streets further along was the street where Kit Carmichael lived with his mother.

Maggie made herself go on, fighting for every breath

now, her hair hanging loose and her coat stained with mud.

Every single house was in darkness, and she felt a recurring wave of panic. Oh, dear God, what was she doing out in the streets, in the dark, in the rain at this time of night?

Was she going to be like her father with his black depressions, his slipping mind? She put out a hand to steady herself against a window bottom before moving painfully on.

No, it was not that. There was blackness in her mind, it was true, but now she could see the substance in the darkness. She was ill. Ill in her body, not her mind. And yet if that were so, how did she come to be out here, walking when she had no strength to walk, burning hot and shivering with cold at one and the same time?

She would never get to the bottom of Kit's street. Never cross over the wider one, never make her way along the flat to Foundry Street. She lifted her head and saw, through the mist before her eyes, that she was directly opposite to Kit's house, and through the black square of window she saw the soft glow of lamp-light shining through from the back room.

Kit . . . kind, considerate Kit Carmichael.

He was there, only a few steps across the street, and behind that closed front door would be warmth, and a drink, a hot soothing drink to hush the pain burning her breathing away.

The door was not locked.

Feverishly Maggie's mind registered surprise at this. The town people always locked their doors at night. But it was too late to wonder. Too late even to bang the heavy knocker against the door in case she woke the street up.

All she wanted was help and warmth, and a drink. . . .

She was inside, groping with outstretched hands to the light, going towards it, stumbling, falling through the dividing door, and seeing the old woman with black picking eyes and the skin of a wrinkled crab apple, staring at her from the high-piled nest of white pillows. . . ,

The rain had stopped, and the sky was slowly changing from black to a sombre grey when Kit decided there was no point in searching the surrounding streets any further. No point in standing on the canal bank and once rather foolishly calling Maggie's name, his eyes narrowed as he tried to identify the floating debris in the murky water moving sluggishly against the canal banks.

Clara had kept a solitary vigil back at the bottom house, dozing in the rocking-chair, and going through into the parlour every now and again to stare through the window at the glistening cobblestones and the sleeping houses across the street.

'There's nowt else you can do, Mr Carmichael,' she told Kit when he came in defeated and wet to the bone. 'You've let the constables know, and they'll send word if owt turns up.' Her left nostril twitched upwards in a resigned sniff. 'They always let the families know first.'

He glanced towards the table where Maggie's sodden hat still covered the telegram, and a great knot of sadness tightened itself round his heart.

'But Maggie has no family, Mrs Preston. She hasn't got anybody, and it's killing me to think she had nobody to turn to.' He shook his head from side to side. 'Oh, I know there was you, and there was me, but she didn't come to us, either of us, did she? Not even when she was – you know.' He gave her a piteous glance which pleaded for under-standing. 'I stopped seeing her, Mrs Preston, because I thought she never wanted to see me again. I'm not much of a catch, Mrs Preston. I've always been *torn*, you see. I've not wanted to upset my mother, and then I've ended up up-setting everybody. For as long as I can remember there have been terrible rows and scenes if I tried to get friendly with anybody. She's always been delicate, you see. . . .'

He had been up all night without sleep; he was wet through, muddy and anguished, and his exhaustion led him to admit something he had never admitted before.

'I've always been a bit afraid of her, my mother, you see. Not physically afraid, not when I could pick her up with one hand, but afraid of the "bother" she makes.' He rubbed a hand over his curly hair in an apologetic gesture. 'My mother can make bother quicker than anyone else I know, but it's only natural when she had my father to put up with. I used to hear her shouting at him when he came in the worse for drink, and I got frightened. He hit her once.'

Clara nodded. Maggie had been right about this man. He had a heart as big as a football – a great soft football at that. He'd be like a piece of putty in the hands of a woman like old Mrs Carmichael, old witch that she was.

Leaning forward, she raked the slack over the flames, and pulled the guard round the fire. When she looked at him the dough-like features of her flat face were softened into compassion.

'You're tired out, lad. Go back home and get some rest, and see to your mother. She'll be wondering what's been going on. I'm going in to see to me husband's breakfast, but me mother will take over here. There's got to be somebody here when Maggie comes back.'

'You're very kind, Mrs Preston.'

Kit put out a hand and laid it gently on her shoulder, almost as if he would draw her to him, and Clara was only mildly surprised to find that she had no instinctive urge to flinch away from his touch. This was no man with wandering hands. Kit Carmichael's touch was the touch of a woman comforting another woman in their mutual distress. She would tell her mother that Mr Carmichael was a gentleman. A proper gentleman.

'Get off with you, then,' she said, and her voice held a gentleness Arnie had never heard.

When old Mrs Carmichael opened her eyes and saw Maggie come through the door, the jealous hatred smouldering in her mind enveloped her in a flame of white-hot rage. She would never have believed that Kit could leave her all alone and neglected to go off with that peculiar little man from down Foundry Street.

It was as though Maggie Craig had appeared like a vision in direct answer to the evil dwelling of her thoughts. It was as though she had managed to conjure her up herself out of a filthy cloud of ectoplasm.

So overwhelming was her uncontrolled rage that it failed to register on her mind for the first minute that the girl swaying on her feet, clutching now at the bedpost to keep herself upright, was ill.

And when the anger blotting Maggie's features out from her sight cleared a little, she saw the straggling wet hair, the fever-flushed cheeks, the chest that heaved and rasped with the effort of breathing.

'You're drunk, you little dirty whore,' she said, and even as she said it she convinced herself that she could smell the drink on Maggie.

Raising herself in bed with an ease that would have astonished her son, had he been there to witness it, she pointed a finger, jabbing it into the air.

'How *dare* you come into my house at this time of night? How dare you, without even as much as knocking at the door? This is a decent house. Get out! Get out back on the streets where you belong. Get out!'

There was a chair over by the window, and Maggie saw it through a mist of pain. If she could just manage to get there, she could sit down, and she would be warm, and Kit would come. He would come downstairs from his room the way he'd done before, that other time. She could almost hear his footsteps on the stairs. Light, tripping footsteps for so big a man.

Yes, it had all happened before, just like this.

The old woman had been shouting at her, just as she was shouting now, and Kit had come . . . as he would come now.

Holding a hand straight out in front of her, like a sleep-walker, Maggie took one step, then another towards the chair. She felt for the arms with her hands, and lowered herself into it.

It was a hard chair, and the arms were wooden, but she laid her head back and closed her eyes with thankful relief.

Now there was no more rain on her face, no tearing wind chilling her very bones. She was warm and safe in Kit's house, and she could sleep, and when she slept she would be better. 'Sleep is her salvation,' someone had said once, a long long time ago.

'Kit?' she whispered before she drifted into unconsciousness. 'Kit?'

The old woman pushed at the bedclothes, pushed at them with scrabbling hands so that she could swing her feet slowly round and place them on the floor. She stared at her feet for a moment, at the bent toes, the ridged yellow toe-nails, then raised her eyes to stare at the girl lying back in the chair.

Even with her hair hanging in wet rat-tails round her face, Maggie Craig was beautiful. She was beautiful, and Mrs Carmichael was ugly and old. Sonny had left her all alone, with the heavy rain beating down and bouncing off the corrugated roof of the shed outside. He had left her to go after that girl, but she would show him. She would show him . . . and her. . . .

She advanced towards the chair, and stretched out her hands.

'I'll do for you,' she muttered. 'You'll not get him. I know your sort. I'll kill you with me own bare hands before I'll let you get him!'

But even as she reached out for Maggie's throat, her

hands were stayed as her wandering mind registered the fact that this girl was ill, not drunk. She was running a fever so high that the heat from her face could be felt even before she had touched her.

Maggie Craig's lips were dry, and she was mumbling something, turning her head from side to side, her breath coming up from her chest as if it was being forced through a bag of rusty nails.

'Kit . . .' she was saying. 'Kit. . . .'

Mrs Carmichael stepped back a pace, her own breathing, in spite of her agitation, as free and easy as that of a healthy child.

She knew what she had to do now, and it was going to be so simple she had to chuckle at her own cleverness.

It was a struggle unfastening the catch on the sash window, then sliding the window up from the bottom, but she managed it.

The rain and the wind rushed in, and a pile of papers on the dresser fluttered to the floor. The old woman grunted her satisfaction, but Maggie did not move.

She never thought she would have had the strength, but it seemed as if something outside of her was pouring strength into her, giving her the feeling that she could have put the flat of her hand on the wall, and given no more than a little push for it to have crumbled away.

Even the pan of water poured on the fire, sending a cloud of smoke out into the room, failed to make her cough. True she was shivering when she climbed into her bed, and pulled the blankets up over her head, but the shivering was with excitement and not with cold.

It was like a cocoon of comforting warmth inside the bed, and the feather mattress seemed to come up and wrap her round. She reached to the bottom for the copper hot water bottle, and it was still hot. With a sigh of contentment, Mrs Carmichael placed her feet on it.

She could be warmer though, much warmer. The old woman chuckled as she stuck a skinny arm out from underneath the bedclothes, and groping around on the bedside table, felt her fingers close over a small bottle of brandy.

'If you hadn't been in such a hurry to go out and leave me, you would have put it away in the cupboard like you always do after I've had me hot milk with two teaspoonsful in it, wouldn't you, Sonny?' she whispered.

Then back inside the warm tent of heavy blankets, she tipped the bottle, and felt the fiery liquid stream in glowing comfort down her throat.

'When you were born,' she muttered, 'I used to cuddle you up, young Kit, nice and warm, just like this. I suckled you for two years, and even when you were a big boy, we would sit on the couch, just you and me, and you would put your arm round my shoulders. We would sit there of an evening when your father was out doing God knows what. Spending good money on beer; money what should have been for providing us with a good meal.'

A tear ran down her cheek, and she tried to lift a hand to wipe it away, but the hand had grown suddenly too heavy. She was crying in earnest now, just letting the tears fall.

'What about that time the man came down from the Guardians and said I would have to go up to the Committee after your dad had gone and left us and we had no money? Do you know what he said, that man from Guardians when he saw we had proper chairs and a table instead of orange boxes with covers on them? "You're not quite destitute, Mrs Carmichael" he said. He had a walking stick, and he pointed it at you. "He looks well nourished, doesn't he?" he said. So I didn't waste me time going up to the Committee after that, did I, Sonny? No, I took work in and trimmed hats till me eyes were coming out at the back of me head. I remember one hat took me five hours, and she give me twopence for it. . . . And her in the chair thinks she has more right to you, Sonny, than what *I* have?'

The brandy bottle was empty, and with her case made out and now rested, Kit's mother slid comfortably into sleep. . . .

She was abruptly jerked awake to see Kit's face staring

down at her. Whimpering, she reached out for the bed-clothes he had wrenched away.

'Don't do that, love. You're making me cold.'

But the beloved face, the face she only knew as a smiling face, was contorted with an anger so terrible, she could only shrink back and close her eyes again.

'Get me stuff,' she gasped, clutching her throat, and disciplined by years of ministering to her, Kit thrust what she wanted into her hands.

'Now get out of bed!' he said, 'and put this round you.'

The shawl he gave her was torn from its nail behind the door. She heard it tear, and when the inhalant dropped from her fingers, he made no attempt to pick it up.

'Kit . . .?' she whispered, and it was flung on to her lap.

'See to yourself,' he said. 'It would serve you right, Mother, if I let you choke yourself to death.'

And the way he said the word 'Mother' was an insult in itself. . . .

Faces came and went each time Maggie opened her eyes. Hands held her, stripped off her wet clothing, wrapped her in blankets, and piled yet more blankets on top of her. A hand smoothed the hair back from her aching head, a voice bullied her; more hands held her head over a steaming bowl with a pungent aroma that made her turn her face weakly aside in useless protest. Held her there and made her breathe. Forced her to take one rasping breath after another.

Once she thought she saw Clara, then Clara's mother, sitting by the bed, and once an unknown face above a bib of a white starched apron lifted the hair from the back of her head. She heard and felt the snip of scissors.

'It was taking your strength, love,' an unfamiliar voice told her, and she submitted because she was in too much pain to do anything else.

'Kit?' she whispered, and he was there, always there, holding on to her, tucking the blankets round her chin when all she wanted was to push them away. He stripped them off when the crisis came, and she sweated so much it ran down her sides, into her eyes, stinging with the saltiness of it, running down her legs and soaking the sheet.

'The fever's broken,' she heard Kit say, but he was saying it from a long way away. The room was filled with steam from the steam kettle set permanently on the kettle-stand at the front of the fire, and Kit was sponging her naked body, patting her dry, sliding a clean sheet beneath her, murmuring all the time.

'It's all right, Maggie, love. You are getting better. Do you hear me? You are going to be well and strong again. Soon. Do you hear me?'

Into sleep and vaguely out of sleep again. Too weak to smile or speak, or even think. Opening her mouth obediently so that the carefully held spoon could trickle broth into it. Beef-tea. She recognized that, and it tasted good.

'Good,' she managed to say, as a child would say it, then she drifted into her first real sleep for days, a healing natural sleep with her breath coming even and unforced.

'Hello,' she said, and Kit's face was there, close to her own, and there were tears streaming down his cheeks.

'Don't cry,' she thought she said, before she fell asleep again.

'She's been sleeping all day,' Kit said when Clara came in, appearing through the door with a covered basin in a basket. 'No, I won't go up and get some rest, Mrs Preston. She is going to need me here when she wakes up and finds out she is in my mother's house, in my mother's bed. I've got to be here to tell her that they took my mother away.'

'To the loony-bin,' Clara said with relish, speaking in what she considered to be a whisper. 'And what else could they do with her carrying on like a mad woman? What else was there for it when you'd found that poor lass half dead with the double pneumonia sitting half dead in a chair by an open window? A window your mother had opened with her own two hands? And the fire out,' she added, moving over to the hearth and setting the covered basin down. 'A nice drop of pigeon broth here, Mr Carmichael. That man that's a blacksmith striker across the street wrung the neck of one his own birds specially. All the street keeps asking about Maggie. Knocking on the door all the time for news. Seems some folk have short memories seeing what they was like with her in the summer.'

'I could not have done anything else but let them take my mother away,' Kit said, putting a square slab of coal on the fire, then tipping what was left of the coal bucket round it. 'I wasn't thinking straight. Maggie would never have lasted as far as the Infirmary. It was warmth she had to have, and her wet things off. There wasn't time to waste.'

Clara's good eye held a sly expression; the other one seemed to be non-committal.

'People will talk all the same. You know what they was like when she . . . when she had that other trouble. The poor lass is after getting herself a bad name without deserving one. An' what about your job, Mr Carmichael. How's the old gentleman you do for managing?'

Kit smiled as if it was of no consequence whatever. 'Oh, he's told me not to go any more. Said he had got someone more reliable. A younger man, a boy straight from school, but I'm not bothered. Shop work's what I've always wanted, and there might be, there might just be an opening . . . but I'm biding my time.'

'She's still a terrible colour,' Clara said, shaking her head at Maggie lying quiet on her pillows.

Maggie was awake and yet not awake. She could open her eyes if she wanted to, but the effort was too much. The lids felt as if they were weighted down with pieces of lead.

'Kit?'

But before he had time to move over to the bed and take her hands in his own, she was properly awake. Terror made her cry out as she saw she was in the downstairs room of

Kit's house, the dark brown room, and oh God, help her, she was in his mother's bed!

Suddenly the sweat was breaking out on her forehead, pricking in her armpits as she tried to raise herself up. When she lifted her head from the pillow the ceiling dipped towards her, and Kit's face blurred out of focus. Her heart began to beat wildly as memory flooded back. The telegram, the pain in her chest, the rain and her hair straggling dripping over her face, the feel of the slimy wet cobblestones against her face. A woman at a door with children clutching at her skirts. The telegram, and old Mrs Carmichael pointing at her with a bony accusing finger. Shouting at her to go away when all she had wanted was to sit down and close her eyes.

'Last night,' she gasped. 'I came looking for you . . . oh, Kit.'

She was held safely in his arms, held up against his shoulder, and he was all warmth and softness, and somehow it was as if she was back in the kitchen at the Schoolhouse, held in the cushiony comfort of her mother's arms. Having her hair stroked back from her face, and being promised that there was nothing to be afraid of.

'There's nothing to be frightened of, Maggie, love,' Kit said. 'My mother isn't here. She has gone away. To a special kind of hospital.'

'She's fallen asleep again,' he said, and laid her gently back on the pillows. 'She'll sleep herself right,' he added, then as Clara nodded, putting a finger to her lips, and picking up the empty basket, he followed her through into the parlour, and ever polite, stepped in front of her, and opened the door on to the street.

'Thank you for the broth, Mrs Preston. I know I don't need to ask you again not to repeat what you know about what my mother did.' He pulled the lapels of his jacket together, and it was a gesture that said plainly, 'I *forbid* you to gossip about what happened. You did enough damage with your clacking tongue before.'

123

'As if I would talk,' Clara said insincerely. 'Things is bad enough as it is.'

She walked flat-footed down the street, going over in her mind the things she had to tell her mother. It was a right to do an' all. The Chapel lot would have something to say when they found out that Maggie Craig was stopping at Kit's house, just the two of them. And with his mother screaming and tearing her hair out in a padded cell. It was a real caper, it was 'n all. . . .

Two days later Kit pulled up a chair to Maggie's bed and sat down. She looked, he told himself, about twelve years old. Her eyes were enormous in the small oval of her face, and her cropped hair curled round her ears and fell over her forehead in a fringe.

'Well, love?' he smiled, and suddenly shy, Maggie smiled back.

She knew he was going to ask her to marry him, and there was a little niggle in her mind that kept her wondering if he would have asked her if his mother had not gone away. Or if she had gone on and had the baby?

And yet it had seemed to her, lying on her side these past days, too weak even to lift a hand to brush her short hair, too weak to hold a spoon at first without Kit guiding it to her mouth, that here in Kit Carmichael was all the kindness she could ever ask from life.

Someone she could rely on, not someone she was responsible for.

He spoke into her thoughts, 'Maggie, I am old enough to be your father, I suppose.'

'You'd have to have started a bit young, Kit.'

He rubbed a hand over his clean-shaven chin. 'Aye but I didn't, did I, lass? I wish I could make you see what my mother was like in those days. She could have been a very different woman if she had not married the wrong man. She told me once he made so many promises to her about the way it would be if only she married him. Went down on his knees, she said, with tears rolling down his cheeks, swearing he would give up the drink and go to Chapel Meetings, and sign the pledge.'

'What a prospect,' Maggie said, and when he saw the twinkle in her eyes, Kit shook his head and smiled.

'Aye, put like that, it does sound a bit sanctimonious, but it wasn't long before he lost his job at the factory.'

'What for?'

'He turned up for work dead drunk and pushed his foreman's face into a vat of water kept for tempering hot steel.'

'Why?'

'Because he said he hated the man's guts. Then he got taken on at the Brewery, and they had to wheel him home one day on a handcart, so drunk he could not stand. That was when my mother started taking work in from the big Manchester shops. She lost three babies before I was born, you know.'

Maggie put out a hand, and Kit covered it gently with his own, rubbing his thumb up and down the thin blue vein at the front of her wrist in an absent-minded way.

'Aye, she had a rough time, my mother did. Then she took to having her bed downstairs because of her chest, and he took to going with other women. He was too uncouth to realize that after three dead babies, and a delicate son like me, any man with a decent bone in his body would know that his wife had had enough.'

Maggie blushed and hoped Kit would not notice. She wished he would stop telling her about his mother's life, and making excuses for her. She wished he would talk about *them* for a change.

She hoped he wasn't going to try to get her to say she was sorry for his mother, and that they could have been friends if things had been different. Nobody but a saint straight down from heaven could have made a friend out of Kit's mother, and she doubted if even an angel could have managed it.

'Nobody would believe what it was like during those years, Maggie. Once, when the hat trade fell off a bit she opened a shop through in the front room. She sold candles and odd bits of grocery – things I could fetch from the warehouse on a handcart. She used to have customers from down Montague Court way.' Maggie caught her breath, but Kit wasn't looking at her. 'Real rough they were, and some of them so poor they had to take the stuff home held in their pinnies because they couldn't afford the price of a basket. At one time the shop was open sixteen hours a day, closing Christmas Day, and that was all. And do you know what my father did? He took the tin where she kept the takings, and ran off and drank it away. He'd found that tin where she had hidden it away, and through it all she insisted I went to school, refusing to send me into the mill when I was nine, then even when the little shop had to close she went on with the hats and went out and scrubbed other people's floors.'

He gave her a pleading glance. 'So what I mean is, I don't want you to think she was all bad, even though what she tried to do to you was so terrible, it doesn't bear thinking about.'

'What *did* she do, Kit?'

He winced away from the softly spoken question, but it had to be told. Told now and never referred to again. He squeezed Maggie's hand hard.

'She opened the window, love, and she unbuttoned your coat, and then she put the fire out, and got back into her own warm bed, and if I had not come in when I did, back from looking for you, you would have died.'

His voice was very low as he told her, and his head was sunk deep on his chest. 'So if you can't forgive her, love,' he said as if reading Maggie's horrified reaction into her silence, 'at least I hope that some day you will learn to forget.'

He touched her cheek lightly with his forefinger. 'What I have been leading up to, really, is trying to make you see that I'm hoping that in spite of what my mother did, you can still find it in your heart to be fond of me.' He nodded as if to give added importance to his next words. 'Aye, I am asking you to marry me, even though I have lost my job, and am not qualified for anything but a glorified nursemaid.' He turned his head and stared steadily through the window.

'And there's something else that must be said. I am not like my father. There is nothing in me that comes from him, thank God. What I am trying to tell you, Maggie, is that I won't *bother* you if you don't want me to.' His back was now almost turned on her. 'There is more to a marriage than what I just said. There is friendship, and tolerance, and pulling together, and even though you could have anybody with looks like yours, there is nobody in the whole world who could think as much of you as I do. Nobody, not even that other one . . . that Joe,' he added softly.

'And your mother, Kit?'

It had to be said. There would never, she felt, be another time, and so she had to say it now.

'Suppose she gets better and comes out of that place? There's not the room for both of us under one roof, you must know that.'

A shadow crossed his face. 'She won't come out, Maggie. I am afraid that my mother is less than an animal now, crawling about in her own dirt on a stone floor, with her food pushed at her in a wooden bowl. She eats it as if she was a pig at a trough.'

'Oh, my love. . . .'

With an effort, Maggie held out her arms, but ever considerate, he shook his head gently at her.

'You look tired out, love. I've talked too much. Just slide down again, and when you wake up I'm going to try you with a bit of steamed fish.'

He stood up, tucked her hands in beneath the blankets, and bending down, kissed her forehead.

'And you will marry me, Maggie? Sweet Maggie?'

She nodded. 'I will marry you, Kit . . . yes I will. . . .'

Even as she spoke the desire to sleep was overwhelming, and it was surely the distorted meandering thinking of a dream that made her start awake, and ask herself the question again:

Would Kit have asked her to marry him if his mother had not gone out of her mind and been put away? Would he even have come to *see* her again if she had not run out into the wind and the rain?

And perhaps the most important question. Would she have agreed to marry Kit if she had had the slightest hope that Joe Barton might come back some day?

7

'I wish we could do something to make the wedding a bit more of a *cheery* occasion,' Maggie told Kit. 'Mr Marsden says that music at a Chapel wedding is a manifestation of idolatry, but you know, for two pins I'd take the black ribbon off my hat and put the daisies back on.' She sighed deeply. 'Nothing can bring Father back, or the boys, or undo what has been done, so why can't we be happy about the one nice thing that's happening?'

Kit looked away from her and coughed gently.

'Maggie, listen to me. I'm going to say this once, then never again, because it pains me. When we're wed I never want to hear the name of a certain person mentioned again. What was done can't be undone as you rightly say, but I want you to know that I have forgiven you from the bottom of my heart for . . . for what you did.'

'With Joe?' Maggie said quickly, her eyes widening with an expression that would have halted Kit's fumbling flow of words had he seen it.

He stared through the window. 'You were . . . you are . . . not much more than a child. He knew he had to get away from the town or be sent to prison, and yet he had his way with you, even knowing he would never see you again. You were more sinned against than sinning; you must always try to remember that.'

Maggie felt her face flame with anger. 'Kit. Kit Carmichael. It takes two to do what we did, and I can't, I won't marry you with you thinking I was set on by a lust-crazed boy fleeing from justice.' She went to Kit and put her hand on his sleeve. 'We were *unhappy*, love. So very very unhappy. Me because of what Father had done to himself, and Joe . . . oh, Kit, I know you and your mother had to struggle, but have you any idea how some of the people in this town have to live?'

She twisted him round, forcing him to look at her.

'Like pigs, Kit Carmichael. His mother was a drunken *whore*, and don't flinch away because you're surprised I know what the word means. There was no money coming into that hovel but what Joe earned, and his mother spent that on drink most of the time. He tried to set her weekly payments out and she took against him for that, and his sister looked as if a puff of wind would blow her over. That house smelled, Kit! It smelled of other folk's bugs in the walls, and I'll tell you something else. There was a man there, a big man on leave from his ship, and he'd tried to touch Belle. Oh, Kit, there were rough men working the harvest where I came from, swearing sweating men, but they wouldn't have laid a finger on a child. Because that's all Joe's sister is, even though she's gone living-in now and left school.'

Maggie felt the tears swim in her eyes. 'Joe took that money because his mother had pinched what he'd saved for his sister's caps and frocks and aprons. That was why he had to run.' Her voice dropped to a whisper. 'And he'd nowhere to run to, Kit. So when he came here it wasn't me and him being wicked. It was him and me putting our arms round each other and trying to make things right just for a bit. We were heartbroken, Kit, each in our own way, so we forgot ourselves and just comforted each other, that's all.'

She lifted her head high. 'Is *that* what you're so set on forgiving me for, Kit? Because if you can't accept the truth, then there's no chance for us, is there?'

Every feature on Kit's face seemed to be working with emotion. His Maggie was too honest. Couldn't she see that he *wanted* to believe his own version of how she had been ravaged against her will by a brutal boy running from the police? Why did she have to make him face a truth he did not want to face? She was brave as well as honest, this bonny Maggie. Even though the long speech had drained her face of colour she was still strong. Like his mother had been strong.

Kit lowered his head and kissed her tenderly on the forehead, leaning without knowing it, on the strength that came from this young brown-haired slip of a girl.

'I'm sorry, lass,' he said. 'And we'll not talk about it any more, I promise. It's me what should be forgiven for upsetting you.'

Maggie's smile was tinged with irritation.

'Now, there's no need to go *that* far, Kit Carmichael.'

He only saw the smile, so he smiled too. If Maggie was happy, then so was he. For Kit Carmichael it was as simple as that.

They were married quietly one blustery Saturday morning, wearing black arm-bands round their coat sleeves. The Chapel was so cold that Maggie could actually feel her nose turning red, and behind her, Clara's mother sobbed noisily into her handkerchief all through the simple ceremony.

Clara and Arnie stood in for them, and after Mr Marsden had pronounced Maggie and Kit man and wife, he gave a quite uncalled-for little homily on the evils of drink, trusting they would enter their new life together in a state of sobriety and with due regard to the solemnity of their union.

Kit had found a job as a grocer's assistant in a flourishing little corner shop in an area crowded with back to back houses and pawn shops. It was no more than twenty minutes' walk away from Foundry Street, and he was to be left in sole charge for most of the day.

They had decided to live in Maggie's house, not only because the rent was a shilling less a week than for the one he had shared with his mother, but because it had a bigger backyard, and fitted cupboards flanking the fireplace in the living-room.

'Small details, but worthy of consideration,' he had said, believing it was his idea and not Maggie's.

'I'm sure I'd have seen his mother bobbing out at me from every cupboard,' Maggie had told Clara, 'especially when I was on my own at nights.'

'I wish we were going away to the seaside for a bit of a honeymoon,' Kit said as they walked back to Foundry Street arm in arm after it was all over.

Maggie gave his arm a little squeeze against her side, and told him it didn't matter.

'It was very good of Mr Yates at the shop to let you have the morning off, especially as you've only just started there.'

'Yes, and Saturday is a busy day,' Kit told her, 'we get a lot of women coming in and stocking up a bit with food before their husbands can get their hands on what's left of the money.'

'Terrible,' Maggie said, so automatically that Kit looked at her with concern. She was still so very pale, and her face, beneath the wide-brimmed hat, was all eyes and dark shadows, with little hollows where no hollows had been before.

Without telling anyone, the week before starting his new job, Kit had paid a visit to the doctor's surgery, to reassure himself that Maggie's recovery was complete.

'She still coughs a lot. Especially in the mornings, Doctor,' he said, standing in front of the wide-topped desk, twisting his cap round and round in his hands.

'Bringing up phelgm?'

'Aye.'

'Streaked with blood at any time?'

Kit flinched away from the inference, hating the doctor for putting it into words. Consumption was more a way of life than a disease in the network of streets with their sunless houses, but the doctor shocked him by voicing his own terrified suspicions and anguished fears.

'No blood, but she is not getting any fatter, Doctor, and she always seems to be cold, even when I build the fire halfway up the chimney. She doesn't eat enough to keep a bird alive, no matter what I tempt her appetite with.'

The doctor stared hard at Kit. Then he got up from behind his desk and took up his stance by the window, hooking his thumbs into the lapels of his waistcoat, and watching Kit through narrowed eyes.

Dammit, he might just as well have been listening to a worried mother talking about a sick daughter. He turned his back and stared out at the view of a brick wall pitted with holes. Dammit, the man was an old woman, if not an out and out homosexual, and no more cut out to be the new husband of a young and spirited girl like Maggie Craig than a boy child recently breached.

The whole thing was obscene somehow. He tapped on the window with a short clean fingernail. At the moment the girl was weak, run right into the ground with the shock of all that had happened to her. How she had pulled through he would never know.

But what would happen when she fully recovered and looked around her and saw the world was full of men who were real men, not soft flabby mother's boys, like the man standing quietly and patiently behind him.

Sighing he turned round and caught the look of anguished anxiety on Kit's big face as he waited to hear what he had convinced himself must surely be bad news. News the doctor was steeling himself to give.

'The poor bloke is looking for another mother,' the doctor told himself silently, and shook his head sadly from side to side.

'Miss Craig has been very ill,' he reminded Kit. 'But I am sure there is nothing that good food and rest won't put right. She comes of fine country stock remember, and that will put her in good stead, but I would recommend that she stays away from the mill for a while.'

He sighed and asked himself what was the use? They

killed themselves, these working-class wives, running back to work before they were fit, having babies one after another, wearing themselves out before they were thirty years old. Oh, he knew poverty was to blame, and dirt, and apathy, and ignorance, and stupidity, but it was something else, something his training had not prepared him for.

It was a grit these Lancashire women possessed, a determination that kept them going on and on, as if they never knew when to call it a day.

'Miss Craig will not be going back into the mill, Doctor,' Kit was saying, in that tiny voice so much at variance with his size. 'I've got a job with long hours, but I'll still have time to help round the house if I can see she's not resting enough.'

Then he asked a question quite simply, taking the doctor by surprise.

'Shall I keep on with rubbing her chest with goose-grease every night? She says the smell makes her feel sick.'

'Then stop doing it.'

The doctor watched Kit leave his surgery, stepping as neatly as if he were avoiding the cracks in the oilcloth, then before he slammed the bell with the flat of his hand to summon the next patient, he leaned back in his chair, crossed his hands behind his neck, and addressed the ceiling:

'Oh, my sainted aunt! Rubbing that little lass's chest with goose-grease every night, and never, I'd stake my life on it, letting his hands stray as much as an inch. I thought I'd heard it all, but I was wrong. God help that bonny, funny, normal little lass. That bloke's still married to his mother, and always will be.'

And even though it was his wedding day Kit was there behind the counter of the corner shop until an hour before midnight. In the last two hours he had sold a dozen candles singly to the same number of customers, a paper of pins, and a jar of milk, remembering from his boyhood to tip the jar first so that the coin fell out.

'Once I had to scrape a jarful of jam off a penny,' his mother had said, and her warning came back to him so vividly that he could almost sense her presence. He could feel her standing there in the darkened shop, watching him, instructing him, praising him, devouring him with her smothering attention, so that in the end, all initiative wiped out, he would turn to her to ask how to do the simplest things.

But now his mother had gone, and soon if she kept on refusing to eat, and throwing her food at the walls, she would die, and he would have to will himself to remember her as she used to be, not as she was now.

Kit glanced at the round clock on the wall, longing for the time when he could put the shutters up outside, lock the door, and go home.

There was no way he could have closed early, even if his conscience would have allowed him to, not with his boss, Mr Yates, living in the two upstairs rooms.

Though you'd have thought he would have come down and stood in for me, just for tonight, Kit told himself, then immediately reminded himself how lucky he was to have a job at all.

'What can I get you, love?' he asked a spare little woman approaching the counter with her purse clutched tightly in her hand. 'We've some nice bacon pieces going cheap. Make a tasty Sunday dinner if you boil them up with a handful of peas. . . .'

It was a dark night, a night entirely without stars, when at last he stepped out into the street. It was the hour when the only people he would be likely to meet would be the tramps, the homeless, those without the twopence it would cost for a bed and a pot of tea in the dosshouse.

Turning up the collar of his jacket, Kit increased his pace, and when he saw the candlelight flickering in the upstairs room at the front of the bottom house in Foundry

Street, he knew that his bride was lying in bed waiting for him.

Maggie had ironed her long calico nightdress frilled at the neck and round the cuffs, as carefully as if she was going to wear it for a walk in the park, and had brushed her hair till it stood out round her white face like a halo.

'Hello, love.' Kit put his curly head round the door. 'Have you had your cocoa, or shall I bring some up? I know what you're like for neglecting yourself when I'm not there to see to things.'

Maggie smiled at him. He really was the kindest man she had ever known. Not a grumble about having to stand on his feet serving groceries on his wedding day, just a touching concern for her and her nightly mug of cocoa.

He took off his jacket and hung it carefully over the chair-back, pulling the sleeves down and smoothing the lapels with his fingers. Then turning his back on her, he slipped first one brace, then the other off his shoulders, unbuttoned the front of his trousers, and dropped them round his ankles.

Politely Maggie stared at the window, concentrating on the yellow blind, but when she felt the mattress move she shot a startled glance in his direction and saw that Kit was laying his trousers neatly underneath the mattress.

'A habit of mine. Saves a lot of pressing,' he explained, then, holding a fold of his shirt decently between his legs, he came round the bed, blew out the candle, and got in, causing the mattress to sag down heavily, and sliding Maggie straight into his arms.

For a moment she panicked, holding herself stiffly against him, and moving her feet away from the hard hairiness of his legs. Then as she felt the familiar touch of his hand on her hair, and heard his whispering voice telling of his love, she relaxed against him, and buried her head in the warm smell of him, a smell tinged now with cheese and salt and scrubbing soap.

'He's a funny man that Mr Yates,' Kit said. 'Hardly human if you know what I mean, but he told me today he has three shops altogether. Three shops and he dresses like a tramp, and when I took the money upstairs he was sitting in a room with just the one candle and sacking tacked over the window.'

'Do you see much of him?' Maggie asked, wondering when what was going to happen would begin.

Kit stroked the hair away from her face with an absent-minded gesture, then casually rubbed one foot up and down her leg.

'No, I don't see all that much of him, considering it is his shop, but if it was mine there are a lot of things I would change.'

'Mmm?' Maggie felt her eyelids droop, and quickly opened her eyes and stretched them wide.

'Mmm?' she said again as Kit moved her head a fraction to one side to ease his arm into a more comfortable position.

'Well, for a start off I would be more lenient with tick. Mr Yates says I must not hand over even a penny paper of pins without catching hold of the money first. He says the previous owner of the shop went bankrupt through handing over food in exchange for clothes which customers promised to redeem the next week. But of course more often than not, they never did. It's a poor district, Maggie, but the biggest part of them are God-fearing folks. So if a customer's money runs out before Friday, and if she has been a good payer and keeps her word about paying back, well, I feel we would attract more customers by showing we have a bit of heart.'

It was no good. Maggie was so warm, so relaxed, so comfortable, that Kit's words were blurring into a maze of sounds, like a soft and lazy lullaby. Her eyelids drooped, her breath came softly and evenly, and Kit, realizing that she was dropping off to sleep, turned her over gently and fitted her on to his ample lap.

'Spoons in a box, love,' he whispered. 'Sleep tight, and if I snore, just give me a nudge.'

He tucked the bedclothes in carefully round her neck.

'Good night, Mrs Carmichael,' he said.

Within seconds his leg jerked against her own, and perversely, the minute Kit fell asleep, Maggie was suddenly wide awake.

This was her wedding day. The only wedding day she would have, come to think of it. There had been no flowers, no music, no dressing-up even. She stared wide-eyed into the darkness.

But that was how they had decided they wanted it, under the circumstances. She sighed, and instantly Kit's hand clasped her own. There had been two rows of women at the back of the Chapel, two full rows, and every single woman come to gape, to gossip in the street after it was over. To pity Kit's poor mother shut away in an asylum, and to pity her big son for being such a fool as to marry Maggie Craig, a girl who had gone tarnished to her own wedding.

But Kit had forgiven her. He had said so, and she had shouted at him and defended herself, Maggie remembered with a touch of shame. She had told him how it had been with her and Joe, and she had seen the way his eyes had clouded over with pain. She squeezed Kit's hand.

This was the second time she had lain with her body stretched close to a man's. She closed her eyes and remembered how Joe's hands had caressed her, starting with her face, then tracing the outline of her mouth. How slow his movements had been, stirring her into an aching response. Then he had pushed her blouse from her shoulders, tearing at the buttons, and fastening his lips hungrily over her breast. . . .

Maggie sat up suddenly, staring down at the humped shape that was Kit.

In another minute she would have turned and covered his face with kisses, but it wouldn't have been her husband she was thinking about, it would have been Joe Barton.

Kit was sleeping so soundly, so exhausted, so kind, so *good*. Maggie bet he had never had a wicked thought in his mind, whilst she. . . . Carefully she lay down again, fitted herself back on to his lap, closed her eyes and willed a sleep that would not come. An hour later, with Kit snoring gently into the back of her neck she faced a bewildered truth.

It was her wedding night and her husband was not going to make love to her.

He did not want to, and nor was he going to. He had acted as if they had been married for years and years and were past it.

'I'd think it was funny if I didn't know it wasn't,' Maggie told herself, then she slid quietly out of bed.

Padding bare-footed over to the window, she pushed a corner of the blind aside and looked down into the dark street. Making love wasn't the only thing that mattered, she was ready to admit that.

With Joe it had been wonderful, and joyous, and filled with the ecstasy of giving. Tonight she had not expected or even wished for that. No, it was just that the whole day had been grey, and drab, with no excitement in any part of it.

She rubbed a place clear on the window and narrowed her eyes. For a moment she had thought that someone, a man, had turned the corner from the canal bank . . . but it was a shadow, a trick of the shifting clouds wisping across the dark sky. Maggie let the blind drop back with a click, and immediately Kit was calling out to her.

'Come to bed, lass. What are you doing standing there? You'll catch your death.'

Maggie, shivering now, crept back into the warm hollow she had recently left, facing the window, feeling Kit tuck her in for the second time.

She was the luckiest girl in the world to be married to a man as unselfish and kind as Kit Carmichael. She was . . . oh she was. After what had happened about the baby that nearly was, it would have served her right if no man had ever looked her way again.

And yet, even as she counted her wedding day blessings, she knew that if the shadow down in the street had been a man, and that man had been Joe, then she would have run out of the house in her nightdress to meet him.

There were no two ways about that. . . . .

8

'I'm only human,' Kit told himself aloud when the letter with the London postmark came for Maggie the next week.

Insisting on her lying in bed in the mornings – just till she got her strength up – he caught the postman actually in the act of raising his hand to the door knocker.

'I'll take that,' he said, his pulse beating quicker as he pushed the envelope in his pocket. Then he walked with his light springy step up the street, muttering to himself as he went.

Kit knew who had sent the letter. Maggie had told him that Joe Barton had said he was going to London to seek his fortune. Besides, it was addressed to Maggie *Craig*. He patted the pocket as he crossed the main shopping street, then turned into the hilly web of streets he used as a short cut to the shop, passing late stragglers as they clattered their way down to the mill.

Once in the shop, he went straight through into the back, a small room kept for stores, and bending down set a match to the pile of shavings and wrappings in the grate.

He slid a finger under the flap of the envelope, took out a closely written sheet of paper, saw Joe's name scrawled at the bottom, and tore and tore until the letter was shredded into pieces not much bigger than confetti.

'And that's where they'll go till he stops sending them,' he said aloud, his anger as white-hot as the ashes which crumbled before his gaze. 'Every man Jack of 'em. Every single one!'

Although Wednesday was supposed to be Kit's day off, Mr Yates sometimes sent him down to the wholesale warehouse at the back of the station, preventing him from catching the train to the gaunt asylum built like a medieval prison.

When Mr Yates relented enough to allow his assistant to take what was, after all, no more than his due, three weeks had gone by since Kit's last visit.

'Let me come with you,' Maggie pleaded. 'I would wait outside, but at least I would be with you. I feel strong enough now. An' just look at my hair! It's growing fast!' She pulled hard at a strand. 'I'm getting fat on all that cocoa and the bits you bring home from the shop.' She patted her flat stomach. 'Fat and a lazy so-and-so, that's me.'

She stood in front of him, laughing. 'Do you know, Kit, I've never been as idle in the whole of my life. If the weather turns warm I'll be taking a chair outside and sitting on the flags with Clara and her mother.'

Kit smiled, adoring her, knowing that his Maggie would never do that. She was too ladylike to sit out at the front, and his mother had been just the same. In some ways Maggie reminded him of the way his mother had been a long time ago.

His mother had devoured the newspapers, every single word, and her movements had been quick and certain like Maggie's.

He watched her as she bustled about the room, laying a white cloth over the red chenille on the table, setting out knives and forks, her cheeks pink from the oven.

Aye, she was a grand little wife, and he wasn't going to have her upset by going with him this afternoon. He wasn't going to have her upset by anything, not if he, Kit Carmichael, could help it. . . .

Three hours later, Kit walked back down Foundry Street, a scarf held over his face, praying he could get into the house without being seen. Hoping he could clean himself up a bit before Maggie saw him.

They had tried to make him say he would stop the visits, but he could never say that. How could he when the emaciated, desperate, vicious little creature who had rushed at him, raking her nails down his cheeks, biting, mouthing obscenities, had once been his mother. So caring that she would take him into her own bed, soothing him with whispered words of love when he had the toothache bad?

But it was no use. Maggie was there even as he put his hand on the latch, drawing him inside with a smothered exclamation of horror.

'She did not know what she was doing,' he kept saying, as she bathed the long weals with water, dabbing at them gently. 'They told me she had been quieter for a while, that she had been eating better, and so they stopped giving her the dope for a while.'

Maggie winced as she bathed a nostril that looked as if it had been half torn away.

'You look as if you've been attacked by a wild animal,' she whispered, horrified, shuddering at the clear marking of teeth bites at the side of his neck. 'Maybe she is not as insane as they think? Maybe she has found out somehow that you have married me?'

'How could she do that, love?'

Maggie laid the damp cloth tenderly over a deep scratch. 'I don't know, but they say there's none as astute as the daft.'

Kit bit his lip. 'Sometimes I blame myself for her being in there. Perhaps I should have . . .'

Maggie suddenly exploded. Throwing the cloth down into the bowl of warm water, so that it splashed over the side, she said in her clear voice:

'That is rubbish, Kit! As far as your mother is concerned you have done nothing to reproach yourself for. Nothing!'

Making a mistake, turning his swollen face towards her, Kit tried to explain.

'But I have, love, don't you see? Many a night, without you knowing it, I've laid awake going over what happened that night.' He tried to find the right words. . . . 'To begin with, I was so upset when Arnie came round, I left her all alone in the house, with hardly a proper explanation as to how long I would be.' He put up a hand to his cheek and, wincing, took it quickly away. 'I was that upset, you see.'

'Go on.' Maggie's voice was ominously quiet.

'Then you walked in, hours later. Soaked to the skin and ill. But it must have frightened the life out of her, seeing you. As far as she knew, you had come to torment her.'

Now Maggie's hands were on her hips. '*Torment* her?'

'Aye, it wouldn't have been the first time. There was a girl once, a long time ago, a rather forward sort of girl, and she stopped my mother on her way to the butcher's, and said some awful things. Dreadful, hurting things. My mother had a terrible attack that night.'

Maggie walked over to the fire, bent down and picked up the poker, and found to her surprise that her hand was actually trembling. She dropped it into the hearth with a clatter.

'True things, I suspect, Kit. True, just the same.'

His swollen mouth dropped open into a wide O of amazement.

'What did you say?'

Maggie lifted her head. 'I suspect that girl said a few of the things I should have had the courage to say to you long ago, Kit. Listen to me. . . . Your mother tried to kill me that night. She was out of her mind with fear and jealousy because she thought I was going to take her precious son away from her. She wasn't daft enough or ill enough not to know what to do, was she? If you had not come in when you did I would have died, you've told me that yourself. And she would have won.'

Maggie started to pace up and down, almost beside herself with anger and frustration.

'And I'll tell you something else, Kit Carmichael. I am sick and tired of listening to stories about how wonderful your mother was, how self-sacrificing, how good. How she struggled to make ends meet. Wouldn't any mother do that for her child? Yes, she would, but she would never leave that child her slave for the rest of his life. She would do all that for nothing. *Nothing.* Expecting nothing in return, not even love if it wasn't freely given!'

Kit shifted uncomfortably in his chair, the blood oozing from his nostril again. So overcome with shock to hear her talk like that he let the blood trickle over his chin without raising a hand to mop it away.

Illogically the sight infuriated Maggie even more.

'You know something? You've told me how inconsiderate your father was. How he drank and went with other women; how he used to recite in pubs, and how he went off with a loose woman in the end?'

She gave a fierce little nod of the head. 'Has it ever once occurred to you, that between you, you and your mother emasculated him so much that he had to get away or be diminished?'

'He was a bad sort, Maggie. A real bad penny.'

So worked up that tears of frustration filled her eyes, Maggie stamped her foot.

'Well, it may surprise you to know that from the things I've heard about your father, I've decided I would have liked him. Yes, *liked* him, Kit. An' admired him an' all. An' I hope he spent years and years making passionate love to his lady friend. I hope she had bright red hair, and wore green corsets just to cheer him up, an' I hope they laughed and kissed so that he soon forgot the domineering old cow he'd had for a wife! That's what I hope, Kit Carmichael!'

There was silence for a long moment, then Kit shook his head at her in genuine and honest bewilderment.

'You don't mean any of that now, Maggie. It's upset you seeing me like this. It shows you're nearly better. . . . My mother always used to say that when . . .'

The bowl of water was on the table one minute and in Maggie's hand the next. Then the water was sloshing over Kit's head, running down his scratched face, dripping in rivulets down the towel she had placed with such concern round his neck not ten minutes before.

She stared at his astonished face, at his mouth, wide open like a fish gasping for air. But her anger was not ready to evaporate, not quite yet.

'If I hear once more what your flamin' mother used to say . . . if just once more you try to praise her to me after what she tried to do . . . the next time you'll get the bowl as well!'

Leaving Kit dripping, but with her own dignity intact, Maggie ran upstairs to sit on the edge of the bed, clenching and unclenching her hands, far too upset to cry. When Kit followed her upstairs, leaving the upturned bowl and the pool of water untouched on the floor, there was a new and unexpected urgency in the way he took her in his arms.

'Don't ever shout at me like that again,' he said, laying his swollen cheek against her own. 'I won't go and see my mother again if that is what you want.'

'It isn't what I want,' Maggie said wearily, but now, replacing her spent anger, was a languid tenderness, a floating weariness so filling her with pleasure she lay back and closed her eyes.

'Take my dress off for me, Kit,' she whispered, and his hands undid the buttons neatly, slid the dress from her shoulders, held it as she kicked her legs free of it.

'Now my bodice,' she said, and he started on the smaller buttons, feeling the silkiness of her warm flesh against his fingers.

'I love only you, little sweetheart, you know that. You must know that,' he told her.

'Kiss me here!' Maggie whispered, throwing her head back and pressing his curly head down on to her breasts. 'Kiss me here, *please*.'

And now as his lips caressed her nipples with an exploratory circling movement, the aching weariness spread to her stomach, to her thighs, so that with a fiercely desperate longing she pulled him over so that he lay on top of her. Then she tangled her fingers in his hair and murmured brokenly that she was sorry, that she was truly sorry. . . .

Almost, but not quite, he stopped what he was doing by repeatedly asking her if he was hurting her. Whispering he would stop if he was.

And hearing the apology in his voice, sensing the reluctance in his fumbling movements, Maggie held him tightly, willing him to forget himself and take her properly. Telling him to hurt her, pleading with him silently to assert his manhood, to stop, even in the act of making love, being so . . . maddeningly considerate.

When it was over, and he rolled away from her, still whispering shamed apologies, Maggie closed her ears to him and curled herself up into a ball. His hot face pressed into her neck as he slept, and she tried to remember, to recapture the floating quiet, the gentle feeling of tenderness she had felt for Joe when their love-making had ended. He too had slept, but that was the time she had held his dark head close to her breasts as a languid sweetness flowed through her.

This time she felt unclean, God forgive her. This time she wanted to slide away from him and wash herself all over at the wash-stand in the corner of the room

9

When Maggie told Kit she was sure, quite sure that she was going to have a baby, it put, as he said straight away, a stop to a lot of things.

It put a stop to her going back to the mill as she had been determined to do, and it put a stop to lifting anything heavier than a saucepan – at least when he was around to see.

And it stopped his sporadic attempts to make love to her.

Three or four times, since the row they had had about his mother, since her frustrated rage had forced him to lose control, he had made a valiant attempt, but his heart was not in it.

There was too much of the role of aggressor in the act for him to enjoy it, and the fumbling flabbiness of the part of him that should have been hard and erect, made Maggie imagine that the first time had been a figment of her imagination.

Yet somehow she had conceived, and Kit was showing almost childlike joy in the prospect of being a father. He worked even longer hours, for sometimes as little as an extra shilling in his wages, and his Wednesday afternoon visits to his mother were few and far between now that she no longer recognized him.

When she died, half-way through Maggie's pregnancy, his sadness was tinged with relief, and he told himself that she was better off, that it was a merciful release, repeating to himself the trite phrases trotted out by the Chapel members who remembered her as she used to be.

Considerate and kind as ever, he was careful not to grieve openly in front of his wife, even though she held him in her arms and comforted him. Not because the old woman had died – she was not such a hypocrite as that – but because if Kit was sad then she was sad also.

Yet it seemed to her that old Mrs Carmichael was still there, influencing her son from beyond the grave, Maggie thought one night as Kit held her close to him in bed. He had formed the habit of burrowing his head between the soft curves of her breasts, kissing each one in turn, gently caressing with his hands, groaning with pleasure, but making no attempt to carry his love-making any further.

So Maggie held him, telling herself that as usual, Kit was being his over-considerate self. She held him close, stroking his hair, totally unaware that he was reliving the times his mother had taken him into her bed as a small boy to relieve the stabbing pain of toothache.

'Mother . . .' he whispered to himself.

'Maggie . . .' he sighed aloud.

Three more letters came with the London postmark before Maggie's baby was born, and Kit destroyed each one of them. He burnt them without guilt in the fire at the back of the shop, and when they stopped coming he rejoiced.

'I've done the right thing, the only thing. No good upsetting her while she's like she is,' he muttered.

So fascinated was he by all the medical details of her pregnancy that he would kneel down on the rag rug, and lay his head against her stomach as she sat by the fire.

'I can feel it kicking!' he would say.

'The very minute you start in labour you must send to the shop for me,' he told her over and over again. 'I want to be there to look after you before the midwife comes. Think on and don't forget then.'

Maggie promised, but when, on a cold morning, with the wind rattling the frames of the sash windows till she thought they would drop out, her first pains began, the first thing she wanted was for Kit to be gone from the house. She managed somehow to keep her expression calm when the dragging sensation in her back made her want to moan. She prayed for it to be time for him to go downstairs and light the fire, and when he brought the usual cup of tea upstairs she took it from him and smiled.

'You had a bad night, didn't you, love?' he said, his face anxious and worried.

'The wind kept me awake,' she told him.

When he had gone she got out of bed, pulled a shawl round her shoulders and going downstairs knocked on the wall for Clara.

'It'll be a long time yet,' Clara said with the wisdom of a woman, with the know-all of a woman who had never given birth to a child.

'It won't.' Maggie shook her head, holding on to a corner of the table, her face draining of colour. 'I've been at it a long time.'

'And Kit's gone and left you to go to the shop?' Clara's eye shot straight down into its socket. 'That doesn't sound like him. You'd have thought it was him having the baby the way he's been carrying on.'

'I didn't tell him. I don't want fussing.' Maggie opened the bottom drawer of the chest and took out a pile of baby clothes, setting them out on the fireguard to air. 'And I don't want the midwife yet either. All I want at the moment is a nice cup of tea, Clara.'

'He would only have been in the way,' she told Clara's mother three hours later in the little front bedroom, clenching her teeth as she pulled hard on a roller towel fastened to the bottom of the bed.

'No, he's done his bit, and anyway it's no place for a man,' Mrs Hobkirk agreed, wiping the sweat from Maggie's forehead then going to sit by the fire.

The fire had been lit in the tiny grate in honour of the occasion, a smouldering fire that did little else but belch clouds of smoke into the room.

'You're going on nicely, love,' Mrs Hobkirk told Maggie from time to time. 'It's with being country bred like as not.'

Maggie caught her breath as pain gripped, and clamped her teeth down on her bottom lip to stop herself from crying out.

What she could not accept, what she must *not* accept, was that the other baby, Joe's baby, that half-formed embryo, had meant more to her than this full-term one did. Then, that awful time, she had been alone, all alone, not surrounded by attention and care, with the baby's things airing downstairs and a binder all ready to be wrapped round her stomach once the baby was born.

This baby had everything, and Joe's baby, the little one that had never had a chance, had had nothing. She drew up her legs and whimpered as another pain caught her unawares.

'I think it's time to send for the nurse,' she said quietly, 'and then perhaps Arnie could go and tell Kit. He'll never forgive me if it's all over when he comes home.'

'I was a full two days with our Clara, then it had to be the forceps,' Mrs Hobkirk said, but when Nurse O'Mara came into the house, taking charge even before she had climbed the stairs, she was able to tell Maggie that her baby had black hair.

'You left it long enough,' she scolded Mrs Hobkirk, then she turned her attention to Maggie.

'Right, love. Hang on to my pinny if you want to. Come on now! Right! That's a good girl!'

And as Kit opened the front door, the first real sound that Maggie had uttered, froze him to the spot with terror.

'How long has she been like that?' he demanded, glaring at Clara who was taking the kettle from the trivet, and starting with it for the stairs.

'Give that to me,' he ordered, his manners forgotten completely.

He had just reached the tiny landing when he heard the baby cry, a full-blown howl of outraged fury. Stopping transfixed in the doorway, the kettle still miraculously in his hand, he saw the nurse holding his daughter by the ankles and giving her a resounding slap between her shoulder blades.

'Get that man out of here!'

Nurse O'Mara's voice had the authority of a woman doing a woman's job, and Clara's mother, enjoying every minute, walked over to Kit, took the kettle from him with one hand, and with the other firmly closed the door in his face.

'How *dare* he!' Nurse O'Mara said, handing over the baby, and bending over the bed again. 'In all me born days that's the first man, not counting the doctor, who has ever set a foot in his wife's room before I've got her all tidied up like. Whatever is the world coming to?'

'Is the baby perfect?' Maggie's voice whispered from the rumpled bed.

'A fine girl, love,' the nurse said. 'Now just do as I tell you, and then you can see for yourself.'

'It wasn't all that bad,' Maggie said, lifting both arms above her head only to have them smartly pulled down by the nurse.

'No raising your arms my goodness me,' she said, reaching for the pile of newspapers at the foot of the bed. 'If all my mothers had an easy time as you've had, love, there'd be nothing for me to do. May you go on and have a dozen if they all come as easy as this one.'

'Catholic,' Mrs Hobkirk said with a sniff when the nurse had gone downstairs with the baby in her arms, bound and swaddled so tightly her tiny face had turned purple. 'A dozen indeed! They'd like that just so they can take us over. I've never had a good word for the Pope ever since that Bernadette Cleary from the top house used to cross herself every time she saw our Clara.'

Maggie raised heavy eyelids in silent enquiry.

'Because of her eye,' Mrs Hobkirk explained, tucking the bedclothes in so firmly that Maggie feared her ankles would never revert to their normal position again. 'Superstitious rubbish, that's all their religion is.'

'It's a girl, Mr Carmichael,' Nurse O'Mara said, standing before Kit and showing him the baby. 'A bonny little girl. Small to be sure, but with a pair of lungs on her like the six o'clock hooter.'

Kit looked at the tiny squashed face, at the blood-red pressure marks on the snub nose, at the forehead creased into lines of anxiety. Tears gathered in his eyes and rolled down his cheeks. All along he had been convinced that his Maggie would have a girl. He had seen himself walking up the street with a bouncy little girl holding on to his hand, staring up at him in adoration.

Kit didn't like little boys. The boys who played out in the street round the lamp standards were dirty and noisy, and often shouted rude things after him. They had black fingernails and permanent bruises on their knees and they played all the rough and tumble games he had never wanted to play.

'When can I see my wife?'

His tone was suitably humble and Nurse O'Mara, knowing she had asserted her authority and won, said he could go up straight away.

'We will call her Rose, because that is what she is, a perfect pink beautiful rose.' He looked at his wife and his daughter with the expression of a man who has just seen a miracle, and Maggie looked down at the tiny face, at the twitching eyelids and the furiously sucking lower lip.

There was nothing rose-like about this baby who stared cross-eyed up at her with the picking glance of the dead and buried Mrs Carmichael.

'She's like your mother,' she said, then closed her eyes before she could see the pleasure on Kit's happy face.

10

When the baby was almost four months old, the annual fair came to the town, and Maggie, on the evening of Kit's Wednesday off, suggested that they took the sleeping baby next door and then walked down to the market-place.

'Fairs are filthy places, full of gyppos,' Kit said, busy with the pipe he had taken to smoking, striking one match after another instead of using the tapers Maggie had placed in a jar in the hearth.

'Kit Carmichael,' she said, standing before him with her head on one side, and her eyes bird-bright. 'If I do not get out of this house I will die of boredom. No, I won't. I will run round this room pulling the pictures down from the walls. I will take the pots from the dresser and smash them one by one on the floor, and I will jump on the table and do a clog-dance in my bare feet. I will!'

She plumped herself down on his knees, setting the rocking chair into motion, leaning back, the narrow band round the neck of her dress unbuttoned to reveal the line of her throat, and the soft swell of her breasts.

'Kit, oh, Kit, do you never want to burst out of yourself and *do* something mad? Anything? Just to relieve your feelings?'

'Not really,' Kit said honestly.

He glanced down at her with affection, and thought what a child she was. In spite of her baby daughter asleep in her cradle upstairs, in spite of her growing hair pinned up into the semblance of a tiny bun with little tendrils escaping from it. As unlike most of the women who came into the shop as chalk from cheese.

Drabs most of them, with shawls round their heads and clogs on their feet, their babies fed on condensed milk at two tins for threepence-halfpenny. Terrible managers of money, unlike his Maggie who could make fourpence do the work of a shilling, and then have something left over.

He bent his head, and holding his pipe well away, kissed her gently at the side of her mouth.

'Kiss me *properly*!' Maggie gripped him fiercely to her. 'Pretend I am a beautiful woman with long red hair.' She pulled at a strand of her shortened hair and found that it just reached her mouth. 'This is the way I measure it every day. Look, Kit, soon it will reach my right ear and then soon I will be able to put it up into a proper bun, not a little scraggy thing like a hen's backside.'

He pretended to be shocked and failed.

'What if Clara comes in?' He shifted uncomfortably. 'She's in before you can blink.'

'She always calls out first,' Maggie reminded him. 'Yoo-hoo!' she called, in such an exact imitation of Clara's loud and ringing voice that Kit laughed in spite of himself.

Maggie got up from his knee, unkissed and restless.

'I don't like the way Clara comes in like that,' she confessed. 'I never have, but she has been so kind to me I would not dream of saying anything. Once I even tried putting the bolt on the front door, but she just came round the back.

' "What have you locked the door for? You been up to summat I don't know about?" she asked me, straight out. Kit. Let's go to the fair. Just to look, then?'

Knowing when he was beaten, Kit knocked out his pipe and went to fetch his jacket.

'All right then, Maggie, but not for long now. Bring the baby down and we'll go to the fair.'

Then, as he was enveloped in a bear-hug that almost knocked him off his feet, he smiled.

'I don't know about you wanting to put your hair up. It strikes me the way you behave it would suit you better floating down your back. Strikes me you're not old enough to behave like a married lady. . . .'

There was no need to risk waking the baby to take her in next door, because Clara offered at once to come in and sit.

'Arnie's gone out again,' she grumbled. 'So I might as well sit in your house as in me own. He's gone up to the Mother Redcap, to play dominoes he says, but he'll come back smelling like a brewery and swear he's had nowt but a pint of ale. I'd think he'd got himself another woman if I thought he had it in him.'

'Poor Clara,' Maggie said, as with her arm linked into Kit's, they set off for the market-place.

It was a warm evening, an evening anticipatory with the soft warmth of the summer yet to come. Maggie wore the hat with the daisies sewn back on to the wide brim, her navy-blue coat, and her much darned gloves buttoned neatly into place. Her eyes sparkled with excitement, and when they saw the fair, lit to splendour by naptha-lights, and when they passed the caravans and the weather-stained tents, she gripped Kit's arm even more tightly.

'Once, when I was a little girl, my father took me to a fair, and one of the fair-ground men took us inside his caravan, and I have never forgotten it. There were white muslin curtains with pink bows, and the beds were like berths on a ship.'

Then as the thought of ships came into her mind, her face was still, all the vivacity gone from it. 'Do you know, Kit, there are whole days now when I never even think about my brothers. I don't want to forget them, but I will, I know.' She looked up at him earnestly. 'Oh, Kit, doesn't it make you think that we owe it to ourselves to make the most of every day, of every minute, because we never know what is going to happen, do we?'

Used to her rapid change of mood and unable to follow

her swift and emotional reasoning most of the time, Kit
patted the hand that lay on his arm.

'What a life for the fair people,' he said, wishing he was
back home already. 'Packing all night, then moving on to
another town. Collecting the horses from the inns they've
been stabled at, and moving on. Not putting down roots,
like us.' He smiled at his wife's glowing face. 'Not lucky
like us.'

He held even more tightly to Maggie's arm, afraid to let
her move away from his side by as much as an inch.
Convinced that all the riff-raff of the town and the surrounding countryside were there that evening at the fair.
Men with weasel faces, caps pulled down over shifty eyes,
factory girls with their high shrill laughter as they moved
from one side-show to another, linking arms. Fathers, who
should have known better, in his opinion, with small boys
riding piggy-back, the night women with raddled faces,
and over there by the Bioscope, a woman known as the
town's oldest whore, with only half a nose.

Maggie was pulling him towards a pea-boiling cart, the
steam rising from its cauldron, then on to a hot-potato cart,
the coals glowing red and the box of salt suspended from
the side.

'Please, Kit,' she pleaded, and much against his better
judgement, Kit handed over a penny and received in a
double fold of newspaper, six small potatoes, roasted in
their skins.

Then, as a father would indulge a beloved child, he
watched as his wife unbuttoned her gloves, handed them
over to him for safe keeping, and smiling broadly at the
man in charge of the cart, put her hand into the salt-box
and sprinkled the potatoes carefully, one by one.

'Oh!' she fanned her mouth with a hand. 'They're red-
hot, but you don't know what you are missing, Kit.'

Just to please her, he took one, averting his eyes from the
potato man's dirty hands, their nails broken and black-
rimmed. His fastidious nature winced at the indignity, and

what his mother would have called the 'commonness' of it all.

Never taking his eyes from Maggie's straight little back, he followed her reluctantly to a side-show where the dancing ladies shook their tambourines and wiggled their hips in time to tinny music from the hurdy-gurdy.

There was a man, a young, bold-looking man with a shock of jet-black hair, and a face as brown as a hazel-nut, standing on the makeshift platform, calling out to the crowd.

'Feast your eyes, ladies and gentlemen!' he shouted. 'What you are seeing now is nothing to what you will see if you come inside the tent. Straight from a London music-hall every man Jack of 'em. Chorus girls, ladies and gentlemen, in between their London engagements, and here to delight you with their abandoned dancing!' He winked at Maggie. 'Talk about the Can-Can. This little lot make the Can-Can seem like a ruddy minuet done in their sleep.' Unable to take her eyes off him, and seeing Joe Barton in the tilt of the black head, the boldness of the laughing eyes, Maggie pulled at Kit's sleeve.

'Let's go in,' she said, a hot potato half-way to her mouth.

Kit took her arm and tried to pull her away, but she stood firm.

'There aren't any ladies going in,' he pointed out, trying not to look at a blown-up picture of a girl lifting her skirts to show a wide expanse of bare leg encircled by a frilly garter.

'I've heard they don't wear no bloomers,' a man's voice said into a sudden silence, and the dark young man threw back his head, showing a strong line of throat as he burst into uninhibited laughter.

'Come in and see for yourself, mister,' he called out.

Although Maggie had given no sign of having heard, Kit saw that she had turned scarlet, and made no protest when he led her away.

'They're not like the Romanies who used to come round

to the house selling pegs,' she conceded, and Kit, taking advantage of her hesitation, handed her his clean handkerchief to wipe her hands, then the gloves, pulling her into the shadow of a tent as he helped her to button them on again.

'I *told* you you wouldn't like it, love,' he said.

She lifted her head and stared straight into his eyes.

'I *could* like it,' she flared, then biting her lips, was silent again.

What she had almost said was: 'I could have liked it if you had not been here spoiling it all for me.'

For a long moment they stood together, Kit miserably uncomfortable in surroundings he hated and mistrusted, and Maggie restlessly defiant, craving something she could not put a name to. Something far more than the loud blaring music, the happy, pushing crowd, the vulgarity of it all.

'Go home!' she wanted to shout at Kit. 'Leave me to be myself again! To be young again. To be winked at by the man with black hair who reminded me of Joe, to eat hot peas doused in vinegar, and brandysnaps straight from the bag.' She clasped her gloved hands together, the music filling her senses, almost as if it were a part of her.

'Let's go on the horses, Kit . . . oh, please. I haven't been on a roundabout since I can't remember.'

'It's coming on to rain,' Kit said, presenting his face with relief to the sky. 'I said it would.'

Even the fair people raced for shelter as the cloudburst caught them unawares, and within minutes the whole glittering display of stalls looked like some dingy squalid ruin, with tent flaps whipping back against the canvas in the strong wind. Girls squealed as their boots slithered and slipped over the greasy cobblestones.

Quickly Kit, with his arm protectively round Maggie, guided her across the road flanking the ground, and pulled her into the shelter of a wooden booth, specially set up for the three days of the fair.

'Let's go inside,' Maggie said, clinging on to his arm with one hand and hanging on to her hat with the other.

'Oh, Kit, it's not a public house. It's only a place set up just for the fair, and anyway, I haven't signed the Pledge, remember?'

'It's not right,' Kit kept saying, as sitting opposite to his wife round an upturned barrel, he watched her sipping a glass of ale, her eyes blazing with excitement, missing nothing as she watched the people crowding in out of the rain, the men shaking the raindrops from their caps, and calling out to each other.

'To think all this is going on while I sit at home with my sewing round the fire!' she marvelled.

'This place only has a three-day licence,' Kit reminded her, his face registering a mixture of pride in the attention she was attracting, and apprehension at what she might do next.

'I know. I know, Kit. But look over there. That little man hardly able to stand up is one of the door-keepers at the Teetotal Mission! It is him, it is, and oh, Kit, he's as drunk as a lord. Don't you think that's funny?'

'No,' Kit said, jumping up with dismay as the man, an old soldier, and a supposedly reformed character, started to weave his unsteady way towards them. 'Come on, we're going home,' he said.

The rain had stopped as quickly as it had started, and the stall-holders were taking the covers off the trays of ginger-bread, the Eccles cakes, the nuts and the brandy-snaps.

'Let's buy some and take them home for Clara,' Maggie said.

But Kit had had enough.

'We're going home,' he repeated stubbornly. 'How you could think that old man in there was funny, I don't know. He was maudlin and slavvery, and he reminded me of the way my father used to look when he had been drinking. Leering and then being sick over everything, and my mother having to mop up after him. You don't know what it was like, or what we had to suffer because he went in places like that!'

Maggie stared at him in astonishment.

'But we weren't going to get drunk, Kit. Just because you don't approve of something doesn't mean you have to run away from it.' She tripped and would have fallen but for his steadying hand.

'Not so quickly, Kit. I can't keep up.'

'That man made me feel sick,' Kit said.

Maggie stared at him. 'Kit, what's wrong? How do we know what that poor old man went through when he was serving his time in the army? He's old enough to have fought in the Crimean War. How do we know that just for once he wanted to sing and shout and pretend he wasn't cold and alone, with nobody left to care for him?'

'You just don't know what you are talking about,' Kit said.

He was walking along with his head bent as if the rain was still beating down. 'And look at you, Maggie Carmichael. Sitting there amongst them. *Enjoying* yourself!'

Maggie stopped dead so that he had to turn and face her. In her anger she slipped into dialect.

'Aye. Enjoying meself, Kit. Just for once enjoying meself.' She stamped her foot. 'I know what you would like to do.'

'And what is that?'

'Wrap me up in cotton-wool, and shut me up in the house like a prisoner. You don't even like me going to the market. You'd like me to be like me father, sitting by the fire, and only smelling the fresh air when I put me nose outside the back door. Wouldn't you?'

'Don't talk daft.'

'You're the one what's daft, not me,' Maggie answered childishly, hearing herself being childish, and not being able to stop herself.

Now the sounds of the fairground were receding, and

Maggie turned her head once or twice, but in silence, with his hand firmly on her arm, Kit urged her along.

His sense of what was right and proper kept him talking to Clara after Maggie had rushed upstairs to the bedroom.

'Had a few words, have you?'

Kit nodded miserably, knowing there was no point in taking offence at Clara when none was meant.

She came over to where he sat slumped in his chair and patted his shoulder.

'Aye, well, she's young, Mr Carmichael, and she's had a rough time taken all in all. She's different, tha knows.' Clara touched the side of her head with a stubby finger. 'Plenty up there, tha knows.'

Kit raised his head and stared at Clara's bland uninteresting face set above her thick neck, and saw the compassion in her sliding eye.

'I can't seem to follow what she's getting at sometimes, Mrs Preston,' he confided.

Clara sniffed. 'If she wants to go back in the mill I'd allus have the baby to mind. We'd manage her between us, me mother and me.'

Kit shook his head. 'There's no need for that, Mrs Preston. I'm not having my wife going out to work, not as long as I can provide.'

'Suit yourself,' Clara said, huffed, but determined not to show it.

When Kit went into the bedroom Maggie was undressed and sitting up in bed with a grey-fringed shawl round her shoulders, feeding the baby.

He hovered in the doorway, uncertain what to say or do next, getting no lead from his wife, her face hidden by the fall of brown hair, long enough now to cover her eyes.

'I'll take the nappy downstairs and put it on soak, and fetch your cocoa,' he said in a humble tone.

'Thank you,' Maggie said. 'You are very kind.'

The completely detached tone of her voice hurt him so much that he went to sit by her on the bed, his weight causing the mattress to sag down as usual. He stared at her in misery, biting his lip.

It was no good, he could not bear it when she was funny with him, like this. He had not been able to bear it when his mother had been cross with him either. It left him stranded and unsure of himself, unsure of anything.

'Are you not speaking to me?' he asked, putting out a hand towards her. 'Are we not friends, then?'

Maggie sighed and took her time about prizing the fiercely sucking mouth from her breast. The blue veins contrasted with the whiteness of her skin, and in spite of his misery Kit felt the stirrings of a kind of desire. He knew a sudden sharp jealousy, a hatred almost for the baby, its head lolling back on a neck that appeared to be broken, milk dribbling down its rounded chin.

'All right then, I'll tell you,' he said, his voice sounding alien even to his own ears.

'Tell me what?' Maggie said with studied indifference, moving the baby over to the other side.

'I'll tell you why I wanted you home, and quick. Because I saw that gyppo looking at you and winking at you. Him shouting the odds about those girls being chorus girls and coming from London.' He snorted with disgust. 'London! That lot have never been no further than Todmorden. Dirty fast little pieces, and as for him, I saw him staring at you with his eyes standing out like chapel hat-pegs, an' I saw you smile at him, and wink back. So don't deny it. An' another thing. He reminded you of someone, another one with a cheeky grin. You think I've forgotten, but I haven't. You think I'm daft, but I'm not. I have feelings like anybody else.'

'Oh, Kit. . . .' Maggie smoothed her daughter's round head, her hand moving in a gentle circular movement that quickened Kit's heart-beats. 'That boy reminded me of when I was a little girl and the Romanies used to camp on the edge of the wood.' She refused to meet his eyes lest he saw that she was lying. 'I remembered a young man just like him who rode with his family on a cart pulled by a painfully thin donkey. I was fetching the milk and he winked at me, and when I tried to wink back he burst out laughing.' She lifted the baby and held her over a shoulder. 'There now, she's drunk herself to sleep.

'Never be jealous, Kit,' she whispered later, 'but I like it when you are. I do.' She wound her arms round his neck, and bewildered by the frenzy of her passion, half aware that even as he struggled to comply, she was thinking of the man at the fair, Kit moved away from her as soon as it was over.

He didn't want to look at his wife, because he did not like what he saw. This was not the young girl with daisies on her hat, and the demure expression that could change in a flash to twinkling mischief. This was a flushed and beautiful woman, eyelids heavy over dream-filled slumbering eyes.

'You won't have another baby on account of you're feeding,' he muttered, backing away from the bed, and tripping over the worn oilcloth by the door. 'But we'd best be careful . . . I'm not having you knocked up again, not just when you're picking up.' He rubbed his finger across his chin, wondering how he could put it best.

'So I'll go through into the back. The bed's made up. It's only fair . . . only fair.'

And as he slid between cold sheets in the single bed in the room where Thomas Craig had killed himself, he failed to hear his wife's muffled sobs as she wept for a man she never thought to see again.

Only one letter came from Joe Barton during the next year, and Kit marked the envelope NOT KNOWN AT THIS ADDRESS, and posted it back into the letter-box.

Rose walked before she was one, but made no attempt at

talking, and Maggie, exhausted by the tantrums of the little doll-like child who would throw herself on the floor, kicking and screaming if her will was denied, took her to the doctor to ask him if her daughter was tongue-tied.

'She'll be talking your heads off. You won't be able to get a word in edgeways,' the doctor reassured Maggie, smiling at her anxious concern.

'Her father seems to be able to understand the sounds she makes,' Maggie told him, prizing a pencil from off the doctor's desk out of Rose's twitching fingers.

Darting a look of uncontrolled fury at her mother from beneath black eyebrows, Rose immediately flung herself backwards on to the doctor's carpet, kicking her heels in noisy fury.

'Sometimes I think the devil himself gets into her,' Maggie apologized, scooping up her daughter and carrying her, still kicking, out of the surgery.

I I

The death of Queen Victoria in 1901 – t'owd Queen, as Kit's customers called her, was commemorated by every column in the local paper being outlined with a thick black line.

'Today,' the paper's readers were told, 'the nation is mourning the loss of the best Sovereign in British History.' They were also told that when the Queen came to the throne sixty-four years ago, her people were neither educated or free.

'Aye,' Kit said when Maggie pointed that bit out to him. 'That's true enough.'

Her answer was to raise her eyebrows in eloquent exasperation.

'Kit Carmichael! When will you learn not to swallow every word you see in print? Do you really believe that the majority of the people in this town are both educated and free? What chance have most of your customers had to take advantage of what little knowledge they got from school when they go straight into the factory to work as unskilled labourers?'

She faced him squarely. Up on her soap-box, he thought with amusement, eyes flashing and determined chin jutting forward.

'How much do you get for the hours you work in Mr Yates's shop? A pound for six days a week from seven till sometimes eleven o'clock at night!' Her fierce expression softened as she looked at him.

It wasn't fair to shout at this mild and gentle man, whose

voice was so rarely raised in anger that she had to laugh out loud when it was.

She sighed. It was just that it got her down sometimes thinking of that Mr Yates with his long face and a beard on him like a billy-goat, counting his takings in the upstairs room.

'Most weeks, like last, we only took eight pounds,' Kit reminded her, 'and most of that in halfpennies and farthings. It's a right run-down area, Maggie. Most of the men, even when they are in full-time work, don't bring home more than fifteen shillings.'

'And some of that gone in the pub on their way home of a Saturday dinner-time,' she said, quick as a flash.

Kit sighed at her, loving her even as he sighed. His mother had been right when she had weighed up his future wife at that very first meeting round her sick bed.

'A bonny lass, but too cheeky,' she'd said, and yet, if she had still been alive, surely she would have had to agree that little Maggie Craig had made him a grand wife.

Not a needlewoman by nature or inclination, Maggie had borrowed a barrow from a man across the street, and trundled a second-hand sewing-machine home from the market. From then on she had made all their clothes, even his shirts, and even if they never seemed to fit properly round the neck, who was he to grumble?

She was so restless she had to be doing something, and if it had not been sewing for them and plain sewing for the neighbours, it might have been putting the child out to mind with Clara next door while she went back in the mill.

He had put his foot down about that, right from the beginning.

If only she didn't have such radical ideas. Kit sighed again. He himself was a staunch Conservative, his principles being nurtured by the contempt his mother had passed on to him for the large community of Irish Catholics living

167

in the area round the shop. They, almost to a man, supported the Liberals, whilst Maggie, refusing to conform as usual, supported a party of her own.

The 'Underdogs', Kit called them privately.

At the moment it was the poor bedraggled British Army fighting the Boers, staining, as she put it dramatically, the hills and plains of South Africa red with their flowing blood.

'It is not a matter women should concern themselves with,' Kit had said, shamed into remonstrating one summer evening when they came back from a meeting of the Chapel Elders.

To his horror his wife had stood up and asked in her clear cool voice if it was not a cause for the deepest concern that over sixty per cent of the recruits to the army from the north of England had been turned down because they were not physically fit?

'Sixty per cent!' she declared. 'And what do they mean by physically fit but suffering from malnutrition? You should ask my husband here about the tramps who come into his shop of a night pleading for a penny, whilst there are those who can eat twenty-one courses at one meal. Boasting of it whilst their fellow-men die of hunger in the streets! A fine start to the twentieth century for a country that is supposed to be the finest in the world!'

'Why do you bother yourself about things you can do nothing about?' he asked her, puffing at his pipe, only to find it had gone out.

At once Maggie leaned forward, lighting a taper at the fire and passing it over to him, the wifely gesture giving him the courage to say what he had had a mind to say for a long time.

'Maggie, lass. Why do you have to be at everybody's beck and call in the street? Why is it they come for you when they can't afford the doctor? We've got a child of our own,' he went on, retiring behind a screen of smoke. 'Running about as fit as a fiddle. But for how long? How long when you spent all one night last week sitting up with that little lad in the end house, knowing all the time he was dying of the cough?'

He was trying very hard to make her see, but without the sensitivity to choose the right words.

'Surely you remember what happened with your own mother? She picked up the diphtheria from somebody else's child and went on to die through it. My mother always used to say that charity began at home.'

Too late he knew he had gone too far. He wished with all his heart he could bite back what he had just said, and he knew too that to say he was sorry would only infuriate Maggie more.

Walking with her light step over to the dresser, she took down two pots for their nightly cocoa. Carefully she stirred sugar, cocoa and a drop of milk into each pot, mixing them to a smooth paste. Then she lifted the heavy black kettle from the fire, and filled them up to the brim. He waited, outwardly calm, knowing inwardly the explosion that must surely come.

'No, I don't forget my own mother, Kit Carmichael,' she said, handing over his drink, 'and by all that's holy you don't forget yours either, do you?'

Sitting down opposite to him Maggie curled her hands round the pot. 'Though how can you be expected to forget yours when Rose is turning into the living spit? I'll tell you something I've never said to you before, but sometimes when she looks at me it is as though your mother has come back in her. In fact if I were a fanciful sort of woman I'd say that was exactly what has happened. She's only a bairn, but already she knows how to play me off against you, and you fall for it. Every time. I tell her she can't have something; she runs straight to you and you give her what she wants . . . oh yes, you do.'

'I don't see all that much of her, not with the hours I work, do I, lass?'

Kit's voice was mild. He knew, and secretly rejoiced in

the fact that his little daughter was the image of his mother. Small-faced and gypsy dark, it was as though some mischievous plan had reproduced his mother in exact miniature. Like his mother, Rose was afraid of nothing, would stop at nothing to get her own way, and like his mother, bestowed on him an adoration it would have taken a stronger man to resist.

Maggie was banking up the fire for the night, taking it for granted that was her job, but he could see from her back that she was still angry.

'I wish you wouldn't encourage her to come into your bed, Kit. Now she's in her own little bed she's out and across the top of the stairs into your room before I can stop her.' Maggie pushed her hair away from her fire-flushed face. 'It's not right a bairn sleeping with her father. It's not healthy.'

'I'm just going out to the back,' Kit said, taking the easy way out as usual. 'You go on up. I'll see to the door and the fire-guard.'

Once again, by taking the line of least resistance, he had won. Maggie braided her hair in the front bedroom, still from force of habit tugging at it to make it grow. She noticed that even in her sleep Rose twitched and jerked, as if wondering what mischief she could get up to next. Holding the candle-flame well away, Maggie stared down at her small daughter.

Could people come back from the grave to torment the living? Was the dead Mrs Carmichael trying to punish her for daring to marry her beloved son? Frustrated once in her attempt to kill Maggie, was she now here again, living with them in the house, making trouble between them the way children could alienate husband and wife?

Blowing out the candle Maggie got into bed, heard Kit come upstairs with his light tread, and heard him go into the room that had been her father's. She heard one boot drop to the floor, then the other, heard the springs of the bed creak as he got into bed, and knew that for the first time since their wedding day he was going to sleep without having said goodnight.

A funny old marriage theirs was turning out to be. Wife in one room, and husband in the other. Their child, and what promised to be their *only* child, growing up disliking her own mother. Because it was true . . . God help her, but it was true.

Tears gathered in Maggie's eyes to roll sideways into her hair and on to the pillow as she faced the truth. Always one for facing the truth she faced it now. The dislike between them, mother and child, was mutual. God forgive her, but it was. There were times when she understood how mothers, unable to stand the screaming tantrums, the whining defiance, landed out and half killed their own child.

She wondered how it would have been with the other one, the child who had died before it had had a chance to live: Joe's child. But the thing was settled. No baby and no Joe, and she was wasting her time crying because crying never got nobody nowhere.

12

In 1905, when Rose was a sullen and secretive child just starting school, Joe Barton came back to the town to see his sister Belle.

When she first opened the door to him, she wanted to cry. She was wearing the white cap and apron her mistress liked her to wear, even though the house was only a semi-detached villa at the end of a cul-de-sac. Joe thought she looked even more washed out and servile than she had as a child.

She fidgeted nervously with the corner of her apron as she stood aside to let him in.

'Mrs Armitage has gone out for her tea, so she said we could sit in the parlour when I told her you was coming. Come in and see how nice everything is, but rub your feet on the mat first.'

She led the way down a narrow hall, made even smaller by a round table bearing an assortment of plants, into a room at the front of the house, a room with a bay window shrouded by net curtains.

If she had not said that about him wiping his feet on the mat, she would have broken down and flung her arms round him, but the only time she remembered having physical contact with her brother was when they had slept together. In houses where they had stayed only long enough to get into arrears with the rent before doing a moonlight flit.

'Sit you down then.' She pointed to a chair covered in plum plush velvet. 'It's nice, isn't it?'

Obligingly Joe looked round the over-furnished room, at

the oilcloth patterned with squares filled with baskets of flowers, and at the mantle-cover scalloped and bobbled.

'Aye, it's nice,' he said, then he smiled directly at her, and it was still the same Joe, the same laughing teasing Joe, who had stolen the money just for her, then had to go away rather than face the consequences.

'You got my letter?' she asked, sitting down opposite to him with her hands folded in her lap. 'The minister wrote it for me.' She frowned. 'Well, at least the minister's *wife* wrote it for me.'

'Aye, I got it.'

It was strange, Joe thought, how in spite of the fact that Belle had received practically the same intermittent schooling as himself, she had never managed to pick her letters up.

There was a sadness filling his heart that made him want to clench his fists and beat them on the arms of his plush chair. She was so *old*, this little sister of his. His half-sister from what his mother had once let slip. So prim and proper, with her small feet in their laced-up boots crossed at the ankles. So much a stranger. He smiled at her again.

'Our mam went quick-like,' she said. 'It was the drink. She choked in her sleep.'

Joe stared at the brightly coloured flooring.

'I never wanted to go away, Belle. You know that.'

She shook her head. 'You had to go, Joe, and from how you look you're doing all right. That suit didn't come from no pawn shop.'

'No, it didn't, love.' He smiled at her again, thinking that was all they seemed to be bloody doing, sitting smiling at each other and thinking of things to say.

'I have me own room,' she said, and he saw the pride shining in her pale eyes.

'Want to take me up to see it, love?' His eyes teased. 'I am your brother, you know. It wouldn't be rude.'

Belle stood up, the desire to show off the first room of her own she had ever had too much for her.

'Carpet on the stairs,' she pointed out, bending down to feel it as she went before up the narrow stairway. 'There's a WC downstairs, just through the scullery. You don't have to go out to the back.'

She opened a door off the landing into a room sparsely furnished by a bed, a wardrobe, a chest of drawers, and a wash-hand stand with a towel on the rail and a jug and soap dish standing on top. On the wall was a framed text bearing the words: 'Be sober and hope to the end. (Peter 1 Verse 13)', and on the floor a rag rug, pegged by herself, she told him.

'I come up here after I've cleared the tea-things away, then I am free until it's time to go down and make Mr and Mrs Armitage their bedtime cups of Horlicks.'

'And one for you?' Joe asked.

Her eyes opened wide with surprise.

'Of course not, our Joe. Do you know how much Horlicks costs?'

He shook his head at her. 'What you want to do is make enough for two do for three. Mrs Armitage doesn't mark the bloody jar, does she?'

Belle put her finger to her lips, staring at the open door, a door she had left open deliberately, for it would never have done to close it, not with a man in the room, even if he was her brother.

'Ee, I couldn't do a thing like that, Joe. It would be like stealing.'

Joe scratched his head. 'Belle Barton! What about all those times we pinched things off the stalls down the market? You could shove an apple under your shawl quicker than anyone I know. And what about that time when some of the neighbours hived off a sheep from the flock passing the end of our street? Who was it held our back door open? And who was it went round selling cut pieces of lamb till all the street reeked of the smell of roasting meat? You gone holy or something?'

'The Lord Jesus has saved me,' Belle said, folding her top lip tightly over the lower. 'Mr and Mrs Armitage would never have taken me on if I hadn't come from a good Christian family.'

At that Joe threw back his head and laughed out loud.

'A good Christian family? Well, bugger me. That takes the bloody cake that does!'

'You still swear too much, our Joe,' Belle said, more in sorrow than anger.

Just for a minute Joe thought she was having him on, until he remembered that this slight serious little sister of his never had anyone on. He stared round the tiny room, at its stark respectability, at the framed text on the wall, at Belle's house slippers sitting neatly by the side of the bed, and at the Bible he knew she could not read, placed dead centre of the bedside table, its marker spilling out on to the lace-edged cover.

His sister's blue eyes were searching his face, pleading with him not to spoil all this splendour for her, beseeching him not to make fun of her. Willing him, he had to accept, to go away before her precious Mrs Armitage came back.

'You haven't even asked me where I'm stopping,' he asked with mock reproach. 'Or even how long holiday I've got.'

'Where *are* you stopping, Joe?'

She was leading the way downstairs, running her hand lovingly over the highly polished wood of the banister rail. Showing by that give-away gesture that this little house with its modest furnishings had filled a void in her heart that nothing in the whole of her life had managed to fill before.

Suddenly he was reminded of how one afternoon, when she was about eight years old, Belle had helped him to build a puny little fire in a tip used for storing bricks. The fire had been built with sticks, odd bits of wood, old papers, anything that would burn, and Belle had crouched over it pretending to be stirring broth in a pan.

'Your dinner's ready, husband,' she had said, and to humour her he had cracked on to be rolling up his sleeves before washing himself at the slopstone, before sitting down at an imaginary table.

'By the gum, but this tastes good, wife,' he'd said, and her face had gone pink with pleasure.

'It was a nice piece of beef I got cheap from the butcher. Don't forget to mop up the gravy with your bread, there's a good husband.'

Poor little Belle, wearing an old tattered coat, seamed up the front to make a dress, with bare legs permanently navy-blue with chilblain scars. With a nose that always ran a candle, even in summer. No wonder this place was like heaven to her. An' he wasn't going to put no spoke in it for her, not in any way he wasn't.

'I've got to get back, love. Tonight,' he lied. 'Being a business man means you have to be on the spot. I've got four men working for me now. What d'you think about that? This carpet cleaning lark is a cinch, a bloody cinch.'

He glanced down at the hall carpet, and grinned. 'This 'ere carpet of yours could do with a bit of a clean, madam, and no need for it to be taken up and beaten in the garden, madam. Just give me a date and I'll send round one of my men with one of my vacuum cleaners, and we'll have the dirt sucked up and carried away without you even having to get your maid to dust the skirting board. Shall we say next Tuesday, madam?'

Belle's eyes grew round. 'You mean no dust brushed up nor nothing?'

Joe described a shape with his hands. 'About that big and worked with bellows, so all the muck goes into a bag. Into the bag, out to the bin, a pound in Joe Blob's pocket, and there we are!'

'A pound? For cleaning carpets?'

'Five shillings to the operator of course,' Joe said grandly, 'but when you reckon I've got four of them on the go, it adds up . . . aye it adds up.' He tickled Belle underneath her chin. 'Where there's muck there's brass, love, you know that, and some of them ladies down in London like to boast to their friends that they've had their carpets professionally cleaned. I'm in the middle of negotiating a contract for a row of offices in the West End, one of them posh places where they have carpets in the boss's rooms just to show how flourishing their businesses are.' Suddenly serious he jerked his head towards the stairs.

'I've left a bit of something under the cover on your bed-side table, love. And you're sure you are proper settled? Certain sure? Because if not you can go up and pack your bag this minute and I'll take you back with me.'

'To London?'

Joe nodded. 'Where the King rides by wearing a top-hat and smoking a dirty great cigar.'

'You've *seen* him, our Joe?'

'Many times,' Joe lied. 'Once he raised his hat to me.'

Belle wrinkled her small nose. 'Oh, our Joe, you haven't changed. But I wouldn't leave this place, not my room. Not the Chapel and everyone what's so kind to me.' She was opening the door on to the quiet cul-de-sac. 'You'll keep on writing to me?'

He nodded, wanting to bend his head and kiss the soft pale cheek, but knowing there were net curtains twitching behind the windows of the neat little houses. It would never do for the Armitage's maid to be seen being kissed by a man. So he raised his hand, then walked away with his jaunty tread down the short path.

It was raining now, the mucky clinging rain sifting its way through smoke-filled air as he walked away from the newly built box-like houses into the streets he knew. Rows of houses, and still more, down to the railway arches, past the canal, down on to its banks where the oily water lapped.

Joe walked on the balls of his feet, walked like a cat. Up and back on to the road again, past the gasworks, into the labyrinth of streets, alleys, the murky courts he had been reared into.

Leaning against a wall, he felt in his pocket and took out

a crumpled packet of cigarettes, flicked one out and felt for a match.

'Blast!' The word came out as a groan. That was all it bloody needed. A fag and nowt to light it with.

Walking on he saw Kit's shop on a corner, with its cardboard cut-out window display of curly-headed girls in red-riding hoods and its little boys in velvet suits blowing bubbles. He went inside.

There were three women in the shop, all with shawls over their heads, and one of them was feeding a baby underneath its concealing folds. They turned around and stared at him, decided they did not know him, and continued talking to each other in loud strident tones.

Just for the hell of it, Joe winked at the youngest of the women, the one suckling the baby, and smiled to himself as she twitched the shawl over the baby's face.

'What can I get for you?'

The man behind the counter was smiling at him, a big fat man with short-cropped curly hair, and an indefinite chin. The front of his hair was combed up into a sort of quiff, and his voice was pitched as high as a woman's.

'These ladies here are not in any hurry,' he went on, still smiling, a tiny hammer in his hand held poised over a tray of glistening brown toffee, patterned with nuts. 'A quarter, did you say, Mrs Parkinson?'

'Tha knows I said two ounces, Mr Carmichael. I'm not made of brass,' the smallest of the three women said. 'By the gum, but tha'd sell a quarter'n of potted meat to one of them vegetarians, tha would.'

'That's a long word for a Thursday morning,' one of her companions said, and Joe smiled to himself.

He was back home all right, even if it was for less than a day. He'd always known that for quick-fire give-as-good-as-you-get, you'd go a long way before you could beat a Lancashire working class woman.

'A box of matches, please,' he said, 'and I'd better light my fag in here, it's coming down like stair-rods.'

'I've seen him afore,' the oldest woman said, when the shop door had closed behind Joe.

'Looks a cheeky type to me,' the girl with the baby said, letting the shawl drop down again because it didn't seem to matter in front of Mr Carmichael.

'Now then, Mrs Parkinson,' Kit said, tapping with the little hammer, then twisting a piece of white paper into a perfectly formed poke as he dropped the pieces of toffee in one by one.

'A nut in every piece, love,' he said. 'And you can fetch it back if there's not.'

Joe walked down the hill, past the house where Kit had lived with his mother, along the main street of shops to the top of Foundry Street.

All right, so he was being a bloody fool. Maggie had not answered his letters, and the last one had been returned with the message that she had gone away.

But whoever lived there might know where she was. They might tell him and he would go and find her. He would demand to know why she hadn't written, because surely, even if she had never wanted to see him again after that last night, she owed him some explanation?

All right, so he had taken his time about writing to her, but he had said he was going to get a job first, and that was what he'd done.

At the bottom house he lifted his hand and rapped smartly with the knocker. He felt the palms of his hands break out into dampness, and his heart was beating with staccato jerks beneath the narrow stripes of his dark grey suit. Waiting only a few seconds, he knocked again, then looked up at the windows. Aye, it looked just the same, but then all these bloody houses looked just the same. Disappointed he turned away.

There was a full hour to go before the hooters went, and apart from a cat slinking across the street, everywhere was deserted. He was standing there, just standing, wondering what to do next when a door across opened, and a youngish woman came out carrying a bucket and a mop.

'Better late than never!' she called out cheerily before getting down on a strip of matting to mop the step. Joe crossed the street.

'Number two, missus? A Miss Craig. I know she doesn't live there any more, but perhaps you . . . do you know where she might be?' He coughed to hide the sudden tremor in his voice.

The woman sat back on her heels and stared up at him. She had lived down Foundry Street for twelve months only, but she knew who he was talking about, and a glimmer of excited suspicion narrowed her eyes.

'Maggie? You're talking about Maggie? Father did away with himself a while back?'

He swallowed hard, feeling the blood rush to his face. He nodded.

The kneeling woman dipped a piece of grey cloth into the bucket, then started to wring it out with hands as red as a lobster's claws. Her mind working overtime, she was trying to remember what she had been told . . . something about a scandal . . . something about Maggie Carmichael having got herself into trouble and not with the man she had married.

'Maggie's still there,' she said at last. 'But she's Mrs Carmichael now.' She let the cloth drop back into the bucket with a resounding plop. 'She's up at the shops as like as not.'

Thanking her with a downward jerk of his dark head, Joe turned on his heel and walked quickly away.

He knew he had been ungracious, even rude, but how was she to know, that sloppy young-old woman mopping her step, that what she had just revealed had been like the shaft of a dagger slicing into his guts? His Maggie married?

He was going to be sick. He could have been sick right there, and it was all his fault, wanting to be somebody, wanting to have something to offer before he came back for her. But she might have answered his letters. She might have told him herself that she had met someone else. She had forgotten him and who could blame her? Who could bloody blame her?

Joe walked with head bent, striding out, past the draper's shop where Maggie was choosing a supply of bobbins of cotton, whilst Rose, unseen by her mother, was emptying a box of pins on to the floor.

So engrossed in his thoughts that he reached the boulevard leading to the station without knowing how he had got there.

'I thought as how Mrs Carmichael was going to faint,' the woman across the street told her husband that evening as he was sitting down to his tea of tripe and onions. 'I told her there had been a fella asking for her, and she went as white as a sheet when I described him. I always said she was a dark horse in spite of her toffee-nosed ways. I wonder if it was him what got her into trouble afore she got married to that nice Mr Carmichael?'

'This is a bit of all right,' her husband said, mopping up the thick grey gravy with a slice of bread. 'Goes right to the spot this does.'

13

Joe Barton paid no more visits to his home town after that rainy afternoon. For a while he left his digs and lived with a widow in Acton, making it quite clear from the start that marriage was not on the cards.

His business flourished, and now he stopped doing any of the cleaning himself, merely visiting housewives in their homes and charming them into agreeing to having the work done by his increasing number of employees.

He wrote fairly regularly to his sister. She was, after all, his only relative, his next of kin, the only link he had with his home town. And when he received a letter one day, written in careful script by the minister's wife, informing him that Belle had married, he was glad for her sake.

Will Hargreaves, the letter said, was a milk roundsman, and he and Belle had managed to get a tiny cottage to rent at the top of Steep Brow, one of a cluster of small tenements, previously lived in by the town's hand-loom weavers.

'There's a loomshop tacked on to the side, and we're turning it into a parlour,' the letter went on, and through the pen of the minister's wife Joe could read the pride in his sister's quiet voice.

She was still working for the Armitages' on a day to day basis, and though she said little of Will, a whole page was devoted excitedly to the rugs she had pegged, and the shiny oilcloth her new husband had tacked to the floor.

Joe immediately sent a cheque of such a high figure that Belle cried for a day after receiving it.

He received in return a brief note of thanks from his new

brother-in-law, writing on Belle's behalf, assuring him with obvious insincerity that there would always be a bed for him, should he chance to be passing through.

'Passing through!' Joe muttered to himself, memorising the address before tearing up the letter. 'That is telling me bloody straight not to make a habit if anything is.'

He worked even harder, banked a good part of his earnings, and told himself at least once a week that his inability to forget Maggie Craig, now Carmichael, was maudlin sentimentality.

He had money, he had power of a sort, and he had women if and when he felt like it. What more could any man want?

Now, as the years passed Maggie was beginning to be worried about the rising anti-German feeling in the country. It was taking the place of bad feelings about the Russians and the French, and Kit told her such topics were none of her business.

'It's not *seemly* to be fashing yourself about such things. Politics are the government's business, not yours, love,' he said.

'But they are my business. And they should be yours!' Maggie cried. 'It's wrong to generalize. There's good and bad in every race, every creed. My father taught me that, and what's more he said we can be *taught* to hate. That's why he was such a good teacher, though I doubt if even he could have taught our Rose much. She doesn't give a damn about her book-learning. I try to help her but she won't let me, an' I could . . . oh I could.'

Kit listened with tolerant affection. He didn't doubt that his Maggie could do anything if she set her mind to it. She never wasted a moment, nor an opportunity. Always think-up schemes to make a bit extra to ensure that Rose was the best dressed kid in the street. Never grumbling about the meagre wage he took home of a Friday. He would watch her sort it out into a box she had made into sections. So much for the rent, so much for the gas and the coal, and never once getting behind with anything. And she was right about Mr Yates at the shop, he had to admit that.

'He's a proper miser,' she said. 'Three shops he has and all he does is count his money in those awful rooms over your shop, sitting there with the damp running down the walls as if he hadn't two pennies to rub together. Why don't you ask him for a rise, Kit? You run that place single-handed now he lets you do all the ordering. It's a wonder he doesn't ask you to bring the stuff back from the warehouse on a barrow. That would save the old skinflint a bob or two on deliveries.'

'He gave me half a crown extra last Christmas,' Kit had reminded her, worried lines creasing his face into a mould of acute anxiety. 'I'm not getting any younger, love. What's to stop him sending me packing and taking on a much younger man? He could get away with paying less than what he gives me, you know.'

Immediately Maggie saw, not only the logic of what he said, but what was more important to her, his real distress.

'You're a soft aporth, Kit Carmichael,' she smiled. 'I only wish our Rose had a bit more softness in her. She's as hard as nails that one.'

For a long time that night Maggie lay awake worrying about Rose in her bed on the other side of the plywood partition now dividing her father's room into two.

It was no good denying it. The years had not mellowed Rose. Far from it. She was old Mrs Carmichael to the life, and she had that way of staring at her mother as if silently promising herself that she would get the better of her one day.

Maggie tossed and turned, wondering . . . was there, *could* there be a hint of the instability that had boiled over into madness in Kit's mother?

'Oh, dear God,' she prayed, turning, as she always did, to prayer when she felt in dire need of comfort. 'Let Rose be happy, because she is not a happy girl, I know that.

She's at some sort of war with herself all the time, an' no matter what I do, or how much I try to get close to her, it's impossible. It's not true, Lord, that love begets love, because I ache to put my arms round her and tell her how much I love her. I want to *ask* her what gets into her, but she would wither me with one of those looks of hers. . . .

'Oh, Rose,' she whispered. 'There's one thing you're not going to get the better of me about. You might not be much of a scholar, but you're never going into the mill like I did. Never!'

Rose went straight into Dobson's mill the week she turned thirteen. There was nothing Maggie could have done about it apart from beating her over the head, and the constant arguments were beginning to wear her down.

She managed to pass the labour exam, and told her mother in no uncertain terms that she wasn't as daft as the scholars who were staying on till they were fourteen.

'I'm fed up with books,' she told her mother. 'I want some money of me own, and I want to learn dancing like me friends do. Besides, I'm not clever and you can't make me no matter how hard you try.'

She walked over to Kit's shaving mirror fastened at an angle over the slopstone in the living-room, and adjusted the stiff ribbon bow at the back of her small head. '*You* went in the mill, Mam, and it didn't do you no harm.'

It was no good trying to correct the way she spoke. Maggie had given up trying to do that long ago. She put her sewing down in her lap and rubbed her fingers over a jerking pain throbbing over one eyebrow.

'I went in the mill, Rose love, because I had no choice. I had your grandpa to see to, and there was three and sixpence to find each week for the rent.' She picked the shirt up again and started to unpick a frayed cuff, pulling at the cotton with her fingernail, unravelling it, then starting to pick again at the other side. 'But you have a better chance to make something of yourself. I am sure I could get you an opening with the milliner in the Hat Market. She goes to Chapel and I could have a word with her.'

The cuff came away from the sleeve, and turning it over she started to tack it back in position. 'You'd have a trade in your fingers,' – she swallowed hard – 'like your father's mother had, and if you get married then you could trim hats at home to bring in a bit extra.'

Rose's scorn brought the swift colour to her mother's cheeks.

'Bring in a bit extra! That's all you think about, our mam. I'm not going in the Hat Market working in the evenings, and I'm not going in no shop neither. I want to have a bit of fun when I finish work, not come home like me dad, flaked out every night.'

Maggie forced herself to keep her voice low. Her face was white now and knowing she was on the verge of losing her temper, excited Rose somehow.

Maggie spoke quietly, fighting for control.

'If I had spoken to your grandpa like that at your age, even though he was a sick man, I'd have been sent straight to bed and made to stay there till I was ready to apologize.'

'There's someone coming in,' Rose said, her voice tinged with relief, knowing she had gone too far with bringing her father into the argument. Thank God for nosey Clara next door. . . .

Clara came straight through, sitting down without being invited to, in Kit's rocking chair.

'He's gone!' she said, pulling a screwed-up handkerchief from her apron pocket and bursting into loud tears. 'He's gone to live with another woman, and he says if I want any money I'll have to have him up for it.' She dabbed at her streaming eyes. 'He said such awful things me mother's taken to her bed. Oh, Maggie, you wouldn't believe some of the things he said. I just could not repeat them, not to a living soul.'

Knowing she was about to do just that, Maggie nodded her head at Rose, but before she could tell her to go up to her room, Rose took swift advantage of the situation.

'Can I go round to Mavis's house, Mam? I'll not stop more than half an hour. Honest.'

She was gone before Maggie could open her mouth to reply, long black hair flying, snatching her coat from behind the door and her tammy from out of the pocket.

Maggie sighed, and turning to Clara, said, 'I'll put the kettle on and then you can tell me all about it over a pot of tea.'

'He called me mother a pissed-out old faggot,' Clara said, setting the rocking chair into frantic motion. 'And what he called me I can't bring meself to repeat. . . .'

Arnie was back within a month, but Clara's mother never spoke to him again. Now widowed mother and daughter slept together in the marital bed whilst Arnie was banished to the back bedroom.

There he could lie and listen to them talking to each other at the tops of their clarion-call voices, referring to himself as ''im in there', and letting him get up to make his own breakfast before he went off to work in the mornings.

Arnie found that in a strange way he was happier than he had been for a long time. There was a kind of peace in knowing exactly where he stood. He could tend his little back-yard garden, and he could sit in his chair by the fire knowing he had won. They had had a taste of missing his money, and once, when the Workhouse had been mentioned, he had seen a flicker of fear in his mother-in-law's eyes. Money was power, Arnie was discovering, and as long as he gave them enough after he had taken out his beer money, they seemed willing to call an uneasy truce.

He was quite insensitive to the spite-filled atmosphere, never having been much of a talker, and if he felt a bit belligerent and did not like what they gave him to eat, he merely pushed his plate aside and said he knew where there was a good meal waiting for him anytime.

Then he would see the swift look of apprehension exchanged between mother and daughter. . . .

Aye, things had changed all right, and they weren't to know he had been chucked out by the woman he'd taken up with when she got fed up with his silences, and his way of staring at nothing for hours on end.

And the next time he got a rise of eightpence a week in his wage he handed it over to Clara with aplomb, just for the sake of seeing the expression on her face.

'Well?' he said, monarch of all he surveyed.

'Ta very much,' said Clara from behind clenched teeth.

When Rose had been working for a year Arnie went on munitions, making big money, as Clara said, and the war in France broke out.

At Chapel the very next Sunday the minister preached a sermon based on what Saint Paul had said:

'He who is not with me, is *against* me!'

'To hell with Saint Paul!' Maggie shouted. 'It made me blood boil when I could see that most of the congregation were siding with the minister. Saint Paul never meant it like that. Taken out of context you can make things mean anything. Does nobody remember the last time? What about all those lads killed in South Africa? What about Benjamin and Jonathan? Do we never learn nothing?'

'This war will be over by Christmas,' Kit soothed. 'That is official. The boys will be back afore we know they've gone, you will see.'

But by the end of that year, the majority of the warehouses in the town were forced to close, and Mr Yates lost two of the shops he had built up over the years. The papers were full of long casualty lists, and Maggie read with horror that one hundred and four thousand men had been killed, gravely wounded, or were missing.

That Christmas Clara, giving her weekly order to Kit, asked for a tin of lobster.

'Sorry, love, but we've no call for that sort of thing in my shop. You will have to go to one of the downtown shops,' Kit told her, and Maggie bent her head over her knitting, working furiously at a khaki scarf in between long sessions at her sewing machine.

'Lobster!' she muttered, then she counted her stitches as if she was telling her beads. 'Let the men come home safe from that terrible war,' she prayed.

The only person who might have prayed that Joe Barton had an easy war was his sister Belle, and she was too busy polishing and sweeping her tiny cottage in the evenings after working at the Armitages' house all day.

Will had left his milk round and gone, like Arnie, into the more lucrative job of working on munitions, even opting for work miles away from home. A wispy and lithe little man, with legs bent like a jockey's, a legacy of rickets from an impoverished childhood, he swore that the army would never catch up with him.

'Strikes and wars will be the downfall of this country, mark my words,' he told Belle, a doting Belle who hung on to his every word in gratitude for him having married her and given her a home of her own.

'Think of them poor sods marching to their deaths. I'm going to die in me own bed, with me hands crossed over me chest, then buried with a nice tongue and ham spread, all civilized, like, that's me.'

'Oh, don't talk about dying,' Belle cried, flinging herself into his arms. 'Please, Will. Promise me you'll never die!'

Joe, her brother, marching at that very moment along a treeless road towards the Ypres Salient, thought about the possibility of dying every minute of his waking hours. He was thinking about it now as he plodded one foot gingerly in front of the other, swearing loudly with every step he took.

'You've had your chips if you fall off these sodding duck-boards,' he told a private following behind. 'That mud will suck you down before you can say "Jack the flamin' Ripper."'

'Welcome to this stately home,' he told the private as they climbed down into their dug-out. 'Come on, lad. You'll feel better after a brew-up, you'll see.'

The private stared around him with startled eyes bulging from a dome-shaped forehead. A lad of no more than seventeen who had lied about his age to get into the army, he was doing his first stretch in the forward trenches, and Joe Barton, *Corporal* Joe Barton, looked as if he might be laughing at him.

'What's that shocking smell, Corporal?' he asked, then jumped a foot in the air as a cat-sized rat ran from one corner of the dug-out to the other.

Joe, busy with the task of pouring chlorinated water from an old petrol tin, pretended not to have heard the whispered question.

If the poor little beggar did not know that what he was smelling was dead bodies, men and horses, lying just over the top in no man's land, then he was better left in ignorance for the time being. He would learn soon enough . . .

Joe passed over the tin mug when the tea was ready. It tasted of petrol and was sweetened with tinned milk, but the private drank it down quickly.

'Are there many rats?' he asked, wincing as another scuttled from the shadows. 'That's the second one since we got down here.'

Joe shook his head. 'Rats is nothing to worry about, lad. Don't you bother about them. I've caught more of them than what you've had hot dinners.'

'How?' The pale eyes protruded more than ever. 'I once heard that rats go for you if you get them in a corner.'

Joe grinned. 'We don't make no attempt to corner them,

lad. When we sometimes get a bit of what they like to call meat, we *bait* 'em with it.' He made a throwing motion with his hand. 'We fasten it on to the end of summat – anything does – then we chuck it over the top, and rats, having no brains, sink their teeth in it. Then we pull quick and bonk it one afore it knows what's hit him.'

The private, his eyes looking as though they were about to leave their sockets, stared at his Corporal as if he could not believe the evidence of his toby-jug ears.

'Then we skin them and eat 'em,' Joe teased, relenting when he was aware that the not very bright young soldier was taking his every word literally.

'That were meant to be a joke,' he said.

'All the same I don't think I am going to like it here,' the private said, and thinking he was showing a welcome touch of humour, Joe slapped him on the back, almost causing him to lose his balance.

'I'll watch out for you, lad,' he said. 'It's getting used to it that's the worst, but give yourself a week and you'll feel as if you've been living down here for bloody years.'

The nights were the worst. Accustomed from his furtive, nomadic childhood to walk like a cat, eyes and ears alert for danger, Joe took to soldiering like a duck to water. As a Very light shot into the air he could freeze into the stillness of a marble statue. He could hurl himself forward into the sticky mud, burying his face into the overpowering smell.

Once, to his horror he had found that he had fallen on to the decaying corpse of a soldier, decomposed too far for him to know whether the man had been British or German.

Out in no man's land it could have been either. . . .

And because of his could-not-care-less attitude, Joe's Sergeant, a veteran of the Boer War, found his Corporal what he considered to be a 'natural'. Joe could outswear him, and did so often, as hearing the whine of a heavy shell hurtling death at top speed towards them, Joe's colourful language peppered the air like gun-fire.

When on a night raid the Sergeant was killed with a

bullet smack between his eyes, Joe stepped neatly over the body and carried on moving forward.

The object of the exercise was to demolish a pillbox manned by Germans wielding stuttering machine guns.

'And the main object is to bring one of the blighters back,' his Lieutenant had said.

'As if we was going pheasant shooting,' Joe muttered, moving ever forward into the staccato firing, and believing every tortured moment to be his last.

Not ten yards from the pillbox, he threw himself flat on the ground, and thought wildly of praying. But to whom? To God?

It did not seem possible that with men falling all around him, screaming with pain, bleeding and dying – how could it be possible that God was there?

But if he was going to die, then surely he should be thinking of someone, or something?

Of Belle? Joe tried to bring her pale little face into his mind, seeing her as he had seen her last when she had almost pushed him through the door in case Mrs bloody Armitage came back.

Of Maggie Craig?

Of Maggie who had married someone else, and likely forgotten he ever existed?

'Oh, Maggie! Maggie!' Joe cried her name aloud over and over, because damn it, there had to be *someone* he could call on.

'Bugger and sod everybody!' he shouted as standing up he hurled his bomb in the vague direction of the pillbox.

When his Lieutenant, holding his bayoneted rifle up against the backside of a petrified German, prodded his prisoner back in the direction of the dug-out, Joe was lying once again, face down in the evil-smelling mud.

14

That night Maggie dreamed of Joe. It was as though he was there, in a corner of the room, calling her name. Calling it angrily, not with love. *Cursing* her, Maggie thought, sitting up in bed, shivering, then lighting the candle and reaching for a book.

Across the postage stamp of a landing, Kit slept the sleep of the physically tired, whilst at the other side of the plywood partition Rose coughed and turned, tossed and twitched the blankets over her, then pushed them back as if they were suffocating her with their weight.

Maggie could hear the vague sounds telling her that Rose too was finding it hard to sleep, and she imagined her daughter lying with her black hair spread over the pillow, staring up into the darkness, thinking her private thoughts, dreaming her private dreams, as alienated from her mother as she had been as a child.

The war would soon be over. All the signs were there, and then, please God, there would never be another . . . Maggie laid down her book, blew out the candle, and Joe was there again, back with the darkness, like a ghost refusing to go away.

Maggie got out of bed, then padded silently to the top of the stairs.

'Rose?' she called softly. 'I'm going down to make a pot of tea. Would you like a cup?'

'No, thank you.'

Rose's voice sounded thick as if she had been crying. Maggie hesitated, a hand actually on the door knob, then fearing the inevitable rejection, she carried on downstairs, vaguely worried and disturbed.

If Rose wanted to tell her what was bothering her then she would tell her or not tell her, all in her good time. And besides, Rose never cried. She sulked and winged; she complained and went through black periods of depression, but she never cried.

Maggie sat in her chair by a fire that had almost died, a terrible weight of sadness in her heart, a sadness that she knew was only a small part of her daughter's rejection of her.

And the next day Rose got up heavy-eyed, went to the mill, came home for her dinner as usual, then without speaking to Maggie, went up to her room.

Sitting on her bed she stared at the dividing partition until her eyes glazed over. She knew she should be shaping herself, but she also knew that by running like mad across the back, over the spare ground and the bridge, she could get there just in time.

She sat there for another minute, then, as if a time spring had been released inside her, she flew downstairs, taking her coat from behind the back door, and saying briefly that it was time she was off.

Clara was hanging her washing out on a line stretching from her own yard wall to a post set in the ground.

'Let's hope it keeps fine, Rose,' she shouted, the timbre of her voice only fractionally reduced by the peg held firmly between her teeth. 'I've fetched this lot in twice this morning.'

Looping one end of a flannelette sheet over the line, she pegged it into scallops, giving the fresh wind a chance to billow it out.

'Yes,' Rose said, and ran on.

'Yes' was a useful word to bring out now and again. It did not matter whether she listened to what the other person was saying or not. Yes brooked no argument at the best of times. . . .

Clara watched her go as she hooked a prop into a space between Arnie's long underpants and her mother's button-through flannel nightie. Even Rose's hurrying back looked sly, she decided.

'I would not trust that girl as far as I could throw her,' she told her mother in ringing tones. 'And that's not far with this awful rheumatism in me shoulder.'

'She's a bad lot,' Mrs Hobkirk agreed. 'Going off to the pictures with that Mavis girl out of Henry Street, with muck on their faces. What can you expect?'

'She's learning dancing in the rooms over the Emporium. Half a crown for twelve lessons, paid in advance.'

Clara walked over to the window, feeling cross for a reason she couldn't fathom.

'It's time Rose Carmichael got herself one decent fella and settled down. The war started her off young with boys. She had too much freedom and too much money. There's bad blood there. I've always said so. She's even stopped going to Chapel, and Maggie doesn't go as often as she used . . . Oh, heck, it's started to flamin' rain again.'

After a week of living with a silent Rose who for some reason had stopped going dancing almost every night, Maggie felt the need to go to Chapel.

Yet the minute the choir stood up to sing the anthem she decided that the choirmaster, beating time with his left hand, had a definite look of Joe Barton about him. There was something about the way his hair grew down into a point in the nape of his neck.

'Oh, Lord,' she prayed, using the words she had been taught as a child. 'Oh, Lord, I am sailing on the wide sea. Please guide my little boat for me.'

It was strange though how just these past days Joe had been more in her thoughts than ever. Every other man she saw seemed to remind her of him.

She had seen it in the milkman's grin as he ladled the

milk out of the churns on his cart. When the doctor's man came for his weekly sixpence last Friday she had thought how his smile had the same teasing quality about it.

Maggie opened her hymn book and sighed. She was tired, that was the explanation; she was doing too much sewing, taking too much on, and the mind played strange tricks when you were constantly tired.

The voices of the congregation rose and swelled. No holding back when Methodists sang.

'Once again, 'tis joyous May. Birds are carolling all day. . . .'

But not round here they aren't, Maggie thought, trying to remember the last time she had heard a bird sing.

Then she sat down and closed her eyes as the minister folded his hands over the edge of the pulpit and said: 'Let us pray.'

Obediently Maggie bent her head, willing herself to concentrate, as speaking to God in his simple language, the new minister spoke straight from his heart. No set prayers, dulling the senses with their familiarity. Just a talk to God and his son Jesus, mentioning by name the sick members of the Chapel, thanking for blessings received, and conceding that blessings not received were all part of his perfect plan.

There was a young-old man in the pew to the side of Maggie. When he got up to sing the last hymn she noticed the haggard stoop and the dull vulnerable expression she had seen on the faces of so many men back from the trenches.

The minister himself had lost a fine boy, a young officer who used to stand with his mother in their pew, finding her place in the hymn book and smiling down at her. Maggie turned her head and saw her now, singing as if she meant every word. Blaming God for nothing.

Clara and Arnie were waiting for her outside in the street, and Maggie hoped the surprise at seeing them out together did not show on her face.

'I didn't see you come in,' she said.

Clara nodded seriously. 'No, we sat at the back because Arnie's having trouble with his stomach rumbling.'

Arnie looked affronted, but smiled at Maggie. 'Rose not here tonight then?'

Maggie fell into step beside Clara. 'No, I think she was glad to stop in, she doesn't look all that well. I'm a bit bothered about her.'

Clara, walking next to her husband, was being firmly nudged. He was telling her to keep her mouth shut, she knew, telling her not to interfere in matters that were none of her concern, but she wasn't going to take any notice. Fiercely Clara nudged him back, almost knocking him off the pavement.

She was going to speak her mind, and nobody was going to stop her, so after they turned into the long street of closed shops leading to Foundry Street, she did her sideways sniff before saying:

'Did you know that your Rose went to Doctor Leyland's surgery on Friday morning? Not to your own doctor's surgery up Mercer Street. To Doctor Leyland's where I go?'

'I'll walk on in front,' Arnie said at once, almost breaking into a run.

'He's huffed because I've told you,' Clara said, 'but I think you ought to know.'

'Rose is not a child,' Maggie said slowly. 'She can go to any doctor she chooses without telling me first.' She felt a faint stab of fear. 'She was sick last week, but she soon got over it.'

'Sick first thing in the mornings?' Clara persisted.

Maggie stopped walking so abruptly that a man a few paces behind almost fell over her.

She put a hand to her mouth in a small inadequate gesture of comfort, whilst little things, things she had not considered of importance, flooded her memory.

And because Rose had always been secretive, her behaviour lately had meant no more than possibly the rejection by a friend, one of the many imagined slights Rose took so bitterly.

Then Maggie remembered her suspicion that Rose had been crying to herself in the night.

'Oh, God, dear God!' Her eyes widened with shock. 'I must have been blind. I never thought . . . well, how could I? Oh, Clara, it can't be. She's never kept a boy for long, you know what she's like. Oh, no, we mustn't jump to conclusions. We could be doing her a terrible injustice. She's not that sort of girl. She isn't!'

Both Clara's nostrils twitched in unison.

'You're far too trusting, Maggie. You should have seen her face when she saw me at the surgery. I'd gone for a bottle for Arnie's stomach. Your Rose nearly died when she saw me.'

They started to walk on.

'She'd been in with the doctor a long time,' Clara went on with grim persistence. 'An' when she came out her face was as white as bleached twill. She never even looked at me. Oh, yes, there's summat up all right.'

Maggie walked so quickly that Clara had to take little running steps to keep up with her. In Foundry Street two children played round a lamp-post, swinging from a piece of rope dangling from the short arm at the top as they made fruitless attempts to climb up it.

Maggie turned to Clara. Somehow she had to get rid of her. Knowing Clara she would be likely to follow into the house, not wanting to miss the drama she sensed was about to be played out.

'You did right to tell me. Thank you, Clara,' Maggie said.

But Clara had cottoned on to the fact that she wasn't wanted, and anyway Maggie looked so small, so *defeated*, she almost wished she had kept her big mouth shut.

'Ta-ra, then, love,' she said, and before she had closed her own front door, Arnie was there, his usually passive expression contorted with anger.

'You can't let be, can you? That girl would have had to tell her mother all in her own good time, and how do you know you're right anyroad? She could just be having a bilious attack or something like that.'

'You don't go to another doctor when your mother thinks you're at work, and you don't get bilious attacks with carrying on like Rose Carmichael's been carrying on. I wasn't born yesterday, you know.'

Arnie looked at the thin greying hair, the sagging chin and the lines running from nose to chin on his wife's flat face.

'You don't have to tell *me* that,' he said.

Ever since her early morning visit to Clara's doctor, Rose had been numb with a terrible aching despair. It had been a long wait, standing there across the street waiting for the door of the surgery to open. Even when she had been let in, there had been another long wait while the benches filled up with coughing people, clutching empty medicine bottles and trying not to look at each other, but keeping a silent count in order not to miss their turn.

For over two long months now she had kept the awful fear to herself, persuading herself that it was worry, reminding herself that the boy she had done it with had said she would be all right. She wiped a tear away on the fringe of a grey woollen shawl.

He had been so nice, so *different* from all the other boys she had known. So much more the gentleman, and yet . . . she shivered . . . he had managed to persuade her to let him go further than she had ever let any boy go before. Rose faced the truth squarely. It wasn't as if she was a young girl who didn't know what could happen if you egged a boy on. She should have known better than go with him in the park. Mavis had paired off with his friend, but she hadn't done anything so daft; she couldn't get over Rose having done it either.

He hadn't talked much, but as they went through the big ornamental gates he had put his arm round her, and then at the top of the park, past the duck pond, he had led her over the grass and laid his raincoat down on the grass in the shelter of a rhododendron bush.

She was used to boys fumbling with urgent fingers at the buttons on her blouse, used to the power she felt when their trembling legs pressed against her own. It was the one time she felt important somehow. She wasn't pretty, she knew that, too small and too sallow of skin, but at times like that the boys she had been with seemed to think she was a bit of all right.

'You're a bit of a dark horse,' they would say, and she would smile, thinking of nothing at all except the pleasure of moving hands exploring just so far and no further.

Silent tears ran down her face. He was from the park end of the town, she guessed, although he had told her less than nothing about himself. His Lancashire accent was far less pronounced than her own, and the cigarette he smoked was a De Reske and not a Woodbine. She knew and was impressed that he had paid two shillings for the packet of twenty-five, so she asked for a puff just to see if she could tell the difference.

He told her his name was John, but that could have been a lie, just as her telling him she worked in an office had been a lie.

'Which office?' he wanted to know.

'That would be telling,' she said, and he told her she was a little tease, then he kissed her in a searching way, awakening a response that no other boy had ever aroused in her.

It was a response that destroyed his own intention of keeping everything well inside the limits of control. . . .

What happened he had never meant to happen, but this girl was like no other he had kissed. Fierce and dark, with glistening dark eyes, she was clinging to him, and *asking* for it. She should have *stopped* him. All the others had stopped him. It was her fault, her fault entirely.

It had been over so quickly he could not believe that was all it was about. All the jokes he heard at school in the sixth form, the sly winks, the nudges . . . for this?

Leaving Rose at the park gates he ran all the way home, then locked himself in the bathroom to wash all over before taking a book down from his father's study shelves and looking up the symptoms of a certain unmentionable disease.

He was ashamed and terrified, at one and the same time. . . .

If anything happened now to stop him going up to Oxford at the end of the summer, his father would kill him. And his mother . . . oh God, it would break her heart.

Would that girl who had said she worked in an office find out his real name and where he lived? Would her father bring her up to the house and force him to marry her? Would she be waiting for him when he came out of school?

He actually beat his forehead with a clenched fist, beside himself with shivering horror and disgust.

Rose shivered. Even if she went looking for him she could never hope to find him. She remembered that he had been tall, and that, passing a lamp, the light had shone down on to a fair head, but she could not bring his features into even a semblance of recognition. Mavis, who seemed to know about such things, had said he would deny it, even if they found him.

'I'll get you some stuff from a herbalist's shop. Pennyroyal syrup mixed with turpentine. They say it works every time.'

'Have you ever. . . ?'

Mavis tossed her head. ''Course not. I just keep my ears open, that's all.'

Dr Leyland had heard her out in silence, called his wife in from the back of the house, and examined her briefly.

'There's a lot worse things you could be having than a baby, believe me, dear, I know,' he said. He stretched out a hand to the bell on his wide desk. 'Come and see me again in a month, and by that time your young man will have put a ring on your finger, and we'll have a laugh you and me about you thinking this is the end of the world. All right?'

The doctor was a kindly, compassionate man, but his surgery was full of waiting patients, and when it was over he had to go and tell a woman in Marstone Road that the tests sent on from Manchester showed that her husband's illness was incurable.

And this war would not end with the defeat of the Germans. He could prophesy that more than half of the men who were lucky enough to come back from that hell on earth would have the stamp of it on them till the day they died.

Besides, he wasn't getting any younger, and he knew he ought to have talked to that young lass a bit longer. She had a strange look about her.

But there wasn't the time . . . there never was enough time.

So Rose walked away, down the short passage and past the dispensary where she handed over her shilling consultant fee, avoiding Clara's eyes as she passed through the crowded waiting-room.

Back at the mill, she stood at her looms, willing her mind into a blankness . . . as she was trying to will it now.

When Maggie came upstairs wearing her Chapel best hat and coat, she found Rose hunched up and desolate on the edge of her bed.

'Rose?'

The swollen eyelids were raised as Rose registered her mother's flushed cheeks, her unbelief, her pleading look that said she wanted to be told it wasn't true.

Defiance and shame turned her face to the wall, then she jerked a finger.

'She's told you then? I'm surprised she waited till now.'

Maggie put out a hand and trying hard to say the right thing, said the wrong.

'You must tell me, love. Is it right that you're in trouble? We must talk before your father comes in from the shop. He'll be late tonight because he's setting out the window ready for next week.'

'Clara Preston's a vicious old cow.'

The words were almost spat out, reminding Maggie of the old woman in the bed, the bitter woman with a tongue like a whip-lash. She sighed and tried again.

'Rose? Rose, love?'

The softly spoken words, the lack or reproach shocked Rose as badly as if her mother had struck her, and she rolled away to the foot of the bed. When hysteria took over it came as a relief. It cleared at last the dead feeling she had had inside her for the past worrying weeks as she gave way to loud sobs that seemed as if they might shake her body in two.

'Tell me who it was, Rose.'

The next words were screamed at the top of Rose's lungs.

'I don't *know* who it was! It was a boy I met just once, and I don't know where he lives or even what he's called. I saw him *once*. That was all! Now be kind to me! Just try to be kind to me now!'

Maggie stood quite still, listening, but not allowing the shouted words to register.

Rose was a strange girl, but she could never have done that. Not gone with a stranger. That was the sort of thing the night women did.

She was shocked to her soul, yet all she wanted to do was to put her arms round her daughter, but if they had had no real communication before, how could she expect there. to be any now? She tried to move and found that she was quite unable to move from the spot where she stood.

She wanted to keep calm, to speak quietly, to go on speaking quietly, but it was as though someone else's voice had taken over.

'You're not like that!' she shouted.

Rose turned a blotched face towards her.

'But I am! You don't know me. You've never known me. Everybody can't be like you, all holy, holy, holy.' She bit hard on her knuckles. 'Always going to Chapel and singin' hymns and prayin'.' Now her voice held the bleakness of a dreadful despair. 'Go away, Mam. Just go away. . . .'

Maggie moved at last. She went to sit on the edge of the bed, careful not to make any attempt to touch the hunched form curled up by the wall.

'Rose,' she whispered. 'Don't shut me out, not now, not at this important time. We have to talk before your father comes home . . . Rose, love. He has to be told, and he'll understand. You know he will. As I'm trying to understand. Just give me a little time.'

Rose turned and the look she gave her mother was so like the look, the never to be forgotten look on old Mrs Carmichael's face that Maggie flinched. Even the voice was the same:

'*Understand?* Me dad understand a thing like that? If he was a proper man he might just *try* to understand, but he isn't, is he? He wouldn't be sleeping on his own in a separate room if he was, would he?'

Maggie tried to control the shaking of her whole body. She had to stay, to listen, to comfort. And yet it was all the same. . . .

But it could not be. It was a trick of the imagination. And could it be that she herself had made Rose as she was, because she could never blot the memory of that night from her mind?

Had the ghost of old Mrs Carmichael merely come

between her and Rose, not been faithfully reproduced in this girl who was her own daughter? Maggie made one of her sudden decisions.

'Rose, listen to me,' she whispered.

And it wasn't easy to tell her child the way it had been with her and Joe. The fumbling words sounded all wrong.

What she wanted to do was to tell, to show Rose, that once, a long time ago, her own mother had been far from holy, holy, holy . . . that she had let a boy make love to her, *wanted* him to make love to her, *needed* him, as perhaps Rose herself had needed comfort.

'I lost the baby in the room across the landing, with no one to tell, and no one to understand. So you see, sweetheart, I *do* understand. I loved this boy, but nobody ever tells us how easy it is to let go, just for a brief moment.' She leaned over to touch Rose gently on her shoulder.

'I love you, Rose. I've wanted to show you before, but there was always . . . always something stopping us getting close.' She closed her eyes. 'I'll face this with you, love, and it won't be easy, make no mistake about that, because folks can be cruel, even those who go to Chapel twice on a Sunday. An' you won't be alone like I was. You'll have me to fight for you, and your father, because he stuck up for me when folks turned on me . . . oh, yes he did.' Her voice softened. 'I think that was what made me decide to marry him in the end. . . . Oh, Rose, little love, don't cry like that. I'm here. I'm right here.'

When Rose came into her mother's arms, it was as though Maggie was holding her child for the very first time.

As though the ghost of Kit's mother had been exorcised, to disappear for ever.

15

When Kit came in that night, it was near to midnight. He was actually stumbling with exhaustion, his face clammy with a thin film of sweat.

'Mr Yates wanted everything down off the shelves and all the stuff in the back room checked, then he asked me to re-dress the window to show off some of the posh foods he's bought in. You'd never think there was a war still on.'

Because Maggie was dreading what she had to tell him, her voice was sharper than she had intended.

'Posh foods? What do you mean by posh foods?'

Kit, bending over with difficulty because of his rapidly increasing waistline, began to unlace his boots.

'Oh, you know, love. Tins of pineapple chunks, and tins of what they call After Dinner Mints. Half a crown a tin they are. He's gone off his chump I reckon. He forgets that most of our customers are like old Mrs Bradshawe coming in begging bacon scraps to stuff a cod's head with.'

'To feed seven of them at that.'

Maggie knelt down and unlaced the second boot. Kit's weight had increased so that his stomach hung like a bladder over the tops of his trousers, and the stiffly starched collars he wore pushed his neck up into a fold as red and loose as a turkey's crop.

'That awful man exploits you!' she burst out, dreading what she had to tell him. 'An' you just let him.'

Rose's cruel words came back to her, making her sharp and irritated, because she knew in her heart there was more than a hint of truth in them.

But Rose had meant what she said in a cruel way, and this man was so good, so good . . . Maggie stood up, ready to do battle on his behalf, still putting off what she had to tell him.

'You ought to try to stand up to him a bit more, Kit. He'll never find anyone like you, and you know it. Where could he find a young man to do the buying as well as the selling, plus keeping an account book, and keeping his shop going when the others have closed?'

Her hands were on her hips now. 'Look what happened early on when so many customers took their coupons to the bigger grocers down town. You hardly lost a single one. They all brought their registrations to you because they remembered how you've helped them and been fair. The old goat knows that, the miserly devil.'

Kit did not bother to respond. For one thing he was too tired and for another he knew his Maggie. She was working herself up because something else had upset her, and she would tell him in her own good time.

All her anger stemmed from concern. She was like his mother in that way, but he wasn't daft enough to tell her. His Maggie had exactly the same mother hen attitude to life – let anyone hurt her family and she would spit in their eye.

And he loved it. Her fighting spirit made him feel safe; it was like warm syrup, soothing and comforting.

He stood up and yawned. 'I'll just go out to the back, love, then I'm off to bed. Rose all right?'

Men *did* cry, Maggie reminded herself as she lay in bed an hour later, as wide awake as if it were the middle of the afternoon. She had felt Joe Barton's cheek wet against her own that night, after he had made love to her, and before he went away.

Kit was an easy crier, she knew that, but his anguish had been so great that he had sobbed in her arms on the sofa downstairs, sobbed like a child with a disappointment so overwhelming he could not bear it.

Now he was asleep. She could hear the rhythmic rise and fall of his snores from the back room, while her own thoughts darted like a fire-fly from one subject to another.

Clara would have plenty to say because she had never liked Rose.

'Bring trouble to your door that one will. There's bad blood somewhere in her and that's not kidding.'

Maggie turned and tossed. Where had they gone wrong with Rose? Was it their fault? Kit's for being too soft by half, and hers for being over-strict?

No, Rose had just seemed as if she wanted to be awkward all round. There were days when if Maggie had said it was a Monday, Rose would have declared it to be a Tuesday.

Maggie pulled the clothes up round her neck. Poor Rose. Believing she was so unlovable she had let a stranger make love to her.

At least she had loved Joe . . . loved him so much that even now the thought of him flooded her body with the ache of remembering.

Maggie sat up suddenly in bed, her long hair falling round her face. . . . She was hearing Joe's voice again, calling out to her in anger. . . .

'Oh, Joe,' she whispered. 'If you need me, tell me where you are. . . .'

Moved from the field hospital in Boulogne, shattered in both mind and body, with a leg wound that refused to heal, Corporal Joe Barton was sent first to a hospital in the south of England, then because his sister Belle was down on his papers as next of kin, to the Royal Infirmary in his home-town.

The week before Christmas in 1918, sleeping fitfully in his narrow bed in the ward filled with wounded soldiers, he dreamed he was standing-to on a trench fire-step.

Dimly he saw the Passchendaele night turn into a pink-tinged dawn. Through bleary eyes he saw the corpse-strewn waste of no man's land. When the order to stand down came he dropped exhausted back into the dug-out.

To Joe the beautiful rosy early morning was nothing more than a hypocritical mockery. It was merely the beginning of yet another day of undiluted horror.

It took him a good three minutes to realize that the dawn he was seeing now was seeping through the tall window behind his bed, and another three minutes to realize that the war in France had been over for more than a month.

Sister Fletcher walked with her springy slip-slap walk down the long ward and stopped by his bed. She was carrying a blanket-wrapped bundle in her arms, and if Joe had not known her as well as he thought he did he might have suspected that there were tears in her voice.

'Mr Barton?' she whispered. 'Are you awake? I wonder if you would do something for me?'

With her free hand she pulled the covers out at one side of his parcel-neat bed.

'Will you take this newborn baby into bed with you and keep it warm? We've just done an emergency in the theatre, and the baby's mother has unfortunately died.'

'Well bugger me!'

Joe pushed himself up on an elbow and blinked, but for once the Sister did not stop to reprimand him for his language. She merely deposited the small bundle beside him, tucked the covers back again, and walked back down the long ward. She lingered for a whispered word with the night nurse, who was cocooned in her own little pool of light at her desk, looked back in Joe's direction, then vanished.

Joe heard her springy footsteps turn into a rapidly receding and totally forbidden run. . . .

The rest of the ward was in complete darkness, but the cold grey light from the window showed him a small round face, no bigger it seemed than a man's fist. It showed him a pout of a pink mouth with the chin sucked in as though the baby knew it was off to the worst of starts, and a surprising shock of jet-black hair growing straight up from a worried, lined and puckered forehead.

'Well bugger me!' Joe said again. 'You poor little sod. You're the baby Nurse Gallagher told me about. The one what the surgeon was going to have to bring on by operating – the one belonging to that lass with no husband.'

Carefully he raised himself a fraction.

'There's not many babies *born* orphans, but I reckon that's what has happened to you, young fella-me-lad.'

He peered intently into the tiny sleeping face. 'That's if you *are* a fella-me-lad. By the left but I've got to watch I don't squash you, little chuck. There, just let me move one arm a bit. There, that better?'

The baby fluttered mauve eyelids, then began making soft little sucking noises, turning its head into the swaddling blanket. Gingerly, scarcely daring to breathe, Joe loosened it with his hand.

'Now, don't go and smother yourself, you little codger,' he said.

He cradled the baby into the curve of his arm, the womanly smile on his thin face at comical variance with the overnight growth of dark stubble on his chin.

'A right bloody turn-up for the book,' he chuckled.

Joe Barton, ex Corporal Joe Barton. Bolshie in outlook, even though back in civilian life, before he joined up, he had been well on the way to being a capitalist. Trusting in nobody and with good reason. . . . Putting out a finger he traced the baby's rounded chin with a feather-light touch, then he grinned to himself as the blob of a nose gave an irritated twitch.

'Sharp little sod, aren't you?' he whispered, so engrossed that he failed to see the way the night nurse approached his bed, then as silently crept away.

He could guess what the rest of the ward would say when waking-up time came at half past five:

'Always suspected old Joe had lost more than his knee-cap and half his brain in France. But we'd never have thowt he was expectin', would we, lads?'

That would be Nobby Clark, shell-shocked on the Somme in March, and still not able to face the outside world. Poor Nobby, still thinking he was in the hospital in Rouen; not able to believe the war was over.

Joe held his breath as the baby sighed, a soft little sigh ending on a whimper.

It was the day the vicar made his weekly round, always stopping by Joe's bed and beaming at him. As if there was summat to beam about, Joe thought bitterly.

'Now then, Mr Barton,' he'd say. 'Sister tells me you've been up on those pins of yours a bit more this week.'

The vicar's cheeks glowed shiny and red, as if he had been at them with a scrubbing brush. They moved up into little round cushions of fat as he smiled.

'Keep it up, man! There'll be no holding you back soon!'

'Holding me back from what?' Joe had asked once. 'From going down to London and trying to do me rounds on crutches? From convalescing with me sister, who doesn't want me anyway? At least her husband doesn't. Holding me back from trying to forget that men I knew well died with their faces shoved in the mud, or their bellies ripped open with pieces of shrapnel? Is that what you mean?'

The vicar's cheeks had glowed redder than ever as he had wished Joe a rapid 'God bless you, my son' before moving quickly on to the next bed.

Joe shifted his position with care. It wasn't fair baiting the little man. He always felt a pang of shame when the vicar had gone on his way down the ward, his Bible tucked neatly underneath his arm.

But what did a man like that know about owt?

Fair enough he must have been too old for active service, but Joe knew he had lived out his war in the northern town, with nothing to upset him but the reading of dispatches. The Rev Shuttleworth had not seen men screaming as their wounds turned gangrenous from the Salient's mud. He had not heard them, some of them, crying for their mothers before they went over the top.

He tightened his arm round the baby, holding it close, willing his own warmth into the tiny body, assuaging the choked-up feeling in his throat by a speech he would have ready for the luckless vicar:

'Right then, sir. What I would like you to tell me is how that oh so merciful God of yours can allow a young lass to peg out, leaving her baby with neither a mother nor a father? Would you not have thought that Him up there would have looked down and decided that she had been bad enough done by by some sod who wouldn't marry her, and seen to it that things would go right for her from now on?'

Joe nodded to himself, satisfied with the neat way he had phrased his speech, then shushed indignantly at the occupant of the next bed, who was snoring rhythmically up and down the scale.

'I haven't minded you keeping me awake all night, old pal,' he muttered, 'but this little whipper-snapper here has to be kept warm and quiet, see? He's going to wonder what sort of a place this is when he wakes up to find there's no titty milk for him.'

Suddenly to his surprise, an amazement tinged with shame at his unexpected weakness, Joe felt a tear ooze out from underneath his eyelids and roll slowly down his cheeks. Putting out his tongue as the tear meandered past the corner of his mouth, he tasted the sad saltiness of it, then he felt the familiar pain run like burning quicksilver down the back of his leg.

For the sake of the baby nestling close to his side, he decided to forgo his usual loud moan, which sometimes resulted in an extra early cup of tea if he could make the moan loud enough to reach the ears of the night nurse sitting writing out her reports at the desk at the far end of the ward.

Instead he thought about the baby's mother, the young black-haired woman lying dead now somewhere down the long echoing Infirmary corridor.

She had been a good looker all right. Sister Fletcher would have skinned him alive if she had known how many times in the past few days he had been on his crutches as far as the side ward where she lay. Oh, she would have been pleased with his progress all right, but shocked out of her starched pinny at the idea of a man patient daring to venture into the women's wing of the Infirmary.

'Nasty mind you've got underneath that apology for a cap, Sister,' he'd told her when she had ticked him off for winking at a buxom ward maid. 'You ought to know better than most that I haven't got the strength at the moment for more than a bloody wink.'

Uttering a sound somewhere between a pshaw and a snort of disgust, Sister Fletcher had flounced around and slapped her flat-footed way back between the rows of beds and out of the ward.

But he had seen the woman through the open door into the small side-ward. He had seen her lying back on high-banked pillows, her long hair lying in two never-ending plaits over the sheet. White as chalk her face with the freckles standing out like spots of undissolved Horlicks on the top of a glass of hot milk. And even in that quick glance he had seen the way the half-moon curve of her surprisingly dark eyelashes lay on her cheeks. He almost risked a whistle, just to cheer her up, because the baby was still inside her then. He had seen the rounded mound pushing the bedclothes up as if somebody had clamped half a barrel on her stomach.

'What is she doing up this end in Women's Surgical if she is in here to have a baby?' Joe had asked little Nurse Gallagher when she came on duty.

'She's going to have her baby by caesarian section,' the nurse had told him, full of importance because she was going to be allowed to watch as part of her training. 'The surgeon, Mr Cardwell, is coming in specially to do it, because there is something wrong with the mother's heart and she can't be allowed to go on and have her baby normally.' Nurse Gallagher's blue button eyes had sparkled with anticipation, then she had gone on to tell Joe that caesar babies were beautiful babies as a rule.

'Their heads aren't pointed like normally born babies, because they haven't had to struggle to be born,' she'd said, then scuttled away before Sister Fletcher caught her gossiping with the patients again.

Joe glanced down at the perfect curve of the rounded head nestling in the crook of his arm. Nurse Gallagher had been quite right. This little head certainly came to no point. Tenderly he traced its shape, feeling the silky hair whisper through his touch.

Poor little Nurse Gallagher, with her pale piggy eyes, and her big red conk of a nose, and her bare arms as mottled as a slab of potted meat.

It would have upset her proper seeing the young woman die on the operating slab, if that was the way it had been. The little Irish girl hadn't been nursing long enough to get used to patients dying. Not young and lovely women like the beauty in the side ward. Joe doubted if Nurse Gallagher would ever consider it all a part of her day's work, as he was sure po-faced Sister Fletcher did.

They could have done with her at the hospital at Boulogne, what with soldiers dying right, left and centre. Or better still, they could have sent her up the line. One look at her horrible miserable face, and even a German minenwerfer would have changed direction – may even have turned back and blown some of its own side up. . . .

'Well, Mr Barton? Tired of holding the baby, are you? I've come to take her away now, thank you very much.'

'What's going to happen to it?'

Joe had never thought Sister Fletcher would answer him, but she did:

'We're keeping her in for a few days, but there's a

grandmother going to take her. She's just arrived with her husband and they want to see their grand-daughter.'

Swiftly she removed the bundle from his grasp.

'Now don't forget it is your morning for helping with the teas; the night staff have been run off their feet what with everything happening unexpectedly.'

And before Joe could say even as much as a 'damn' Sister Fletcher had been and gone, taking the baby with her.

His left arm was still curved round the empty warm space in the bed. It had all been as quick as a trench raid, target reached, mission completed. Yes, sir, please sir, three bags full sir. . . .

But oh, bloody hell, it was terrible this emptiness he felt. He could still smell the new-born smell of the baby, a sweet soft scent, far different from the stink in his nostrils every time they changed the dressing on his leg.

He would never forget that dreadful smell . . . but that was when they had thought his leg would have to come off.

Joe buried his head in the place where the baby had been. By the left, but he had told that still wet round the ears apology of a doctor in France where he'd got off. He had told the bloody lot of them that if they cut off his leg he would do himself in at the first opportunity.

He wasn't going back to Blighty with one trouser leg flapping. He wasn't 'one of our gallant defenders' as a sickening headline in a newspaper had described him and his like. He wasn't cut out to be a cripple, not Joe Barton. Not even Joe Barton, son of a drunken whore, father unknown. Always he had had to fend for himself, just as that poor little sod of a baby would have to.

And that bonny little lass with her gypsy colouring, never knowing that she had a perfect baby with a face as round as a miniature full moon.

It wasn't fair. Nothing in the whole bloody rotten world was fair. . . .

Joe turned his face into his pillow and wept. Quietly at

first, with subdued sobs, then with an abandonment to grief that left him without even the semblance of control. Shaking with unmanly sobs, crying his terrors of what had passed away, crying as he had never cried before, not even as a child.

When the night nurse, going off duty, told Sister Fletcher about it, she nodded with satisfaction, her eyes starting from her head with exhaustion.

'So it worked then,' she said, her plain dedicated face flushing with an emotion which should have made her look beautiful in its compassion, but because of the unfortunate set of her features, made her look merely blotchy and ugly.

'Mr Barton will start to improve from now on. That leg wound of his is only half his trouble. I'm sure you realize that. He just needed to crack, that was all. That swearing and carrying on is all part of his loneliness.' She pinched the bridge of her nose as if she would smooth her exhaustion away. 'Finding out there is always someone worse off than yourself is often the best medicine, human nature being what it is.' She straightened her already straight cap, pushing back a strand of mousy hair.

'Everybody has to crack sometimes, even the toughest nut of all.'

Then, having worked a full night on top of a full day, she went off duty for a few hours, her back ramrod straight, and her feet slapping the polished floor in their quarter to three position.

'She actually looked part way to being human,' the night nurse told her friend as they ate stringy sausages flanked by watery cabbage downstairs in the nurses' dining-room. 'I even dared to ask her what would be happening to the baby, and she said we would be keeping it in for a few days before the grandmother took it home.'

'The mother's mother?'

'There never was a father, if you know what I mean.

216

Seems the girl, Rose Carmichael, insisted on staying on too long at one of the mills, when she should have been resting with a heart condition brought on by her pregnancy.'

She shovelled her food in from force of habit. 'It won't be easy rearing a baby that size.'

'Especially for a grandma.'

'Oh, she's not in the least *old*. Not white-haired and doddering,' she said, yawning as she stirred sugar into a thick white mug of tea.

It did not occur to Maggie that there was anything extra-ordinary in the fact that she was walking alone the three miles from Foundry Street to the Infirmary, wheeling an empty pram.

Kit had accepted that they would bring up Rose's baby as a matter of course, had taken two hours off from the shop for the funeral, and had agreed with Maggie on the in-scription for the wreath of white and red chrysanthemums:

'The Lord giveth, and the Lord taketh away.'

'Though I'm not too sure I believe that literally,' she said. 'Not if I set me mind to it. Rose died because she was stubborn, right to the end. I don't feel the Lord had much part in anything that happened to Rose. . . .'

She levered the heavy pram down off a kerb, across a street and up on to the opposite pavement, stopping now and again to feel the blanket covers to make sure they were still dry.

They had been airing over the fire-guard and on the string across the fireplace since six o'clock that morning, and still felt warm to her touch.

She adjusted the storm apron, frowning at the frayed elastic holding it in place. The half-crown she had paid for it had been more than enough for a third-hand pram, she decided.

Guiding the pram across the tram-lines, Maggie turned into a side street leading to a short cut underneath a railway arch. A sudden gust of wind lifted the brim of her hat a little, and she stopped to pierce it more firmly to her up-swept hair with a long pearl-ended hat pin. Then, for the second worrying time, she pushed a hand inside the pram to feel the blankets.

'And there's nobody going to feel sorry for you, little love,' she told the empty interior. 'I'll see you go nothing short somehow or other. You're going to have your own little kit of milk every day from Mr Ainsworth's best cow. I've arranged that. There's not going to be any of that skimmed condensed muck for you. You are going to grow up just the same as if everything was as it should be. Your grandma will see to that.'

Her expression was very fierce, the well-defined eyebrows drawn together, and the small chin jutting out, as Maggie continued on her way. It looked like rain and she lifted her face to the sky and dared it to do any such thing.

'You can just wait till I get the baby safely back home,' she told a lowering cloud, then as a tram clattered past, rocking along its rails, she bent her full weight over the pram handle, pushing it up the long steep slope leading to the Infirmary.

The baby was ready, dressed in the long feather-stitched petticoats, one of flannel and two of cotton underneath the pin-tucked nightdress, the hand-knitted jacket made by Maggie during Rose's waiting months.

Everything was too big, she noticed; even the bonnet she had sworn would have been too small for a doll when she stitched it up.

She watched silently as Sister Fletcher wrapped the baby in the grey shawl with darns worked in wool pulled from its fringes, the shawl Rose had been wrapped in as a baby.

Maggie swallowed hard. She had no intention of showing herself up in front of this hatchet-faced nurse, so she blinked and stared at the far wall with its top half painted a sickly green and the bottom a bilious yellow.

'It looks a bit like rain,' she said in a casual-sounding voice.

'Yes it does.'

Sister Fletcher tied the bonnet strings with a ferocious bow, and Maggie winced.

She would throttle the little thing if she wasn't careful, then to take her mind off the lump in her throat she narrowed her eyes and gave the Sister what Kit would have called one of her 'summing-up' looks.

By gum, but she looked a hard one all right. She would not fancy getting the wrong side of *her*, Maggie decided. A bad enemy the Sister would make. She stared at the nurse's ringless left hand. Yes, Sister Fletcher would likely be one of the women who would claim to have lost a sweetheart in France, and God only knew, there would be plenty of them about now. . . .

She held out her arms as the Sister passed the bundle over to her, and marvelled how any woman could look so forbidding when they were handling a baby. Why, even Clara would have smiled if she had looked down at this tiny round-faced scrap with her tuft of black hair showing where the bonnet wasn't pulled down far enough.

Maggie adjusted the frill until it almost covered the baby's eyebrows.

Sister Fletcher was feeling as grim as she looked. Personally she did not give this particular baby much of a chance. She had sent far too many babies out into the world, only to see them return as undernourished infants, bowed with rickets, heads alive with nits, middle-aged before they had even gone off to school.

'She'll have to be fed every two hours I'm afraid, Mrs Carmichael,' she said, 'and that includes during the night for the first few weeks. She's not sucking strongly enough to get all she needs at one feed. You'll find that she gets exhausted then falls asleep.'

The deep resigned sigh showed Maggie that the nurse considered what she was going to say next was possibly a waste of time, but she waited patiently, ready to give as good as she got.

'She will also have to be kept very warm, Mrs Carmichael, and that means keeping her in a heated room all the time. Are you all right for coal, because if not I might be able to put you in touch with an organization. . . .'

Maggie nodded quickly, her dignity at stake.

'The coal shed's that full it's spilling out into the back-yard, thank you very much all the same, Sister. I've been stocking up for weeks.'

She felt the hardening of the lump in her throat. The time for crying was not here. If there was such a time it was when you were alone, shut away behind a closed door so that nobody could see you giving in.

Giving in was a waste of time; she had decided that a long long time ago.

'Thank you for all you and the other nurses have done for my daughter, and for the baby, especially for keeping Rosie here till we got things sorted out an' . . . an' the funeral over with. It's been very good of you, it really has. . . .'

Sister Fletcher waved the thanks away, walking to the door of the little side-ward with her starched apron crack-ling as she went.

'You know your way out, Mrs Carmichael?' she asked over a disappearing shoulder.

Then she took out her jumbled feelings on the first nurse she met, a young probationer who was doing nothing more revolutionary than carrying a bed-pan to the sluice.

Joe Barton, trespassing yet again as he swung his way along the stone-flagged corridor on his crutches, saw the soberly clad back of a small slim woman carrying a baby in her arms.

She did not need to turn round for him to recognize her. He would have recognized that walk anywhere, that straight back, that brown hair slipping its bun and wisping down her neck.

'Maggie!' His heart was beating so fast, beating right up in his throat so that his voice came out as no more than a croak. 'Maggie . . . oh, Maggie!'

The more he tried to hurry after her, the more the crutches got in his way, and when Maggie turned a corner and disappeared from his sight Joe slumped against the wall, drained and exhausted.

He stood there, head bowed, saying her name over and over to himself . . . Maggie Craig . . . *his* Maggie. So that was the grandma little Nurse Gallagher had spoken about. His Maggie, his own love, and they had been within yards of each other, and because of this blasted leg he couldn't even get her to turn round.

Joe raised his head, suddenly filled with an elation he didn't know how to control. Bugger the man she had married, and bugger the fact that she hadn't answered any of his letters. That one glimpse of her had told him something he had known all along. All those terrible months and years in France, she was the only woman he had dreamed of, still was the only woman he dreamed of.

And that baby had been put in his arms because it *belonged* to him. That baby was a part of Maggie, and he had cuddled it and kept it warm right after it was born. No wonder he had felt like he did . . . it was fate, it was a miracle, and the sooner he got out of this damned Infirmary the better. To see Maggie again, that was all that mattered now.

16

Will Hargreaves, Belle's husband and Joe's brother-in-law, viewed Joe's impending release from the Royal Infirmary with the gravest trepidation.

'Don't commit yourself as to how long he can stay, that's all I'm trying to say,' he warned, walking on his bent legs down the stone corridor in time for the Sunday hour of visiting at three o'clock.

'Tell him he can stop for a bit when he comes out next week, but have the sense to emphasize the bit. If you don't, then I will.'

His size seven shoes, tipped with heel protectors, made ringing noises on the floor as he bounced along, narrow shoulders hunched, and small fists buried deep in the pockets of his Sunday jacket.

'We might find ourselves landed with him for good.'

'He *is* my brother,' Belle said weakly, 'and anyway, our Joe will be off back to London as soon as he can. He's much too independent to be beholden to anyone, least of all to you. He's not short of a bob or two remember, and he'll want to get his affairs sorted out once he's found his feet.'

'But he never is going to find his feet, is he? From what that Sister told me he'll always have to walk with a stick.'

'That doesn't make him a *cripple*,' Belle said faintly. Arguments always had that effect on her. She sighed as they turned right into another long bare corridor.

'Please, Will, try and talk to him just a little this time.'

Then Belle walked on, the worriting nature of her thoughts wrinkling her forehead. Because it wasn't merely Joe's leg that was bothering him. It was his *nerves*. Sister had said so.

And Will had no patience at all with nerves. Belle had tried to make him *see*, but it was no use.

'Oh, aye? Your Joe might have been in the trenches, but tell me summat? How could our lads have even begun to fight in France if it hadn't been for folk like me providing them with munitions? Tell me that to be going on with.'

'I wasn't getting at *you*, Will,' Belle said gently, but it was no good.

There was no besting Will. . . .

To get to Joe's bed they had to walk past a bed with a red screen round it. Belle averted her eyes, and closed her ears against the sound of a hollow groan.

'He's just coming round from the chloroform, missus,' a soldier in hospital blue told her, trying to reassure. 'He'll make more noise than that when he finds they've taken another chunk from his leg.'

Belle felt the colour drain from her face, but Will took her by the arm and moved her on quickly. They found Joe sitting on a bed playing cards with a man with large sad eyes set in a long drooping face. He struggled to his feet when he saw them, and put a hand on the man's shoulder.

'Better luck next time, old pal,' he grinned, scooping the kitty of halfpennies from the bedcover.

'Nice of you to come,' he told Belle and Will, then he escorted them over to his own bed and indicated two hard little chairs already hopefully set into position.

'Have a chair. I can come home next Tuesday.'

The word 'home' had been a mistake, and Joe knew it at once by the way Belle flinched, and the way that pint-sized husband of hers shot her a warning glance.

Will at the same time was wondering if he could give Belle a warning kick without letting it show? He and this so-called brother-in-law could never share the same roof and he was astute enough to realize it. It was time Belle knew it too.

Working with gunpowder had not been exactly a bean-feast, but not to be considered of course with charging about in France with a fixed bayonet. Joe was obviously far from well, you only had to see the nerve jumping at the side of his scarred face to see that. And it wouldn't be no bloody picnic having a bloody war hero sitting opposite to him on the other side of his own fireplace, wincing every time he struck a bloody match, and jumping a mile when a lump of coal back-fired. He stared anywhere but at Joe and said a deliberate nothing.

'That's right good news,' Belle said after far too long a delay, and when they had gone, back home to their neat little cottage and their Sunday tea of cold ham and toma-toes, followed by a treat of a tin of pineapple chunks swimming in a sea of Bird's custard, Joe lay back on his bed, remembering the sudden exhilaration he had felt when he had seen Maggie again.

Exhaustion, Maggie knew, was something you learned to live with after a time. Lack of sleep was another.

Not able to take more than a few ounces of cows' milk at a time, the baby woke regularly every two hours, crying with a thin wail, and jerking Maggie out of a twitching sleep on the hard and slippery sofa.

Sometimes she heard it when the baby was fast asleep, she told Clara.

'You look shocking,' Clara said kindly.

So tired was Maggie that she was sure she nodded off for odd minutes, even when she was putting the nappies through the mangle in the yard, or even queueing up in the Fish Market as she was now, leaving Clara to keep an eye on the baby.

The main thing was that Rosie was thriving. She still

cried a lot, still sicked up a goodly part of her bottle, but now she would stare up into Maggie's face with a sort of cross-eyed resignation. And Clara she seemed to adore, a feeling that Maggie knew was mutual.

There was something strangely soothing about the long nights dozing fitfully on the sofa downstairs, the firelight softening the contours of the dark furniture as the fire struck sparks from the burnished steel fender. Maggie drifted in and out of dreams. . . . Once, half awake and half asleep, she imagined that Rose was standing by the dresser smiling at her.

Moving up in the queue Maggie shifted her weight from one foot to the other, and made up her mind not to faint. She was not going to faint in a fish queue, not her. . . .

All the same, it was good to get out into the open again, away from the overpowering smell, out on to the cobblestones of the market-place. She glanced up at the round clock set high in the market house tower, and saw that it was almost time for the baby's next feed.

She would have to hurry. . . .

'It's all right, she hasn't moved a muscle,' Clara said the minute she walked in, then her eye slid down into its corner.

'There's a man been. A tall fella with a walking stick, and no hat on. I told him you'd gone out, and he said he would come again.' She sniffed her disgust at the caller going away without stating his business and saying who he was. 'I can't think who it might be, love. I knew it weren't the Insurance man or the Doctor's man with it not being a Friday, but he asked for you by name so he must have come for summat.'

Maggie was taking the parcels of fish from her basket and handing one to Clara.

'Pay me later,' she said. 'Isn't that your mother knocking on the wall?' She smiled. 'Thank you for letting me get out a bit. I really enjoyed it, there's a lovely fresh wind.'

'It's time you had a bit of life,' Clara said kindly, then

raising her voice and startling Maggie she walked over to the dividing wall and banged on it with a clenched fist.

'I'm coming as fast as I can!'

Her voice dropped two octaves. 'I never thought the day would come when I would admit it, but me mother's really getting on me wick.' She glanced at the baby. 'Oh, I've wakened her up,' she said in a surprised tone. 'She's a light sleeper, isn't she?'

Before she took off her coat, Maggie set the milk to warm, smiling to herself. Yes, she had enjoyed being out on her own in the fresh air even though the wind had been a bit parky. She puffed up the front of her hair with her fingers. And the baby was gaining weight, and the sewing orders were coming in, and even if Kit was laid off from the shop they would manage somehow.

With secret pride Maggie had, for the first time in her life, opened a bank account.

'One of these fine days we'll move,' she'd told Kit. 'We'll have a garden with a swing in it, an' when I hang the washing out it won't bang against a sooty wall. An' Rosie will run to school down a leafy lane. . . .'

She stirred sugar into the milk and began to fill the bottle, then started as the knocker banged three times, making her spill some of the milk over the table.

Telling the baby to be quiet for a minute, Maggie walked through the parlour to the front door.

She could not believe it . . . this man, this thin pale man with the dark hair that flopped down over his forehead had been in her heart and her mind for so long, and yet she could not bring herself to believe that he was standing there.

'Joe! Oh, Joe.' She held out both hands towards him, and he hooked the stick over his arm and took them, and they gazed into each other's eyes, all attempt at pretence forgotten.

'Joe . . . I never thought to see you again. I never . . .'

Joe was the first to recover. 'Well then, Maggie love.

226

Aren't you going to ask me in?' He glanced up and down the street. 'There's eyes boring in me back. I can feel them. Dozens of them.'

Maggie stood aside, held out a hand to help as she saw the awkward way he negotiated the step, then drew it back when she saw the expression on Joe's face. Then she led the way through the parlour into the living-room, to where Rose's baby slept peacefully, tired after her crying spell, in the clothes basket to the side of the black fireplace.

'My daughter's baby,' Maggie said, overwhelmed now by an unexpected shyness which she tried to hide by bending over and tucking the blankets in more firmly. A hairpin loosened itself and fell with a tinkle to the floor as it bounced off the fender.

'My hair's a mess,' she said stupidly, putting up a hand and trying to secure the straying wisps.

'Maggie, lass. . . .' Joe came up behind her, stooped down to lay a gentle finger on the baby's head, and saw the floor coming up to hit him smack between his eyes.

Taking a deep breath he straightened up, feeling the sweat break out on his forehead as the entire room swam round and round. Groping behind him he felt for the edge of the table.

'I think mebbe I walked a bit too far,' he said, and his voice was a shaky echo, as if it came from a far-off place.

Then somehow, he never knew quite how, he was sitting in a chair, and his head was being held down between his knees, and from the same far-away place a sympathetic voice was saying:

'You'll be all right in a minute . . . oh, Joe, love . . . take a few deep breaths . . . that's right. Now just sit there quietly and I'll make a pot of tea. I've got some tea you'll like. It's special for nowadays.'

Joe fumbled in his pocket for a handkerchief, only to be handed one, neatly folded and ironed into a triangle.

'Now slip your coat off. This room's too hot, but it has to be for the baby. It must be a day for dizzy spells,' Maggie went on, talking quickly and not looking at him, giving him a chance to recover. 'I thought I was going off meself in the fish market earlier on, so I know how you feel.'

He put his head back and found that the room had stopped whirling round, then he watched her as she lifted the black kettle from the fire and poured the boiling water into the tea-pot standing in the hearth.

'Here you are then,' she said a few minutes later as she handed him a cup of tea, sweet and hot. 'Now then, tell me where you've walked from, and where you've been. . . .' She sat down opposite to him, and saw him sitting in Kit's chair, and it was as if there were no years in between; as if nothing of importance had happened since he went away. It was uncanny, but it was true.

'I've walked from Steep Brow,' he told her, answering a question she had already forgotten she had asked. 'It was hard on the knee coming downhill.' He leaned forward, putting the cup of tea on the table. 'Maggie, lass. I know a lot you think I don't. I know about your girl dying, and I know that baby very well.' He nodded towards the basket. 'I saw that baby before you did. I've been in the Infirmary a long time because some compassionate sod of a captain saw it was my home-town, and sent me here to be near my kith and kin.'

He gave a twisted smile. 'And I saw you taking the little nipper out, but I couldn't make you hear when I shouted after you.'

Suddenly he raised his voice, startling Maggie out of her dream-like state.

'An' the first thing I've done is to come and find you, *Mrs Carmichael*. Why did you never answer my letters, Mrs Carmichael?'

Maggie's eyes widened with shock.

'Letters. I got no letters, Joe.'

'One of them came back with NOT KNOWN AT THIS ADDRESS written on it,' he said more quietly. 'So somebody was getting them, weren't they?'

Maggie flared up then. 'But you took your time in writing, didn't you, Joe? It was just after you'd gone, for weeks after you'd gone, that I needed a letter bad. I'll tell you how bad, Joe Barton.'

She was hating him and she was loving him. She could not take her eyes from his face, from the fading scar on his cheek, from the nose, more hawk-like than she remembered it, from the gaunt expression he never had before.

He had been through hell, she could see that and she could not bear it. He had suffered and she had not been there to smooth the hurt away. . . .

Maggie, quite without volition, got up from her chair, knelt down by Joe's chair, laid her head on his lap until she felt the touch of his hand on her hair, and cried without restraint. She was crying the years away, but she did not know it; this was happiness if she had recognized it, and Joe's broken words were like healing balm to her ears.

'Don't cry, little love,' he murmured. 'It was my fault, all my fault. I sent for you when I was beginning to be somebody, when I'd started putting a bit by. . . .' His hand, stroking the hair away from her forehead, was suddenly still.

'Oh, Maggie Craig . . . why did you have to go and get married?'

For a moment Maggie too was quite still, then she raised a tear-washed face.

'I'll tell you why I got married, Joe Barton. I married a man who was probably the only man in this town who would have me, knowing that before my own father was cold in his grave I had started to have a baby.' Her gaze was steady. 'Our baby, Joe. An' I lost it upstairs in this house, crying for you. For a letter that never came, and when you did write, Joe, it was too late, and though I never would have thought Kit could do such a thing, I can't find it in my heart to blame him. Not at this moment I can't blame him. One day I might, but now. . . .'

She could hear the ticking of the clock on the mantelpiece. The baby made a snuffling sound, then was quiet again.

'Oh, God!' Joe's voice was ragged, filled with hurt. 'Oh, God . . . what a mess. What a terrible bloody wasted mess.' He gave the arm of the chair a derisory slap with the flat of his hand. 'I never thought . . . I never once thought . . . Maggie. I was nineteen!'

'I know.' Maggie sighed. 'We were both there, Joe, but it's all over a long time ago. I've got my life now, and you've got yours, and maybe it is all God's will.'

Joe jerked her shoulders so that she was staring into his blazing eyes.

'It's not bloody God's will, Maggie, it's not! I doubt if there even is a God, and don't look at me like that. I've had the chance to wonder these past few years out there in France. I'm living with Belle till I'm fit enough to go away again, and she goes on about God's will all the time. What's happened to me and you is me not writing early on. You can't blame God for that. For once I'm sticking up for Him!'

'I'm saying nothing, Joe,' Maggie said wearily, 'but all I know is that if I hadn't had a God to turn to at times I shudder to think what might have happened.' She stood up, small and dignified, smoothing down her unruly hair, and moving so that she stood well away from him.

'It's Wednesday, Joe, and Kit's half-day. I don't want you here when he comes in for his dinner. He'll know who you are straight away, and I can't face that.'

Her face crumpled.

'When they came to tell me that Rose had died, do you know what I did? I went out into the yard and banged my head against the wall till the blood came. Then I came in and started to get Kit's breakfast. So you see I do know how to carry on . . . and, Joe, I'm glad to have seen you again, and I'm so very happy that you came through the war alive, but now you must go.'

Joe got up from the chair with difficulty and came towards Maggie, but she held up a warning hand.

'Now this minute, before Kit. I'm not in no fit state to make polite introductions and neither are you.' The glance she gave the clock on the mantelpiece was full of wild entreaty, and even Joe could see that her control was ready to snap.

'I've never stopped loving you, Maggie Craig,' he said clearly, then turning his back on her he limped towards the door, raised a hand in a mock salute, and was gone.

When Kit came into the house, exactly four minutes after Joe had left it, he went straight to his chair, slumped down into it, wrenched off his tie, and unbuttoning his high starched collar, threw it on to the table as if it had been choking the life out of him.

If Maggie had looked at him properly she would have seen the utter desolation on his round face, the dejection in the droop of his shoulders. But she was rushing around, pulling a white cloth over the red chenille, setting out knives and forks, nervous at the way Kit had just missed seeing Joe, and hearing Joe's last words to her, hearing him say them over and over again.

'I've never stopped loving you, Maggie Craig . . . never . . . never . . . never.'

Bending down to the fire-oven she took out a dish of well-browned hot-pot, and set it on a mat.

'It's ready,' she said, crimson-faced, knowing she would be quite unable to touch a mouthful.

Obediently Kit took his place, then sat with head bowed as Maggie spooned the food on to his plate.

'Aye . . .' he said, then again, 'aye.'

'Kit! What's the matter?'

Maggie saw him for the first time. 'What's wrong?'

Wearily Kit pushed the untouched plate of food away.

'I've been given the sack,' he said in a low voice. Even as

231

he spoke his hands were outstretched to his wife for comfort, just as he had stretched them out to his mother when things went wrong.

Maggie did not fail him, she never had, but this time her pity was tinged with despair. Standing behind his chair she tangled her fingers in his curly hair whilst he leaned against her, his eyes closed.

Then she was angry, so angry that for a moment no words would come.

'You mean that old skinflint has done what he's been threatening to do for years? Taken on someone younger for lower wages? Kit, he can't have! He wouldn't! Not after you keeping that shop open all hours, working out the rations and doing most of the buying? I won't let him!'

She gave Kit's shoulders an exasperated push.

'I could kill him, that's what I could do. The old goat, the mean, spiteful, miserable old goat.'

Kit shook his head from side to side.

'Nay, love. It's not what you think. He's selling up, lock, stock and barrel, and going to live down south. He's seventy years old, Maggie, and he's made his pile. He says he's earned his place in the sun . . . those were his exact words.'

'And what about *your* place in the sun then?'

Maggie faced him now, hands on hips. 'Does he not think about all the years you've been late home, after slaving behind that counter to help him make his pile? The times before the Act came in and you were working from six in the morning till the last customer came in, and then sometimes for no more than a candle?' Her voice rose. 'And what did you say to him when he told you, Kit? Did you just listen and say nothing at all? Nothing at all?'

Kit spread his hands wide.

'Don't take on so, love. I did let him see that I was cut up about it, of course I did. I even asked him if the new owner might keep me on to manage the shop. I reminded him that I knew where every last matchbox was kept, and that I knew all my customers inside out, and I told him I knew who could be trusted to have a bit of tick. But he said he was sorry.'

'Sorry? I should just think he *was* sorry. An' that's all he was, just sorry?'

'He told me he was selling it to a man who wanted to set his son up in business.' Kit looked away from her. 'He wants me to keep on for a few weeks, to show this lad the ropes . . . just till he gets used to it, you know?'

Maggie felt the injustice of it deep inside her, but what she felt she could not even begin to stomach was Kit's attitude. This time he had gone too far. She felt physically sick.

'And you agreed? You actually agreed to that?'

She wrenched a chair from underneath the table and sat down, not trusting her legs to support her. 'You mean you let Mr Yates persuade you to do *that*? Oh, Kit, where's your pride? Do you know what I would have done? I'd have told your miserly Mr Yates exactly what I thought about him, then I'd have marched outside and thrown a flamin' stone through his flamin' window . . . that's what I'd have done!'

Kit got up, leaving his meal on the table. 'Then I would have got myself arrested, wouldn't I? No, there was nothing I could do, and I'm hurting no one but myself if I refuse to help the new lad coming in. I'll find meself another job somehow. Things are sometimes for the best.'

Maggie stared at him. He was so kind, so good, so weak, so much less than a man that she wanted to cry. No, not cry, but beat her fists against his chest, scream at him and kick him for being as he was, for putting her into this position of being the stronger. For making her responsible for him. She stared at him, her hand over her mouth, seeing the defeated droop of Kit's head, seeing too in her mind's eye, the cheeky, almost arrogant lift of Joe Barton's head as he had left her not half an hour ago.

Joe would have stood his ground. Joe had come through

experiences which Kit could never even have imagined, and he was still a fighter. . . .

Maggie made up her mind the way she always did, quick and swift, before she had time to change it:

'How much is Mr Yates asking for the shop?'

Kit mumbled his reply. 'A hundred pounds. He told me he considered it a fair price, with the two rooms above and the one at the back, even though it is used mainly as a store room. He said that . . .'

But Maggie was not interested in what else Mr Yates had said. She was doing quick sums in her mind, and any minute now she would regret it and it would be too late.

Going over to the dresser drawer, she rummaged beneath a pile of tea towels and took out her bank book. She flicked over the entries, one pound, three pounds, and once when she had sewed for five weeks on the linen of the hotel near the station, an unbelievable six.

She held out the book to Kit.

'A hundred and ten pounds, six shillings and fourpence. Do you think Mr Yates would change his mind for ten pounds, six shillings and fourpence?'

As though he had suffered a sudden stroke, Kit sat without moving a muscle, staring at the bank book.

'Open it, Kit!' Maggie was shouting, forgetting about the still sleeping baby. 'Open it and see for yourself. It's all down there, every single saving. Look at it if you don't believe me!'

He stared at the closely figured pages as if in a trance, running a finger over the column, shaking his head, then when he spoke at last it was to say something that made Maggie want to pick up a knife from the table and stick it in his chest.

Shaking his head in infuriating bewilderment, he said:

'But it would be a dirty trick, lass. What about the man who wants to buy the shop for his son?'

Maggie clenched and unclenched her hands, feeling the nails bite deep into her palms.

'Has anything been signed?' She marvelled at the calmness of her voice.

'No. Mr Yates said it was just a gentlemen's agreement as yet.'

'Then as Mr Yates is no gentleman, there's no problem, is there? That shop is *yours*, Kit. Without this money it is yours the way you've worked it up, and you know it.'

Still he argued. 'Maggie, love. I can't take this. I'd no idea you had saved so much, but I know what you were saving for. You hate the town, you've hated it all these years. Anyway, there's the baby now. It's no fit place for a baby apart from the fact that it would take more than one pair of hands to make that place decent enough to live in. The back is just a store room, and upstairs there is damp running down the walls, and the floorboards are giving. There's mice and cockroaches . . . oh, Maggie, it's a *terrible* place. This house is a little palace compared.'

Maggie's eyes flashed.

'Do you *want* the shop, Kit Carmichael, or don't you? I know what it's like, and I know it's no place for a baby, but Clara will take little Rosie for a while. She'll jump at the chance. So just for once, will you be decisive and tell me what you really want to do?'

He did not need to tell her, one look at his face was enough. Slowly despair was being replaced by hope, and more than hope, a wonder in his wife's capability, a marvelling at the way she could always be relied on to bring order out of chaos. Defending him, shielding him from trouble, the way his mother had always done. . . .

And almost *killed* Maggie at one time, his conscience was reminding him, but Kit had long ago put the memory of that night from his mind. He'd had to in order to replace his mother on her pedestal.

'It's not as nice a district as this,' he said again, his hand over the bank book as if he had already transferred it into his own keeping.

'Do you really think Clara will have the baby to mind?

There's sacking over the windows, love, and plaster peeling from the walls, and I won't be able to help much if I'm in the shop and doing the buying and everything.'

'If I warm your dinner up, do you think you could eat it?' She was too tired to talk about it any more. It was done, and that was that. As he ate she sat straight in a corner of the sofa, watching the years fall away from his face as he waved his fork about to emphasize a point, to illustrate what they would do to make the upper rooms habitable.

Maggie knew that the rest of her life was being mapped out for her, because she knew that the post-war boom would be over almost before it began. There would be unemployment, and when the house was clean there would be days, months and years of standing behind the counter, selling a poke of sugar here, and a bundle of firewood there.

Kit wasn't getting any younger, and there was Rosie to bring up. . . . Maggie sighed. Oh, yes, she could read all the signs. Most of the town's mills needed new methods and new machinery. India's import of cottons had begun to fall off, and she had read that the Japanese weavers were willing to work even longer hours and for far less pay.

Her dream of moving to the country might never materialize, and little Rosie would have to grow up with the street for her playground, and the dirt and the grime as her heritage. . . .

That night Maggie went to Kit and whispered that she would like him to sleep with her.

'I have a great need of you, a greater need than you know,' she said.

He stared, shocked by what he considered to be her un-womanly behaviour, then he turned his head. 'You'd never sleep a wink with my snoring, lass,' he said.

Maggie felt her face sting as if he had slapped her. 'Good night, Kit,' she said quietly.

17

The climb up Steep Brow was easier than walking down. Seeing Maggie again had, Joe felt, done more for him than all the weeks and months he'd spent in hospital.

When Will Hargreaves came home from his milk round Joe was sitting by the fire, whistling and looking pleased with himself. He had gone through a bad few moments when he thought about Maggie going through what she had been through and all his fault, but that was done and past and what mattered now was their future together.

For they were going to have a future together. He had made up his mind about that.

'You happy or something?' Will asked, peeved because Wednesday was baking day at the Armitages' neat little semi-detached, and that meant Belle would not be home till later.

'Mrs Armitage likes her kitchen left clean and the oven done. She's very proud of that oven,' Belle had told him, smiling.

'Silly faggot,' Will had said, hating Wednesdays from then on.

Joe put down the paper he had been skimming through, and grinned, not unaware that his brother-in-law was regarding him with something akin to loathing.

'Not been a bad sort of day, has it?' he remarked for something to say.

'Not for *some* it hasn't,' Will said pointedly.

Joe merely laughed. Then he lit a cigarette and flicked the spent match into the fire, where it struck the bars of the grate then fell into the hearth.

'Pick it up.'

Will's tone was even, but frustration was rising thick in his throat. 'You wouldn't be smoking down here if Belle was at home,' he said, small eyes narrowing with dislike.

Joe did as he was told, still grinning.

'Oh, come on now, Will. You're not past having a crafty fag yourself now and again.' He held out the packet. 'Come on. Have one. We can waft the smell out before she comes home.'

'No, thanks.'

Will felt at that moment as if he could sell his soul for a smoke, but he was in no mood to be patronized by the man sitting opposite to him, the man so obviously chuffed about something.

He unbuttoned his waistcoat one button at a time, slowly and deliberately.

'Feeling up to getting back to London, and all them mucky carpets yet, Joe? You'll not earn much brass sitting on tha backside.'

Joe shook his head. 'All in good time, Will. I know it's not right me being here with you and Belle, but I try to keep out of your way as much as I can.'

'And I more than pay my way,' he added silently to himself.

He clenched his hands, dismayed to find that the palms had grown clammy. The little pulse at the side of his head had begun to throb again. 'It's not easy settling after all this time.'

His brother-in-law unfastened the top button of his trousers, and sighed with relief, as if their tightness had been straining over a billowing paunch.

'So we're back where we started then, are we?'

'What do you mean, back where we started, Will?'

The small eyes narrowed. So he had managed to ruffle the tall self-satisfied bloody hero, had he? Good! It was time Joe Barton realized he couldn't just walk into his house and behave as if he belonged. He belonged nowhere, this arrogant thin-faced so-and-so, with the twitching scar on his face, and his assumption that he had the right to get his big feet under their table.

From what Belle had told him, Joe Barton had cleared off pronto when he had found things getting too hot for him, and if he had found somewhere to go then, he could find somewhere to go now. Him and his big talk of a flat in London and his own firm, what did he know about having to get up at four o'clock of a morning and work for a boss who wouldn't give the skin of his rice pudding to his starving grandma?

Aye, Joe was ruffled all right. He'd wiped that grin off his face, that he had.

'Just how long *are* you reckoning on stopping here?' he asked, then before Joe could answer he got up and went out to the back, leaving him to think that one over.

Slipping his braces down as he went into the yard, Will felt mightily pleased with himself. He'd put his spoke in, and he knew Joe would not repeat what he had said to Belle. Just for a split second he felt a stab of shame when he thought what Belle would say if she knew he had been getting at her precious brother.

'He's all I've got, Will. The only family in the world,' she would say.

Still it had needed saying. Will lifted the latch of the privy, then jumped away as a thin grey cat streaked past him to disappear over the wall into the next yard with the speed of light.

'Thought I saw a rat out there,' he said, when he went back into the house, his humour partly restored, and quite prepared to say no more.

What he wasn't prepared for was the swift reaction to what he considered to be an innocent remark. . . .

Immediately Joe sprang to his feet, the colour draining from his cheeks, leaving him grey and shaking, with his eyes starting from his head.

'A rat? Did you say a *rat*?'

Will studied him intently, realizing he had at last found a way to ruffle his brother-in-law's composure.

'Aye,' he said distinctly. 'We did have some at one time. They come from the tip over the field. Great big rats, as big as cats. What's the matter?' he asked in mock innocence. 'You frightened of them or something?'

Joe felt for the chair and sat down, sweat standing out on his forehead like glistening globules of rain.

It was Ypres again – the first, second, and the third battle, and Passchendaele, and Verdun, and there was a rat nibbling away at the dead hand of a soldier lying across his feet. And he could not move . . . he could not bloody move. . . .

Will pressed home his advantage, a faint niggling guilt at what he was doing spurring him on.

'You're all the same, you lot,' he said. 'Making out that your nerves are shot just to get some sympathy.' He sat down again, dismayed in spite of himself at Joe's pallor, but stung into bravado.

'It weren't no joke for me either, I can tell you, working with TNT. And there weren't no ruddy medals given out either.' He stabbed a finger in Joe's direction. 'I'm not like some who yell out in the night, but I could tell you things, aye that I could. There were times when me chest was so tight I was coughing up yellow phelgm, and me skin was yellower than a ruddy canary's.'

He raised his voice. 'Aye, and there weren't no leaves tickling up French tarts, not even after one of the buildings filled with nitro-glycerine blew up in a ruddy sheet of flame.'

Joe tore at his collar, finding it as hard to breathe as if his lungs were being filled with poison gas. He was no longer in the cosy living-room of Belle's cottage, with the ornaments on the mantelpiece, and the rugs laid out in a neat pattern on the floor. He was picking his terrified way along a duck-board over a stinking mud-flat, his equipment weighing a ton across his sagging shoulders. He was seeing the man in front of him slip from the track and die gasping for breath as the mud filled his mouth and eyes.

He was on his way struggling towards the front line, and the trenches where rats . . . he reached out for Will, lifting him out of his chair, and holding him suspended, his tiny feet swinging clear of the floor.

'Oh, I'm sorry for you, Will Hargreaves,' he said through clenched teeth. 'Heart sorry I am for you that your face turned yellow. Have you ever been so frightened that you shit yourself, Will?'

From his undignified position Will stared straight into Joe's eyes, and the glimmer of tears he saw there restored his bravado.

'It was only a cat, you filthy devil,' he said clearly, and staggered to recover his balance as Joe let him go.

Yet somehow he had won. He was not quite sure how, but he knew that he had won. Now he and Joe Barton could never live under the same roof again, and he was glad. And Belle would be glad, though she would never admit it.

Joe backed towards the curtain at the foot of the stairs, his limp more noticeable than ever. Then he drew the curtain back and stumbled up to his room, his shaking terror and his anger evaporating, leaving him weak and filled with self-loathing.

He ought not to have said that. He could scarcely believe he had said what he had. Sitting down on the edge of his bed, he dropped his head into his hands.

Tomorrow he would go back to London. When his hands had stopped their shame-making trembling he would start packing his few things, then he would be off. Sister Fletcher might have said that he wasn't fit to be on his own yet awhile, but even old po-face didn't know everything.

And he would take Maggie with him. And the baby. She wasn't happy in her marriage, he knew that, even if she hadn't said so. They belonged to him, the both of them, because why else had that baby been put in his bed if it hadn't been a sign?

A sign from the God Maggie believed in. The God he himself wasn't all that sure about.

'It's folks what make happiness, not God,' Joe told himself, levering himself up from the bed and starting to pack.

When Joe went downstairs again Belle had come home, pale and tired from the Armitages'.

He found her in the scullery peeling potatoes ready to drop them into the stew she had prepared the day before.

'Will's told me you're going, Joe,' she said, too tired to pretend that she did not know it was for the best.

'That's right, love, and I appreciate what you've done for me. It's just that, well . . . you know me.'

She nodded. 'It would have been nice if you could have stayed somewhere near. It would have been nice to have a bit of family living near.' She dug at an eye in a mis-shaped potato, taking out her feelings on it so that Joe would not see how upset she was feeling.

'Not enough folks with carpets, nor the money to have them cleaned,' Joe said, then he lowered his voice.

'Besides, love, Will is your family now, and you'll be having babies some day when you get a bit put by.'

Her face flamed and she averted her face as she answered him with quiet resignation.

' I don't think so Joe. They would have come afore now if God had meant me to have any.' She moved to the slopstone. 'You see, I'm not quite like other women in a certain way. The doctor told me it was because I was not fed well enough when I was a child. It's a sort of anaemia, if you know what I mean?'

'Oh, Belle. . . .' Joe picked up the knife and jabbed it into the potato peelings. 'Why must you always be so un-complaining? You make me feel ashamed. Surely some-thing can be done? Maybe if you went to one of them specialists in Manchester? You know, one what deals with women's complaints? I'd give you the money, love.'

Her cheeks glowed red again.

'It wouldn't do no good, our Joe, and anyway Will doesn't want no children,' she said simply, and bowed her head, resigned quite passively to the inevitable.

'Then I'll be off in the morning,' Joe said, and they stared at each other, each wishing there was more they could say, but knowing equally that there was nothing.

18

In the long wakeful stretch of the night, propped with a pillow against the bed-end, Joe smoked one cigarette after another, remembering the way Maggie had looked when she had opened the door to him.

There was something about her, something he couldn't put a finger on. She had seemed as untouched as when he had laughed with her as a young girl, as vulnerable and trusting as a young lass in love for the first time.

He narrowed his eyes against the upward curling smoke as he recalled, for some reason, the lonely housebound women he had often met on his rounds before the war. Hungry-eyed and nearly asking for it, and though God forbid his Maggie was not like that, there was something not quite right. She had been terrified of him touching her, and the conclusion he was coming to was that it had not been him she was frightened of, but herself. . . .

Joe drew too deeply on his cigarette and started to cough.

And it wasn't easy walking all that way downhill, carrying a case and managing with his stick, but he stopped now and again pretending to be looking in a shop window, or waiting for a tram. By the time he reached Foundry Street he was hot and sweating, and his knee was aching with the familiar throbbing grind.

He did not attract all that much attention in his badly fitting suit, but one woman, standing on her doorstep gossiping with a neighbour, said:

'That man is back from France. You can tell by his face, even without seeing his stick. It's awful to see them so pulled down. What they must have been through is hard to realize.'

Her neighbour nodded. 'Aye, it was a terrible war, but it's over now, and there will never be another, that's one blessing.'

'You look ill,' Maggie said when she opened the door to him, just as if she had known he would be coming; as if they had arranged it all the day before.

'You don't look all that well yourself, love,' Joe told her, and she led the way through into the living-room, pushed the kettle over the flames, and set the tea-pot down to warm in the hearth.

'I didn't get much sleep,' Maggie said, being careful not to look at him, not wanting him to see the joy just having him there shining from her eyes. 'Sit down, then, Joe.'

He put his case down by the dresser, and lowered himself stiffly into the rocking chair. 'And you sit down, lass. There's something I have to tell you, and I want you to take it all in, every word.'

Maggie did as she was told, then folded her hands in her lap and waited, her head dropping so low that all he could see was the top of her piled hair.

'I had a bit of a dust-up with Will,' Joe said. 'I only just stopped myself from belting him one. So I can't stay there any longer. I'd outlived my welcome there, anyroad.'

Just for a moment the memory of what Will had said about the rat in the yard caused a spasm of pain to cross his face. Maggie glanced up briefly and saw it, and her own heart contracted in sympathy.

'Joe Barton,' she said, trying to make her voice light. 'You seem to make a habit of setting yourself against somebody, and running away. *And* calling here to say goodbye first.'

As she spoke it came to her that she never seemed to have a normal conversation with this man. When they had been young it had all been teasing and laughter, and now, after all these years apart, they still talked with an intimacy as if the years between had never existed, as if all the trivia of politeness and small talk had been dispensed with, leaving them free to say exactly what came to mind.

She got up and got down the cups from the shelf. She got out the big glass sugar-bowl and clattered teaspoons into saucers, keeping her back carefully turned to him.

'So I won't be seeing you again, then?'

He came and putting his hands on her shoulders turned her to face him, standing so close she could see the puckered line of the scar, and the way his dark eyes were flecked with green.

'I've told you to *listen* to me, lass,' he said, and all at once she was aware of the excitement in him, the barely controlled violence.

'Don't touch me, Joe,' she said, and even as she said it she was aching for him to pull her close, to hold her face between his hands, and to kiss her with the mouth that was not fleshy as Kit's was fleshy, but firm and strong.

'Stop messing about with those bloody cups. I don't want a cup of tea. I'm not here to be soothed with tea,' he said. Turning round he picked up the poker and pulled the stand away from the flames. 'Tea's not what I've come for, and you know it.'

He came close to her again, and putting his arms around her, held her close. She could feel the heat from his face, and she knew that she was powerless to push him away.

'Joe,' she whispered. 'I'm not that young girl you came to say goodbye to long ago. It's not the same, an' it's not going to be the same. Go and catch your train, and be happy, and, Joe . . . you'll take care of yourself? You're not fit to be on your own, not yet.'

He gave her a little shake.

'I've been taking care of myself all me life, love. All my life. You know that.'

'Yes, I know that,' she whispered.

246

And then he kissed her. Gently at first, with his mouth softly covering her own, searching with sweetness, tracing her face with his lips, murmuring her name.

'Maggie! Oh, lass, you're so beautiful. So bloody marvellous and beautiful. You know that I love you . . . you must know that I've always loved you.'

He kissed her with passion, tangling his fingers in her hair, then letting her go so violently that she groped behind her for the arm of the chair.

Sitting down, she buried her face in her hands, but grasping her by the upper arms, Joe pulled her to her feet again.

'An' don't go and tell me I shouldn't have done that, because you wanted it as much as I did,' he said brutally. 'Tell me, Maggie, because it matters. It has a lot to do with what I've come to say. Has your husband never kissed you like that? Ever?'

For a long moment she was silent, then she shouted:

'No, no, no!'

And she was crying, openly in front of him, crying her shame away, feeling the hot tears run down her face. Sobbing her rejection of the night before away even as she despised herself for her disloyalty.

She raised her face.

'Joe. Don't ask me to talk about it. Not about Kit. He is the kindest, the most considerate man in the whole world. He hasn't done the brave things you've done, Joe, but in his own way he's been brave.' Her breath caught on a sob. 'I'm the wrong one, not Kit . . . He can't help being . . . being different. It's just that he's not made that way, that's all. He can't help not having *feelings*, Joe.' She was talking wildly, agitated and uncontrolled, and giving herself away with every word she spoke.

'And now you must go. Take your case and go. Please.'

Joe cupped her face in his hands, and Maggie even in her distress thought they were the kindest eyes she had ever seen. There was a tender sympathy there, an understanding, and a love that made her close her own eyes against it.

247

Joe spoke quickly and with urgency. . . .

'Now listen hard, Maggie love. If I could, and if there was time, I would get down on me knees to the bonniest, the bravest woman I've ever known. But I'm down on my knees in me heart, lass. An' that's the way it's going to be from now on.'

He let go of her, and limping back to the chair sat down and felt in his pocket for a cigarette. She saw that his hand trembled as he held the lighted match, and knew she would have to hear him out.

It was no good though. There was no 'from now on' for either of them, but she had the sensitivity to realize that what Joe was about to say had been well rehearsed in his mind. And when he began to speak she knew she was right.

'In two hours from now there's a train to Preston. That train goes to Crewe, Maggie love, and from there on to London. It's a long journey, lass, but it won't seem long, because you are going with me.'

Maggie shook her head violently, but Joe put up his hand for silence.

'You and the baby. *Our* baby, because that's what she is. It all fits like a pattern. You losing ours, then me coming back here and Rosie being put in my arms just after she'd been born. Me coming to find you. Will forcing me to act quickly. I thought it all out in the night and there's no other explanation than that it's a sign. Maybe from that God you're always on about.'

He nodded towards the basket by the fire. 'You can wrap her up well, and there are . . . there's a place at Crewe where you can get warm milk for her bottle.'

He had gone very pale, but Maggie let him carry on.

'We'll get her there all right. She won't come to no harm, an' we'll go to an hotel till I can get my place fixed up nice. Then it will be you and me and her, just like it was meant to be. You'll never want for nothing, Maggie, not for the rest of your days.' He stared down at the cigarette smouldering away in his hand, as if wondering what it could be.

'So just you go upstairs and get a few things together, not much because tomorrow you can go out to a fancy London shop and buy yourself and Rosie anything you need . . . no, not anything you *need*, anything you want.'

He grinned. 'And I won't take no for an answer, Maggie lass. You gave yourself away when I kissed you. You feel just the same way as me, and don't go saying it would be a sin, for staying apart would be a greater sin. Love, the kind of love we feel, doesn't come all that often, and what I saw in France taught me one thing:

'You have to take what you want from this life, 'cos nobody is going to hand happiness to you on a plate. Nobody.'

His face darkened. 'And it's our turn, Maggie. It's *our* bloody turn.'

There! He had said what he had come to say, but he had never dreamt it would take so much out of him. Drained and spent, he put his head back, closing his eyes, so that Maggie saw his face as she imagined it would look when he was dead. White and still, with the only thread of colour the pink scar tissue running down one cheek.

It was very quiet in the little room, quiet with the hush that came at that time in the morning. When Clara began raking the ashes from her fire-back at the other side of the wall, Maggie jumped as if someone had suddenly prodded her in the back.

'But I can't come with you, Joe,' she said. 'I can't leave Kit. He needs me. You don't know just how much he needs me.'

'And don't *I* bloody need you?'

Joe opened his eyes and stared straight at her. 'I need you in a way he has never needed you. You said so yourself, Maggie. Oh, Maggie love, you are still a young woman. You can't live out the rest of your life in this house, in this town. There's another side to life down there.'

He leaned forward, his thin face serious and intent.

'Do you want to grow like the rest of them? Like my

249

sister Belle? She was a washed-out child and now she's a washed-out wife. Maggie? Do you really want to turn into a worn-out drab, waiting on a man what needs a mother more than he does a wife?'

Joe threw the half-smoked cigarette into the fire.

'Oh aye, I know his sort. There were some like your husband in the army. Soft mammy's boys who should never have been breached. Show them a woman, a real woman, and they'd have run a mile. You can't stay here with a man like that, little love. You need someone to care for *you*. Not t'other way round.'

Maggie shook her head sadly.

'Now it is your turn to listen, Joe Barton. Even if I wanted to leave Kit . . .' She lifted her chin. 'And I can't and I won't. It could never be as you say. For one thing, I burnt my boats yesterday after you had gone.'

She glanced over to the dresser drawer where the bank book no longer rested beneath the pile of tea-towels.

'Kit came home and told me his boss had sold the shop to somebody else so that he could retire on the proceeds and the pile he's made over the years. Kit had worked that shop up from nothing, doing all the buying and the figure-work, besides working all the hours God sends for no extra. Yet that mean old goat of a boss gave Kit the sack. Just like that.'

Maggie nodded towards the drawer again. 'I'd been saving up, bit by bit, not much, but it was all money I had earned with sewing, every penny of it. I gave it all to Kit and told him to go and buy that shop for himself. I said I would ask Clara to have Rosie to mind till we got things straight. I told her about it early on this morning, and she's over the moon about it. She reckons she never wanted babies, but to see her with Rosie is a revelation.'

She nodded. 'So I am committed, Joe. That shop is in an awful district – nearly as bad as Montague Court – but there are two rooms above, and I'm sure I can make something of them. It's a *challenge*, Joe. I can decorate those rooms myself, and in between I can help Kit in the shop.'

Twice again she nodded her head. 'So that is what I am going to do, and even if I was the sort who could just walk out on her husband I can't now. Because it is too late.'

'Come here.'

Joe spoke quietly, but the command rang out like the crack of a whip.

'Come here, Maggie. Over to me, and kneel down by this chair, then look me in the eyes and tell me you don't love me. Never mind what you have just been saying – them's only excuses. Just come and tell me that one thing.'

Slowly Maggie obeyed. She got up from her chair, walked across the front of the fireplace, then knelt down by Joe's side on the pegged rug.

There were tears glistening in her eyes, but she wasn't going to let them fall. Crying was a waste of time. Nobody knew that better than she did, but she had to try to make Joe understand. This time he would go away for ever, so what she had to say was important, because she wanted him to remember her words.

'Joe . . . oh, Joe. I can't tell you that I don't love you, because it would not be true. I don't think I have ever stopped loving you and wanting you. Even on my wedding night I stood at the window upstairs and looked up the street, wishing with all my heart that you would come round the corner. I saw a shadow an' I thought it was you. I *made* it into you before it disappeared for ever.'

She blinked the gathering tears away.

'You are my only true love, Joe. I think, like my mother, I was only meant to love one man, and that one is you. But, Joe . . . dear Joe. Nobody has things just the way they want them. Nobody. Life is a compromise for everybody in some way or other. Even Kit has to make do with me when probably he would be happier with someone who didn't blow their top as often.'

She dashed a tear away from the corner of her eye.

'Kit will come home tonight, and the shop will be ours. I know what I have facing me. I know that all right. I have years of serving in the shop, fighting to bring up little Rosie decent, looking after Kit when he is too old to work such long hours, and yes, you were right. I will probably grow old before my time. . . .'

Now the tears were rolling down her face. 'My father used to long for what he called a "glimpse of green", and there's none of that where I'm going to live, Joe, I can tell you that.'

'Where is the shop?'

Joe's voice was cold and he was looking at her as if not a word of what she had been saying had penetrated.

Maggie told him the name of the street where Kit's shop stood on the corner, then she drew back on her heels startled as he banged angrily on the arm of the chair with his fist.

'And you talk about bringing a child up round there? I know you, Maggie. I know you of old. What will you do when Rosie wants to go out and play in the gutter with the rest of the kids in that neighbourhood? Will you lock her up in her room and hope she ends up talking as nicely as you? Will you wash her hair every night to keep the nits out of it?'

Joe thumped the chair arm twice more. 'What sort of a man is this Kit who would *allow* Rosie to be brought up round there? And where do you come into it? Strikes me he's a selfish bastard as well as a . . .'

Maggie put up a hand to cover Joe's mouth, and he took it, and turning it palm upwards, bent his head and kissed the blue veins on her wrist. Immediately she tried to pull away, but he held fast.

'Look, lass. I'm going now. I am going down to the station on me own, because I know you have a lot of thinking to do, then at twelve o'clock I am going to send a taxicab for you and Rosie. If it comes back without you then I'll know. But talking's not my way, and we've said all we need. . . .'

He jerked her to him and kissed her hard, so hard that

she felt the pressure of his teeth. So long that when at last he lifted his head she opened her eyes and saw the ceiling dip and sway towards her.

'It's me or him, Maggie. A straight choice. One or the other. You'll not be fulfilling your part of the bargain you made when you got wed, but then he's not fulfilled his either, has he? If I go alone this time it will be for ever. I will never come back to this town again. Ever. . . .'

Maggie felt him move away from the chair. She heard him unhook his stick from the dresser, and she heard the front door slam behind him.

Too shattered, too filled with emotion to get to her feet, she stretched out her arms across the seat of the chair and gave way to wild and anguished weeping.

It was a cold, bitterly cold day, with the sky hanging low with the threat of snow. Joe walked slowly, past the statue of Queen Victoria on the Boulevard, past the tramcars with their overhead cables, and across the wide stretch of road to the station forecourt.

He spoke briefly to a cab driver who nodded and wrote down his instructions, then in the entrance hall he walked over to a window and booked two tickets for London.

Then he sat down on his case to wait. . . .

He was quite calm, as calm as he had always been when waiting to go over the top in the trenches. He was so pale that one or two people, rushing for their trains, glanced quickly at him then looked as quickly away.

There were so many men like Joe Barton in those early months after the war had ended, hanging about at stations, wearing suits that did not fit right, looking as if they were waiting for nothing, with nowhere to go.

War did that, they told themselves, and there was nothing anyone could do except feel pity, and a sort of shamed gladness that it was all over without having affected them directly.

And Joe, sitting as still as Queen Victoria's statue, saw none of them. Every muscle in his body, every nerve inside him tuned into waiting for what might be.

What *had* to be, he told himself, praying to a God whose existence he had never even acknowledged.

There were only five minutes to go when he saw the taxi-cab turn in a wide circle and chug into position at the front of the station.

When Maggie got out wearing her long dark coat and a small velvet hat pulled well down over her forehead, he saw that she was carrying a brown paper parcel, and nothing else.

'The baby? Where's Rosie?'

Joe hurried her towards the ticket collector's box, then up the slope to the platform, so overwhelmed at seeing her that he could talk only in jerky syllables.

Maggie shook her head, not looking at him.

'I couldn't bring Rosie. She is too little. Joe, you know that.' She glanced up at him. 'You knew that if I came it would not be with Rosie.'

She was as deathly pale as he was himself, and when he tried to take the parcel from her, looping the stick over his arm as he tried to manage without it, she clung to it.

Walking by his side, and looking straight ahead, she said:

'I've left her with Clara. But only for a few days, Joe. An' I want you to know, before we get on the train, that I am coming back. I am definitely coming back. I cannot leave Kit. You have to know that.'

As they reached the top of the second slope up to the platform, the train was in, bursting with great clouds of steam which rose and dissolved against the filth of the high glass roof.

The guard, his whistle already in his mouth, had his green flag at the ready, as he stood by his van, watch in hand.

'We are going to miss it,' Maggie said, but Joe stopped dead, staring at her in blank amazement.

'You mean to tell me you are just coming away with me for a holiday? A ruddy flaming holiday?'

The whistle blew. Joe wrenched open a door, almost pushed Maggie inside, then with a strength he had not known he possessed, dragged himself in after her, throwing the case in first.

A porter, running alongside the train, slammed the swinging door, his mottled elderly face scarlet with anger.

'Tha silly buggers!' he shouted. 'What's t' trying to do? Commit bloody suicide?'

The compartment was empty, and as the train drew slowly out of the station, they sat opposite to each other. Joe with his case on the seat beside him, and Maggie with the neat brown parcel tied with string held carefully on her knee.

'Well,' she said. 'I never thought I'd manage it, but I have, and we're off, aren't we? Aren't we then?'

Joe stared at her. He had imagined that the first thing he would do would be to take her in his arms and kiss her, and never stop kissing her till they got to Preston.

But this wasn't the Maggie he had left sobbing on the floor only two hours before.

This was a Maggie he had never seen before. This was a woman with fierce determination in her expression, a woman who knew what she was doing and exactly why. A far far cry from the joyous vulnerable girl he remembered best.

'I wrote a letter for Kit to find when he comes home tonight. I propped it in front of the clock like they do in all the best stories,' she said.

Her head was up and her voice rang clear over the sound of the train wheels.

'I had a long think after you had gone, Joe. I had a long look at myself, and at what was in store. I weighed up the consequences, and I came to the conclusion that a few days out of my life was not going to change things too drastically. If Kit were stronger – if I thought he would come after me and try to find me and knock you about – then I might have thought different. But in this case his weakness has turned out ironically to be my strength.'

She unbuttoned her carefully darned gloves and frowned at the stitches along one finger.

'I told Clara some cock and bull story about a sick relative down in London, and though she knew I have no relatives, sick or otherwise, she was too busy settling little Rosie into her house to be over-inquisitive. . . . And in the letter I told Kit the truth.'

Joe's mouth dropped open.

'You told him you were coming away with me? And you think he will have you back?'

The head in the small velvet hat nodded.

'He will have me back, and worse than that he'll forgive me, Joe.'

'And what about me? Where do I come into these calculations? Might I ask that? Have you got me weighed up an' all?'

Maggie put the parcel down beside her, then came to sit beside him. There were tears sparkling on the ends of her long eyelashes, betraying her calmness.

'Joe, dear Joe. All I knew was that nothing, no power on earth, could have kept me off this train. You see I tried to see how it would be with you gone. For ever this time, just as you said, and I couldn't face it. I couldn't let you go. Oh, Joe, if I have to spend the rest of my life paying for what I am doing, I don't care. Not at this moment I don't. The future was so bleak, and I love you so much, so very very much. . . .'

Then she was in his arms, and he kissed her, and then they were silent. As the train rocked and swayed, and the fields, hoary with frost, flashed by the windows, Maggie snuggled closer and began cautiously to dare to accept the faint beginnings of happiness. Of a joy she would only have dreamed about had she stayed.

There was a dreadful aching weight of guilt on her, but

as she told herself with her usual practical northern common sense, if she really was sincere in her guilt, then she could get off at the next station and go back.

And she was not going back. For just a little while she was going to be the woman she might have been if she had married Joe Barton and not Kit Carmichael. And she was going to give as well as take. She was going to take that dreadful suffering look off Joe's face, and make him smile at her the way he used to do before their long separation and the war.

When they changed trains and were standing on the platform, it came to her that she was wicked. Really wicked, so that, according to her Chapel upbringing, all she could expect was a burning in hell's fires. Maggie had never believed that merely to confess to some misdeed put it right with God, the way Catholics did.

For a minute she shivered, only to feel Joe's hand firm on her arm.

'Will you never stop surprising me?' he grinned.

Once more they changed trains, and by the time the main line train pulled into Euston station, Maggie was asleep with her head on Joe's shoulder.

It was only as they got down from the taxi-cab and Joe propelled her through the revolving doors of the big hotel in Paddington that she really became aware of her surroundings.

'I must have been tired,' she whispered, and Joe smiled down at her telling her to stop where she was for a minute.

The foyer was wide, and so were the flight of steps straight ahead. There were potted plants everywhere, and it was all so huge and impressive that Maggie felt she wanted to turn and revolve herself back through the doors again.

Telling her again to stop where she was for a minute, Joe went over to the curved reception desk, then came back to her smiling.

'They've had a cancellation, so we can have one of their

best rooms,' he told her. Then they followed an ancient hall porter along a wide corridor to the right.

Surely the corridor was as wide as Foundry Street? There were lights set high in the red-flocked papered walls, and a marble surround either side of the crimson carpet.

She hid a smile at the grand way Joe tipped the porter, then as he left them alone, she stared around her in amazement.

'You could fit the whole of our upstairs into this room,' she cried. 'Oh, Joe, just feel these curtains, and this bedspread! Lined both of them. Oh, I'm not used to materials like this. Beats cotton fent, doesn't it?' As she stroked the spread she was doing rapid calculations in her mind.

'It must have cost a fortune, an' it's not skimped, neither.'

She opened the wardrobe door and it swung back, revealing a cavernous interior. 'Oh, Joe, my two clean blouses are going to look a bit lost in there, aren't they?'

'See through here,' he said, opening a door, and Maggie stood on the threshold of a high-ceilinged enormous bathroom, and clasped her hands together, like a child who has suddenly seen riches beyond her wildest dreams.

'A proper bathroom! An' taps! Hot and cold! Just look at that marble surround, and feel these towels!'

She picked up a white and fluffy bath towel and held its softness to her face. 'This beats bringing the bath in from the yard on a Friday, and filling it with jugs and heating the water up with pans and the kettle off the fire. Oh, Joe. Can I have a bath right now? Right this minute?'

He smiled on her with love. Now he had got his Maggie back. This was how he had always remembered her. Laughing, joyous, cheeks flushed, hair wisping down from its slipping bun as she darted from one thing to another, exclaiming, incredulous, eyes sparkling.

'Just a minute,' he said, pulling her to him, and tilting her face with his finger so that he could look deep into her eyes.

Then suddenly he threw back his head and laughed out loud.

'Well, bugger me! You've got odd eyes, Maggie, lass. There's one brown and one with green in it. You should be in a circus alongside the bearded lady, or in a tent on the fair, did you know that?'

'The odd-eyed woman from the north,' she agreed, and then they held on to each other, rocking and laughing, then as quickly serious and intent as he bent his dark head and kissed her mouth.

And later, when they had bathed, and sworn that neither of them was hungry, they made passionate love, with Maggie's white cotton nightdress tossed to the floor in a heap of white.

Maggie buried her hot face in Joe's shoulder and sighed.

'Why is sinning so lovely?' she wanted to know.

And uncomfortably but cosily, they slept in each other's arms all night and woke up so hungry that they were first in the dining-room.

'You are so beautiful it hurts my eyes just to look at you, lass,' Joe said.

'If I am then it's you what's done it,' Maggie replied, and they ate bacon and eggs, sausage and tomatoes, and when Maggie wondered aloud how such food could be Joe wrinkled his nose at her.

'Money buys anything, lass. I learnt that a long time ago. You can be happy without much brass, oh aye, but with it you can be doubly so. Especially when you have known the other way. That is one advantage of coming up the hard way, you never take nothing for granted.'

They got their coats, and he took her outside into the cold frosty morning, and as they walked along Maggie had to keep stopping to stare at the tall buildings, and to watch the traffic streaming by.

'Why does everything move so fast? Even the people? Where are they all going to, Joe?'

He touched the tip of her nose. 'I know where we are

259

going, love. Into that shop over there to buy you a dress. A brown dress trimmed with green to match your eyes. Both of them.'

'No!' Maggie's face changed its expression to one of dismay. 'I can't go home with a dress bought by you, Joe. You must see that. I don't think even Kit would stand for that.'

But they were already in the shop with its lavish Food Hall on the ground floor, and Maggie forgot her dismay as she left Joe's side to move rapidly from one counter to another, eyes sparkling as she pointed out one display, then rushing over to the next.

'Look at that tea, Joe! Oh, my goodness, half a pound of that and you would have to starve for the rest of the week. And that coffee! Oh, it can't cost that much. It can't possibly!'

There were biscuits in shiny brightly coloured tins, succulent whole hams laid out on marble slabs. Oranges in flat boxes, with every other one wrapped in silver paper, and chocolates in boxes as big as trays, with pictures on the front of the Tower and Buckingham Palace.

'That's what we are going to do tomorrow,' Joe told her. 'This leg of mine won't stand up to much walking yet, so we are going to hire a taxi-cab and get the driver to take us round to see the lot. The Palace, and the Tower, and Oxford Street, Trafalgar Square, Piccadilly Circus . . . everything!'

Then because she was adamant about the dress he took her into the fur department and bought her a muff. It was soft brown fur, and lined with silk with a pocket inside, and she couldn't get over it.

Privately Joe thought she was splitting hairs about her acceptance of the muff and her refusal of a dress, but he said a diplomatic nothing, not wanting to spoil her pleasure.

Maggie kissed him thank you, right in front of the smiling saleswoman, and when they came out into the street again, he bought a bunch of early primroses from a flower girl, and Maggie pinned them in front of the muff, and insisted on wearing it there and then.

They slept the afternoon away, and when Joe tried to make love to her and failed, Maggie held him close and told him that it did not matter.

'Loving is sometimes just a holding,' she whispered. 'Like this. It doesn't have to be no more. Just a touching and a holding.'

And when he slept she thought of Kit and the way he always shied away from any physical contact with her.

As though he doesn't like the feel of me. As though my skin is repulsive to him, she thought, sadly.

Then, remembering how the night before, Joe had kissed her all over, lingering at the hollow of her throat, moving his mouth downwards over the slight swell of her stomach, she blushed.

Then the pale winter sunshine, filtering through the tall windows lay like a blessing on their closed eyelids.

There was so much to say to each other, so much catching up to do. Foundry Street was another world away; it was another life, and though there were heart-stopping minutes when she wondered how Clara was coping with Rosie, and when she saw Kit's face as he read her letter, she pushed the thoughts away with a ruthless determination.

'This is to last me for the rest of my life,' she told Joe, and when he asked her if she would like to go and see where he had lived before he went to France, she shook her head.

'That would make it too real, love. This . . . all this is a dream, and though I know I have to wake up, I'm not ready yet. Not yet. Waking from it is going to last me a long long time.'

They walked hand in hand in Hyde Park, and he showed her where the toffs rode, and where, in summer, lovers sat on the grass.

'It's all so *light*,' she told him. 'It is as though the sky is higher than it is at home. I thought the Corporation Park was lovely, but this is so fresh and clean, and yet there are

motor buses and charabancs not far away. Open charabancs, even at this time of the year.'

'Aye, winter doesn't seem to *dwell* so much down here,'
Joe agreed, then she ticked him off for talking like a south-
erner, and teased him for turning into a toffee-nosed snob.

'I am never going back, all the same,' he said seriously,
and they sat for a while on a bench for him to rest his leg,
whilst London sparrows pecked hopefully round their feet,
and two men in top hats walked by, twirling silver-topped
canes.

That night their love-making was ecstatic. They were
becoming more used to the needs and desires of their bodies,
and Joe was filled with surprised delight at the way Maggie
responded, and sometimes even took the initiative. So
natural was her giving, so completely without shame that
he realized this was the way God had intended her to be,
as she expressed a love that had been kept in check for all
the barren years of her marriage.

When, around midnight, she said she could just do with
a cup of tea, he immediately rang for the chamber-maid.

'Joe!' Maggie reached for her nightdress. 'You are
terrible. What will she think, us wanting a pot of tea at this
time?'

'Just put it down there, and thank you. My wife will
pour,' he said grandly when the tray arrived.

The pride in his voice, and the possessiveness turned
Maggie's heart over, and her hand as she picked up the
pretty flowered tea-pot, was far from steady.

'One more day,' she said. 'It's got to be faced, Joe. I
have to go back, you know that.'

He was so thin, sitting up in bed, holding the gold-fluted
cup in his hands, so vulnerable, so much younger looking
than his years now that his face was gentled by love, that
she felt the tears spring to her eyes.

'I can't leave Kit,' she said quietly.

'No,' Joe agreed equally quietly. 'You can't leave Kit
because he needs you. You've told me that over and over.'

He looked at her with anguished eyes. 'He needs you to mother him and to slave for him in that bloody awful little shop. Kit Carmichael needs you to keep him going, and to be his strength and his bloody rod and his bloody staff. But what about me? What about me, Maggie? Don't I count for nothing? Aren't my needs as great as his?'

Maggie put her cup down, and going over to the dressing-table, sat down and stared at herself in the walnut-framed mirror.

She had shed ten years over the last few days. Her hair was softer and curling more. Her skin had a luminous quality about it, and her eyes were bright, with the whites shining clean. Joe's love had transformed her; she was fulfilled and replete with the kind of love that rarely happened between a man and a woman, the kind that had happened for her and Joe.

'I married *Kit*,' she repeated. 'And even if he did destroy your letters, I was married to him when they first came. He stuck by me, Joe. In the Chapel, in front of everybody, he came and stood by my side when they turned on me. I cannot forget that.'

She turned round to face him.

'Kit could be a drinker; he could beat me. He could be mean and selfish and cruel, but he is none of these things. He nursed me, Joe. When I would almost certainly have died, he sat up with me day and night, and sponged the fever from me and saved my life. I wouldn't be here with you now but for Kit.'

Her head drooped.

'And he married me, knowing I had lost a baby to some-one else. . . .'

She got back into bed and tried to pull Joe down beside her, but he resisted.

'Aye, you've told me the credit side. Now tell me the other.'

He took his cigarettes from the bedside table and lit one before he went on:

'Tell me now about how he has never been a proper husband to you, Maggie. Tell me how he worships you with his body, because that is what it says in the marriage service.'

His voice rose. 'With my body I thee worship . . . How often has he fulfilled that side of the bargain? And while we are at it, how ever did you come to have Rose? Was it another immaculate conception or something?'

For a moment Maggie felt the awkward fumbling flabbiness that had been Kit. She shuddered.

'There's more to life than that, Joe. More to a marriage. That is only a small part of it.'

'But it's not!' Joe exploded, stubbing out the cigarette and reaching for her. 'It's a *need*, Maggie my own love. It is this and this and this . . .'

And this time his loving was brutal and selfish so that she cried out, but when he slept at last it was to sink into one of his fighting screaming nightmares.

He was drowning in a sea of mud. He was crossing no man's land, his bayonet at the ready. There were shells bursting all around him, and the staccato putter of machine gun fire was in his ears. The air was silvery green with the glow from Very lights, and his sergeant had dropped dead at his feet with a bullet through his head.

Maggie held him, whispered to him, smoothed the hair back from his sweat-soaked forehead. Then when he slept again she crept from the bed and went through into the vast marble bathroom with its gleaming taps.

She sat there on the edge of the white bath and faced up to her own particular hell.

Never in a million years could she leave this man. He needed her just as Kit needed her, and oh God, there was no way she could split herself in two.

She shivered as the cold marbled floor struck icy cold into her legs and feet, and she rubbed at the tops of her arms as though the chill had reached up to there.

She could go back to Lancashire, and she could bring Rosie back with her. She could live with Joe, and Rosie would be brought up as a Londoner. Joe would make more money, she knew that. Joe was on the up and up, she could sense that when he talked about what he had planned to do.

There would be no more sewing at turning sheets and replacing frayed cuffs on shirts, no more counting every penny. They would walk in the London parks, and Rosie would learn to talk differently, and Joe would be the father she would never have known.

They would be happy. Without certain knowledge of that, Maggie knew this would be so. Joe Barton was her man. If things had been different he would have been the only man in her life. Like her mother with her father, they would live out their lives together, not without tiffs sometimes, because loving somebody did not mean, in Maggie's code, that you always had to agree with them.

But Kit was there. Gentle, kind, affectionate Kit, who without her would be a nothing . . . a great soft nothing.

Slowly Maggie walked back into the bedroom. She got into bed and Joe's arms immediately closed round her, straining her close to him, even in sleep.

She felt the strength of his arms, and knew that where Kit would give up without her by his side, Joe Barton would not.

Oh, Joe loved her, she knew that. He loved her desperately, and he would grieve for a while; he would be angry and lost for a while, but he would survive.

And survival seemed to be what it was all about.

Joe bought a shawl for Rosie the next day. It was a whisper of a shawl, worked in cobweb scallops, and Maggie knew that the baby's tiny fingers would soon be caught up in it, but she said nothing.

She was living on borrowed time now, every hour and every minute ticking away, and that night, their last night together, Joe took her to a music hall.

'You won't need your muff, lass,' he told her, but she could not bear to part with it. She sat with it on her lap in the hot smoky atmosphere of the little theatre, stealing glances at Joe now and again as if she would remember every line of his thin face.

The music was loud, and a big woman with tightly curled hair sang at the top of a powerful voice, while the audience stamped and cheered her on.

A tall man in a red lined cloak made a woman disappear into thin air, and when she appeared from the wings everyone stood up and yelled aloud their delight.

They drank stout, and when it was all over they decided it wasn't much of a walk back to the hotel.

'It's a bonny night,' Joe said, and Maggie took his arm as they strolled back along the wide pavements.

'Just look at those stars,' she said.

'Aye, it's a bonny night,' Joe said again.

It seemed there was nothing left to say, or at least nothing they dared to say, and Joe ordered whisky to be sent to their room, and for the first time in her life Maggie tasted the fiery liquid, feeling it run smoothly down her throat and warm the place where her heart seemed to have frozen itself solid.

'You are really going back then?' Joe said when he had drained his glass twice. His voice was slightly slurred and his eyelids drooped, concealing the expression in his dark eyes.

'Methodists don't drink,' Maggie said, holding out her glass for more. 'Drink is the scourge of mankind.'

'And the source of all evil,' agreed Joe, holding his own glass high.

When they got ready for bed Maggie laughed at Joe in his long underpants, army issue. She had seen them before, but now with the drink warm inside her everything seemed silly and funny.

Joe laughed at her when she tripped over the hem of her long white nightdress.

'Whoops a daisy!'

'No, whoops a Maggie!'

They made love to mingled laughter, and then fell

asleep with the suddenness of a stone flung down the well of Maggie's childhood.

Breakfast was a solemn occasion, with Maggie settling for toast and tea, and Joe pushing his poached haddock to the side of his plate and leaving it there.

Back in their room Maggie unfolded the brown paper she had laid neatly in a drawer, and wrapping her few belongings in it, tied it with the same piece of string.

'My mother used to have a box with all different lengths of string stored away, some too short to be used for anything at all,' she told Joe, trying not to look at the empty coat hangers swinging in the dark recesses of the huge wardrobe.

He looked at her without a smile.

'Oh, aye?'

And the last thing she did was to go into the bathroom and look around. She ran a hand over the marble surround of the wash-stand, and she turned on the hot tap and let the water trickle over her fingers.

She looked up at the dark green patterned wallpaper stretching away to the high ceiling, and she picked up one of the big white towels and reminded herself that somebody else would be washing them. They wouldn't fill a living-room with steam as they dried over a clothes horse round the fire.

'I am not going to kiss you goodbye,' Joe told her, taking his stick and his case and somehow managing to open the door for her.

Maggie tried to keep her mind on the towels.

'That's all right,' she said.

Joe paid the bill, then out in the wide sweep of the fore-court he hailed a taxi-cab, and helped Maggie inside.

'It would have to be raining,' he said.

He sat back, his head sunk deep on his chest, and his hands resting on the curved handle of the hospital issue walking stick. Then at the station he booked a single ticket for Maggie, and walked her towards the barrier.

'If you want me, I have written Belle's address down here,' he told her, giving her a slip of paper which she concealed in the fur muff. 'I won't be settled in a place for a while. I have a lot of things to see to first.'

Maggie nodded. Politeness, it seemed, was all that was left, all they had to cling to.

'Thank you, Joe. Thank you for giving me the best, the very best time of my life,' she whispered. Then her face crumpled. 'Oh, Joe, what can I say?'

'Nowt!' he said sharply, lapsing into dialect as he always did when troubled. 'There's nowt at all to say now, is there, lass?'

'God bless you, Joe,' Maggie whispered before she turned and walked away, handing her ticket to the man at the gate, having it punched, putting it away safely in the pocket her muff, then walking away down the long slope to the train.

She dare not turn round. If she turned round and saw him standing there, the dark hair falling forward over his forehead . . . if she saw him she would have to run back.

And there could be no running back. . . .

When the guard blew his whistle and waved his green flag, the train moved forward slowly, out of the station, past the tall grey lodging houses shrouded in a mist of fine rain.

Putting her head back Maggie closed her eyes.

She had done what she had done, and when Kit came home that night she would be there, waiting for him, no doubt with his tea warming in the fire-oven, and little Rosie asleep in her basket.

Kit would cry, oh he would most certainly cry, and she would comfort him, and talk to him, and he would try to understand.

God forgive him, but he would already be trying to understand.

Then when a few weeks had gone by he would tell her he had forgiven her, and she would accept his forgiveness, and in his simple loving way he would never know the truth.

The truth being that she would have preferred him to rant and rave at her, to call her all the names she deserved, and even land out at her and clout her one.

But Kit was Kit, just as Joe was Joe.

The two men, so different . . . the only men she had ever known.

'Oh, Joe . . .' she whispered as the train gathered speed.

'Oh, Joe, my love, my dear, dear love.'

'Mammy, that lady's crying,' a small boy sitting on the opposite seat said in a loud voice. 'Why is she crying?'

His mother put a finger to her lips and shook her head.

'It's rude to stare,' she told him.